DO

KEEF

Matt Bracken

Matt Bracken

6-4-24 Florida

Steelcutter Publishing, Inc.
Orange Park, Florida

DOOMSDAY REEF

First Printing 2024

This novel is a work of fiction. All the events and characters described herein are products of the author's imagination. Any similarities to actual persons are entirely coincidental.

ISBN 978-0-9728310-8-6

Library of Congress Control Number
2024907975

www.EnemiesForeignAndDomestic.com

This novel is humbly dedicated to my wife. Without her constant love and support I would have never completed even a single novel, much less six.

Many thanks to Kirk Kuehl and Liz Elliott for all their help.
Back cover mid-ocean photo credit to Jim Simcox.

No artificial intelligence program or application was used in the creation of this product of a human mind.

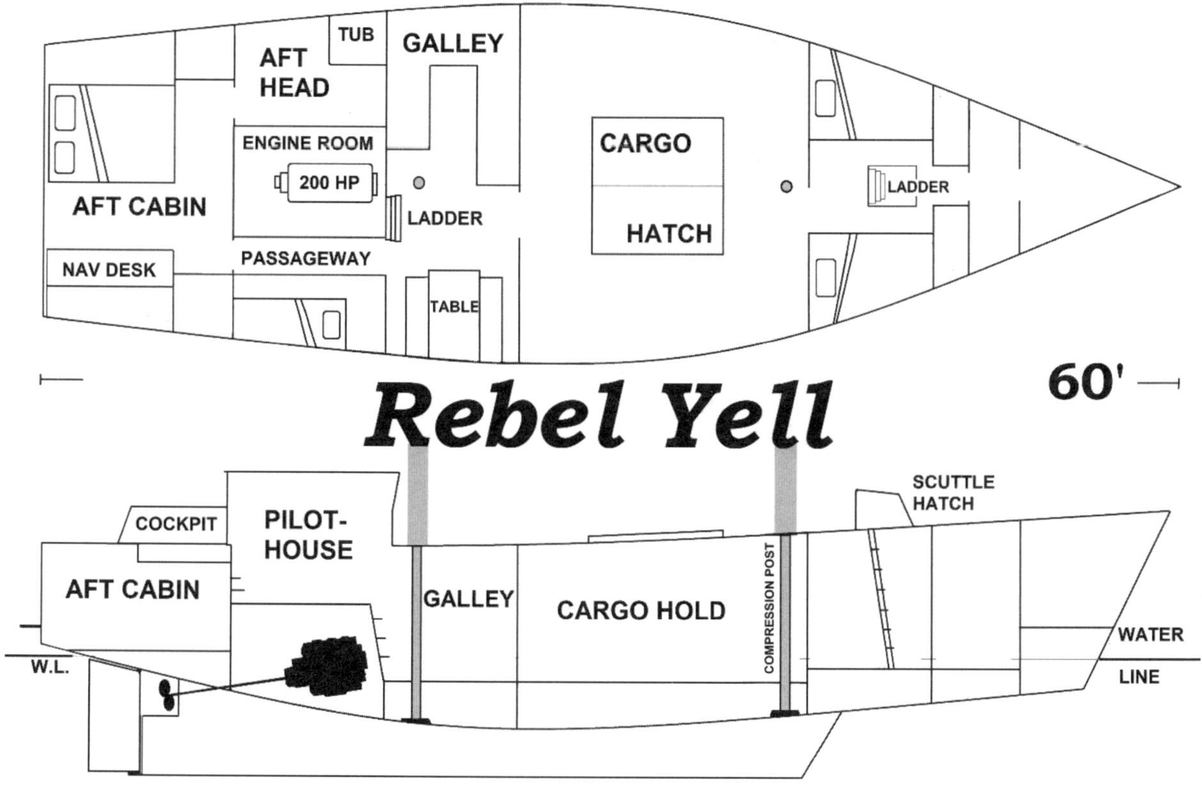
TUB
AFT HEAD
GALLEY
ENGINE ROOM
200 HP
CARGO HATCH
LADDER
AFT CABIN
LADDER
NAV DESK
PASSAGEWAY
TABLE
60'
Rebel Yell
COCKPIT
PILOT-HOUSE
SCUTTLE HATCH
AFT CABIN
GALLEY
CARGO HOLD
COMPRESSION POST
WATER LINE
W.L.

DOOMSDAY REEF

After we dropped the anchor the church bell tolled one time, followed after a few seconds by five more rings. The church bell was the time keeper for the town, noon being determined by a sundial in the parish garden. The bell rang the hours from six in the morning until six at night. Mechanical alarm clocks let them know when to pull the ropes. The bells were audible far out on the anchorage.

If you had a wrist watch or a wind-up clock at home that worked, and you cared about the time between the hours, you set it by the church bell. Cell phones were a fading memory, but some people still had to meet at agreed-upon times and places. I often found myself looking at my watch as the top of an hour approached. Sometimes the bell-ringers were early or late, or they missed an hour entirely. This time the bell and my watch were within four minutes of each other. Plenty good enough.

Hilton Sapelo checked his own watch, and then he pointed a few hundred yards north to the town's public dock. A small red sail was being lifted. "That's Adam. That kid is on the ball."

"How old is he?" I asked.

"He turned fifteen the week before Halloween."

I was standing in Rebel Yell's cockpit just forward of the wheel, so I pushed the kill button on the engine panel to shut down the diesel. The primary feature of the engine panel was its round analogue tachometer, and the needle fell from idle speed to zero as the motor went silent. The engine panel, the depth sounder and the speedometer display were mounted on the back of the pilothouse on the starboard side. The door was hinged open to the port side. The top half of the steel door had a Plexiglas window, so that in rough or rainy weather with the door closed somebody in the pilothouse could look through and communicate with the helmsman behind the wheel.

We'd burned a few gallons of diesel to get my schooner's compass tuned up for a long ocean voyage. Hilton Sapelo was the best compass adjuster on the island, and this is why he'd spent Friday with us. "The island" was how locals referred to Beaufort, Port Royal, St. Helena and a few other islands that were separated from the South Carolina mainland by tidal salt water. This collection of dry land, marshes, rivers and creeks was roughly fifteen miles by twenty, or about as large as all five boroughs of New York City—but with only a few thousand inhabitants instead of millions.

The little pram with the red sail was Hilton Sapelo's ride back to shore. Gino Bracciano and Rita, Gino's stepdaughter, joined us in the cockpit as the dinghy approached. They'd been up on the bow for the anchor detail. Gino normally did this by himself, or he steered and I did it, depending on our moods.

I think thirteen-year-old Rita had been with Gino on the foredeck to escape babysitting the twins. We'd been too busy swinging the compass to deal with Jonathan and Christopher on deck underfoot. It was hard enough to understand Sapelo's compass correcting magic as we motored back and forth across the sound without also hearing *But why, Daddy*? from five-year-olds with no real concept of north or south.

(Alone among Rebel's crew my sons were not volunteers, so I won't describe who was more outgoing, or more pensive, or even who had green eyes and who had brown.)

Adam tacked over toward us, cutting between some of the other anchored boats, and steered his dinghy up to our stern. It was ten or eleven feet long with a flat pram bow, and it was sprit-rigged with a four-sided sail that was loose footed. This meant there was no boom at the bottom to smack your head when you were tacking over. Instead, there was a sprit pole along the top of the sail where it crossed the stubby mast.

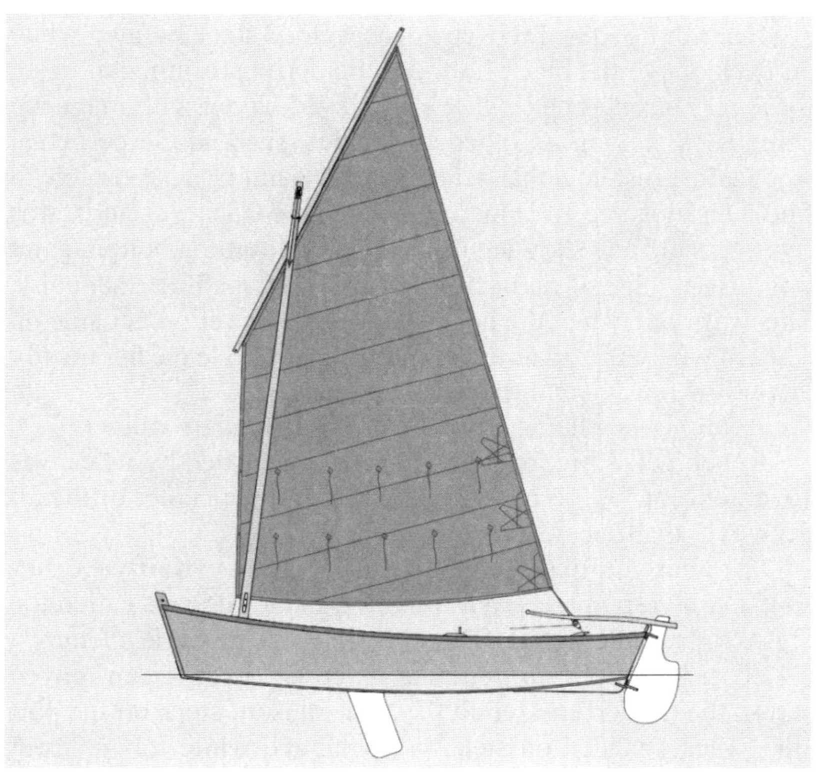

A fuel can was lying in the bottom of his boat. He grabbed the boat's bow line and the jug and hopped over onto our swim platform. This was nearly two feet above the water when Rebel Yell was at rest. He left his boat's red sail up, but unsheeted and flying free. This was no problem for a small dinghy in the wind shadow behind Rebel Yell's transom at anchor.

Adam's chin reached Rebel's aft deck, so he was tall for fifteen, with wind-tousled blonde hair, blue eyes, freckles, and a smile revealing a few crooked teeth. He tied his boat's bow line to a deck cleat one-handed, passed the empty five-gallon fuel container up to me with his other hand, and then grabbed onto Rebel's toe rail. This was a two-inch-high steel bar running all the way around my sixty-foot schooner.

Everything joined to Rebel was welded steel, painted white on deck above the black hull. All this ferrous iron metal made for a very strong boat, but it also played havoc with magnetic compasses, among its other downsides, such as the perpetual war against rust now that usable marine paint was impossible to find. Our most recent paint job, done in the Canary Islands, was five years old and showing its age. Our antifouling bottom paint was just as old, so barnacles had to be scraped off manually. This was done when the boat was careened over on her side on a beach where the tidal range was sufficient to leave her mostly dry at low tide, cleaning one side per day.

Adam looked up and asked me, “Is that a fifty caliber?”

Rebel Yell’s big machine gun was concealed by its canvas cover, except for the tripod legs welded to the center of the aft deck over the transom.

“No, but you’re close. It’s basically a Russian fifty caliber, so it’s twelve-point-seven millimeters. The Russians called it a Dushka for the letters D, Sh and K. In Russian, Sh is a letter.”

“Can I see it? Can you take its cover off?” Adam moved across the platform to climb the four transom steps on the port side. These welded-on steps were painted white to stand out against the vertical black steel wall. Sand had been mixed with the paint on top of the foot-wide steps to make them non-skid.

“Not now,” said Hilton Sapelo. “We’re not quite finished. We still have some more work to do.”

I said, “You can both stay for supper if you’d like. We can finish our business down below.”

Rita leaned over the rail, studying Adam and his boat, and she said. “I’m not hungry, so while it’s not raining, I’d rather go sailing. I mean, if you’re not hungry, Adam, and you don’t mind. Our dinghy is a little too big for me to sail by myself, but I think I can handle yours with some practice.”

He looked up. “It’s okay with me, if it’s okay with them.”

Rebel’s fiberglass launch was stowed on a pair of chocks between her two masts. It was sixteen feet long, and it could be sailed, or it could be rowed by one or two men, but it was more often pushed by its four-horsepower outboard motor.

This hard dinghy had replaced my worn-out Avon RIB and its ancient 70-horsepower Evinrude motor. Eventually both of them were beyond our ability to repair. The inflatable was cut into scrap, the rubber saved for future projects.

I traded the old two-stroke Evinrude, (along with some gas and oil), for the little Honda at an outboard motor exchange in Morehead City. Even in its decrepitude the Evinrude retained value in its parts. A random piece here or there could finish up a 'project' engine and restore it to working order, so almost nothing mechanical was ever thrown away.

Gino Bracciano was Rita's stepfather, but we never used that term. Rita had been part of the deal when Gino had met and married Sofia Burgos back in the Canaries, when Rita had been no bigger than my two boys were in Beaufort. Now Rita was a teenager, already over five feet tall and just beginning to fill out—although her new maturity was not evident beneath her sweater and rain jacket. She was dressed for the damp, chilly weather, as we all were on that late November afternoon.

Rita turned to Gino and asked, "So, can I go sailing?"

We had all seen how well Adam had handled his dinghy and his agility in springing onto Rebel's swim platform.

Gino said, "Oh, sure, why not? Just bring her back before it gets too dark. Do you have a light?"

"Yes, sir, I have a good lantern." Flashlights and anything else that ran on AA and AAA batteries were another memory of the bygone era. Over time even the so-called rechargeables had become useless. Now boats normally showed a white light at night, and on the island that meant a kerosene lantern of some kind. It wasn't the law, but the law had little to do with much of anything anymore. It was simply a matter of common sense to make a boat visible during the hours of darkness, to prevent it being run over by a larger vessel that couldn't see it.

Seconds after receiving permission Rita climbed down the transom steps and hopped onto his pram, sitting down facing aft on the plank bench beside the mast. Adam untied the bow line and followed her aboard, his boat drifting back away. He sat in the stern steering with one hand and pulled in the sail's sheet with the other. There wasn't a lot of breeze, but enough to send them gliding through the anchorage.

We had no reason to worry about them. Rita's coat had built-in flotation, and she was a strong swimmer. Adam had grown up on the water like most Beaufort kids. Although Rebel Yell was home-ported five miles south in Port Royal, my black schooner had become an icon in the local waters, from her long bowsprit to the big machine gun on her stern. Adam and Rita could find refuge on any of the anchored boats if they had a problem either with his boat or the weather, but a look at the sky showed no chance of a late afternoon squall.

The leaden overcast was changing from gray to silvery orange. Hilton Sapelo likewise surveyed the sky and water all the way around. He said, "We were lucky it didn't pour today. It's been a week since we had a full day with no rain. Or even snow flurries, like we had last week. I can't ever remember snow before Thanksgiving, and I've lived here all my life." He was around sixty judging by his gray hair and beard, so his perspective meant something.

"I think it's the volcano," Gino suggested. "The one they call Laki, up in Iceland."

We had been discussing this theory for a few months, and I wanted to hear what a life-long resident thought. There was no denying that it had been a cold summer, and who had ever heard of snow flurries in coastal South Carolina in November?

Hilton Sapelo agreed. "Right, it's Mount Laki, that's what the Gunny says on 77." He was referring to VHF channel 77, one of the unofficial local news and chat radio frequencies.

Most of the boats at anchor or tied up at the nearby docks and marinas still had some kind of a working VHF marine radio.

If you could maintain and charge your boat's deep-cycle 12-volt lead-acid batteries, you could still use your VHF radio, as well as your boat's lights, pressure water system, fridge and some music systems, at least for as long as they kept working. Solar panels and home-made wind generators could keep the batteries charged on boats without a working diesel engine or generator, or the fuel to run them. Many of the people living ashore also had VHF radios powered by car and truck batteries connected to solar panels. CB radios were also popular.

Gino said, "The gunny is full of shit most of the time, but I think he's probably right about the volcano."

Retired USMC Gunnery Sergeant Morton Haddock lived aboard Ooh-Rah Two, an ancient Morgan Out-Island 41 ketch that was permanently moored down the river in the shallows. By the Gunny's own account he scanned the short-wave bands all night, culminating in a one-man news program that began every morning at seven sharp. Haddock read through his take on world events in a staccato drill-instructor style, which was sprinkled with stale jarhead humor. We could receive it all the way out to the ocean, a dozen miles away. According to the Gunny and a few other local short-wave-radio buffs, the Icelandic volcano had been blasting out lava ash, sulfur, and even fluorine gas since last year. According to the theory, Laki's ongoing eruptions were the reason for the cold summer, the seemingly constant rains, the freakishly early snow flurries, and the spectacular sunsets and sunrises.

Other radio channels were dedicated to seeking, selling or swapping goods and services from A to Z. Another channel shared weather and agricultural news. Some of the frequencies were open party lines, but by long tradition channel 16 was reserved only for hailing and emergencies. The hailing part of this protocol meant that you would initially try to connect with another boat or a person on 16 before switching to a working channel. Helpful local voices often chimed in with ideas about where somebody was located or headed.

The downside was a total lack of privacy. The radio traffic was all unregulated, but it worked out pretty well. When some of the locals became too drunk, obnoxious, or otherwise made jackasses of themselves they were dressed down on the air.

I went through the pilothouse and down the ladder into the galley. Sofia was stirring a pot of soup; seafood chowder by the aroma. Fish, oysters, clams, potatoes, carrots, onions and a few other staples were still plentiful, but we were conserving our propane, so we cooked a common meal only once a day.

By mutual agreement, Gino's wife Sofia and my wife Tala took turns preparing our suppers, with Gino filling in when both ladies were busy at other tasks. The galley was to port of the pilothouse ladder, and the dinette table and bookshelves were to starboard. The engine room bulkhead was behind the ladder, and a few steps forward of it was the sliding door into the cargo hold. It was closed in order to contain the warmth of the galley within the most comfortable crew area on the boat.

Gino followed me down and joined his wife in the cook's space behind the gas stove. They embraced as if they had been apart for days, and not only a few hours. There was just barely enough room for two adults in the little galley alcove, but only if they were cozy in tight quarters, and those two were.

Sofia was about an inch shorter than Tala, with brown hair and blue eyes of the same shade as her daughter. Sofia and her first husband had been Spanish tourists stuck in the Canary Islands when the big jets stopped flying. Her husband had died in an accident when the minivan he'd been a passenger in had sailed off a cliff. His death was just bad luck; it had nothing to do with pandemics, famines or wars.

When Rita was born her father was already dead. By the time Rebel Yell arrived in Las Palmas for an overhaul, Sofia Burgos had been a single mother for seven years, and meeting

Gino Bracciano was the answer to her prayers. She had readily signed on for the adventure aboard Rebel Yell.

Gino told his wife, "Rita is out dinghy sailing with Captain Sapelo's grandson."

Hilton Sapelo spoke as he came down the ladder from the pilothouse. "Actually, Adam is my grand-nephew. He was my sister's grandson, and his name is Adam Selfridge. My sister is deceased, but his mother is still living."

"He seems like a nice young man," Sofia replied. She'd already met Captain Sapelo. He'd been aboard Rebel Yell all day, but she had no interest whatsoever in magnetic deviation, variation, or adjusting compasses for optimal accuracy.

"You heard us talking?" I asked her.

"Yes, and I saw them in his little boat. I saw them out the back." Rebel Yell had a pair of brass portholes in her transom. They were spaced seven feet apart and looked like golden eyes when seen from behind, because they were oval shaped. Each was a foot across and eight inches high. One was on the port side over the end of the double bed where I slept, and the other was to starboard between my bed and the navigation desk. Anyone in the aft cabin could use this one to look out astern.

Sofia and Rita had the run of Rebel Yell, and they moved through the aft cabin at will when its door was latched open during the daytime. This was the only way for them to get to the larger and nicer head, or bathroom, of the two on Rebel Yell. It even had a sitting bath tub. The aft head occupied all the space between the engine room and the port side of the hull. Forward of the head was the galley, with a solid bulkhead separating them. A louvered door connected the head to the aft cabin, which had been my bachelor's lair until I'd met Tala.

Gino still only used the crew's head up forward, and its more Spartan shower. This compact head was located in what had originally been the crew's berthing compartment, and then Victor's stateroom, and was now configured to accommodate Gino's little family. This was forward of the cargo hold that occupied the space between the schooner's two masts.

When the hold was empty, or it was at least clear enough to enable a pathway through it, you could walk from one end of Rebel Yell to the other below deck and out of the weather. The forward compartment had its own ladder and hatch ahead of the foremast, providing access up to the deck when the hold was full to its ceiling.

Tala and I would latch our aft cabin's louvered door closed when we wanted privacy, but when it was open, Sofia and Rita freely passed through it to use our nicer head. So it was natural that Sofia had gone back there to take a look at Adam through the transom porthole, and then to watch her daughter sailing off with him on his dinghy. This was all normal life aboard Rebel Yell at anchor in Beaufort and Port Royal.

"So, one more for dinner, yes?" Sofia asked me.

"Yes, one more. The kids will be out for a while, so they won't be joining us." This was just as well. The dinette could comfortably seat six, but seven required a stool to be placed at the end of the table by the ladder, blocking the path over to the galley. This arrangement could work well enough at anchor, but never at sea unless in a flat calm.

I sat facing forward, and Hilton Sapelo sat across the table from me facing aft. He tilted his head to study the titles of the books on the shelves behind me. Not much light was coming through the Plexiglas top of the small hatch above the table, so I reached up and switched on the dome light. It had separate buttons for white light and for red light. The red light was used when we were underway to save our night vision. There was a matching hatch and dome light over the cooking alcove.

The brass ship's clock and barometer were mounted on the bulkhead above Captain Sapelo's head. The mechanical clock had to be wound every other day. On the bulkhead between the clock and the door to the cargo hold was a small bulletin board where items of interest to the crew were posted. Recipe ideas, chores, shopping lists, witty sayings copied from books and other miscellany were pinned to it with tacks. These notes were written in pencil, since all of our ink pens had dried up. Our last pencils were used judiciously and sharpened with care.

Tala came out of the passageway to the aft cabin and said, "The boys are sleeping on our bed." At night the twins slept in the cabinette across the aft passageway from the engine room.

This mini-cabin had been Tran Hung's domain for nearly a decade until my elderly Vietnamese sea-cook, boat guard and shipmate had left the world of the living. When the boys were sleeping further aft on our bed in the captain's cabin they were less likely to be awakened by our talking. I moved over a bit more to my right and Tala slid in beside me.

2

Tran Hung had disappeared on the Atlantic crossing from the Canaries to Virginia. Hung had always been reckless on deck, never wearing a safety harness no matter how rough it got, so it was impossible to know how he had gone overboard. Maybe he had decided it was time to rejoin his ancestors.

Rebel's rusted and nameless steel hull was already at least thirty years old when my Uncle Jeff had found the derelict in the back lot of a South Florida boatyard. Jeff Kilmer had died before Rebel was relaunched, after falling from a scaffold.

Doctor Victor Aleman, my other long-term shipmate, had not made it out of Morocco alive. Victor, Hung and Uncle Jeff were only three of the spirits aboard Rebel Yell. I didn't know the ghosts from Rebel's first three decades, from before she'd been found by my uncle and we'd rebuilt her, but they visited me nonetheless. I'd often had the feeling that her first Dutch captain was trying to offer me useful hints and warnings. I'd felt his presence from the time of Rebel's boatyard rebirth and through every storm and trial since then.

Gino Bracciano replaced Victor in the crew berthing area ahead of the cargo hold, but the Italian bachelor had the place to himself for only a few months before Sofia and Rita joined him there on a permanent basis.

Tala Abidar, who had become Tala Kilmer, moved into the captain's cabin following our escape from Port Zerhoun. Less than a year later we'd been blessed by the arrival of our twin boys, Chris and Jon. We were hoping for more children, but it hadn't happened. We didn't understand why, except that we had both been deathly ill with typhus fever during our horrible year in Virginia after crossing the Atlantic. There was really no way to know if the problem lay on my side or hers, but more children seemed unlikely—although not for our lack of trying.

Sofia not having children after Rita was a private matter

between her and Gino. She was still in her early thirties, nearly the same age as Tala, so she was not beyond her child-bearing years. Her womanly figure and overall fitness indicated robust health. If their lack of new children was a personal decision or a biological matter, well, that was between the two of them.

One thing was certain: overpopulation was no longer a problem, if it had ever been. There was no reliable information on a national or even a state level, but there was no ignoring the fact that there had been a dramatic population collapse in the formerly once United States of America following a decade of anarchy, violence, famine and disease. There was no way to know the extent of the population drop with anything close to certainty, but ninety percent was a frequent guess. According to Gunny Haddock, most of America's cities were virtually uninhabited no-go-zones, with just a few exceptions.

But on the island there was no disease and there were few empty stomachs. Beaufort and Port Royal seemed to be in a just-right Goldilocks zone between Savannah and Charleston, with their far worse post-urban problems. The island had its own potable water supply, which was fed from rivers upstate, and enough arable farmland to grow its own food crops, with some surplus to export to the nearby coastal cities—or what was left of them. The fact that smaller populations had smaller needs was an undeniable reality of the new era.

Another local advantage was the island's close and easy access to the ocean, with both inshore and offshore fishing, as well as readily available oysters, clams and crabs in the bays and estuaries. With only one intact bridge over to the South Carolina mainland, the island's security had been preserved during the worst of the chaos that had swept the country. This is why we'd made the island our home base, with my schooner filling a niche transporting cargos up and down the coast—but not for much longer. Our time there was drawing to a close.

Hilton Sapelo seemed to be reading my mind. He smiled and asked, "So, where are you sailing off to? Where are you going to find that's better than here? You know that we turn people away at the bridge every day, and you make a nice living with your boat. So why leave?"

I compared Captain Sapelo to the Doctor Aleman of my memory. My old friend Victor had sat across this table from me thousands of times. Captain Hilton Sapelo was shorter, and with a rounder face, but he wore similar wire-rimmed glasses, and he also had a closely-trimmed gray beard.

"Who said we were leaving?" I replied.

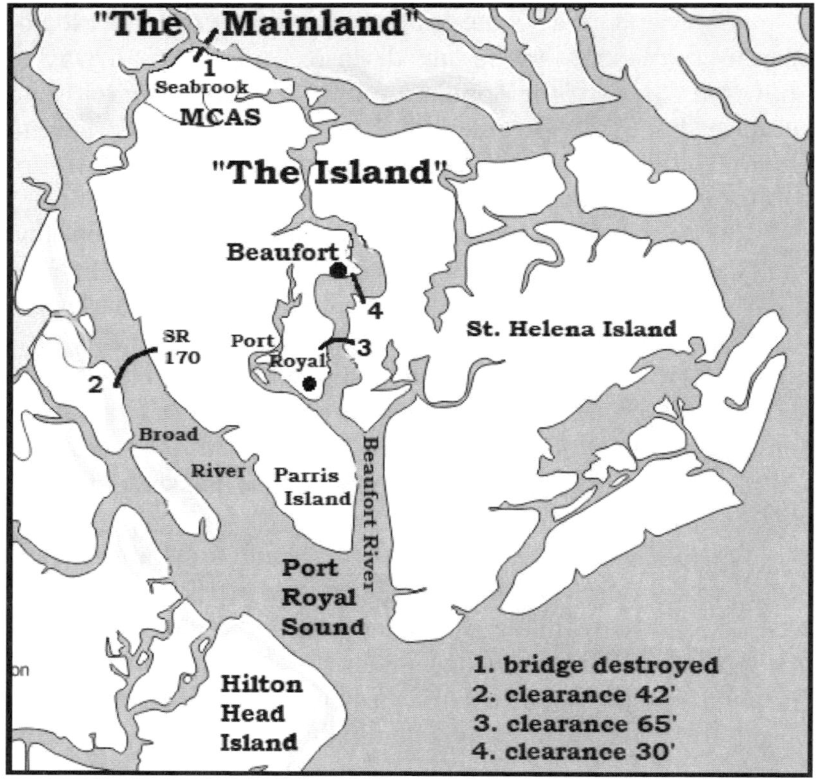

"Who said? Well, for one thing, in over twenty years I've never had a client who was fussier than you about his compass deviation. And not only in my adjusting it, but in learning how to adjust it yourself. My other clients are happy to let me do it again in a year or two. And there have been a few rumors."

"Oh? Rumors? What kind of rumors?" I'd been careful to avoid telegraphing any advance notice of our plans.

"Well, let's just say there's a few people who think your schooner might not be around the island much longer."

He wasn't wrong, but how could he know this? In fact, there were two families I'd been in discussions with. Couples with children, and one young couple with no children, at least not yet. The final decisions hadn't been made. Mostly it had been in the realm of the hypothetical, with broad hints being dropped while I'd been feeling them out. Plus, I didn't want to leave before the end of the hurricane season, not when we were going to sail straight out into the Atlantic. But I couldn't make a flat denial; Hilton Sapelo knew too much for that.

"Okay, there might be something to it, but I hope you can keep this between us, all right? Yes, it's true. We're leaving."

"I thought so. And you're taking the machine gun, right?"

"Of course I am. Why wouldn't I?"

"Well, the militia might have another idea about that."

This new angle was completely unexpected. "Hilton, I'm not part of the militia. Sure, okay, I fly the South Carolina flag—but that's it. I never joined the militia."

The flag on our stern was indeed the white-on-blue South Carolina palmetto tree with the white crescent in the top left corner, and now a white five-pointed star hand-stitched in the top right, signifying the independence of the Palmetto State. (As if anybody outside of South Carolina gave a single damn about its modified flag in the absence of a functioning federal government. Or even a functioning state government, for that matter. But for some reason it mattered to the locals.)

To me, flying the blue palmetto flag simply meant fewer hassles when anchoring or tying up at various public docks, and for moving about freely when sailing between Savannah and Charleston. Some boats flew other flags, such as those of Texas or Florida. The red Marine Corp flag was still seen a lot, owing to the many USMC veterans living on the island that had long been home to the Parris Island boot camp and the Marine Corps Air Station. Some boats flew the flags of other nations, or even the old Confederate battle flag. This had become a symbol of resistance to the federal government, which, of course, was by then a moot point, a dead letter.

(One flag almost never seen in South Carolina waters was the stars and stripes of the old U.S.A. There was still too much bitterness, even anger, following America's collapse, and the terrible years that had followed its disintegration.)

Sapelo said, "You might not consider yourself part of the militia, but there are those who disagree. 'Every armed vessel in these waters,' and so forth and so on."

"You mean Colonel Dalton Dorchester's militia? I heard he got out of the Marine Corps as a major, so who promoted him to full-bird colonel? Himself? His drinking buddies? Who put him in charge of the whole damn county?"

"Dan, at this point, what difference does it make? I guess his guns put him in charge, because his men got to the armories first. That was smart, you have to admit. You weren't here, but the fuel from the air station kept us going during the worst of it when the electrical grid went down. Major or colonel, it was Dorchester who took control when the U.S. military folded up and all those fancy generals disappeared in the tall grass. What matters is that he believes his militia has the authority, and so do all his men. They have the gun trucks and the gunboats, and they control all the bridges. That's why he's in charge."

"Well, they don't control *my* boat."

"Maybe not while you serve their interests, and certainly not while you're donating a drum of fuel every time you come back from Charleston. But if they knew you were leaving here for good, well, that might be another matter."

"How do you know all of this?" I had told nobody about our fuel contributions to the militia. These were made on the quiet on the Port Royal wharf, when Rebel was tied alongside being unloaded. It was just good politics, that's all. In some ports it was called *baksheesh*. In others it was called *mordida*, or "the bite," but by any name it was the universal grease that kept the wheels of commerce turning.

"Dan, there aren't many secrets that can be kept on the island. For instance, I know that you traded a drum of gasoline for two hundred rounds of ammunition for that machine gun. You got the ammo from a friend of mine who used to run the ordnance depot at Parris Island. So maybe you're not actually in the militia, but there are those who hold that every belt-fed machine gun in Beaufort County is militia property by eminent domain, just because they say so. Including yours."

"The hell it is! I bought that twelve-point-seven in Beirut fifteen years ago. The militia must have at least a dozen fifty-caliber Brownings they took out of Parris Island. They even have one on the bridge not two miles south of here. I see that gun truck parked on the bridge almost every time I go under it. What's my old Russian Dushka got to do with them?"

"It doesn't matter, Dan, it's just what they believe. They believe that every belt-fed machine gun in the county belongs to the militia. One way or the other."

"Not this one. I brought it here with me, and I'm taking it out when I go. I never got to vote on any damn militia. They're just a bunch of low-country redneck yahoos. So as far as I'm concerned, the Beaufort County Militia can all go to hell."

"Slow down, Dan, slow down. That's too simplistic. You have to look at the big picture. There's a reason why the island is doing as well as it is, and that reason is the militia. Without the militia, we would have been overrun the first year. Even now the militia keeps out the refugees, except for the ones that we want. There's no disease on the island, and there's no bandit gangs, and that's only because of the militia. It's not as black and white as you make it out to be."

"Black and white? That's pretty funny. You know, Hilton, over the past two years I haven't seen one black face on the island. Not one! So tell me just how the hell did *that* happen?"

He sighed, and spoke quietly. "It was a lot worse on the mainland. Charleston and Savannah? You can't even imagine what happened there. This was before you arrived. It was ugly, and it was racial. Oh, yes, it was racial—among other things. There were massacres and atrocities. Nobody's denying it. But it wasn't nearly as bad down here on the island."

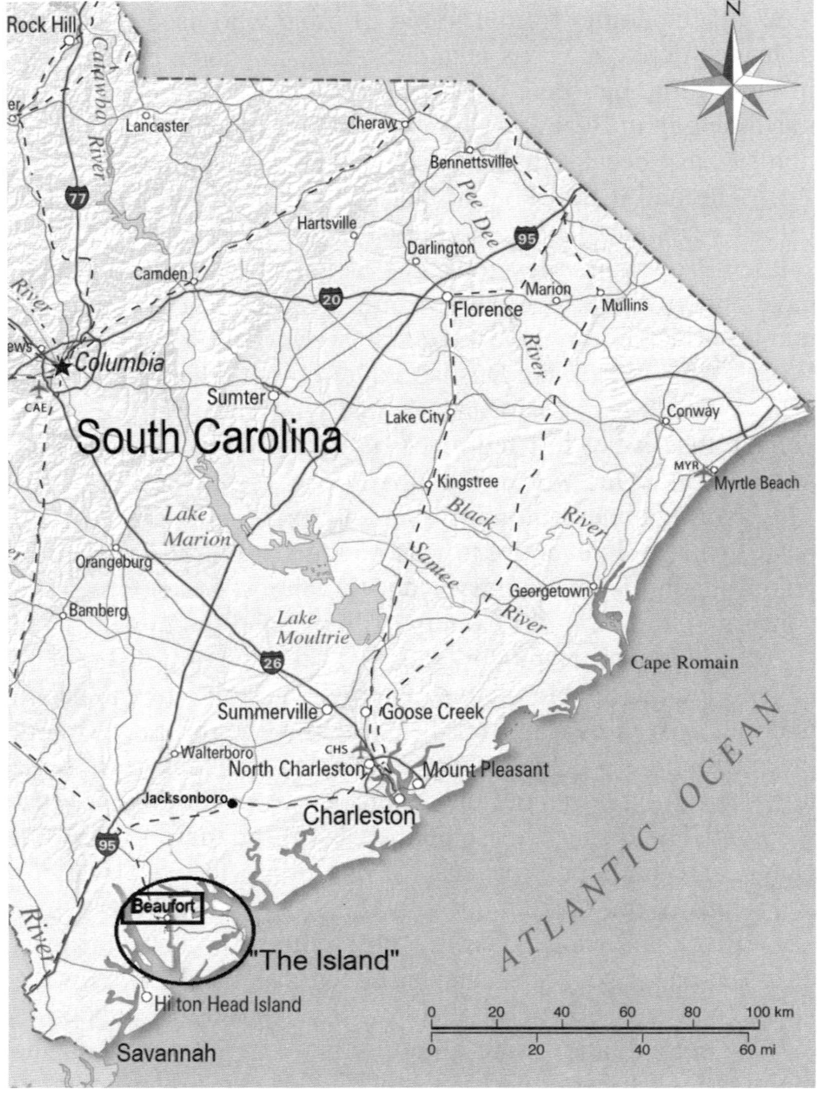

"People say that there was a lot of . . . cannibalism."

"Not on the island. Well, maybe a little, but what can you expect with no food coming in? I mean zero food, nothing, so who knows what people did in their own homes? The real cannibalism was all over on the mainland, in Charleston and Savannah. All the big cities, I suppose. In some places it actually became organized. People were rounded up and kept in pens like sheep or cattle. White people, mostly, or so they say. So what would you expect after that? People turning the other cheek? Showing forgiveness? No. It's impossible. That kind of rage, stacked up on top of constant fear and starvation? It burns like a wildfire. It has to burn itself out, there's just no other way. Anyway, what happened back then, it's all in the past, and now things are a lot better. These days it's safer for everybody, for blacks and for whites both."

"But just not on the island—not if you're black."

He sighed again. "You weren't here, Dan. Whatever happened—and it was bad—it's all in the past now. Let the dead bury the dead. Life goes on for the living. Think of the kids. These days the militia keeps the peace, or at least they keep the refugees off the island, and that keeps out the gangs and the diseases. And it was Colonel Dorchester who helped get the militias up and running in Jasper and Hampton County—and that's why we have safe, clean water on the island. Where did you think our water comes from? From magic? Well, it's not magic. I'm telling you: no militia, no safe drinking water."

Hilton had a point there. Between Virginia and Beaufort it was extremely rare to find readily accessible potable water. Anybody who has tried to live off captured rainwater for all their needs for any length of time knows what a struggle it is.

He continued. "You've only lived here for what, almost two years? Then you know it's better here on the island than almost anywhere else, so what good does it do to bring up the past? Anyway, you should know they consider this vessel to be part of the militia's reserve auxiliary because of two things: the belt-fed machine gun on your stern, and the blue palmetto state flag flying above it. 'Every armed vessel in these waters,' it's all in their charter. I'm just telling you how it is, Dan. That's all. Don't blame the messenger."

"Well, I never voted on any militia charter."

He sighed, exasperated. "What does that matter? You're here now, so in their eyes you're under their jurisdiction. Just be careful, that's all I'm telling you. If it gets around that you're planning a horizon job, you might get a visit from the militia—and it won't be so friendly. Dan, I've known them peckerwoods since they were boys, and they've got hard heads."

This was a lot to digest. "Well, thanks for the warning."

"Anytime, skipper. So, now that *that's* behind us, where are you heading off to—if I may be so bold as to ask?"

Gino and Sofia had paused in their galley work, listening carefully to our cross-table conversation. Tala hadn't spoken a word since sitting down beside me. I couldn't see any harm in telling him. Beyond the fact that we were leaving—which he obviously already knew—what did our destination matter?

"We're aiming for Argentina or Uruguay. Things seem to be stabilizing there. That's what I've been hearing." Meaning, that's what I'd been hearing on my single-sideband before the transmitter had blown a capacitor and half died. These had just been some rumors supposedly between boat captains, none of them personally known to me. Not much to go on.

He replied, "Dan, things seem to be stabilizing here, too."

"That may be true, but there's another problem now: the volcano. You even said it yourself, Hilton; when did you ever have snow here this early? When did you have a hard freeze in October? They say there was snow up in Boston on Labor Day, and the harvest was ruined across the entire north."

"Yes, that's true, but we got our harvest in on the island."

"This year, maybe, but it was only half of last year's, and

Laki is still erupting. It's even worse in Europe, but it goes all the way around the northern hemisphere. That means there's going to be another famine, worse than ever this time, and that means another wave of refugees will be heading south. Armed refugees, better organized, maybe even whole refugee armies. And tougher this time, smarter, because they're the survivors. Maybe more than your militia can handle. Everybody in South Carolina knows that there's food on the island. Refugees from up north will be coming even if they have to walk it, and it's only ten miles from the interstate to the top of the island."

"Dan, Dorchester's militia blew up the Seabrook Bridge at the beginning of the troubles, thank God, so they can't just walk in. Now the only way onto the island is all the way around and across the bridge from Hilton Head. The river is a mile wide there, and the militia controls every inch on both sides."

I knew the bridge carrying the four-lane State Highway 170 over the very aptly named Broad River by sight. It was over a mile across from shore to shore, but the bridge was low, only forty feet from the water up to the road deck at its highest point in the middle. This was as far as Rebel could navigate up Port Royal Sound on the western side of the island.

Rebel's tall masts similarly prevented her from traveling any further up the Beaufort River because of another bridge just a quarter mile east of the anchorage. The old iron swing-bridge from Beaufort over to Saint Helena's Island was permanently stuck in the closed position. Most of the half-mile-long bridge was supported by concrete pilings, but the section in the middle was built of riveted-iron cantilevers. Road traffic could still use it, but no vessel higher than thirty feet above the water could pass under it. This bridge joined the two biggest parts of what locals called "the island."

As it was, Rebel Yell could just manage to fit under the high bridge across the Beaufort River two miles south of the anchorage. Like the old swing bridge next to Beaufort, this concrete span connected different parts of the island. Its 65-foot clearance made it a critical choke point for my schooner.

There was usually a militia gun truck parked right on top, armed with a Browning 50-caliber machine gun. And as if that wasn't enough, the militia had outboard-powered runabouts carrying pintle-mounted belt-fed 7.62mm machine guns. Their mission was to prevent outsiders from sneaking onto the island anywhere except across the only remaining connection to the mainland, the mile-long State Road 170 Bridge over to Hilton Head. According to local lore, the militia did not fire warning shots. If they caught a mainlander sneaking in, they were used for target practice. The sharks and the crabs did the rest.

These militia boats didn't stay out on the water running patrols; there just wasn't enough fuel to allow them that. They were docked where they could get underway quickly in response to any reported incursion attempts. Their militia crews lived nearby. These boats passed us fairly often, but we just waved and moved along on our own separate missions.

Most of the island's surrounding coasts consisted of tidal mud flats and sawgrass marshland that not even the toughest Marines would attempt to cross. Shallow-draft boats could drop somebody off near the shore, but that would not prevent them from sinking waist-deep into the black glue-like "pluff mud." Even if they somehow managed to crawl through the mud, they would then face hundreds of yards of razor-edged sawgrass, and more mud in the tidal streams and creeks interlaced through the marshes, before they ever touched dry land. Mother Nature had provided the island with formidable natural defenses.

Most of the mainland refugees who'd been allowed onto the island were put to work as field labor to earn their keep. Farmers were relearning how to work the land with manpower and animals replacing lost technology. It was common to see horses and mules pulling plows, but always with men steering them up and down their furrows. Another common sight was long lines of men and women working the fields with hoes, in between planting and harvesting by hand in the spring and fall.

But in my view, the nearly constant autumn rains, and the shortened growing season from the increasing cold, could only mean renewed famine and starvation in the coming year. The island's fallow fields were flooded, and still the rain fell nearly every day. And if the growing conditions were going to be bad the next year in coastal South Carolina, then they were going to be much worse further north up the east coast of America.

"Hilton, that volcano shows no sign of letting up. Laki can erupt for months, even for years. It did this in the 1780s, and a lot of historians think that it caused the famines that led to the French Revolution. No, I'm done here. I've seen enough. We're sailing down to South America. That Laki hasn't affected the Southern Hemisphere at all. That's why I needed our compass to be as accurate as possible: without GPS, it's all we have for steering, and as we both know all too well, getting a compass corrected on an iron boat is a real bitch."

"Yes," Hilton replied, "steel boats are a challenge, even for me. So, how are you with a sextant?"

"I'm pretty good. At least, I'm as good as I can be just shooting noon sights without a chronometer. I've been trying to find a station for a time signal, but now my single-sideband is crippled. Jesus . . . I thought we'd put this behind us centuries ago—and now we're back to sailing latitudes."

This was why the church bells and all of our mechanical clocks were set locally. Without trains rolling or planes flying, there wasn't a need for precise time coordination on a regional much less a national basis. But this also meant that boats could only determine their latitude, but not their longitude.

He added, "And now you don't have a working autopilot, and that's why you need more crew, am I right?"

He knew I had no autopilot because we'd been steering by hand all day while swinging the compass. This meant motoring back and forth across Port Royal Sound on precisely mapped courses while he worked his magic on our magnetic compass. Rebel's autopilot and its electronic compass had burnt out three years earlier while we were bashing our way south around Cape Hatteras against waves like green walls.

"Yeah, more crew, because we're going to have to hand-steer every mile of the way. It's over 6,000 nautical miles to Buenos Aires by the shipping routes, but allowing for tacking against the wind, and having to get plenty of easting before we turn south, it's going to be at least 8,000 miles before it's all done. If we average five knots—and that's optimistic—then we're talking about two months at sea. At a bare minimum."

Sapelo whistled softly, and then said, "I heard something at church about the Walkers going with you."

Oh, sweet Jesus, I thought. First the militia was dogging my ass, and now a critical failure of operational security. And were these both connected in some unknown way? I took a deep breath, and said, "Hilton, I'd really rather not discuss it."

I had told Jim and Judy Walker to keep their mouths shut about our evolving plans. Now we were going to have to take off sooner instead of later, before our imminent departure was being announced on every VHF channel, and we had a dozen would-be passengers lined up. And Dorchester's militia might be at front of the line planning to confiscate my Dushka.

I was so angry at hearing the Walker name spoken at my table that I thought of crossing them off the list. But Jim was a physician and Judy was an emergency room nurse, and both could sail. Neither of them got seasick, another big plus. Jim had even made a run up to Charleston with us on the outside.

It was only because of their valuable skills that they'd been allowed straight onto the island as residents, instead of spending at least a year as indentured farm labor, or working on reconstruction projects. The Beaufort Militia and the private Beaufort Farm Council ran the V.I.W. program. This stood for Voluntary Indentured Worker.

Sitting beside me, Tala listened attentively but in silence. This would not be her first time escaping from a hostile port, but she instinctively knew when not to intrude. Gino and Sofia pretended to work in the galley across from the dinette table, but they were also paying close attention to our every word.

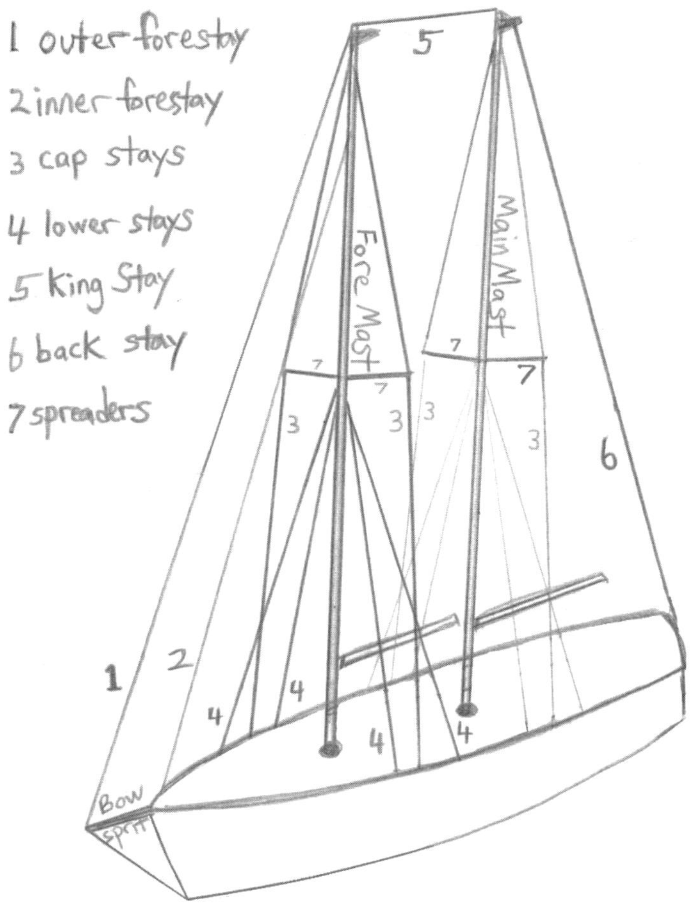

"Dan, I noticed that your rigging wire looks worn out. Is it up to a long voyage?"

"There's nothing I can do about the rigging. I'll try not to stress it too much. Maybe we can get new wire in Argentina."

"I see that you have deck-stepped masts." He pointed to the six-inch diameter vertical section of pipe just on the other side of the pilothouse ladder. This steel pillar was painted white to blend with the white surfaces of the galley area. It was welded to the bottom of the deck and the top of the keel, but only the part between the ceiling panel and the floor was visible. What Sapelo was implying was that deck-stepped masts were not as strong as keel-stepped masts that were supported both at the keel and again at the deck.

"This is how she was set up when I got her. I know they're stronger when they're keel-stepped, but when they're deck-stepped they use a thicker mast and bigger wire to compensate. And there are some benefits too. I don't have two giant holes in the deck for the masts like keel-stepped boats. My entire deck is welded steel, and it's one-hundred-percent watertight from bow to stern. And deck-stepped masts are real easy to pull with any boatyard crane. I've had them off and on at least a half-dozen times, and it's a piece of cake.

"And in the worst-cast scenario, if you're going to be dismasted in a storm, I just want the thing gone. You can cut the shrouds and the lines and the mast will sink, instead of beating against your hull in the waves. I've even seen a boat that had its mast wrapped all the way around its hull when it capsized. They were lucky it happened close to port where they could get help. But I take your point that I'm just relying on that old rigging wire to hold them up. Believe me, I'll be cautious."

"You'll surely need to be. If I was surveying this boat for an insurance company or a buyer like back in the old days, I'd condemn your wire—but I guess I'm not telling you anything you don't already know. How clean is your hull?"

"At least we're good there—we careened her two weeks ago and scraped her bottom. It's about as smooth as it'll ever be until we can find a boatyard with anti-fouling paint."

The tidal range in coastal South Carolina was enough to let boats dry out on a low tide so the barnacles and other growth could be scraped from their hulls. The difference between a smooth bottom and one covered in barnacles and grass could be measured directly in knots of speed gained or lost.

"How are you set for diesel?"

The refined fuel tankers from Louisiana had not come to Charleston since last August. The arrivals of the small ships and ocean barges, which had been coming once or twice a month, were never announced in advance. Instead, they just showed up in Charleston, along with their private escorts, old patrol craft and converted oil rig crew boats, now armed to the teeth. These escort vessels were necessary protection from piracy.

Charleston had been a major fuel distribution point for the region, and the empty tanks at the Cooper River fuel terminal were always ready to accept new deliveries. Businessmen who had survived the decade-long disaster were attempting to re-suscitate a modern economy, and liquid fuel was essential. Over the summer we'd heard that the power grid was up again in Louisiana. There was even some talk of the militia escorting tanker trucks from Charleston to Beaufort. This talk had been a cause for optimism, but since September the fuel shipments to Charleston had stopped. I knew this very well, because drums of fuel had been our most valuable cargo.

Plastic barrels of butter, cheese, corn, peanuts and other local produce went the other way to trade for the fuel at two or three to one. It was always a complicated transaction, and with many shifty middlemen, but it had been profitable. And it was popular: every steel drum of fuel brought to Beaufort and Port Royal was a boost to the local economy. A farm tractor did the work of dozens of men without needing to be fed or housed. A generator could run a machine shop. Kerosene lamps provided light at night. But when the next tanker or fuel barge pushed by an ocean tug might arrive was anybody's guess. Maybe never. All of the talk about tanker trucks delivering fuel to Beaufort had dried up, and last summer's optimism had been replaced by gloom heading into the winter.

Our profit had come in keeping a percentage of our cargo, so we were better set than most would have been to launch an ocean voyage. Hilton Sapelo knew how we earned our living, so I didn't see any reason not to disclose our fuel situation.

"My diesel tanks are more than half full. Plus I have a few drums of gasoline and motor oil for trading purposes." This made me a wealthy man on the island, and this was another reason for the militia to take an interest. And this liquid wealth didn't account for some one-ounce gold coins, or a few plastic jars full of so-called junk silver, mostly pre-1964 American quarters. (Some of the old paper dollars and euros were kept as souvenirs, or curiosities used to educate our children.)

Hilton stared at me as if deep in contemplation. Then he said, "Dan, you were going to pay me five gallons of diesel, and I spent twice as much time here as I planned to."

"So, you want more than five gallons? Okay, no problem, you'll get it when Adam picks you up. He can pump the fuel into your cans." Since I'd told him how much diesel fuel we had on board, I could hardly refuse to give him a little extra.

He took in a breath, and slowly exhaled. "I've changed my mind. You can keep the fuel. I don't want it. I want something else for my work today."

"And what's that?" I wasn't surprised by this latest twist. A deal was rarely concluded on its original terms.

"I want you to take Adam with you on your voyage."

This took me aback. "Adam? What about his mother?"

"My niece? She's an alcoholic. She's not going to make it. No, what I mean is, what I mean is she'll be better off here, and not having to look after Adam. He'll be better off too, a lot better off, if he goes with you. So take Adam with you, when you go. Do that, and we're all square, and then some."

Wow. This took a moment. "What about you, Hilton?"

He settled into his seat and sighed, looking down at his folded hands. "Honestly, I feel like I've pretty much run my course. Dan, I'm plumb worn out. I don't have the energy for another turn around the track. I'll look after his mother, and with the good Lord's help, we'll get by."

This presented a lot to think about. Taking Adam meant another adjustment to the temporary quarters being set up in the hold, minus the space already occupied by metal drums of fuel, plastic barrels of food and other crates and boxes of more food, rigging, engine parts, sails and trade items.

Well, we'd just have to make do, that's all. And young

Adam seemed to be a natural-born sailor, even at fifteen years old. Another steady hand behind the wheel would be a plus, at least in settled weather. He'd also bring the sharp eyes and energy of his youth.

"All right, Hilton, we'll take him. He seems like a fine young man. And he's close to Rita's age: it'll do them both good to have a companion on the voyage."

Then a new idea struck me. "Do you need Adam's sailing pram, if he's gone? Throw in the dinghy, and I'll give you ten gallons of diesel for it." That much fuel would provide Hilton Sapelo and Adam's mother with nighttime lantern light, and maybe even keep them from freezing through the coldest nights of winter if they had a kerosene heater, as most of the locals did. Depending on their intended use, kerosene and diesel fuel were generally interchangeable.

Hilton Sapelo brightened at the prospect, extending his hand. "Make it fifteen gallons, and you have a deal. It's an excellent dinghy, top notch. I rigged it myself."

"Okay, fifteen gallons—but in your fuel cans." I shook his hand across the table while we held knowing eye contact. We were discussing much more than a dinghy and some fuel.

Sofia asked us both, "Does this mean you two are finally finished talking? Are you ready to eat?" She ladled the fish chowder into bowls and Gino carried them to the dinette table, along with a basket of cornbread, spoons and cloth napkins.

I slid all the way in to make room for Sofia next to Tala, and Gino sat next to Hilton facing aft.

The meal laid out, we all took hands around the table and lowered our heads. Gino said the blessing. It was our custom to take turns, but more often than not it was Gino.

It was blessing of gratitude for the hot food before us. A blessing for our good health. A blessing for the voyagers, for the people of the island, and for the people of the world. And especially a blessing for all the children, that in time they might prosper and have happy, healthy children of their own.

In Jesus' name, Amen.

3

Just after dawn I was on deck scanning the anchorage, part of my morning routine. I could tell by lining up various landmarks that we hadn't dragged anchor, nor had any other boats dragged or swung too close to us. Tala and the others were still down below, sleeping or staying warm under their covers. It was gray and misting, almost a drizzle, so I threw our big canvas tarpaulin over the main boom, tying its corners to the lifelines and stern pulpit to form a tent. Even if the rain began to come down hard, and it looked as if it might, it would keep the cockpit area dry from over the pilothouse to the aft deck.

The floor of the pilothouse was two steps below the cockpit, so it had standing headroom inside. This meant that the helmsman behind the wheel could see forward over the pilothouse when he was steering the boat. Our Caterpillar diesel lived in the engine room directly below the pilothouse. The old Cat never bitched about the lack of standing headroom, but the human crew who had to work on her always did.

An island of dryness under the cockpit tarp boosted crew morale on drizzly autumn days. The tan fabric blocked the rain while letting much of the light through. The pilothouse could become cramped, especially when its old Plexiglas windows were fogged with condensation.

The dry cockpit was a nice place to sip hot chicory or mint tea without needing to get into waterproof gear. Real coffee or tea would have been better, but who had any? But even those substitutes would have to wait until somebody lit up the galley stove and heated some water for the morning's thermos.

Before it was even fully light out I spotted Adam's red sail going up at the dinghy dock. After dropping off Rita the night before, we'd put the offer to him to join Rebel's voyage crew, and he'd said yes after only a moment of surprise.

When his boat was ready it only took him a minute to sail it across the anchorage. There was another five-gallon metal Jerry can and two smaller red plastic containers in his boat. He tied off his dinghy and set the jugs on the boarding platform, and then he asked, "Permission to come aboard, sir."

The boy was well trained. I had to credit Captain Sapelo for that. "Permission granted."

He stepped from his bobbing pram over onto the platform and climbed up the transom, ducked under the awning, then stepped down into the cockpit. This was my first look at him face to face. Wavy blonde hair, bright blue eyes and a freshly scrubbed face that had never seen a razor . . . but soon would. He was wearing a green raincoat with its hood folded back, old blue jeans, and ratty sneakers. We would need to find him some better footwear if he was joining our crew.

He had a firm handshake for a boy of fifteen, and held eye contact. Not too skinny; I guessed he had some meat on him, but it was hard to tell in his rain gear over sweaters. I thought maybe he'd go near six feet if he stayed healthy and well fed, but he had a long way to go, and nothing was guaranteed.

"Adam," I said, "you've had the night to reconsider what we spoke of. This is a serious decision, and it's yours to make. Yours and yours alone. Not your uncle, and not your mother."

"No sir—I mean, yes, I understand: it's my decision. So yes, I do want go with you, and I don't care where. I just want to get off the island. There's no future for me here."

His voice was stuck in that awkward phase between boy and man, but it was pleasant enough. He sounded earnest, and he looked me in the eye when he spoke.

"Good. Let me give you a tour of the topsides, and then we'll fill your cans." He followed me around the pilothouse along the starboard side. Rebel's decks were wet from the drizzle. The space between the two masts was occupied by our launch, stowed upright in its wooden chocks. Matching Rebel Yell, it was painted black on the outside, and white around the gunnels and inside, but just then it had a canvas cover over it to keep out the rain. It was tan, like the cockpit tarp.

"This is Whisper, our dinghy. Rebel Yell and Whisper, get it? It's fiberglass like yours. We have a couple kayaks and old inflatables in the hold for backups, but nothing like this one here. We can sail it or row it, but most of the time we use the outboard motor. It's pretty big, sixteen feet, so it's kind of a hassle getting it in and out of the water, but it can carry all seven of us in flat water. Of course, Rita and the twins don't weigh much, they add up to maybe one big adult. We use the foremast boom to swing it out over the water and lower it down. That's why I was interested in your pram; it'll fit across our swim platform flat against the transom. It won't be able to carry all of us, but it'll be a lot handier to get it in and out of the water and stow it there."

"Yes, sir, that makes sense."

I let him "sir" me. He was just fifteen, I was over forty, and I was the boat owner and captain. We continued our tour.

"The mast in the back is called the mainmast, even though it's the same height as the foremast. That's just how they're called on equal-masted schooners, the main and foremast. We raise and lower the foresail and the main with these winches on the masts. Do you know about raising sails like these?"

"Yes, sir. The halyard lines haul them up, and the winches give you the power to get them all the way up when the sails are too heavy to pull up by hand. Each sail has a halyard; they go over a pulley on top of the mast. When you pull the halyard down, the sail goes up, and when you let the halyard go the sail comes down. I know all about sheets and halyards."

"Good. When our dinghy is in the water, we can open the cargo hatch. The cargo hatch is split in two parts and each half swings out to the side: you can see the hinges."

"How big is it when it's open? About seven by seven?"

"That's right. It's just over two meters on a side, or ten feet from corner to corner. Now, that white box in front of the foremast is called the scuttle hatch. That's how we get down into the forward compartment. See how the two little doors are latched open around the sides? That's so the back of the hatch can be left open for ventilation. Then you slide the top of the scuttle forward so you can go down the ladder."

Adam said, "It works like the companionway hatch at the front of the cockpit on a regular sailboat."

"Correct. In rough weather offshore, we seal it up tight to keep the waves out. Down below is where Rita lives with her mom and dad. And up there on the bow is where the primary anchor is stowed on that roller, but now you only see the chain because the anchor is set. And that little machine is the anchor windlass, it pulls up the chain. Simple stuff, right?"

"Yes, sir. Your boat is bigger than what I'm used to, but I've crewed on lots of boats, even on a forty-footer going up to Charleston. I know how your jibs work too: the one here on the bow and the one out on the bowsprit. The jib out on the end of the bowsprit is on a roller-furler and it rolls in and out. It's wrapped around your forestay when it's put away like it is now. The one right here is clipped to the forestay wire and it goes up when you pull its halyard line back on the mast. I've done both kinds of jibs a million times on other boats." He pointed to the various parts as he described them.

"Okay, Adam, you're hired. Welcome aboard. Now, let's go get your uncle his diesel fuel. We have a 12-volt pump with a long hose that reaches down into our diesel tank and back to the boarding platform. I'll get it all set up and show you how it works, and then you can do the pumping. Just try not to make a mess of it, because it makes the boat smell like diesel."

He smiled. "I *like* the smell of diesel, Captain Kilmer."

I agreed with him, although Tala did not. Diesel made the engine run, so it made Rebel go, and it ran the generator that charged the house batteries that ran almost everything else. In those days, what man didn't love the smell of diesel? If you had plenty of diesel fuel, well, you were good to go.

When his full jugs were back in his dinghy, he asked me, "Why is your machine gun on the back, instead of the front?"

"It's a good question. It's because we're slow, and almost anybody out to mess with us is going to be faster than we are. That means it'll always be a chase, and the best we can do is keep our stern to them. That's why the big gun is back here."

"That makes sense. Have you ever had to use it for real?"

"Oh, yeah. You'll hear all about it, but not right now."

"Can I see it? Can you take the cover off?"

"Not in port. In port we always keep it covered, level, and tied off straight back. That shows we have no bad intentions. If I take the cover off in the anchorage, it might upset some of the nervous Nellies." Actually, I doubted that anybody would be bothered, but it might arouse unwanted curiosity about us at a time when I wanted to minimize it.

"Yes, sir, I understand. I'll be back as soon as I can. Back to stay, I mean. I'll be back this morning for sure."

"We'll be here. Give your uncle my best regards."

Adam sailed off toward the dinghy landing a few hundred yards north, just past the marina. I watched him through my binoculars as he carried the fuel containers up the ramp onto the parking lot in just two trips, loaded them onto a wagon, and pulled it away out of my sight. Not a weakling, and a very bright boy. Beaufort's loss was Rebel Yell's gain.

I scanned slowly across the town's waterfront park, from the marina on the west side over to the iron swing bridge to the east. More than a dozen vendors were already setting up their tables and canopies. It was Saturday, the big shopping day in Beaufort, and some drizzle wouldn't stop it.

Market day was locally important both as a commercial and a social event. Boats of all sizes were moving through the anchorage under power and sail. Almost every part of the quay wall along the waterfront was occupied by a trading vessel of one sort or another. We had spent our share of Saturdays tied alongside that quay.

When the church bell rang nine o'clock Rita was in the cockpit knitting away on her newest sweater project. It was unusual for her to be up so early, but I'd guessed why, so I wasn't at all surprised that she was the first to observe a red sail being hoisted over at the dinghy dock. She set aside her needles and yarn and stepped down into the pilothouse and called down the ladder, "He's coming, mother, Adam is coming!"

Few land-dwelling friends ever grow as close as a crew living within the confines of a boat surrounded for weeks on end by the empty horizon. Going for a long walk to get a little solitary personal time is not an option.

Countless hours are spent immersed in deeply personal and even philosophical conversations while standing the night watch in the cockpit beneath a canopy of stars. The shared stress of enduring stormy weather strengthens the bonds that are forged. On the other hand, petty grievances about undesirable personal habits can grow into bitter festering feuds if they are not addressed head on.

It's difficult to convey the significance of a long-time crew member leaving a voyaging boat for the last time. Such a departure can attain the solemnity of a funeral, or of a family member or close friend going off to war. I still felt the absence of Victor and Tran Hung every day. Conversely, a new person joining our seafaring clan was a serious event in the memory log of the old steel schooner that I had renamed Rebel Yell.

So when Adam's dinghy reached our swim platform, all of us were in the cockpit or standing on the aft deck to greet him. He tied off his boat and dropped its sail, then he tossed a pair of duffel bags onto the platform. Then he stepped aboard and looked up at all of us, seeming a bit overwhelmed.

I said, "Well, don't just stand there gawking, pass up your stuff and climb aboard."

Once Adam was in the cockpit, Gino shook his hand and said, "Welcome aboard. I know you're going to like it here."

Rita shook his hand and then stepped behind her mother.

Sofia said, “Adam, we’re home-schooling Rita. How far are you in your studies?”

“I, um, I started school again this year. But I missed some time. Actually, as a matter of fact . . . I missed a few years.”

“Well, don’t worry. Rita says you’re very smart.”

“He is!” she agreed. “I mean, yes you are, you’re smart. And you’ll like home-schooling. We have everything.”

I’d already spent some time with him earlier when he’d come for the fuel, so I said, “Rita, why don’t you give Adam a quick tour of the boat down below. Bow to stern, but just for, oh, ten minutes, okay? We have things to do this morning. He can leave his bags in the hold; we’ll sort all that out later.”

“Come on, Adam, just follow me,” she said. They both disappeared inside and below.

Tala said, “It’s good that they get along. I haven’t seen Rita so happy in a long time.”

Gino added, “And for just fifteen gallons of fuel, we get a dinghy and a sailor. Boss, I think you made a very good deal.”

“I think so too.” Then I addressed the rest of the crew who were still in the cockpit. “We don’t all need to go ashore at the same time. And if we use Adam’s dinghy, we won’t have to put Whisper in the water. If the wind holds from this direction, it’ll be an easy reach to the dinghy landing and back.”

I looked at Tala and Sofia; they were dressed in frumpy frayed robes over their pajamas. I said,“I think you should go ashore first, so you can get the first choice at the food tents.”

Sofia stretched, yawned and responded, “I think we can be ready in maybe a half an hour.”

“No,” said Tala, shaking her head. “At least one hour.”

Sofia nodded her agreement. “Yes, one hour is better.”

It was market day in Beaufort, and the ladies would not be seen ashore if they were not looking their best, even at the risk of missing out on the freshest and best produce. I’d long since given up trying to understand such matters of the female mind.

Gino said, “I need to take the heat exchanger back over to Jersey Girl. I’ll need an hour to get it installed. Adam can drop me off while you two make yourselves beautiful, and then he can pick me up after you go to shore."

"That sounds good," I replied. "Let's do that."

Tala and Sofia went below. I sat down across the cockpit from Gino. "How much work do you have after Jersey Girl?"

"That's the last job."

Gino was a magician at getting engines back in running order without any access to factory-made replacement parts. I could largely thank him for my old Caterpillar still running. His electrical knowledge was also deep, another valuable skill in that era of improvising and jury-rigging systems. He could analyze, dissect and rebuild just about anything small enough for him to haul back to Rebel Yell.

I said, "We're almost ready to shove off for Argentina. But is Sofia ready? Is Rita? This'll be their longest voyage by far."

"Boss, after Cape Hatteras, I think they're ready for anything. But steering in big waves? Tala can do it, but I think not for more than one hour, not even her. Sofia and Rita? No, not sailing in big waves. I think that Adam can steer, he's a good sailor, but he's only a boy. You need to be strong to steer for two hours in big waves."

"I agree. They can be the number-two on watch, but they can't be primary helmsmen. That means we need at least two more strong sailors who can steer for a full watch. We have as much diesel as we'll ever have, so there's no point in waiting around burning fuel in port."

"No, boss, there's no point in waiting. The sooner we go the better. But what about hurricanes? Do you think we can leave before December, with the weather crazy like it is?"

"Honestly, I don't have a clue. It's already cold here for November, but I don't know what that means for hurricanes coming up from the tropics." Like in so many areas, we were flying in the dark. There was no internet to check, no outside expert to offer an opinion. We both stared landward, taking turns with the binoculars. Market day was getting into swing.

"Okay, after Adam drops you off, Tala and Sofia will go

ashore—but they need to keep a low profile. No talk about the voyage. Nothing that looks like we're getting ready to leave."

"They can pay in silver," Gino suggested. "It'll simplify everything if they don't have to take fuel ashore today."

Old plastic soda bottles full of gasoline and diesel fuel were the most frequent trade items that we took ashore. Their narrow mouths meant there was no need for a funnel to pour their contents into a merchant's container. Clear bottles were preferred because the fuel was visible for pre-sale inspection.

Tala and Sofia were used to taking the bottles ashore, but they hated it, because they were heavy and they stunk. Usually they'd hand over a bottle and let the vendor do the pouring.

I said, "Sure, good idea, they can use silver today, as long as they're careful. They know what we need, right?"

"Yes, of course. If they can find it, they'll buy it."

"It's November, so there's not much that's fresh. Butter, eggs, onions, carrots, potatoes . . . they know what to look for. Cheese, honey, jelly, jam, pepper, spices, anything like that. New yeast for baking. Apples, all we can find. We're going to be at sea for a long time."

Gino smiled. "We can do it, boss, we *will* do it, and then, South America! And that means coffee, *real* coffee. Oh, we're going to *swim* in Brazilian coffee!"

"Okay, but now before you go, let's talk about the rest of the day. I'm going to meet Luke and Jessie, and they're going to come out to see the boat before they make their decision."

Luke and Jessie Hanahan were a married couple in their late twenties, fit and healthy, but with no kids yet. In time they could make great crew, even though they had no sailing experience. Jessie looked strong and seemed brave enough to steer out in big waves, but there was no way to know in advance.

"I like them both," said Gino. "And they're musicians, so that's good too. But what do we do if they get too seasick, and they don't get their sea legs? We won't be able to come back."

Chronic seasickness could kill you by dehydration. Some people were unable to retain any fluids even after days at sea, especially in rough weather, and rough weather was absolutely guaranteed on the open Atlantic in November and December.

I said, "We'll take them out for a sail, maybe tomorrow, and then they'll have to decide. That leaves the Walkers and the Edmunds; they're both still maybes. I'll see the Walkers at church tomorrow. They need to know it's time to decide, especially that Judy. But it's going to be tricky, because they don't know about our offer to the Edmunds. I'll have to feel them out. I might see them ashore at the market."

This was the classic pre-voyage crew hunt. If you invited only as many as you optimally desired, you'd invariably have last-minute no-shows, and you'd depart undermanned. But if you overbooked, they'd all show up, and then you'd need to disinvite somebody. And we were dealing with families with adolescent children. The cargo hold was going to be packed.

The situation was made even more difficult by the fact that the militia might be sniffing around. I could not risk making a VHF call to arrange a meeting with any of the potential crew. Not with half the island listening in. We'd have to meet at the Saturday market or after church on Sunday, but all while keeping up our normal patterns of living.

4

Adam dropped off Gino and returned. The pram's slackened spritsail rig was docile behind Rebel's high transom. Tala and Sofia were standing on the aft deck with me, waiting. They were both dressed for the market day ashore wearing colorful scarves, sweaters and skirts. After a few days spent aboard, they were eager to put their feet on terra firma. We all were, especially with the long voyage looming ahead.

Normally I'd be giving them canvas tote bags loaded with plastic bottles of fuel to haul ashore. Instead, I handed each of them a leather draw-string purse containing ten dollars in old silver coins, mostly quarters and dimes. The silver came as a surprise, and Tala gave me a hug and peppered my face with kisses. The drizzle had stopped and the sky was clearing. After looking carefully in all directions both ladies went back down below to modify their attire for the improving conditions.

I took the opportunity to climb down onto the boarding platform to have a word with Adam while sizing up his pram. At eleven feet long and five wide, it could be stowed on edge resting on the platform without jutting out past Rebel's hull to either side. It would be completely secure there when it was lashed in place with its bottom facing away from the transom.

One downside of carrying the pram there would be our inability to look out of the aft cabin's two transom portholes. This wasn't a major loss; the opening ports would still provide ventilation. Another disadvantage would be our inability to get down onto the swim platform when it was stowed there. Even so, it would be a worthwhile tradeoff to have his pram ready to launch in just a fraction of the time that it would take to splash the longer and heavier Whisper, stowed on deck amidships.

Adam spoke first, while I was still studying his dinghy and comparing its size to our swim platform. "Gino told me that I'm going to take the women ashore as soon as they're ready."

"What? Who? I think you mean *Mr. Bracciano.*"

"No, sir. He said to call him Gino."

"He might have, but I didn't! He's Mr. Bracciano to you unless you're off together on your pram, then you do what he tells you and call him anything he likes. But just to be clear: to you, the ladies are Mrs. Kilmer and Mrs. Burgos, or ma'am. And I'm Captain Kilmer, or captain. And 'sir' is always good. But not skipper: you haven't earned that yet. Skipper is only for veteran crew. We're going to sea for a long voyage, and this is serious business, so I don't want to hear *Tala* or *Sofia* or *Gino* or *Dan* come out of your mouth—is that clear?"

I wasn't being harsh without a good reason. Always using the proper names aboard ship was essential to maintaining an unambiguous understanding of the chain of command. Adam had to know his place in the pecking order, which was near the bottom. And if this demonstration of my authority was going to cause him to have an emotional meltdown, I wanted to find out now, when I could send him home. On a voyage, orders had to be carried out immediately and without discussion.

Adam just smiled and said, "Yes, sir, that's what my uncle told me, to always call you Captain Kilmer. I understand, sir. It's like in the Navy, or the Marine Corps."

"That's affirmative, son. Now today I'm putting you right to work. You're going to be our water taxi today. The wind is fair, so it'll be an easy reach both ways."

"Yes sir, and it's clearing up. It's going to be a fine day."

"And just how do you know that?"

"Uncle Hilton taught me how to read the weather."

"Oh, he did, did he? What's the wind going to do next?"

"It'll keep clocking around from northeast to east."

"Hmm . . . yes, I'd say so too. And we might even see the sun by the afternoon. Now, once you drop the ladies off at the dinghy landing, swing on over to Jersey Girl, tie off, and wait there. They'll probably give you a tour of their boat, but don't ask them if you can come aboard. You let them ask you—or not. That's just how we do it, that's boat courtesy. You don't ever invite yourself aboard, okay?"

"Yes sir, I understand, I know how it works."

"And don't talk to anyone about joining our crew, or the voyage. Not a word, not to anybody. Not a single word."

"Yes sir, I understand that too. I do."

"When he's finished his work, bring Gino—I mean—Mr. Bracciano—back here. He'll need to clean up before he goes ashore, but that's okay, because I don't think we can both fit in your pram with you. But what do you think?"

"Taking both of the ladies will be easy. And you and me will be okay, but not you and me and Mr. Bracciano. This boat is rated for five hundred pounds maximum under sail. That's what Uncle Hilton said, and I think that's about right. But less is better, because with three you're always getting in each other's way, banging knees and elbows and heads. And lighter always means faster. With just me in it, I can make it plane out if there's any breeze at all, and then she'll really fly."

The boy knew what he was talking about. He might have missed some years of organized schooling, but it was obvious that Captain Sapelo had given him another form of education. Maybe one that was better suited for the time and place. Rita was right: Adam was smart. School, or no school.

I said, "It's going to be too crowded for you to stay at the dinghy dock all day. You have to just get in and out on market day, but I have a friend whose boat is on the outside corner of the marina. It's called Texas Belle; it's a 36-foot Cheoy Lee trawler. Rap on the hull, tell him you're from Rebel Yell, and tell him that Captain Kilmer sent you to wait there."

"I know the boat, but only by sight."

"Good. Herman will let you tie off to his swim platform. From there you can see the dinghy dock, the waterfront, and out across the anchorage. Keep an eye out for the ladies when they come back from shopping, so they don't have to walk all the way over to the marina and out the docks to Texas Belle."

"Yes sir, I will."

"They'll probably need to make a few trips with all the food they're buying, so it might be best to just load it up, bring it here, and then go back and get them on a separate trip. I'll leave that kind of decision for you to figure out when the time comes. If you do a good job at this, I'm going to make you my dinghy master, and you'll be in charge of our small boat ops. Is that something you'd be interested in?"

"Oh, yes sir, I'd be *very* interested. I'm good with boats."

"Good. Once you bring the ladies back safe and sound, I'll let you go sailing with Rita again, and you can go ashore with her later in the afternoon. Would you like that?"

I heard a girlish squeal coming through the open portholes from the aft cabin, and Rita said, "Well, I'd sure like it!"

Adam's face went red, and after a moment he said. "Yes sir, okay, I guess that sounds all right."

I crouched and looked into the starboard transom porthole. "Have you been there the whole time, you little snoop?"

Rita's face appeared behind the opening. "I'm babysitting the twins, remember? Jonathan, say 'Hi' to your daddy."

"Hi, Daddy!" A little waving hand and arm extended out through the port, so Rita was holding him up by my navigation desk. Then another small hand came out of the other porthole, so Christopher had climbed up onto the aft cabin's double bed.

My speech to Adam about the gravity of being a member of the crew of Rebel Yell was blown out of the water. Try as I might, at times it was impossible to be serious on a boat full of women and children, including my five-year-old twin boys.

And I loved it. I absolutely loved it.

Adam dropped the ladies ashore and came back to fetch me. They both looked smashing, making a big splash anytime they went ashore together. Where they found makeup on the island was a mystery, but they did. Lipstick, eye shadow—the works.

Sofia's hair was pulled back in a ponytail, while Tala's was in a single French braid. One lady was Spanish and the other was French and Berber, but they might have been sisters.

Rita was briefed as both babysitter and anchor watch. I was ready to go ashore by the time Adam returned, and he didn't need to tie off. Instead, he just grabbed the outermost teak slat of the swim platform and let go of his sail's sheet to spill the wind. Spritsails were good that way. It had no boom to smack our heads flailing about, just the sprit pole that was attached to the top of the mast and sail.

"Where should I sit?" I asked him.

He said, "Sit by the mast or sit on the middle seat, it all depends. If we're going to tack, I'll tell you when to move."

"Adam, on this boat, you're the captain."

He smiled, showing his crooked teeth for just a moment before hiding them again. "Thanks, Captain Kilmer."

"Well, you know your boat and I don't. At least, not yet."

I tossed my nearly-empty pack aboard and stepped down inside. The pram rocked and rolled with my added weight, and I quickly sat down by the little mast to steady it. A hole in the center of this gunnel-to-gunnel bench near the bow formed the upper support for the mast. The butt of the mast was planted in a matching step in the bottom of the boat. My weight seemed too far forward, so I moved to the middle seat.

Adam said, "We can make it back to the landing on one tack, but it's to windward, so I'll drop the board. It's made of steel so it goes down by itself." He uncleated a line attached to the top of the centerboard trunk and eased it down. When it was raised, the centerboard occupied a narrow housing about three feet long running down the middle of the boat. The plank I was sitting on crossed the boat atop the middle of it; this seat would also be the rowing position. Oars were stowed along the bottom of the boat on either side of the centerboard trunk. You had to watch where you put your feet.

I said, "Your centerboard is about the same as the one on Whisper, it's just smaller."

"Right, it's the same principle." He let go of the boarding platform, tightened his sail while pulling the tiller, caught the wind, and we took off through the anchorage. We made it in a few minutes, both of us still dry, with no spray coming over.

He nosed into an opening and I stepped over the bow onto the floating dock. He handed up my daypack and I removed my holstered Glock 19 from it, then I attached its clips to my belt so that it rode high on my right side, outside my pants.

Adam stared at it. "Do you always carry a gun ashore?"

"In Beaufort I do. Doesn't your Uncle Hilton?"

"Sometimes, but not usually."

"Well, if you don't exercise a right, it can disappear. Bad people will get the wrong idea, and the next thing you know, it's against the law. It's just like muscle atrophy, it's all about exercise. Use it, or lose it."

Maybe half of the men and fewer of the women openly carried firearms on the island. More folks might have had guns concealed on them. I left my dark blue windbreaker unzipped. It covered my pistol, but I didn't care if anybody saw it or not.

"Do you think Beaufort is dangerous?" he asked me.

"Nope, and I want to keep it that way. Now, scoot on back to Texas Belle and wait there. Keep an eye out for us on shore, and keep an eye on Rebel Yell. When we're all done shopping and everything is back on the boat and put away, you can take Rita ashore, all right?"

"Yes, sir!"

5

I slung on my daypack. It was mostly empty except for a water bottle and a few small items. I walked from the floating dock up the ramp onto the parking lot. The silver coins in my front pocket could fill it with new purchases several times over, but my plan was to use it to help Tala and Sofia carry what they'd bought back to the boat. Unless I found something unexpected that was worth buying—and I was always on the lookout.

That market day I was dressed to blend in and keep a low profile. Other than my jacket, everything that I wore had been bought since returning to America: a hunting-camo ball cap, black sweater and jeans. On the island, a clothing store meant used clothes. It was impolite to ask where they came from, but traders did forage over on the mainland.

Shoes and boots were especially problematic. I wore so-called "half-breeds" that a cobbler had made by stitching new cowhide uppers onto old rubber boot soles that still had plenty of tread. I could pass for a local, which was my goal.

On market day the marina parking lot was given over to vendor's canopies and tables. The expression parking lot had lost its old meaning. On the island almost nobody drove cars simply for personal transportation. Such an ostentatious display of wealth could have been met with some hostility.

Anybody driving a vehicle with extra passenger space was expected to stop and offer to pick up the nearest or the oldest pedestrians. That seemed to be the unwritten rule, but it was rarely put into practice, because if a motor vehicle was going somewhere, it was almost always fully loaded to make the trip worth the fuel. This included piling extra cargo on the roof, on top of the trunk, and on trailers.

Horse-drawn hay wagons that had been converted to carry passengers on benches made daily trips between the island's communities. Bicycles were also in common use, often pulling small trailers of their own. Most of their tires were solid, the last irreplaceable rubber tubes having failed years before, but even so, bikes were still faster than walking any distance. That being said, people of all ages routinely hoofed it the four miles between Port Royal and Beaufort. This included old folks and toddlers, usually while pulling or pushing wagons and carts.

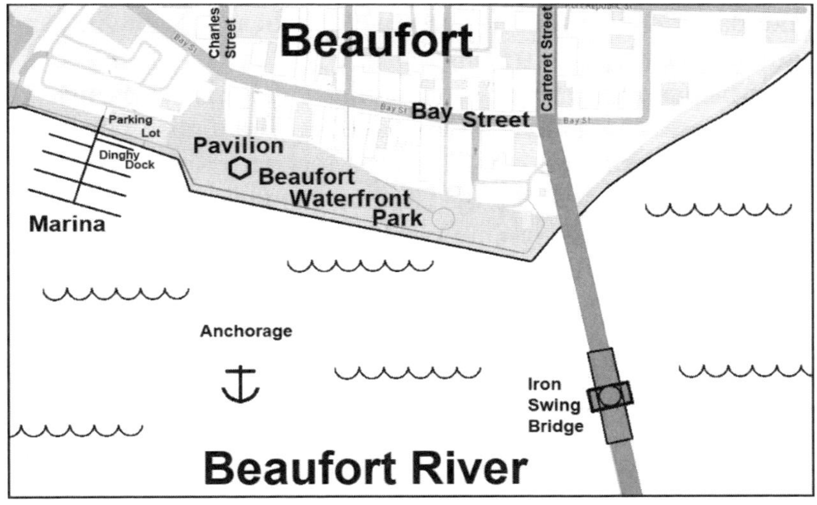

Due to its location by the marina, the asphalt lot tended to specialize in items of nautical interest. 12-volt batteries up to golf-cart size had their own section near the ramp. These were arrayed on the ground due to their weight. Their simple lead-acid technology went back to the 19th Century, and there was a thriving industry in refurbishing and charging them, but I was not in the market. Our house batteries were good to go.

Jerry cans of diesel and gasoline and smaller containers of motor oil were also sold around the marina. I knew some of the retail sellers because they had bought drums of fuel from me in the past. I was already familiar with most of the stuff displayed on the tables, and so I gave them only a quick look in passing, but I did spend a few minutes at a chart exchange. Nautical charts always merited a look; you never knew what might have just been traded in. Seeing no charts I could use, I moved on, always keeping an eye out for Tala or Sofia.

From the marina's parking lot over to the swing bridge, Beaufort's waterfront park ran eastward for more than four hundred yards. Before the recent bad years it must have been a wonderful place for both locals and tourists to enjoy a stroll, walk dogs, have picnics, or toss Frisbees and footballs. On that Saturday in November its acres were dedicated to buying and selling, shopping and trading.

The part of the riverfront park that was closest to the marina was occupied by an open-sided pavilion with a raised floor. Its metal roof was more than a hundred feet across and supported by widely-spaced columns. The surrounding walkways were brick paved. In passing I noticed hand-painted posters nailed to nearby trees that read LIVE MUSIC TONIGHT!

The Beaufort park pavilion had obviously been built in more affluent days, constructed to a hurricane-proof standard that had stood the test of time while still being esthetically pleasing. Being rainproof in everything short of gale winds, it was by default one of the town's primary meeting places.

Boat captains, farmers, property owners, businessmen and other groups met there to discuss issues of concern, choosing the times and topics by VHF radio. A weekly Beaufort town meeting was held each Sunday at two pm, with the public all welcome to attend. More than a hundred local citizens could stand under the open-sided pavilion, with many more outside beneath the open sky within earshot. The mayor of the town of Beaufort was selected there by a voice vote and was subject to replacement the same way.

In truth the mayor had little power. Almost every decision being taken up at the weekly public meeting was settled by a voice vote, with popular consensus always the goal. Somehow it worked, but this was in a small community that was very homogenous, both racially and culturally. Shouting matches or other obnoxious behavior were not tolerated. Repeat offenders were socially ostracized and could be barred from attendance, again by a simple voice vote.

Showing up at a town meeting with a band of allies to try to steamroll a position through to approval was not illegal or banned, but this kind of effort was always resisted by a solid majority, so it was considered to be a self-defeating strategy. Political parties and factionalism were considered to have been major ingredients of the toxic brew that had led to America's destruction, and to all the misery that had followed.

"What are you trying to do, be a party boss?" was usually enough to head off political alliances. "If you don't like it, you can always leave the island," was frequently heard.

Maybe this open-air self-governance wouldn't work on a larger scale, or with a more ethnically diverse population, but it seemed to suit the island, with each village and community mostly running its own affairs. Only a few subjects of mutual concern required the consensus of the whole island, such as extending the militia's operational area out onto the adjoining mainland counties to secure access to water, and the digging of drainage canals and irrigation projects, which were mostly done by indentured laborers overseen by the Farm Council.

Surrounding the pavilion and running all the way along the riverfront quay wall was a wide paved walkway. This path was kept clear of vendor's tents and stalls and was reserved for the use of pedestrians. In Ireland the word quay had been pronounced *key*, here in Beaufort, it was *kway*, but I didn't care either way. Same difference: it was a seawall that boats could tie alongside. Beaufort's history as a seaport went back centuries, and I often imagined the generations of vessels that had been tied up there during the last age of sail.

It was mid-tide, so depending on their size and their draft, the decks of the boats tied alongside the quay were almost at the level of the river walk. About half were sail and half were powered, running from thirty up to eighty feet in length. Some shrimpers had been stripped of their rigging to haul dry cargo. Former cruising sailboats had changed from pleasure craft to workboats to take advantage of their thrifty diesel auxiliaries and the free wind. Rebel had been tied along that quay many times. We were always ready to swing a drum of fuel over to a buyer's wagon, which was often horse drawn.

These quayside spots along the seawall were prized, and the early birds got the best locations. Later arrivals were tied outboard of those along the wall. The quayside boats had the easiest access to customers, but by common rule they couldn't prohibit folks from crossing their decks to visit boats tied to their outboard side. In some places the boats were tied three deep, with their crews sharing lines and fenders and jokes.

The rain had quit and the ground was drying, making it an ideal market day. With the sun trying hard to burn through the overcast, that Saturday felt like a festival. The girls seemed prettier and livelier, wearing their best outfits, and the young men were all laughing and showing off to catch their attention. And everywhere folks were running into old friends, and then stopping to engage in cheerful conversations.

On the lawns behind the river walk, tents and tables were arrayed in random rows and aisles, along with the horse carts and pickup trucks of the vendors. The vendors occupied all the green space from the walkway to the backs of the brick-and-mortar shops along Bay Street, which ran parallel to the river.

From the quayside path I could see Rebel Yell at anchor. My black schooner was the biggest sailboat in view out there, easily recognizable because of her two equal-height masts and long bowsprit. If there was a problem aboard, Rita would run a red signal pennant up the mainmast's flag halyard. Our green flag was still flying, indicating there were no problems aboard.

I leaned out over the water and I looked back toward the marina. I could see Adam's pram behind the Texas Belle, its red sail lowered. There was no sign of Tala or Sofia among the shoppers crowding the vendors' tables.

It seemed like another lifetime when we had all carried cell phones and hand-held VHF pocket radios to get in touch anytime we liked. But it was a workable alternative to keep an eye out for our flag turning from green to another color, each signal pennant conveying a different message. In the case of a warning flag going up, I could step aboard one of the vessels tied along the quay and ask to use their installed VHF marine radio. This courtesy would never be refused to a fellow boat captain. Rebel's decades-old VHF radio was left on channel 16, listening watch we called it, and Rita knew the protocols.

So I continued walking eastward along the waterfront. I came to a pilothouse ketch I recognized, maybe fifty feet in length. Battle Wagon IV was stenciled across her transom, her homeport Norfolk. Was she a transplant to South Carolina, or was she carrying some cargo worth braving Cape Hatteras? I vaguely recalled her from the Willoughby Bay anchorage near the old Norfolk naval station, where we had spent some very bad weeks deathly ill with typhus fever.

A hand-painted sign leaning against her pilothouse said "All Radio Gear Etc—Military & Civilian." That went with the insulated wire running from the top of its mizzen mast up to the top of its main mast: this was an antenna used for long-range high-frequency radio transmissions.

I waited until the young crewman finished talking with a potential customer, and I asked him if the skipper was aboard. He looked plenty salty, in his twenties and fit, but he clearly wasn't the boss of the boat. I was advised to check back in an hour or two. Captain Stark had some shopping and business of his own to attend to, but he'd be back.

The young sailor measured me as I measured him, eye to eye across the gap between boat and land. Everything about him, from his self-assured physical presence to his casual and carefree smile indicated a high level of cool competence, and I thought: I'd sign him on as crew here and now.

The truth was that every seaport afforded a sailor a fresh cut of the cards from a clean deck. Only when offshore and out of the sight of land was a crew arrangement inviolable, for better or for worse. Perhaps a trip down to Argentina might appeal to him? Trade the North Star for the Southern Cross? I moved on as a more likely customer sought his attention.

Without an autopilot, I needed to find sailors who could handle two hours behind the wheel in big seas. I needed men fit and able enough at that singular task that I could sleep soundly below their feet. Tala could take a turn at the wheel in rough weather to spell Gino or me, but that was not enough. Rebel Yell needed burly sailormen who could steer through the big waves until they were relieved, or until hell froze over.

As the saying went, the only weather you can choose is the weather you leave port in—but that might take a while. The same went for finding enough crew—and strong helmsmen in particular. Once you launched out into the briny blue, you could neither choose your weather, nor find additional crew.

And our time in Beaufort was running out.

I turned away from the river to scan across the market tents. I was still looking for Tala and Sofia but I didn't spot them, and so I continued down the paved walkway. As the day's weather improved, jackets and sweaters were being peeled off to be stowed in packs and bags, wrapped around waists, or slung over shoulders. Beaufort's young ladies were out in force, and I had ample opportunity to appreciate their youthful smiles and trim figures. My blue eyes were no longer quite as sharp as they'd been, but they were still around 20-20.

The almost complete absence of overweight people, far less any in the morbidly obese category, was striking. Either they had not made it through the population collapse, or they had permanently shed their excess pounds during the famine years.

By all reckoning the island was doing much better than the mainland, but food was still tight. Counting calories had come to mean trying to find enough food to stave off hunger.

Then I spotted Jim Walker from some distance away, and he was coming toward me. Judy was not with him. I continued toward him, the gap between us closing, but he seemed not to notice me, so I raised my hand to wave. At maybe thirty feet away his face was still set straight forward. Without making eye contact he seemed to give a little shake of his head, as if warning me off. I dropped my hand to my side, my eyes also forward, and we walked past one another without slowing.

That was sure weird, I thought, and nothing at all like the gregarious Jim Walker that I knew from church and socially. The man had sailed up to Charleston with me! Clearly he'd been spooked by something, or someone. Normally we'd have stopped for a friendly chat, and probably to arrange a luncheon together with our wives. But not that time. Hilton Sapelo's recent warnings returned to my mind.

Well, I'd see the Walkers at church tomorrow, with an entirely natural reason for a face-to-face meeting that could not be seen as anything other than innocent. Or maybe I'd see Jim later around the riverfront or over on Bay Street, and he'd offer some reason for brushing me off.

I was more than halfway along the seawall when I heard a rising chorus of shouts from up ahead, and the repeated cry of Stop Thief! Heading straight toward me and barreling through the shocked pedestrians burst a skinny young man who looked to be in his twenties or thirties. He was wide-eyed and open-mouthed, running at full speed, and close behind him was a pack of men in hot pursuit.

Luck had placed me in an opportune location as most of the other onlookers had melted back in alarm. I took a half step back toward the quay like many others, and then at just the right moment I stuck out my leg. The runner hooked my calf with his ankle and went flying through the air, landing on his back after an unplanned summersault. The pursuing group was on him in a second, their hands and knees holding him pressed to the ground as he regained his senses and his wind.

An older man caught up to the scrum, red faced and out of breath. He looked down and pointed at the captured runner's face, which was being pressed hard against the paving blocks.

"That's him," he said, "That's the thieving little bastard all right! Check his pockets—you'll see!"

The presumed thief was jerked up to his feet, eyes darting, insolence and fear flashing across his face. Medium height and scrawny but rather fit looking. He had a deeply tanned face and close-cropped hair that might have been blonde or light brown, and about two weeks of whiskers on his cheeks.

Angry hands clenched both his arms and shook him by his jacket collar. He was surrounded by men forming a tight circle around him, and I had a close view. He had pale blue eyes, and he gave me a direct look that told me that he knew that I, among them all, was the one who had tripped him. He had a daypack on his back, and it was yanked off.

Some of the men wore holstered pistols, but no guns were drawn. The situation didn't call for that escalation. Hard fists and strong hands were all that were required.

The white-haired man who had identified the thief fished into his pants pockets and pulled out some items, declaring, "Ah-Ha! So, you thought you could pull one over on me, eh? You think because I'm old I'm blind too, eh?" With each hand he held a silver Zippo lighter up high for any witnesses to see.

Another man opened the thief's daypack and dumped its contents on the ground. A clear plastic jar of peanuts, no label, of course. A fist-size hunk of cheese wrapped in paper. Water in a two-liter plastic bottle. Two glass mason jars of preserves, a sheath knife, and other items I couldn't identify. Something in a case with a strap, maybe a small pair of binoculars.

One of the men holding the thief said, "Well, it won't take long to find out who he stole the rest of it from."

Another said, "Look at his hair: it ain't even long enough to grab. I'll bet he's a farm runaway, a V-I-W. They shave their heads to keep 'em clean. Yeah, look at those hands, look at those calluses; he's a runaway for sure. And those pants are what they give 'em for farm work."

The thief was wearing torn and faded woodland pattern camouflage trousers from the twentieth century. Mainlanders seeking to remain on the island were stripped and had their heads shaved by the militia as an initial step of their delousing process. Head lice, also known as cooties, often carried deadly typhus, of which I had more than enough personal experience. The shaving and medical inspection was done at the militia checkpoint atop the four-lane state highway 170 bridge, which was the only official entrance onto the island.

If would-be islanders passed the militia's initial screening process, they were disinfected and given clean uniforms. Prior generations of military fatigues were available in abundance on the island after the evaporation of the Marine Corps. These newcomers were taken to the old Parris Island USMC recruit barracks, and after a month for quarantine and evaluation, they were assigned to farms as voluntary indentured workers. If at any point they failed to pass muster, these aspiring island residents were unceremoniously thrown back onto the mainland.

The same man who had noted the thief's short hair asked, "Where you from, boy? Off island? Where you been living at? Do you have papers? You're a V-I-W, ain't you?"

Another man said, "Who cares? He's a thief and we caught him red-handed. I'll bet he stole the backpack too. Let's chuck him in the sound. He can swim on back to the mainland, or he can wash out to sea, and I don't care which."

Another replied, "No, let's tie him up and hold him for the militia. Let the militia decide what to do with him."

"Oh, fuck the militia! We'll take care of this ourselves, like always. Those militia boys have been getting on a mighty high horse lately, and we don't need them turning into police. They can guard the bridge and keep out the mainlanders, but they don't guard *us*. We sure as hell don't need *that* shit again."

A different man leaned in close, and marked a letter T on the thief's forehead with two strokes of his index finger. "I say we brand him first. Once a thief, always a thief. Brand him with a big old T. Let honest folks see him coming before he can steal anything else. Brand him, then we'll kick him off the island—and we don't need no goddamn militia to do it. I gotta boat just the same as them."

"Naw, Fred, we're not branding them anymore, not just for stealing. For rape, yes, of course, and for cannibalism, but not for stealing. Anyway, not for small stuff like this."

"Well, you got anything to say for yourself, boy? Like, 'I'm sorry?' Now's your chance to say your say. Speak up!"

The thief barely lifted his face. "Okay. . . I'm sorry, I'm really sorry," he stammered. "Just don't put me off the island."

The right side of his face was deeply abraded and weeping blood where he'd been held down. It'd be purple tomorrow. There was no need to brand him, not for the next week or two.

"You a farm hand? A V-I-W? Where? Better tell us, boy, because we'll find out anyway. Or maybe you just want to get off the island? Well, we can arrange that too."

The thief mumbled, "I work for the McAllister's, down Fishing Pond Road on St. Helena."

"I know the McAllister farm," someone else said. "Tie him up; they've got a truck here today. I've seen it parked over by the bridge. He must've come in for the day with them—and just look how he repays them for their kindness! They'll tote him back to the farm sure enough."

The older man who had identified the thief said, "Well, son, I'd say you just earned yourself another year on the farm, and for sure they won't let you ride the truck into town again. You'll be lucky if they don't put you in leg irons this time."

Somebody produced a piece of cord, and the thief's hands were bound behind his back. I'd seen enough, and veered off the quayside path onto the lawn between the vendor's stalls. It all struck me as funny, somehow. The thief wanted to stay on the island, even as forced labor, and I wanted to get away. So which was the frying pan, and which was the fire?

A hundred feet further on into the crowd, and as far as I could tell the entire drama had passed unnoticed. Shoppers were still haggling with merchants over shoes, eyeglasses, guns and ammo, locally manufactured gunpowder, homemade charcoal water filters, antique non-electric hand tools, used clothing, soap and candles, new-spun wool yarn, empty plastic bottles and glass jars, books, leather goods, hunting dogs and ducks and geese in cages. Herbal potions, powders and poultices promised to cure what ailed you.

This market business was further complicated by the fact that it was mostly all done by barter, with buyers and sellers comparing the relative values of their own wares to the items they wished to trade for. This meant that elaborate three-sided deals were often required to complete a transaction.

Rebel Yell's usual two-liter bottles of gasoline or diesel were convenient "cash" by comparison. The silver coins in my pocket put me into an elite status. Seeing nothing I needed, I continued onward, winding through the canopies and stalls.

The bell tolled, and after a pause it rang twelve times. I was only a few blocks from the church, so it was louder than out on the anchorage. It was high noon on Saturday. Today my watch, also theoretically set for local time, was five minutes fast. Or was the church bell five minutes slow? Or was there a combination of errors? It didn't really matter, not when local noon was recalibrated from a sundial.

The best farm produce was usually sold on the paved lots and streets around the end of the non-swinging iron bridge, where it landed in Beaufort and became Carteret Street. This was because the big farms brought their produce to the market on trucks and wagons, and they took up more space. I steered over in that direction and I finally saw Tala and Sofia, who were recognizable through the crowd and across the tables in their colorful outfits. They noticed me as I came closer.

When I reached them I gave Tala a quick hug and kiss, and she said, "Oh, Danny, look at everything we find today—even honey and eggs and butter. Oh, and rye flour, much rye flour! And cooking oil, and a cheese as big as your head! And even some bars of lavender soap. Yes, we had a good day shopping. We have too much to carry, so we pay this boy to follow us."

A scrawny red-headed teen dressed in oversized rags stood behind a pushcart filled with their day's purchases. He carried the unmistakable stamp of the starvation years about him—his size did not match the age of his freckled face. He was short, with a sallow complexion and sunken cheeks, but he had bright green eyes and he looked directly at me.

His handcart was obviously homemade, screwed together from salvaged plywood and lumber. It was supported on a pair of bicycle wheels that had rope around their rims instead of rubber tires. An old military camo parka lay across the cart's handles by the cargo box. But I had to give him credit. Despite the unlucky timing of his childhood growth years, which was no fault of his own, he was out hustling to make a living.

His wagon's cargo area was about four feet on each side and two feet high. It was loaded with the canvas tote bags that we always took ashore for shopping. Taking bags full of bags, that's how we went shopping. You had to provide your own.

Sofia waved a hand over the wagon's contents and said, "I think this is enough for taking to the boat."

"Have you two eaten lunch yet?" I asked them. We usually treated ourselves to a nice meal ashore on market day. Besides the cafes on Bay Street, instant restaurants were set up under canopies on the weekends. Fresh seafood was cheap because there were no freezers or ice to keep it chilled, and hence no export market. What was caught was consumed as soon as possible. If the island ever restored enough electric power to run big commercial freezers, the local fishermen would make a better living selling it to the outside world. But until then, the island's residents would feast like kings.

Chickens, ducks and wild waterfowl were also plentiful, but the beef was wretched. Screwworms infected the island's cattle, and without any access to medicines or antibiotics, they were emaciated and the meat needed to be cooked to death. Any good steak or hamburger was considered more of a delicacy than fresh-caught crab, oysters, mahi-mahi or even snapper. Supply and demand. Go figure.

Sofia exchanged looks with Tala and replied, "Lunch? No, Danny, we are shopping until this minute now. You and Tala enjoy a nice lunch, I'm sure we'll have too much time together on the way to South America. Don't worry, I can take this to Adam's boat, it's really no problem. We'll put everything away, and then I'll return later with Gino."

She would not need to touch a single bag until she was back aboard Rebel Yell. Adam's little sailing pram would cost her nothing, of course, and the pushcart service maybe a quarter. Or even two, if she was feeling especially generous.

So while pretending to look into one of the bags, I palmed a silver fifty-cent piece from my pocket by feel, and I placed it down into the back corner of the boy's home-built wagon. The ginger-haired kid would find it when he was unloading the cart and handing the bags to Adam over on the dinghy dock. Charity? Pity? Call it what you want. The kid had earned it.

One boy was throwing his dice on a desperate voyage into the unknown with strangers, and the other was trapped on the island pushing a handcart for those who still had a little money or extra food to give him. Pondering the fates and fortunes of the two, and of the thief, I counted my blessings.

The two ladies exchanged air kisses, and then Sofia turned toward the riverfront walkway. She had a very nice figure seen from behind, but not as nice as Tala's. The skinny teen huffed, and then lifted the two handles of his pushcart and followed behind her. So much for keeping a low profile. But what could you do? Classy ladies like them enjoyed shopping in style.

And I'll admit that it was a major boost for my male ego to stroll through the market day crowd arm-in-arm with Tala, a decade my junior. She was practically as slim as when I'd first set eyes on her back in Morocco, and her form-fitting red and gold jersey accentuated her curves. This knit sweater extended to her hips, covering the top of her black leather skirt. A black belt fit snugly around the narrowness of her waist, matching her red and black shoulder bag.

Even though the day was a bit chilly, she wore her favorite wedge sandals, showing off her red-painted toenails, matching her fingernails and lipstick. She had had them made by the same cobbler who had done my shoes. With the extra inches, her shoulder almost reached mine as we walked together.

I enjoyed observing the reactions of both men and women as Tala passed through any crowd. Men's eyes would flicker from her ankles up to her face, then hover over her torso, but what always fixed their attention was the dagger tucked under her belt on the left side. The damascene steel blade inside the curved sheath was ten inches long and razor sharp. Its knobby black grip had been carved from the horn of a desert ibex back in Morocco generations before.

Plenty of men and more than a few women carried pistols and revolvers on the island, but Tala's heirloom Berber knife captured attention like no handgun ever could. It did not seem in any way to be an affectation or a fashion accessory; rather, it bespoke deadly purpose. And in reality, it had been blooded.

One thing I knew for sure: since I had met her in Morocco, no other man had ever laid a hand upon her. The long curved dagger on her hip clearly indicated that you may look, but you must not touch. This made being with her in public even more delicious, because Tala was mine and mine alone—and every other man who saw us together and desired her knew it.

6

Different trades clustered in their own areas on market day. The sellers of the big, heavy deep-cycle batteries were located back on the parking lot near the marina, for example.

The block-long extension of Bay Street on the east side of Carteret was the weekend location of a few micro-restaurants like the one that Tala had chosen for our lunch. Carteret Street was the north-south road that ran over the old iron bridge connecting Beaufort and Port Royal to the rest of the island.

Our little eatery was set up on a grassy area with a river view. A canopy covered two portable tables, but with the day so nice, we moved one of them a few yards out from beneath it to sit in what was almost sunshine. It was still hazy, but the disc of the sun was occasionally visible.

A pleasant woman in her middle years told us the two menu choices: red snapper or stuffed flounder. We both selected the flounder with crab meat inside, cooked in seasoned butter in a covered clay pot. The owner, chef and waitress placed it in coals that were glowing at the bottom of an iron box. Tala said the clay pot cooking reminded her of Morocco.

The panorama of boats moving under both motor and sail made the time spent waiting for our meal pass quickly. It was interesting to watch the part of the Beaufort River where any vessel higher than thirty feet above the water was filtered out.

A few cars and trucks moved over the bridge, but there were just as many horse-drawn wagons, people on horseback, bicycle riders and pedestrians. Nothing moved faster than the horses in the constricted space. Most of the tires for bikes, cars and trucks were so threadbare that people were not interested in testing their top speeds. The pedestrians had their own lane, separated from the two-lane road by a permanent barricade. The bridge was old, but it had been well engineered. Island life moved at a slower pace, but it was still moving.

If not for the inoperability of the bridge's iron section, Rebel Yell would have been able to motor up the old Intra-Coastal Waterway to Charleston on the inside route. But this also would have meant burning diesel for most of the distance, so the bridge's closure didn't mean much to me. After all, a cargo schooner's biggest advantage was using the free wind.

I wondered if the iron section of the bridge would ever be able to turn its designed ninety degrees to permit the passage of loftier marine traffic. I supposed that this would depend on the restoration of the electrical grid, and who could tell when, or even if, that would happen? In any case, it wasn't going to be my problem. Soon we'd be thousands of miles away in another hemisphere, facing new challenges and opportunities.

After baking in their own juices, our chef transferred the steaming entrees onto china plates, along with rice and coleslaw and glasses of mint tea. I wondered what fine Beaufort house the china had come from. Was our lady chef formerly a society maven? Did she live in one of the antebellum glories on the streets behind us? It would not have surprised me. All the ingredients for the meal were local to the island. The lump crabmeat inside the delicate flounder was beyond description.

Between bites Tala said, "I forgot tell you—I saw Jessie a little time before you came. Jessie Hanahan."

"You did? What did you tell her? What did she say?"

"I told her they should go sailing with us, to decide if they want to go to Argentina. I said maybe tomorrow, and she said yes they would do it. Oh, and she said they are playing music tonight on the pavilion. She said they are making the electric rock music, and we can come to hear their music band."

To my knowledge this would be the first time amplified music would have been played for a crowd in Beaufort since before our arrival. This was a touchy subject, because many people still associated the old pop culture with America's spiritual decay and agonizing collapse. Everything connected with the bygone era's degenerate culture, including Hollywood movies, television, pop music, the internet, computers and even cell phones had disappeared during the catastrophe, and many people never wanted them to return.

Computers boosted by networked artificial intelligence were compared to the biblical tree of knowledge. The widely held opinion was that mankind had tried to assume the mantle of God, leading to humanity's downfall. After the collapse it was difficult to avoid the comparison to Adam and Eve being driven out of the Garden of Eden to suffer in the wilderness. Video screens from smart phones to wall-mounted televisions were called "Satan's windows," and they had all been smashed during and after the collapse by the survivors. (With the grid down for good, the screens were dead and blank anyway, so this was an easy outlet for unfocused rage.)

Now church services were conducted without amplified speakers and microphones. They would require generators and fuel, so it was simpler and cheaper to get along without them. Pastors with booming voices, and there were many, benefited the most. This dynamic had curved back around into a mainly religious disapproval of amplifying the human voice in order to reach an audience larger than a typical church congregation.

This was especially true when it came to the low purpose of mere mass entertainment, as opposed to the glorification of the word of God. It was the old slippery slope argument again. Not everybody agreed with this, and it might not have been the prevailing opinion, but those who held it were influential.

Two-way VHF and CB radios had escaped condemnation. They were among the few electronic technologies which had for the most part continued working through the worst times, and their usefulness to the community was undeniable.

"So, Danny, can we come to see their music band?"

"That's what Jessie said? Electric music? Are you sure?"

"Oh, yes, I'm very sure. She said electric rock music and lights. She sings in the music band, you know. To enter under the pavilion roof we will need to pay something. Jessie said maybe a little gasoline for the generator is good to bring, and then we can be under the pavilion if it's raining."

"I don't think it's going to rain. Look up, honey, what's that yellow thing way up there?" I squinted and pretended to shield my eyes. The haze had burnt off, revealing blue sky. "The sun is out! I think maybe it's going to be dry tonight, and if the sky is clear we'll even see the moon."

"Jessie said the electricity is going to begin at six o'clock. Then the lights and the music. Electrical rock music! Danny, we can do *dancing*, me and you."

"Go dancing, we can *go* dancing."

"Yes, we can go dancing, me and you! So, you are going to tell me yes, and we are going to bring the gasoline and go dancing under the pavilion?"

It was tempting. When would we ever get another chance for some real fun like this? Electric music, electric lights, and dancing? Probably never again in Beaufort, at least, not for us. And also on the plus side, this event would give me a chance to have a longer discussion with Luke and Jessie about their making the voyage. If they could come out tomorrow for a day sail, it would be convenient to pick them up here in Beaufort.

And I'd see the Walkers at church on Sunday morning, so maybe Jim and Judy could also come out sailing, and they'd get to meet Luke and Jessie. It was time to finalize the crew.

"Sure, honey," I told her, "we can do that. I have a little shopping to do on Bay Street, and then we'll go back out to the boat. Then Gino can come ashore with Sofia, and I told Adam and Rita they can go sailing later this afternoon, and we can stay aboard with the twins. It's only a little past noon, so there's enough time, and then we can come back tonight and hear Jessie's band and go dancing."

Tala reached across the table and took my hand in both of hers, her tilty eyes flashing like amber jewels in the sunlight. "Oh, thank you, Danny. Only just *thinking* about dancing with the electrical music makes me *very* happy!"

The thought made me pretty happy, too. I was so pleased with myself and how the day was going that I overpaid for the meal, leaving two dollars in silver. Our chef seemed almost as excited as Tala was when she eyed the stack of eight quarters I'd left on the table. Mr. Big Spender—that was me.

Argentina seemed just over the horizon.

Back across Carteret, Bay Street was lined on both sides with two- and three-story commercial buildings for the five blocks back over to the marina. I'd seen enough of the chaotic market day crowds on the green space and along the river walk. It was far more pleasant to walk back with Tala on Bay Street.

Before the catastrophe the buildings had been occupied by realtors, art galleries, boutiques, salons and ice cream shops. Now they were places where you could have an electric motor rewound, purchase a bicycle built from scrounged parts, trade guns and ammo for lead bullets and gunpowder, buy books or try on some eyeglasses to read them, get a haircut and a shave, or have a troublesome tooth extracted.

A few pubs and restaurants had sailed right on through the transformation unchanged in their basic functions. The ancient secrets of distilling liquor, winemaking and brewing beer had not been lost. Life went on without ice cubes in drinks. And I never heard an island resident express any desire to create a government agency to regulate alcohol, tobacco or firearms.

The storefront windows facing Bay Street were still intact, evidence that the mayhem that had plagued the mainland had never reached the island. My destination was Burton's Marine Chandlery, two blocks over. It occupied the bottom of a two-story brick structure; the owner and his wife lived on the upper floor. Nautical wares were visible through the front windows. A bell jingled when I opened the door for Tala.

The proprietor himself was sitting behind a counter near the entrance. He was hunched over a book, using the daylight. Short, bald and bespectacled, Harry Burton rose, smiling.

"Well, if it isn't the skipper of Rebel Yell! And thank you, Captain Kilmer, for bringing your lovely bride to brighten up my day—and a sunny day at that! Tala, dear, you must have brought the sunshine ashore with you."

She smiled and blew a kiss, which he pretended to catch. For some reason the happy little toad charmed the ladies.

"Harry," I said, getting to business, "any new charts since last week?" New meaning newly traded in to the shop. Charts had not been printed in a decade, and electronic chartplotters were useless without GPS, so southbound vessels exchanged paper charts with those northbound, and east with west. Every boat captain sought information about what lay ahead on their route, and was willing to trade what lay in their wake to obtain it. Hunting around for useful charts was always on a skipper's to-do list, especially before a voyage.

"I don't think so," Harry replied. "I still have Northeast Brazil, in case you've changed your mind."

"Nah, I'll pass, I've got all the Brazil I need."

"Hmm. . . Well, it's not a chart, but somebody brought in Jimmy Cornell's World Cruising Routes, it's the 9th edition. Now that book is a real treasure. Whenever I have one, folks come in just to study it and take notes. I should charge them."

"I already have a 3rd edition, it's almost the same."

"Yeah . . . okay . . . well, just look around, then. Oh, say, there was a fellow in here a half hour ago who had something you might be interested in seeing. It was too pricey for me to buy, and he wouldn't let me take it on consignment. He said he's not sticking around long enough for that."

"Okay, Harry, I'll bite. What did he have?"

He leaned across the glass counter and said, "He has an actual chronometer. Accurate to seven seconds a month."

This grabbed my full attention, but I soon dismissed the idea. "Even if I believed it, what good is that kind of accuracy if you can't get a time signal to set it?"

"That's just the thing, Dan, it is set. He said he tested it all around the Chesapeake Bay from known positions, and he can fix his position to under ten miles."

That was fantastic celestial navigation . . . if it was true.

"Who is he? Where is he now?"

"He's Captain Peter Stark off the Battle Wagon, it's a—"

"I know the boat. I was just over on the quay, I saw it."

"Well, he said he's going for a haircut, so you might catch him down the street."

"What did he ask for it?"

"Oh, far too much! An ounce of gold, cash and carry. No holds, no layaways, and no consignment."

"Hey, thanks for the tip, Harry."

"Don't mention it."

I went right back out the door, Tala following me.

The barber shop was a block west and across Bay Street. When I entered I saw the likely Captain Stark settling his bill by pushing silver dimes across the counter. He was a bit older than me, maybe fifty, a bit shorter, and weather-beaten with reddened skin and deep facial creases. His gray hair was cut short; his beard was trimmed and edged, leaving his upper lip bare. He wore a black sweater over khaki trousers.

Tala followed me inside, so the barber and the captain both had someone prettier than me to glance at while they finished their business.

I asked him, "Are you by any chance Captain Stark?"

He redirected his eyes from Tala to me. "It depends who's doing the asking."

"Dan Kilmer, captain of the Rebel Yell."

"Do we know each other?"

"We were both in Norfolk a few years ago. Willoughby Bay, between the Willoughby Spit and the old Navy base."

"So, that's your black schooner at anchor? I remember her now." He had a northeastern accent, Massachusetts or Maine. We'd never had a conversation, but we had probably crossed wakes a dozen times over.

"I just came from the chandlery. Harry said that you might have an item I'd be interested in."

"He said that, did he?"

"Yes, he just did. Maybe we can walk back over there and discuss the matter? It's a comfortable place for a chat."

"Then I'll see you there in five minutes, captain."

I left the barber shop with Tala, and standing on the sidewalk I reached into my pocket and grabbed some silver.

"You know the dress shop that's around the corner from McNally's Pub? Why don't you go see if you can find a new outfit for tonight? And maybe get a present for Sofia. I'll meet you there when I'm done at Harry's."

I poured the coins into her hand, about five dollars' worth. Serious money. She looked at it and smiled, gave me a kiss on the cheek and spun on her wedge sandals.

Back in the chandlery, I said, "Harry, I just caught up with Captain Stark. Can we use your library for a little parlay?"

Near the back of his shop was a reading room surrounded by floor-to-ceiling bookshelves. In the middle of this dimly-lit space was a table made from an antique timber hatch cover. A brass anchor light hung by a wire above the table. I switched it on and held it steady to keep it from swinging.

Away from the front windows, the artificial lighting in the shop was powered by a solar panel on the roof. Like distilling liquor and beer making, the 19th-century alchemy of lead-acid batteries had not been lost after the collapse. Electric light was the result when these batteries were coupled with solar panels and LED bulbs. I pulled up a chair and sat facing the front of the shop with my daypack at my feet.

After a few minutes Captain Stark joined me there, placing a sailcloth tote bag on the table and pulling up his own chair. We shook hands below the hanging anchor light and sat down. It was protocol to exchange a few pleasantries before business.

"That's a beautiful woman you have, Captain Kilmer. I'm thinking that you're a very fortunate man in that special way."

"That woman is my wife, and I'm very fortunate to have her in my life. But please, Captain Stark, call me Dan."

"And my friends call me Pete. I'm thinking that she isn't from around here, is she?"

"Not even close. I met her in Morocco."

He chuckled. "Morocco? I'll bet there's a yarn in there."

"Oh, there's a few yarns in there. Good yarns."

"Maybe you'll write a book about it someday."

"Maybe I will, Pete."

"Well, the last I heard—and correct me if I'm wrong—you had typhus on your boat. Quarantine flag and all. Typhus fever was going around Virginia something terrible back then."

"That was three years ago, and only two of us had it." Tala and I had spent a month confined in our aft cabin, with Gino and Sofia caring for us and tending to our children. For some of that time I was sure we were both going to die. Without any antibiotics, all we could do was ride out the fevers.

He said, "Rather unusual to hear of typhus aboard a boat at anchor." Typhus, which is often confused with typhoid fever, was carried and spread by head and body lice.

"That's what I thought, too, but we caught it anyway. We must have picked up the cooties when we were ashore. But we survived, and now here we are."

"And may we praise the good lord for his infinite mercy."

"Yes, praise the lord. So, were you recently in Norfolk?"

"Aye. We left the Chesapeake in October."

"How was your trip around Hatteras? Cape Hatteras nearly did us in a few seasons back. As it was we lost our autopilot. It burned out fighting those head seas, those square waves."

"Then we were lucky, or the good lord was looking out for his fools again. Ten days from Norfolk to Morehead City. We made plenty of easting; we tacked far out and back in to avoid those Gulfstream waves. A late October hurricane would have done it for us, but we had no damage to speak of. So you have no autopilot, eh? Sorry, but I can't help you out there."

"I'm sorry too. But Harry says you have a chronometer?"

"Aye, that I do." Captain Stark smiled, and patted his tote.

When GPS failed, celestial navigation suddenly came back into fashion, but it all depended upon having a timepiece set to Coordinated Universal Time. (This had been called Greenwich Mean Time in the last century.) Antenna towers in Colorado that had been continuously transmitting time signals allowed the precise synchronization of all of the chronometers in the world—until the grid went down and it didn't come back up.

A few other atomic clocks around the world were used for academic research, and foreign military outfits might have used systems that were not publicly available, but WWVB, broadcasting from Fort Collins, Colorado was the master clock that set the official time for the world via the radio waves. That is, until WWVB went silent amidst the violent chaos that had overtaken Colorado and the rest of the United States.

So I asked him, "How did you set it? I haven't found a trustworthy time signal in more than two years."

"It was set last spring, by me, and I checked it all through the summer. It gains seven seconds a month, no more, no less. There's a page of my own log notes that comes with it."

"How could you set it without a time signal?"

"Well, that's just the point, Dan; I *did* have a time signal. Tokyo University was broadcasting a time tick for almost two years after Fort Collins went down. You didn't hear about it?"

"Tokyo? No, I didn't. My single-sideband is ruined, kaput. I think it's a blown capacitor, but I can't fix it. Tokyo, huh?"

"Yep, Tokyo University. Weak but readable. And we keep checking, but we haven't heard it since last August. Say, why don't you swing by the Battle Wagon? I can set you up with a good single-sideband for a fair price. Should be an easy swap-out if the rest of your radio gear is good to go. We could even take your old set in trade for a discount. One of my crew was a Navy E.T., a Senior Chief Electronics Technician. Why don't you come by the boat and tell him about your radio problem? If it's just a blown capacitor, maybe he can fix it. He brought loads of that kind of stuff with us from Norfolk."

"I'd love to, Pete, but I can't today; I've got to get back to my own boat right after this."

"I'll tell you what, then: come on out to the Battle Wagon tomorrow. No, make it Monday. We'll be anchored out near you. And even if I can't sell you a radio, we can still compare notes. Tokyo might come back on with a new time signal, and there's some talk about a time signal in Switzerland too. I'll give you any help I can."

"Thanks, captain, I'd really appreciate that. And I'd sure like to have a working single-sideband again."

"Yeah, I can imagine. So, Dan, do you want to see it now? The chronometer? That's what we're here for, isn't it?"

"Oh, it sure is." I struggled to restrain my anticipation.

Stark unzipped his tote and removed a blue box about five inches on a side. It was hinged in the middle. He opened it and set it on the table in front of me so I could see the face of the watch mounted inside. It was stainless steel. Its second hand was silently ticking ahead in perfect little jumps. Its hour and minute hands announced that it was fourteen minutes after five o'clock at the zero longitude meridian in Greenwich England.

"Pretty, isn't she? It's a solar-powered Citizen Eco-Drive. I found four of them in Boston last year. New in the box, still wrapped in factory plastic and never opened. They never saw the sun from the factory in Japan until I opened them. As good as new and sure to keep wicked good time for years and years to come. This one gains seven seconds a month. A month!

"I couldn't be sure about the Tokyo time signal, so I tested it by taking fixes at charted locations and working backwards. I've nailed six-mile positions around the Chesapeake Bay, just *nailed* them, and so I *know* the Tokyo time signals were right. They brought us straight to Morehead City after ten days out."

"Well, Pete, that's damn fine navigation."

"I'll say it is. So, what are you using for nav tables?"

"Back when I still had a working chronometer, I was using Kolbe's Long Term Almanac."

"That'll do. You won't get a ten-mile fix using Kolbe, but fifteen is better than guessing, and Kolbe will work until we're both dead. Then somebody else can figure it out." He laughed.

"Right on, Pete. So now all I need is a chronometer." The self-winding Seiko diver's watch on my wrist was useless as a chronometer without a time signal to reset it, because its loss and gain were erratic and unquantifiable, up to minutes a week plus or minus. This was good enough for "church bell time" set from a sundial, but not for celestial navigation.

Captain Stark said, "Well, then right here is just what you need. I'm keeping two of the original four for myself, so I can check one against the other. This is the last one I'm selling."

I knew the next part was going to hurt.

"So, Pete, what do you want for it?"

"I'm just a plain and simple man, so I like to keep things plain and simple. One ounce of gold for the best chronometer on this side of ocean. And probably on the other side too."

An ounce of gold for a Japanese wristwatch! Ordinarily I'd haggle, get up as if to walk out—but I might have lost my only chance at the Citizen if I did. His Battle Wagon could be over the horizon, and I'd curse my stinginess if I hesitated.

"Well, Captain Stark, I just so happen to have one of those on me—but I need to dig it out of its hiding place." I stood and removed my Glock from its holster with just my thumb and a finger, and laid it on the table pointed away from us at a book shelf. I watched him closely as I did it, and he kept a poker face all through my display. Then I unclipped the black Kydex holster from my belt, and sat down again.

"Harry," I said aloud, "Harry, do you have a screwdriver handy? A Philips head screwdriver, about a medium size?"

In less than a minute he brought one to me without saying a word, and then he left us. I unscrewed and disassembled the adjustable parts of my Kydex holster, exposing part of a gold coin inside a double layer of the black plastic. I'd heated the Kydex there to soften it, and I'd press-melted the coin right in, forming its own semi-permanent nest.

I figured that if anybody took my pistol and my holster, I'd already be dead, and the gold coin would be of no further use to me. Or, in another scenario, I might be able to make a deal with the boss of any gang that held me captive, a gang who had no idea of the full value of the plastic holster they'd taken from me. Not even Tala knew about it. She couldn't be tricked (or tortured) into revealing a secret that she didn't know.

Using my own folding pocket knife, I carved the plastic back from where it curled over the coin and freed it, and then I handed it to him. While he examined it, I screwed my holster back together and put away my Glock.

"Oh, a good old South African Krugerrand." Captain Stark hefted its weight on his fingertips, then put on reading glasses and closely examined both sides of it.

"That's right, a Krugerrand. One ounce of pure gold. Plus a little silver and copper to harden it up for rough use."

He pushed the watch box toward me and said, "Well, don't you want to inspect it?"

"Oh, you bet I do." I slid its stand up and out of the box and unfastened the strap. The watch had a nondescript black diver's band, but I didn't care about that. It looked legit on the front and on the back, and I was certainly never going to test it to its claimed 200 meter working depth. (At least, not while I was still alive to personally verify it. Otherwise . . . possibly.)

Inside the box under the watch stand were a few tags and certificates of authenticity, a folded multi-lingual instruction sheet, and Captain Peter Stark's own page logging its seven-seconds-a-month gain in time. This known error rate would be subtracted to obtain the best estimate of the current UTC required for the most accurate celestial navigation. The time on the watch would never be adjusted unless and until I found another reliable time tick being broadcast. Until then, the last Tokyo time signal would be considered sacrosanct.

I put it all back in the box and snapped the lid shut. We were both taking a chance, him that my Krugerrand wasn't a gold-coated slug, and me that his story about the watch being set from a Tokyo time-tick was bullshit. But in this game, a man's reputation was everything, so I reached across the table and shook his hand. The Krugerrand had already disappeared.

He said, "Now you know that it's far too valuable to wear, but it does need some light to keep it running. Just fasten it in a safe place in your pilothouse. That's worked for me."

"Thanks, Pete, I'll do that."

Then he leaned closer over the table and lowered his voice. Harry was somewhere in the front of the store, out of our sight but not necessarily out of earshot. As we both knew.

"So, Captain Dan, where are you heading? You don't need that pricey timepiece just for coastwise sailing, and that means you're going a far distance. So where are you aiming to, if you don't mind my asking?"

Captain Stark was blunt and to the point, like other Yankee sailors I'd known. I didn't mistrust him, and I might even have bought a replacement single-sideband radio transmitter from him, but I didn't want to confirm to him or to anybody that I was leaving the island for good. But Stark would never believe that I'd given him an ounce of gold for a chronometer just to gunkhole around Georgia and the Carolinas, so I fudged my departure date and ultimate destination.

"We're going far, very far. At least to the Windwards, and maybe to Trinidad. It all depends on what we find along the way. But we're not going to be ready for a few more weeks."

"You're worried about that volcano too? Laki? Boston's under a foot of new snow, and there was skim ice on the docks in Norfolk. The Battle Wagon is heading south, but just how far south, I don't know. Down island, like you. Most of them are a wicked mess, and some more than others. Martinique sounds promising. Of course it's just radio chatter, and maybe even lies. Maybe they're just trying to lure foolish sailors into a trap. It wouldn't be the first time it happened. We can talk it over when you come out to buy your new radio on Monday."

"Well, Captain Stark—Pete—until Monday, then."

The watch box went into an inside pouch in my daypack. We shook hands across the table and then I rose and left first, thanking Harry for the use of his reading room on my way out. I wondered just how much he'd heard. In any case, it wouldn't take Sherlock Holmes to deduce the meaning of my paying an ounce of gold for a Japanese wristwatch. An ounce of gold!

7

Tala could cut my hair, and she did from time to time, but Sofia was better at barbering and she didn't mind doing mine as well as Gino's. When she felt like it, we'd all get haircuts one after the other in the pilothouse swivel chair, including the twins. She would shave Gino with a straight razor maybe once a week, but I shaved myself or let my beard grow as my mood struck me. With a big night out on the town to look forward to, I bathed and gave myself a close shave at the sink.

Adam brought Rita back soon after five o'clock, using the church bells for his time keeper. I'd given him three dollars in silver to show Rita a fun time ashore, and to find better boat shoes. This was also a test of his financial judgment. When he returned he was wearing canvas sneakers that had once been white, but they were a vast improvement over the trash he'd been wearing, and the canvas would dry quickly.

Both kids looked happy after their time ashore, and happy crew are the best kind. Rita went below to take over the baby sitting duty, that was part of our deal, but Adam stayed on the swim platform with me. I wanted to see how his pram worked with our four-horsepower Honda outboard. His boat's transom was not very different in its thickness or its height above the water than Whisper's. This was going to be my big date night out with Tala, and I wanted to make the ride as comfortable for her as I could, so we were going to use the motor.

I also wanted to see how good Adam was with outboards, and he turned out to be quite knowledgeable. He was for sure going to be our dinghy master. This would be a job he'd both enjoy and excel at, and it would also take the hassle out of my hands and Gino's. A win-win all around.

The sky was mostly clear, the breeze fresh. I didn't mind sailing to shore and back, I knew his boat was easy to handle, but the wind was continuing to clock around toward the southeast, and I didn't want to be tacking home in the dark, not if the water was choppy. Nothing would change Tala's mood for the worse like returning her to Rebel Yell doused in salt spray.

Adam removed the pram's rudder, slipping its stainless-steel pintles out of the matching mounts on the transom, and clamped the little outboard in its place. He put the red gas tank aboard, attached and pumped the fuel line, adjusted the choke, and had the motor going after just a few pulls of the rope. We let it run a while to warm it up.

An advantage of his boat's spritsail rig was that both the mast and the sprit were each short enough to fit within the pram when they were taken down. Tonight they would just be in our way, so I had him take the entire rig off the boat. He wrapped the sail around the two little spars, tied it up with its sheet line, and he left the bundle on Rebel's aft deck.

Without being asked, Adam removed the pram's kerosene lantern from a dry-bag beneath the forward plank seat. Its base fit into a recess just behind the bow. The lantern's glass wind break was protected by a metal cage that hinged to the side for lighting. Adam lit the wick with a Zippo from the dry bag.

Tala was in our cabin getting ready, keeping me informed of her progress through the starboard porthole. She had bought something at the ladies clothing shop on Bay Street, but she wanted it to be a surprise. The transom portholes were hinged on top and opened inward to adjust the air flow, or they could be closed tight to keep out rain, cold air, or diesel smoke when the engine was running.

I was wearing one of my nicer cool-weather outfits, that is, my least stained and frayed khaki trousers, my best boat shoes, and a gray sweater. I was also taking a navy-blue blazer, but it was folded in my pack. (And my holstered Glock, of course.)

Tala gave me a five-minute warning through the porthole. The pram was ready, so I told Adam to find the first mate and ask him about setting up a bedroll for the night in the hold.

When Tala announced she was ready it was half past five by my watch, just after sunset. After a few more minutes she was coming through the pilothouse. She told me to face away: she didn't want me to watch her climbing down the transom. That rear view of her wasn't the first impression she wanted to make on me. Who was I to complain? I turned away.

Finally she said, "Okay, you can turn around."

In another era her fawn-brown dress might not have set the Paris runways ablaze, but it looked fabulous to me. V-necked in front, the elbow-length sleeves were full and loose. The knit dress fit snugly from her shoulders to her waist, but had plenty of extra material in pleats from her hips down to the hemline just above her knees. She wore the same wedge sandals as before: Rebel Yell's slatted boarding platform was a notorious destroyer of spike high heels.

"Danny, I am buying this dress especially for dancing, so please you will see." She executed a pirouette while raising her arms like a ballerina, and the skirt spiraled out in a fan shape before swirling back down around when she stopped. Her long brown hair was brushed out, and because it had been braided before, it lifted in waves when she made her spin.

I stepped across the teak platform to embrace her, and I did, but she turned her face away from me saying, "No Danny, no kissing, not now—my face will be ruined."

"You look beautiful, honey, just beautiful. Adam's boat is a little tippy, so be careful getting on."

She grabbed her small cosmetics purse from where she'd left it in reach on the aft deck. "Oh, more tippy than Whisper? This is not a problem for me. I can climb up castle walls, did you someday forget?" I knelt and held the pram steady as she stepped aboard and sat on the middle seat facing aft. I tossed my daypack over, and then placed a canvas bag holding a pair of two-liter bottles of gasoline aboard, and then I got on. The warm engine fired on the first easy pull of its rope.

I cast off and steered for the dinghy landing. The captain and his lady were going out for a night of music, dancing and fun. My boat was secure at anchor, the twins looked after, friends and family safely tucked aboard, and a promising young man had been added to the crew. The world was my oyster.

On the way, Tala placed her small cosmetics purse inside a compartment on the outside of my pack and zipped it shut. I didn't mind toting her lady stuff around, because a hands-free Tala left her with an extra hand to pull me in close to her, and one more arm to wrap around me.

With the little four horsepower Honda we weren't going fast enough to make spray, not in the slight chop and random wakes from other boats. Adam's pram rode them like a duck under sail or power. Rebel's new dinghy with the little motor wasn't even remotely in the league of my old Avon RIB and its 70-horse Evinrude, but it beat sailing or rowing to shore when we were dressed for a night out in our best clothes.

I only wished I'd had a camera. The half-moon was high in the west, the sky changing from pink to silver to gray. Tala was facing me from just a few feet away, our knees nearly touching. She was silhouetted against the last twilight, the knit fabric of her dress snug against her body like a second skin. If she was not quite as slender as she'd been when we'd met in Morocco, five years and twin boys earlier, she was even more voluptuous, and to me, that much more beautiful.

The breeze lifted her hair and I wanted to capture the precious moment. But where had all the cameras gone? The same place as the cell phones, consigned to the keepsake box. I had taken hundreds, maybe thousands of digital photos and videos before everything had come unraveled. All those images had disappeared into the ether, or they were trapped in useless hard drives and memory sticks. The film needed for old-fashioned photography had vanished with the digital revolution, so that option was also gone. I didn't even own a working camera, so I could only save this image of her in my memory.

My right hand was on the tiller, so I put my left in front of my face and I mimed taking a photo of Tala with an imaginary camera, clicking my tongue to make my meaning clear.

She took my left hand in both of hers, and kissed each of my fingers, her eyes shining.

I said, "Tala, honey, no matter what happens, I'll always love you, and I'll never forget this perfect, perfect day." Then I noticed something different about her. "No knife tonight?"

"The knife belt looked ugly on this dress. You have your pistol, and you will protect me."

"Yes, I will, I'll protect you forever."

When we reached the landing it was nearly dark at about quarter to six. Most of the dinghy dock was empty, market day over, boat folks gone home for dinner. I was able to tie the pram right alongside the dock with fore and aft lines.

Tala blew out the lantern, but we didn't bother to chain the dinghy to a dock cleat. Stealing another man's boat just didn't happen on the island. Where could a thief take it, either to use it or to sell it, that he wouldn't be found out? The community was too small for that, and theft was not tolerated. I grabbed my pack and the canvas tote bag with the gasoline and stepped over onto the floating dock. When Tala was also on the dock we walked over to the ramp and up onto the land.

There were only a few vendors left on the marina parking lot, and they were packing up their wares. The big deep-cycle batteries were left there on the ground covered with tarps. I remembered how the thief had been chased down for a pair of Zippo cigarette lighters, so who in his right mind would try to steal fifty- and hundred-pound lead-acid batteries?

Crossing the lot toward the river walk and the pavilion, I heard a voice from the landward side calling me by name.

"Captain Kilmer, can you wait up for a moment, sir?"

I had no idea who it was, so I positioned myself in front of Tala with my right hand on the grip of my pistol. Peering into the darkness I could see someone coming our way. There were no streetlights, the moon was providing the only illumination, and it brightened or darkened with each passing cloud.

A boy in an oversized parka approached us, with his hands held far out from his sides to show his peaceful intent. The parka's sleeves were rolled up, its hood was thrown back, and its hem reached past his knees.

"You remember me, sir; I brought the food to your dinghy this morning. I helped your wife and the other lady. That's my wagon over there, you remember?"

"Of course I remember. What can I do for you?" Even in the dim light, Tala and I made a recognizable couple.

"I just wanted to thank you for the extra silver you put in my wagon. You didn't have to do that."

"Oh, you're very welcome. I can tell you're a hard worker. Did you make that cart yourself?"

"Yes sir, I did. But there's something else, sir, something else I wanted to tell you." He looked around and lowered his voice to a whisper. "There might be trouble tonight."

"Trouble? What kind of trouble?"

"It's about the music, sir. The electric music, the amplified rock music and the lights. Some people are upset about it."

"How do you know this?"

"Well, sir, it's like this: I hear things all day, from all kinds of people. They talk around me like I'm a donkey or a mule, like I don't have ears or a brain, oh, but I do! And that's how I know you're Captain Dan Kilmer, and your ship is Rebel Yell. That's how I knew you were coming here tonight; your wife and her friend were talking to the blonde lady from the band. I just wanted to warn you to be careful. And please tell the band to be careful where they put their generator, and who they let into the pavilion. There might be trouble tonight."

The teenager was a runt, he didn't look like much, but he had earned my respect. "Well, thanks for letting me know." I reached into my pocket for some coins, but he held up a hand.

"No sir, that's not necessary. You already did enough for me today. A dollar in silver for just one trip to the dock, that's more than I make on a good day. And if there's ever anything I can do for you, sir, my name is Will Padgett. They call me Wagon Will, like wagon wheel, just ask around. Anything I can do for you, I'll do it. You're a good man, sir, and better than most around here, I can tell you that."

"Thank you, Will, and I do appreciate the information. I'll let the band know what you said."

It was fully dark and nearing six o'clock. We walked along the quay wall toward the river side of the pavilion. There was already a crowd there, the fine weather bringing the people out, or maybe just holding them over from the market day. And it was a beautiful night for a change, after so much rain. The half-moon turning the clouds silver above the palm trees along the river walk, the boats at anchor across the water . . . It was quite romantic, and I pulled Tala close to me, my free arm around her waist, walking hip to hip.

Some vendors were still out, selling local whiskey by the shot, or by the bottle, and pumping beer from aluminum kegs. You could have your own mug filled, or buy it in a cup for an extra fee. Candle makers would sell you one of their lit table samples, and many passers-by were carrying them, adding to the charm. There was no barter at these nighttime tables—it was all cash silver. Some of the dimes and quarters might have begun the day in my pocket. The velocity of real money.

Strings and wires were wrapped around the pavilion's outside pillars, surrounding it from knee to shoulder height, dividing inside from outside. Closer examination showed that many of the ropes and wires were unlit strings of Christmas lights. The covered area of the pavilion was raised a few steps above the brick-paved walkways and lawns that surrounded it, further distinguishing inside from outside. I had brought fuel as our donation, so we were going inside with the high rollers.

The space between two front pillars on the river side was left open; the only unlit light strings were above head height. Tables had been placed where people were leaving various contributions as their entrance payments. Kerosene lanterns and candles on the tables provided illumination. The donations consisted mostly of cakes, pies, loaves of bread and cookies, but I also saw pairs of gloves, knitted socks and caps, unlit candles, bars of soap, and jars of preserves. There was also a change box for cash donations. Cash, again meaning silver.

I pulled out my two-liter plastic bottles of gasoline, and a young man said, "No fuel up here, Captain Kilmer—it's a fire hazard. I'll take it—the fuel goes over there. Oh, and thanks a lot. That much gas will run the generator for a long time. Not for tonight—we're covered—but for the next show."

I didn't know the guy at all, but he knew me. A schooner captain with an old battle scar under his eye, with a beautiful and somewhat exotic wife at his side, well, I supposed that we might stick in folks' memory. There couldn't be many couples fitting our description on the island. Low profile, we were not. But what was the harm? The world was my oyster, right?

A young lady behind the table looked up at me and said, "Give me your hand, captain; it's how we're keeping track." She tied a piece of red knitting yarn around my wrist, and then Tala's. She tightened their knots so that they could never be untied. They would have to be cut off, or left on.

She said, "Now you can come and go as you like. There's a table inside where you can leave your bag and it'll be looked after. We're taking all the food that's donated inside. Some is going to be for everybody to eat, some is going to the church, and some will be for door prizes. Now the beer and whiskey, that's all sold outside, but if you get too drunk you can't come back in. Okay, captain?"

I agreed to her terms, and Tala dragged me up the steps to the main floor under the pavilion's roof. There were already more than a hundred people inside, mostly couples, and more than that number outside on the lawns and under the trees on blankets. The amplified music wasn't going to stop at the edge of the open-sided pavilion, and, for a change, there looked to be almost no chance of rain.

Tala pulled me through all the people toward the back of the pavilion, away from the river, where a stage had been erected. Lanterns were hanging above it to provide some light while the band made their preparations. I stashed my pack under the open front of the stage where I could get it easily. Luke and Jessie were up on the platform; Luke was wearing a red-and-black plaid shirt and blue jeans. His normally wild and bushy beard had been trimmed down to under an inch in length. His black hair was still long enough to tie off in the back.

Jessie's blonde hair was tied in two braids. She wore a light-colored sweater and a dark vest over a leather skirt and cowboy boots. Seeing us, she jumped down from the stage and gave Tala a hug, released her, and then grabbed my hand and twisted my wrist around to look at my watch.

"Four minutes to show time!" she announced to anybody in earshot, and then in a normal voice she said, "We're starting on the six-o'clock church bells, but I guess you knew that."

Luke hopped down and put an arm around Jessie. He was a solid-looking guy about thirty, give or take, and maybe five-ten or eleven in height. With his broad shoulders, plaid shirt and beard, he could have been taken for a lumberjack if you handed him an axe. Jessie's cowboy boots had plenty of heel to them, so she was standing nearly at Luke's height.

We shook hands and I said, "Luke, we need to talk."

"I know, Jessie told me—we're going sailing tomorrow."

"Yeah, that's right, but that's not what I need to tell you. Somebody told me there might be some trouble tonight. Some trouble about the music."

"Trouble? What kind of trouble?"

"I don't know, he just said to watch out where you put your generator, and to be careful who you let inside."

"The generator is in a good place. It's in a fenced-off area that was made for a dumpster, and somebody will be watching it." He moved closer, only inches away, and said, "We've had some other warnings, and we've taken precautions. But I'd appreciate it if you kept an eye out, and let me know if you see anything you think is weird, you know, out of place."

"Yeah, Luke, of course I will." Then I asked him, quietly, "Are you carrying?" Meaning, carrying a concealed handgun.

"Hell yeah, I am, just like you. But mine's hidden better."

He glanced down at the grip of my Glock. I swung off my pack, removed and shook out my dark blazer, and put it on. It was getting cooler, and the jacket would cover my pistol.

Jessie asked me, "So, Captain Dan, what time is it now?"

I checked again. "I've got two minutes after, but my watch never matches the church."

Luke said, "As soon as the bells ring, we're firing up the generator. We've been practicing in a barn, but it's still going to be a little crazy getting our sound levels right because this place has a metal roof and it's wide open. No walls."

I looked past him up onto the stage, which was a few feet higher than the floor of the pavilion, which was itself a few feet higher than outside. There was no piano or keyboard I could see, just string instruments propped up on stands. These included a few electric guitars and a bass, and a raised drum set in the back. I counted three higher microphones on stands in front, so there were at least that many singers, and some more microphones at waist height for the acoustic instruments.

There were unlit spotlights rigged onto a ladder that was attached horizontally to the bottom of the pavilion roof, and tall speakers in the back and on the sides of the stage. Wires snaked across the stage floor and off the back. Behind the stage, just outside the pavilion, were some hedges and trees, and somewhere back there was the waiting generator.

"What time is it?" Jessie asked again.

"Four after, but sometimes they forget, or they're late. The bells aren't on a timer. Somebody has to look at a clock and pull the rope. Sometimes they even miss an hour. They're only human, Jessie. Sometimes, somebody forgets."

She shook her head. "No, not tonight. They didn't forget." She paced nervously, and whispered something to Luke.

"What time is it now?" she asked again.

"Six after," I replied.

It was fully dark outside, the last glimmer of twilight gone, and still no church bells rang. There was more unease, and some murmuring in the crowd. Those who had watches were checking them and repeating the times to their friends.

Luke said, "That's it. At ten after we're kicking it off, bells or no bells." He climbed back on stage, pulling Jessie up after him. Then he picked up an acoustic six-string guitar and lifted its strap over his head. Jessie grabbed a mandolin and did the same. Alongside them other members of the band got ready with a banjo, an electric guitar, and a bass.

A dark-haired girl no older than twenty grabbed a fiddle and bow, waving them over her head, getting the attention of somebody back in the audience. The drummer was behind his drum set, twirling his sticks through his fingers like batons. He was around my age, wearing farmer's overalls over a red shirt and a ball cap on backwards.

Tala and I were standing closest to the stage, in touching distance of the first row of microphone stands. Luke looked at me and said, "Just tell me when it's ten after." The crowd had grown hushed, every ear straining to hear the first chime of a church bell announcing six o'clock. It didn't come.

I checked my watch again, looked back up at Luke, and I announced, "I've got eleven after, right now."

Jessie turned and looked at Luke, and he nodded to her. She put two fingers in her mouth and made a long piercing whistle. After a moment I heard a gas generator firing up somewhere back behind the stage. Jessie jabbed both of her arms straight out, and the overhead spotlights came on, flooding the band in colors and turning the stage into a blazing island of light.

Then Jessie brought her hands together in front, paused, and then slowly spread her arms wide again, and from pillar to pillar all of the way around the pavilion the dark wires flared on in strings of light. Red and green Christmas lights, blue and white lights, Japanese lanterns, and color-changing LEDs in clear tubes. In string after string they came on, encircling the pavilion in electric light, and the crowds both inside and outside erupted in cheers. The church bells were forgotten on the rising tide of excitement.

Jessie put her lips up to her microphone and her amplified voice said, "Now I hope y'all understand that we didn't have a chance to do a sound check in this wonderful Beaufort pavilion, but at least I know this mic is hot, right? So just give us a minute here—sound check, please. Sound check."

The drummer beat a tattoo on his snare followed by a bass thump and a cymbal strike, and the other band members tested the strings of their instruments and adjusted the knobs of their amplifiers as the singers repeated "check-check-check" into their microphones, looking around and nodding to the others.

The electric guitar player appeared to be the third singer, because he was standing behind his own microphone on the other side of Jessie from Luke. He was about my age or a little older, with long blonde hair down over the shoulders of his red cowboy shirt. I had the strong impression that this wasn't his first time on stage with his red Fender Stratocaster.

Jessie's voice blasted out again, crisp and clean. "Wow! Hey, that sounds pretty good, doesn't it?" and the audience cheered. "And if you're wondering about the songs we're playing tonight, well, they're mostly old stuff we found on vinyl.

You know, old-fashioned L. P. records, because that's all we could find that still worked. For some of them we found sheet music, but mostly we're just faking it from the records, but I think we sound pretty good, and I hope you think so too."

She laughed, and the crowd clapped and laughed with her.

The bass player, who was over sixty judging by his gray ponytail, long beard and wrinkles, held up two record albums, and the crowd erupted in cheers again. I recognized one of them as The Eagles Greatest Hits.

Jessie's amplified voice said, lower then, "Well folks, it sounds like everything is working, and if the band is ready—and I *know* they are—well, keep your fingers crossed and let's see what happens."

The first song began with Luke playing a hauntingly familiar guitar riff followed by his amplified voice, with Jessie and the young female violinist singing counterpoint harmony behind him. She had a microphone on her fiddle.

All the leaves are brown, and the sky is gray,
I've been for a walk, on a winter's day,
I'd be safe and warm, if I was in LA,
California dreaming, on such a winter's day

The crowd's cheering dropped down to a hush. Some of the people around me seemed to choke up, and even to weep. I was probably getting a bit misty too. It had been so long since I had heard that song, much less played live on stage.

Tala buried her face against my neck as the song played out and we swayed together. She said, "You know, my brother Kam went to California. He was surfing with Americans. And now I don't know if he is living or no."

What could I say to that? Old songs triggered memories, and everybody's memory was different. Their next song began with ringing guitar chords, and Luke singing lead.

Well I'm runnin' down the road,
Tryin' to loosen my load,
I got seven women on my mind,
Four that want to own me,
Two that want to stone me,
One says she's a friend of mine

After the second verse the audience began to join in. Don't let the sound of your own wheels drive you crazy.

Take It Easy ended with a banjo solo that carried the band into a bluegrass set. One song I remember was about good old Rocky Top Tennessee, and that tune continued straight into a bluegrass rendition of Dixie.

Oh I wish I was in the land of cotton,
Old times there are not forgotten,
Look away, look away, look away, Dixie land

I was not a native son of the South, but even so it was emotionally stirring to be in that crowd with everybody else singing along with the band, stomping their feet, clapping, and hollering. Tala didn't understand the lyrics but it didn't matter, she was there to dance, and dance she did, copying the moves of the other ladies around us.

It had been years since Rebel Yell's CD player had eaten its last compact disc and died. Speakers also had a short life span on board an ocean sailboat, but I resolved that I'd look into getting an old-fashioned turntable record player. It would be simple to run it off 12-volt DC using our AC inverter. I put buying a record player on my pre-voyage shopping list, along with vinyl records and 12-volt speakers—if we could find any.

And just maybe Captain Stark on the Battle Wagon had a working CD player and speakers for sale along with his radio gear and other electronics. I'd hung onto a bunch of compact discs after the demise of our last CD player. They didn't take up much room, and I couldn't bring myself to toss them over.

The next song was a bluegrass instrumental. I didn't know its name but it transitioned into an old country hit by Alabama.

Play me, some mountain music,
Like grandpa and grandma used to play,
And I'll float, on down the river,
To the Cajun hideaway

By then everybody in the pavilion was clapping, spinning, stomping, hooting and whistling, and the even bigger audience outside was too, when the stage lights went dark. The music stopped except for the band members' unamplified voices and guitars. The lights around the pavilion went out at the same time. The only light came from the lanterns hanging above the stage. The band looked around in confusion and stopped playing. I couldn't hear the generator running. I looked down at my watch: it wasn't even seven o'clock.

Some people in the audience booed and yelled out their disappointment at the abrupt termination of the concert, but my initial sense was that the problem would be sorted out, the power would come back up, and the show would go on.

8

Instead, a brilliant white spotlight flashed through the front of the open-sided pavilion and across the audience all the way to the stage, its beam sweeping side to side. Another spotlight penetrated from another angle. Both of them were originating from the river side, crisscrossing back and forth through the pavilion. An amplified voice boomed from a loudspeaker, from the same direction as the source of the powerful lights.

"This is the Beaufort County Militia. This is the Beaufort County Militia. You are holding an unauthorized and illegal event. I repeat, you are holding an unauthorized event and you are disturbing the peace. You are hereby ordered to disperse and go home. You are ordered to disperse and go home. Go on home, everybody, go on home. Disperse and go on home."

Luke handed his guitar to the older bass player and jumped down from the stage, followed by the drummer and the other guitarist. Luke Hanahan was absolutely livid, but all three men seemed seriously angry as they pushed through the audience toward the riverside entrance. I followed them to the steps of the pavilion and toward the sweeping spotlights, shielding my eyes with my left hand.

The loudspeaker voice continued making demands. "This is the Beaufort Militia. You must disperse immediately. This is an unlawful event. You are disturbing the peace and you must disperse immediately. This is an unauthorized event."

Outside the pavilion I saw two pickup trucks parked on the paved river walk about a hundred feet apart. Both pickups had a man standing in the bed near the cab holding a spotlight. I knew the lights well, corded million-candle-power jobs. I had similar ones on Rebel Yell that were still working years after the last so-called "rechargeable" spotlights had died. As long as they were plugged into a 12-volt outlet, they could light up a ship's bridge on a black night from a mile away. They were blinding when they were aimed at close range through the pavilion, and disorienting given that the beams were randomly sweeping from side to side.

About twenty-five uniformed soldiers were spread in a line in front of and between the trucks with a few yards between each of them. The side-shine of the two spotlights lit them up well enough to study them in detail. They were all wearing an old uniform I knew well, USMC desert digital camouflage, but with tan ball caps on top instead of Kevlar helmets.

Each man was wearing a hard-plate armor vest with extra magazine pouches in front to feed the M-4 carbines they were cradling. These weapons were all carried level in front on two-point slings. Their carbines were aimed to the side, but they had mags loaded and it would only take a second for them to turn and open fire if they were given the order.

Luke and I saw the man who was doing all the talking. He was standing inside the open door of the pickup closest to the front of the pavilion. He continued barking out his demands.

"You heard me! This is an illegal unauthorized event. You are disturbing the peace and you have to leave right now. This is an official order. The party's over, folks. Now, go on home, everybody. You have to go on home right now."

Luke marched right up to him in a fury. I thought he'd go right for the man's throat, but he stopped short. When we were just a few yards from the white pickup its searchlight beam, originating from above its cab, shined over us into the open-sided pavilion but not directly into our faces.

The drummer, the other guitarist and the banjo player were standing beside Luke, and I was just behind them. I did a slow 360-degree turn, not wanting to lose my all-around situational awareness. Tala and Jessie were on top of the steps near the entrance to the pavilion, protecting their eyes while watching the unfolding drama along with most of the audience.

Luke continued to within a yard of the militiaman with the microphone, and in a loud voice he said, "Well, well, well, it's Bobby Ray Aikman—I should have guessed! Bobby Ray, you were a douchebag in high school, and you're still a douche. When did you make captain, you asshole? Who authorized the railroad tracks on your hat, Dalton Dorchester? Who made Dorchester a colonel? Weren't you just an Airman in the Air Force? And tonight you're pretending to be an officer in the circle-jerk Beaufort Militia? Jesus. . ."

Captain Aikman, clearly stunned, replied, "L-Luke, you didn't get approval for this rock concert—it's unauthorized."

"What? You know that's all bullshit. We signed up for this time slot last Sunday, just like anybody else could have done."

"But you didn't get approval for amplified music. You're disturbing the peace, and we've had complaints."

"So who said we needed approval for amplified music? Where's that written? Show me. And you got complaints from who? Name them! Who are they?"

"B-but Luke, nobody has ever done this before. Something like this, a big change like this, it has to be approved."

"Approved by who? Who died and made you the king of Beaufort County? Bobby Ray, this is all bullshit and you know it." Luke stepped even closer, moving into shoving range.

A militia soldier near Aikman with three black sergeant's chevrons on the front of his ball cap said, "Luke Hanahan, you better stop right there—I'm warning you!"

Luke turned to the NCO and said, "Ben Cardin—what the *hell* are you doing with these assholes? You can go ahead and play the militia hero on the bridges, but don't you *ever* get the idea you're going to boss us around like you're a cop again. No way. Those days are over, and you ain't no kind of a cop."

The militia sergeant wasn't carrying a long gun, but he had a handgun holstered on his belt. He looked at Captain Aikman, who nodded back to him, and then he turned back to Luke and moved his hand toward his hip.

The drummer said, "Ben Cardin—you ain't a cop no more. There ain't no cops on the island. But you pull that pistol, and I swear to God almighty it'll be the last thing you ever do."

The line of troops spread between the two pickups seemed frozen in place, their carbines held horizontally in front but not pointed at the people. I turned again, and from both sides of the pavilion the crowd that had been listening from outside on the grass was inching forward. Against the two dozen militiamen were hundreds of islanders, with the angriest men in the front. I guessed that half of them were carrying pistols.

Captain Aikman, if that was a real rank, seemed to notice them too. His microphone was connected to the inside of the vehicle's cab with a spiral cord, and he turned and set it down on the front seat so his back was to us. When he turned toward us again he was holding a cylinder as tall as a can of spray paint, but thicker. By the red stripes and the lettering on it, I recognized it as a military-issue CS canister, or what we used to call tear gas back in the day.

Luke didn't back down at the sight of it, but said, "Bobby Ray, you must surely be mentally retarded. Did that Colonel Dorchester send you down here tonight, or did you initiate this cluster fuck all on your own?"

Aikman moved the canister to his right hand and put his left index finger into the ring that, when pulled, armed it. In a quaking voice he announced, "Everybody has to go right now. We're not joking around. This is an unauthorized event, and you all are disturbing the peace."

Without the loudspeaker his voice was unimpressive, but more importantly, he needed both hands on the canister to pull the pin, and he could not pick up the microphone again unless he let go of the ring. It was obvious that he had not thought this all the way through. I did another look all around. The two spotlights were no longer sweeping the crowd, but were aimed over the roof of the pavilion. They still threw off plenty of side light, but without being shined aggressively at people's faces.

By then the front edge of the crowd, almost all men, had walked up to within bare yards of the line of militia troops. Many of these civilians had their hands on their pistols, but none had been drawn, at least not that I could see. The ratio was obvious to everyone. The militiamen were outnumbered at least twenty-to-one. Even with their loaded thirty-round magazines they would have no guarantee of ultimate success.

Luke turned to face the crowd, and in a commanding voice he said, "Stand down, men, everybody stand down. Nothing's going to happen tonight, nothing is going to happen."

Then, turning back to Captain Aikman and his sergeant he said, quietly, "Bobby Ray, if you throw that canister in among our wives and girlfriends on a happy night like tonight, you'll be lucky to make it to the mainland alive. And even if you do, you'll never be able to show your face on the island again. Are you hearing me, Bobby Ray? Do you copy what I'm saying?"

Luke was getting right in the militia captain's face, leaning in, quite furious but still maintaining his composure. Speaking in a lower voice, just to Captain Aikman and his sergeant, he said, "There's only two ways this can end. One way is you're going to climb into your trucks, and you're going to drive on back up to the air station and call it a night—and we'll try to forget this ever happened. That's one way."

The crowd kept inching nearer, almost close enough to touch the line of militiamen, or grab at their slung carbines.

"The other way is we're going to take your guns from you and roll your trucks into the river, and then you're going to have to walk back to the air station to give your after-action report to Colonel Dorchester. Those are your only two options, Bobby Ray: you drive out, or you walk out. Because you are never, *ever*, going to run this town like you're some kind of a police chief. We're all done with that here. Those days are all over. So you can go back to guarding the bridges and keeping out the mainlanders—and we're fine with that. But if you pull the pin on that CS, well, Bobby Ray, I'd seriously advise you not to do it. So it's your call: you drive out, or you walk out."

Captain Aikman stood frozen for long seconds, leaning against the pickup, trying not to tremble, but then he removed his finger from the canister's arming ring and said, "Sergeant

Cardin, tell the men to mount up. R.T.B. We're going to return to base." He got into the cab of his truck and closed the door.

The sergeant hollered, "Okay men, mount up! Mount up! Tonight's exercise is over—return to base. Return to base!"

The two dozen militiamen turned and walked past the front of the crowd accompanied by boos, jeers, and insults. They got into the cabs and climbed into the backs of their trucks, which reversed down the river walk to the marina parking lot, turned around and departed, heading north in the direction of the old Marine Corps Air Station.

It had been such a shocking five or ten minutes that I didn't notice the generator firing up again, but we all saw the lights come back on, and then we heard Jessie's amplified voice.

"Well, come on back everybody—we're not even halfway through our song list!"

Those of us with red yarn bracelets went back inside, and maybe some without them went in too. Nobody was checking. Tala found me by the front steps, hugged and kissed me, and dragged me by my hand back toward the stage. The generator was growling and the spotlights were back on.

Jessie, up on the stage, said to the audience, "Well, folks, I don't know about you, I sure didn't expect *that* tonight!"

Before Luke climbed back onto the stage, an older man in a black suit and white collar spoke to him, and Luke asked him if he'd repeat the same thing to the crowd. Jessie removed a corded mic from its stand and handed it down to him.

The man turned and faced the audience, saying, "Hello, everybody, I'm Pastor Bill Keller, and maybe you know me, at least I hope some of you do! I'm real sorry about tonight, but I just wanted everybody to know that we were going to ring the bells at six o'clock like always, but, uh, a few fellows from the militia visited us just before then and they wouldn't let us. So if you heard a rumor that we have a problem with the music, well, it's just not true. And that's all I wanted to say."

The audience applauded respectfully, and somebody called out, "You're a good man, Reverend Bill!" Then Luke passed the mic back up to Jessie and he climbed on stage and huddled with the band. Some were nodding yes, and some seemed unsure. Luke put the mic back in its stand and said, "Okay, we haven't practiced this one as a band, but Jessie and I know it, and the rest of them will fake it." Luke and Jessie both began to play and sing, the others joining in.

Just a closer walk with thee, Grant it Jesus, is my plea,
Daily walking close to thee, Let it be, dear lord, let it be

The audience inside and outside was quiet until the end of the song, then erupted with Amen, Praise Jesus, Glory Be and Hallelujah. And so the concert continued, with Jessie right in the middle switching between her mandolin and her acoustic guitar, and sometimes just singing, playing neither instrument.

I can't remember all the songs, but the band played some more Eagles hits, and some Fleetwood Mac, and Johnny Cash, and Creedence Clearwater Revival, and Marshal Tucker, and I remember John Denver's Country Road. But for me the highlight of the evening was slow dancing with Tala while Jessie sang one of the last songs of the night.

I feel so bad, I've got a worried mind,
I'm so lonesome, all the time,
Since I left my baby behind, on Blue Bayou

Finally Jessie announced, "Now listen folks, and I mean it this time, this really is our last song. I think everybody has had enough excitement for one night, and we're awful tired." Then she turned to Luke and the other members of the band and she mouthed a song title them.

She lifted her guitar off and placed it on the stand behind her, then took her microphone out of its stand and held it in both hands. She nodded to Luke, and the band began to play the first notes at a slow tempo.

Somewhere, over the rainbow, way up high,
There's a land that I heard of, once in a lullaby.
Somewhere, over the rainbow, skies are blue,
And the dreams that you dare to dream,
Really do come true . . .

As the last notes faded the spotlights went out, leaving the stage in darkness except for the hanging kerosene lanterns. The generator and the lights surrounding the pavilion were left on to provide light for the audience on their way out. Tala and I continuing our embrace long after the music ended.

I thought: by the time we get back to Rebel Yell, the twins will be sound asleep in their passageway berth, and if we tiptoe past them, I'm going to lock our cabin door behind us, peel this soft new dress up and off Tala's soft, curvy body and . . .

She pushed away from my embrace, hauling me back to reality. The band had to break down their equipment, and we needed to help them. I checked my watch: it was only a little after nine o'clock, but it felt much later.

Jessie jumped down to the floor and said, "Luke doesn't think we should go home tonight. We'd better let that jerk Bobby Aikman cool off some first. I can't believe I ever dated him. We live up north too, and we don't want to run into him. Can we stay on your boat tonight, until we go sailing tomorrow?"

"Well sure, of course," I replied.

Luke asked me, "Do you mind if we bring our guitars and Jessie's mandolin? I don't want to leave them here over night. Do you have room?"

"Luke, it's a sixty-foot schooner. There's room. We'll help you carry everything over to the boat landing. But we'll have to make two runs out to Rebel Yell. Our new dinghy isn't big enough to take the four of us and all of your stuff in one trip. I'll take Tala and Jessie first, and then I'll come back for you."

The drummer volunteered to camp out on the stage under the pavilion roof, guarding the speakers, the amplifiers and the generator. There wasn't much theft on the island, but this principle could not be extended out to infinity. Tomorrow morning some of the band and their friends would take the stage apart, bring down the strings of lights and clean everything up. They had a horse and wagon lined up to get all their band equipment back to the barn where they practiced.

Finally the generator was switched off, and the strings of lights went dark. Luke and Jessie spent a minute or two with each member of the band, telling them that it was a night they would never forget for the rest of their lives. The audience was gone when we finally walked out of the pavilion.

And standing there by the bottom of the steps next to his cart was Wagon Will, wearing his too-large military parka.

I said, "Have you been waiting here all this time?"

"Oh, no sir, no. I've been keeping busy; I made some good tips tonight. I hauled the empty kegs back to McNally's; jobs like that. The concert was amazing. I've never heard anything like it in my life. Nothing like it, not ever. The lights too, they were just beautiful, beautiful. It was like magic."

I introduced him. "Luke, Jessie—this is Will. Will hauled our groceries to the dock with Sofia this morning. Will, do you want to make another wagon run tonight?"

"Of course, Captain Kilmer, anything you say. Anything."

We loaded his cart with the guitars and the mandolin in their black cases, a few bags that Luke and Jessie had brought with them for the concert, and my daypack. We could have carried it all by ourselves, but Will's wagon was right there.

Jessie said, "My throat is so sore. I never thought we'd play for that long. And I'm so tired I'm ready to fall down."

Tala leaned against me, Jessie leaned against Luke, and we set off across the marina parking lot to the dinghy landing, with Wagon Will following us with his cart. After we walked down the ramp to the floating dock Will turned his cart around so that he could back it down, keeping it under better control from below. When we were all on the dock he spun it around again and followed us out to the pram.

I looked at the passengers and the baggage, and suggested that the ladies should go with me on the first trip out to Rebel Yell, and then I'd come back for Luke.

Tala stepped on and clambered forward, the dinghy rocking madly. "What about the lantern?" she asked casually.

I said, "There's a Zippo in the bag by the mast." She was still the lead climber. Fortress walls, cliffs, or anything else.

In a minute she'd lit it, its oil lamplight providing enough illumination for Jessie to board and for us to load the boat.

Luke passed over their instruments, and I climbed aboard and got the motor going. He cast off our lines and we motored back out through the anchorage. By then the half-moon was two hand-widths above the western horizon, and the stars were visible where the sky was not blocked by passing clouds.

The wind had dropped and Rebel Yell was resting easy at anchor, but now with her bow pointed south, down river, and her stern facing back toward town because the flood tide was coming in. Rebel's white masthead anchor light and stern light were on, giving me a clear target to aim for between the other anchored boats. Like all the lights on Rebel Yell they ran on 12-volt current, so we had plenty of juice to run them anytime we needed to—at least for as long as their LED bulbs lasted.

Gino and Adam were standing on the boarding platform to catch our lines when I coasted in parallel and put the outboard in neutral. Tala and I passed our lines to them and they cleated them off, holding the pram in position parallel to the platform with the current trying to pull it away.

Adam said, “We knew you’d be coming back after all the lights went out. That was a great concert, it was awesome!”

“You heard it all the way out here?” I asked him.

“Oh, yeah, sure, I mean, yes sir. It was great, just great. Except when the music stopped in the middle. What happened then? We couldn’t make any sense of it.”

“We’ll tell you about it later.”

Tala passed their bags and instruments across to Gino, and then she stepped onto the platform. She was barefoot, holding her sandals. Like a cat, Tala always landed on her feet.

Adam took Jessie’s hand and steadied her as she stood up in the pram to step across. He told her, “You have an amazing voice, ma’am. I mean, the whole band is great, but your voice, I think your voice is the best part.”

She looked at him a little uncertainly, not knowing who he was, and I said, “Jessie, this is Adam, the newest member of the crew. He’s going with us on the voyage.”

She laughed and said, “Well thank you, Adam, it’s always nice to meet a new fan.”

“What’s the name of your band?” he asked her.

“We don’t really have a name, not yet.”

I said, “Adam, Jessie is Mrs. Hanahan, all right? Mr. Luke Hanahan is still back on the dock because there wasn’t room for him on this trip. The Hanahans are staying aboard tonight.” I wanted to reinforce my policy about how he was to address the adults on my schooner.

Tala said, “Come on Jessie, let’s go down below where it’s warm. Do you like some hot soup? We have so much.”

“Oh, hot soup—that would be perfect for my throat.” The ladies climbed up the transom steps and disappeared. Gino went up last of all, and Adam passed the baggage to him.

I told Adam, “I’ll be right back in a few minutes with Mr. Hanahan.” The motor was running, and he cast off the lines.

When I returned to the dinghy landing Luke was not alone. Wagon Will was still there, keeping him company. Then it hit me—I hadn't tipped him for the last trip from the pavilion. I said, "Luke, climb aboard and sit in the middle, and just hold onto the dock. I'll be back in a minute."

I left the motor going, and stepped off as Luke got on. I was already getting used to the balance points of the pram. Will was standing about twenty feet away, probably too shy to ask for payment. It was unlikely that Luke was carrying any silver on him, and Will had probably not asked. So I went over to him, thinking about our interactions from around noon on. Before reaching into my pocket, questions formed in my mind.

"Will, do you live in Beaufort?"

"Right now? No sir, I live just outside on a little farm. On an orchard farm. I only come in for the weekends."

"Do you have somebody you're looking after? A mother, a sister, anybody like that?"

"No sir, it's just me. I live in a shed, but I fixed it up nice and I'm getting by just fine. They treat me all right there."

"How old are you, Will?"

He looked down. "I'm sixteen, sir, if you can believe it."

The famine had done this—blighted his most important growth years. The lost years could not be made up with more food and better nutrition later on.

"How is your eyesight?" Stunted growth often manifested in other ways, but at least his mind seemed sound.

"I'd say my eyes are sharp, sir. I can usually spot things far off before most others do. Birds, things like that."

"No family at all?"

"None on the island. I don't know about back on the mainland, my cousins and such, but my close family is all passed."

"Can you read and write, Will?" Nothing could be taken for granted in those days. Nothing.

"I can read okay, I suppose, but I'm not so good at writing. I've really had no schooling since before, you know . . ."

This was not unusual for the time and place. Adam had truly been blessed to have a man like Captain Hilton to tutor him.

"Do you get seasick much?"

"Seasick? No, I don't think so, but I really haven't spent much time on boats. Why?"

I stared at him, almost disbelieving what I was about to say, an inner voice urging me to stop . . . shut up . . . don't . . .

But I did. "Will, how would you like to leave the island, and sail to South America with us?"

"Sail to South America, sir?"

"That's where we're going, and I'm short on crew."

His eyes pinched, his lips pursed and quivered. "You're not joking on me, sir? You wouldn't do that, would you?"

"No, son, I wouldn't do that. Not even a little bit."

After a few fast short breaths he said, "Then I'm your man, Captain Kilmer. Until the day I die, I'm your man."

He thrust his hand out, and I shook it.

"Well, I hope that day is a long way off, for both of us. Sit up there in the front and we'll shove off."

He left the wagon and climbed aboard. The outboard was running so we were underway in a few moments. From the middle seat Luke gave me an inquisitive stare. I just shrugged.

As soon as I'd made my impulsive offer, and Will had immediately accepted it, I'd had misgivings. It wasn't likely, not on the island, but he could be carrying some dormant disease or virus. Or he could be some kind of an emotionally damaged psychotic. God knows there were enough of them.

And he was a famine runt. He wouldn't be able to handle Rebel Yell's wheel in anything but a flat calm. From the look of him he barely broke five-foot-three and a hundred pounds, but what there was of him had muscle. He'd demonstrated that by lifting his cart handles when it was heavily loaded with our groceries, and pushing it across the ground behind Sofia. He was coordinated, too. I'd seen that when he'd turned his cart around and backed it down the ramp from below.

And he'd sought me out to thank me for the extra silver, and he'd given me the warning. Even if he'd been starved in childhood, and left alone in the world, somehow his gratitude and sense of morality had developed and flowered. Once again it seemed as though the good lord still had a few mysteries to toss my way, and for most of them I was grateful.

To have survived through the catastrophe as a famine runt and an orphan, and a ginger-haired runt at that, he must have had a strong will to survive, and inborn native smarts. He'd built his own wagon and carved out a niche in Beaufort. And if his eyes were as sharp as he said, then he could stand watch as a lookout as well as anybody of any age or size.

In a minute I'd be back on Rebel, and I was wondering how I was going to explain the unexpected arrival of a new member of our crew to Tala, Gino and Sofia. They'd probably think that I'd lost my mind. Maybe I had. Probably I had.

9

The breeze had lessened and the river was calm, so we had a smooth ride back out to the boat. The half-moon was lower. Despite the lack of wind the anchored boats were pulling hard against their chains, the flood tide trying to drag them up river.

On the way through the anchorage I told Will that he'd have to hand over or toss the bow line to whoever was waiting for us, and if there was nobody, he'd have to hop off and tie the line to one of the cleats on the aft deck. I expected help to be there waiting, but Will had to learn the duties of the dinghy crew anyway so I told him.

When I slid the pram in next to the boarding platform, only Adam was there to meet us. The stern light on the back of Rebel's transom provided illumination. We'd turn it off once we finished with the dinghy and were all down below.

Will handed the end of the line to Adam, and he tied it to a cleat on the port side of the aft deck, the side near the transom steps. The current caught the dinghy and swung it away from the swim platform. The tide was running at a few knots, and the line was put under some strain, but we were secured to the mothership and I killed the engine. We'd be using it again in the morning, so I left the propeller down in the water instead of tilting the little motor up. Home again, Finnegan.

Adam pulled the dinghy in close by its bow line until its stem was against the swim platform, showing off his strength, which was considerable for a fifteen-year-old. He registered some surprise at seeing an unexpected passenger in the bow of his pram, but he held at his task.

All the baggage had gone aboard on the first trip, so I told Will and Luke it would be quicker to scramble over the bow. There was no need to bring the dinghy alongside fighting the current just to get aboard. First Will and then Luke clambered over and onto the swim platform, and I followed them.

Once we were all aboard, Adam let the rope slip back out until his pram was trailing in the current a few yards behind, while still secured at the deck cleat. I checked it, just to be sure. He'd wrapped the cleat with several figure eights and a locking turn at the top. Captain Sapelo had trained him well.

Adam and Will seemed to recognize one another, but that could wait until later. The boarding platform at night, even on calm water, wasn't the best place for a reunion.

I said, "The dinghy can stay here. It's not going anywhere, and the current will hold it off. My pillow is right under that porthole, so if anything changes, I'll come up and take care of it. Adam, you go up first, and then Will."

As the boys climbed up to the aft deck, a light came on in the aft cabin and Tala asked, "Is everything okay, my love?"

"Of course it is. I'll see you in a minute."

She reached a hand out through the open starboard-side transom porthole, and I gave it a squeeze. She said, "We're eating soup. I just came back to see you. The boys are asleep."

"We'll be right there. I have a surprise." I was thinking of how to introduce Wagon Will to Gino. At least Tala and Sofia already knew him as the wagon boy from their shopping trip ashore. The aft cabin light blinked out.

Then I heard the roar of an outboard motor, and not far away. Some idiot was out joyriding through the dark anchorage, wasting gasoline, and probably drunk. The sound of the engine was off from Rebel's port side so I didn't see the boat until it passed our stern and carved a turn in toward us. Then a spotlight switched on, flooding us in a brilliant glare and rendering the approaching motorboat invisible to me.

Nobody I knew would ever pull a stunt like this. This was major-league asshole behavior at night in an anchorage. Then a voice over a loudspeaker screamed out, "This is the Beaufort

County Militia—put your hands up or we'll open fire! Hands up, or we'll open fire! Do it now, or we'll open fire!"

And that voice was familiar—I'd heard it only a few hours earlier. Our stern light plus their searchlight reflecting off our transom lit them up as they drew near. My hand was on my Glock when I saw the machine gun on the bow of the gunboat.

I knew the boat by sight; we'd passed it dozens of times over the past two years. It was an eighteen-foot Boston Whaler with a belt-fed thirty-caliber M-240G machine gun on a pintle post ahead of the center console—and the business end of that machine gun was aimed at my chest!

The voice on the loudspeaker demanded, "Put your hands up, Hanahan, and you too, Kilmer! Do it now, or we'll open fire—no more warnings!"

I did as the voice ordered. The boat slowed, coming down off plane and gliding up to our stern. The handheld spotlight went out, glowing orange for a moment then leaving a black mark on my eyeballs until they recovered some night vision.

I knew the voice and now I recognized the one who held the light: it was Captain Aikman. Four men were aboard the Whaler. They were wearing the same desert digital uniforms and tan ball caps as before, but this time without their chest rigs. One man was standing in the bow manning the machine gun; the others were beside the center console. Then I heard, without any loudspeaker amplification, "Put us up against him and keep us there until we're tied off."

The coxswain inched the boat forward until its bow was nudging against the boarding platform, and then he held its position against the force of the tidal current with just a little forward thrust. Adam's pram had been pushed over so that it rode against the Whaler's port side.

Aikman said, "Cooper—tie us off." The militiaman on the port side of the center console had been aiming his carbine at Luke. He let his rifle hang by its sling, then he moved forward and stepped over the Whaler's bow and down onto our swim platform. He took their boat's bow line with him and secured it to the middle cleat on our aft deck, leaving a little slack.

My hands were still straight up. I edged over toward the starboard end of the platform away from the bow of their boat, and the machine gun followed me. Luke was across the platform on the port side, where he'd been about to climb up the transom steps. His arms were also all the way up.

Captain Aikman set his corded microphone and spotlight down on the top of the console and said, "What's the matter, Luke? Cat got your tongue, tough guy? All out of tough guy talk without your mob behind you? How about it, tough guy—you're not feeling so tough now, are you? Yeah, well, I guess we're going to see who's the tough guy now!"

Luke didn't say anything in response, and neither did I. What could I say? The machine gun was still trained on me.

The militia captain drew his pistol, then he moved around the center console and past the machine gunner and up onto the Whaler's bow, ready to step down onto Rebel's boarding platform. This would put two of them on Rebel Yell and leave two on their boat, the machine gunner and the coxswain.

This wasn't much of a boarding party to attempt to take control of a sixty-foot schooner, but then I hadn't been very impressed by Captain Aikman's talent for mission planning earlier that night. That aside, the belt-fed M-240 aimed at my chest from only a couple yards away did have my full respect.

Maybe they were about to be joined by more militia boats, in which case we were flat plain screwed. Or maybe this was a case of Captain Aikman going rogue and ordering a mission out of angry revengeful spite after his public humiliation at the pavilion concert. In this case, maybe we'd get an opening when they tried to take Rebel Yell with such a small force.

Or, more likely, they were going to handcuff Luke and me and force us onto their boat, take us ashore under some kind of arrest, and then send a bigger force out to seize Rebel. There was so much to process in so little time, in such a small space, and it was hard to think clearly with that gun aimed at my ribs.

At close range a belt-fed thirty-caliber can cut a man in half—and you don't ever forget the sight.

I spent a moment studying the machine gunner. He was up against his gun's stock, his right hand on its pistol grip, his finger curled around the trigger. I looked at his face, trying to read his eyes to gauge his intent, when a black hole appeared in the middle of his forehead and he fell backward.

Captain Aikman clutched his chest as he was stepping down onto the swim platform. He twisted and fell against the bow of the Whaler, looked at me in passing, and then he rolled and plunged head first into the river and disappeared. All this happened in a few seconds, and I never heard a gunshot.

The Whaler's coxswain thrust his arms straight up; it must have seemed like the smart thing to do. With his hand off the throttle the boat slipped back a few feet in the current, but it was caught there by its line so that its bow was about two feet behind and above our swim platform.

I finally remembered my own pistol and drew it, but the other militiaman in the middle of the platform also had his arms straight up by then. My ears started working again, or maybe it was my brain, in either case I heard him shouting, "Don't shoot! Don't shoot! Don't shoot!"

It took a few moments for me to put the pieces together. I could see across the aft deck all the way to the back of the pilothouse. Adam and Will were taking cover low in the cockpit. This meant that the gunshots whose results I had seen but not heard had come through one of the transom portholes. This was actually an anti-boarding contingency that we had planned and trained for. This is why I had instinctively moved to the outside of the swim platform, to give a shooter inside a clear field of fire. I'd done this without conscious thought.

Luke was on the other side of the teak platform from me,

the other militiaman was standing between us with his hands straight up. Then Gino was looming above me, pistol in hand, yelling and cursing nonstop in fast Italian, and I saw Adam's face appear up there too. I tried to pull myself together but I was still pretty shocky. Tala was behind Gino, she was also armed with a pistol, and behind her were Sofia, Jessie, Rita, and Will, all wide-eyed.

Somebody had to be in charge, and that somebody had to be me. I forced my brain to stop whirling, like jumping off a spinning playground merry-go-round. I kept seeing that hole appear in the machine gunner's forehead, and Aikman's boots disappearing into the river. Deep breath. Focus. I directed my attention to the militiaman on the platform between us.

"Luke, take his rifle." He lifted the sling over the man's head while I aimed my Glock at him. Luke handed the carbine up to Tala who set it down out of sight. The man's arms were at the level of our machine gun's tripod legs, making for an easy solution. "Gino, tie his hands behind the Dushka. Luke, stay here in case I need something else."

This only left the boat's coxswain to deal with. What next? Think, Dan, think! Captain Aikman is in the river so he's dead or he's dying. No, he's dead. He was shot center mass and he went into the cold black river head first, and you don't survive that. So he's dead all right, and this means the machine gunner might as well join him.

I holstered my pistol and climbed over onto the Whaler. I grabbed the dead man by the collar and belt of his uniform and dragged him to the starboard side. There was no exit wound and not much blood but he was as dead as a stone. I heaved him up on the gunnel of the boat and rolled him into the river. The tidal current carried him back about twenty feet before he disappeared into the dark water below the setting half-moon.

The two dead militiamen were being swept inland up the Beaufort River. One or both of them would fetch up on a sand-bar or in a marsh, and whatever the crabs didn't want might eventually be found and identified by the uniform. This meant that we couldn't stick around the island. I had zero interest in attending a town meeting under the pavilion to explain what had just transpired on the back of my schooner to the brothers, cousins and uncles of the two dead local militiamen. No way.

It was time to get out of Dodge.

"Gino, start the engine and be ready to haul up the anchor on my word. Take Adam and the other new boy with you, they might as well learn the ropes and help out."

My first mate went to the engine panel on the back of the pilothouse, and in a few moments I heard the 200-horsepower Caterpillar rumbling, and soon after that diesel smoke and salt water began to hiss and belch out of the exhaust pipe beneath the middle of the swim platform.

A new plan was forming in my mind. The first and biggest problem was going to be sneaking Rebel under the high bridge two miles south of the anchorage. A militia gun truck with a mounted fifty caliber would in all probability be parked right smack over the boat channel at its center. There would only be a scant few feet of clearance between Rebel's two mastheads and the 65-foot-clearance bridge. The militia squad could stop us with a grappling hook dangled in our rigging. The channel that we had to take under the bridge was less than a hundred feet across between its supporting pillars. If the militia were alerted to our escape attempt, they could easily prevent it.

Then an idea struck me: why not use their gunboat as an escort? If the outpost on top of the bridge wasn't put on alert, the addition of the Whaler would make no difference during our passage beneath them. But if they were on alert, maybe the militia gunboat could be used in our favor, somehow.

After deep-sixing the machine gunner, I held a grab-bar on the starboard side of the center console to steady myself. I was standing only a few feet from the coxswain. His hands were still up so he was leaning forward against the console with his hips to keep his balance. He was a young man, clean shaved with a mustache. He could have been Hispanic, or not, it was hard to tell in the white monochrome light. A new plan began to form in my mind. First, I'd have to put him at ease, and this was not going to be a simple matter after what he'd just seen.

"So, what's your name?"

He half-turned to look at me. "What? Oh, Mike Ortega." He had a single black chevron, point up, on his tan ball cap.

"Okay, Private Ortega, let your hands down slowly. Just keep them on the wheel, all right?"

"Thanks." He lowered his arms.

"Quite a night so far, wouldn't you say, Mike?"

"Oh, yeah. Quite a night."

"Tell me something: was this Captain Aikman's idea, or was it Colonel Dorchester's, or somebody else's?"

"Which part? At the pavilion, or here?"

"Both."

"Colonel Dorchester knew about the pavilion. Nobody else knew about this thing here. Only the four of us."

"Was the pavilion raid Dorchester's idea, or Aikman's?"

"I have no idea. Probably Captain Aikman's. I had no idea the pavilion was going to turn out the way it did, with Captain Aikman trying to shut the music down. And I don't think that Colonel Dorchester knew about it either. They just told us it was going to be a routine exercise."

"They hand out live ammo for a routine exercise?"

"Sometimes, sure. We do live-fire drills where they put a target out on a marsh or floating on a creek and we light it up."

"So you think attacking my boat was Aikman's idea?"

"Oh, I'm pretty sure it was."

"Who else knows about it?"

"Nobody else. Well, maybe they know something at the bridge marina—that's where we keep this boat. I mean, they know when we take it out, but that's all they know. They don't know where we're going, or what we're doing."

The other big marina near Beaufort was located practically beneath the high bridge we still had to sneak under. It was on the west side, the Port Royal side of the river. "So, Mike, is there a gun truck on top of the bridge tonight?"

"There was when we got the boat. They normally leave the truck there at the change of shift. The duty squad gets dropped off and picked up, or they just walk there or ride a bike. We're assigned near where we live, to save gas."

"Would they know that Captain Aikman checked this boat out from the marina?"

"They can see the marina from up on the bridge, but we didn't contact anybody on the radio. They wouldn't know who took the boat out, or where it was going."

"What radio frequency do they use?"

"We use VHF 82 for unclassified stuff, like talking to the marina office during the day. Channel 16 for hailing. Between militia units it's encrypted. It's our own system. Military."

"These radios right here?" I gestured to the back of the console where their face panels were lit up.

"Correct. On the left is VHF, on the right is our own."

"I haven't heard a squawk out of your radios yet, Mike. Is anybody on the militia net tonight?"

"Not since that pavilion fiasco, but a duty section is always on listening watch in case there's an attempted incursion. You know, anybody sneaking over from the mainland."

"You're the regular boat driver for this Whaler?"

"No, not always, but I'm qualified on our boats. Captain Aikman picked me because I was already at the pavilion."

"And you're qualified on the radios too?"

"Yeah, it's part of the same job description."

"Where are the rest of the troops from the pavilion? There were about a dozen men in each truck."

"We took Captain Aikman's car—he drove us. He has a militia car, I mean, he gets a gas allotment. The Aikmans are rich, he's real connected. Was connected. He chose us for this operation because we were at the pavilion and we're qualified on boats. The rest of them went back to the air station on the trucks or they got dropped off at their homes. Aikman drove us down to the bridge marina in his car, we got the Whaler, and we waited for you to come out to your boat."

"Mike, it's practically pitch dark out. How could you tell it was us from across the water?"

"With Captain Aikman's NOD. He has a PVS-14. Had."

"Where is it now?" A PVS-14 was a single-tube night observation device. It was spelled NOD and pronounced nod.

"It's under the console in the bin. We were watching the dinghy landing from the west, over by the shoreline. Captain Aikman didn't even know Luke Hanahan was coming to your boat. You always rubbed him the wrong way. He says you're too rich for an outsider. I mean, he said you were."

"He knew me?"

"Oh, everybody knows you, Captain Kilmer. He was super pissed at both of you after what happened at the pavilion, but he didn't know where Luke Hanahan went. He was going to grab you first since he knew where to find you."

"Grab me for what? For a shakedown?"

"Yeah, I guess that's what I'd call it, a shakedown. I didn't really understand that until now, but it's the only thing that makes sense. But then he saw Luke Hanahan, and he kind of lost his mind."

"Yeah, I noticed."

"Captain Aikman dated Jessie back in high school. Now she's the lead singer from the band at the pavilion, and she's married to Luke Hanahan."

"I know. Okay, Mike, here's what we're going to do. . ."

10

We had done the anchor drill so many times under so many conditions that it was second nature. The electric motor that powered the windlass was working, and Gino had our anchor up and stowed on its bow roller in under five minutes.

I gave the crew a half-minute introduction to Will, and told him to follow Adam's and Rita's lead, and left them to it. Just stay below, that's it. There wasn't any extra time to deal with kid problems—we already had our hands full with adult ones.

Gino was driving Rebel, because after a quick planning session in the cockpit I was back on the militia Whaler. I was wearing our other prisoner's desert camo uniform top and tan ball cap. My khaki trousers were close enough in appearance that I left them on, our time being short.

The tarp was still over the main boom since the morning, covering the cockpit and aft deck. It would obscure the cockpit from the militia outpost on top of the bridge as we drew near. Our 12.7mm Dushka heavy machine gun was uncovered and loaded. If it came to a fight, Gino would man the Dushka and Tala would steer Rebel Yell. Luke would stay in the cockpit but keep a constant eye on me in the militia gunboat trailing behind, because we couldn't use the VHF radios.

Once I was back on the Whaler Luke uncleated its bow line, tossed it aboard, and we dropped a hundred yards behind Rebel. As we'd planned, Gino was making RPMs for six knots through the water, which would be even less over the ground against the inflowing tide. Rebel's speedometer didn't work, and GPS was a distant memory, but we knew how many RPM equaled how much speed. Mike Ortega understood what he had to do: just maintain the interval. The Whaler's hundred-horsepower outboard motor was very quiet at that low speed.

I stood to his left side and behind him, covering him with my pistol. Mike seemed like a pretty reasonable guy, that is, he wanted to live. He'd just seen two of his militia boat team killed, and he wanted to avoid that outcome. Cooper, our other prisoner, was bound and gagged in our pilothouse. I informed Mike of my intention to let them both go once we were near the ocean, in order to encourage his cooperation.

The eighteen-foot Boston Whaler was too heavy to tow offshore or to lift onto Rebel. If I could have found a way to keep it, I would have. Even its hundred-horsepower outboard would have made quite a valuable prize, if we'd only had the time and a safe place to hoist it aboard.

Rebel's running lights were on: red and green on the bow, a white steaming light halfway up the foremast to indicate we were under power, and the white stern light on the transom. I thought running darkened ship would only draw suspicion as we approached the militia outpost atop the bridge.

I could see Gino's back because he was standing behind Rebel's wheel. The tarp over the boom did not block my view of him from the Whaler. It was two miles from the anchorage to the high bridge, our most dangerous choke point, and then ten more miles to the open ocean.

The river between the anchorage and the bridge was only a quarter mile wide at its narrowest and over fifteen feet deep in the channel, so I had few worries there. One of the electronic devices that still worked on Rebel Yell was its depth sounder, and even in the dark Gino knew the way from experience. The river made a gentle S turn running southward, but the land was so low that I could already see the unlit high bridge.

The single-tube NOD was attached to an external battery with a cord, and it powered up. Rebel Yell's white stern light ruined most of its effectiveness when looking forward, so I left it on the console dash ahead of the wheel. But I was so used to the river that even with just my bare eyes I could make out the arc of the bridge in the moonlight. There were no headlights visible moving over it in either direction, but this was normal.

When I checked my watch again it was after ten pm. There was no other boat traffic on the river. With any luck, the duty section assigned to the gun truck would be fast asleep inside of it. There was no reason for them to be outside keeping a look-out on the empty river on such a quiet night, and especially not toward the north, since their mission was to detect and prevent incursions from the ocean. I wondered if I should signal ahead to Luke to turn off our running lights to sneak through unseen. It was under a mile and a half to the bridge.

Then a voice crackled out from a speaker on the console.

"Whiskey Two, Whiskey Two, this is Sierra Hotel—over."

Mike turned to me and said, "We're Whiskey Two. Sierra Hotel is the duty section at the air station."

"Don't answer. We'll be at the bridge in twenty minutes."

"Okay, it's your decision, but I think it's a mistake. The only reason they'd be calling us is because they know this boat was taken out of the marina. They wouldn't be calling if they thought it was just tied up for the night."

The radio crackled again. "Whiskey Two, Whiskey Two, this is Sierra Hotel. Request sit-rep—over."

"He's asking us for a situation report."

"I know what a sit-rep is, Mike. Don't answer it."

Then the radio spoke again, but with a new voice. "Bravo Three, Bravo Three, this is Sierra Hotel Actual—over." The new voice repeated the message several times before finally getting a response.

Then we heard, "Sierra Hotel Actual, this is Bravo Three, over." The new voice had a pleasant South Carolina drawl.

Mike said, "Bravo Three is the gun truck on the bridge." We could only listen, and wait, while motoring closer to it.

"Bravo Three, Bravo Three, this is Sierra Hotel Actual. Do you have contact with Whiskey Two, over?"

"Ahh, Sierra Hotel Actual, this is Bravo Three. Negative radio contact with Whiskey Two, over."

I asked Mike, "So, who is Sierra Hotel Actual?"

"He's the duty officer up at the air station. That's militia headquarters. That's Major Macgregor, I know his voice."

The radio spoke again. "Bravo Three, Bravo Three, will you please try to contact Whiskey Two? Over."

The voice from the gun truck outpost on the bridge replied, "Sierra Hotel Actual, this is Bravo Three. Affirmative, I'll try, sir. Wait one. Out. Break. Whiskey Two, Whiskey Two, this is Bravo Three, Bravo Three, radio check, over."

Mike said, "I have to answer that. They know something's up. Captain Aikman should be back at the air station by now. We'll have to come up with a story."

I had to think. Should we continue our radio silence, or attempt a ruse? "Okay, but we're not going to reply to Sierra Hotel, only to the bridge. Let Sierra Hotel think they can't contact us directly. That'll buy us more time for stalling. So go ahead and make the radio check with Bravo if they call again, and I'll tell you exactly what to say. Repeat it word for word, and don't try anything smart." I didn't need to tell him what had happened to Captain Aikman and the machine gunner.

"All right, no problem. And I'll put the set on low power. On low power we won't reach the air station, but we'll still be able to hear them."

The radio squawked again. "Whiskey Two, Whiskey Two, this is Bravo Three, radio check, over."

Mike reached down and pushed a button on the radio by feel, then unclipped its spiral-corded microphone and held it about a foot from his face, steering with his left hand. Quietly he said, "Bravo Three, this is Whiskey Two, I read you weak and broken, how me, over." While he spoke he moved the microphone from his mouth to an arm's length away.

"Whiskey Two, I read you weak but readable. Sierra Hotel Actual is trying to contact you, over."

Mike waited and then replied, "Understand Sierra Hotel Actual is trying to contact us, what is the message, over?"

I said, "That's great, Mike, that'll eat up a lot of time with them relaying everything back and forth."

The radio spoke again. "Sierra Hotel Actual, this is Bravo Three, I have comms with Whiskey Two, over."

"Bravo Three, Sierra Hotel Actual. Instruct Whiskey Two to put Charlie Alpha on the radio, over."

(Mike said to me, quietly, and with his thumb off the transmit button, "Charlie Alpha is Captain Aikman. Was.")

"Roger, Sierra Hotel. Break. Whiskey Two, did you copy the last transmission from Sierra Hotel, over?"

I told Mike what to transmit. He nodded and then he said, "Negative, Bravo Three, negative copy. Whiskey Two has negative copy from Sierra Hotel."

Again Mike moved the microphone from close to far from his mouth. It wouldn't make sense that we would be unable to hear the much more powerful transmitter sending out Major Macgregor's voice from the militia headquarters on the old Marine Corps Air Station, but strange things often happened with two-way radios, and while they were baffled by these mysteries, we were getting closer to the bridge.

However, simple logic would dictate that Whiskey Two must be further away from the air station than the gun truck on the bridge, if the bridge needed to serve as a relay. In other words, the Whaler must be on the ocean side of the bridge, and further to the south, and not on the north side, and closer.

"Whiskey Two, Whiskey Two, this is Bravo Three. Sierra Actual requests you put Charlie Alpha on the radio."

Mike waited, and then he replied, "Say again, over, I did not copy your last." Once again he played the in-and-out arm trick. He was getting into the spirit of the game.

The voice said, "I say again, Whiskey Two, this is Bravo Three. Sierra Hotel Actual requests you put Charlie Alpha on the horn, over."

This was going to be a problem, because Captain Aikman was at that moment at the bottom of the river behind us. I had to think of a new ruse. We were less than a mile from the bridge. I told Mike what to say, and he did.

"Bravo Three—Whiskey Two. Charlie Alpha is unable to get on the radio because he is not aboard Whiskey Two at this time, over."

Mike did more microphone arm and mouth distance play, while also pressing and releasing the transmit button. Bravo Three reported that the previous message was garbled, and this required Mike to repeat it, eating up more time and distance before it was fully understood.

As I hoped, the bridge outpost relayed this information to Sierra Hotel, instead of just asking us directly where Captain Aikman was, if he was not on the militia gunboat designated as Whiskey Two. When Sierra Hotel came back, he sounded frustrated. We could, of course, hear him perfectly well, while pretending that we could not hear him at all.

"Bravo Three, this is Sierra Hotel Actual. Kindly please ask that Whiskey Two where in the *hell* Charlie Alpha is, if he is not aboard that goddamn Whiskey boat! Over!"

"Uh, Roger, Sierra Hotel Actual. Break. Whiskey Two, Whiskey Two, Sierra Hotel Actual requests the best current location for Charlie Alpha, over."

I was beginning to like the radioman in the gun truck up on the bridge. He was keeping the same calm and unhurried Southern drawl through it all. It was my sincerest hope that he and his buddies, who I was sure were all listening intently to every single word being exchanged, would not be given orders to open up on us with their Browning fifty caliber.

I'd been under that bridge dozens of times. The gun truck would be parked alongside what was essentially a concrete Jersey barricade that formed a lip on both sides of the four-lane road. His barrel would be depressed over that barricade like it was a castle's parapet, able to shoot us to pieces, while our return fire could only hit the bottom of the bridge and the outside of the concrete barricade.

That is, except for maybe a quarter mile to the north and south of the bridge, where the Browning's long barrel could not be sufficiently depressed, but once we were that close, we would be in small arms range. And there was always the risk of grappling hooks being swung into Rebel's rigging as her two masts passed only feet below them. And, God forbid, they could simply drop grenades down onto her deck. These were some of the dark thoughts that tormented my mind as we motored south down the river toward the high bridge.

We had to modify our gambit. Stalling wasn't going to work forever, or Sierra Hotel Actual might order the bridge to prevent any and all traffic from going under it, and they could do this easily. I told Mike exactly what to say next.

"Bravo Three, Bravo Three, this is Whiskey Two. Current location of Charlie Alpha is aboard the fishing trawler Fujimo Two, Fujimo Two, spelled Foxtrot, Uniform, Juliet," and so on through all nine letters. When he was finished, Mike was actually smiling, which was an amazing mood transformation since only a short time earlier, when he'd seen the machine gunner and his militia officer shot dead right in front of him. Humans are nothing if not resilient, and soldiers more so than most. Anyway, you can't fix dead. You just have to move on.

The bridge gun truck outpost painstakingly relayed all of this new information to Sierra Hotel Actual, and when Major Macgregor responded, he was not a happy man. "Bravo Three, for the love of God, son, *please* ask Whiskey Two what in the *hell* is Captain Aikman, I mean, Charlie Alpha, doing aboard that goddamn Fujimo trawler?"

"Ahh, Roger, Sierra Hotel Actual. Break, break. Whiskey Two, Sierra Hotel Actual requests to know why Charlie Alpha is aboard the fishing trawler Fujimo Two, over."

The bridge was in clear sight. It was unlit and no moving vehicles or headlights were visible. There was a stationary mass atop the center of the span. I told Mike what to say.

"Bravo Three, Bravo Three, this is Whiskey Two. Charlie Alpha is currently aboard the fishing vessel Fujimo Two with a boarding party. The fishing vessel is being taken to the Port Royal ship pier for inspection and possible impoundment."

This was laboriously relayed to Sierra Hotel Actual, who after half a minute of radio silence replied, "Bravo Three, this is Sierra Hotel Actual. Interrogative follows. Please request the following information from Whiskey Two. Number one: why is the fishing boat being taken to Port Royal? Two: where was it boarded? Three: why was it boarded?"

Confusion and delay were our best allies. The questions from the militia HQ were repeated.

"Whiskey Two, Whiskey Two, this is Bravo Three. Sierra Hotel Actual requests the following information concerning the boarding of the fishing vessel Fujimo Two. Number one: why is it being taken to Port Royal? Number two: where was it boarded? Number three: why was it boarded?"

I fed Mike his next lines.

"Bravo Three, Whiskey Two. I read you weak and broken. Repeat all after 'fishing vessel Fujimo,' over."

The bridge was much closer, looming above Rebel Yell up ahead of us. The half-moon was nearly touching the western horizon, the clouds around it were backlit in pale orange.

Macgregor broke in next, not waiting for the questions to be repeated. "Bravo Three, this is Sierra Hotel Actual. Listen to me closely, son. I am getting in a car and I am driving down to Port Royal right goddamn now, do you read me, over?"

"Ahh, Sierra Hotel Actual, this is Bravo Three. I read you loud and clear, Major Macgregor, sir."

"And when I get to the Port Royal ship pier, I expect your truck to be waiting for me there, and I expect Charlie Alpha to be standing at attention on the pier right next to that goddamn Fujimo fishing boat, do you read me, Bravo Three? Over!"

11

The high bridge was less than a half mile south when I saw lights coming on at the top center. Headlights then swung in a circle against the dark sky, and descended heading to the west. The moon was gone, leaving only a smear on the horizon.

I said, “Good job, Mike. Now, speed it up and bring us to about twenty feet back.”

He goosed the throttle ahead, and then eased off again.

Luke was in the cockpit facing aft, keeping watch on us trailing astern. We couldn’t use Rebel’s VHF radio, only hand signals. I waved for Luke to get Gino’s attention.

We were still lit by Rebel’s stern light, so they could see us clearly. I held up eight fingers and yelled “Eight knots! Eight knots!” The bridge was clear. The time for stealth was over. Then I told Mike to drop back to a hundred yards behind my schooner again. Adam’s pram was bucking and rolling, unhappy to be dragged on a short tow line with the outboard’s propeller still down in the water.

Five minutes later Rebel Yell passed under the high bridge at the best speed I reckoned she could make without risking an engine casualty. Her two masts rose sixty-three feet above the water, almost scraping the bottom of the bridge. Rebel drove between the concrete pilings and timber side-boards at her full speed, framed for long seconds in my view, and then she was through the trap. Oh, what relief! There were still ten miles to go until the ocean and real safety, but it was only a mile and a half to where the Port Royal ship channel split off to the west from the Beaufort River.

Major Macgregor was going to be out of his mind with fury when he arrived at the ship pier and met the gun truck, but with no fishing trawler Fujimo Two and no Captain Roy Aikman. I knew there was another militia gunboat kept in Port Royal, and it would not take them long to get it manned up and out in hot pursuit. The detail from the gun truck could run the boat even if nobody else was available.

I told Mike to get close again, and I yelled to Luke to kill Rebel's running lights. There was no reason to make it easy for them to spot us now. When our stern light went out Rebel became a black shadow, and I picked up the PVS-14. It had a power cord instead of an internal battery, so I had to stand by the console, but that was no real impediment.

It had been years since I'd held a working NOD. The last time had been just before Morocco, when the Atlas had gone down in the Atlantic. Before that had been back on Castigo Cay, with my own old PVS-14. This one had a white phosphor tube, not green, and with it against my eye I could see the docks, trees, and houses on each side of the river.

Once beyond the high bridge it didn't make sense for the Whaler to be trailing behind Rebel Yell, not when I had night vision, so I told Mike to get close again. I held up the NOD so Luke could see it, and I yelled over to him that we would lead them out to the ocean. One of the last remaining risks to our escape was Rebel running aground on the sand bars and mud flats that flanked the channel on both sides. If that happened, we'd almost certainly be captured.

We left the Whaler's stern light on for Gino to follow, and we moved out in front. Using the NOD, up ahead of us I could make out the familiar Green 41 buoy that marked the entrance to the Port Royal shipping channel. A decade earlier it would have had a green light blinking on top, but now it was unlit like all of them. I was grateful that it was still there at all.

After looking ahead with the NOD and then down at the Whaler's compass with my bare eyes, I told Mike the bearing to follow. I even let him take turns with the night vision so we would both have the same mental picture. With the moon gone and just some starlight left to amplify, the NOD only turned night into grainy twilight, and that was enough. I scanned all the way around 360 degrees, because I wasn't only concerned about what was out in front of us.

"Mike, there's another militia boat at Port Royal, right?"

"Yeah, and it's bigger, it's not just a Boston Whaler. It's a 28-foot Mako with twin 200s. It's up on a trailer, but they can launch it in ten minutes. We practice that, launching it fast."

"What's it have for guns?"

"An M-240, just like that one."

"Will they chase us? Will they try to stop us?"

"It all depends," he said.

"Depends on what?"

"Does your big machine gun really work?"

"You're damn right it does."

"What is it, a fifty caliber? It looks funny."

"It's a Russian fifty caliber."

He said, "A fifty caliber against a thirty caliber? That's no contest. If you put a few bursts in the water around that Mako, I guarantee they'll head for home and call it a night. But I'll bet they're still trying to figure out what happened to Whiskey Two, Captain Aikman and Fujimo Two. And that Mako is a fuel hog. They won't waste the gas on a wild goose chase. But that's just my opinion; who knows what the hell they'll do?"

I kept a sharp lookout with the NOD both ahead of us and behind, but it worried me that Rebel Yell's eighteen-foot beam might hide the Mako's approach from my view. I was thinking the Mako would also have night vision to make their stealthy approach. But without night vision, Luke and Gino would not see the Mako creeping up behind them in the dark until it was well inside M-240 range. The Dushka might win that battle, but a belt-fed thirty-caliber could do a lot of damage before it was all over. The Mako's M-240 might even kill everybody in Rebel's cockpit with its opening bursts.

So which presented the greater risk: a stealthy attack from behind, or Rebel Yell running aground without a guide leading it through the winding channel? Should the Boston Whaler be out front on point, or in the back on rear security?

Our next five miles were in the relatively constricted Beaufort River, with Parris Island off our starboard side and St.

Helena Island to port. This part of the river was about a mile wide, but the navigable channel was only a fraction of that, so great care had to be taken not to run Rebel aground, or have her to collide with any of the unlit channel markers along her path. These floating steel buoys were substantial, weighing tons and rising a dozen feet above the water. The Whaler's depth sounder was working, so together with the NOD to see the channel markers we could stay in deep water, keeping us—and Rebel Yell—out of trouble. So we stayed in front.

Once past Parris Island the river opened up into the Port Royal Sound, several miles wide. Some swell was coming in through the wide ocean mouth between St. Helena and Hilton Head Island. According to the sounder the water depths were deepening into the thirty-foot range. The ocean swells were not enough to bother the Whaler, not when we were loafing along at only eight knots, but they were enough to start my schooner rolling, and I could see her masts beginning to sway from side to side behind us.

An hour after passing under the high bridge, we led Rebel Yell toward the ocean gate formed by the paired red 24 and green 25 buoys, well known to us from our many daytime passages and our paper charts. I could see both of them ahead with the NOD but Gino could not, so I used the Whaler's handheld spotlight to illuminate them. The last hand that had held the light had been Captain Aikman's. I knew that when Gino saw their red and green reflectors glinting up ahead he would know his precise location. This was confirmed when I saw Rebel's own million-candlepower spotlight shining on them.

Once Rebel Yell was through this pair of buoys Gino only needed to hold the same course for a few miles. He knew the rest of the way out to the ocean as well as I did, and he'd have the paper chart in the cockpit giving him each new magnetic bearing to steer. But as the land became less of a danger to us, the ocean increasingly made its power felt. The swells grew in both their height and their steepness, pushed up by the shallow bottom after being born far out to sea in deep water. Then it occurred to me that I had never seen Rebel depart the land for the ocean without me aboard her. This was a first, but I only had the camera of my memory to record the event.

Now it was time for me to get back aboard Rebel Yell and let our two prisoners go, but first I'd remove everything useful from the Boston Whaler. I told Mike to slow down and let the schooner pass us close along our starboard side. As she went by I yelled up to Gino and Luke to hold their course, and they yelled back that they understood. The Whaler rose and fell on the waves next to the steadier sixty-foot steel boat. I knew that the next part was going to be very tricky with the two vessels moving closely together, because they would behave radically differently in the same waves. We dropped behind Rebel, and Adam's pram was nowhere to be seen!

Mike noticed its absence at almost the same time. "Hey, what happened to your dinghy?"

I scanned behind us with the NOD, but saw nothing. "It's gone. Forget it, there's nothing we can do. Put our starboard bow along Rebel's port quarter."

If the pram had flipped over in Rebel's churning wake, the sudden drag as its bow dug into the water would have snapped the tow line like a thread. I'd lost dinghies that way before, and usually they could be recovered. But not on that night. We couldn't stop or go back. We weren't in the clear yet, not yet.

I waved Luke down onto the swim platform. He noticed the dinghy's absence and asked about it, and I yelled the same answer to him: It's gone, forget it! I mimed throwing and catching things from boat to boat, and he nodded and shouted that he was ready. I told him to tell Gino to put the stern light on; we'd need illumination for the next event.

This message was relayed to the pilothouse and in a few moments the transom light came on again, bathing the swim platform, the waves and the Whaler in white light. My Glock was holstered because I needed to use my hands. I unplugged the PVS-14's power cable from its battery pack, took them both to the bow of the Whaler and tossed each part to Luke. He caught them and set them on Rebel's aft deck. Next I unplugged the spotlight, wrapped its spiral cord around the hand grip and threw that over too.

There was no mistaking Luke, not with his dark beard and his red and black plaid lumberjack shirt lit up by the stern light like he was on stage again. I had the thought that he was used to working close to the edge, and then I went to get the M-240. The machine gun had a full box of ammunition in the carrier loaded and ready on its left side. I lifted the gun's feed tray cover and removed the linked cartridges, dropping the end of the belt back into the ammo box.

Then I reached under the machine gun and pulled out the two steel pins that secured it to the pintle mount. They were each a few inches long, with a pull-ring attached to their ends for removal. I hadn't done this in twenty years, but it came to me as naturally as if I'd done it the day before. Once it was freed I carried the M-240 the two steps over to the starboard bow. Moving like this without my hands for balance was a challenge because we were in some waves, with the Whaler rising and dropping behind Rebel's port quarter.

Luke leaned out from the platform, and when we were close enough I passed the machine gun over to him. He grabbed it by the barrel end and swung it up on the aft deck. Next I lifted the open ammo can from the carrier on the side of pintle mount, and passed it to him carefully because its hinged lid had been removed and it wasn't worth the time to look for it. A machine gun was just scrap metal without ammunition.

Behind me, Mike said, "There's three more in front of the console." I flipped up what looked like a hinged seat and there they were. I grabbed the ammo cans by their top handles, still so familiar after all those years, and tossed them across. They were hard steel and heavy, with 200 linked cartridges in each box, but Luke caught them like they were bean bags.

The radios installed on the Whaler could be of no further use to us; the time for bluff and fakery was over. I yanked the microphones out of both and threw them overboard, then reached under and ripped out every wire I could see or feel. I was tempted to put a few rounds of 9mm into each of them to make sure they could not be used to betray our escape, but I didn't, not with Rebel in front. A shiny pair of handcuffs were dangling from a hook on the back of the console, and they went into my pants pocket.

I went onto the Whaler's bow again, yelling to be heard. "Luke, go get the prisoner. We're going to let them go."

He absorbed my message, had no questions, climbed up the transom and disappeared forward into the pilothouse. In a minute he was back with the man whose camo shirt I was wearing. His hands were free, he was not tied. He'd be plenty cold in just his t-shirt and trousers, but he was going home.

I told Mike, "Put your bow alongside the platform same as before." This required skillful boat driving because the Whaler was rising and falling several feet as each swell passed below us. The last thing I wanted was to wreck our teak-slat swim platform, or even worse, snag the Whaler's bow beneath it and swamp or capsize us.

We were getting closer to the ocean. Port Royal Sound was much wider there. It was three miles between the ends of St. Helena and Hilton Head Island, with nothing but the wild Atlantic out in front. The Whaler's bow was a moving target for Cooper, but when he judged it was the right moment he sprang over onto the boat, landing on his chest. He slid, kicked and crawled the rest of the way aboard, and then stood on the other side of the console from me holding its grab rail. The two militiamen were in no mood to fight, not when their freedom was close. I still had a pistol, and so did Luke. Mike bore off and dropped back a few yards.

I said, "I'm going to let you go now, all right?"

“All right, yeah, thanks for sure, but can you tell me one thing first? Is there really a fishing trawler named Fujimo Two? What was that about?”

“Fujimo Two? Oh, Fujimo stands for ‘Fuck you Jack, I’m movin’ out.’ It’s an old joke. It was stupid of me. They might have known the joke and figured out they were being punked.”

Mike Ortega said, “Well, Captain Kilmer, I’d say you’d better not come back to the island anytime soon.”

“Oh, trust me on that, I don’t plan to.”

“I suppose you won’t tell me where you’re heading next?”

“Why the hell not? South America, Mike, we’re going to South America. You can tell Major Macgregor and Colonel Dorchester that’s where we’ll be if they want to find us. And tell them that Captain Aikman was a real asshole, and he got what was coming to him. And the other guy, well, fuck him too.” I could still see that machine gun pointing at my chest, and the black hole appearing on his forehead. No regrets.

“South America? For real?”

“Yes sir, for real. Next stop, Buenos Aires, Argentina. Or Montevideo, or Punta del Este. Some place around there.”

“Buenos Aires, Argentina? You know, that sounds pretty damned cool. Hey, listen, how are you set for crew?”

“What did you say?”

“Captain Kilmer, I can’t go back now, not after what I did on the radio. They’ll kill me, they’ll literally kill me.”

“Nah, you were transmitting under duress. I had a gun on you, just tell them that.”

“No, they’ll never buy it. Not after what happened at the concert, and on your boat. They’ll never buy it, never. Captain Aikman’s family is too important. They’ll kill me, or they’ll put me to work on a farm. So, what about it, skipper, do you need more crew?”

After about five seconds to think it over, it was decision time again. “Yeah, Mike, as a matter of fact I do. Are you volunteering?”

“Hell yes, I am!”

"What about you, Cooper?"

"No, sir, I have a family back there. A wife and a kid."

"Can you drive this boat, Cooper?"

"Not as good as Mike, but yeah, I can drive it okay."

"Then drive it. Let him have the wheel, Mike."

He moved out from behind the console as Cooper took over the controls. Eight knots was nothing for the Boston Whaler, even in some waves. It was parking lot speed. But a lot of accidents happened on parking lots due to bad or even just careless driving. A little too much gas could launch the Whaler straight into Rebel's transom like a rocket.

I coached him back in closer, his left hand on the wheel, his right on the throttle. "You've got this, Cooper, do it just like Mike did. Slide up the port side real easy, that's it, that's good; now just ease in closer, that's it. Okay, Mike, it's your turn—if you're going, go!"

He nodded to me, put a foot on the gunnel and leapt across onto Rebel's swim platform, and was caught by Luke. Then Mike slid behind Luke to the other side of the swim platform to make room for me.

Luke kept his right hand locked onto the aft deck toe rail, his left arm was held out to receive me. When the Whaler was close enough I pushed off from its gunnel and landed on the swim platform. Luke grabbed me by my collar and reeled me in, and just like that we were finished with Whiskey Two, the militia's Boston Whaler gun boat. With our former prisoner at the wheel it bore off and dropped away, and then made a wide turn and headed north for home.

Unlike back on the calm water of the Beaufort River, the swim platform was a wild and wet place to be standing when Rebel was pitching in a seaway. Salt water slapped its bottom and sprayed up through the teak slats with each swell that passed below. Hot diesel exhaust from the Caterpillar hissed and spat out beneath it, sometimes underwater and belching bubbles into our wake, all of it lit by the transom light.

The three of us were hanging onto the toe rail welded to the top of the transom, riding the schooner like a sixty-foot surfboard, with just our heads and shoulders above the aft deck. I yelled, “Hey Gino, it’s a beautiful night to be out on the water! Look, I found us another crew!”

He turned around and saw three faces instead of two, and he said, “You’re crazy, boss, you know you’re crazy!”

Mike Ortega reached around Luke and grabbed the right shoulder of my new-old militia uniform shirt. “It’s a beautiful night to be alive, skipper! It’s a beautiful night to be alive!”

Luke slid a hand over the golden letters that were painted in script between the portholes. “Rebel Yell—oh, I just *love* that name!” He clutched the toe rail with both hands, leaned far astern with his head back even further, and let out a long, howling scream, a real rebel yell!

Gino said, “You’re all crazy—now get up on the boat.”

In the cockpit, I briefly introduced our newest crew addition to Luke and Gino. Luke had been watching the events on the Whaler, so he understood more of what had been happening, but there wasn’t time for our life stories. We’d have weeks for that, but even at the edge of the ocean we were no match in speed for what the militia could send out to chase us down. It wouldn’t take Major Macgregor long to suss out our trickery, our true identity, and our ocean destination. A Mako 28 with twin 200s could handle the open ocean with no problem at all.

I plugged the PVS-14’s cord back into its power supply, this looked like a motorcycle battery with an external voltage transformer attached. I stood up, looking forward over the pilothouse, searching ahead for the next channel buoy to give Gino his new compass heading, and then astern, looking for signs of pursuit. We were passing from the realm of the land dwellers over to Neptune’s kingdom, but there were miles of shoals and breakers on the north side of the channel extending far out to sea. This was normally a terrifying prospect at night in the post-GPS era, but with the NOD it was just a matter of spotting the next unlit buoy and holding an already-charted compass course.

Gino was standing at the helm with both hands on the leather-covered wheel. The glowing compass appeared to float in space just above and in front of the hub of its spokes. The liquid-filled hemispherical glass compass was mounted on top of the same round pillar that supported the wheel. The floating compass card inside the glass said that we were steering 150 degrees magnetic, or south-southeast. The compass was old, but after Hilton Sapelo's work it was as accurate as it could be made to be on a steel boat. On this voyage the helmsman and the compass would be constant companions.

Tala came out of the pilothouse. "What's happening? I see from the cabin porthole that the two boats are gone, the militia boat and Adam's boat. Now everybody wants to know what is happening? And who is this new man?"

"We're almost to the open ocean," I told her. "Everything is good. This man is Mike Ortega, and he's coming with us. We still need to get past the north breakers out to deep water. Just tell them everything is good, but they need to stay below tonight, okay?"

The very last thing I needed to deal with was women and children on deck and underfoot in the dark. They had to stay below and we needed to work. And this would also be a good time for Gino and me to get to know Luke Hanahan and Mike Ortega without women and children playing twenty questions. I just couldn't deal with that now. Even soaking wet from my waist down in the chilly breeze, I was so jacked up with adrenaline that I knew I'd get no sleep, and in that condition I was prone to being short-tempered. Most men could take my outbursts in stride, but often women and children could not. I didn't want to let myself be provoked into angrily snapping at somebody and starting the voyage off on a sour note.

So I said, "Maybe later, honey, after the sails are up, okay? But not now. Please, not now."

"Not even me?"

"Maybe later, when we're sailing, okay? When the motor is turned off. But only you and Sofia tonight."

When she was gone again Gino said, "So, we lost Adam's dinghy? I think he's going to be angry."

I asked him, "So, do you want to go back and look for it?"

"Go back? No, boss, there's no going back. But I think he's going to be unhappy that we lost his uncle's dinghy."

"He'll get over it. It's not the first dinghy we've lost, and it won't be the last. We still have Whisper."

Gino shook his head ruefully. "We have the Whisper, but we lost the Honda. I loved that little Japanese motor."

"I liked it too, but it's a good trade for a machine gun and eight hundred rounds of ammo." Rebel's new M-240 was tied to the aft toe rail, between the Dushka's tripod legs. The four ammo cans were nested side by side down in the very back of the cockpit foot well. Luke had done a good job of stowing them without being told how or where. They were secure, but could be put to use in under a minute if they were needed.

"So, Gino, who shot those two assholes? You or Tala?"

"Oh, that was me, boss. I don't like it when he pointed the machine gun at you. That was right over my limit."

"Well, nice shooting, and thanks."

He held his right hand and index finger out as if it was a pistol. "It already had the suppressor on it, and the subsonic bullets. And I'm glad I didn't shoot that Cooper—I think he's an okay guy. I couldn't see him, so he was very lucky."

Mike Ortega said, "I'm glad you didn't shoot me too."

"Hey man, you put your hands up—I'm not a savage. But it's a good thing you did, because you were next."

"Gino," I asked, "did anybody see you do it? Shoot them?"

"Only Tala. She wanted to shoot them too, but I got there first, and my gun had the can. Nobody else saw it."

"Good. Don't tell them. They don't need to know, not yet. Maybe later, but not the details."

I made a careful scan behind us with the NOD, looking for a pursuing militia speedboat, but Port Royal sound was clear of any other vessels. We were the only ones out on the water, so I said, "Okay, there's nobody following us. We have the whole ocean to ourselves, so it looks like we're home free."

Gino, standing behind the wheel, turned to me and said, "Home free? Boss, it's six thousand miles to Argentina!"

"No," I replied, "We're already home. Rebel is our home. Rebel Yell, and the ocean. That's home."

Mike Ortega said, "Rebel Yell. Home free. I like that."

"I like it too," said Luke. He was standing at the back of the aft deck while leaning against the stern pulpit railing. I handed him the NOD and its tethered battery, so that he could experience the magic of night vision, even under a moonless sky, and watch for pursuit.

I stood and faced astern and said aloud, "The wind is backing to the northeast, so on port tack we'll be able to lay this course all the way out to deep water." Deep water meant beyond where our fathometer's pings could reach the bottom and bounce back up to be shown on the LCD display. For our depth sounder anything deeper than 500 feet was considered "off soundings." It was showing numbers in the thirties and low forties, so we were on soundings.

The depth sounder was next to our matching but broken speedometer display. The pilothouse was painted white, but the two small round displays and the larger rectangular engine panel were black. Five hundred feet or five thousand, it was all the same to Rebel's depth sounder, and to me. Only when we were off soundings would I be able to sleep soundly, way out on the deep blue and far from the land and all its worries.

Gino said, "Let's raise sail, boss. No point wasting fuel."

"Sure, let's give the old Cat a rest. It's a long, long way to Argentina."

12

After the tarp over the boom was taken down, Gino turned our bow into the wind and we raised sail, beginning at the back with the main. With no moon and the sky overcast we turned the mast spreader lights on so that we could see what we were doing on deck. Once the main was up I had Mike and Luke winch up its twin, the foresail, and after that the two jibs were set. Before midnight all four of our working sails were up and the diesel was shut down.

When we were beyond the last sea buoy, with nothing out in front but ocean, I went below to change into dry clothes. Tala met me in our aft cabin. The gooseneck lamp over the head of our bed was aimed down at my pillow, providing enough light without ruining my night vision.

When I leaned against the side of our bed and peeled off my wet khakis and the new desert-uniform top, she sat beside me and said, “Sofia and I made a new crew list. Do you know how many persons we have on the boat now?”

I was too mentally fatigued to run through all their faces, counting them in my mind. “No, I don’t. Please, just tell me.”

“We have twelve persons. This is the most of forever.”

“No, honey, it’s not the most. From Ireland down to the Canaries we had fifteen, and they were all grown men. Three crew and twelve soldiers. But that was only for a short trip, ten days.” I didn’t tell her how many had made it out of Morocco.

“Yes, Tran Hung and Doctor Aleman. I always remember Victor, even that I only knew him for some few days.”

“Even *though* you only knew him for a few days.”

She tossed her head in irritation. “That or though? I think that you thought? And there and their and they’re? Who can remember every small letter of this stupid nonsense?”

Many of the subtle mysteries of English still eluded Tala, but considering that it was her fourth or fifth language, I rarely corrected her anymore. I understood her well enough.

She said, "I have talked with Sofia. We are changing the beds where the new persons are sleeping. Jessie and Luke can live up in the forward cabin; they can share it with Gino and Sofia. And now because of this, Rita can move to the back."

"Rita? Move to the back? Move to *where* in the back?"

"Rita will sleep in the passageway cabin. She is only very small, smaller even than was Tran Hung. She is a girl but soon a woman, and she can have the privacy in that cabin."

"Wait a minute—so what about the twins?"

"The twins can sleep here in our cabin again, like as when they were small babies."

"Tala, honey, they're not babies now. There's no room for them here. And what about *our* privacy?"

"Danny, there is not another way. It is decided, by me and by Sofia. Rita does not want to walk through the cargo where now the boys are sleeping. And now you don't need the table here for making the navigation. The radio can't work, and you can make the navigation on the galley table. So from here you can take away the chair and put it in the cargo like as before. The boys can sleep here until South America."

"But Tala, honey—that will be months!"

"Jessie has moved to the front. Gino and Sofia will stay on the port side, and Luke and Jessie will be on the right side, and they can put a curtain between for the privacy."

The forward cabin had originally been set up for the crew of a cargo schooner, with a wide berth high on each side, and a narrower berth below them.

The four bunks each had sturdy canvas lee-cloths, so that no matter which way the boat was heeling over, sleepers could not roll out. These lee-cloths were only needed on one side, depending on which way Rebel was heeling over. On the low side, sleepers rested comfortably against the hull with the sea rushing past a few inches away. On the high side, the lee cloths kept a sleeper from falling several feet to the deck. At anchor, or with the boat not heeled over, they were not needed at all, and they were stowed flat under their mattresses.

The upper berths were wide enough to accommodate a couple if they were both fairly slim and enjoyed spooning and turning over together. When that wouldn't work, one of them could take the lower berth to get a good night's sleep. During the day, or when they were not occupied, the lower berths also served as sofas. On an ocean voyage when the boat was heeled over, the "downhill" settee was especially desirable as a sitting place, with one's back pressed against the lower side.

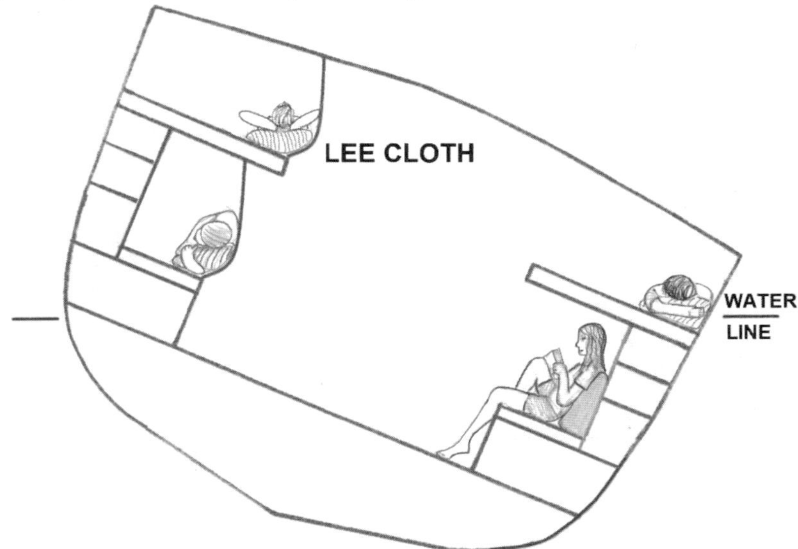

Now there would be two married couples up forward, and Rita would be living in the narrow passageway cabin that had been Tran Hung's quarters before it had been inherited by the twins. This compact compartment was on the starboard side between the galley dinette table and the aft cabin. Its louvered sliding door was across from the engine room, and it occupied the narrow space from the passageway to the hull side.

As far as I was concerned everything was fine with this new berthing arrangement—except for the twins moving back into the aft cabin! The captain's cabin had been my retreat for almost twenty years, with only occasional female companions, and none of them lasting longer than a few months. But it's not that I'd been a bachelor by choice. No, I just hadn't found the right woman, one who was both smart and attractive, and who could take to the rootless life of an ocean nomad. That is, not until I had met Tala Abidar in Morocco.

I certainly hadn't minded the sexy half-French and half-Berber runaway moving into my cabin and sharing my bed, for all the obvious reasons. Our honeymoon had lasted over a year before the twins had arrived, and sharing our cabin hadn't been much of an imposition when they were infants. Since the two boys had graduated to the passageway compartment, we'd had the captain's cabin all to ourselves again.

Tala read the disappointment on my face. "Danny, on the deck you are the captain, I know always you are the captain. But down the below, it's better when Sofia and me decide the places for sleeping. You men can sleep any place, but not the ladies. The boys, they can live in the cargo, they can make the beds, or they can sleep with the hammocks, it's not to matter. They are men, and so they are like soldiers. They don't care. But the ladies need the privacy. Even Rita."

"But Tala, honey, what about *our* privacy?"

"Danny, don't I make you happy?" She snuggled against me and squeezed my thigh.

"Yes, but *the twins*? Those monsters? Right here in our cabin?" I waved my arm over the small open area between the navigation desk to starboard, and our own double bed which occupied the port side of the aft cabin. There was a few feet of space between them, with a swiveling captain's chair bolted to the deck smack in the middle. This would have to be removed again, as it had been when the boys were infants.

"Tala, if they're sleeping here, I'll have to get on and off the bed over the foot, at the bottom. Sometimes I need to roll off in a hurry, and I might step on them."

"No, you won't. Sofia will make a new bed almost like a hammock from canvas. It will be on the floor but it will go up both sides, and they can sleep no matter the side the boat is leaning. And we will put up the lee cloth on our bed, and that will give us the privacy." She rubbed her shoulder against me, and squeezed my leg again. The heavy canvas lee cloth was installed when Rebel was heeling far to starboard on passages, to keep us from being rolled off our double bed. Now it would also prevent the twins from seeing—well—never mind what!

"You and Sofia already had this planned out, didn't you?"

"Danny, please don't worry about the boys sleeping again in our cabin. Don't I make you happy?"

"Yes, but *the twins*? Sleeping right here?"

"When they are asleep, they sleep very strong. And many hours every day they are not in our cabin. And there is our own toilet, with a bathtub and a door we can close."

"Yes, but—"

"Danny, it was already decided with Sofia and with me."

And that was that. To think that three men had managed to run this sixty-foot schooner for more than a decade. Three men, and an autopilot that could steer Rebel Yell for day after day and week after week, fed only with electricity. And without ever attempting to rearrange my life.

But there were also undeniable benefits to having my life rearranged by the addition of a wife and children. Before I put on dry trousers I pushed Tala down onto her back and rolled onto my side, facing her.

"And do I make *you* happy, Tala my love? Do I?"

"Oh, *yes*, Danny, you make me *very* happy." The light from the reading lamp reflected the amber of her eyes.

When I awoke the glowing hands of my dive watch said it was almost 0400. Rebel Yell was heeled to starboard, so she was still on port tack. Pitch and roll were minimal. On our first night offshore, I'd slept for a glorious three straight hours. Most of my state of deep relaxation could be credited to Tala, still sleeping beside me. But the loss of the old autopilot also came with a benefit: I didn't have to endure the constant creaking groan of its hydraulic piston working below the cabin sole.

Who was on watch, who was steering? I was the captain, and I didn't even know—but what a blessing to sleep for three uninterrupted hours! But if there was a problem, whoever was in the cockpit only needed to rap hard on the aft deck to get my attention. And with no autopilot, I knew for sure that *somebody* was up there steering.

I left Tala sleeping, pulled on dry pants and a sweater, put my feet into my boat shoes and padded out of my cabin. Its louvered door was latched open for easier movement fore and aft. The sliding door to the passageway cabin was partly open. A nightlight showed that Jon and Chris were fast asleep.

Sofia was in the galley, sleeping at the dinette table, her face on her crossed forearms. She had slid across to starboard so she was resting against the hull with the boat heeled to that side. The door into the cargo hold was slid open. I took a look inside; nighttime LED footlights showed that all the drums, barrels and crates were chained securely. I couldn't make out each of the sleeping figures, but everything was silent and still in there, so I left well enough alone.

I climbed the ladder up into the pilothouse, and because the cockpit door was latched open, I went straight up the two steps and outside. Gino was standing at the helm, his face and hands were illuminated by the glowing compass.

"Did you get some good sleep, boss?"

"Three straight hours—a miracle on a first night out."

I yawned and stretched, holding the grab rail on the back of the pilothouse, looking all around and forward over Rebel's bow. I felt about fifteen knots of breeze on my face. No rain, but no stars either. The diesel was silent so the engine panel was dark. The fathometer was indicating more than a hundred feet of water below us, its lit digital display changing every three seconds: 127, 130, 129, 131. We were still on soundings over the continental shelf.

"Have you been steering the whole time?" I asked him.

"Sofia steered for an hour while I slept here." Here meant on the cockpit bench on the comfortable low side, where you would be cradled securely against its backrest.

I said, "Sofia is asleep at the dinette table."

"Oh, she's an angel, that woman."

"What's been going on?" More stretching and yawning. On such a nice night it took me a few minutes to fully awaken.

"We're just sailing, boss, just sailing. No ship contacts, no lights, no nothing. Wind is northeast, and we're sailing southeast. Best I can make close-hauled is one-twenty magnetic, but we lose speed, so I'm steering one-thirty. Our average speed has been dropping from about five knots down to four. We have over a hundred feet of water. We're not sailing our best direction yet, we want more easting, but we're getting away from the coast. I would say it's a good first night, especially for the new sailors."

I had to agree with him on that. Easy sailing during the first days of a voyage meant fewer problems with seasickness, especially with untested crew. Rough weather right out of port could send them into miserable retching agony. A severe case of mal-de-mer could lead to dire outcomes, even to death by dehydration when a victim could not retain fluids. We didn't have a doctor on board any more, we had no I.V. setups, and no matter what, we couldn't go back. So an easy transition to offshore sailing was a blessing, and once again I thanked the man upstairs for his large and small favors.

"Where are the new crew?" I asked him. I had gone below and slept with a lot of business still left undone, and I needed to get up to speed to take over from Gino on watch.

"Jessie is forward, and Rita is up there too. The new men and boys are in the hold sleeping rough. Sail bags and blankets are good enough for tonight." Sail bags meant our spare sails folded up in their Dacron canvas bags. These could be moved around to serve as makeshift mattresses.

"Tala told me that Luke and Jessie are going to move up forward, and Rita will move to the aft passageway berth."

"Sofia told me the same thing. You know, when those two agree on something, we can't stop them."

"What do you think about it?"

"Oh, I guess it's the best way. Rita wants to have her own cabin. Hung was taller than Rita, and he lived there okay."

"That means Jonathan and Christopher will move into the aft cabin with us, but there's nowhere else for them to go. I'm not crazy about it, but Tala is set in her mind."

"Sofia is too, boss. And it won't be so great for us either. We'll only have a curtain between us and Luke and Jessie."

Working out the new accommodation arrangements was typical for the start of a voyage. A familiar routine.

I asked him, "What do you think about Mike Ortega? Do you trust him? He was in the militia until a few hours ago."

"Well, he burned that bridge. Oh, I think he's okay. He's strong, and he already knows how to sail. I let him steer for a while; he knows what he's doing. We'll have to teach Luke how to sail, but that won't take long. They can both steer."

"I'm thinking we'll run a four-section watch. Two hours on and then six hours off. You, me, Luke and Mike. But every watch will need a number-two, and that can be Rita, Adam, Will and Jessie. Tala and Sofia will just cook."

When the autopilot had worked, standing watch basically involved just that: watching. Watching out for ships and boats, and watching for bad weather and adjusting the sails according to the changing conditions. Now, standing watch meant somebody keeping two hands on the wheel and both eyes on the compass. Before, with the autopilot, it had been possible for the watch stander to sneak below for a snack, or another layer of clothing, or to use the head. Without the autopilot this was impossible, so a second person was required. The number-two was also a second pair of eyes, and helped to keep the helmsman awake and alert with quiet conversation at night.

Thinking aloud, I said, “Tala and Sofia will cook and run the galley. Rita can watch the twins when Tala is busy. Sofia will run the home schooling and Spanish class. We’ll keep our routines as much as we can. Can you think of anything else?”

“Yeah, boss—sleeping. I’m thinking about sleeping.”

“Okay, I’m ready, I’ll take the helm.” I moved past him and put a hand on the wheel.

As he left he asked, “Can I get you anything?”

“I forgot my water bottle. It’s in the galley.”

“You got it.”

“Hey, on your way forward, wake up Mike and tell him to come up and see me. In fact, have him bring me my water bottle. You can show him where everything is, and I can start teaching him our routines.” I looked at my watch. “It’s after four, so I’ll take it until at least six. And pass the word to anybody you see who’s up: we’ll have an all-hands meeting here at nine, weather permitting.”

“All hands, including the twins?”

I thought for a moment. “Yes, even the twins. They’re not babies anymore. Oh, and fill in the log for each hour since we reached the ocean: our dead-reckoning needs to be sharp until we can get a celestial fix. All right?”

“You got it, boss.” Gino ducked inside and below.

The moon had set, and searching for stars revealed only an overcast sky. This meant it was too dark to make out any horizon, so Rebel was sliding through a dimensionless black void with no top and no bottom. I couldn’t even see the ocean sliding past our hull, so I could only guess our speed. We were running darkened ship, and the brightest light in our world was the glowing compass atop the pedestal in front of the wheel.

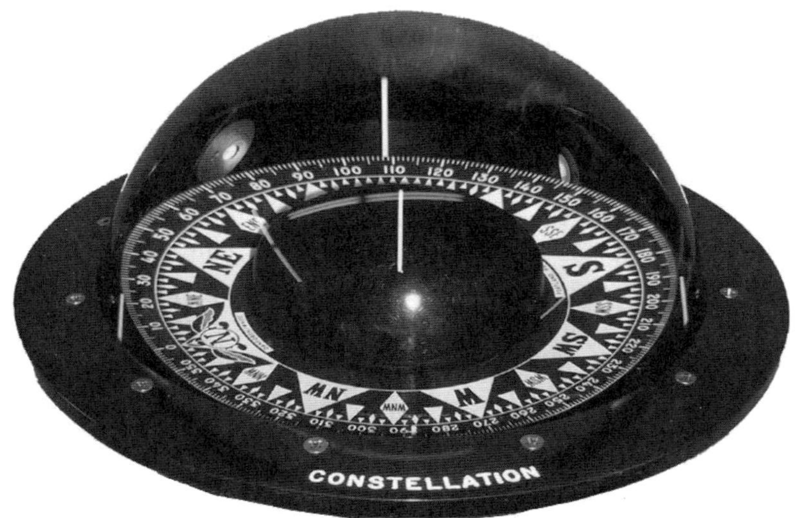

A decade ago the same real estate had been occupied by an electronic "virtual compass" and a GPS chart-plotting unit with a dozen screens to select with just the touch of a fingertip. For a while in the more distant past we'd even had radar, but one by one most of the old electronics had failed.

My single-sideband radio transmitter was crippled. On the back of the pilothouse to starboard by the engine panel was the working depth sounder, next to the matching but dead speedometer. Both had come out of the same box back in the Florida boatyard where Rebel Yell had been reborn with a new name.

Rebel's 200-horse Cat diesel still ran like a Russian tank engine, thanks to Gino's mechanical finesse, but it was leaking motor oil out of its front seal at an increasing rate, and even he couldn't repair that without a boatyard overhaul and parts that were impossible to find. The Caterpillar had been brand new when it was delivered to the boatyard in a factory crate.

What added value do you place on the things that last?

Five minutes later Mike joined me in the cockpit and handed me my water bottle. Once in the distant past it had been filled with a green concoction called Gatorade, now it held a pint of Port Royal's best South Carolina river water. Mike was still in his militia-issue USMC desert cammies, minus the ball cap.

"Did you get any sleep?" I asked him

"An hour, maybe. What time is it?"

"A little after four. Get in the habit of looking at the clock when you come through the galley. It's over the table, and we always leave the red light on when we're sailing at night. We do everything by the hour, so you need to know the time."

"Okay. Clock—galley. Got it." He yawned while looking all around. There was nothing to see beyond the cockpit.

"Gino said you steered for a while."

"That's right. Sailing is just sailing. Big boat or small, one mast or two. It's like riding a bicycle once you know how."

"Yeah, that's true. Listen, Mike, when you came aboard things were pretty crazy. I'd understand if you've had second thoughts. We're going straight over the Bahamas. There won't be many chances for you to get ashore."

"What? No, skipper, I've had no second thoughts, and no regrets. Even if you could turn around, I wouldn't go back."

"Since you already know how to sail and run small boats, I'll bet you had a lot of boating experience as a kid."

"Sure, we all had boats growing up. Power and sail."

"Was that on the island?"

"You mean Beaufort? No, I grew up on Kiawah Island."

"Kiawah? Your family must have had money if they lived on Kiawah." This was a barrier island south of Charleston.

"They did, but in the end, money didn't matter. Not when the power went out and the water stopped. All our water came from the mainland, so Kiawah sort of died on the vine." He sat down in the front of the cockpit facing me, his back against the latched-open door of the pilothouse, his feet in the cockpit well. This spot kept him out of the wind.

"We had a second home in North Carolina, way up in the mountains. You might say my dad was a prepper. We always planned that the cabin would be our bugout location, but it just didn't work out that way. At least, I couldn't get there. When the power went out, that was it. No banks, no credit cards, no ATMs, no gas stations. No nothing. You basically couldn't go anywhere unless you had your own airplane."

I didn't push any further. We'd have weeks and weeks to share our stories. "Okay, Mike, here's my plan. We have four helmsmen now, so we're each going to pull two hours behind the wheel. Two on, six off. Can you steer for two hours?"

"Do you mean right now?"

"No, not now, I've got it now. I mean starting tomorrow."

"Sure, I can steer this thing—if I can get some sleep first."

He was yawning heavily. Even in the weak light cast by the compass and the depth sounder I could see he was fighting to stay awake. One of my purposes in asking Gino to awaken Mike and send him up on deck was to see how he would do when he was forcibly dragged out of his slumber. He'd passed the test, a test I had used on new crew many times before.

Some potential crew just could not be forced awake, either because they could not *or they would not* get out of their racks. In either case the result was the same. Some malingering crew even faked seasickness to avoid doing their duty and remain in their bunks. I thought about asking Mike to send up Adam or Will, but I decided not to. The young ones needed sleep more than they needed another test from the captain.

"Gino says you know how to sail pretty well."

"Sure, growing up on Kiawah we all had boats. Maybe not everybody, but somebody always had a boat. Ski boats, fishing boats, sailboats . . . just about anything that floated from surfboards on up. I learned to sail in summer camp when I was a little kid. We had a real nice life on Kiawah. That's how I got to Beaufort: I took a Hobie Cat and I sailed there."

"What about your family, your parents?"

"My parents were up-state when the power went out. I was a senior in high school and my sister was in college. She went to Clemson and my parents were visiting her. Cell phones kept working for a while, off and on—and then just off. My dad told me they were heading for our place in North Carolina, and that I should try to get there too. But that was impossible. Every road was jammed when the gas stations went dry. It was pure mayhem. People shot each other over a gallon of gas. I haven't heard a word from them since that last phone call.

"After that I had the whole house to myself, so I had all of my dad's guns and prepper supplies, but you just couldn't live on Kiawah when there was no drinking water. Then I started hearing gunfire and smelling smoke all the time, and I knew it was time to haul ass. The people from Charleston were heading to where the rich people lived, I guess. I heard it was better in Beaufort, so I went for it on a Hobie eighteen, but the militia grabbed me and they robbed me of all the stuff I had. Man, they just robbed me blind. Guns, gold, silver—everything.

"I did my time on a farm, and then they let me join the militia because of my boating experience. I guess that's what you call ironic, after they robbed me first. Most of the time I was crewing on a fishing boat and the militia thing was just a sideline, but fishing was better than farm work. You know, I saw this boat all the time back on the river, but even in my wildest dreams I never thought I'd be on it."

I could see him smiling by the glow of the compass.

"Your name is Ortega, right? Do you speak Spanish?"

"Spanish? Me? Barely. My dad is third-generation Cuban and he married an American. We didn't speak it at home. My dad was an architect and my mom was an attorney."

He'd switched from present to past tense when describing his parents. He spoke about them with almost no emotion, as if he was discussing last week's weather. People's emotions had in many cases been bulldozed flat. There was no point in more probing. We had weeks together ahead of us.

"Okay, Mike, just so you know, we're going to have an all-hands meeting here in the cockpit at nine. You can hit the rack now. That means you can go below and go back to sleep. I've got it under control up here."

He didn't need to be told twice. I spent the rest of the time before dawn trimming and adjusting the sails, trying to get her so well balanced on the wind that she would keep tracking in a straight line without a hand on the wheel. Three minutes was my record, and that was not good enough.

Building a self-steering wind vane capable of handling a heavy sixty-footer would require access to a machine shop and a long list of parts that were not available on the island. Tying off the wheel and leaving the helm unattended could result in going far off course and into an uncontrolled gybe that might result in irreparable damage. Rebel's two booms would swing out of control all the way across the boat, gaining speed until they slammed hard to a stop on the other side.

With the rigging wires holding up our two masts as old as they were, this could even result in Rebel being dismasted. An unplanned gybe could also result in crew being struck in the head or even knocked off of the boat. As a result, I concluded that Rebel would have to be hand-steered for every minute.

The danger of a gybe was captured in a macabre saying: "paid off by the boom." An often-repeated legend held that unwanted crewmen, (perhaps unfortunate souls who had been shanghaied after being slipped a Mickey in a sailor's dive bar), would be called on deck and given a task that would put their back to the boom that was on the other side of the boat. The helmsman would steer to cause an intentional gybe. The boom would sweep across the deck and knock the poor unsuspecting sailor overboard. There would be no need to pay him his share of the voyage profits after he had been "paid off by the boom." Maybe this story was a myth, but it underscored the danger of an unplanned gybe.

13

At nine o'clock we were still on port tack sailing southeast. It wasn't raining, we weren't healed over steeply and the motion was easy, so we held our first all-hands crew meeting.

Gino was at the wheel again, because he could steer and follow what I was saying. The crew meeting was mostly for our new hands. Normally all this information would have been shared back in port, and then on a series of coastal shakedown sails. This time we didn't have that luxury.

When I had their attention I said, "Now, first things first: I'd like to begin our voyage with a prayer. The coming weeks and months are going to test us to our limits, and a positive and spiritual attitude will help us to get through the hardest times. Please feel free to join in, but I leave it up to you. I only ask that you be respectful, even if you're not a believer."

I lowered my head and then began. "Our father, who art in heaven, hallowed by thy name. . ." I didn't look up to see who was praying. This was up to each person. After the final amen, and some time for quiet reflection, I opened my eyes and said, "We're very fortunate to have nice weather our first day out, so we can get our sea-legs. We have some new crew members, so can you introduce yourselves? Let's start with Adam."

Adam Selfridge, Will Padgett, Mike Ortega, and then Luke and Jessie Hanahan each told us their names, their ages, their home towns of origin and a few facts about themselves.

I asked Gino, "First mate, what's our course and speed?"

He glanced down at the compass, then back up. "Our course has been averaging 125 degrees magnetic, which is 118 degrees true. Our speed has been about four knots."

I translated this for the non-sailors. "Okay, that's roughly southeast, and we want to sail more eastward than that, but we can't because the wind is from the northeast and we can't sail straight at the wind, right? We could run the engine, but we have thousands of miles to go and we need to make the fuel last. We'll sail until we're making less than two knots. What this means is, we're going to keep sailing even if we're not sailing fast, so just be patient. We're in this for the long haul."

Every eye was on the captain—me—standing in front.

"We don't have an autopilot, so somebody has to steer every minute. Rebel Yell has a long keel and she tracks pretty straight on most points of sail, but it's dangerous to let the wheel go unattended, because a gybe could break something that we can't fix. I'll explain what that means later when I'm teaching you about sailing. This means that there will be two of you in the cockpit for every hour of the day and the night. We'll be splitting this work into four duty sections, so you'll be on watch for two hours and off for six.

"Each duty section will have a primary helmsman and a number-two. The helmsmen will be me, Luke, Gino and Mike. We'll do them in that order, so that Luke and Mike will have an experienced coach during the turnover at each end of their watch. The watches will change every two hours on the even hours, except for between four and six in the afternoon when there'll be one-hour watches. This is called the dog-watch, and what this does is shift the times so nobody is stuck pulling the same hours every day. Every fourth day you'll see a sunrise, and every fourth day you'll stand the mid-watch, that's from midnight until two am. And this way, everybody will get to sit down for supper between four and six."

I'd written the watch schedule in pencil on an old piece of note paper, and I held it up to show them. "This will be on the bulletin board by the dinette table. Today is Sunday, but it's also the first Day One on this four-day watch rotation. Take a good look at this paper. We'll still have seven-day weeks like we do on land, but we're also going to live by these four-day watch rotations. The watches are on twenty-four hour time, so get used to hearing sixteen-hundred for four in the afternoon. Midnight is zero-zero, so we just call it midnight."

I handed it to Luke, who glanced at it and passed it along.

	Day 1	Day 2	Day 3	Day 4
0000	Dan	Luke	Gino	Mike
0200	Luke	Gino	Mike	Dan
0400	Gino	Mike	Dan	Luke
0600	Mike	Dan	Luke	Gino
0800	Dan	Luke	Gino	Mike
1000	Luke	Gino	Mike	Dan
1200	Gino	Mike	Dan	Luke
1400	Mike	Dan	Luke	Gino
1600	**Dan**	**Luke**	**Gino**	**Mike**
1700	**Luke**	**Gino**	**Mike**	**Dan**
1800	Gino	Mike	Dan	Luke
2000	Mike	Dan	Luke	Gino
2200	Dan	Luke	Gino	Mike

"During the day when most of us will be awake, we don't have to be real strict about who is steering. If you need to use the head or get something down below, or even if you just need to stretch and move around, you can have somebody else take the wheel for a couple minutes. Gino's steering now, and by the schedule it should be my turn, but we need to finish this meeting first. Gino steered a lot last night and this morning, so Luke, why don't you take the helm?"

Luke was wearing the same red and black plaid shirt he'd been wearing on stage. It seemed impossible that the concert had only been the night before. He wasn't a sailor, not yet, but with his black beard and wild untied hair he looked the part.

He stood behind the wheel and Gino took his seat in the crowded cockpit. I was curious to see if Luke had the ability to balance steering by the compass course and laying the best track to windward, while also being distracted by the meeting. Some non-sailors got the knack of it in a few minutes, and some never did. Luke couldn't get us into too much trouble in broad daylight with the other helmsmen watching and ready to grab the wheel to prevent a serious mistake, like a gybe.

After a few minutes the handwritten watch schedule came back around to me and I said, "Once the meeting is over I'll take the helm and finish the 0800 eight-to-ten watch. Then it's Luke, then Gino, then Mike again. This will go on around the clock, so catch some sleep any chance you can. And if somebody is sleeping, don't wake them up unless it's time for their watch. Sleep is like having gas in the tank. You'll understand how important this is when we get into rough weather.

"These are going to be two-man watches, and we'll switch these pairs around as we see how it's working, but for now I'll take Will, and Adam will be with Luke. Even though Adam's young, he's already a good sailor, so he can teach Luke how to trim the sails. Rita will be Gino's number-two, and Jessie will be with Mike to start out. Mike knows how to sail, and he can teach Jessie. We'll switch the teams around as we see how things are working out. Luke, once you're up to speed Jessie can be your number-two. And the number-twos should get as much practice steering as they can—you never know what'll happen on a voyage. The more helmsmen we have, the better. Oh, and the number-twos also have the very important job of waking up the next duty section if they're sleeping."

I held up my left arm. "I have a watch, and there's another watch tied to the wheel on top of the hub." This was Sergeant Major Tolbert's self-winder. The old SAS trooper hadn't made it out of Fort Zerhoun in Morocco. His watch had been passed to Victor, and now it belonged to Rebel Yell. It didn't keep better time than my own self-winder, but it would be close enough for the watch standers to know the top of the hours.

"There's a clock in the galley over the dinette table, so get used to checking the time there. There's a red dome light over the table and we leave it on at night when we're at sea. It's red light so it doesn't ruin your night vision. It has a white light too but that's for when we're in port. The barometer is next to the clock, and you should always check that too. The time and the barometric pressure are both important. If the pressure is dropping fast, that means trouble. We have a new timepiece, a wristwatch that's supposed to be accurate enough for celestial navigation, and we'll use that one to reset the others.

"Now, Tala and Sofia aren't on the watch rotation because they're our sea-cooks, and being a sea-cook is a full-time job. They'll also be looking after Chris and Jon, and so will Rita. Tala and Sofia are in charge of the galley and all of the food, and they'll ask you to help them with meal prep. That means peeling potatoes and carrots and chopping onions, that sort of thing, so be a good sport and help out."

Gino added, "After a few weeks at sea you'll be so bored that you'll *want* to peel the potatoes. Once Rita made a whole chess set out of dried carrots and potatoes."

Rita shook her head, laughing. I took back control of the meeting. There was still important information to convey.

"Right now I need to be serious about something. I can't emphasize enough that if you fall overboard, you're probably a goner. Even if somebody sees you go over, by the time we can get this big old boat stopped and turned around you'll be hundreds of yards behind, and probably a lot further. If the waves are any bigger than they are right now, we won't be able to see you unless it's by pure luck. And if you go over at night, you can forget it. Same deal if nobody sees you go over during the day. What I'm trying to tell you is that if you fall overboard, we'll probably never find you. This means that you should treat the deck of Rebel Yell the same way that you'd treat walking near the edge of a cliff, or working on the top of a skyscraper: if you fall off, you're probably a goner.

"Now, that said, if you do see somebody fall overboard, start yelling 'Man Overboard!' and don't stop yelling until everybody is on deck. Keep your eyes on the person who went overboard, and nothing else. We'll do some man-overboard drills once things have settled down. My point is, don't be casual moving around on deck. If you fall off the boat, you can pretty much kiss your ass goodbye. I don't mean to scare you, but that's just the reality. As you can see, Jonathan and Christopher are wearing life jackets. They always wear them on deck, and they don't go forward of the cockpit unless it's with an adult and their safety lines are clipped on. They grew up on Rebel Yell, and they know the deal—right, boys?"

Taken by the gravity of the moment, they both nodded and Chris said, "Yes daddy, we know the deal." Jonathan added, "Stay on the boat, or you're a goner."

It was a solemn moment. We knew a cruising family who had lost a child overboard. It was heartbreaking, and their self-recriminations were never ending. It destroyed their marriage.

After a moment for reflection I said, "Water is another serious topic. Fresh water is only going to be for drinking and for our meals. When we get some heavy rain we'll rig tarps to catch water off the sails and collect it in jugs, and you can use that water for washing up. And we might get enough hard rain to wash the salt off the deck so we can run it into the water tank, but we can't count on that. It almost never happens.

"We're lucky we filled our tanks last week in Port Royal, so we have about five hundred gallons on board. If it takes us sixty days to get to Argentina, that comes down to about eight gallons a day. Those eight gallons are for our meals and for our drinking water. Call it two gallons for cooking and six for drinking. Six gallons divided by twelve of us is a half-gallon, and that's your daily water ration."

Jessie asked, "What about water for washing up, and for showers, and for brushing our teeth, things like that?"

"I'm sorry, but we have thousands of miles to go and only a limited amount of fresh water, so that means it just can't be spared for taking showers or washing your hair. For washing up it'll have to be buckets of sea water on the aft deck, or on the swim platform when the conditions allow it. Put a little of your drinking water in a cup to brush your teeth. The sinks in the heads are going to be secured, that means turned off. Fresh water is too valuable to waste any running down a drain. The only fresh water source will be the tap in the galley. I know it sounds harsh, but we've never made such a long voyage with so many people. We have to plan to go the whole way on what we have on board right now, today. It would be foolish to do it any other way, and I'm not foolish."

"What if we stop along the way?" asked Luke, who was steering while also looking at the compass, up at the sails, at the horizon ahead, and at me.

"We can't plan to stop anywhere from here to Argentina. They never had any water to spare in the Bahamas, so they're not even worth considering. There's plenty of water in the Dominican Republic and Puerto Rico, but we don't know the conditions there and it'd be much too dangerous to just drop in to find out. The same goes for Brazil or anywhere else before Argentina or Uruguay.

"Our safety depends on being far out at sea and out of the sight of land. Pirates don't roam around out on the ocean; they lurk around coastlines and ports. Almost any ship or boat we come across will be faster than us, so we need to keep out of their sight. This means we can't plan for a water stop, so we're going to stick to a half gallon a day per person until we get a feel for how it's going. It'll be better to ration our water from the start than to run out of it half way. A lot better. If we get some big rain and we can put some water in our tanks, we'll make another calculation, but don't count on it."

Nobody appeared shocked or dismayed. One benefit of everyone having lived through the hard times was that I didn't need to explain the requirement to restrict our water intake, so I could speak frankly. Even the twins, five years old, already understood that drinking water was a precious commodity.

"Tala and Sofia are in charge of the galley and the food stores, and by that I mean *completely* in charge. Gino and I run the deck and the engine room. I'm the captain and Gino's the first mate, and we're in charge of the watch rotation, and the sails, and running the engine and the generator, but otherwise Sofia and Tala are in charge down below. This means nobody else goes into the galley area except to fill their water bottle.

"The next rule goes for the food stored in the cargo hold, and it's the same as for the food in the galley, and the rule is *no pilfering*. This includes me. Only Sofia and Tala can go into the barrels and crates in the hold to restock the galley. We only eat at meals: breakfast, lunch and dinner, and then we eat together. It's the only way to be fair; there just isn't enough food to eat what you want anytime of the day. If you want a snack during your watch, you have to save it from your meal. You can get a plastic jar to keep your leftovers in, but it has to stay in the galley area or up here in the cockpit.

"You'll each get a water bottle to keep for your own use. What we have the most of are sixteen-ounce bottles, so they'll be the standard issue." I held up my own. It was clear plastic, about three inches in diameter and seven inches tall, with a wide screw-on cap. "When you get your bottle, personalize it with a piece of string, maybe with some beads or knots in it. Rita can give you some colored yarn for this. As long as you can tell your own bottle from the others, that's good enough. For now, we'll fill our own water bottles on the honor system. If you have a sixteen-ounce water bottle that means you can fill it four times a day. Our tank water doesn't taste great but it's safe. It goes through a charcoal filter that Gino designed.

"Other than for filling your water bottle, nobody goes into the galley cooking area except Tala or Sofia, or me or Gino or Rita when we're helping to cook. What this means is if you're in the galley alone, other than for getting water, well, it won't look good for you. 'Lead us not into temptation,' right? Now, on the starboard side of the pilothouse ladder, on the dinette table side, you can hang out there any time of the day or night. You can sit there to read, or work on a puzzle. We have some board games too, and cards and a magnetic chess set. But stay out of the cooking side unless you're getting water.

“This afternoon we’ll start reorganizing the cargo hold into crew quarters for our three bachelors. Luke and Jessie will be all the way forward with Gino and Sofia. We have hammocks for the cargo hold, and when you get used to sleeping in them you’ll be better off than sleeping on top of the cargo. Now, the heavy barrels and crates are chained to the hull sides to keep a passageway down the middle open, so no matter what, don’t mess with those chains and timbers! If something as heavy as a drum of oil gets loose down there, people can get killed, or our food stores could be ruined. So don’t mess with the cargo, but if you see something that looks like it needs attention then get me or Gino: don’t try to fix it on your own. Keeping heavy cargo secured in rough weather when we’re heeled way over is serious business, and we both have a lot of experience at it, so come to us if something doesn’t seem right.

“It’s going to be a difficult trip, but we’ve all been through hard times and we’re still around. We’re all survivors. We just have to be patient and kind to each other, help each other out, and overlook our rough edges. My only goal is to get us safely to a new place where we can raise our families and live better lives. Right here and now there are twelve souls on this boat, an even dozen, and with the good lord’s help, there are going to be an even dozen of us on board when we reach Argentina.”

I looked at all their faces. It had been a very serious crew meeting, but it was better to set the correct tone right from the beginning. Strict discipline that was established at the outset of a voyage could always be relaxed as conditions allowed.

When I was almost ready to close the meeting, I heard a male voice from behind me. Behind me? Who? What?

“Ahh, umm, no, Captain Kilmer, I’m afraid that you’re off by one. There are thirteen souls on board. Thirteen.”

I turned around and looked forward over the pilothouse, and there, standing by the foremast on the far side of Whisper, was the thief from the Beaufort market!

14

He made his way around toward the cockpit on the port side, the high side on port tack. His left hand was on the pilothouse grab rail for balance; his right hand was held out from his side to show it was empty. He was wearing a green t-shirt and the same 20th-Century woodland-pattern camo pants as before, but this time he was barefoot.

He stopped by the corner of the pilothouse, and after a moment he said, "I'm sorry to break in on you like this, but I had to come out sometime, and I suppose now is as good a time as any. So, hello everybody, my name is Barry Conway. When I hid on your boat I thought you were just going to Charleston or Savannah. If I'd known different, I would have picked another boat, and you can believe me on that!" He smiled awkwardly at his own weak attempt at humor. Nobody smiled back at him. We were all in shocked surprise.

I said, "Luke, hold your course. Rita, take the twins below. Everybody else, the meeting is over." Then I turned again to the stowaway, pointed my finger at his chest and then toward the front and said, "You and me—we need to talk. Up on the bow, in front of the foremast."

After a brief hesitation he turned and went forward.

Gino asked me, "Do you know this guy?"

"We, ahh, sort of met yesterday. It's a long story."

I went up forward to confront the thief. The two jibs were stretched tightly back along the starboard side, the low side on port tack. The boat was pitching a bit on the swells, but not enough to send water over the deck, just a little spray now and then. The scuttle hatch was open in the rear for ventilation.

The stowaway stood easily on the slanting deck, holding the inner-forestay wire and looking aft while waiting for me. The front edge of the working jib was attached to the forestay wire every two feet with bronze spring clips called hanks. A man with good balance could stand upright on the open deck, but some extra support always helped, and made it safer.

The right side of his face was bruised and scraped where he had been held against the ground. With his arms exposed, I could see that he had burn scars on both of them.

"So, where were you hiding?" I asked him.

"In the boat between the masts."

I looked behind the foremast at Whisper. Its canvas cover was in place, but it looked loose and unfastened in the front. It had seemed fastened correctly earlier. I pressed my hip against the side of the scuttle hatch so that my torso was vertical over the slanted foredeck. It was a comfortable and secure standing position in those fairly mild conditions.

Leaning back against the pulpit railing in the very bow, the thief kept hard eye contact with me. He was about five-ten in height and weighed maybe a hundred and fifty pounds. To get any further forward he'd need to climb out on the bowsprit.

"Is Barry Conway your real name?" I asked him.

"What difference does it make? I don't have any ID."

He had a point there. My most recent official government-issued documents were more than a decade out of date, but I'd been out of the country for almost that long, at least officially. As far as I knew, from what I'd heard on the island, there had been no functioning American government anywhere at any level issuing new documents for the past five or more years. On the island any push to issue identification documents had been fiercely opposed as a dangerous first step on the road to tyranny. Some locals called identification, taxation, regulation, vaccination and conscription the five deadly *'tions* or "shuns" that must be shunned forever. It hadn't even occurred to me to ask the other new crew members to prove who they were.

"How old are you, Barry? And where are you from? I take it you're not from the island, not originally."

He waited to answer, seeming to measure me just as I was measuring him, and then he said, "I'm twenty-six, and I grew up in North Charleston."

His pale blue eyes were about the same shade as mine, not the vivid blue of Adam's. Once his hair grew out from its current buzz-cut it might be a light brown or blonde.

I said, "They tied your hands behind your back, I saw them do it. So how did you get away?"

He hesitated, and then answered. "I had a little pen knife in my back pocket. Real small and flat, but sharp. They missed it. It's one of the tricks I learned. They left me in the truck tied to some pallets, and when nobody was looking I was gone."

"Did you steal that too? The pen knife?"

"What difference does it make?"

"So how in the hell did you wind up on my boat?"

"How? You're the one who tripped me on the Beaufort landing—do you think I'd forget your face? Then after you left they were talking about Captain Kilmer and his schooner. They even pointed it out, the black sailboat with two masts. They said you sail up to Charleston and down to Georgia. After I got out of the truck I hid in the marsh under the bridge freezing my ass until the tide was running out. I figured your boat was my ride off the island. I'm a fair swimmer but the current did most of it. I climbed up onto your back porch, and when nobody was on deck I got into that boat. I fixed up the canvas and I waited inside there. Your meeting seemed like a good time to come out. Can you get me some water, please?"

He folded his arms across his chest, getting into a more secure position by leaning back against the bow pulpit with his legs spread, his toes wedged under the stock of the stowed main anchor. It was chilly in the breeze, and goose bumps were raised on his arms except where they were scarred by burns. His camouflage trousers were too long for him, and their frayed ends covered his feet. The deck was wet where some spray came across when a wave slapped the hull.

"Get you some water? You sneaky little bastard, I should just throw you overboard and be done with you!"

He shook his head. "Oh, no you won't, Captain Kilmer. Not a good Christian man like you. 'Forgive us our trespasses, as we forgive the trespasses of others,' isn't that right? Well, here I am. No, you won't throw me off, and you can't go back. I heard enough last night to know you're never going back."

"Then I'll put you off at the first island."

"But you're not stopping at any islands, you just said so."

"Then I'll have you tied up. I can't trust a thief."

"A what? A thief? No, Captain Kilmer, a runaway slave, that's what you really mean. Everything I took was to help me escape from the farm. I had way more than that coming to me after more than a year of forced labor with no wages. A slave has the right to run away, don't you agree?"

"But you're not a slave if you volunteered. Weren't you a voluntary indentured worker?"

He snorted. "Sure, captain, call it voluntary if it goes easier on your conscience. But I just call it what it is: slavery."

"But didn't you volunteer?"

"Do you think I volunteered for *this*?"

He lifted his right pant leg. His ankle had an iron shackle around it, padded in places with pieces of dirty rag. His skin there was scabbed and calloused.

"That's been on me since the first time I tried to run away in July. Since then I've been chained at night like a cur dog. If they'd seen this yesterday and chained me proper, I'd be back on the farm today. Them not seeing it was my lucky break."

"But didn't you volunteer, though? Originally? Didn't you come to the island of your own free will?"

"Do you call it free will if you're starving to death and you can't walk one more mile? If you've been passing out from hunger and dehydration and fever, and sometimes you wake up with no memory of the past days and weeks? When you don't know where you are, when you can't even remember your own name? Somewhere along the way I heard that things were different on Beaufort Island. Things were better there. So yes, I walked over that bridge of my own free will—if that's what you want to call it—and I walked straight into slavery.

"They put me in the old Marine barracks for a month to get me strong enough to work. Quarantine and selection, that's what they call it. They give you a month of good food and clean sheets, showers and soap even—but it doesn't last. Just when you almost feel like a human being again, you're sent to a farm. On McAllister's they work you like an animal from dawn till dusk, and you're fed slop you wouldn't feed hogs—and not enough of it. At night you sleep in a barn under shared blankets, and you're so dog-tired you don't even care about the chiggers and the bedbugs and the lice. And every time you get an infraction they whip you and they hold back your food, or they add months to your 'contract.' There's some 'volunteers' at McAllisters that have been there for more than two years, and they came in on one-year contracts the same as me. Plenty of them are buried back at McAllisters, that's how they finished their contracts. Captain Kilmer, you didn't know this?"

Barry extended his right foot out toward me, resting his heel atop the anchor windlass. The ankle scars were at least several months old. The burn scars on his arms were even older.

I said, "I didn't know anything about that. We were on the island two years but I didn't know. I heard it was rough on the farms, but I didn't know how rough."

"Sure, you were up in Beaufort with the free islanders, living off the fruit of our slave labor. Life was a little different down on St. Helena for us 'volunteers.' So, Captain Kilmer, now that you know my story, what are going to do?"

"I don't know yet. I have to think it over."

We just stared at one another for most of a minute, Rebel surging along to windward, rising and falling on the swells.

"Well, captain, it's your ship, so you do that, think it over. The only thing I ask is this: don't tell them how we met. Tell them I'm a runaway slave, a runaway VIW, I don't care. I'm not ashamed of that. And I'm not ashamed of what I took for my escape, but the rest of your crew, they won't understand. If you can do that, I swear I'll be the best crew you have. I'll outwork any man on this boat, and it'll be a holiday vacation compared to what I've been through. But my feet are freezing and I could sure use some water, and maybe something to eat. Just let me know what you decide—I'm not going anywhere."

He turned away from me to face into the wind, both hands on the bow pulpit, nothing but clouds and white-capped waves all the way to the horizon in every direction. There were some breaks in the overcast where beams of sunlight turned the sea radiant blue, but they were rare, like sapphires scattered on a dark rug. It was going to be a real trick to catch a noon sight.

I returned to the cockpit. Luke was standing behind the wheel, so he could just see over the pilothouse, but mostly he was watching the compass while trying to make the best speed to windward. Gino was leaning against the stern rail and hanging onto the backstay wire with one hand. Mike was sitting at the back of the cockpit on the high side, his feet braced against the opposite seat edge. There was nobody else.

I understood from experience that Tala and Sofia had cleared everyone else from the topside so that an important discussion could be held between the men. She had meant it when she said that Gino and I ruled the decks, just as she and Sofia ruled the galley and the berthing arrangements down below. This was a fair arrangement, and frankly it took a lot of stress off my plate. For one thing, when mealtimes came, I just sat down to eat. So God bless them, and their division of labor.

It also occurred to me that perhaps they'd cleared the topsides of all but the adult men so that if we were going to pitch our unwanted guest into the drink, there wouldn't be any extra witnesses, and particularly not among the youngsters.

My mood was grim when I sat in the front of the cockpit facing the three men, my back to the latched-open pilothouse door. I was at a loss for words, and I was grateful when Gino asked, "So, where in the hell did *he* come from?"

After a little more time to think, I told them Barry's story, skipping the part where I had tripped him while he was being pursued as a thief. I abridged the story to make him a runaway V-I-W swimming out to the anchorage looking to become a stowaway, because he'd heard waterfront scuttlebutt that we sailed the coast. He'd used our swim platform to climb aboard, and then he'd used Whisper as his overnight hiding place.

Gino asked me, "So, what are we going to do with him?"

I sighed, unsure. Stalling. "Put him to work, I guess. He looks fit enough, and he's not stupid, I can tell that already."

Mike said, "I spotted him for a runaway just as soon as I saw his pants. Those old woodland camos are what they give the VIWs for farm work." He pronounced VIWs as *views*.

"He told me he tried to run away last summer, and they put a shackle on his leg, and they kept him on a chain at night."

"A chain?" Mike replied, "I spent my time as a VIW—and it was no fun—but I didn't see anybody in chains."

"Well, Mike, he has a shackle on his foot. I saw it. And it wasn't put on yesterday, I could see that too."

Luke said, "Mike, you were in the militia, so you handled the off-islanders. How could you not know about chains and shackles, if this guy has one on him?"

"We just take them in for processing, the ones who pass the initial selection on the bridge. I don't know what happens after that, after they're assigned to farms—but I never heard about anybody being chained up. At least, I never saw it."

I said, "But doesn't the militia run the quarantine at Parris Island? Doesn't the militia assign them out to the farms?"

"That's between the militia brass and the Beaufort Farm Council. That was way above my pay grade, which was room and board. Hell, I just got my first stripe."

He pointed to the single black chevron sewn on his tan ball cap. Weirdly enough, I thought it sort of matched his trimmed black mustache. Private Ortega had a couple days of whiskers, and a military haircut too—but maybe that was a militia thing.

He said, "Back when I was at Parris Island, I wasn't in the militia. No, when I got to the island I was sent to a farm as a VIW, the same as this stowaway. Even after I got off the farm and I joined the militia, I was mostly working on fishing boats. The militia's not a full time job except for a few specialists, and the brass. But I never saw any VIWs in chains."

Again, Mike Ortega pronounced VIWs as *views*.

"Well," I said, "you should take a look at his shackle. It's iron and it's riveted on, so it's permanent."

"Just a thought, skipper," he replied, "but did it ever occur to you that maybe this guy had a shackle put on him for some other reason, and not just because he ran away from a farm?"

"What are you suggesting?"

"I'm not suggesting anything, but it makes me wonder. Three years on the island, and I never saw anybody shackled. It makes me wonder, that's all. Maybe each farm is different, and I just didn't see it. So, I guess we're keeping him, huh?"

"Well, Mike, we can't just throw him overboard. Anyway, I won't. So here's the deal: he's one more mouth to feed, and one more man living with you in the hold, but now there's also one more crew. He'll work. Everything happens for a reason, right? I'll make him my number-two along with Will until I figure out what he can do. Neither of them is a sailor, so I can train them both at the same time."

Gino said, "Boss, remember when you rescued me? I had a chain on my foot and I was a slave for those moslem pirates. But I wonder about it too, what he said: what does a shackle mean on the island? And I like twelve—the even dozen. Like the twelve apostles. I don't like thirteen. Thirteen is bad luck."

"Oh, that's just a superstition. Thirteen is just the number between twelve and fourteen." I stood and turned around to get Barry's attention, and waved him back to the cockpit. He stopped short by the side of the pilothouse when he saw Mike sitting in the back of the cockpit wearing his militia uniform, including a tan ball cap with a black chevron, and with his hair and mustache cropped to military standards. Private Ortega.

In his own turn Mike's gaze took in Barry's green t-shirt, burn-scarred arms, and woodland camo pants. By then we all understood what they meant: the wearer was a runaway VIW. I wondered if this was going to be an issue between them. How could it not be? On the other hand, Mike had just told us that he'd spent time as an indentured farm hand on the island. At least they had that experience in common.

I made the introductions. "This man is Barry Conway, our stowaway. We can't take him back, and we won't throw him overboard, so get used to him. On the plus side, he's another man to share the work load. Okay?"

Next I half-turned to address our stowaway, still standing by the port side of the pilothouse. "Barry, the man in the back is my first mate, Gino Bracciano. The first time I saw him he had a chain on his leg, a chain put on him by jihad pirates. The one with the moustache is Mike Ortega—he just deserted the Beaufort Militia. Luke Hanahan is steering. Gino and Luke are married men like me; our wives are below. Come around and show them your leg iron."

He moved the few steps aft and lifted his right pants leg. It was pure ugliness, there was no denying it. The rusty ring had been made from a piece of iron flat bar, heated and formed into a C-shape by a blacksmith. The two ends of the bar were turned out so that they could be clamped together, with an iron rivet passed through matching holes. The ends of the rivet had been hammered into flattened mushroom caps. The C-shape and the outward-angled ends and the holes could be made on a forge, but the clamping and riveting and hammering had to be done on the prisoner's ankle while the rivet was red hot.

Next to the rivet there was a large hole through the mated flanges where a chain could be attached with a lock. Rags had been twisted around the shackle to provide some padding, but they did not hide the band of scar tissue, welts and scabs.

I said, "Barry, we're going to cut that thing off you right here and right now. There's never been a slave on Rebel Yell."

Tala was coming up through the pilothouse, and I told her, "Well, it looks like we have one more man in the crew. Tala, this is Barry Conway. He was hiding in Whisper. Barry, this is my wife, Tala Kilmer."

He was standing by me and he said, "Hello, Mrs. Kilmer," and put out his hand, which she briefly took, then let go.

"Tala, each of these men will need a water bottle, so you might as well find them and fill them up. But get some water for Barry first—he hasn't had anything to drink since yesterday. After that, find him a sweatshirt and a jacket, and some socks until we find something for shoes." She knew what was in our grab-bag collection of left-behind clothing better than I did. On a voyage, the only goals were functional warmth and staying dry, so rips and paint stains meant nothing at all.

Tala took in the cockpit scene, measured Barry with her eyes, and went back down through the pilothouse and below. Distributing gear to new crew was a routine practice at the beginning of every voyage. What wasn't routine was dealing with a stowaway, and a thief at that. But I felt a demonstration of trust would be my best approach, at least initially. I'd make a show of accepting him—while watching him like a hawk.

But really, how different was Mike Ortega from Barry Conway? Both had come to the island as V-I-Ws, and a day earlier, neither man had planned to leave it. And how about Wagon Will? He was another I'd never laid eyes on before yesterday. And Adam? I'd known him for only a day longer. Exactly what did I know about any of them? I just had to trust in the lord—and sleep with one eye open.

Because he'd originally leapt across onto Rebel Yell with a chain locked around his ankle, I thought my first mate should be the one to remove Barry's shackle. "Gino, do you think we can get it off with the blowtorch?"

"I don't know, boss, we're almost out of acetylene."

I glanced at Barry to see his reaction, but he showed none. I was just joking about the blowtorch; we had neither oxygen nor acetylene on board. Gino went below to find the tools and returned in a few minutes. Barry lay on his back on the low-side cockpit bench for the operation.

After a brief attempt with a hacksaw, Gino pronounced the steel too thick and the blade too dull. I thought: add hacksaw blades to our Argentina shopping list. That is, if blades were made there, or were being imported from somewhere else.

Gino said, "This is a five-minute job if we have a Dremel tool with cutting wheels. Or a reciprocating saw."

"Tell me about it," I replied. The simplest items, things I had taken for granted for much of my life, were simply not available. When consumables like hacksaw blades broke, or they were worn dull, they could not be replaced.

After giving up on the hacksaw, and after wrapping Barry's ankle with towels to absorb as much of the impact force as possible, Gino attacked the rivet with a hammer and chisel. Sometimes the hammer missed or the chisel slipped and bit into flesh instead of metal, but Barry just gritted his teeth. When the chisel was dulled, Gino sharpened it with an abrasive block.

Millimeter by millimeter the rivet's mushroom cap edges were beaten and chipped away.

Attracted by the sound of steel striking steel, the rest of the crew came to witness the shackle's removal. Adam and Will sat on the high side to port, just outside the cockpit. They were more than boys but not quite men. Adam was a couple years younger than Will but he was already significantly bigger.

The twins watched from the pilothouse without asking why this was happening. Why was obvious. No man should have such a wicked device permanently attached to his body. Barry even managed to smile at them and laugh a little from his supine position, his head propped up on a cockpit cushion. Despite the wood blocks and rags for padding his foot was gouged and cut in new places and his old scabs were weeping.

We took turns steering the boat, sharpening the chisels, and hammering at the rivet's edges. Gino finally said that the steel pin could be moved a millimeter, and a few minutes later he turned it with pliers clamped to the opposite mushroom cap. When he judged it could be pushed through and out with only a few more sharp blows, Gino asked Barry if he wanted to finish the job. Our stowaway sat up and knocked the rivet all the way through by hammering it with a narrow metal punch. It fell into the cockpit foot well. Gino picked it up, examined it and handed it to me. The rivet was made of steel round-stock a half-inch in diameter. The second and still-intact mushroom end was almost an inch wide. The iron shackle was intended to *never* come off the man to whom it was affixed.

Even with the rivet removed the shackle did not surrender easily. The two mated flanges had to be forced apart, first with wooden wedges hammered between them, then by twisting and prying with a crowbar, and finally by me and Gino each pulling an end in opposite directions.

When the shackle was finally off his leg and in my hand, Barry looked at it and then at each of us in turn and said, "I guess I picked the right boat after all. No matter what happens now, I'll never forget what you did for me today. Until now, I thought I was going to die and be buried that thing on my leg."

The rusty iron was bright silver around the hole where our chisels had attacked the now-absent rivet. By its heft I guessed the shackle weighed almost two pounds.

I asked Barry, "Do you want to keep it for a souvenir?"

"Me? No. I don't want to see it again. Just get rid of it."

I watched him carefully. Not a tear, nor an expression of joy or even relief. He kept a mostly flat affect during what had to have been a deeply emotional moment.

I'd never been shackled or chained in my life. I'd only been handcuffed once or twice, briefly, so I passed it to Gino. He only glanced at the familiar iron band, and then he tossed it over the side where it disappeared without a splash.

"What about the rivet?" Gino asked Barry.

"I don't want the rivet either."

I said, "Let me have it. It was too much work getting it out to just deep-six it like the shackle."

Barry said, "Sure, captain, sure. That's fine with me. But if you don't mind—I don't want to ever see it again."

The rivet would join Victor's five-shot Smith & Wesson revolver, the broken key from the dungeon at Fort Zerhoun and a few other small but priceless keepsakes. I pocketed the rivet and said, "Let's get your ankle cleaned up and disinfected."

"Captain Kilmer, I'm infection-proof. If cuts like these were going to kill me, I'd have been dead years ago."

"Okay, fair enough, but we'll still get you some soap and water. And we won't even take it out of your daily ration."

I thought about offering him a fresh water bath in the aft cabin's tub. Gino had received that deluxe treatment when we'd rescued him from the pirates on the way to Morocco, but that had been on a relatively short voyage with fresh water to spare. And I also didn't want Barry the thief to ever enter my captain's cabin, much less its private head. My sympathy had limits. Letting our stowaway nurse his ankle with soap and clean water over a basin in the cockpit would be sufficient.

15

The sky was still heavily overcast, so there would be no noon sun sight for a position fix. I'd have to try for a star at evening or morning twilight, or hope for the sun again tomorrow. With Rebel Yell sailing southeast into the northeast-flowing Gulf Stream, our dead reckoning position was going to be a wild guess. But the Bahamas were still five hundred miles distant, so we had a long way to cover before I'd have to worry about hitting a reef. Even so, we needed all the easting we could get to carry us beyond Puerto Rico and the Windward Islands, and then around the shoulder of Brazil. For now southeast was the best we could manage.

A journey of six thousand miles begins with a single step, and we'd taken that step by getting away from South Carolina. This was true even if our departure had not been made on my schedule or with my first choice of crew. And it was still only November, so it was still hurricane season—for whatever that meant in a year of volcano-caused climate disruption.

It was ten-thirty in the morning. I studied the horizon all the way around, and examined our sails and rigging from top to bottom and bow to stern. Small problems could usually be fixed if they were found early. Luke was at the wheel. Adam was behind him, coaching him as he steered closer to the wind and then turned back away in long shallow S curves, trying to make the best speed and gain the most easting.

The two seemed to get along well, and it was good to have another knowledgeable sailor aboard to help train the novices. Thank you, Captain Sapelo, for tutoring Adam so well that he was already capable of teaching others to sail at only fifteen years old. Along with our tuned-up compass, in young Adam Selfridge I felt something of Hilton Sapelo was still aboard. He'd only spent a day on Rebel, but it had been an important one. It was hard to believe it had only been two days earlier.

Barry, Mike and Will observed the sailing instruction and the personal interaction between Adam and Luke. Their male competitive instincts would drive them to learn everything they could about sailing and crewing on an ocean-voyaging schooner. On some level each of them knew that they would be evaluated and ranked according to their ability to perform at the highest level under the most difficult circumstances.

Every boot camp since before the Spartans had employed this dynamic to draw the best out of each recruit and to find the leaders, as well as to identify the problem children. On the first day of the voyage Rebel was their entire universe. There has never been a better sailing academy than the ocean itself.

I pulled the folded watch schedule from my pocket and said, “Luke, Adam—you’re on until noon. Are you good? Can you handle it?”

Luke, his eyes darting between me, the compass and the sails, replied, “Sure, skipper, we can handle it fine.”

Adam gave me a thumbs-up. “No problem, captain. We’ve got it all under control.” Adam was big for fifteen, and in time he’d make a rough-weather helmsman in his own right.

“Luke,” I added, “if you let Adam take the wheel now and then, he’ll be able to show you, instead of just telling you.”

I turned to the other three young men. “Now, let’s get you squared away down below. Follow me, gentlemen.” Adam had come aboard with his own clothes, and Mike had his militia uniform to wear, but Will and Barry needed to be outfitted practically from head to toe.

Tala met us in the galley. I asked her to get the hammocks, and any of our grab-bags of leftover clothes that she thought would be suitable for our new crew. The three young men sat at the dinette and Tala set stacks of t-shirts, sweaters, jerseys, jackets, shorts and trousers on the table. The hammocks were rolled together into one big bundle.

A liveaboard schooner accumulates mountains of clothing over the course of decades. Some of the items are left aboard unintentionally, but most are old clothes considered too worn out, torn up or stained to wear ashore in public. During periods of stormy weather or prolonged precipitation, the only way to get dry after your watch is to have plenty of towels and spare clothing stored away, as day after day they all become soaked in salt water. Afterwards, when sunny weather returns, laundry is done on an epic scale, with towels, bedding and clothes drying on all of Rebel's lifelines and deck. Once dry, everything is stored away again to await the next storm.

The three new crewmen rummaged through the piles, each taking what they needed to make a few sets of clothes. Each was given his own canvas bag in which to store his wardrobe. Faded, stained and torn shirts and jerseys ironically bore the famous designer logos of companies that were long extinct.

Next, Tala produced a plastic laundry basket full of worn-out sneakers, half-broken sandals, sun-bleached reef-runners and even neoprene wetsuit booties. It would be up to them to find out what suited their feet. Another box was packed with ball caps, straw hats, boonie hats and canvas sailor hats.

This wasn't my first go at dressing new crew from scratch, but it was the first time we'd had so many to deal with at once. At least when the Brits and the Irish had come aboard for the Moroccan picnic, they'd come fully kitted out. Not so this rag-tag crew of last-minute volunteers, plus a stowaway.

Luke was still up in the cockpit steering, so he'd have to choose from the leftovers. I wasn't worried. Tala would make sure that Luke and Jessie were well turned out, even if some of their 'new' clothes came from our own drawers. Adam was a separate case; he had brought his own clothes, and he had a 'new' pair of canvas deck shoes that he had purchased at the Beaufort market with my own silver coins.

When each of them had filled their ditty bags with what they thought they needed, I said, "Okay, let's get you set up in your new quarters." I picked up the bundle of hammocks and slid the door to the cargo hold to the side. This opening was in front of the ladder up to the pilothouse.

When we were all inside, I said, "Rebel's hold is sixteen feet fore and aft, and a little more from side to side. This is what makes us a cargo schooner. Our internal volume is the same as a thirty-foot cargo container. The heavy stuff is always in the back, where it's the closest to the middle of the boat. The steel drums are full of gasoline and motor oil, and the blue plastic barrels are mostly full of food. More food is in the wooden crates on both sides of the passageway, along with our tools, spare parts, lumber, extra sails, spare anchors, anchor lines and a few tons of other stuff."

The cargo hold wasn't finished with teak and mahogany like the rest of Rebel Yell. It was all just white-painted marine plywood, with plenty of protruding ring bolts and metal cleats for attaching chains or tying ropes. These strong points were welded or bolted to hull frames. Daylight and ventilation were provided by four small opening hatches through the deck, two on each side of the cargo hatch. The two leaves of the seven-foot by seven-foot hatch were sealed tight for the ocean. More light came through four non-opening Plexiglas skylights, two in each half of the cargo hatch itself.

"Everything is held in place with these big timbers on the sides of the passageway. Chains hold the timbers to the hull, and the timbers hold back the cargo. If anything breaks loose there'll be hell to pay, but compared to a lot of trips this is a light load. When the hold is full there's no passageway in here at all, and you have to go on deck to get from one end of the boat to the other. Right now there's enough space above the cargo for four hammocks, two on each side. Mike and Barry will be back here, and Will and Adam will be up forward.

"You can use the head in the forward cabin if you need to take a crap, but just between you and me, you'll find it's a lot easier to use a bucket in the cockpit. Just catch some seawater in it first. I'll teach you how to catch water in a bucket with a rope, it's easy. You'll be amazed how your body adapts to the new routine. For taking a leak, just piss over the side, but the low side, downwind, right? Just lean against a rigging wire or the stern pulpit so you don't fall overboard. You'll figure it out. If you see any women up on deck, just say, 'Checking for reefs astern,' and believe me, they'll look somewhere else."

I unrolled the bundle of hammocks and gave one to each of the three, keeping one. "I'll put up Adam's. Nine men slept in here from Ireland to the Canaries, right on top of the cargo, and believe me, hammocks are a lot better. I had these custom made when we got to South Carolina."

The canvas-and-rope hammocks had a crescent-shaped wooden spreader bar at each end. The spreader kept a sleeper comfortably in the middle, but without squeezing him at each end the way that rope-only hammocks do. These spreader bars had a strong attachment rope at each end meeting at a metal snap link forming an inverted V.

Halfway down the hold on each side of the big overhead cargo hatch there was a stout ring bolt protruding through the plywood ceiling panel, and there were two more ring bolts at each end of the hold. I had installed them specifically for these four hammocks. The port and starboard hammocks shared a common middle ring bolt.

I clipped each end of Adam's hammock to a ring and the job was done. "You can adjust the end ropes if you want your hammock looser or tighter, but they'll work okay the way they are. Sleep with your feet in the middle and your heads at each end. This way you won't hear as much snoring."

To prove it could be done, I climbed atop the cargo to the high side of Adam's hammock, and then I shinnied into it. The three new crewmen followed me up the passageway to see how I did it, while I continued the lesson from my back.

"Once you get used to your hammock, you'll sleep like a baby, and it won't make any difference how far the boat is heeled over. It'll take a while to get the hang of it, but there's a reason why sailors have slept in these things since forever. Just be careful you don't fall when you're climbing out."

I rolled over and down, and by sheer luck I landed on my feet in the passageway, making my dismount seem easy. And if I could do it, these youngsters would have no problem.

"At sunset when the cockpit compass light is turned on, little LED nightlights will come on too. They're on the same circuit; I'm sure you saw them last night. They're down low so you don't trip and fall in the dark. There's also a light at each end of the hold over the sliding door, but they're too bright and they'll ruin your night vision, so we don't use them when we're sailing. They're what we call working lights.

"When it's time to change the watch, if you're on duty as the number-two you'll come down and wake up the next duty section. Just shake them by the shoulder, tell them what time it is, tell them it's their watch and let them know if they'll need foul-weather gear. That's it. When it's your turn, it's up to you to get out of your hammock, get dressed for the conditions, and get topsides. Do you all understand this?"

Each of the three nodded affirmatively, and I put out my hand and shook all of theirs in turn, right there in the cargo hold passageway, making eye contact with each of them.

"Now, to get my attention, or when it's my turn on watch, just rap on the aft deck behind the cockpit. If it's an actual emergency, bang like crazy and yell and holler about exactly what's going on. Don't be shy, yell it right out, and you'll get lots of help in a hurry. Mr. Bracciano lives up forward, but I'll be right under your feet and I can get to the cockpit faster.

"If you need a foul weather coat, that means a rain jacket, the off-going watch will give it to you. I'm sorry, but we don't have enough good ones to go around. They get worn out, and then they leak. They'll stay in the pilothouse. Now here is the important part: everybody on this boat is a volunteer, so when it's your watch, you have to roll out of your rack and turn-to. Turn-to means you do your job, and you do it like a man."

I held up my right hand, making the V-for-victory sign—or the peace sign—with my index and middle fingers, and I rotated my wrist. "This means turn-to. Turn two, get it? It means you do your job and you don't bitch and moan about it. Not for seasickness, not for fear of big waves or other scary shit, not for *any* of that. When it's your watch, you turn-to and you're up on deck and you do your job like a man. Don't be a load that the rest of us have to carry. Don't be the weak link. Don't let your shipmates down. All right?"

I had their full attention. Three young male faces nodded yes to me. Every boot camp drill instructor had pulled this act since time immemorial. I almost felt bad using it, but I had a job to do too, and my job was forming a crew that would take Rebel Yell all the way to the end of the voyage.

"Okay, my little pep-talk is almost over. The beatings will continue until morale improves, right? Any questions?"

Mike asked, "About the foul weather coats, what if one of them fits somebody better? Can they just keep it if there's enough to go around?" Mike was a bit heavier and taller than Barry, and a lot bigger than Will.

"You guys figure it out. I'll bring you all the extra foul-weather gear we have, and we've got some plastic tarps and some ponchos, stuff like that too. We're all men in here, so we'll work it out. One hand for yourself and one hand for the ship. All for one and one for all, that's the name of the game."

I pulled the schedule from my pocket. "Luke and Adam are still on watch until noon. Then its Gino and Rita—Rita's his daughter—from noon till two. Then Mike and Jessie. Once everybody knows how to sail, we can change the watch teams around, but this is how we're going to start it for now. The watch schedule will be pinned up on the bulletin board by the dinette table. That's also where the ship's clock is, so get used to checking the time when you pass it. You're responsible to know when your next watch is coming up. No excuses.

"You can spend your off-duty time in your hammock, or anywhere you can make yourself a comfortable spot here in the hold. You can drag some sail bags around and make a nest on the low side if you want to. And you can spend your off-duty time at the galley dinette table, or up in the pilothouse or in the cockpit."

Barry asked, "What about the rest of the deck?"

"Anywhere on deck is fine during daylight hours in nice weather, but at night and in rough weather, stay behind the pilothouse. It's just safer. But down below, the aft passageway from behind the dinette table to my cabin is off limits unless it's a real emergency, or if I invite you back there. Okay?"

I knew from long experience that it was better to lay down the rules and the expectations right at the beginning, so there would be no misunderstandings or hurt feelings later on.

"My bed is under the aft deck behind the cockpit, so when you're on watch don't stomp around like elephants, don't drag anything across the deck, and don't drop anything heavy, or it'll wake me up. But if you need me in a hurry, just bang on the aft deck real loud and I'll come flying up fast. And if you need more clothes or different shoes, anything like that, just find Gino or me. I'll put all the foul-weather gear together and you can sort through it."

Will said, "I think my Army parka is good enough."

"I think it should be. Oh, and we have some toothbrushes and combs, things like that. Hygiene, you know the deal."

Mike asked me, "What about shaving?" Alone among the male crew, his hair and mustache were well trimmed. Only Barry's hair was shorter, but that was due to his V-I-W status.

"Shaving's a hassle, and it's even worse with salt water and no shaving cream, and really no razors, so we don't bother on a voyage. Trim your beard with a comb and scissors and a mirror if you want, it's a lot easier. Just do it on the aft deck so you don't leave whiskers everywhere. You only get a half gallon of water a day, so you can't waste it. Any more questions? No? Then welcome aboard, shipmates."

I put out my hand and shook each of theirs again, making firm eye contact and maintaining a serious demeanor, because this was meant to be a serious talk. My expectations had been laid down, and my authority as captain had been established, with each man bearing witness to the agreement of the others.

Even if they didn't fully understand it yet, Mike Ortega, Barry Conway and Will Padgett had just signed their voyage contracts. Adam Selfridge had already agreed during our one-on-one time, and Luke Hanahan, I already knew that Luke was a fighter and that he would never let me down. He'd already shown me what he was made of. Captain Aikman had been right about one thing: Luke Hanahan *was* a tough guy. Tala and Sofia would take care of breaking in Jessie Hanahan.

Rebel Yell's crew was all set. Argentina, here we come.

After exiting the cargo hold I pinned the watch schedule to the bulletin board. Sofia was in the galley, Tala was folding up the extra clothes. What I wanted next was some sleep, but first I went up to the cockpit. Adam was behind the wheel; Luke was sitting in the cockpit behind him across from Jessie and Rita. The sky was still solid overcast.

Since Adam was steering, I asked him, "Everything still under control? What's our course and speed?" Another test. Always another test. It was in the captain's job description.

"The wind backed around to the north, and we're steering about a hundred degrees. We're making about the same speed as before, so I'm guessing four knots. Depth is just starting to drop to over three hundred feet."

"Good, that's good. East is what we want. The other guys are getting settled into the cargo hold, they're putting up their hammocks. I already set yours up, so when your watch is over you can try it out. It's port-side and forward. Where's Gino?"

Jessie said, "He's up forward. He's sleeping, I think."

"So everything is under control?"

Luke replied, "Everything is under control, skipper."

"Okay, I'm going to get some shut-eye. If it looks like the sun is going to come out, wake me a quarter of an hour before twelve so I can try for a noon sight. If it's hazy but you can make out the disc of the sun, even part of the time, that's good enough, that's all I need. If not, let me sleep. Gino and Rita will take over at twelve. When you finish your watch, fill out the D.R. log for both hours. D.R. means dead reckoning. Our course, speed, wind speed and direction, the air temperature and the barometric pressure. There's a block for each one of them. Anything else I should know?"

Luke said, "I think we're good. Adam and I have it."

"Good." I went below and aft down the passageway. The door to the twins' cabin was slid aft partly open and they were both inside, their life vests off. Chris was asleep; Jonathan was leaning back against the starboard hull side, the low side, busy with a plastic dinosaur in each hand.

Tala had set up the canvas lee-cloth on the downhill side of our double berth to prevent me from rolling off and onto the cabin floor (or sole) a yard below. This reminded me that I needed to unbolt and remove my navigation desk swivel chair, so the boys could move back in with us, but that could wait. I went to the foot of the bed, which was a yard from the engine room. I kicked off my deck shoes and crawled into my rack. My face hit my pillow and I was gone.

After about two hours in and out of sleep I was up again. I unscrewed and lifted out the cabin floor panel beneath the nav station swivel chair, unbolted it from the steel hull frame, and carried it up the cargo hold. With the floor panel reinstalled and the space freed up, Sofia laced a square of old sail cloth from the side of our double bed, across the floor, and up the side of the nav desk, forming a U which would accommodate the twins on either tack. A folded blanket wrapped in a sheet at the bottom of the broad U became their mattress.

It looked fine to me, and I could still walk across it to look out through the starboard transom porthole, or to open or close it. Had it really been less than a day since Gino had shot Captain

Aikman and the Whaler's machine gunner through it? A black hole in a forehead, and boots disappearing into a dark river. Was that possible? Was that in another life?

Yes, and it was more than possible. It had happened.

You can't fix dead, and you can never go home again. So you sail on and on, and you welcome the knowing smiles of your ghostly shipmates, the crew who truly understand you.

For the duration of the voyage the captain's cabin—my cabin—would be divided down the middle by the canvas lee cloth. Tala and I would sleep on the double bed to port, but now the twins would be in with us. With the boat heeled to starboard the canvas was needed anyway, so it was no big deal to get used to entering and leaving the bed over the foot again. On other voyages I'd done it for weeks at a time.

This arrangement did have the advantage that the twins were safely out of the way when they were back there. There were many times when I had to charge through the boat like a raging bull to get to the scene of the latest crisis. "Coming through!" or "Make a hole!" meant get out of the way, or risk being trampled underfoot or body-checked into a bulkhead.

The one-hour dog-watches beginning at 1600 and 1700 were our suppertimes. The later watches ate first, the earlier watches ate last, with 1700 being the dividing time. The dishes would be washed by the number-twos for each meal sitting. Steering was much more physically demanding than serving as the number-two on watch, so I considered this to be fair. Since I was the captain and my word was law, this became our new voyage protocol. Tala and Sofia would direct the galley slaves, so this was another task off my plate.

Eating didn't take an hour, so there was plenty of time to clean and dry the dishes for the next sitting. There was a 12-volt seawater pump faucet for the galley sink. Fresh water could not be wasted on dishes. Gino said the salt added flavor.

It began to rain after the second dog-watch, when Gino and Rita were on watch. He was behind the wheel, she was in the pilothouse. With the mainsail up, we could not put a tarp over the boom to keep the cockpit dry. Under most circumstances the helmsman had to endure the elements in the best foul-weather gear available. It had not always been this way.

Rebel Yell had no name when my Uncle Jeff found her high and dry in a state of derelict abandonment in the back lot of a South Florida boatyard. As near as we could figure she'd been built in the Netherlands in the 1970s on a limited budget. To simplify her original construction, Rebel had wire steering cables running from the wheel to the rudder quadrant beneath the floor of the aft cabin. While this was simple and efficient, with excellent feedback and feel, there was no secondary helm inside the pilothouse.

This hadn't mattered during all the years that Rebel had a working autopilot. If the weather outside was wet or stormy, we let the autopilot handle the steering while we stood watch from inside the dry pilothouse. This had worked like magic.

This happy era ended when the autopilot died rounding Cape Hatteras. Now somebody had to have his two hands on the wheel every minute that the boat was moving underway. A woman or a youth could handle this job in mild conditions, but not during all the worst rigors of an ocean voyage. Then you needed a bear of a man behind the wheel, the driving rain and lashing spray notwithstanding. And you needed another bear of a man down below to take the helm after his watch ended.

16

At 2200 Will and Barry were already in the cockpit when I took over from Mike. The scrapes on the side of Barry's face were less conspicuous at night. We were still guessing our position by dead reckoning, but we had plenty of Atlantic out in front. The rain was just a drizzle, a nuisance to be ignored. We were still on port tack, heeled over to starboard, the wind coming from the north. We were sailing east by the compass. I only knew the half-moon was out there by the murky gloom behind the overcast behind us to the west.

Barry was behind me in the cockpit while I steered. Will sat in front, his back against the latched-open pilothouse door. His face was shielded from the drizzle by his parka's hood. Its sleeves were rolled down, enveloping his crossed arms within them. His Gore-Tex military parka was zipped up in front, and he had drawn his knees up inside. I recognized the neoprene reef runners peeking out from the bottom: Gino had bought them for Rita. I knew they were red even though they looked brown in the dim light. My permanent crew was looking after the new guys without my even asking. A good sign.

Will said, "Captain, we're not showing any running lights. Is that to save electricity?"

"Partly. But if anybody's out there, I don't want them to see us at all. I'd rather take our chances on a collision than be seen by another boat. We're only about a hundred miles from land, and any powerboat can catch us if they see us. We could cross the whole ocean and not see another boat or ship, but you never know what's just over the horizon."

From behind me, Barry said, "And that's why you have this machine gun, I'm thinking." As he spoke he moved past me to sit just ahead of the wheel, his feet braced across the cockpit foot well on the opposite side. Now I could see them both while looking down at the compass and over the top of the pilothouse.

Barry was wearing a yellow raincoat with a hood, and matching rain pants. Just a cheap vinyl suit with plastic buttons and snaps, not even zippers. It had already been repaired in several places with duct tape, back when there was duct tape. On his feet he wore an old pair of rafting sandals over thick wool socks. Wet or dry, wool was warm.

"That's right, Barry, that's why we have the machine gun, and that's why we always keep a sharp lookout all the way around. Now, even when we're keeping a lookout we could still run into floating debris, something low in the water, but I'm not too worried about that. Rebel's hull is quarter-inch steel, and that's almost as thick as your shackle was."

Barry made no reply, but after a few minutes of silence he asked me, "How long have you had this boat?"

"You said you're twenty-six?"

"That's right."

"Then since I was about your age. That's if you count the time I was working on her before she went back in the water."

"Really? How did you manage that? This is a sixty-footer, right? Was your family rich?"

"Rich? No, nothing like that. My Uncle Jeff found her in Florida. She was abandoned in a boatyard, propped up on dry land. He thought he could buy her cheap and fix her up and go sailing, but it was a lot more work than he figured. After a year he was ready to quit, and that's when I came in. I did an enlistment in the Marine Corps, and then I was in college but it didn't work out, so I moved to Florida to help him. It was a *huge* project. We even put in a new engine, the Caterpillar we still have now. I spent two years helping my uncle . . . and then he died a month before Rebel Yell was relaunched."

Barry said, "Well, that sure sucks. What happened?"

"He fell off a scaffold and landed on his head. Broke his neck. He left the boat to me, and I've had her ever since."

"That's too bad for your Uncle Jeff," said Will.

"Yeah, it's too bad," I replied. "All that work and he never even got to see his boat in the water."

"But," said Will, "at least you finished his dream and went sailing in his place. I'm sure he'd like that."

"Yeah, I like to think so, anyway. Wherever he is now."

"You mean like heaven, like the afterlife?"

"Yeah, Will, like up in heaven, looking down. Of course, on a night like tonight all he'd see are clouds." I wanted to lighten the mood and change the subject. I'd seen religious differences split crews apart, and I wanted none of that. The others could debate religion and philosophy to their hearts' content, and if they argued, that was their problem. But as the captain I just couldn't do it. My saying the Lord's Prayer at the beginning of the voyage, and taking turns giving a blessing before our meals, that was as far as I'd go down that path. The captain had to stay above religious frays to retain his authority, which depended on a shared perception of strict impartiality.

But the genie was out of the bottle.

Barry said, "Personally, I don't believe in any of that after-life stuff, but if you do, that's fine with me. I mean, I really do think Christian values are good as far as they go, at least when everybody believes in them. But I've seen way too much evil to believe it for myself. Any God who would allow what I've seen is a goddamn bastard—you can just take my word for it."

I wanted to steer the discussion away from religion. "Will, you weren't born on the island, were you?" I didn't want to embarrass him, but from what I'd heard, runts like Will could not pass the selection process for admittance onto the island as V-I-Ws, voluntary indentured workers, so I was curious.

"No, sir, I was raised in a little town called Sheltonville. It's a few miles north of Beaufort Island."

"You had family there?"

"That's right. I had a family there, a really good family. A really good Christian family. Yes sir, I did."

"So, what happened?"

Will sighed, leaning back and looking upward, his eyes closed. His big parka enclosed him almost like a tent. Now its extra-big size on him made perfect sense. "My dad had a shop, a garage. He worked on cars and he repaired engines. He rebuilt pumps and fixed generators, outboard motors, that kind of thing. It was a one man operation, but sometimes he hired another man or a couple of men to help him on a job. He also, what do you call it? He subcontracted out for other companies. And then the money was no good, or you just couldn't get it, and then everything pretty much stopped. I was real young, so maybe I don't know the right words for what happened. Food, gasoline . . . they just ran out. And finally, the power went out.

"They were the most hungry years. My mother and my little sister, Martha, they died of the fever—that was, four, no, five years ago? I can't remember exactly. . . The fever didn't touch me or my older sister at all. My pop got real sick but he lived. When he was okay again he went out on jobs, but he only rode a bike because there was no gasoline. I don't know where he went, I didn't go with him, but he'd take some tools, what he could carry on his bike pulling a little wagon trailer. When he was out we had to stay in the house most of the time.

"I'm not sure what he was doing for work, but he'd bring some food back to us, to me and Sarah. And we had neighbors with a water well behind their house, a hand pump water well, so that was good. The Soddermilks, that was their name. They were old, and they both died. They just stayed in bed and they died, that's what my pop said. He buried them but we still got water from their well. We had to be real quiet pumping water because that well squeaked, and we had to keep it hid from strangers. Then my pop didn't come back from one of those jobs. He just didn't come back. Then my sister Sarah went out looking for him, and she didn't come back neither. That was about three years ago, and since then I've been alone, mostly."

Will sighed deeply several times, his voice faltering.

"Most of the people in Sheltonville, they were dead by then, dead I reckon, or they'd just up and gone, and I was too afraid to go around and see who was living in whose houses to ask them for food. People died and new people just moved into houses. Strangers. There were rumors about, you know, about people who—people who were eating people. I mean, those days, people were just crazy. I heard gunshots all the time. 'Pop-pop-pop-pop.' And screams. I hid in a secret place in our house until there was nothing more to eat. Not even a bread crumb or a grain of rice. Not a squirrel or a mouse or a cat to catch. Not even a root to gnaw on.

"Sheltonville was on the old railroad line that runs down to Beaufort, and I thought maybe it would be better down there because of all the Marines and such. I walked it in one night, down the old railroad right-of-way. The track is mostly gone but you could still follow it because it was built up high where it went over the swamps. I went on a clear night, so I kept the North Star behind me. At the end was the Coosaw River, but it's real narrow there, and I swam it."

Barry said, "So I swam to get off the island, and you swam to get onto it."

"Yeah. And now we're both on the same boat and we're both leaving Beaufort Island. Now how about that? Huh?"

"What about the militia?" I asked Will. "Did the militia catch you?"

"No sir, I never even heard of the militia until later. After I got onto the island I kept walking down that old railroad line. When it got to be daytime I come to some little farms, like big gardens really, and I went up to a house where I saw laundry on a line. I went up to the back door and I just knocked and a nice lady finally opened the door, and well, she fed me at least. Fed me bread and something like I think was gravy.

"She fed me and she gave me water, but she couldn't keep me. She was all crying, and I know she was a good woman. I seen she had a picture of Jesus up in her kitchen, and a cross. She said she didn't have any work, but she sent me to where I lived since then. I work, I mean, I *worked* in orchards and such like that, but I'm pretty handy, too, and I think that helped me some. No, it helped me a lot. Maybe I got that from my father, from always being in his garage when I was little. I'd fetch him a tool so he didn't have to roll out from under a truck. He said that helped him a lot, and it made me real happy too. I learned the name of every tool and what it's used for. If you can figure out how something works, most times you can fix it, one way or the other. That's what my pop always said.

"So I made that push wagon, and they let me go into town on market days to earn my own money, and well, now I guess you know my whole story, my whole life story, such as it is. But Captain Kilmer, I do believe your Uncle Jeff is up there, somewhere. Somewhere up there in heaven. And so is my pop, and so is my mom, and my little sister Martha and my big sister Sarah. And the old Soddermilks with the water well, the water that kept us living even after they had passed on. Good people like that who never harmed nobody, they got to be up there in heaven, right? If they're not up there, then just what are we all? Just animals that walk on our two back legs?"

After a few more sighs, Will continued. "Barry, I've seen a lot of bad things too, real bad things, but those people where I worked in the orchard, they could have turned me over to the militia and got me thrown off the island anytime—but they didn't. They fed me, and they gave me a place to live, even if it was just sort of a shed, and they taught me about orcharding fruit trees. And now here I am on this great boat, sailing off to Argentina, so maybe somebody *has* been looking out for me. Somebody or something. God, or Jesus, I heard a lot of names for him, and maybe I don't know which name is right, but I believe in him just all the same.

"And maybe someday I'll see my family again. Up there in heaven, I mean. But I hope so, and I do believe so. I mean, just look at everything that happened to my family, and to me, and now look at where I am on this great boat. Even after everything bad that happened to my family I'm still alive, and I still remember them every day all the time, and I still love them. And now I'm the last one, the last of the Sheltonville Padgetts. So just being on your boat, Captain Kilmer, instead of back there in a shed—and I was grateful for it—well, this is pretty great if you ask me. It's a plain old miracle is how I see it."

I was steering by the glowing compass and the feel of the wind on my face, and I had to blink away some tears. Wagon Will was a green-eyed ginger-haired famine runt, but he was a born survivor with a beautiful soul. Where most people would have surrendered to despair, he had just kept pushing forward, if only to keep the memory of his family alive in the hope of an eventual reunion with them in eternity.

After a few quiet, deep breaths to steady my own voice, I said, "Will Padgett, I'm glad we met yesterday. And I'm glad to have you aboard, shipmate." There was no denying that the ways our paths had crossed had been more than coincidental, but I kept those thoughts to myself. How could I explain my chance meeting with Wagon Will without comparing it to how I had met Barry the Thief only a few minutes earlier and a few hundred yards away? Who could ever believe it? Who?

I spent the rest of the hour teaching Barry and Will what I'd learned from years of ocean sailing. Tricks of the trade, subtle tips I'd never read in a book. Ocean voyaging had been much easier with GPS chartplotters and a working autopilot, but my instinctive feel for sailing was actually better without them. I could close my eyes and steer Rebel Yell just by the feel of the wind on my face, the sound of the sails, the lift and turn of the waves, the changing angle of heel, the rudder pressure giving feedback to the wheel, and subtle indications of slowing or accelerating. My new crew would learn this holistic style of sailing without the technological shortcuts of the bygone era.

Barry explained to Will that our sails were like airplane wings aimed at the sky, so he must have picked up this useful analogy from Mike or even Adam, who might have heard it from his Uncle Hilton. He said that the curved front edge of a sail was like the curved top of an airplane wing, and that was what created lift when air flowed over it. Steer too close to the wind and the sailboat's fabric wings would flap and stall, steer too far off the wind and the fabric wings would be square to the wind and lose their power, stalling the other way. The goal was always maintaining laminar flow, with the wind gliding smoothly along the sails to generate the maximum pull in the forward direction. You steered the boat where you wanted to go, and then you trimmed the sails to achieve the laminar flow that would create the most lift and then power you forward.

(An exception being that you could not sail directly toward the wind. In that case you had two choices: run the engine, or make a series of tacks, sailing at angles back and forth across the wind to eventually arrive at your destination.)

I knew the waxing half-moon had set when the last hint of gray in the west turned black like the rest of the sky and sea. The only visible light in the cockpit came from the glass dome on top of the compass, and the lit depth sounder on the back of the pilothouse. Sergeant Major Tolbert's dive watch was tied with parachute cord between spokes across the wheel's hub. When the rudder was amidships, the watch's face was straight up. The wheel's movement kept the self-winder ticking.

Steering by the compass meant making constant wheel movements of a quarter or a half turn to compensate for the swells pushing Rebel around on their own rhythm. Our path through the water was really an average, the boat continuously moving five or ten degrees to each side of our ideal course. The lit compass was the brightest thing in our world, so it was easy for the helmsman to become hypnotized by it and lose all-around perception. On a clear night I could also steer by getting the boat on course and then aiming for a star, but on an overcast night there were no stars. I didn't even bother to have Will or Barry bring out our new PVS-14. The light-amplifying NOD would have been disappointing on such a black night, with nothing to see beyond the cockpit.

My eyes were so well adjusted to the darkness that I could easily see the luminescent hands of the watch down on the wheel hub as well as the ones on my own wristwatch. Their times already varied by more than a minute, even though I had set them both from our new chronometer only that morning.

Barry was still conversational, which helped me stay alert, but Will was beginning to nod off. When the minute hands of both watches had made a circle around to the top I said, “Will, it’s twenty-three-hundred. If you want to knock off, you can lay below and hit the rack.”

He made no protest. He just nodded, withdrew his arms from within his crossed sleeves, rose within his parka-tent and disappeared down inside without another word. I was glad he left the cockpit because I wanted to spend some time alone with our Beaufort Island stowaway, Barry Conway.

After a few minutes of silence Barry said, “He’s a starveling for sure, but you have to admire his spirit.”

“A starveling? What’s that mean?”

“Kids like Will, kids that grew up through the worst of the famine. You didn’t see many starvelings where I was. Before the island I mean. They didn’t make it. How old is he?”

“He said he’s sixteen.”

“Yep, a starveling. He’s only as big as if he was eleven or twelve. Some people think starvelings are good luck, that they bring good luck, but I just think they *had* good luck.”

“Good luck? You think Will had *good luck*?”

“Sure, he’s on this boat, isn’t he? That’s lucky. Same as me—lucky. Lucky now, I mean. But I wouldn’t say they *bring* good luck. No, that’s a whole different kettle of fish.”

“You actually think Will has been *lucky*?”

“Don’t take me wrong, Captain Kilmer, I get what you mean. It’s too bad he was starving when he should have been growing, and he wound up a runt like he is. But he had to have been in a really lucky place to survive, that’s all I meant. With people to take care of him right through it all. Where I was, you didn't see any starvelings. They're so rare, maybe that's where the whole lucky thing came from."

"You said you came from Charleston?"

Barry laughed. "Charleston? Me? Charleston? No, sir, I'm from *North* Charleston, and that's a *whole* different town. I was living in a trailer park between I-26 and Rivers Avenue. And let me tell you, you don't get any more poor white trash than poor white *trailer* trash. Especially a mile outside an Air Force base in South Carolina. Nothing but tattoo parlors, strip clubs, fast-food joints and used car lots as far as the eye could see. That's where I was when all the shit went down, and we didn't see any starvelings in that zip code. You either survived until you got out, or you wound up on somebody's menu. Little kids didn't make it. Kids, babies, women with nobody to look after them, old people—they didn't make it."

Barry stared into the lit upper hemisphere of the compass. Sitting across from it he was too low to read the numbers, but it was still the mystical glowing ball that defined the center of our universe. On an overcast moonless night it was not only our sole source of direction, it was our direct connection to the planet beneath us. The floating compass card was always level with the surface of the ocean, which we could not see at all.

I was thinking about Mike Ortega, who had grown up on Kiawah Island among the wealthy elite, the top one percent at least. No way was I going to mention his background to Barry.

"You said people wound up on somebody's menu. Are you talking about . . . uh . . . cannibalism?"

Barry didn't take his eyes off the side of the compass. You could sometimes see weird and distorted inverted reflections of the compass card within the liquid-filled glass hemisphere from different angles. It could be mesmerizing, like staring into a fireplace. Finally, he said, "The what? Did you say the C-word, captain? What else would I be talking about? Where the hell have you been for the last five years?"

Conversations were unhurried on night watch, with long pauses between questions and answers. We were trying to pass through a hundred and twenty minutes of time as well as the next ten or twelve unmarked miles of ocean, so there was no point in rushing to offer a reply. There was all the time in the world to ponder a question and formulate an answer. The outer limits of the galaxy might have been one mile or a million light years away. Deep space could not have been any darker than it was for an ocean voyager on a moonless overcast night.

I finally answered him. "Where have I been? Well, I was on the other side of the Atlantic. We sailed back a few years ago, and we spent the last two years on Beaufort Island."

"Then you were damn lucky to miss those years on the mainland. Damn lucky. So, why the hell did you come back?"

"Well, Barry, I couldn't come back while the government was still up and running. The old federal government, I mean. The one that used to run everything from Washington D.C."

"Why couldn't you come back? Were you a fugitive? An outlaw? What did you do?"

"I didn't 'do' anything, but they would have taken my boat for back taxes. That's why I couldn't come back. I owed taxes even for all the years I never put a foot on American soil. But once America fell apart and broke up into states again, I hoped things would be better for us. And we did all right the last two years, you know, doing the trading schooner thing along the Carolinas and down to Georgia and Florida."

"Well, I can certainly understand how that would work out well for you, with this boat. Captain Kilmer, Beaufort was the luckiest place I've been to since everything went to shit, or at least it was if you're not a slave. And let me tell you, captain, Beaufort looked *very* nice to me on market day, and that's the truth. All those pretty girls just walking around, laughing and happy, free as a breeze, not a care in the world. Does it get any better than that? Does it? I mean, if you don't have a shackle on your leg to remind you who you are. No, I can't see how it gets any better than market day in Beaufort. Will was talking about heaven above. Captain Kilmer, if you ask me, Beaufort *was* heaven—at least for a free man."

After some time staring down at the compass I said, "Oh, it's true. We were very happy there."

Barry didn't hurry to reply. "I'm sure you were, captain. A sixty-foot schooner, a beautiful wife, healthy kids. . . But me? Me? Then somebody stuck out his foot—and here we are."

Whew. "Yeah, Barry, here we are. What are the odds?"

"Oh, and thanks again for getting that goddamn shackle off." He leaned forward and stroked his ankle with both hands. "For most of the last four months I thought I'd be buried on the farm with that goddamn leg iron right here. So thanks."

"No problem. You were starting to talk about the C-word."

"The C-word. Oh, yeah, the C-word. . . So, how long is it going to take us to get to Argentina?"

"Six weeks, two months . . . maybe even longer. Or maybe we'll end up somewhere else. Only God knows the answer."

"Yeah, only God knows. But does God give a goddamn?"

"Well, I hope he does. So what about *the C-word*, Barry?"

He was staring into the side of the compass. "Can we talk about that some other time? I don't want to ruin tonight, and that would ruin it for sure. But do you know what I want to do tonight, instead of talking about the C-word?"

"No, Barry, what?"

"Captain Kilmer, I want to steer this boat. If Adam can do it, I know I can do it too. I was right about the wings sticking up vertically, wasn't I? Lift and pull and laminar flow?"

"Yeah, you were right. Did Adam tell you about that?"

"Yes, he did, and it all makes sense. So please, captain, let me steer for a minute. Nobody else is up here, and if I start to screw it up you can just grab the wheel. Captain Kilmer, you just have no idea how much I want to steer this boat. No idea."

But actually, I did have an idea. Being a passenger on an oceangoing sailboat can be very enjoyable. But taking the wheel and turning the rudder with your own two hands, controlling sixty feet of schooner and the four sails spread across two masts, well, to me that was an incomparable experience. The moment you took the helm the vessel came alive in your hands. You became an integral part of it, just as much as the masts, the sails and the rudder. You became the schooner's living, breathing human guide. This was a feeling I had almost lost during all the autopilot and GPS chartplotter years.

So I said, "Be my guest, Barry. You get behind the wheel and I'll sit behind you. Just remember one thing—and this throws a lot of people off—especially on a dark night with no stars and no horizon—but the wheel turns the boat, *not* the compass. The compass never turns. North is always north. It's easy to get it backwards in your mind, and then every turn you make to correct it just makes it worse. North is always north."

I kept a hand on the wheel as he rose and stood behind it, grasping its leather cover at the ten-and-two position. When he said he had it, I let it go. I slid a little behind him on the high-side cockpit bench, where I could keep an eye on the always-level compass card.

Barry made some slow half-turns of the wheel to get a feel for the rudder feedback and the lag time in turning the forty-ton schooner. He steered gradually to port, edging toward the wind until the sails began to luff, and then he eased back off to starboard. Adam had to have taught him to do this. He glanced down at the compass and then over the pilothouse, his face set with determination. A half smile pursed his lips and turned up the corners of his mouth.

And just like that, I had another helmsman. Barry Conway would still need to learn all the rest of sailing, but the airplane wing analogy proved to me that he understood the principles. He might have been a stowaway, a runaway, and maybe even a thief—but stupid he was not. And more than willing, he was.

And that was enough.

17

The second day out I had the watch with Will and Barry again from 0600 to 0800. It was still overcast and cool but at least it was dry so our foul-weather gear was unneeded. Barry was wearing a set of the old British Army desert camo utilities that had been left aboard Rebel after Morocco. After receiving his new outfit he'd flung his woodland pattern trousers into our wake. Barry's new outfit was roughly the same tan and brown colors as Mike Ortega's USMC-surplus desert digital uniform, but the two were easily distinguishable, coming from different countries and even different centuries.

Will was going to be harder to outfit. This was the first time I'd seen him without his oversized military parka. He was wearing his tatty rolled up jeans and a too-big gray sweatshirt with cutoff sleeves. He was sixteen, but not much bigger than Rita, and we had almost nothing for a boy his size. This meant that Tala, Sofia and Rita needed to get involved on his behalf. With scissors, needles and thread they'd be able to modify the clothes from our grab-bags to fit him, and not shame him.

The sun rose, and then it "set" five minutes later. That is, it rose above a clear part of the horizon and sent its full power across the ocean at us only briefly before it disappeared again into thick overcast.

Our breakfast was bowls of hot cereal eaten in the cockpit. Barry steered while I ate. Barry and Will had their own water bottles, marked with different colors of yarn wrapped around them. They were both adapting well to the ocean, but this was not surprising. The era of needy crybabies was far in the past.

There was plenty to teach them about ocean sailing, and they were eager to learn. After eating I took turns at the wheel with Barry. Both of us encouraged Will to give it a try, but he declined. Will was in the cockpit for both hours, so I had no opportunity to reopen last night's discussion with Barry.

Luke and Adam were next on watch, with Luke steering. Barry went below, but Will stayed in the cockpit, and so did I. After its brief appearance at dawn the sun was gone, but at least it wasn't raining. Since Adam and Will were both in the cockpit, and they were the two youngest of our new crew, I asked them, "Do you guys know what a collateral duty is?

Their expressions were blank, as I'd expected.

"Well, boys, a collateral duty is an extra job that you don't get paid extra for. But since you're not getting paid anyway, what's the difference, right? A collateral duty is another job that we give you on top of standing watch. Like cleaning the galley and washing the dishes. Are you following me so far?"

Both of them nodded affirmatively.

I asked them, "So, how did you like dinner last night?"

"It was pretty good," said Adam. "I like beans, and there was even butter for the bread."

I said, "We have some canned chicken in jars, but we have to save it for special occasions or we'll run out too soon. But if we're lucky, maybe we'll have something better than chicken. Today you're going to learn how to fish the Rebel Yell way. And after I show you how, you two are going to be in charge of fishing. Fishing is going to be your collateral duty."

After that, I had their *full* attention.

"What are we fishing for?" Adam asked.

"Anything that's good to eat. Mahi-mahi, some kinds of tuna, kingfish, snapper—it all depends on what's down there."

I dug into a locker under a cockpit seat and pulled out a pair of my fishing rigs. Years ago they were plastic peanut jars about ten inches long. Nylon cord was wrapped around them. Mike Ortega was off watch, but he had come back up to the cockpit and he was also watching my tutorial.

"We're not sport fishing, we're meat fishing. We don't use rods and reels when we're sailing, we just drag a line. Back in the old days sport fisherman tried to catch a big fish on a light line, but we don't care about that. We just want to hook 'em up and drag 'em aboard. Sport has nothing to do with it."

I handed Adam and Will each a cord-wrapped plastic jar.

"There's a hundred yards of nylon wrapped around them. The lure is inside so the hooks don't catch on everything. I'll set one up the first time so you can see how we do it."

I took the rig from Will and went to the port-quarter, the corner of the transom that was on the higher side on port tack.

"First, you take out the lure; it's got a stainless-steel hook inside a rubber skirt. The rubber fringe wiggles like a squid and it makes the fish want to zoom up and eat it. These hooks will take a fish up to twenty or thirty pounds, and that's what we're after. You just take out the lure and unwind the leader and throw it back in our wake, see? Then hold the jar like this and the line will run out on its own. Nothing to it. Just don't let go of the jar and lose it overboard, all right?"

I handed the jar with its diminishing windings of line to Will, and he let it run out over the stern pulpit rail.

"The end of the line is tied to the jar, but if you let it go, if you drop it, it's gone. When you have a few yards left, you tie off the line to this little cleat on the corner of the pulpit. That's good, Will, cleat it off. This means make some figure eights."

He did so. The empty peanut jar hung from the rail.

I asked them both, "How fast do you think we're going?"

Will guessed ten miles an hour, and Adam said six knots.

"Adam is closer. We're making about five knots, which is around six miles an hour. Knots refers to nautical miles, which are longer than land miles. It's going to be important to know how to estimate our speed because we have to keep a dead-reckoning log in between getting real positions with the sextant. That's assuming the sun ever comes out."

Adam said, "There's a speedometer right next to the depth sounder, how come it doesn't work?"

"It hasn't worked in a few years. It runs off a tiny paddle-wheel sticking outside the hull about a half an inch, and it got broken and it's not something we can fix. This means we have to estimate our speed and write it down hour by hour. That's going to be one of your jobs when you're on watch."

Will said, “I can see the lure back there, it’s skipping along the surface. Shouldn’t it be underwater? Can a fish catch it if it’s up on top like that?”

“That’s just how they like it. They think it’s a little squid or a flying fish jumping between the waves. Once they get the hook in their mouth they take off running, but they can’t break the line because it’s too strong and it’s too stretchy.”

“So how do you reel them in?” asked Adam.

“We don’t reel them in. We just pull them in hand-over-hand. If they’re small, like under ten pounds, we usually just pull them right up onto the aft deck. If they’re big, we try to land them on the swim platform first. Now, Adam, it’s your turn. You set yours up on the starboard side just like I did.”

“How often do you catch a fish?” asked Will.

“Sometimes not for days and days. Sometimes it’s like a fish desert down there and you don’t get a bite for weeks at a time, but sometimes you get a bite the minute you put out a lure. You just never know. We’d usually catch a mahi-mahi or some snapper on the Charleston run, but sometimes it’s a trash fish like bonito, what they call the false tuna. Then you just want to get your hook out and throw it back, unless you’re going to cut it up for bait. And sometimes a shark eats the fish before you can get it up on the boat. It’s different every time. We’re in the Gulf Stream now, so we should do okay.”

Mike was also watching intently, and I could tell he had a lot to say, but he was keeping his counsel and allowing the skipper to give this class without throwing in his two cents. Luke was steering, but glancing behind to watch us.

Adam was letting his line out, so the second rubber squid was also trailing in our wake but from the starboard quarter.

Will, looking aft, said, “Is that normal, sir?”

I looked far astern. The port-side line was stretched taut by the pull of the moving ocean so that it didn’t even touch water until it was about a hundred feet behind us. You could follow the next two hundred feet of line when sections of it popped clear of the sea between waves.

Then Will said, “There’s something on it, underwater.”

The rubber squid was a hundred yards back. The lure was connected to ten feet of hundred-pound monofilament leader, then to a swivel where it joined the nylon cord. My vision was still very good, but I couldn’t see what Will was reporting.

Our attention was astern. From behind my back I heard the jibs begin to luff at the other end of the schooner, and I said, “Luke, your job is steering, so just steer. Mike, do you see it?”

He stood by the Dushka, one leg bent and one straight on the slanted deck. “I think I see the lure, but that’s it.”

Then the water exploded a hundred yards back, a shadow flashed through the air and landed with a cascade of spray and I hollered, “Fish On!”

Will looked up at me. “What should I do now?”

“For now, just watch the show. Watch, and learn.”

Gino came blasting through the pilothouse and up into the cockpit after hearing the call of Fish On. He looked far aft and said, “Big fella, looks like. You want some gloves, boss?”

“Not me—this is Will’s fish all the way.”

Gino tossed him a little bundle of gray leather; it was a pair of fingerless sailor’s gloves.

He put them on and asked, “Now what do I do?”

I said, “Now you pull it in, hand-over-hand. That little gadget on the stern pulpit with the black plastic teeth is called a cam-cleat. Springs inside it keep it clamped on a line. Drop your line in it between the teeth. Perfect. Now, when you pull it in, the line can’t slide back out. Remember—this is why it’s called meat fishing. We’re not in it for the sport.”

Will began to haul in on the line, his legs wide apart on the slanted aft deck. He pulled it in faster when the line was slack, slower when it was tight, and not at all when the fish tried to run away from us against the unbreakable nylon line. The line piled up in loops and curls between his feet. The fish was still struggling, but in a losing battle as its energy waned fighting the stretchy nylon. By then Gino was standing ready by one side of the Dushka, and Mike was standing on the other side. Each of them held a wooden pole like a harpoon. Both poles were aimed down toward the boarding platform.

When the fish was a few yards behind the boat, weaving side to side in weakening efforts, I grabbed the line behind the pulpit and heaved the fish onto the teak slats. It lay still for a moment and Gino speared it through the gills before it could try to rejoin the ocean. Then Mike hooked him through his jaw with the gaff hook and pulled him upward, lifting the pole and fish hand-over-hand over the stern pulpit onto the aft deck.

"Is it a barracuda?" Will asked.

Adam replied, "No, it's not a barracuda, it's a wahoo. I've seen wahoos, and I've eaten wahoo, but I never caught one."

"It's one of the best fish you'll ever eat," said Mike.

It was a beautiful fish. Not huge but about a five-footer, so it would go around thirty pounds. More than half of that would be tier-one fish steak on any menu anywhere back in the old days. Gino handed me our fish billy, an ashwood club with a weighted metal end, and I finished the job. By then we had an audience in the pilothouse, the cockpit, and on the side decks.

"What do I do now?" asked Will. The nylon cord had been pulled in haphazardly and lay in piles of loops on the aft deck.

I said, "Just wrap the line around the jar and we'll do the rest. And Adam, you bring your line back in too. This wahoo is all the fish we'll want today."

Mike offered, "I'll fillet it, unless somebody else wants to. I'm pretty good at it; I've had a lot of practice. This is one fine wahoo. I've seen bigger, but not many, and this one is primo."

Gino brought out our filleting board and knives and Mike dissected the fish. Its blood streamed down the slanting aft deck, then ran back along the starboard toe rail and off the transom. Gino took one of the first fillets below, and in a few minutes he returned with a wooden serving tray piled with red cubes of meat. There was a bowl in the middle of the tray that was filled with dipping sauce. These were just the appetizers while our two sea-cooks got busy in the galley.

Will asked, “Is it safe to eat raw fish like that, uncooked?”

I answered him. “From the deep ocean it’s all safe to eat, except sometimes maybe barracuda.”

When the tray of wahoo sashimi was gone it was replaced by another, while more trays of fillets were being taken below. Twenty minutes later plates were coming up with grilled and blackened wahoo, home-fried potatoes and cole slaw.

By one in the afternoon we were all drowsy with fullness, unable to eat another bite. Kings and billionaires had never eaten any better. Rebel’s navigator—me—missed his chance at a noon sight because of the fish feast. Instead, the day took on a festive atmosphere, and how could it not? During the feast the helmsmen took turns steering. Since it was dry out, with Rebel sailing steady on course, Luke and Jessie brought out their instruments. I had forgotten about them.

Everyone made room as they settled down onto the low side of the cockpit aft of the wheel. They tuned their guitars by ear from string to string. When they were ready to play, Jessie and Luke whispered to each other, and Jessie said, “This is an old song, but we think it’s pretty cool.” They strummed the opening chords and then sang together.

Long as I remember, the rain been coming down,
Clouds of mystery pouring, confusion on the ground,
Good men through the ages, trying to find the sun,
And I wonder, still I wonder, who’ll stop the rain?

They ran through some of their pavilion play list, the rest of the crew finding comfortable places to watch and to listen. Rita asked Jessie if maybe she’d teach her to play the guitar, and Jessie told her she’d try to find the time to work it into her busy schedule, and we all had a good laugh at that. Will asked her if she could teach him, too, and Jessie said of course she would, and gave him a hug as he leaned over her guitar.

All the terrifying storms with towering waves that lasted for days and nights and more days, all of the infected cuts from scraping barnacles off the propeller and the rudder by feel in freezing black water on breath-hold dives, and all the searing burns and scrapes from dealing with engine room emergencies in tight channels with ships bearing down on us blasting out the danger signal, well, they were all worth it for a few hours like those. No boat captain was ever better paid, not in dollars and not in gold, and I wondered yet again what I had ever done to deserve such grace. It was a complete mystery to me.

Because the navigation desk in the aft cabin was not going to be useable with the swivel chair in the cargo hold, I decided to move the single-sideband up to the pilothouse. The SSB radio couldn't transmit, but it could still receive. My next watch was going to begin at two in the afternoon, 1400, so I had the time.

On the port side of the pilothouse and forward was a chest of drawers with a flat surface on top that was usually occupied by charts, books and papers. The chart desk was chest-high, or at the level of the bottom of the pilothouse windows. A two-inch-high teak rail around its top kept things from sliding off when the boat was heeled over. I couldn't claim credit for the custom teak pilothouse furniture because it was already on the boat when we'd found her. I only needed to screw a pair of stainless-steel eye straps to its top to make a new home for my receive-only SSB radio. Cord lashed over and across the radio to the eye straps would keep it secured in its new place.

The SSB's coaxial antenna cable ran up into the ceiling from the aft cabin, then beneath the pilothouse and up inside the mainmast, so it wasn't hard to splice into it. Splicing into the antenna cable took more time than connecting it to power. This was simple because there was already a light mounted on top of the chart desk. This gooseneck lamp had taken on great importance in the years since the last flashlight batteries had died, even the rechargeables. Its red LED bulb was shielded by a cone and could be aimed down so that ones night vision would not be ruined while examining a chart in the darkness.

I had a decent set of headphones that still worked, and when the radio was powered up I plugged them in. Daytime generally meant poor radio reception, especially when there were so few stations broadcasting in the first place, but since I heard the same static as before, I figured the radio would work in its new location as well as it had in the aft cabin.

Will and Barry were getting ready for their next watch with me, and they observed what I was doing with interest, asking me questions and listening to my ideas. There was a swiveling pedestal-mounted chair in the front of the pilothouse on the port side near the chart desk, with a padded back and armrests. In port or at anchor, or on flat water when underway, you could turn the seat to obtain a 360-degree view from the pilothouse. It could be locked in place facing in any direction to prevent it from swinging around when we were heeled over.

In Rebel Yell's distant past there had been two matching swivel chairs in the pilothouse. They had been purchased as a set by my Uncle Jeff, but in time I decided the pair took up too much of the limited real estate. The starboard pilothouse chair had been reassigned to duty in the aft cabin for my navigation and radio desk, and now it was back in the cargo hold.

With the pilothouse door opened to the port side in good weather, the helmsman could communicate with his number-two when he was in the pedestal seat about eight feet forward. I told Barry and Will to cover one ear with the headphones if they were on watch, so that they could hear the helmsman calling to them if he needed something. I told them that they shouldn't spend their entire watch in the pilothouse monitoring the radio, but if they weren't on watch, they could sit in the chair and search the airwaves to their hearts' content.

Adam and Rita came up from the galley to the pilothouse during this class, and they also paid close attention. Barry was twenty-six, but the other two boys were teenagers, and Rita was even younger than them. The three had only fading childhood memories of the internet and television. The very idea of listening for live human voices from distant continents seemed to fascinate them. I gave them a quick tutorial on scanning the frequency bands, and how to use the radio's memory features to save any promising stations they found, and I advised them that reception would be better at night. I left a notebook and some handwritten cheat-sheets near the radio for them to use.

18

My next watch began at 8 pm. This time was written on the schedule as 2000, but it was said as twenty-hundred. Mike stayed in the cockpit to give Will and Barry extra lessons on sail trim, and I didn't mind a bit. I never held myself out as the ultimate authority on the subject, and new students learn better when they are exposed to a variety of teachers.

The wind had swung around to the west and dropped to about ten knots of true speed, so we were only making about three knots through the water. If we didn't have thousands of miles ahead of us without a realistic chance of refueling, I'd have run the engine. The moon was more than half full and the overcast had thinned, so our night-adjusted eyes could make out the sails. This made it a perfect night for giving sailing lessons, beginning with Mike as their instructor and ending with me.

My watch was over at 2200, but I stayed in the cockpit to see how Luke was doing as a helmsman. The greatest risk was an unplanned and uncontrolled gybe, which meant letting our stern turn through the wind, causing the two booms to swing violently across, ending with a slamming crash on the wrong side of the boat. Even in light winds this could result in serious damage to Rebel's old rigging hardware and wire, already in precarious shape. There was also a grave danger to anybody standing in the path of the booms when they swung across.

After his watch was over Mike said he'd stay on with Luke to coach him and make sure everything would be alright. Gino came up to the cockpit for a look-around, and he said that between them all they'd ensure that Luke had a safe and instructive tour of duty behind the wheel, and that the skipper should lay below and get some much-needed sleep.

Around 2230 I finally went down. The galley was cleaned up, everything put away. Adam was sitting at the dinette table with Cornell's World Cruising Routes open before him. With his young eyes the red light was sufficient for him to make out the book's tiny print. The wisdom of generations of mariners was contained within it. It was what captains needed to plan a voyage between any two points on the globe in any season. Even back when there had been an internet, I always deferred to Jimmy Cornell. Now, long after the internet, the knowledge contained in his World Cruising Routes was beyond priceless.

I passed Adam with a nod, that he returned, and I headed back to my captain's cabin. Footlights made our movement through the boat in darkness safe without ruining our night vision. The louvered sliding door to the aft passageway cabin was closed all the way, and it was dark inside. When the twins were there it was always left partly open with a nightlight on.

This meant that Rita was in the passageway cabin, and the twins had moved into mine. Tala and Sofia had accomplished this switch while I was on deck. Rita was thirteen, and I knew that she was delighted to have her own cabin, however small, as long as it was away from her parents, and private.

The aft cabin door was latched open so that I wouldn't blunder into it going in either direction. The twins were asleep in their new nest between my former navigation desk and the double bed. The lee cloth was tautly laced between the side of our bed and the ceiling, dividing the aft cabin into two parts.

There was about a yard between the foot of the bed and the engine room bulkhead. The engine room door was always closed unless it was opened for maintenance, for inspection, or for when we needed to tackle a problem while the Caterpillar diesel was running, (which actually was pretty often.)

I sat on the foot of my bed and removed my deck clothes, and then Tala pulled me back and down into our own nest. I had hoped that she was going to make it up to me for moving the twins back into our cabin, and she did, *but very quietly*.

A four-section watch, two hours on and six off, was a luxury I was still getting used to. Hand-steering a forty-ton schooner was much more physically demanding than just sitting in the cockpit or the pilothouse keeping watch as the number-two, so our helmsmen required another level of rest and recuperation.

As the skipper I rarely slept for four straight hours, and I was awake again before my 0400 watch and my turnover with Mike Ortega. I could feel that Rebel Yell was only heeled over a few degrees, and even before I went on deck I could tell by her easy motion that the wind was behind us and we were not setting any speed records.

When I climbed up into the pilothouse Jessie was in the swivel chair with the radio headphones on. When she saw me coming up the ladder she took off the headset. Her blonde hair was still done in braids. I recognized her blue zipper jacket as one of Sophia's. Rebel's new crew was settling in.

"Find anything to listen to?" I asked her.

"I heard some people speaking Spanish, but no music. It's mostly all static. Some Asian stuff, I think Chinese, but I can't tell what it is. Nothing in English that I can understand."

"Well, keep trying, you might find something good."

"Captain Kilmer, please don't think I've just been sitting here the whole time. Mike has been teaching me about sailing. He knows a whole lot about boats. And so does Adam."

"Jessie, why don't you call me skipper now?"

"That's fine . . . skipper. Thanks."

"You and Mike finish at 0400. Who's on watch with me?" Always a friendly test. Skipper's habit.

"Barry and Will are with you next."

"Right. Roger. Wake them up ten minutes ahead of time. You know where they sleep?"

"Will is in the front hammock on the right side. Starboard. Barry is in the back hammock on the same side."

"That's right. I'll tell you when it's time to fetch them.

I stepped up into the cockpit. The half-moon was gone, and stars were visible among the cloud cover. Still it was a black night, with the glowing compass the center of our world.

"Greetings, captain," Mike said. He looked relaxed behind the wheel. He was a sailor all right, no doubt about it.

"How goes the night, Mr. Ortega?"

"Wind is light from the northwest. As you can see we're on port tack, and we're making about three or four knots on course due east, zero-nine-zero."

"Jessie says you're teaching her how to sail. Luke is plenty strong enough to handle the wheel, but I don't like the idea of two non-sailors standing watch. They might make a mistake by accident and break something we can't fix. But on the other hand, I'm sure they'd like to be on the same sleep schedule. What do you think?" I had my own ideas, but I wanted to hear Mike's opinion. Not so much because it might affect my own decision, but as a test of his judgment processes.

"Hmm. . . I'd say start them together on daytime watches. Switch Adam and Jessie during the day. Put Adam with me, and Luke with Jessie, and then we'll see how it goes. I think Luke has got it down pretty good, and Jessie's coming along. During the daytime we'll be around to coach them until they really get it. And I think we should do some sail reefing drills while the conditions are this easy."

It was good to hear him suggest the drills unprompted. "I was planning on it. Man overboard drills too. That fish kind of took over today's schedule."

"Perfectly understandable. Wahoo is right up there with swordfish in my book, and it doesn't get any fresher."

I checked my watch: it was ten minutes to four. "Jessie," I called to her softly. She slid out of the pedestal chair and came to the cockpit door. I said, "It's time to get them up."

She disappeared down below.

Mike said, "Skipper, you've been on watch with Barry, and I haven't, not one-on-one, but I've got to tell you—there's something 'off' about him. I just don't trust him."

"Well, he's picking up sailing really fast. He's smart."

"Maybe he is, but I still don't trust him."

"How is he to live with in the bachelors' quarters?"

"He mutters a lot in his sleep, and sometimes it keeps me awake. He's not a happy camper, I can tell you that much."

"How do you like sleeping in a hammock?"

"The hammock is fine. It's good. No problem."

"How are Adam and Will doing in there?"

"I think they're doing okay. They talk to each other a lot when they're in their hammocks, but they're at the other end and I can't make out what they're saying. It doesn't bother me, not like Barry's muttering, and I guess his bad dreams. They all seem to get along well. And we made a big sofa out of sail bags. It's on the low side on top of the cargo against the hull so we can chill out there when we're not in the hammocks."

"That's good. Anything else?"

"We don't want to use the forward head. It's just not a good match, us four guys up there with two married couples. We'll use the bucket in the cockpit, like you said, and we'll piss over the side. And there's no reading lights in the hold. The nightlights are okay, but there's no reading lights. There's a light over the door at each end, but they're not where you can use them for reading in your hammock."

"I'll get Gino to fix something up on a long wire that you can use for reading. Maybe one at each end, so he can branch them off the light circuits. We never had four people sleeping in hammocks, so this is new to us too."

"I sure do miss flashlights, skipper. Do you think they'll have batteries in Argentina?"

"I hope so, Mike, I hope so. I miss flashlights too."

Flashlights and about a hundred other things, I thought. Including a competent dentist near the very top of the list.

Barry Conway came on deck just before the top of the hour. There was no greeting between him and Mike Ortega. The night was dry but chilly, and Barry was wearing one of my old wool sweaters which had been demoted to storm-duty status. It was torn and frayed, with reminders of old paint jobs on it, but it looked as warm as ever. He wore the same British desert camo pants, sandals and socks as before. He passed us both and went to the stern to take a piss over the rail.

Will came up next, again in his big military parka. I told Mike I was ready to take the wheel, and he said goodnight and went below. With Mike gone, Barry joined me and Will in the cockpit. I asked them how the hammocks were working out, and about life in the cargo hold in general, and they both said everything was okay. I knew it would take them a few minutes to fully awaken. I gave them the run-down on our course and speed, and how we set the four sails for the wind at its current velocity and relative angle to the boat.

I explained to them that Rebel didn't like running directly with the wind, or as sailors called it, dead downwind. "So, just like we can't sail straight toward the wind, we don't normally sail straight with the wind either. We usually steer off about thirty degrees so all four of our sails can catch some clean air."

"That's called a broad reach, right?" said Barry.

"Almost. It's a far reach. Steering as close as we can to the wind is called close-hauled. Then as you steer away from the wind you have near reaching, then broad reaching, then far reaching, and finally you're sailing dead downwind. We call it D-D-W for short. Sailing dead downwind doesn't work on a schooner because the sails block each other. Our best point of sail is broad reaching, that's when the wind is coming right at our side. That's also called beam reaching, because the side of a boat is called the beam."

After some more instruction Will asked, "Is the only thing wrong with the speedometer the little paddlewheel thing?"

"The paddlewheel thing is the impeller. Yeah, it's trashed. The unit still powers up, if you want to see it. Go ahead, turn it on." The speedometer was next to the lit depth sounder. Both displays were about four inches in diameter. Will cupped his hand over the depth sounder to throw enough light onto the speedo to find the power button. It lit up with the same yellow hue as the depth sounder, but its LCD display read 0.00 knots.

Will said, "It would be helpful if it worked, right? I mean, for the dead reckoning. It would be better if we weren't just guessing our speed, right?"

"Sure it would, but the impeller got all smashed up in the Canaries. We were hauled out for anti-fouling paint, and the whole bottom was covered with barnacles. I forgot to warn the boatyard guys and somebody ruined the impeller with a hull scraper, the big kind on a long pole. The scraper broke off one of the impeller blades."

"Is it still down there, down there in the water?"

"No, I pulled it out. There's a through-hull fitting that it slides into. It's under the deck up in the forward cabin. You can pull out the sensor unit with the impeller on the end, and then you put in a dummy-plug that's the same diameter. You want to see the old impeller?"

"Sure, why not?"

I said, "Barry, take the wheel. Hold us due east, and I'll be right back."

"Yes, sir," he replied, springing past the wheel on one side as I headed toward the pilothouse door along the other. Adam was no longer at the dinette table, the galley area was empty. There was some illumination down the aft passageway from the footlights, but I could have found the cigar box under the navigation desk with my eyes closed. The broken speedometer impeller, the size of a large grape, had earned a place in the box to remind me not to overlook small but important details.

I was back in the cockpit after less than a minute. Barry was standing behind the wheel, his shoulders back, elbows out, smiling. I sat across from Will at the front of the cockpit and handed the ruined impeller to him. He held it in front of the lit speedometer display to study it. It was formed from a single piece of white plastic under an inch in diameter. Two of the six blades were cracked and mangled, and one was gone.

I said, "When it's working, it's half outside the hull."

Will asked, "I suppose you tried gluing a new blade on, and gluing the busted ones back in place?"

"No, I didn't. Epoxy won't stick to nylon plastic; it's too slick. And now we don't have any waterproof glue anyway."

"Then why don't you make a new one?"

"A new what? A new impeller? How?"

"Just carve a new one from plastic. Do you have a piece of plastic big enough to make a new one?"

The five remaining blades were about three millimeters thick, each of them about as big as little pieces of an old Popsicle stick. Two were torn and bent. After the impeller had been destroyed by the steel scraper, I hadn't given it a lot more thought. But at least it had earned a place in the cigar box.

"Will, I know it doesn't look like much, but that impeller was made in a factory. Precision made. The nylon was cast in a mold, and then the six blades were machined out of it. One of the blades even has a little piece of titanium in it. That's what the sensor counts when it's spinning in the water, a little piece of metal going around and around. It all has to be perfect to the millimeter or it won't work, and that titanium was put in at the factory. I can't even tell if the titanium was in the blade that's busted off or not. It's too small to see it because it was molded right inside, I think. I can't even tell."

Will said, "I understand that, I do, but do you have some plastic that's big enough? Big enough to whittle a new one, blades and all? We can figure out the titanium thing if we get that far. It can't hurt to try, can it?"

I had to admire his optimism. "You're right, Will, it can't hurt to try, and we've got all the time in the world. I'll look for a piece of plastic tomorrow." I was already remembering a chunk of scrap Delrin nylon that was thick enough, a piece of one-inch flat stock that was left over from a rebuild of the rudder's bottom bearing. We *never* threw out stuff like that.

Will asked, "Can I hang onto this to study it some more?"

"I don't see why not. Knock yourself out."

"Do you have a drill bit the same diameter as the hole through the middle?"

"I'm sure we do. Gino will find you anything you need."

He studied the white plastic paddlewheel ball a while longer, and asked, "Should I turn off the speedometer light?"

"Sure, turn it off."

He did. Its fathometer twin was still dutifully reporting the feet of ocean under our keel. 453. 451. 449. 452. 454.

"You know, Will, I showed you how to use the radio, so why don't you try to find a station that's broadcasting tonight? Nighttime is the best time. Check the frequencies that are saved in memory first, and then scan around. Anything you hear might be important. News about the volcano, news about South America—anything could be important."

"Yes, sir, I'll let you know." Will stepped down into the pilothouse, stripped off his parka, climbed up onto the swivel chair and put on the headphones. The front of the radio lit up when he powered it on. It was facing sideways to starboard, not back toward the cockpit, so while it made his face visible, it didn't bother my night vision.

Barry asked, "Do you want to take the wheel again?"

"No, you're doing just fine. Why don't you keep at it?"

"Glad to! And thanks. Thanks a lot. I mean it."

"What, for the shackle job?"

"That too, of course, but mostly for trusting me to take the wheel when you went below. And right in front of Will! Let me tell you, Captain Kilmer, that means a lot to a slave. Just one week ago I was sleeping in a barn with a chain on my leg, like a dog, and look at me now! There's even stars out tonight. So thanks for not throwing me overboard like trash."

I looked up at him, and he looked down at me. His face was lit by the compass between us. "Barry, I was never going to throw you overboard. The thought never entered my mind."

He held our eye contact, and then went back to checking his course. "Well, I'm just glad you didn't put it to a vote. I think the jury was leaning against me." He snickered, and not in a humorous way.

"Well, Barry, I'm the captain, and this is my boat. There are some things I don't put to a vote."

"Forgive us our trespasses, eh, captain?"

"That's what the man said." Whew.

After a few minutes of silence between us, listening only to the ocean flowing along the hull, and the wind humming through the rigging and wafting across the sails, Barry said, "I think we're going to have a clear day tomorrow."

"What makes you think so?" I was curious why Barry had said this, because I had already come to the same conclusion.

"Captain Kilmer, I didn't learn anything about sailing back on the farm, but I learned a lot about the weather. I was out in it every day, and the only rain gear I ever had was a dirty piece of canvas that I made into a poncho, and a piece of trash that I made into a hat. That poncho was also my winter coat and my blanket, and let me tell you, captain, I learned to study the sky like a preacher studies sin. It's going to be clear tomorrow."

"You might be right, Barry, you might just be right."

Nobody understood weather forecasting by the clouds and the wind like sailors and farmers. I was sitting across the front of the cockpit facing north, trying to identify stars in the parts of constellations that appeared to be sliding across openings in the overcast. Then looking far behind us and low I could just make out an unbroken horizontal line of stars. A section of the western horizon was becoming discernable between the black ocean and the equally black sky because of that thin edge of stars. And the stowaway had noticed it before I did.

I pointed past him astern. "There's tomorrow's weather, all right. Nice catch, Barry. Well done."

19

Barry seemed in a good mood, and Will was in the pilothouse with the headphones on, so I thought I'd revisit our previous night's discussion. I was trying to think of a way to bring it up when Barry surprised me and raised it first.

"Captain Kilmer, last night I didn't want to ruin my first try at sailing by talking about what you called *the C-word*."

"I remember. You said that some people wound up on the menu, but you didn't explain what the menu meant."

He closed his eyes, turning his face slowly side to side to feel the wind. "I've been trying not to think about it for a long time, but since last night, I'm thinking about it all the time. So I guess that means this is a good time to talk about it."

Because of all the normal boat sounds, even under sail, the wind in the wires, random pieces of metal rigging hardware creaking and clicking, and the ocean gurgling along the hull and slapping under the transom, I couldn't have heard him if he whispered. He had to speak in a normal voice.

"Do you want me to take the wheel?"

"No, it'll be better if part of my mind is on holding the course. Are you sure you want to hear about it? It's not pretty, and I'm not proud of some of it. A lot of it."

"Oh, I can take it. I've been to war. I've seen ugly. Who knows? It might make you feel better."

"Confession is good for the soul, is that it, captain?"

"I'm not your priest, far from it. Tell me if you want to."

"Okay. I do want to, but don't ask me about it again after tonight. One and done, all right? Deal?"

"Fair enough, shipmate. Deal. I agree to your terms."

"Shipmate? Shipmate. . . Thanks, captain. Okay then. But I can only tell you what I saw with my own eyes. I can't tell you what happened in the next county over. Anybody could have had a totally different experience than I did."

"Like Will Padgett."

"Right, just like Will. He was close enough to Beaufort to walk there, and he was lucky not to get thrown off the island by the militia, or to be put to work as a VIW on a real farm. That's what they call the farm slaves on the island—VIWs. Voluntary Indentured Workers. But there's nothing voluntary about it, no way. Not after you walk across that long bridge."

(I noticed that Barry, like Mike, pronounced it *views*, and didn't spell it out as V-I-Ws like the men who'd caught him.)

"Being a starveling, Will wouldn't have made the selection for farm work anyway. Before I got to the island I starved, oh, I starved plenty, but I'm not a starveling because I was already a full-grown man when it all went down. And now I'm just a survivor, but I guess I'm not real happy about it."

"Why not?"

Barry looked upward, leaning back with his hands on the wheel and sighed. "Because I'm not proud of *how* I survived."

"Because of the C-word?"

He said nothing for at least a minute. "The C-word. That, sure, but not only that. That was a part of it, but that wasn't even the *worst* part. There was worse. Much worse."

"Look, Barry, if you don't want to talk about it—"

"I don't *want* to talk about it, captain, I really don't, but I feel like I *have* to talk about it. I have to tell *somebody*."

On night watch there were always pauses between replies.

"Well, it's just you and me out here on a big dark ocean."

"If you hadn't of tripped me, I wonder where I'd be now? Thrown off the island? Or back on the farm with two shackles, instead of one? You don't get a third shackle. You get buried."

Whew. "Now you have no shackle, and you're steering."

"Steering to Argentina. Sometimes in my hammock I think it's a dream. Or in my dreams, I'm back on the farm. Then I feel my ankle, with no iron on it, and I know I'm not."

Some more minutes passed. We were still surrounded by the same black ocean, but the narrow band of stars across the horizon behind us was widening.

Barry asked me, "Are you *sure* you want to hear it?"

"If you want to tell me, then I'll listen."

"Yeah. Okay then. So last night I told you I lived in North Charleston, in a trailer park. I lived there for a few years after my mother died. She died even before the shit hit the fan."

"What did you do for a living, I mean, to pay the bills?"

"Oh, I was trained in HVAC. I did the vocational-technical track in high school, 'vo-tech,' but my best job was installing satellite TV antennas. I installed the dishes and I got peoples' connections set up, and I did troubleshooting when they didn't work. We subcontracted for the satellite cable network. That lasted for about three years until the installation company went bankrupt. After that I did part time work: HVAC, electrical, hell, plumbing, anything to make a few bucks. They were all side jobs for cash. Everything was going downhill for a long time before that, but then it all came apart at once.

"When it happened it was almost like overnight. The credit cards, the ATMs, the gas pumps—nothing worked. It was cash only—only there was no cash! People who could get away, I guess they got away, but I don't know where they got away to, or how far they got. Every food store was looted in the first week. It started in the black neighborhoods and it just spread out from there. The government put on curfews, and then they declared martial law, but that's just a lot of empty words when all the police run away too. Who's going to die to keep hungry people from taking food out of a supermarket when the credit cards and EBT cards don't work? *Nobody*, that's who.

"I lived in sight of I-26, and pretty soon that highway was gridlocked as far as the eye could see. Every truck was busted open and looted, so maybe you got some of that if you were right there and you were lucky, but what did that get you? A week? Some people set up black markets with what they stole, but that didn't last long. Credit cards and debit cards didn't work, and neither did the ATMs, so who could pay? How?"

"What about the banks?" I asked him.

"The banks were closed, and then they were burned. There was like one day of bank runs, you know, people in long lines down the street, and then all the banks were closed. It turned out there's no money in banks, not really, at least, not enough. But one thing we all learned real fast is that people who are starving get pretty goddamn mad at anybody who's sitting on a pile of food and trying to sell it back to hungry people. And not normal angry mad, I mean *crazy* mad, like homicidal mad! And there were a lot more guns and ammunition around than food after all the supermarkets were looted and burned.

"All of this happened at almost the same time. The money stopped and the food was gone, and then the shooting started. Shooting all the time. It was constant, like a war. But being in a poor white trash trailer park, I guess we weren't exactly the first place that hungry people would go to look for food. It was more the other way around, with people going to the rich neighborhoods. It was actually kind of lucky I was in a trailer park. My neighbors were what you might call the hard-luck cases—but at least they were *hard*. They'd all been hungry before.

"You know—bikers and ex-cons and fired cops and mean drunks. Well, those kinds of guys can put a guard on the only way in and out of a trailer park like right off the bat. There was a big chain-link fence around the whole place and there was only one way in and out, off Rivers Avenue. Old soldiers and ex-cons and ex-cops—they know how to do security. And you never saw so many Confederate flags in your whole life as when all that was going on—it was like people were marking their territory. *Just stay the fuck out*, right? That's why I liked *Rebel Yell* as soon as I saw the name. So, Rivers Avenue is the main drag out of Charleston other than I-26, the interstate."

"I know, I've been there a few times. How did people get to the nice neighborhoods if it was all gridlock?"

"This was before the gridlock. I'm sort of jumping around the times in my mind. But people just walked, they met up in groups and they walked. With guns. Or they rode bikes. Bikes are great; they don't get stuck when cars are jammed up. The bottom line is there's no reason to stay where you're at when you've got no food. So you might say the looting and robbing started the panic that started the permanent gridlock. Even if you just wanted to stay home and mind your own business, how can you, when you have no food? And the water stops?"

"What about the preppers, you know, the survivalists, the people who already stored up a lot of food?"

"In a white trash trailer park? I didn't know any. And after you eat every old rusty can of corn, and every MRE you find stashed somewhere that you forgot about, then what? You'll dig up roots and boil them, but roots won't stop your hunger. Do you think you've been hungry before, captain, *really* hungry? *Starving*? No, you haven't. This is different. I heard somebody call it *wolf hunger*. You see anything warm that's moving and you just see meat. You can smell it. You can taste it. They live and I die. They die—and I live. That's *wolf hunger*. And after the electricity goes out and stays out, and then the water stops, how can you stay put? With no food? You can't."

"So what did you do?"

"Some of us tried to go to the Air Force Base. My father was in the Air Force when I was a kid. That was before he ran off and left me with my mom, but I still knew my way around the base. For a while after he split she still had a dependent's ID card, and sometimes we shopped there. So some of us from the trailer park thought they had to have some food on the base, for emergencies, because it was the government, right? They used to fly charity missions out of there in the C-17s, the Globemasters, so they had to have a lot of food there, right?

"But by the time we got there the Air Force security force was keeping people out with machine guns, and there were bodies just all over the place. All over the place! Piled up by the main gate, and along the walls and fences. So when we went up there looking for food, we got grabbed by Air Force security instead, and they told us if we worked on a sanitation detail they'd feed us. And it wasn't a choice, it was an order. Working on the sanitation detail meant throwing dead bodies on the back of a flatbed trailer behind a pickup. Two men, one on each end, just throwing them up. One-two-three: heave-ho.

"So you're taking bodies to be piled up to be burned way out in a field past the runways, and at the same time you're starving to death, and something just clicks. You make a new equation in your head: A plus B equals C. And you're not the first one. Some other people are already at it. You didn't kill anybody—they were already dead, right? You didn't know them, right? And those Air Force boys are nowhere to be seen, no sir. They want nothing to do with the sanitation detail out in the field with all the burning bodies. So what do you think happens next? Well, I can tell you what happens next. You're not starving anymore. That's what happens next.

"And you didn't do it! You didn't kill anybody, you didn't carve anybody up, no, it was just *there*. Take it or leave it. Eat or keep starving. Well, Captain Kilmer, I didn't see anybody say 'no' and leave it. Not when you've been starving more than two weeks. Not when people are dead all over the place, and you didn't kill them either. But you can't just pull something to eat out of a big funeral pyre, no, that won't work. For one thing, the smell. Oh, you'll never forget the smell! It's not just muscle that's burning, oh, no! It's guts, it's blood, it's hair, it's clothes, it's shoes—everything's burning, everything at once. No, you have to take an arm or a leg, and you have to take it somewhere else. And somebody else did it first, so you're just sharing, at first. And then you're not hungry. You're a wolf."

Barry went quiet. I let it hang there for a long minute, looking behind him at the band of stars on the western horizon.

"Did everybody do it?" I asked him.

"Everybody . . .who? Everybody, where? For me it started with the sanitation detail, but I'd say anybody who tells you they didn't is a liar, at least where I was at. You eat or you die, and you can't live on dandelions and fresh air. After every cat and dog and squirrel and rat is eaten, after you try to eat roots and weeds and the wheat off the top of tall grass, well, what do you think happens after that? What? When there's already dead bodies everywhere? The Air Force just made it easier for us by putting us on the sanitation detail. We were early adopters.

"And away from the Air Force Base a lot of people killed their own selves anyway. You've got no food left at all, not a grain of rice, not a crumb, but you've got a bottle of pills and vodka? Well, a lot of people took the easy way out, and who can blame them? And after you run off from the base and you make it home and you find your next-door neighbor dead in his trailer, well, there's thirty pounds of meat lying right there on the floor—and there's still propane in the tank for his grill.

"Let me tell you, people go out of their mind when they're starving and there's dead bodies every place you turn. In cars, in stores, hell, up in trees! Anyplace. It's just pure crazy town. Anything you think you know about human nature goes right out the window. I've seen a boy kill his brother with a hammer fighting over one red apple. I've seen a mother boil her own littlest baby in a pot to feed her other babies. And once people get past—you know—the cannibal thing—there's no limits at all after that. People who will boil and butcher up a little baby will do anything at all after that. Anything. That's *the menu*.

"And everybody is going crazy not just from starving, but from the bodies everywhere, the smell, the smoke, the gunfire, the fear. It's *worse* than hell. Much worse. Half of Charleston burnt to the ground just from people setting fires for no damn reason at all. Even normal people go crazy out of their minds. So the people who were still alive past the first month, well, they're operating on a whole new plane of reference.

"But by then you're not starving anymore, so at least that part is over. Then your whole life splits into two parts: the part *before*, and the part *after*, and your life before is gone, gone like a nice dream you woke up from, but this time you woke up in hell, and there's no place else to go because *everywhere is hell*.

And if you want to get out of hell, you don't have any good choices left. No good choices. You can kill yourself—or let yourself get killed—and then you're on the menu. Okay, so you learn there are new rules in hell, and rule number one is *eat or be eaten*. Either you write the menu—or you're on it.

"But after a while all the bodies from the early days are gone. Or they're too rotten and putrefied to—you know. And nobody is doing any more sanitation details, no sir, nobody is collecting those bodies. There's no more Air Force security, and there's no more police and there's no national guard, and where there's no food and there's no water but there's bloated rotting bodies everywhere, well . . . you just can't stay there. You have to move on. You have no other choice. And do you know something really weird? Every dead body is black after a week. Everybody is equally black in death."

My mind drifted back to Morocco, to the holiday feast we'd shared in the walled compound before the rescue mission to Fort Zerhoun. All of the food had been grown within the range of a small truck or even a wagon pulled by a donkey. I'd seen some of the terraced farms from atop the rock pinnacle where Tala had taken me to see both the blue Atlantic and the Atlas Mountains from the same perch. There were no distant supply chains to break down and cause immediate mass starvation.

After a few minutes, Barry went on with his story.

"So, I fell in with a little pack of survivors from the trailer park and the sanitation detail. They were bikers and veterans, and we moved up the interstate on foot to get clear of the city. A car couldn't get two blocks the way the streets were then."

"Wait, you said that bikes could get through. Bicycles."

"Bicycles? Yeah, I guess I meant maybe in the first week or two. After that, anywhere you went, you had to move in a super sneaky stealth mode. In the city, I mean. By the time we left, you'd get picked off if you were riding a bike. Ambushed. Somebody puts a rope or a chain between some cars, or a car and a tree, and you've got to get off the bike to take care of it, right? Bang! You're on the menu. So we had to walk, always keeping cover on each other. I had a 12 gauge pump and a bag full of shells. Everybody in our squad had some kind of a long gun, mostly AR-15s and AK-47s. There were seven of us when we left our trailer park.

"Sometimes we walked on the interstate, right up the line of cars, and sometimes we walked in the tree line off to the side. Almost everything in that gridlock was already picked clean, picked clean of food, I mean, but you could still find things to use. Like, say, a crowbar is real useful, that gets you into car trunks. We were moving real slow and careful, like soldiers. The boss of our squad was an Army Ranger. He was in Somalia and Panama and some places like that. He was old but he was hard, and he taught us about squad tactics. That's what he called us, a squad. You don't all move at the same time like in movies. You get behind cover, and you take turns moving. You plan it out and you cover each other. The old Ranger had a pair of binoculars. The binoculars helped him to plan things out so we wouldn't get ambushed."

"So there were seven of you in your squad. What about women and children? Were there any other survivors?"

Barry paused before answering. "There were no women and children. The squad was seven men. I was the youngest."

I almost asked him what happened to the women and the children in the trailer park, but I was afraid of the answer I'd get. A mother putting her own infant in a pot to feed her other children was still in my head. And after that, what came next?

"Sometimes we stayed in houses that were already picked over. Only places we could check out for a long time, to make sure nobody was around. The Ranger was real careful about that. But we never stayed for long, usually just a day or two. Or maybe we'd lay up for a few days when it was raining real hard, but we always kept moving west."

I asked him, "Why west?"

"Partly it was because of the sun. We'd always move out before dawn. The old Ranger said that moving west, the sun would be behind us in the early morning, and that gave us an edge if we ran into anybody. We'd be able to see into where they were hiding, and they'd be looking at the sun and we'd be in the shadows. This was before that Iceland volcano fucked everything up even worse so it's raining almost all the time. Well, anyway, we'd make good time in the first light, just a couple hours, maybe make a few miles, then we'd slow down and move real careful, or we'd lay up during most of the day. The old Ranger had a South Carolina highway map, and one of the men in the squad said he had friends out west around Jacksonboro. But one way was as good as another to me. The squad was going west, so I was going west.

"And then we got ambushed crossing a fallow field. It was just dirt and mud. It was a rifle ambush. There was no cover, but it was right at dawn, first light, and the Ranger said it was safe enough and we had to chance it. There were no houses or anything like that in sight. No sign of anybody. We mostly stayed in woods and tree lines, but sometimes you just had to cross a field because there was no other way around. I never even saw who was shooting at us. I think maybe I was the only one of us who wasn't shot, but I don't know. I ran like hell and I made it to a ravine and then into some woods, and that was the end of the old Ranger's squad from the trailer park. After that I was going solo. I kept moving west, I guess because I was used to it. I had no map or compass, and no binoculars. I was just traveling by the sun. I'd fill a water bottle from streams. At least there was plenty of water.

"Sometimes I had to use a road, or walk just off to the side of the road because there was no other way to go, so I walked mostly at night. Everything changed all the time—the terrain, I mean. Roads, rivers, farms, towns—it always changed. Sometimes it was wide open, and you could see for miles ahead, and sometimes it was pinched in tight. Sometimes there were woods and tree lines, and sometimes nothing but open fields. You had to study each new situation and figure out the best way to go. The old Ranger used to say, 'terrain and situation dictates.' So sometimes the best way was to follow behind another group of travelers. Let them walk across a danger zone first."

"So there were other groups moving too?"

"Not many, but some."

"Did you ever try to join one of these groups, for safety in numbers? Like with your squad from the trailer park?"

"No, never. We talked about it, before the ambush, about joining another group, but one of the guys told us about this gang in India called the Thugees. The Thugees are like killer gypsies, and they have their own secret culture. Their main trick is to make friends with travelers on the road and gain their trust, you know, just like you said: for the safety in numbers. So the Thugees would act real friendly, real helpful, and when everybody was asleep at night they'd strangle the people they joined up with. So when I was moving solo I never tried to join another group. After what I'd seen, I figured that gangs of killer gypsies like the Thugees would be next for sure. So I'd just trail along behind them, like when they'd cross a danger area like a little town that looked all abandoned.

"Or they'd come to a road block, or maybe a bridge across a river, or maybe some cars and trucks were pushed together across the road to make a wall. Sometimes the locals would put up a roadblock after a turn so you couldn't see it from far off. And the easiest scam in the world is to put up a sign that says there's food at some U.N. refugee camp just up the road. I think a lot of people fell for that one, but not me. No way. I'd always circle back around and try a whole different route."

20

I remembered something I'd seen when Barry had revealed himself to us as a stowaway. "So, how did you get the burn scars?" There was no denying he had been through many trials and tribulations. The scars on his ankle and his arms were permanent. The scrapes on his bruised face would fade with time.

"Oh, yeah, the burns . . . I'm getting to that. So I'd try to hang back behind a group of travelers, right? But one time I wasn't back quite far enough. A group I was trailing walked into a trap, and I walked into it too because I was too close to them. It was just some little farms, and then a little town but it all looked like it was deserted. Well, the whole setup was like a fish trap, but for people. Do you know how they work, fish traps? They're like V-shaped funnels put in a stream. They're made out of sticks and nets, one after the other, like funnels, but getting smaller and tighter. That's what they walked into. It all seems natural and normal, just a regular fence here and there, or a hedgerow, or maybe a stone wall, and nobody is around, there's no sign of life—and then you're in the trap. When I figured this out, it was too late. When they sprung the ambush I was in one of those funnels, and you can't run back out of the funnel when there's men behind you with guns.

"No, then it's too late. You just drop your gun and you put up your hands, or you die right there and that means you're *on the menu.* So then I was put on a pickup truck with the rest of the group I was following, out to like a ranch, and I figured I was going to be on the menu for sure. The gang that trapped us was called the Templars of Christ, and their leader was a real trip, man oh man, he was something! Simon Templar was his name. I know it was just made up, but that's what they all called him, Simon Templar, or Simon Peter, and he was the boss. He was a big man, real big, six-six easy, with long hair and a beard. He'd lay his head back and howl, and all the other Templars would join in like a pack of wolves. That was really something to hear, let me tell you."

"They were Christians, and they howled like wolves?"

"They weren't like normal Christians. I saw some crosses but I never saw a Bible. They said they were still in stage one, and stage one was just survival, and after stage one they'd find the pureblood women and rebuild the true church. They had their own customs, like the wolf howling. One of them would start, and then they'd all go off howling."

"So, what did they have to do with your burn scars?"

"Well, the Templars didn't tolerate tattoos, no sir. Some of it's kind of mixed up in my mind, the Templars of Christ and the howling wolves, and some things might not be in the right order, but man, I'll never forget their leader, Simon Peter, and how they'd howl like a wolf pack. I guess I was already pretty goddamn crazy by then, but even so, it'd make the hair stand up on your neck hearing thirty or forty of them all howling."

"But what did that have to do with your scars?"

"Oh, right. The Templars didn't tolerate tattoos, no sir. So when they trapped me and the group I was following they said just strip on down and let's see what kind of new meat we got. This was at the first selection, after they unloaded us at their ranch. That's what they called us when they caught us in their trap: new meat. There's rifles aimed at you, so you just do what you're told, or you die right there.

"The Templars hold that tattoos are a desecration of the temple of Christ, and so they must be removed. They said it was my choice, but I knew what it meant if I said no. It meant I'd be on the menu. So that's where I got the scars, and I'm lucky I only had a few tats they could cover with an open hand. That was their rule, the one-hand rule, and none of my tats offended the Templars much. Some tattoos would get your throat slit like a hog right on the spot even if they passed the one-hand rule. This happened to a man right in front of me in the line. We were all bare-ass buck naked, arms straight out."

"What was his tattoo that offended them so much?"

"I never saw it. I think that it was on his chest, and I didn't look, but it sure riled up the Templars. Later I found out that anything with Satan or devils would set them off, and some other things. Hex signs, things like that. So after they cut his throat right in front of me, I figured I'm on the menu too, but when they looked at my tats they weren't bothered by them, and they passed the one-hand rule, so they gave me the choice. They did it with an iron pipe that was red hot from a fire. They tied my arms around a tree real tight, and they rolled that hot glowing pipe over my tats real slow, back and forth. Then they left me tied there onto that tree for three days with no water. Bare-ass buck naked. They called it the tree of life.

"I was still alive after three days, and as you can imagine I was mighty goddamn thirsty. I was already pretty far out of my head but there was some kind of a psychedelic potion in that tea or whatever it was they gave me. They called it the cup of life. I think the cup was made from a human skull but that might be a hallucination I had. From what they said later I think the tea was made from magic mushrooms and toad skin, and I had visions. I flew around outside my body, and after all the visions I was numb for a week and I could barely move, but they fed me, and they howled over me, and after that I was a howling wolf Templar. I was the only one they kept alive out of that group who walked into their human fish trap. Like I said, captain, it was pure crazy town, but it turned out they liked people with blonde hair and blue eyes. And I'd survived the tree of life and the cup of life, so I was in, and they told me their secrets. At least, I think they did, most of them."

Barry rubbed his bristly head and whiskers. I tried to picture him with long hair. No wonder he muttered in his sleep. He would require close watching, that was for sure.

He said, "The howling wolf Templars went out on raiding parties, only they called them rescue missions. They said they were rescuing the purebloods from the mud people. And they did, they did rescue people. This was a few years ago, and they still had one of those quad-rotor camera drones, so they could see what was out the next couple miles past their pickup trucks when they went out on missions. They were picking up territory and looking for purebloods to rescue, and looking for new meat. You have to understand, this wasn't normal times. And by then you weren't starving anymore, because by then you were a hunter—only I'm not talking about hunting deer.

"I went on a rescue mission where we found about twenty children kept in a chain-link pen like they were sheep. None of those kids were bigger than Rita. It was men from the Middle East somewhere running that camp. God knows how they got into America. . . No, I guess we let them in, and then they built their own camp. Anyway, we killed all of them we could find, those Arabs or whatever they were. Most of them never even saw us before we dropped them. The Templars were real big on their rifle shooting. They'd pick out their targets and count down together, three-two-one, and then they'd open fire at the same time. Gino said you were a Marine Corps sniper?"

"When I was a young man, even younger than you."

"Well, that was the first time I saw a rifle ambush from the other side. The other time was when my squad got ambushed. Anyway, after we took that place we killed every one of those Arabs, or whoever they were, that was still alive. They'd rape those poor little kids, and then they'd cut them up and cook them and eat them. Bones and leftovers down to little babies. Little baby hands and feet and little baby heads. Their butcher table was next to the pen. It was crazy town, right? Captain Dan, what happened made *everybody* crazy, even the normal people. So if some people were already crazy even before all this happened, well, then you just can't *imagine* how crazy the crazy people got when they were starving to death."

"So what happened to the little kids in the sheep pens?"

Barry sighed, and let out his air slowly. "The children we found, we couldn't do anything for them. They were like paralyzed mutes. They just shook. You couldn't get them to move. You couldn't get them to look up at you. You couldn't even get them to stand up with their cage door wide open."

"So what happened to them?"

Barry looked down and shook his head. "I don't want to talk about it. It wasn't up to me. I was just the fucking new guy. The Templars said they were beyond salvation, and that it wasn't decent Christian mercy to leave them there like that. Even killing can be a mercy, a mercy, that's what they said. And after you've seen little kids kept in pens, right next to the rape bed and the butcher table and the cooking fire with the iron grill on top . . . any last shred of humanity just goes right out of you.

"So on top of everything else it becomes a race war. The Templars were shooting every black or brown face they could see, and from as far away as they could see them. It was the cleansing fire, they said. No, that went back to Charleston. Before we left, half the city was on fire and it just got crazier than hell. Smoke on the water, and fire in the sky. And not just normal smoke, not just wood smoke. That's when I had the shotgun. But you go from eating those who were already killed, to killing people to eat. It takes some time, but you get there. And everybody had a reason to do it. Boomers? They already lived too long in those nice big houses. Bang! Then just people with gray hair. Bang! You don't speak English? Bang! Wrong color? Bang! Don't like your face? Bang! And a lot of people blamed the Chinese for taking down the power grid, so you didn't see many Asians once the dust settled. Or blacks or Mexicans for that matter. At least, not where I was.

"Remember, captain, this is all happening after you wake up in hell, and your old life is already over. And when your face is your uniform, it's a lot easier when you can see their faces from five hundred yards away—and eight hundred yards is even better. That was the Templar way. I think I was with them for a couple of months, wolf-howling right along with them. My hair was long then, and they were into the blue eyes and blonde hair thing. So that gave me pureblood status with them, and that's why they kept me around after the tree of life. Simon Templar said that after the survival stage was over they were going to find pureblood women and start the true church all over, but without the mud people to drag us down again.

"Then on a rescue mission—but it was really just a hunting party—the squad I was with got ambushed. Simon had stayed back at the ranch; he wasn't with us that time. They had a video drone, but it happened in a place that they thought was safe. There were about a dozen of us in two trucks, and we got ambushed where the road went through some woods.

"Whoever ambushed us had fully automatic weapons and grenades. I bailed out of the truck in back and I hid in a culvert pipe under the road. It had bushes growing out of each end and I crawled way inside. I barely fit, it was tight. It was pure luck I made it in there, because in a few minutes the ambushers went around and they scalped all the Templars, dead or alive. Scalped them like Comanches. I heard it all from not thirty feet away. Scalped them and took their limbs and left the rest for the buzzards. They took one of the trucks, too, the one that would still run after the ambush. I saw it all when I crawled out of the culvert. One night you're wolf-howling with the Templars, and the next night they've got no arms or legs, and they're all scalped, and it's all under the same full moon.

"And after that I was all finished with the Templars. My burns were as healed as they'd get, and I wasn't starving, and I had a rifle they gave me. They didn't entirely trust me, so they only gave me a 22 rifle with a scope and a box of fifty bullets for that mission. This was just to see how I'd do with it, but it turned out that was lucky because that 22 rifle was real quiet.

"I'd already learned how to be sneaky. How to move in the woods by day or night, and how to cross fields and roads the safest way. How to find water, and how to hide. Finally I came across a group that didn't do the cannibal thing. They were all living on a farm that was in its own little valley, real hidden. I crept around and I watched them for two days before I approached them when they were working in a field. They were growing their own food, and they had some goats and pigs. I walked up to them real slow with my hands straight out. I didn't think they were like the Thugee killer gypsies because they weren't travelers; they had their own place already. It was men and women and some kids too. That pulled me to them, their women and kids. They seemed normal, like before. I hid my rifle where I could fetch it later if it didn't work out.

"They didn't let me in their house, but they let me stay in a shed with another man who was retarded. We had to stay in the shed from dusk till dawn—that was our deal. We'd get fed if we worked. That's where I heard about Beaufort Island, and how it was there. They said they heard that on Beaufort Island if you worked on a farm you could live free just like anybody else. Well, I was working on a farm and I had to live in a shed, so Beaufort sounded better. I guess they were okay as people on their little hidden farm, but I think they had too many men and only a couple women and it was a pretty bad scene.

"The men were always fighting over the women, and I was one man too many. I know they were Christians, I could hear them pray together, and I suppose they tolerated me, but I still had to sleep in the shed with a retarded guy. They never let me inside their house to sit down and eat with them, not even once. I could tell the men didn't want me there. The men were always watching the women to see who they were talking too. It was always very tense. I think the fact that I had found their hidden farm freaked them out. Right after I got there, the men started carrying guns all the time.

"So I left the farm and I got the stuff I'd hidden and I just kept walking, shooting game like woodchucks until my bullets all ran out, and then I was back to eating frogs and turtles. But after I left the farm I was heading south because of what they said about Beaufort Island."

"How did you start fires for cooking?"

"Fires? I didn't make any fires. Cold camp all the way. That old Ranger taught us that. Fires would give you away for sure. Hungry people can smell meat cooking from miles away. I could start a fire with a flint and steel, but I knew it was too risky. By then I could eat just about anything, cooked or not.

Even so, pretty soon I was starving again, but I wasn't going to kill anybody just to eat. I wasn't going back to that way.

"My last selection was on the long bridge over to Beaufort Island. That's where I ran into the militia and I 'volunteered' to be an indentured farm slave. Now you know the rest of my story, at least what I can remember of it. I know some of the time I was out of my head, I know that now, and I'm not sure what happened when, or even where, but it all happened, all of it. I didn't dream it." Barry pulled his right sleeve up, showing me the burn scars on his arm. They were as real as the scars around his ankle where we'd removed his shackle.

I said, "Something I've been wondering about: I didn't see any blacks at all on the island. Some up in Charleston, but not on the island. Were there any blacks working as farm hands?"

"Blacks? I wondered about it too. A foreman I trusted said no blacks were allowed on the island, not even as VIWs. And I didn't see many blacks on the mainland either, not after a few months. Captain, it was real ugly—and blacks were easy to spot at rifle distance. I only had a shotgun, but I saw it. After the C-word, all the rules are different. After you've seen what people can do to people . . . there's no rules after that."

I'd been looking at Barry while he was steering and telling his story, or I'd been gazing behind us at the widening band of stars marking the clear western horizon. After he was finished speaking I turned to check inside the pilothouse. Will was still in the pedestal seat, but it was facing toward the cockpit and he was staring at us.

There were no radio headphones covering his ears.

I didn't know how much Will had heard, or how he would react. When he saw me looking at him he slid down from the chair and stepped up into the cockpit. He went past me and faced Barry across the compass and wheel and he said, "I saw terrible things like that, too. There were some things I didn't say last night. People did terrible things to survive, but Jesus will forgive you. Jesus will forgive all of us, if we just promise to do the best we can. He'll forgive us, I know that he will."

Barry looked at Will and he made a slight nod and shrug. "You know, I sort of envy your belief, but I just can't share it. I just can't. Not after what I've seen. Not after what I've done. And even if there was a God, and even if God would forgive me, why should I forgive God? After all the evil he allowed to happen? After everything he did to people?"

"But God didn't do it, people did it. People fallen in sin."

"Not everybody was a fallen sinner, not by far, but your God punished them all. He punished the good along with the bad, and the good suffered the most. And there weren't many good survivors. I know that much for a fact."

Will sat and slumped down across from me. "I don't think God abandoned us. I think we abandoned God."

Barry said, "Will, I envy your belief, your faith. At least you believe in something. I don't think I believe in anything now. Not that higher-power stuff, anyway."

"You don't believe in God? Not at all?"

"I'll tell you what I do believe. I believe in this compass: it points the same way no matter how I turn the boat. I believe in the electricity that's lighting up the compass, the electricity that's made right on this boat. I believe in the steel boat hull that's holding out the ocean, and the four sails that are pushing us across it. All of these things were made by ordinary men, and not by any God. And it was ordinary men who screwed everything up back on the mainland, and it's ordinary men who are going to fix it—if it can ever be fixed again."

"Good men didn't mess it up, Barry, evil men did. Sinners against God. What's the difference between the good men and the evil men, if it's not a belief in something higher and better than just men? If there's no God over us all to guide us, then what'll stop the evil men from doing it all over again?"

Barry steered in silence for most of a minute. "Will, I envy your belief, your faith in God—but I just can't share it."

Even for an after-midnight cockpit conversation, this one was particularly deep and dark. I thought it was good that Will and Barry were both in my duty section. The two would have many more night watches to explore where both of them had been, and where they were going. Geographically, physically, mentally and spiritually.

Will and I were in the small space between the pilothouse and the compass pedestal. A few feet from the two of us and behind the wheel Barry was the third corner of our triangle. It was time for me to say something, but not in order to take sides between them. "Will, everything that Barry said, every word of it, it has to stay between the three of us, all right? Just between the three of us. Do you understand, son?"

Will looked me in the face and smiled. "Oh, I understand better than you'll ever know, captain. Better than you'll ever know—and count your blessings for not knowing! But I most surely do know we're going to heaven, Barry and me, because we've already been to hell, and we come back out. So even if you don't believe it, Barry—I do. Jesus won't give up on us."

21

Barry was right, the sky was clear the next day. There was just some high cirrus, and the sun turned the Atlantic electric blue. The wind was from the north at about fifteen, so we were able to broad reach to the east at around seven knots of speed. The air was fresh but chilly; it was a sweater and jacket day. The swells weren't bad, only about six feet high and wide apart, their tops beginning to blow off. Bigger than whitecaps, they were what old sailors called white horses. A fine sailing day when the wind is broad on your beam. Only Jessie was complaining of seasickness, but we advised her to get up on deck where she could watch the horizon. She brought up her mandolin, and her mild seasickness was soon forgotten.

In the morning we held our first man-overboard drill, which, on a sixty-foot schooner with all four sails up, was no trivial thing. After throwing a cardboard box over the side to represent the man overboard, step one was to head Rebel Yell into the wind to stop our forward progress away from the box, and get the engine running to assist us in maneuvering back under sail. I steered and Gino started the engine. The event was largely a fiasco, requiring almost fifteen minutes to get us back to the box, which was waterlogged and sinking by the time we were close enough to throw a life ring on a rope to it.

I told the new crew that this drill was a best-case scenario, done in broad daylight with all hands waiting at the ready, and not coming by surprise during a storm or at night with most of the crew below deck asleep. However, the man-overboard drill did serve one good purpose: it reinforced the point that if you fell off the boat, you were in all likelihood a goner.

I was finally able to shoot a noon sight using the new Japanese wristwatch chronometer and my old sextant. With so many new crew members on board the noon sun sight became a class in celestial navigation, and I had assistants calling out the times and writing down my marks, which recorded the precise angle of the sun above the horizon at exact times.

The class followed me to the galley dinette table, and when I finally drew our position on the chart we were near 32 North and 76 West, or roughly 270 nautical miles east of Savannah. This was the first real position of the voyage plotted on Chart 11009, "Cape Hatteras to the Straits of Florida." I compared our position to the lightly-penciled dead-reckoning plot. Our D.R. had us fifty miles to the southeast of our true location.

Will asked me why the two positions were so far apart, and I explained that we could only guess at the Gulf Stream's overall effect. Our speed through the water was only an estimate, and even our recently adjusted magnetic compass was going to have some serious errors on a steel boat. However, we were out of the Gulf Stream's grip, and we'd have a better understanding of our compass deviation as we sailed along the route between our future celestial fixes.

I said, "There are four things you need to know for dead-reckoning. First, you need a fairly accurate timekeeper, and that's easy with any clock. You don't need a chronometer for D.R. Two, you need to know the true course you're steering, and that's a little tricky with a magnetic compass on a steel boat. Three, you need to know what the ocean current is doing, how it's pushing you off course, or slowing you down or speeding you up. Sometimes you can estimate this, but you can see how far off we were crossing the Gulf Stream. And number four, you need to know how fast you're going through the water.

"This was easy back in the GPS days, because GPS gave you your speed over the ground—that's the ground under the water—and your boat's speedometer gives your speed *through* the water. When you compared these two speeds, you had an idea of what the current was doing. But now we don't have either one, because we have no GPS and no speedometer. We were safe to use dead-reckoning out of Beaufort because we had nothing out in front but ocean for hundreds of miles.

"But when we're near land, we'll have to be a lot sharper with our dead-reckoning. Especially when we're around low islands and reefs that you can hardly see before you're almost on them. When the sky is cloudy we might not get another celestial fix for days at a time, so D.R. is all we'll have. This is why you all need to be as precise as you can with what you record in the D.R. log. This is no joke. Mistakes can stack up over a few days—and then we're piling onto a reef."

Will asked me, "Did your speedometer only measure your boat speed, or did it measure distances too?"

"Good question. It had a lot of functions. It could count your miles run for a day, or for a voyage, it did a lot of things. And one of the best things was letting you know if something you did made you faster. Trimming sails, or changing course, did it help or did it hurt? Yeah, speedometers are great."

He said, "I still want to try and make a new impeller, like we talked about last night." Will opened his hand, showing the rest of the crew around the dinette table the busted impeller I'd given him. It was smaller than a golf ball, and a tiny fraction of the weight.

"Do you really think you can make one?" I asked him.

"I can only try," he answered.

"All right, Will. I'll tell Gino, I mean, Mr. Bracciano, to get you anything you need." At least, I thought, this impeller project wouldn't require a lot of working space. It's not like he'd be trying to rebuild an engine.

We had to shift things around in the cargo hold to get to the box containing the leftover block of Delrin. The cargo-hold boys moved things around under my direction.

Their help was needed because the crate in question was at the bottom on the low side, and a dozen other items had to be shifted into the passageway or set on top of other cargo for them to drag it out for inspection. The wooden shipping crate had rope handles and a hinged lid like a foot locker. Inside it was packed like a 3D puzzle with scraps of pipe, tubing, hose, plastic, wood and metal from projects done over the years.

The Delrin was there. It was black, a little bigger than two decks of cards stacked together. Will held it next to the white impeller: it was just thick enough. He rooted around in the box and extracted some other random items: blocks of wood scrap, some stainless-steel rods, a thick piece of plywood the size of a notebook and a few other items.

It took most of an hour for our four bachelors to extract the crate, retrieve the small piece of plastic, and then repack and secure all the cargo again. This work included re-lashing the heavy timber boards that held all the cargo against the side of Rebel Yell, and prevented it from shifting into the passageway down the middle. The cargo that had to be moved was on the low side of the boat on port tack, but would be on the high side and straining hard to break loose once we tacked over.

Will, being a starveling, didn't do very much of the heavy lifting. Barry and Mike seemed to go out of their way to avoid personal contact, not an easy feat in the confines of the cargo hold. Adam was cheerful and got along well with everyone. I tried to imagine the four young men in a decade. Will was as big as he'd ever get. I thought that Adam would eventually be taller than the others, but he was only fifteen, so humor and a pleasant smile were his most effective social tools.

Gino wandered from the forward cabin into the hold. With the Delrin block retrieved and all the cargo restowed, he asked Will, "So, what's your plan?"

"It depends on the tools we have. Do we have a drill? Do we have a saw? First we have to cut it down to just what we need. I was going to drill a hole through it first to be the guide for everything else."

"We have an electric drill that runs off 110 AC power. It has a cord, not a battery, it's that old. Our generator has a 110 outlet. And we have an electric jigsaw, too."

Mike asked Gino, "If you have a jigsaw, then why didn't you use it to cut off the shackle?"

"The metal-cutting blades are too dull, just like our hacksaw blades. But we have some wood-cutting blades that'll cut plastic, even Delrin—at least I think they will. Delrin's pretty hard, but it's not metal. We can re-sharpen the wood-cutting blades because the teeth are big enough to file."

I asked Gino, "Do you need me for anything else?"

"No, boss, I think I know where everything is. Our tools aren't buried like that box of cut-offs."

Will said, "I'll need small drill bits and wood screws, and a screwdriver, and files and chisels, small ones, and, um, sandpaper. Can I see what we have, Mr. Bracciano?"

"Sure, Will, no problem."

I said, "I'll leave it up to you two. Gino, if there's anything you can think of that you can't find, just ask me. I've stashed things in some pretty strange places over the years."

I was tied to some kind of a table. I knew this because there were mirrors up on the ceiling. My arms, feet and head were bound with leather straps. My mouth was held open by metal clamps. A man dressed in white entered my field of vision; his face was hidden behind a mask. He held a drill in front of my face. In a German accent he said, "Now, Mr. Kilmer, this is what happens when you don't see your dentist for more than ten years! Now you will pay the full price for your neglect!"

I could only move my eyes as he lowered the spinning drill into my mouth. It made a nightmarish screech when it cut into a nerve. The mirrors exploded into white light and I was falling through space, but I was still strapped to the table when I awoke in bed. Tala was looking down at me, not a German dentist. The electric whine didn't stop, but sometimes dreams are like that.

You think you are awake but you have entered a different room in your subconscious mind. But I knew I was awake because Tala was holding me down, not leather straps. And I could smell her. You can't smell in dreams.

Yet the shrieking whine from my nightmare continued. I pushed Tala to the side and slid down off the foot of the bed. It took me a few panicked moments to realize the sound wasn't the Caterpillar diesel screaming its death throes with a busted timing belt. The generator was running but the hideous noise was not coming from the engine room, it was originating from further forward. Coming fully awake I lurched through the aft passageway toward the source of the infernal screeching. It was worse than a metal rake scraping a blackboard, unless the rake was attached to a jackhammer.

I looked up the passageway, the cargo hold door was slid open and nobody was visible inside, but the shriek continued. The sound was closer and as I entered the galley I turned to my right, to starboard. Will was sitting at the dinette table with his back to me, and in front of him was my ancient Black & Decker jigsaw, upside down and backwards! Blocks of wood were clamped to other blocks of wood that were attached to the table with my biggest C-clamps. The saw was bound with wire and lashed with cord and held in place on both sides with smaller blocks of wood. The entire crazy contraption was held together with more of my C-clamps.

The jigsaw's blade was pointing toward Will's nose from just a few inches away. He was holding a tiny black ball with his fingertips, focused entirely on his work, lifting it up into the moving blade, then down for inspection, then up again. An orange power cord ran from beneath the pilothouse ladder to the saw's black power cord, and where they were joined by my feet I yanked them apart. The shriek ended instantly but I could still hear the generator running in the engine room.

The jigsaw stopped and Will froze, and then turned to look down at the power cord, and then up to my looming face.

"Will Padgett, what in the *hell* are you doing?"

“I’m—I’m making the new impeller, captain.”

Gino came through the cargo hold. “What happened to the jigsaw?” Then he saw me holding its black power cord in one hand and an orange one in the other. He said, “It’s okay, boss, we’re not hurting the table, I promise. Everything is padded where the saw is clamped to it.”

The faces of more witnesses appeared, looking down from the pilothouse and back at us from the cargo hold. The picture came together. The jigsaw’s on-off trigger had been locked on to run continuously. Will had used it to shape the plastic cube into a ball, and now he was beginning to carve its six blades. The jigsaw had been running nonstop while he worked the black plastic up against the blade.

Gino said, “I helped him to set it up. I think he’s doing a good job so far.”

I tried to fake calm nonchalance. “Yeah, okay, all right. It looks good, Will, but the next time, let me know before you use a power tool, okay?”

Gino replied, “But I thought we did tell you? In the cargo hold, when we found the black Delrin.”

“No, I mean, like right before you turn on a power tool, let me know. Right before. Especially if I’m sleeping.”

Will added, “I’m real sorry for all the noise, captain. But it looks okay so far, don’t you think?” He held the old white impeller in one hand and the unfinished black one in his other.

“Sure, sure, it looks fine. Carry on.” I plugged the black cord back into the orange one and the jigsaw’s shriek began again. And I really did need to see a dentist.

That was the end of my nap, so I went up to the cockpit to see how Luke and Jessie were getting along on watch together. Mike and Adam had been coaching them, and they said that they thought were ready to stand night watch. So did I.

The next time I saw Will and the impeller it was mounted on a small piece of plywood that was resting on the dinette table. The black and white plastic balls were sharing a stiff piece of wire running through both of their centers. On either side of the two balls the wire axle passed through blocks of wood that were screwed to the plywood.

"I'm getting closer, captain. It's not very pretty but I don't think the water will know the difference. Take a look."

"What's that wire that they're on?"

"It's an old bicycle spoke; you can tell by the ends. I'm glad you saved some of them. Bicycle spokes are just about perfect for a lot of things. They can even work like a drill bit if you sharpen the tip just right. They're good for drilling wood and plastic, not metal. I used it to drill the Delrin because your really small drill bits were broken. I used it to drill through the wood support on each side too. Anyway, I'm all done with the jigsaw and I'm sorry about waking you up. Now it's just quiet work with chisels and files and an X-acto knife. When I lay this card between the old impeller's blades it lines up with the new one and I can see how much more I have to take out. I take it off the spoke to carve it."

He handed the foot-wide piece of plywood containing the wood support blocks, the stiff wire and both impellers to me. I spun them both with my finger, and turned the plywood ninety degrees so I could look down the length of the black and white paddlewheels. The broken and missing blades on the white impeller didn't matter because the three intact ones were all symmetrical and could be used as perfect models for all six of the blades on the new black one.

What a clever boy, our starveling. It had never occurred to me that a bicycle spoke could be filed at its tip to create a new 1/16th-inch drill bit that was useable for soft materials. Will was right, all of our tiny drill bits were broken; they were inherently fragile. Busted drill bits aside, why hadn't I thought of fabricating a new impeller from scratch? Or Gino? Well, at least I hadn't thrown out the old impeller, or the scrap of black Delrin. Without them there'd be no new impeller.

When Will came on watch at 1800 he said, "I think it's ready, sir. Here's the old one and the new one." He handed the black and white impellers to me on their shared bicycle spoke. Tiny chisel marks were visible between the new black blades. I noticed a bit of white plastic smaller than a kernel of corn inset into one of the black blades. "Is that the metal bit?"

"That's right; the titanium is in that white piece. I found it by holding the old one up to the sun. It was molded right into one of the broken blades. I carved a slot for it in the new one. I angled the edges so when I popped it in it won't pop out again. I think it'll work. I mean, there's no reason why it shouldn't, but we won't know until we try it out, right?"

"That's right, Will, we won't know until we try it out. So let's go see if it works, okay?"

Like sharpening the end of the spoke into a drill tip, the work on the inset white plastic containing the tiny bit of metal was exceptionally minute and precise. How had he cut a hole through the black Delrin blade? And so exactly that the white plastic became a press-fit? There appeared to be no working room between the blades, but there it was. These were jobs for watch makers or jewelers with magnified goggles and special tools. Will Padgett had done it all by eye at our dinette table.

Mike said, "I'll keep steering while you go check it out."

"No, that's okay. It's after eighteen-hundred, so it's our watch now. I want you and Adam to come down and see how the speedometer and the depth sounder are hooked up. Barry can steer while we go see if this thing works. Will, turn on the speedometer, and Barry will let us know what happens."

The display came to life, but showed that our speed was 0.0 knots. Barry moved around the wheel, standing behind Mike. This was the first time Mike and Adam had seen Barry take the helm. Before, he had only steered at night after they had gone below. And not only that, he would be taking the wheel without anybody else in the cockpit. Mike raised his eyebrows and gave me a look that said *are you sure*?

I said, "That's right, Barry can steer. Come on; let's go test the new impeller." Mike gave up the helm without saying anything to Barry, and the three followed me through the pilothouse and down the ladder. Tala and Sofia were in the galley putting away the dishes from the evening's meal when we trooped past. Jon and Chris were across from one another at the table building forts out of Lego blocks. Soon they would be attacked by Lego tanks. They had created their own rules for Lego warfare.

As we filed through the cargo hold I could hear the sound of guitar chords being strummed in the forward cabin. Up in the bow, Luke, Jessie and Rita were sitting on the starboard-side settee berth. This was the downhill side on port tack, so it was like a cozy recliner sofa for them. Rita cradled a guitar across her lap and stopped playing when we appeared.

I said, "Sorry for the intrusion, folks, but Will finished his speedometer impeller and we're going to try it out." Gino was lying on the upper berth to port. This was on the high side, so he was mostly hidden behind its canvas lee-cloth. He looked over it and down at the mob invading his domain. The forward cabin had been his and his alone for only a matter of months before he'd met and married Sofia in the Canaries. Now most of the crew was crowded in around the forward ladder.

I knelt down and unlatched and lifted out a teak cabin sole floor panel. It was a yard wide and ran from the ladder to the front of the cargo hold bulkhead. Luke took it forward to get it out of our way.

We were all looking down at the raw inner hull of Rebel Yell, welded together from steel plates and flat bars at least a half century before. The steel transverse frames that were the ribs defining Rebel's hull shape were spaced a half meter apart from one end of the boat to the other, but they were only visible when a floorboard was pulled up, or in the engine room where there were no wood floors. Throughout the rest of the boat the frames were hidden beneath the floors and behind plywood panels on the hull sides and ceilings. It was dusty down there but not too rusty, not where it mattered. The paint was still protecting the steel, and the quarter-inch-thick hull plates were still doing their job keeping out the ocean.

I said to all the observers, "The keel starts right there. In front of the keel it's just two steel plates joined in a V all the way up to the bow. These black wires go to the depth sounder on the left and the speedometer on the right. The speedometer's through-hull fitting has a plug in it now."

I lifted the speedometer's insulated wire; it terminated in a black plastic cylinder less than an inch in diameter and three inches long. It was about the size of a roll of quarters. I held the speedometer sensor up to show it to them. The end where the wire came out had a T-shaped handle for pulling it out of the permanently-mounted through-hull. At the other end from the handle were two thumbnail-size ears with a silver pin between them. I removed it carefully; it was basically a bigger version of a wristwatch strap pin.

"Okay, Will, let me have it."

He handed me his homemade impeller. I slid the silver pin through it, and then pressed the pin and the impeller between the two ears at the working end of the sensor unit.

I said, "When I pull out the plug some water is going to shoot into the boat, but it runs into the bilge and gets pumped overboard so don't worry." The black plastic through-hull fitting was the size of a small jelly jar attached to the steel hull plate a foot from the boat's centerline. I'd installed it decades ago during Rebel Yell's reconstruction, and I'd had no reason to mess with it ever since. The only part that had failed had been the impeller, the most vulnerable part of the system.

To remove the plug I had to first take out a stainless-steel safety rod that ran through both it and the through-hull fitting. The plug also had a T-handle on its end like the one on the actual sensor unit. I'd done this swap-out a few times and it was always impressive to see how much seawater would shoot out of a one-inch hole a yard below the waterline. Another reason for bringing Mike and Adam down to see Will's new impeller going in was to impress upon them the speed with which flooding would occur after a collision or other accident that breached the hull below the waterline.

I was sitting under the ladder on the port side with my feet down on the hull plate on each side of the through-hull. With the safety rod removed, I pulled on the plug's T-handle while twisting it. The matching sensor unit with Will's new black impeller on its end was in my other hand. I twisted and pulled the plug until it was almost clear. Both the plug and the sensor unit had rubber O-rings in grooves to ensure perfect watertight integrity when either one was in place.

With only an inch of plug remaining in the through-hull I said, "Okay, here we go." I gave the handle one more pull and the plug was out. A geyser of salt water erupted behind it like a fire hose. I dropped the unneeded dummy plug and used my now-free right hand to guide Will's impeller into the stream of water, trying not to wreck this one too in my haste. Once the cylindrical unit was inside the through-hull the water stopped. I pushed it all the way in and then turned the T-handle so that the impeller's exposed blades would face the ocean rushing across them at ninety degrees.

Then we all heard Barry shouting from the cockpit behind us. "Six-point-seven knots! Six-point-nine knots! Seven knots captain, seven knots!"

Oh, glorious moment! As soon as the safety rod was back in the through-hull and the floor panel was replaced we all hurried to the cockpit to see the result with our own eyes. I went up the forward ladder through the scuttle hatch, some of the crew went through the cargo hold, but in no time the whole herd of us was in the cockpit and spilling across the aft deck. Tala, Sofia and the twins watched from the pilothouse door. This was the first time that most of them had ever seen our stowaway behind the wheel steering, another surprise.

We were finally off soundings, so the depth sounder was showing a constant 500. This was comforting, but not exactly exciting to watch. The matching speedometer display had been the depth sounder's mute companion ever since the Canaries, and now it was showing our speed through the water to the tenth of a knot, updating every two seconds: 6.9—7.0—7.1.

I stood behind the pilothouse on one side of the display, with Will on the other side, and we turned around to face the rest of the crew. I said, "Barry, head up until the jibs start to luff, then fall off again." He steered toward the wind, and our speed dropped into the low sixes and then into the fives, and when he turned back to the original course our speed climbed up to seven knots again.

I told them all, "Having a speedometer is a great help. It lets you know right away if whatever you did is making the boat go faster or slower. And it has an odometer function so we can count the miles between our noon sights. Our celestial fixes are good to about fifteen or twenty miles, and in between it's all dead reckoning, only now it'll be a lot more accurate. Will Padgett, I want to personally thank you." I turned to him, put out my hand, and we shook. I said, "Will, you're the man! If you need anything invented, just ask Will."

He was beaming. My accolades were repeated by the crew. It was a great to see our speedometer working again, but it was even better to see the crew's growing respect for our red-headed orphan starveling, Wagon Will Padgett.

While everyone was still gathered in and around the cockpit I announced the crew change. Adam and Jessie would switch places on the watch rotation. Beginning immediately Luke and Jessie Hanahan would stand watch together around the clock. On hearing this they embraced. Now they could be together both on and off duty. I told them if they encountered a situation they didn't understand, or saw a squall coming, they should just bang on the aft deck to bring me up fast. Mike Ortega and Adam Selfridge would also make a strong watch team. They were both already good sailors, and young Adam would soon be an all-weather helmsman in his own right.

The new watch teams were Dan, Barry and Will, then Luke and Jessie, then Gino and Rita, and finally Mike and Adam. Tala and Sofia would continue to manage the galley, and the twins were still exempt from duty, other than cleaning up their Lego battle debris and the like.

I kept both Barry Conway and Will Padgett as my two number-twos. Barry could steer almost as well as any of the helmsmen, and as captain I could turn my attention in other directions during part of our watch.

	Day 1	**Day 2**	**Day 3**	**Day 4**
0000	DBW	L J	G R	M A
0200	L J	G R	M A	DBW
0400	G R	M A	DBW	L J
0600	M A	DBW	L J	G R
0800	DBW	L J	G R	M A
1000	L J	G R	M A	DBW
1200	G R	M A	DBW	L J
1400	M A	DBW	L J	G R
1600	**DBW**	**L J**	**G R**	**M A**
1700	**L J**	**G R**	**M A**	**DBW**
1800	G R	M A	DBW	L J
2000	M A	DBW	L J	G R
2200	DBW	L J	G R	M A

After the impromptu crew meeting I wrote out the new watch schedule and pinned it to the galley bulletin board. The ship's clock, the barometer and the corkboard were mounted onto the bulkhead between the door to the cargo hold and the table where everyone would see them many times a day. It was hard to believe we were still only on the third day of the voyage, not counting Saturday night when we fled the island.

We continued sailing southeast while trying to get as much easting as possible given the wind direction. As the night came on the wind dropped, and so did our speed, down into the fives. When it grew dark, the lights of the depth sounder and the speedometer were switched on, showing their black LCD numbers against a glowing orange background.

Now changing our course or adjusting our sails resulted in an almost immediately visible gain or loss in speed, providing rapid feedback to the helmsman. This was an especially useful tool for our new sailors. And if our speed changed without a change in boat direction or sail trim, then the wind itself had to be changing. Having a working speedometer was the key to all of this improvement. The crew called it Will's speedometer.

The thirteen of us were all confined to the same sixty feet, either down below or up on deck. The moon was more than half-full, so the decks and cockpit became a more attractive option for hanging out when off watch than down inside the crowded and stuffy interior of the boat. When it was cloudy the moon backlit the overcast and made the sea visible. Where the moon broke through the clouds it cast a silver path across the rolling swells all the way to the horizon.

I had cautioned our new crew to be careful about using the forward ladder and scuttle hatch instead of the pilothouse to come up on deck at night, but I didn't forbid it. After a few days aboard ship restless young people will want to explore their boundaries. It's human nature. They were getting their sea legs and their confidence was growing. I warned them all about the scarcity of old, bold motorcyclists and pilots, and I extended this to ocean sailors, but to little effect. I had been young too, and I would not outlaw what I had done. Each of the crew could choose their own acceptable level of risk.

As captain I would make my rounds both above and below deck and from bow to stern at least every few hours. This was not only my right, it was my duty. So if I found Barry sitting Indian-style staring at the moonlit ocean from up on the bow where we'd had our first conversation, we'd pass a quiet word or two but I'd let him be in peace.

When Mike wanted to be alone he'd often sit on Whisper's gunnel facing into the wind, arms folded, his feet wide apart on deck. Or he'd lean a shoulder against the mainmast's cap stay wire, which ran from the deck edge up over the spreaders to the masthead. Leaning against a leeward stay wire put your head right out over the water rushing by just beyond your toes. This was a somewhat risky but exhilarating experience.

Other members of the crew liked to sit on deck leaning back against the side of the pilothouse. Luke and Jessie would sit together on the windward or high side of the aft deck with their feet against the outside of the cockpit combing. They all found their own favorite places to hang out, or to spend time alone, both up on deck and down below.

Maybe I'd hear whispering through the aft passageway's sliding louvered door, revealing that Adam was in Rita's little cabin. On port tack her berth was on the low side, so it was a comfortable place for them to sit with their backs against the hull. I knew those two children were innocent and I never let on that I heard them in there sharing their secret hopes and dreams, and neither did Tala. Now it was Rita's private cabin, and before her, the twins had shared the space. Before them and for much longer, it had been Tran Hung's domain.

I often wondered who had slept in each cabin before my Uncle Jeff had found the homely hard-chine steel schooner in

South Florida. Freedom-seeking ex-pat runaways? Aspiring adventurers, or paid hands? Hitchhiking vagabond sailors? Dope smugglers? Gun runners? Lovers and other strangers? Dutchmen, Brits, Yanks, Aussies, Krauts, Frogs, Swedes? Where are they now? Still alive, or passed on? Who had welded the steel plates together and dropped her into the water? Who had done the incongruently fine wood joinery down below? And who was the first occupant of the aft cabin? Were they the same man?

So many ghosts for an old schooner. I never regretted the new name that I gave the abandoned hulk before launching her second life. Rebel Yell spoke for all of them, and for me.

22

When I hit the rack Tuesday night I knew that my next watch began at 0200 the next day. Some unusual noise brought me out of my sleep, but at least it was nothing like that shrieking jigsaw. Was it something on deck? In the rigging? They said that Napoleon woke up when the cannons stopped firing, and I understood that completely. Rebel was still on port tack, still heeled over leaning to starboard. I blinked and rubbed my eyes and stared at my watch. The glowing hands were faint, and I was not yet fully awake, so it took me a while to determine that it was in fact a few minutes after two in the morning. I should have been on deck, and on watch, up in the cockpit, *at least* ten minutes before the hour!

Tala mumbled and snuggled against me as I pushed my covers away and rose to sitting, taking deep breaths while forcing yawns. I was still wearing my khaki trousers. Even down below in the aft cabin with both transom ports closed it was chilly, and wearing pants and a jersey to bed saved time when the captain was needed on deck in a hurry. I pulled on my sweater, and slid my feet into my boat shoes. The twins were asleep in their nest, so I staggered up the passageway, hands on both sides for balance, trying to wake all the way up. Missing watch was a dereliction of duty by any member of the crew, but for the captain it was unthinkable!

Nobody was in the galley, so I pulled myself up the ladder into the pilothouse. The pilothouse door was open, Barry was behind the wheel. He was wearing an old field jacket over his British desert cammies and a tan watch cap to keep his bristly head warm. It was all Rebel Yell grab bag stuff.

"Good morning, captain. Our speed is five knots and we're steering 120 degrees magnetic."

"Where is everybody? Why didn't somebody get me up? Where's Will? What's going on?"

“I haven’t seen Will yet. When I came on deck Mike was steering.” Barry looked down at the watch tied on top of the hub of the wheel. “That was about, oh, ten minutes ago.”

“So where’s Mike? Did you do a turnover?” Barry should have known better than to let Mike go before I was on deck.

“He said he didn’t feel well. He asked if I could take the wheel a little early, and I said I could. Then he went below.”

“What about Adam?”

“He was already below.”

“So where’s Will? Will or Adam should have gotten me up ten minutes before the hour if I didn’t get up on my own.”

“I haven’t seen Will, only Mike.”

“Shit! Okay, Barry, just stay on course and I’ll get him.” I dropped down the ladder and went into the cargo hold. On the downhill starboard side Barry’s hammock was empty, which I expected because I’d just been with him. I looked forward and Will’s hammock was empty too. I could tell this by the shape of the canvas, but I went up and looked over and into it anyway. There was just a blanket. No Will Padgett.

I turned across the cargo hold passageway. Adam was in his hammock on the uphill side, his head toward the bow, and I shook its front cross bar. He should have only recently gotten into his hammock after he’d gone off watch, but he was sound asleep. I shook it harder, and then I grabbed his shoulder.

“Adam, Adam, where’s Will?”

He yawned, stretched and stirred, blinking and rubbing his eyes. “Will is up on watch. What time is it?”

“No, he’s not on watch, and I can’t find him. It’s after two in the morning. Get up. Turn-to. On your feet, Adam, get up, get up now.” I moved back toward Mike’s hammock, which was to port across from Barry’s empty one. He was already awake, his feet forward and his head toward the stern as usual.

“What’s the matter, skipper? What’s going on?”

“Will should be on watch, but we can’t find him. Get up. Turn to.” Then I went all the way up into the forward cabin. Gino was sleeping alone on the lower port-side bunk. At sea he always slept on the bottom so he could get out of the rack faster when duty called. I shook the top of his lee cloth. "Gino, Gino, we have a problem. We can't find Will."

He opened his eyes, then he unclipped the lee-cloth and swung his legs over and down. "What? You can't find him?"

"That's right, we can't find him, so we need to search the boat and find him fast. You search from the chain locker and all the way aft down below. I'll look for him up on deck."

Sofia, Luke and Jessie were all stirring. Will could not be found? Rebel Yell was a sixty-foot boat and less than twenty-feet across the beam. Where can somebody go? Only the twins were of an age to play hide-and-seek as a prank. Not Will.

I scrambled up the forward ladder and out the scuttle hatch, which had been left open for ventilation. Even from behind the clouds the moon lit the white deck. Whisper was resting in her chocks between the two masts, and recalling our stowaway, I lifted its canvas cover. Empty. Back past the pilothouse to the cockpit. Still just Barry behind the wheel. It was ten after two.

I said, "I can't find Will—so where the hell can he be?"

"I'm telling you I haven't seen him, captain. Just Mike."

Gino came out through the pilothouse in his gray sweats. "Will's nowhere down below. He's not in the chain locker, not in the cargo hold, not in Rita's cabin, not in the engine room, not in the aft cabin or in the aft cabin's head. So if he's not on deck, then he's—"

"Then he's overboard! Shit! Okay, start the engine. Barry, we're steering 120 degrees magnetic, right?"

"Right, captain, 120 magnetic."

"Turn to port until we're on 300, that's the reciprocal." I threw the outer jib's sheet off its winch atop the combing and hauled in its furling line, winding the sail up around the outer forestay which terminated at the tip of the bowsprit. Dropping the working jib required me to scramble to the foremast. I unwrapped its halyard line from the winch and went to the bow and pulled the sail down the inner-forestay wire until it was on deck, and then I scurried back to the cockpit.

By then our diesel was running, its engine panel lit up on the back of the pilothouse next to the fathometer and speedometer. The engine's control levers were on either side of the steering pedestal beneath the compass, with the gear shifter to port and the throttle to starboard. I pulled the shifter forward and put the motor in gear.

The main and foresails swung behind their masts atop their booms so they were much less of a hassle to deal with than the jibs during sudden maneuvers under power, so they could be left up. As we came into the wind during our U-turn Gino hauled in their sheets, tautly center lining both booms so that nobody would get hurt by them swinging across on their own.

"Barry, tell me when you're on 300 magnetic."

"We're on 300 now, captain. The time is 0215."

I wanted to grab the wheel myself, this was my instinct, but I needed to be free for all the other tasks that were certain to come. I was in front of the wheel and I pulled the throttle lever forward until the tachometer on the engine panel showed the engine was turning at 2,200 RPM.

Because of Will's speedometer I could match our speed to our RPMs again. Three grand was the Cat's redline. We'd make almost ten knots with a clean, slick bottom, which we didn't have, and we'd blow more oil out of the front main seal. The hull wasn't covered with barnacles yet, but slick it was not. In any case, making our top speed was not my goal.

In a minute Mike, Adam and Luke joined us in the cockpit. I knew Tala and Sofia understood that this was a time to stay below with Rita and the twins, so I didn't expect to see them.

I said, "Gino, turn on the steaming lights, and then get our spotlight hooked up. Get the new spotlight too, the one from Beaufort. Mike, do you know where I stowed the NOD? The PVS-14 from your militia boat?"

Before he could answer Adam replied, "I know where it is. It's in the pilothouse in the bottom drawer under the desk."

"Do you know how to hook up the battery and turn it on?"

"Yes sir—Mike showed me how."

"Good. Get the NOD and its battery pack and go up on the bow. Scan forward and out to both sides. After you turn it on, holler back and let us know when it's working, all right?"

"Yes, sir."

"Do it now." He disappeared into the pilothouse.

This left the adult men in the cockpit with me. No women, no girls, no teenagers, no children. Just the men. If I had to do any yelling, at least there'd be no crying.

"Barry, stay on 300 magnetic."

"I am, captain. Steering 300 magnetic. The time is 0220."

I nudged the throttle back until the tachometer needle was showing 2,000 RPMs and the speedometer indicated we were making five knots. The engine was quieter at two grand, and our ability to hear a cry for help might be critical. The wind had dropped after sunset and the waves had also come down some, with no whitecaps on top of the two-meter swells.

There were five of us in the cockpit: me, Gino, Luke and Mike, with Barry steering because it was our watch. If Will had gone overboard, it had probably happened not long before the change of the watch at 0200. I said, "So, who saw Will the last time, for sure? When? Mike, your watch was almost over. You handed the wheel off to Barry a little early, right?"

"No," Mike replied, "I handed over the watch at 0200." He was wearing his militia-issued USMC desert digital uniform, but bulked up with sweaters underneath.

"Adam or Will should have gotten me up at ten-before-two if I didn't get up on my own. So Mike, where was Will when you went below?"

"I haven't seen Will on deck since we did the speedometer thing after supper. I didn't see him on deck at all since then."

"Was he in his hammock when you went below?"

Mike replied, "I didn't check it."

"So where was Adam at the change of the watch?"

"He was tired and I wasn't, so I let him go down early."

"Barry, what time did you come on deck?"

"About five or ten minutes before two, I think."

"Did you see Will?"

"No, I didn't see him."

"What about Adam?"

"I didn't see Adam either. Mike asked me if I could take over the helm early, and I said I could, and I did. Then about ten minutes later you came up on deck. That's it. That's all."

"You never saw Will, or Adam?"

"No sir, I never saw them since I came up here."

"Were they in their hammocks?"

"I didn't check," Barry replied. "I guess I should have."

"Then who woke you up?"

"I was already awake. Wait, Adam did go by me. That's how I knew it was time to change the watch, but I'm not sure how long it was before I went up on deck. It wasn't long."

"Okay, we'll figure it all out later, but right now we can't find Will, so that's our only priority."

From up forward, Adam called, "The NOD is turned on, and I'm looking all around out front."

I yelled back, "Okay, Adam, stay on it!"

Think, Dan, Think! Okay, we're on the reciprocal course, we're making about the same speed under power that we were making in the original direction under sail. But when had Will gone overboard? If he had fallen overboard an hour ago, then finding him would be practically impossible. So, how best to use the *next* hour? How about we motor back for a half hour, to cover the fifteen minutes *after* 0200, plus the fifteen *before*? I had to choose a starting point for the search, so I chose our estimated position back at 0145. Will was always cautious on deck, and there was no reason for him to be up much before his next scheduled watch. He wasn't one to hang out on deck alone at night.

I announced my decision. "We'll stay on 300 magnetic for thirty minutes. We're more concerned about where we were *before* 0200. We turned around at 0215, so at 0245 we'll turn north for five minutes, and then east, and then south, and then west. We'll add five minutes to each leg and do an expanding box search until we find him. Barry, you'll be our time keeper. We'll make our turn to the north at 0245."

He looked down at the watch tied to the wheel's hub.

Gino came out of the pilothouse with two 12-volt handheld searchlights, our old one and the new one, both trailing 12-volt power cords. I said, "Mike, you scan to starboard, Luke, you scan to port. Don't aim straight forward or it'll wash out the NOD. Just sweep fore and aft out to each side, and keep the beam off the boat or it'll ruin our night vision. Shine it out at the water, not at the boat, and not straight forward."

They did as they were instructed, and the two long fingers of million-candlepower light lit the tops of the swells for hundreds of yards out to both sides. Between the crests were black shadow canyons. Luke and Mike's grim faces told me they had little hope of finding Will, but that didn't matter. I was the captain, and Will was one of my crew.

And I knew what it was like to be lost overboard in the ocean, treading water without a boat or even another human in sight. It had happened to me on the other side of the Atlantic, 4,000 miles due east off Morocco. That was when the Atlas landing craft had foundered on the way to Cape Zerhoun.

This time, on this side of the ocean, we still had another hour or so of moonlight before it set. And the ocean, while not flat, was at least calm enough for us to motor in any direction.

I'd been found and saved off Morocco, also under a half moon. The other Atlas survivors in the inflatable zodiac didn't give up, and they rescued me. And Will could swim: he'd said that he'd swum from the mainland to the island. The sea was not so cold that hypothermia would be an immediate threat to him . . . but there was no time to waste.

Falling overboard was a dreadfully real possibility in the mind of every sailor. The ocean flowing past our hull looked soft and safe, but the edge of the boat could be as deadly as the edge of a cliff. There were lifelines on both sides, and steel pulpit rails at the bow and stern, but the top lifeline wire was only three feet above the deck. Moving carelessly and tripping on deck, or thoughtlessly backing up, could even result in the lifelines catching your legs and flipping you over the side.

Even the twins understood that if you went over, you were a goner. Will treading water out there somewhere in the dark was awful to imagine, and not one among us would be the first to suggest giving up the search. What if it was you out there lost in the dark ocean after Rebel had sailed out of sight?

I went into the pilothouse to find a pencil and paper, and I drew out our initial search pattern. I went over the times and courses with Barry, and I showed him the sketch to keep the plan clear in our minds. We finished the half hour motoring to the northwest, and at 0245 we turned north for five minutes, then east for ten, then south for fifteen, expanding the box.

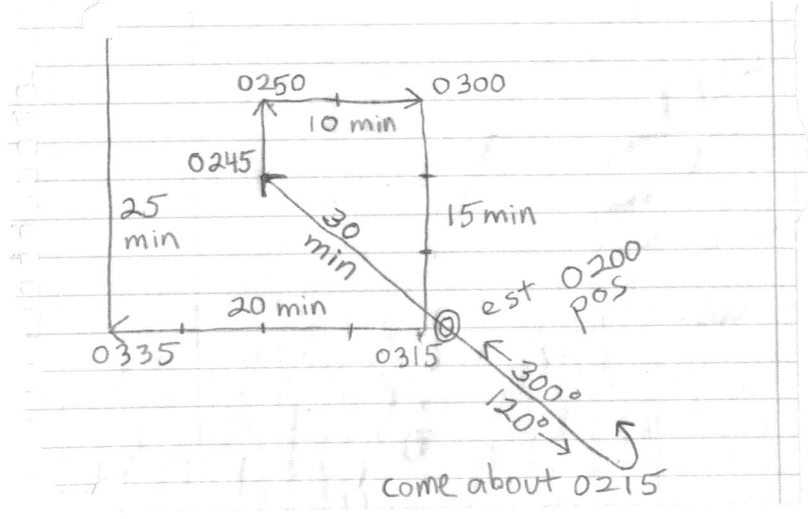

The half-moon was still above the horizon, flitting in and out of the clouds. Next, motor to the west for twenty minutes, and then to the north, adding five minutes to each leg to widen the search box. It was almost 0330. How many hours until dawn and daylight? And then what do we do? Just keep expanding the box? Or start the search again at some arbitrary point?

But without GPS, where would we locate the new starting point? Where had Will fallen over? And when? The odds were astronomically stacked against our finding him, so how long should we keep looking? On a voyage measured in weeks and months, what were a few more hours or days against giving up on finding him, and saving his life?

The swells were widely spaced, no waves were breaking. The searchlights moving out to each side were lighting up the wave tops for hundreds of yards. If, by luck, Will happened to be on top of a swell at the moment a beam swept across him, he might be spotted. But if he was in one of the long, dark valleys in between, he'd be missed.

If we were even within a few miles he'd see our running lights and our searchlights. He'd know that we were searching for him but that we had missed him and continued past. A near miss would be soul crushing, maybe even worse than the constant dread that the sharks would find him before he drowned.

Our second northward leg was penciled in for 25 minutes. It was almost over when Adam called back to us, "I think I see something, maybe. Turn to port about twenty degrees."

Barry swung the wheel over and said, "I'm turning to port, captain, coming to a new course of 340 degrees magnetic."

I shouted forward to Adam, "What do you see? How far?"

"I see something dark that looks solid. I can see it when it lifts up on a wave. I can't tell how far it is, but we're heading toward it now."

"Good! Don't take your eyes off it. Barry, drop us back to fourteen-hundred RPMs. Gino, get the life ring ready."

I told Barry, "Hold this course—I'm going up forward." This was a major advantage to being the captain. I didn't need to seek a consensus or take a vote. I just stated my intention and moved. Adam was sitting on deck beside the anchor windlass, the PVS-14 held to his eye.

I sat on the other side of the windlass and said, "Good job, son. Now, let me have a look."

"There's something out there, captain. A black dot."

He passed me the NOD and I pressed its rubber cup to my eye. Distances were hard to guess with no points of reference, but there was a dark shape at least hundreds of yards ahead of us, but no more than a kilometer away. It was visible for two seconds out of ten when it was lifted up on a wave. As a sniper I'd been trained to estimate distances based on the heights of soldiers, vehicles, doors and other known objects. But a dark spot out in the swells gave me nothing to judge its range.

I called back, "Barry, turn five degrees to port, and slow to twelve-hundred."

In a moment I heard, "Turning five degrees to port, to 335 degrees magnetic. Making twelve-hundred RPMs."

Whatever it was, I didn't want to overshoot it. I kept the NOD's lens aimed at the dark shape in front. It was prominent when it was on top of the swells and it disappeared between them, so it wasn't very high. Then the moon found an opening low to the west ahead of us and sent a beam of light across the sea from the horizon to Rebel Yell. The dark shape grew until it was visible for longer periods between swells, so we were getting closer. Whatever it was, we were going to pass it in about a minute. And now the dark shape was surrounded by sparkling glitter as seen in the NOD's white-phosphor tube.

I turned around and yelled, “Barry—steer ten degrees to port, and slow to nine-hundred. Gino—we have something up ahead. Put the life ring out on the port side and trail it astern.”

They both repeated back what I’d said to make it certain to me that they had understood.

Adam asked, “Do you think it’s Will?”

“We can only hope. And pray.” Or it might have been a random plastic bag of trash, or a half-submerged metal drum. I kept looking through the PVS-14 and saw more white sparkles around the dark blob. No, it couldn’t be an inanimate object. Something was splashing the water around it.

I called back, “Barry, slow to eight-hundred and be ready to go to neutral. Your course is good—hold this course.” The dark shape was only a couple hundred yards ahead at most.

“Gino—is the life ring out?”

“Affirmative, boss. The life ring is out on the port side.”

“Gino, turn on the spreader lights and the aft deck lights.” In a few moments we were lighting up our acre of ocean, and I could see that we were going to pass the shape close down our port side. Now the greatest risk was running it over with our forty-ton schooner. I could see arms slapping the water, the details were becoming clear. It had to be Will! But what was the dark shape that he was clinging to?

I didn’t need the night vision anymore and I handed the NOD back to Adam for him to take another look for himself. At a hundred yards I could see we were going to miss him to port by five or ten yards, and this is what I wanted. From this distance he didn’t disappear in the troughs between the swells.

As we drew nearer I called back, “Barry! Go to neutral, and hold this course.”

After just a moment I heard, “In neutral, holding course.” Even without the propeller spinning our inertia would carry us onward for another hundred yards at least. The dark shape was Will Padgett clinging onto something. We were going to pass him by just a few yards off our port beam while our coasting speed dropped to only about one knot. Without the steadying effects of the wind against our sails or any significant forward speed, Rebel Yell was rolling in the swells and staggering like a drunken sailor.

"Will!" I called out. "We're dragging a life ring—grab the rope and we'll bring you to the boat." The engine idling in neutral at the other end was nearly inaudible up on the bow, so I knew that he could hear me. When Will came under the cone of illumination from our spreader lights I could see him nodding that he understood. His arms were wrapped around the dark blob but he managed to give a thumbs-up as we passed.

I said to Adam, "We're done here. Take care of the NOD, and let's go back." I scurried aft. Gino had taken control of the recovery once Will was visible from the cockpit. Barry was behind the wheel, both searchlights were off. The life ring was being towed toward Will as Rebel Yell made a final slow turn to port. The yellow rope reached him as we came to a stop.

Rebel was bucking like a rocking horse and our bow and stern were alternately rising and dropping in the swells. Luke and Gino climbed down onto the platform. The entire scene was lit in brilliant white light. Will and the dark blob were just a dozen yards off our stern.

Gino pulled in the rope until the orange life ring reached Will and he was able to grab it. Gino continued pulling in the rope until Will was only a couple yards from our stern. Luke told him, "Don't try to grab the boat—we'll grab you."

With the boat pitching and rolling, Will could be bashed over the head by our boarding platform coming down on him. Luke crouched at the port side of the platform while behind him Gino pulled the line in slowly. Luke grabbed the life ring when it was close enough, and when our stern plunged again he pulled Will over onto the momentarily submerged platform. When it came back up, Will was on it!

Luke and Gino pulled him up to his feet and then Adam dragged him up the transom and onto the aft deck, where he collapsed, hacking and choking. I rolled him onto his side so that he could vomit and cough out some of the seawater he'd swallowed and inhaled.

Will wasn't wearing his parka; instead, its dark fabric was pressed against his chest. Adam asked him, "Is this what you were holding onto, your coat all full of air?"

Will coughed again and said, "Yeah—full of air."

The parka's sleeves were tied together behind his back. The hood's string was cinched around the parka's neck. The draws-string at the bottom had also been drawn tight. The blob we had seen was Will clinging to his inflated military Gore-Tex parka, with its sleeves under his arms and around his back.

23

Will began to shiver, his shivers turning into uncontrollable shakes. He had been in the ocean for two hours, barefoot, in a thin shirt and jeans. The water temperature was below eighty degrees Fahrenheit, and the boy had no body fat on his frame. I untied his parka's sleeves and pulled it off him, then scooped him up in my arms under his back and his knees. At sixteen years old he couldn't have weighed ninety pounds. He put an arm around my neck and I carried him like a sleepy child.

I didn't have a plan other than taking him below. Passing the helm and stepping from cockpit seat across to cockpit seat as the boat lurched, I told Gino and Barry to get us back under sail heading east, and to kill the motor when they'd done it.

Tala met me in the pilothouse. Met us both.

I said, "He's so cold—we need to get him warm."

"Put him in our bathtub. The motor is going a long time so we have hot water." She went ahead of me down the ladder, and steadied us from below coming into the galley. I felt the Cat diesel clunk into gear, and heard its RPMs climbing again.

Our hot water tank had a heat exchanger plumbed into the engine's seawater discharge line. Rebel Yell had hot running water in two situations: when we were in a marina hooked up to AC shore power—which was never—and when the engine had been running for a while. So we had hot water.

The bottom of Rebel's sitting tub was above the waterline so that it emptied down a hose into the sea by gravity like any boat's galley or bathroom sink. This left the top of the tub at our chest level. The opposite side of the tub was the hull itself. Three more plates formed its sides, and a curved plate was its bottom. All of them were more or less a meter square.

There were steps for climbing up into it, and this quickly became second nature. Once you were sitting in the bathtub, with its sides as high as your shoulders, there was zero risk of falling out no matter what the boat was doing. And unlike the old dusty steel up in the bow by the speedometer sensor, the sitting tub in the captain's cabin's head was finished in smooth and glossy enamel paint, with rounded corners and edges.

Tala got the warm water running through the handheld nozzle and let it run down Will's shoulders. He leaned against the back of the tub and asked, "Is this heaven?"

I said, "No, Will, you're back on Rebel Yell. You fell off the boat and you were in the ocean, but we found you."

He smiled up at me, his slitted eyes closing. "No, Captain Kilmer, no. I d-didn't fall off the boat. No, I was pushed off."

"Pushed? Tala, can you get some dry clothes for Will?"

"What? *Now* you want me to get dry clothes? And you are joking on me? No, Danny, I am not leaving. Tell us, Will, who pushed you? Who?"

He half-opened his eyes and he looked up at her. "It was Mike. Mike pushed me off the boat."

Mike Ortega, the fortunate son of Kiawah Island.

I asked him, "What happened, Will? We need to know."

"Oh, yes, w-we n-need to know, we *all* need to know. . ."

Tala continued to run the shower nozzle's warm water across his shoulders and back and down his chest while unbuttoning his shirt. I felt the boat's motion changing and we began to heel to starboard, so we were under sail again.

I asked him again, "What happened, Will?"

"M-mike Ortega pushed me off the boat. Mike did it." He was still shivering heavily from his two hours in the ocean.

"When?" Establishing the timeline was critical.

"W-when I came up for my watch. I said Hi to Mike and I went back to take a leak like usual. I was leaning on the stern railing. My pee will hit my parka in the wind, so I have to hold it around my back and under my arm. Then I was pushed real hard in the back—and then I was in the ocean."

"It was Mike, Mike for sure? Who else was there? Where was Adam? Where was Barry?"

"I didn't see Barry. Oh, wait: Adam woke me up. He said my watch was starting next, at two, so I went up to the cockpit but I had to take a leak, and then I was in the ocean. Mike was at the wheel. Nobody else was there, so it had to be him."

I asked Will, "What time was it when you went up?"

"I don't know, I'm not sure. I forgot to look at the galley clock when I went by it. I went up to the cockpit, I said Hi to Mike, I went to take a leak—and then I was in the ocean."

"And you're *sure* it was Mike?"

"Nobody else was back there. Not unless they were hiding on the swim platform, maybe."

Tala said, "I am going to cut him into bait for the fishing." Her eyes were narrowed and her nostrils were flaring.

I said, "Maybe tomorrow, but not tonight. Will, where did you learn how to make your parka into a flotation device?"

"A what? Oh, flotation, I understand. My father had a real old Boy Scout Handbook. I can see it like it's right here. BSA, 1975. It was his father's." Will held up three fingers, with his thumb and little finger crossed in front making the Boy Scout salute, but shaking as he quivered with chill.

"I memorized that handbook, almost. I saw it in there, or maybe another book, about making things into life preservers. Pants, mostly, but it's the same idea. And thanks for coming back for me, Captain Kilmer. Thanks for coming back. Oh, I just *knew* you'd come back. I just *knew* it. I *prayed* for it."

"Were you in the Boy Scouts, Will?"

"No, no, we just had the old Boy Scout Handbook."

His big green eyes were fixed onto mine.

Tala had peeled off his shirt and was running the warm water down his bare chest. Will Padgett was so small and pale. The body of a child, but the soul of a hero. And a survivor.

"Will, you can't tell anybody what happened yet. You can stay back here in our cabin. We'll tell everybody that you have hypothermia and you can't get in your hammock. I'll say that you're in shock and you can't talk. Don't talk to anybody until I say, not a word. Do you understand what I'm telling you?"

He smiled up at me. "Oh, yes, I understand you, Captain Kilmer. I *always* understand you. Even when *you* don't, I do."

"I know you do, son. Now, Tala, honey, will you *please* get Will some dry clothes, and put him in our bed and cover him up and make him warm? I have to go face the music. And no more talk about cutting anybody into bait. Not tonight."

That would be *my* decision. The captain's. Mine alone.

The twins had slept through it all, bless their souls.

I went forward to the galley. The engine was off. We were on port tack and heeled about ten degrees to starboard, so we were sailing, but not fast. The wind pressure on the sails and our forward speed reduced our pitching and rolling to a tolerable level compared to when we were dead in the water.

My first inclination was to charge up the ladder and back to the cockpit. Tala wanted to cut Mike into fish bait, but I was thinking of pushing him overboard the way he'd pushed Will. But there was a lot to consider before I made an irrevocable decision. There were thirteen souls on board, including children. A rash decision might be a bad one for reasons I couldn't even yet fathom.

I looked at the galley clock and then at my own watch. Splitting the difference between them it was 0420. What time had we picked up Will? What time had he gone overboard? My pencil sketch of our search pattern was in the cockpit with the times of our turns marked at their corners. Had I given it to Barry last, or to Gino? I sat down at the dinette table staring at the clock to gather my thoughts.

Sofia came into the galley through the cargo hold. There were so many people to keep track of. So many moving parts.

She said, "We found Will, thank God. What happened?"

"I have some ideas, and I'm trying to figure it all out. Tala is with him in our cabin. He's very cold, he has hypothermia, she's warming him up. Listen, can you do something for me?"

"Of course, Dan, anything."

"Go up to the cockpit, but just to the pilothouse door, and tell Gino you need him down below for something. Think of a reason, but don't tell him it's to see me, okay? Then we'll talk some more." First, I needed to get my first mate on board with my evolving plans. But we had to be on the same page.

She was quickly back with her husband. I gestured across the dinette table and they both sat opposite me.

I said, "I can't remember where I left the search map."

Gino pulled the folded scrap of notepaper from a pocket and flattened it on the table between us, so it was facing me.

"Who's still in the cockpit? I'm trying to make a mental picture, and every detail is important."

He said, "Luke is steering, it's his watch now. Jessie is with him. Barry, Adam and Mike are in the cockpit too. Rita is up forward. She wanted to be with her mother tonight. She was really upset about Will going overboard."

I said, "And the twins are in the aft cabin with Tala and Will, so I that's a full muster, all thirteen. Finding Will was a miracle. We put him in the bathtub to warm him up since we had hot water from the engine running. He told us that Adam came down to get him up for his watch, and when he went up Mike was steering. He said he went to the stern to take a leak, and then he was pushed overboard, and only Mike was there. That's what Will said, and I believe him. But he didn't see Mike do it, because his back was to him."

Gino said, "Then Mike needs to go for a swim, just like Will. But this time we don't go back to look for him."

"Maybe, but we need to know for sure. Will didn't see who pushed him in and he wasn't clear on the time. So far it's just his word, and that's not enough to take a man's life. Barry told me that he went up at about five-before-two, and he didn't see Adam or Will, and Mike asked him to take over. But Mike said the turnover was right at 0200. And Barry shouldn't have taken the wheel anyway; he's just a number-two. They both should have waited for me. Something's not adding up."

Sofia said, "Well, if and when it adds up, then Mike is a killer. But why Will? What does he have against the boy?"

"I can't figure that out. Because of all the attention Will got over the speedometer? Jealousy? Or maybe to try to blame Barry for it? I know that Mike hates Barry for some reason. Remember what he said about Barry's shackle? That maybe it wasn't on him just to keep him from running away? And on the other hand Barry is no saint—I know that for sure. I'll tell you what, Gino—send Adam down. I want to talk to each of them separately. And Sofia, can you see if Tala needs anything? Will needs new dry clothes, and nothing fits him."

She left for the aft cabin and Gino went up the ladder. I switched sides at the table so that my back was to the cargo hold bulkhead and I could see anybody coming down into the galley. I had my dive watch, but I wanted the witnesses to be looking at the ship's clock above my head. In a minute Adam came down. I pointed to the other side of the table and he sat. Nice looking kid. It had been a while since his wind-tousled blonde hair had seen a comb, but what did that matter?

I said, "What a night! But we found Will, and that's all that matters." It wasn't all, but I wanted to put him at ease.

"How is he? Is he okay?"

"He was in cold water for a long time, and he's got hypothermia. He's still in shock and he can barely talk, but I think he'll be okay, at least physically. Psychologically, now that's another question." I pushed the sketch of our search pattern toward him across the table. He studied it, and then he looked up at the galley clock behind me.

"Adam, when I woke you up in your hammock I asked you where Will was, and you said that he was on watch. How did you know this? Did you wake him up?"

"Yes, captain. I woke him up and I told him."

"What time was this?"

"My watch ended at two. Anyway, it was *supposed* to end at two. Mike said I looked tired and I could go down early. He said he wasn't tired, and he could handle the rest of it alone."

"What time was that?"

"Quarter of two, maybe? I went down and I gave Barry a shake and he said, 'Yeah, yeah, I'm awake.' And then I gave Will a push, and he seemed awake enough and I rolled into my hammock. We've done this a bunch of times, but it's always harder in the middle of the night."

"Did Mike ever let you go off watch early before?"

"Maybe a few minutes. Only the helmsman can really see the time on the wheel watch. I mostly go by the galley clock."

"When you were on watch with Mike, did he seem okay? Did anything seem different tonight?"

"No, not really. Some of the time I was in the pilothouse listening to the radio. Oh, I heard something about Texas."

"Texas? We'll get to that later. Did Mike say anything to you about Will or Barry that maybe seemed unusual?"

"Tonight? Not really, but I'd say he doesn't care much for Barry. I'd say he has a very low opinion of him. I try to stay out of that kind of talk, you know, like spreading rumors about people when they're not around. It's not Christian."

"What kind of rumors do you mean? You can tell me. It might be important."

"Oh, just that nobody got a shackle put on them unless it was for a real good reason. Like maybe they were dangerous."

"Okay, Adam, thanks. And you're not in any trouble, not at all. In fact, *you* found Will. *You* found him, so you saved his life. If you hadn't spotted him, he'd still be out there, and as cold as he was he couldn't have lasted much longer. But now I want you to do something for me. I want you to get in your hammock, even if you can't sleep. I'll explain why later."

"Can I have some water first?"

"Yes, of course you can. Just use the cup by the sink. Oh, but before that, I've got one more job for you. Go up and tell Barry to come down."

After Adam returned from that task, he had his drink of water and disappeared behind me into the cargo hold.

Barry came down next. I gestured for him to sit across from me. The scrapes on the side of his face were scabbed over and healing, and the bruising was not as dark. It would take a week to know if he'd be left with more scars. It was going to take even longer for his buzz cut to grow out. I said, "You did a good job on the search tonight. First class. Here's the map we made, it's a keeper. We found Will, and that's what matters."

"How is he doing?" He picked up the notepaper sketch of the expanding box search pattern and studied it.

"He was in cold water all alone and scared out of his wits for two hours, but I think he'll be all right, physically at least. He was pretty hypothermic and he can't talk. He's still kind of in shock. But there's a few things I just can't figure out. You said that when you got up to the cockpit you didn't see Adam or Will, right?"

"That's right, they weren't there. Just Mike."

"You said that Mike left the helm and went down early. Did you ever do a watch turnover early like that?"

"Well, during the day it's more informal."

"I understand that. But did you ever take over the helm early at night? Did Mike ever go below early on night watch?"

"Captain Kilmer, I've only been steering for one day!"

"Oh, right. But didn't you think it was strange, not seeing me or Adam or Will when you did the turnover with Mike?"

"I guess I did, but I didn't know what else I was supposed to do. I steered by myself when you were doing that thing with the speedometer. I guess I didn't really know exactly what I was supposed to do when Mike said he didn't feel good and he was going to go down early. I guess I figured that you or Will would be coming up in a minute. Anyway, I was sitting right there in the cockpit and Mike said he didn't feel good and he was going below. What should I have done? He got up and he left. I mean, I had to take the wheel or we would have gone off course. He didn't ask me, not really, he just said it and then he was gone. Then you came up and we couldn't find Will, and then all hell broke loose."

Sofia returned from the aft cabin and went past us into the cargo hold and forward without saying a word.

We were both silent until she was gone, and then I asked Barry, "Who woke you up for your watch?"

"Adam gave me a little shove when he came down, but I was already awake, just sort of waiting. I get like that when I know I have a watch coming up. Sometimes I can't sleep."

"Adam said that he got Will up after he knew you were already awake. Then why did Will get up to the cockpit before you did? That doesn't make sense if you were already awake."

"Will asked me if I was awake when he passed by, and I said I was, and I'd be up in a few minutes. I was doing a lot of thinking there in my hammock. I wanted Will to go up first so he'd already be with you in the cockpit when I got up there. I guess I wasn't up for another conversation like last night."

"Okay, Barry. Now, to the best of your knowledge, what time did you get on deck? What time did you take the wheel?"

"After Mike went below, when I looked at the watch on the wheel hub, I think it said like ten before two. The hands on the wheel watch aren't as clear as the galley clock, and they're usually a minute or two different."

"When you come up for watch at night, who is up in the cockpit first, usually? Of the three of us in our watch section."

"You're there first, most times. And then me or Will."

Then I thought: we usually go back to the stern to take a leak before taking over the watch for the next two hours. But this time Will had come up first, and early. Then I wondered if Mike would have pushed Barry overboard instead of Will, if Barry had come up first? Was this murderous plan already in his mind when he sent Adam down early? Had he switched his target based upon whoever appeared first? Maybe even me?

"Thanks, Barry. I'm just trying to sort a few things out in my mind, for the record. Some of it's still a little confusing. But you did a good job tonight on the helm during the search. We should be proud of what we did. It's almost unheard of to find somebody who went overboard at night. Will is going to be okay, he's in the aft cabin now getting warm. Adam is up in his hammock. And now I want you to get into your hammock too, even if you're not tired, and then just stay there while I try to figure everything out."

"I didn't push Will off the boat, if that's even what you're thinking. I didn't do it. I swear to— I swear I didn't do it."

"You and Mike don't get along very well, do you?"

"What's that got to do with anything?"

"I'm just trying to see the whole picture."

"Well, if Mike doesn't get along with me, it's not because of anything I ever said or did to him. I really don't care about him one way or the other. We have nothing in common."

"I understand. That's all, Barry. And you did a great job on helm tonight. We found Will, and that was a miracle."

While I was thinking of my next move, Jessie Hanahan came down the ladder. Now only Gino, Luke and Mike were up on deck and presumably in the cockpit, with Luke at the wheel.

Jessie was wearing Tala's red fleece jacket, and black leggings that might have belonged to Tala or Sofia. At least the women were getting along well—and thank God for that. She was holding an empty water bottle, but instead of going to the galley sink to fill it she came over and sat across from me. Her blonde hair was tied back in a single braid, and it occurred to me that Adam and Barry, who had just been sitting in her place, were also blue-eyed blondes. As Luke's number-two, Jessie coming down to fill up his water bottle was routine and to be expected. But sitting down with the captain, uninvited, during a secret inquest, was not. She was visibly agitated.

She said, "I can only stay for a minute. I think we know what's going on. Luke and I thought the same thing as soon as we heard Will was overboard. We didn't say anything before this because we try to get along with everybody, we really do, and telling tales out of school is no way for Christians to act. But we know some things about Mike Ortega that you ought to know, from back on the island."

"Oh, really? Like what?"

"Like he says he was a V-I-W like Barry, but that's not true. He never did any of that indentured farm work. He came to the island on a sailboat, and he was loaded. He bought his way into the top of Beaufort's social crowd from day one. He had lots of guns and gold, that's what everybody said. And I know for a fact he was a big pal of Roy Aikman, Captain Roy Aikman. He wasn't in that militia boat just by the luck of the draw, no. Mike and Roy were buddies. Mike was roommates with one of Roy's best friends in a real nice house in the same neighborhood. Mike even had a car, they all did. I just thought you should know. Now I've got to go back up."

"Wait a minute, Jessie, wait a minute. What do *you* think really happened tonight?"

"I think Will knew all about Mike Ortega, the real story. Will Padgett worked in a little orchard up on the north end of the island. They had a fruit stand, and they sold jelly too, and pies, stuff like that, and sometimes Will worked there. People knew Will. He's kind of unforgettable, like a cute little elf, or a leprechaun, and he knew a lot of the customers. And when he did the wagon thing on market days he probably heard even more stories when he was pushing his cart for people who had money. Maybe that's why Mike did it, and maybe it's not. But no matter why he did it, I think Mike threw him overboard and then he planned for Barry to take the blame. And to me, that's just as bad as what he did to Will. I can't prove a bit of it, but it's what Luke and I think. And that means maybe we're next, because Mike knows that we know all about him from back on the island. And now I've really got to go back up."

She stood, went to the galley sink and filled the water bottle, then climbed the ladder up to the pilothouse.

It was time for an intervention. This poisonous state of affairs among the crew had to be dealt with immediately, like a snake bite, before it spread. I put the sketch of our search pattern in my pocket. But if Mike was physically dangerous, I didn't want to take any chances, so I went back to the aft cabin first. There were a couple items I wanted to have on me before I went up to the cockpit, and I retrieved both of them silently.

The twins were sleeping through it all. Tala was sleeping on the low side of our bed against the lee cloth, under covers with Will so she could warm him with her body heat. I was as quiet as possible in order not to disturb them. Their snuggling together didn't bother me in the least. Hell, I'd cuddled with some damned ugly Marines through bitter cold nights. When you're edging into hypothermia the concept of maintaining a polite social distance is quickly overcome. Then you do what you have to do to keep from freezing, and you're grateful for every square foot and inch of shared body warmth.

I went back up to the pilothouse. Gino and Jessie had spoken to me at the table, but as far as Luke and Mike were concerned I could have been down below tending to Will the entire time I'd been out of their sight.

I stepped up into the cockpit and stood leaning against the back of the pilothouse. Luke was standing behind the wheel. Jessie was sitting just in front of the pedestal on the low side staring at the side of the glowing compass. Gino was sitting behind Luke also on the low side leaning against the back rest. Mike was further back and across from him on the high side to port with his legs braced across the gap between the bench seats. There was no escaping the tension. I stood there, taking it all in. Patches of stars were visible among the broken overcast. The moon was gone.

"How is Will doing?" Luke finally asked.

I replied, "I was just with him. He's sleeping now. Tala is nursing him. He was pretty hypothermic, and he swallowed a lot of salt water, but I think he'll be okay."

"Did he say what happened, how he fell overboard?"

Until that moment I hadn't decided what tack I was going to take. Somehow I knew I'd just have to read the situation in the moment when I was there. And now I was there.

"Yeah, Luke, he told me how he fell overboard. Only he said he didn't fall. He said he was pushed."

"He was pushed? How did that happen? Who did it? Who pushed him over?" Luke didn't seem especially surprised to hear that Will had been pushed over the side. Jessie had just told me they had already come to the same conclusion.

"He said he didn't see who did it. He just said that he was pushed overboard." Strictly speaking this was not a lie, even if it was not the complete truth. I didn't say anything more; I let it hang there. Will had been pushed overboard. This was the action of a would-be murderer who was still aboard. The most improbable part of the entire drama was that we had found Will, and he had not drowned far behind us.

Then Mike said, "Captain Kilmer, you know I hate to be the one to have to say this, but it must have been the stowaway, Barry. I just *knew* he'd be a problem. VIWs don't get shackled unless they're dangerous. This just proves it."

He pronounced it *views*, just like Barry. Everybody else spelled it out, V-I-W. So if Jessie was right, and Mike Ortega had never been a farm worker on the island, why did he say it the same way as Barry, who had been one for sure? And why did he profess to know jack shit about V.I.W. shackle policies on the island? Nobody else had. I sure didn't know.

"Mike, it's really terrible to hear that about him. It's just terrible. So what time did you turn over the helm to him?"

"At about the regular time, skipper. About 0200."

"Was Adam still up here in the cockpit?"

"Adam? No, I think I let him go a little early. He seemed tired, he was nodding off. It was almost the end of our shift, so I said he could go below early. No big deal. I wasn't tired, and I knew you'd be up on deck soon."

"Except I wasn't, was I? I guess that I overslept. So Barry came up, and you turned the helm over to him?"

"That's what happened. I knew you'd be up in a minute."

"And what about Will? What time did Will come up?"

"I never saw Will, not during my watch. Not once."

"So I guess he overslept too. It happens. But wasn't Adam supposed to wake him up?"

"Well, sure, he's *supposed* to, but they're both kids, and you know how it is." Mike chuckled nervously. "Maybe Adam forgot, or maybe Will didn't wake up all the way. But after Adam went down I never saw Will, just Barry."

"So, if Will is pretty sure that somebody pushed him over the side, who do you think did it?"

"Well, when you lay it out that way, I guess it *must* have been Barry. I'd already gone down below. And to tell you the truth, I'm not surprised."

"Why? Because of his shackle?"

"Yes sir, his shackle. And have you seen the scars on his arms? The burn scars? They're not the kind of scars you get from a fire. I'll bet he had criminal gang tattoos burned off. They do that. And what's up with his face? He must have been in a bad fight before he stowed away. Like a criminal. Yeah, I think there's something wrong with Mr. Conway's story."

"But why would he push Will overboard?"

Mike paused before answering. "Well, you got me there, skipper. I guess because he's a psycho, or a criminal. Maybe Will said something that set him off? Or maybe he was jealous because of all the attention that Will got for the speedometer. Who knows how psychos think?" He laughed uneasily.

"Yeah, Mike, I suppose you're right. But there's something I just can't figure out." I pulled the search pattern sketch map from my pocket and held it up. "We turned around at 0215, fifteen minutes after you said you gave the helm to Barry. So fifteen minutes after we turned around, at 0230, we were about back to the same place where you did the turnover. That's when you said Barry took over and you went below.

"But we didn't find Will until almost four in the morning, after we did a whole box search all the way around. But if you measure it out in a straight line back along 300 degrees, we found Will back where we were quite a while before 0200. That's what's got me all confused. If Barry pushed him over after 0200, we should have found him sooner, and not after that whole box search. I'm just trying to understand the whole sequence of events, that's all."

"Well, if Barry said we did the turnover a little bit early, maybe he was right. Maybe it was before two."

"But that still doesn't account for where we picked him up. How would *you* explain it?"

"How? Ahh, well, maybe the currents where Will went in the water were different than the currents where the boat was going after Barry pushed him overboard?"

"No, I don't think so. Not that different." I stared at him.

"Maybe your search map is wrong. I mean, it's really just guesswork, making all those turns. Like dead reckoning."

"No, I think the search map is pretty good." I stared at him, and he turned away. "You know, Mike, I think it would have worked if we just hadn't found Will. That really messed everything up for you, didn't it? Yeah, if we hadn't found him, it probably would have worked. It would have been a toss-up between you and Barry, and who would have believed a stowaway with all those scars, and a shackle on his leg like a criminal?"

"I'm telling you the truth, captain—I'm not lying. I swear to God, captain, I swear to God I'm telling you the truth!"

I drew my Glock from under my sweater and let it hang in my hand. With my other hand I pulled the handcuffs from my left pocket and tossed them to Gino. I'd had a feeling it might end this way when I'd gone back to fetch my pistol.

"Cuff him to the Dushka, Gino. We're going to get all the way to the bottom of this sad, sorry situation. If you're telling the truth, Mike, then you have nothing to worry about."

"I swear to God almighty I'm not lying, captain! I didn't push Will overboard. I would *never* do a thing like that."

"Well, we'll know for sure pretty soon." I stepped around the wheel and past Luke, the Glock still casually at my side, stopping just a yard from Mike and looming over him. "Gino, you need any help with that?"

"No boss, I got this. Make it easy, man." Gino grabbed a sleeve of Mike's USMC desert-digital militia shirt, cuffed his wrist, pulled him back across the aft deck and snapped the other cuff around the Dushka's back tripod leg. Mike appeared to be stunned by the rapid turn of events and didn't resist. My pistol was only there to ensure compliance.

I'd owned the Glock 9mm for years, but the cuffs were a recent addition from the Beaufort Militia. When I'd grabbed the police handcuffs off the console of the militia Whaler last Saturday night I hadn't seen a key, so we'd have to make one. Until then, Mike Ortega was going absolutely nowhere.

"You have it all wrong, captain, all wrong. I swear to God I'm not lying. *Barry* did it, I *know* he did it. He's a sociopath, and you can't believe a word they say! They're all liars!"

"Shut up, Mike it won't help your case. I'm tired, and we all need to sleep. We'll sort it out tomorrow. Well, no, I guess it's tomorrow already."

The horizon ahead of us was beginning to lighten.

I said, "Gino, it's almost time for your watch. You got it? You're good to go? Do you want me to go get Rita?"

"No, boss, it's early, we have time. We'll be ready."

Luke said, "Jessie and I can handle it until six."

I gave one more look back at Mike. He seemed to be in shock while sitting on the deck shackled to the Dushka. Did he present any more danger that night? I judged not. Even if he stretched far forward he couldn't reach the helmsman.

Then I told Gino, "If he gets too mouthy—gag him."

24

Actually, I did have a handcuff key on board, but it took me some time to recall this fact, and even more time to remember where it was stashed. I used to carry them hidden in my pants inside the beltline, but that had been years ago. The keys were the same, because American cops often lost or swapped their handcuffs as prisoners were transferred between them.

After all the hullabaloo of the past night I knew that it was going to be hard for me to sleep much past dawn, but I was tired and I needed some horizontal time. The twins were still asleep in their aft cabin nest. Tala had her back against the lee cloth on the low side, with Will's back curled against her and just their faces visible above the blanket. They'd earned their rest and I wasn't going to disturb it by climbing in to join them. With the boat heeled that way I'd roll down onto them.

That left me the cargo hold. Mike's hammock to port was empty, of course, and to starboard, Barry was breathing loudly while grinding his teeth. Adam was also deep in sleep a dozen feet up the aisle on the port side. I hadn't lied when I had told the cargo-hold boys that if they could adapt to sleeping in the hammocks, that they'd be better off for it. Whether the boat was heeled to port or to starboard, or rolling like a pig dead-downwind, it was all good to a sailor in a hammock.

Since my own berth was occupied, and Will's hammock was vacant, I decided to test it out. I leaned against the cargo on the starboard side and managed to juggle myself one limb at a time up into his hammock and then wriggled myself onto my back. I just needed a nap, and I thought it might be a good opportunity to recap the past night and ponder the coming day.

Will Padgett had nearly died, lost behind us in the ocean. Mike Ortega stood accused of pushing him overboard in what was a clear act of attempted premeditated murder. But he was loudly proclaiming that Barry Conway had done the deed, and that Barry was a dangerous psycho who could not be believed under any circumstance. Barry the thief, Barry the stowaway. Even Barry the cannibal. So there was that. No denying it.

The ceiling was touching distance above me and just visible in the dim light. The hammock barely moved, but the ceiling rolled from side to side like a slow visual metronome.

I slept until eight when Tala nudged me awake. After falling out of the hammock I clambered up the galley ladder. A quick look around from the pilothouse showed me that Gino was steering and the sky was mostly clear. I had missed getting a morning celestial fix on a star but it looked good for a noon sun sight. I downed a bowl of oatmeal mush at the table facing the clock and the barometer while I gathered my thoughts.

The duty roster on the corkboard said that Mike and Adam had the watch. Well, we could cross Mike off the list. And if Mike Ortega was a killer, we had to do something about him and do it quickly. Keeping him handcuffed to the Dushka was only a short-term solution. He'd be a problem and a danger to us all no matter where we chained him, if only by the bitter dissention his words could cause. Mike was smooth, polished, and clever—and his tongue could tear our crew apart.

Delivering him to some land-based police station was out of the question. The only jurisdiction was Rebel Yell, and the only judge and jury were the other twelve of us aboard. Ten, keeping the twins out of it.

On the back of the box-search sketch I wrote down the times when Adam told Barry and Will they had to go up for the next watch, and when they actually got up to the cockpit, according to each of them. According to Adam, Mike said he felt fine and he could finish the watch solo, but according to Barry, Mike said that he didn't feel well and he needed to go down early. That was a major discrepancy. I studied the search map again, and went over the times. And then a new test came into my mind, so I tore two pieces of brown paper from a bag and I found a second pencil.

Then I announced we'd have an all-hands meeting in the cockpit at nine to discuss last night. Each of them that I told was to inform the others of the time and place. This didn't take long on a sixty-foot boat.

We met in the cockpit and on the aft side decks at 0900. Rita was minding the twins in the forward cabin at my own request. I stood by the pilothouse facing Mike, who was sitting on the aft deck handcuffed to the Dushka. Gino was steering.

It was nothing like the atmosphere during our first crew meeting after escaping from Beaufort, or when we caught the wahoo and had the fish feast and the guitar sing-along. It was grim, and I had no law books to guide me through it. The only authority was the authority that I could muster within myself. *God please grant me wisdom.* Deep breath. Exhale quietly.

I began. "We all know why we're here. Will says he was pushed overboard around two in the morning. He says that Mike was the only person in the cockpit, and he was pushed from behind when he was standing at the starboard quarter leaning against the rail there. Is that what happened, Will?"

He replied, "Yes, sir, that's exactly what happened."

As the captain I was both the judge and the prosecutor. I recapped the inconsistencies in Mike's timeline, and how if he had turned over the helm to Barry at 0200 as he said, and not ten or fifteen minutes before that, we would have found Will sooner along our reciprocal course back toward the northwest. Where we had actually found Will was the proof of Mike's lie. And if we had never found Will, then Mike's lie might have been believed, and Barry would have been blamed for Will's death. So not only did Mike Ortega plan out one premeditated murder, he planned to have an innocent man take the blame.

When I was finished I asked Mike to either admit to the charge against him, or to deny it and make his own case.

"It's not true, captain, it's not true at all. I never saw Will last night, not from the time when you put in the speedometer until the time we picked him up out of the water. Okay, yes, I let Adam go a little early, but that doesn't prove anything. And I'm not sure where Barry was all the time anyway. I might have dozed off and he could have slipped by me and hidden down on the swim platform, waiting there for Will. A lot of things could have happened. Even Will says he didn't see who pushed him. Maybe he just fell overboard and he doesn't want to admit it, and he felt like he had to blame somebody else for it. Anything could have happened! The only thing I know for sure is that *I didn't do it*."

I just looked at him for a good half a minute. "Okay, Mike, so your theory is that maybe Barry snuck past you, hid on the swim platform, pushed Will overboard, and then what? Hid on the swim platform again? And then somehow he just turned up in the cockpit and you just turned the wheel over to him like everything was normal? Is that right? And your other theory is that maybe Will fell overboard, and then he decided to blame you for it? That doesn't make sense either. The only story that makes sense is what Will said: you pushed him over, and then you went below when Barry came up, so he'd take the blame."

"I didn't do it. Somebody's lying, and I don't know why."

"You told Adam he could go down early because he was nodding off, and you told him you were good to go for the rest of the watch. But when Barry came up you told him you didn't feel well, and you left the wheel and went below early. Don't you see the conflict there?"

"They're lying. I don't know why, but they are."

"Which one? Who's lying, Adam or Barry?"

Mike didn't respond. I think he felt cornered, but for the sake of the crew I wanted to make the case even stronger. It was time to open up a new approach. To my thinking this was like getting a navigational fix by using more than one or two lines of position. Where all the lines crossed was the truth.

"Okay, Mike, last night I was told that you were never a Voluntary Indentured Worker on the island. I was told that you came to the island with enough gold to buy your way out of being a farm worker, and not only that, but you were a good friend of Captain Aikman. So, is this true, or not true?

He appeared surprised to hear this. "No, captain, it's not true. I don't know why they're telling you all these lies."

"Then you *were* a V-I-W when you came to the island? That's what you told me, that the militia confiscated the guns and the gold that you brought from your house on Kiawah Island, and they put you on a farm as a V-I-W. You already told me you came to Beaufort with gold, your father's prepper gold, and now I've been told that you never worked on a farm. So did you, or didn't you? Were you ever a V-I-W?"

"Of course I was a VIW; everybody has to work on a farm when they come to the island."

Again he pronounced it *view*. And he was wrong about everybody coming to the island serving as a V.I.W. Jim and Judy Walker had avoided the period of farm work because he was a physician and she was a nurse. So why not somebody who arrived with his missing father's gold stash and guns?

"Then you must have gone through quarantine on Parris Island at the old Marine Corps Recruit Depot. In that case this will be real easy for you: just make a map of the place. Draw the barracks, the latrines and the chow hall where you spent your month. Just make a rough sketch, and Barry will draw one, and then we'll compare the two." I handed the pieces of brown paper and the pencils to Sofia and they were passed along until Barry and Mike both had their own.

Barry held his paper down on the side deck and began to draw on it. Mike said, "Is this some kind of a joke? What does this prove? What does this have to do with anything?"

I replied, "It goes to your truthfulness. Let's see a map of where you did your month of quarantine and selection."

He held the paper up, let it go and it blew off downwind. "Okay, so I wasn't a *Vee-Eye-W*. What does that prove? What does that have to do with who pushed Will overboard?"

"It proves you're a liar, Mike."

"No, it doesn't prove a goddamn thing! I didn't push Will overboard. And even Will says he didn't see who did it."

"Is that all, Mike? Are you done? Does the defense rest?"

"You have no right to do this, Kilmer, no right at all."

"I'm pretty sure I do, Mike, I'm pretty sure I do. Are you done now? Anything else you'd like to say in your defense?"

"Not that it'll matter, but this whole thing is a bullshit kangaroo court, and you can all go straight to hell."

I let that hang for long moments. "Okay, Mike. You've had your say. You've made your case. Now I'm going to take the wheel, and I want the rest of you to go up on the bow and come back with your verdict. I'll abide by it, whatever it is."

Tala, Sofia, Luke, Jessie, Barry, Adam and Gino filed past me on both sides of the pilothouse. I took the helm when Gino stepped forward. Will did not go to the front with the jury of seven; instead, he went into the pilothouse and down below.

When they were all gone Mike said, "You think you're pretty goddamn fucking smart, don't you, Kilmer?"

I sat on the high side of the cockpit to port just behind the wheel so I could steer and watch him at the same time. "Mike, it's just the two of us now, nobody else. Just us two. Tell me the truth: did you do it? Why?"

"Go fuck yourself, you bastard. I'll see you in hell."

"Maybe you will, and maybe you won't. It's not up to us."

The jury of Mike's peers came back after only five minutes and took their places around the cockpit again. Gino stood in front by the pilothouse door and announced the verdict. I was steering so he was looking past me at Mike sitting all the way in the back, but it felt like he was looking through me.

"Michael Ortega, we find you guilty of the premeditated attempted murder of Mr. Will Padgett. We have decided that you should be pushed off the boat just like you did to Will."

I remembered our team of ex-SAS and ex-IRA throwing the two surviving Moslem pirates off Rebel Yell on our way to the Canaries. That was the day Gino Bracciano came aboard Rebel for the first time. He had been chained in their engine room with a single mandate: keep the propeller turning, or die. According to Gino, those sea-jihad pirates had spent days torturing and sexually abusing a Swedish girl taken from her family's captured sailboat. He had heard all her screams. Our Dushka sent their converted fishing trawler to the bottom, all of them killed by our guns except for the captain and one of his crew. Upon reflection, their deaths by drowning had been too easy.

"Gino, take the wheel. I'm going to go get a few things." I went through the pilothouse and down below, and was soon back with a big black umbrella, a one-gallon jug of water, a rolled-up inflatable dinghy, the handcuff key, and just in case, my Glock on my belt under my sweater. I blew up the yellow PVC dinghy inside the pilothouse in a couple minutes. Fully inflated, it was about seven feet by four feet. The main tube that encircled the inflatable floor was about a foot in diameter. It could accommodate both of the twins or one adult.

Even with the wind dropping, you had to be careful with such things on deck lest they blow out of your hands. I passed it up into the cockpit and told Adam to take it down onto the swim platform and secure it there. Then I brought out the umbrella and the gallon of water. The key was in my pocket.

All eyes were on the yellow dinghy as it was passed to the stern. I handed the big umbrella and the water jug to Luke and then I went to the stern where our prisoner was sitting on deck cuffed to the Dushka.

I said, "Let's do this the easy way, Mike. We're not going to throw you in the water like you did to Will. You're going to have a chance. We're only a few hundred miles from land, and the prevailing winds are going to blow you there. You can use the umbrella for shade and for a sail and to catch rain. If you take it easy on your drinking water you'll have a chance—and that's a lot more than you gave Will last night."

The judge and jury were gathered around him on the back of Rebel Yell. I held up the key and said, "It's time, Mike. Do it like a man." I was curious to see if he'd crack up and try to prevent me from unlocking the cuff from his wrist, but to my surprise he didn't. I left the other cuff on the Dushka's tripod leg. Gino and I pulled him to his feet by the transom. To his credit he didn't beg or fall to pieces. He didn't resist us at all.

"It's up to you, Mike," I told him. "You can take the raft, or you can just go for a swim, like Will. I'll let you decide."

The folded umbrella and the gallon of water were already in the boat down on the platform. Barry dropped Mike's tan militia ball cap into it. Mike climbed down the transom steps, slid the boat into our wake and in the same smooth motion he jumped aboard it, landing on his back. It was a pretty slick transition, I had to admit. But then, living on Kiawah Island, Mike and his friends had all grown up around boats.

He sat up and hollered, "I'll see you in hell, you bastards!" and gave us two middle fingers. Then he pulled on his hat and opened the umbrella and held it toward the west, I think as an act of defiance. It wasn't much of a sail, but at least the big Irish umbrella would give him hope. But more importantly to me, the rest of the crew would not have the memory of Mike Ortega plunging into the ocean and coming up splashing and yelling to haunt their dreams. I knew too much about those dreams, and I wanted to spare my shipmates from them.

It wasn't an act of mercy to give Mike the yellow plastic raft, the umbrella and the gallon jug of water. Instead of dying in just a matter of hours treading water while waiting for the sharks, he'd die over a few days, much more slowly and painfully, with plenty of time for reflection. The sharks would still find him in the end. That yellow raft was trash, about our fifth-string dinghy, really only fit to be a toy for the twins.

When the yellow dot disappeared behind us, the jury finally dispersed. Mike was gone and Adam was steering. Next man up—or boy. It was Mike and Adam's watch until ten, but now Mike was gone for good. I went down to the table facing the corkboard, the clock and the barometer to make a new watch bill and write something for the log. For the voyage narrative log, and not just for the line-by-line data log which listed our course, speed, the wind's direction and velocity and other dry information. The narrative log was in a spiral-bound notebook, the data log was in a smaller foolscap notebook.

The twins stealthily approached from behind and emerged across the table from me below the clock and barometer. Only their heads rose above the mahogany top into my view, but the five-year-olds were both growing by the week. They were in a somber mood. We all were.

Jon asked me, "Why did Mr. Mike go away on our yellow boat, daddy?"

"I thought you boys were up front with Miss Rita?"

Chris said, "We were, but then we went back to the back and we looked out the little window over the big bed. So why did you give Mr. Mike our yellow boat? It's ours."

"He did something really bad, and he can't stay with us on Rebel Yell anymore. He has to go back to the island now."

Jon asked, "What did he do, daddy? Miss Rita said that he pushed Will off the boat last night."

Chris added, "If he did, then I hope our yellow boat sinks."

"Well, boys, that's up to God. That's only up to God."

And right then and there I was so glad that we hadn't just thrown Mike Ortega into our wake for the twins to witness. Or anyone else, for that matter. Even me.

Maybe Mike would make it back to land. And maybe he'd find Jesus somewhere along the way. And maybe I was wrong about everything. Rank has its privileges, and its curses. What if I was wrong? What if I'd made a strong case, but he hadn't actually done it? Mike was a goner for sure in any event, but if he didn't do it, then whoever did do it was still aboard.

But that couldn't be. The case against Mike Ortega was air tight. The would-be killer was gone. For the sake of my sanity, and for the sanity of my crew, Mike had to be the killer.

But what if he wasn't?

25

One of my top priorities was creating an updated watch bill. Our thirteen had become twelve. I didn't want any lingering reminders of Mike Ortega aboard. But no matter how I tried to rearrange the watch teams to work around his absence, it kept coming back to pairing Barry and Adam. Adam had the sailing skill and the knowledge, and between the two of them they'd be strong enough to steer Rebel Yell for two hours.

But I wondered if Adam could accept being subordinated to Barry, who was older by a decade, but who was only a novice sailor. On the other hand, would Barry be comfortable having fifteen-year-old Adam lead their watch team?

I decided to include Will in the discussion. All three of them would have a lot to digest after what had occurred. Sofia passed by on her way up forward and I asked her to tell Gino that I wanted to see him for a moment. When he appeared I told him that I needed to see the three remaining cargo-hold bachelors. He asked me when, and I said now, because I had the watch starting at ten. He said not to worry about the watch starting at ten, but the sky looked perfect for a noon sight.

Of course I missed Victor, but Dr. Aleman was never a first mate like Gino Bracciano was. But then, with a crew of three men and a working autopilot there wasn't as much need for a first mate. And to be fair, while I was more than happy to let Gino work on our engines and electrical systems, he would not be my first choice to repair a slashed brachial artery that was spurting out the precious red stuff at a disturbing rate.

I switched table sides so my back was to the cargo hold bulkhead, and they would be looking up at the clock and the bulletin board. Almost everything on our ocean voyaging boat had to serve multiple purposes, so now the galley dinette table was also the captain's office. While waiting for them to appear I penciled a new watch bill on a piece of lined notepaper.

Even blank notepaper was growing scarce. The days of walking into a store and casually deciding among many sizes and types of notebooks, well, those days were just as gone as ballpoint pens and the internet. There was practically no such thing as paper trash aboard Rebel Yell. Any kind of paper was repurposed multiple times until it was cut down to postage stamp size. Old pencils were re-sharpened with the greatest of care lest a precious quarter-inch of graphite be broken off and wasted. Pencil stubs were placed in pencil holders made from the plastic and metal shells of pens and markers that had dried up years earlier. Their corporate names and logos reminded me of what had been lost when the factories and the ships all stopped moving. Bic, Pilot, Paper Mate, Sharpie.

I seemed to remember a kind of ink pen I'd seen in an old black and white movie, where you dipped the tip of the pen in a jar of liquid ink and drew it inside with a lever. In the movie, this led to an accident where ink was sprayed on another actor, ruining their shirt. So, was this why they were called "fountain pens?" This was a gag line when somebody's white shirt was ruined, but to me a refillable ink pen seemed like pure genius.

Even decent pencils were tiresome to use, and the words they left on paper were light and difficult to read. Wasn't the Declaration of Independence written in black India ink, using a quill pen carved from a goose or turkey feather? Now I was down to using pencil stubs, and any blank paper I could find. Lined note paper was preferred, and graph paper was reserved for important engineering projects. The data and narrative logs were sacrosanct, and I never pirated blank pages from them.

It was quarter to ten. By the last schedule Mike and Adam had the watch. Now it was just Adam. Mike was out there on the yellow raft pulling a one-man watch for the duration. But the seas were down, and the wind was diminishing. His gallon of water might last him a few days. Maybe he'd catch some rainwater in the umbrella.

At least we hadn't thrown him overboard and killed him fast. Fast? No, fast was the way I had killed foreign men I'd never met from hundreds of yards away. And all because my Uncle Sam had told me I should, after the Twin Towers fell. But fast or slow, Dan Kilmer always got the job done. My not-so-proud legacy? Multi-speed *and* multi-mode executioner.

For sure not all of them were righteous kills, and anyway, who was I to decide what was righteous and not? Well, to be fair, some were more righteous than others, like the gang who had raped and torture-murdered a Christian girl in Baghdad. I lost no sleep over most of them. It remained to be seen where Mike Ortega would fit into my dreams.

Fujimo, baby. Fuck you Jack, I'm moving out. Four days after leaving the island aboard Rebel Yell, Mike Ortega was on a yellow raft all alone on a big ocean. Live and learn. Die and your story ends right there. But at least he had a fighting chance. And no matter what he had done before and after last Saturday night, it had honestly been a blast to spend those hours with him on the Whaler motoring down the Beaufort River behind Rebel Yell, and goofing on Major Macgregor on the radio. Now that terrific memory was shared in exactly two living heads, but only for as long as they retained their body temperature and a pulse.

Then where would all the memories go? What a shame if we were just worm food in the end. Maybe I'd become a new ghost haunting Rebel Yell. But what if Rebel's ultimate port-of-call was a hundred fathoms deep? Not much down there in the cold blackness to keep old memories alive, and no living visitors to nudge and tickle with ghostly pranks. No, there had to be something more, something higher. There just had to be. No wonder I was driven to write, even with pencil stubs. But once these pages were finished, who would ever read them? Somebody? Anybody? Nobody? A concern for another day. . .

The cargo-hold boys came out together and sat across from me, Barry sliding over first, then Adam and Will sitting last. Our hard-to-fit starveling was wearing a maroon sweater that had been one of Rita's first serious knitting projects. The shoulders were misaligned, but it looked warm and cozy.

Adam, in the middle, spoke first. “Mr. Bracciano told us we needed to see you about something. He said that Luke and Jessie would steer and he was going to help them on deck, but please don’t forget about the noon sight.”

I checked my watch and they looked at the clock above me. I said, “It’s not even ten yet. What a night, huh? I guess we should talk about it before any more time goes by, instead of just stewing over it and letting it fester. I know it was pretty heavy for all of us, putting Mike off the boat like that.”

Adam replied, “It was a lot heavier when he pushed Will of the boat. He got what he deserved. I wouldn’t have given him the dinghy.” That harsh tone was a surprise coming from Adam. He was a month over fifteen but he was already more of a man than a boy. If only his uncle could see him now.

“Will, how do you feel about it?”

“Honestly, I’m still all messed up about it. At least now I don’t have to worry about him behind me. And I would have liked to have had that yellow dinghy when I was in the water. That’s a lot more than he gave me.”

“Will,” I told him, “that was real smart, what you did with your parka. Adam found you with the NOD, and Barry was steering and keeping track of our turns. We all helped to find you last night. Okay, we need a new watch schedule and I just wrote it. We’re on Day Four.” I turned over the notepaper and pushed it toward Adam. Barry and Will leaned in to study it.

“Will, you’re going to stay with me, but Barry, you’re going to be on with Adam. I think you two will make a good watch team. The only problem I have is that I don’t know who should be the watch leader, and who should be number-two. Adam knows more about sailing, but Barry, you’re older, and bigger, and you have more, ah, life experience. Honestly, I just don’t know how to skin this cat.”

Without hesitation Barry looked at me and said, “Captain Kilmer, the first day we spoke, up on the bow, I said that if you don’t throw me overboard, I’ll be the best crew you have. Adam *does* know a lot more about sailing than I do, so I'll be his number-two. Don't worry about it—we'll do fine."

	Day 1	**Day 2**	**Day 3**	**Day 4**
0000	D W	L J	G R	B A
0200	L J	G R	B A	D W
0400	G R	B A	D W	L J
0600	B A	D W	L J	G R
0800	D W	L J	G R	B A
1000	L J	G R	B A	D W
1200	G R	B A	D W	L J
1400	B A	D W	L J	G R
1600	**D W**	**L J**	**G R**	**B A**
1700	**L J**	**G R**	**B A**	**D W**
1800	G R	B A	D W	L J
2000	B A	D W	L J	G R
2200	D W	L J	G R	B A

Adam nodded at me, then turned to Barry and shook his hand above the table. Will said, "The good lord has carried us this far, and I think he'll take us the rest of the way. He'll even take Mike, if Mike will open up his heart." Then he reached across the table and grasped my hand and then Adam's. I reached across the table to find Barry's right hand at the same time that Adam took his left. I think Barry was surprised by all the sudden hand-holding, but after an awkward moment or two he relaxed and he didn't pull away from our circle.

Right then and there we formed an unbreakable ring of four, sharing deep eye contact and knowing nods all the way around the table. This was way above and beyond religion, but it was all that too. This was a new brotherhood being forged. Sitting across from them, I squeezed their hands while looking into their eyes. When we lowered our heads, in my mind I saw the moonlight shining our path across the swells to Will. I feel genuinely sorry for men who have never experienced this level of battle-buddy comradeship in a life-or-death arena. And for those who have, well . . . they know what I'm talking about.

I said, "Jesus, thank you for guiding us back to find our brother Will. And please guide us safely to wherever it is that we're going next. In your holy name, amen."

Two hours later the sky cooperated and I was able to snag a noon sun sight. The fun part is done on deck with the sextant, shooting a series of angles between the sun and the horizon. The dull part is done at the table with a pencil and paper. Will sat next to me to learn about celestial navigation. Gino could do it in a pinch, but he didn't enjoy it. And for the past three years we hadn't really needed a sextant much at all, except for keeping in practice on the overnight Charleston run. When I penciled the position on our chart the X was near 31 North and 75 West, or 400 miles east of the old Florida-Georgia border.

In a narrative journal there is no point in writing out exact positions down to the fractions of degrees. It's enough for a reader to know that there are sixty nautical miles between each degree of latitude, from the equator all the way up, and that nautical miles are somewhat longer than statute land miles. Degrees of longitude are widest at the equator, and narrower up toward the poles. In the middle latitudes it's okay to think of either kind of a degree as about sixty nautical miles. This will put you in the ball park, and you will never be held liable for striking a reef because you made a minor mathematical error. That level of stress is reserved for the captain and the navigator. Aboard Rebel Yell, I wore both hats.

After I marked our position on the chart I entered the full latitude and longitude in the log. Each celestial fix restarted our dead-reckoning from that point. The distance between the last two positions on the chart showed that we had made less than eighty nautical miles of progress in the past twenty-four hours.

I attributed this partly to our backtracking to find Will, and also because the wind had been dropping for more than twelve hours. Even sitting at the dinette I could tell by the angle of heel and the lessened sound of the water along the hull that we were moving at only about three knots, if that. I mumbled these musing aloud for Will's benefit. At some point Adam joined us, studying both the chart and my noon sight mathematics.

I scanned the previous columns and rows of numbers in the data log to see what we could learn from the wind speeds and directions that had been recorded since we had reached the ocean. The 0200 and 0300 lines were blank, which was understandable. We were busy on more important business.

The column showing recent barometric pressures caught my eye. The pressure had been steady until yesterday, when it had begun to drop from 1007 down to its current 993 millibars. "This pressure drop bears close watching," I told Adam and Will. We had missed it in the recent excitement. I turned around on the bench seat and twisted the barometer's pointer to align with the new pressure.

I made sure that Adam and Will learned how I put away all of my navigation tools and paperwork, including the folded chart, the data log, Kolbe's Long Term Almanac and the other materials. Neatness and orderliness were hallmarks of every competent navigator, and I wanted to ingrain these habits into both boys. Rebel Yell had one-and-a-half celestial navigators on board, and this was a dangerous deficiency. When the autopilot had died we could still steer by hand. Without a celestial navigator, Rebel Yell would wind up hard aground on a reef.

Now that the navigation center had moved from my aft cabin to the dinette table, I had taken to stowing the nav stuff on the built-in bookshelf that was on the bulkhead opposite the clock and barometer. My pencils and the nav tools, such as the parallel rules, the protractor and the compass dividers shared a zipper case. My sextant lived in a hardwood box that had its own spot on the top shelf. Showing all this to Will and Adam was part of the training of every new navigator. There are no exceptions. An ocean navigator is only as good as his tools, and they must be respected and treated with the greatest care.

With everything properly stowed away we went topside. The wind was from the north at around ten knots. According to the speedometer, our speed under full sail was under three knots, but at least we were sailing east, thanks to the new wind direction. I considered starting up the engine, but our batteries were fully charged after all the recent motoring.

What would our cutoff be? Below two knots of forward speed, it would be hard to keep our sails full enough to keep the boat moving. A minute of inattention by one of my new helmsman, and she'd be dead in the water, and harder to get moving again under sail alone. The cutoff speed between the sails and the motor was a puzzle for every captain. So how far are you going? Oh . . . just down to Argentina. And how much fuel do you have? Enough to motor seven or eight hundred miles. Maybe. Give or take. Plus or minus. No guarantees.

How do captains sleep at all? That's the real mystery.

Then I had another idea. The calm conditions offered a golden opportunity to do something fun and exciting that would be a perfect catalyst to push us past our funk over all the recent drama. Ever since Beaufort we'd had a new gun on board—a machine gun—and it was time to try it out. Gino had overseen stowing it in the cargo hold, so I informed him of my plan. He grinned back at me and agreed it was a fantastic idea.

We had 800 rounds of 7.62mm linked ball-tracer ammo on board. I had to weigh the need for the crew to get in some familiarization fire, against our need to save as much ammo as possible for actual use. I told Gino to bring up the ammo box that had been attached to the machine gun on the militia boat, because its hinged lid was gone, and the brass cartridges were showing some tarnish. Those rounds might have been on the militia boat for weeks, being covered and uncovered.

The off-watch crew assembled between the masts on the port side. To port or to starboard these were the biggest open deck areas on Rebel Yell, with about seven feet of space from either side of Whisper out to the toe rails, and with twenty feet between the masts. Gino set the M-240 on the deck aimed out to port resting on its bipod legs. Adam followed him carrying the steel ammo can. Under Gino's direction Adam placed it on deck on the left side of the gun.

We were still on port tack, so the port side was the high side, but not by much in the dropping wind. But even a little deck slant would make the raised side of the hull into "cover," and make the shooter feel like he was firing from behind a low berm. (Firing from behind any kind of cover beats the hell out of taking grazing fire while caught on flat ground out in the open.) The M-240 was no lightweight, and the only way we'd ever fire it, in the practical sense, was from the prone position using the front bipod. This would also keep much less of the machine gunner exposed to enemy fire.

I had found a few pairs of foam rubber earplugs and two sets of ear muffs that Gino and I used for engine room work. I put in ear plugs, but Gino waved them off. I gave one set of the muffs to Barry and the other to Adam. I had a new plan for them. I gave everybody else a demonstration of holding my ears, and I warned them the machine gun would be LOUD. (I also decided to make enough ear plugs for everybody to use in the future. They just had to be cut out of the right foam stock.)

It was Luke and Jessie Hanahan's turn on watch back in the cockpit. Everyone else was gathered to see the old Marine touch off a few bursts. They rested on Whisper's gunnel, or leaned against the mast or the front of the pilothouse. I proned-out on deck with my shoulder against the butt stock. I pushed the gun forward until the bipod's feet were against the toe rail. The muzzle was below the bottom lifeline, and between the nearest lifeline stanchion posts. There was nothing out to the north but empty ocean. From somewhere deep in my memory I repeated what I had heard more than just a few times. "The M-240G is a belt-fed, air-cooled, gas-operated, fully-automatic machine gun that fires from the open bolt position."

I yanked the charging handle on the right side to the rear and slammed it forward again and it all came back to me, but in my own words. I said, "You can tell it's not an M-240B like the Army used because it has no hand guards on the barrel. Up here gets real hot, so don't touch it until it all cools down or you'll burn your hand, and that's a promise. That's what the carrying handle is for." I grabbed the handle, swung it up and let it back down, and then I pointed to parts that required some explanation. "The M-240 has a cross-bolt safety here behind the trigger. Push it to the right, and it's on safe. Push it to the left, and I promise it'll shoot all the ammo you've got."

I showed them how to open the top feed tray cover, and then the smaller feed tray below it to give them an idea of how the M-240 worked. Today was going to be a Hollywood shoot, with just the rock-and-roll party, and with no dull disassembly, assembly and cleaning lessons to memorize and practice over and over like robots. We only had 800 rounds of ammunition, so there was no point in teaching it. For an M-240, 800 rounds was about a good burp, belch and fart.

"Adam," I said, "I want everybody to see what all 200 rounds of ammo looks like. Pull it out and lay it on deck." It ran nine feet long, in two belts of a hundred cartridges.

"These are disintegrating links, and that means the links come apart when they're coming out. On the Dushka, the links all stay together. Now, here's how you load it. With the feed tray cover up and the little feed tray down, you just grab your ammo and put the first rounds right here like this. Shiny side down, the links go on top. Every fifth round is a tracer; they're the ones with orange tips. The bolt is already locked back to the rear. Close the cover and you're all set. The empty brass drops out the bottom, and the links fly out of this little hole, so don't get scared when you see it."

I pushed the top cover down and pushed the safety to the left. "Don't forget to cover your ears. Fair warning, this is *real loud*. Now, out here on the ocean you aim by your tracers and your splashes. Most of the weight is on the bipod, so you aim with both of your eyes and your shoulder. Use the sights to get on target, then just aim at a wave and pull the trigger. It's not a sniper rifle—it's a machine gun—so don't baby it. When you want to fire, pull the trigger like you mean it, and hold it back.

"Your right hand is on the pistol grip, so reach your left hand back and grab the butt stock from below like I'm doing. Both of your elbows will be on the deck, and keep your feet apart. If you have a target, aim low and to the left because it's going to want to climb to the right. Pull the trigger and let off five or ten, and watch your splashes. That's the key to success on the ocean: following your tracers and correcting off your splashes. Remember—you're aiming with your eyes and your elbows and your shoulder. The bipod just tilts and turns. When you see your splashes, adjust your aim and fire again."

Everything was set: the bolt locked back, ammo in, cover down, safety off. I picked a swell about a hundred yards out and I pulled the trigger. Ba-ba-ba-ba-ba-ba-bam! I waited a second and hit it again, trying to stitch the wave in the same place. The red tracers were still good, flying out to my point of aim. The M-240 ran perfectly, and that was the main thing. I could have easily ripped through two hundred rounds in about twenty seconds, but it would have been a waste. In a gun fight I'd have been back there on the Dushka, not on the M-240. Still, firing those rounds felt great, and they took me way back in time. Who would I see when I turned around? Old ghosts in desert-camo and full battle-rattle? I saw them in my memory.

There were more than 180 rounds left. If everybody fired off a couple bursts, it wouldn't mean much to any of them in terms of training. Even without shooting, they could learn the basics of what to do by watching and listening. I had a different idea about how to use the rest of the day's ammo.

"Barry and Adam . . . I'm thinking that maybe you'd like to be in charge of this bad boy, and be our designated M-240G machine gunners? What do think of that for a collateral duty?

Adam smiled and said, "Hell yeah, we'll do it."

Barry shrugged. "Machine gunners. Sure, why not?"

They both already had ear protection on, so maybe they'd guessed something was afoot involving them. In fact I'd given their selection for this assignment considerable thought. Both were bachelors with no wives and no kids. If it came to a real gunfight, they'd be out on deck in the thick of it. Will and Rita were too small to handle the 27-pound machine gun. Luke and Jessie didn't have any children yet, but they were hoping. (I was too.) So that left Barry and Adam. Both of them were fit and strong enough, especially as half of a machine gun team.

Neither of them was a celestial navigator, a diesel engine mechanic, a cook, or an inventor like Will. They couldn't even sing or play a musical instrument. In short, they were perfect machine gunners—and may God bless and protect them all.

I sat up, turned and faced the crew, but mostly Barry and Adam. "Now, you could just run through this belt in one go, but instead, we're going to use it for training." I dragged the belts closer and broke individual cartridges out of their links to make foot-long sections of about twenty rounds each.

I stood up and said, "Barry, get down behind the gun like I was." He did, squeezing his shoulder into the stock, hands on the gun, elbows on the deck, sandal-clad feet wide apart. His old British desert camouflage took me back to the Brits and the Micks on our ten-day voyage to Morocco. More ghosts.

"Adam, you sit on the left side. You're going to feed him the ammo, spot the enemy for him, and do anything he needs so he can stay on the trigger. If we had a spare barrel, you'd learn how to change them when they're too hot. Today you're going to practice with these short belts, but if it was for real you might have to shoot all 200, and then the next 200. Okay, you were both watching me, now it's your turn. Adam, open it up and load it, and tell everybody what you're doing. This is all part of the training: see it, hear it, say it, do it."

Adam opened the feed tray cover, put the first rounds of the belt in place and pushed it back down, while repeating his own version of what I'd said before. It needed no correcting.

Then I said, "Barry, it's on safe. Push it both ways with your thumb and your knuckle and get a feel for it. Now put it off safe, and you'll be ready to rock and roll. Just pick out a wave, give it a burst, wait a second, and hit it again. Follow the red tracers and watch your splashes. Adjust your point of aim with your eyes and your shoulder."

He was wrapped around the back of the machine gun, his right eye behind the peep sight. "Okay, captain, it's off safe. Tell me when I can open fire."

"Open fire!"

Barry touched off a half-dozen rounds, paused, then let off another burst that crossed his first line of splashes, then did it again, finishing that section of ammo. Every fifth round was a tracer. While he fired the empty brass clattered onto the deck below the gun, and the empty links were thrown out to the right. After that first volley Barry and Adam took turns loading, unloading and firing the machine gun. They practiced de-linking ammo and joining belts for extended firing. I wanted them to be as familiar with the M-240 as they could be, given that they could only fire the rest of the 200-round belt.

They fired every round while proned out using the bipod. It took a real beast to fire an M-240 from the hip, holding its 27 pounds with the left hand out front gripping the carrying handle. Prone would be good enough for Barry and Adam.

It was another fun day, almost like when we had caught the wahoo, and we had certainly earned a good day after the previous terrible night and morning. I hated to burn up two hundred of our rounds, but now I had a machine gun team, and it was a big morale boost for the crew. Even for the audience there was something energizing about hearing and feeling that M-240G ripping off bursts and making splash-lines appear on distant waves a half second later. If you had a pulse, it gave you a viscerally emotional charge.

And I knew that way back in our reptile brains wanton displays of sheer bad-assedness calmed and placated our ever-present worry nerves. Calmness was always to be striven for. This is why Soldiers and Marines occasionally held firepower demonstrations. Seeing and hearing the wall of lead you and your buddies up and down the firing line could lay down on an enemy just made you feel better about your chances.

The M-240 rock-and-roll party turned victim gloom into optimism about our chances. Hey, don't mess with us! We're a big steel schooner, so you'd better give us some room, pal. We have two belt-fed machine guns, plus rifles and pistols. You'll be sorry! So just back off, and leave us in peace.

And I knew it would be an experience beyond compare for Barry and Adam, who had touched off the bursts. For the rest of their lives, anytime they fired a new type of gun for the first time, they would remember the day and grin.

Two hundred rounds were gone, links and empty shells scattered across the deck. I gave the twins the task of picking up the brass and the links. I had each of the boys gather his shells into ten piles of ten. What's ten divided by two? Five. Now make each pile of ten shells into five pairs of two, then two pairs of five, and you can see how many there are without even counting. Always a lesson.

After the machine gun shoot was over I was looking out ahead to the east. The old waves had disappeared as the wind had died down. The air was nearly calm, but the ocean was not. We were only making a little better than two knots, but Luke was doing a good job of keeping our sails full and our forward momentum going between puffs and lulls.

Now with the waves from the west and the north almost totally gone, I could distinguish a long swell coming from the southeast. The southeast? Not too high, maybe five-footers just by eye-balling them from crest to crest. There was almost no wind, and the wind that we still had was coming from the northwest. So what was causing this southeast swell?

What indeed.

Wind before waves, the good ship is saved.
Waves before wind, pray if you've sinned.

26

I let Gino organize getting the machine gun cleaned and put to bed by our two machine gunners, Barry and Adam. A little lube and a wipe-down was all it needed, if that. Drag a snake through the bore. And I asked him to call an all-hands meeting in the cockpit for 1430. As my reason I pointed out the new swells and said, "Waves before wind: that means trouble."

"Oh, there's a storm out there for sure," he replied. "And we're still in November, if that means anything."

I went below and checked the barometer. It was at 991, so it was still dropping. I pulled Heavy Weather Sailing off the shelf and flipped to a couple of heavily-underlined dog-eared pages. It had been published more than a half century earlier, but its lessons were timeless. I studied up and began a sketch that might be a useful teaching tool for the crew.

At 1430 we were all gathered around the cockpit for the second time that day. I told them about the dropping pressure and the waves before the wind that we could now all plainly see. I told them that the current 990 millibars didn't matter as much as the steady drop in pressure. I told them that those new swells are being pushed out from a storm that's already out there. If it was just a normal low passing by, the wind and the waves would be getting here at about the same time, rising more or less together. The almost calm wind conditions we have are the winds from South Carolina being cancelled out by the new winds from the east that haven't even arrived yet. It's a shoving contest between the old and the new systems, and the waves tell you which system is going to win. The dark nimbostratus clouds were also a sign of worsening weather.

I showed them my sketch of what I believed was going on out there: a rotating tropical storm. I had already penciled its basic outline on the next page of my narrative log, because I knew it would be a keeper. An entire clean page dedicated just for a sketch was a lot, but sometimes I had to do it. The page would be more pencil gray than paper white before it was all over. I held the folded notebook against my chest and used my finger as a pointer.

"We are here. Florida and Georgia are here. The big circle is the storm, hypothetically, and it's hypothetically somewhere out to the east of us now. Where I put the circle is just a guess, but if it's out there then it's rotating counter-clockwise, and that means we can figure out how the wind is going to come at us. If the system is heading north we'll be on the weak side, and we'll mostly be getting winds from the north. But if the system is heading our way, it's going to get ugly." I pointed to my sketch, dialing my finger around the circle to show the direction of its winds if the system spiraled off to the north.

"The new swells we're getting are coming from where the center of the storm was maybe six or ten hours ago, but that's a guess too. Now, if it's heading north, then we'll start getting the hardest wind coming from the northeast, because it's spinning counter clockwise, right?"

Adam said, "Captain Kilmer, what you're talking about is a hurricane, right?" Adam didn't beat around the bush.

"Well, I'd say a tropical storm at least. But it's probably way out there, so we should have some time to get ready. Tala and Sofia, let's have our supper early, and cook a couple extra meals. And don't spare the chicken, open a few jars. Fill every thermos with hot water. Make plenty of soup and stew, and put all the cooked food containers down in the old ice box so they'll stay warm. Rita, your job will be helping out in the galley and watching the twins. Jessie, you can help out with the twins and in the galley when you're not on watch.

"We'll be shifting the watch teams around, so be flexible. Any chance you can, get some sleep. Everybody secure the boat for heavy weather. Anything you see, if it looks like it'll come loose in a knockdown, do something about it now. Tie it up or put it someplace better. Something heavy falling across the boat in a knockdown can seriously hurt somebody. Okay? We have to prepare for heavy weather, because it's coming."

Sofia asked, "Will it be as bad as Cape Hatteras?" This was her standing benchmark for what a storm could be.

"I don't know. I'm only guessing how strong the storm is and how far away it is. Going south around Hatteras we were bashing into those Gulf Stream waves head-on. Now we have enough sea-room to run off, so most of the big waves will be behind us no matter what happens. We're about 240 nautical miles from the Abacos in the Bahamas, and that's our closest point of land if we have to run off to the southwest. But yes, it might get as bad as Hatteras. Or maybe even worse."

Rita asked, "Does that mean there's a safe place for us to go in the Abacos?"

"No, that's not what I meant. The closest point of land is a bad thing, not a good thing. If we're driven against the Abacos by the storm, we'll end up on a reef. What we want is lots of sea-room so we can run off downwind as long as possible."

Tala asked me, "How much time do we have for cooking before everything is falling down in big waves?"

"I think we'll have the rest of the day. Until it's dark, anyway." A look at the gray overcast sky told me there would be no twilight stars for an updated celestial fix. Just getting the noon sun sight had been a major stroke of good fortune.

Jessie asked, "Do we have a life raft, just in case?"

"We're on the life raft. Our life raft is made out of steel, and it can't leak when all the hatches are dogged down. This boat is like a bottle in the ocean, a corked bottle. Storm waves might throw us around some, but we won't sink." This was mostly true, and mostly said to give them confidence. I didn't bring up my private worries about our pilothouse windows.

Gino, who was steering, said, "Boss, maybe this is a good time for a prayer?"

"Yes, of course it is; thanks." I reached for the nearest hands by me and we made a prayer circle around the cockpit. I led it off this time. "Our Father, who art in heaven. . ."

When we released hands I said, "First mate, I'm firing up the diesel. No more playing around. We'll want the propeller spinning while we get everything else ready." After it rumbled to life and smoothed out, I told Gino to put it in gear, and then we'd see how she did at 2,000 RPM.

Yes, motor-sailing was a real thing, creating a positive synergy between the propeller's push and the sails. The motor gave you more forward speed, which gave the sails more felt apparent wind, and more lift. Motor-sailing was often a win-win in normal conditions with plenty of diesel on board, but not on a voyage to Argentina without any fuel stops along the way.

Then, you save your fuel and wallow in light air. That is, until the greater danger of a storm is staring you in the face.

"Luke, Barry, Adam and Will: you come with me. We're going to get our sails ready for a blow. Odds are it's not going to be that big of a deal and it'll miss us, but we're still going to get ready. Better safe than sorry, and then all this will just be for practice, and that's good too."

They followed me down into the cargo hold and I directed them while they dragged out our storm jib. This was stowed in a white sail bag that had its name painted in big black letters on every side so that it could not be lost, missed or mistaken for any other sail. I directed them at getting the sail up through the forward scuttle hatch, pulling and pushing it from above and below. We also brought up the empty bag for the working jib. A big man could easily fit inside our sail bags if he was crouching down just a little. They were that big.

The bottom front corner of the working jib was attached to the very point of Rebel's bow, not including the steel pipe bowsprit which extended out for another six feet. The sail was attached to the stainless-steel inner-forestay wire with bronze spring clips called piston hanks. These were spaced two feet apart along the front edge of the sail. Getting the working jib down just involved releasing its halyard on the foremast and letting it slide down the inner forestay until it was all on deck. This was quickly accomplished.

Next, each spring-loaded piston hank was unclipped from the forestay and the big jib was folded up, bagged and shoved down the scuttle hatch. Then we clipped the storm jib to the forestay in its place, attached the halyard line and the two jib sheets and winched it up. Measured in square feet it was only a third the size of the working jib, but it was made of heavier Dacron fabric, and was also much more strongly reinforced at it corners and along its edges.

When it was up, its front-bottom corner (or 'tack') was ten feet above the deck, kept there by a ten-foot piece of rope with an eye splice at the end. I explained to my new crew that this extra space above deck was to prevent sweeping waves from striking the storm sail, and also to keep it up in the wind when Rebel was deep in a trough between waves.

By suppertime the swells were over ten feet high coming from the east, and the wind was coming from the northeast at fifteen. The growing swells were not matched by the wind speed, so we were still in a “waves before wind” situation. We could stay on port tack, with the wind coming over the port side and our sails out to starboard, but only if we were sailing to the south or the southeast. If we tacked over, we’d be heading north, and, I thought, more directly into the path of the storm, but I was only guessing. Sailing to the south, we had about 250 nautical miles of open ocean before we’d slam into the Abacos. This gave us less than two days of sea-room if we were forced to run to the southwest. Everything really depended on the location of the center of the storm, and its direction and speed, and I could only guess at them.

Lord grant me wisdom, and don’t let me show my fear.

Barry and Adam’s one hour dog watch was going to begin at 1600. I wanted to stick to the established schedule for as long as possible, and I wanted those two young men on my hip as we did some more sail changes. It was still Gino’s watch but Rita wasn’t there anymore. It didn’t matter as much during the day, and I’d already informed her of her new primary duties: galley support, and seeing to the twins’ safety. Will was also below. He’d been a vulnerable third wheel on deck when we changed the working jib for the storm jib. I told him he looked tired, and maybe he should hit the rack. His heart was there, but our starveling was never going to be a deck ape.

It’s a good thing I got the noon sight, I thought. At least we have a starting point. The swells were growing and their tops were beginning to blow off; the wind was catching up to the waves. It was always an awesome gut-check to see Mother Nature's pre-attack wave formations, with the long gray lines marching in perfect order, and Rebel Yell motor-sailing over them angling to the southeast. I counted nine seconds between crests. The shortening period between the waves was another indicator. From the top of each swell we could see white lines to the horizon. When we dropped down into the troughs we were momentarily between two sloping gray walls, and could only see up and down the length of that moving canyon.

These well-ordered wave formations would not last. The enemy army was passing in review and reminding us of its power. These were the bagpipes you heard before the wild Scots attacked from all directions, swinging claymores. It was your last warning, but the warning could last for hours.

Luke came up and informed us that the barometer was down to 986. He joined Barry, Adam, Gino and myself in the cockpit. When he was settled in the back I said, "Okay, men, we're going into battle, and there's no sugarcoating it. If the center of this thing runs over us, I mean, if the heavy artillery gets dropped right on our heads, it's going to be a big problem. A real big problem. But as long as it doesn't roll right over us, we can handle it. Next, we're going to reduce sail the rest of the way to get ready. We'll start with the outer jib. We'll roll it up so it has a few extra wraps of sheet around it. It has to stay rolled up no matter what."

I didn't need to tell whom to do what. I sat back and Gino accomplished this from behind the wheel with finger-points and just a few phrases here and there. Luke hauled in the furling line hand-over-hand, causing the outer jib at the far end of the bowsprit to diminish in size until it was just a roll of fabric tightly wrapped around the outer forestay.

"Okay, that looks good," I said. "Next job: the sail on top of us. I don't want to deal with the mainsail again until this is all over. Let's get that thing down on the boom and lashed up so tight a flea can't hide in it. Use all the extra sail ties."

Adam said, “I’ll work the main halyard and ease it down. You guys are taller than me so you can strap it to the boom.” He went around the pilothouse to the mainmast. I could see him there through its open door and front windows.

Gino turned the boat toward the wind until the main was luffing, so that it could be pulled down and tied to the boom. Its full-length battens helped in this matter. It took a good ten minutes for them to get the main secured to storm standards. Then they winched in the main sheet until the boom was on the centerline, but still held above our heads by the topping lift line. This rope ran from the end of the boom up to the masthead, then down to its own winch on the mast. The topping lift supported the boom when the mainsail was down and furled.

Secured as it was only from the top and bottom, the boom could still swing a foot each way as the boat rolled. To prevent it from moving even an inch from side to side, we tied ropes from its end out to the stern pulpit railings on each quarter, locking it in place from four directions. Nobody wanted to be paid off by the boom. They had all heard the sea story from me, and it was an unforgettable reminder to always mind the boom.

When the job was done the boom and the furled mainsail were about a foot over our heads when we were standing in the cockpit well. To steady yourself you could grab one of the dozen or so sail-tie straps that were cinching the white Dacron fabric of the furled main to the top of the boom. If you wanted a better view forward over the pilothouse and you stepped up onto a cockpit bench seat, then you could throw an arm over the furled sail and lean against the boom. In this way the boom, so often a danger, became an extra source of crew security.

In normal conditions I’d throw a small, strong tarp over the boom when its sail was down and furled. It was half the size of the big tarp we’d used on market day in Beaufort. At sea I’d tie the smaller tarp to the pilothouse in front and to the lifeline stanchions on each side to make a rain tent for the helmsman. But not before a storm, not when the rain would be coming sideways. Then, every scrap of tarpaulin canvas would vibrate and shriek like a banshee until a grommet let go, and then even a small tarp would lash around the cockpit like a bullwhip. And in a real storm the helmsman could not have his vision obstrutted, not even by the small tarp. He needed to be able to see every part of the masts, the rigging and the sails. So no tarp over the boom, not even the small one, not for a storm. The helmsman just had to stand there and take it.

I told them to put three reefs in the foresail, which was the twin in all respects of the mainsail, now tied down and at rest. Adam stood by the foremast and lowered the halyard line until the bottom half of the sail could be strapped to the boom by Luke and Barry. This sail-area-reducing deck choreography is known as reefing. I gave them some pointers but I didn't lend them a hand. When Adam winched its halyard back up tight, the triple-reefed foresail looked comically small. I didn't assist them because assistance would only hurt them in the long run. They had to be able to do it themselves. At my suggestion they put double lines over the Whisper. Coming from the captain, a suggestion was the same as an order in such moments.

Everything was finally secure, and with all of the deck apes sprawled in the cockpit again, I went over all our plans and preparations with them, and with Gino who was steering. We only had the storm jib and a third of the foresail up. The sails at each end of the boat were furled and secured. No boom would be swinging over the cockpit, and there'd be no reason for anyone to climb out on the bowsprit to fix some random outer jib roller-furler crisis. Any sail work to be done will be done on deck between the bow and the pilothouse, but no such work is anticipated. The storm jib and the triple-reefed foresail could be sheeted in or eased out from the safety of the cockpit.

I told them, "I used to wear a life harness in a storm, but I got out of the habit. A safety line is always getting caught on something or tripping you, or you get tangled up with somebody else and you have to get untangled before you can even do what you went to do in the first place. But if you just want to tie yourself into the cockpit while you're on watch, that's something else. We have plenty of short pieces of good line for that, and you can all tie a bowline. Now, does anybody want to try on a life harness? Don't let me talk you out of it."

None did. If we went forward of the pilothouse, it would be freestyle. That's what Rebel Yell's toe rails, lifelines and bow and stern pulpits were for: keeping you on the boat. One hand for yourself and one hand for the ship.

"We only have a fraction of the canvas up as usual, but don't worry—it'll be more than enough. Maybe too much. And if this storm doesn't pan out—and you always pray that they don't—then this will just be a good practice. And from now until it's over, every chance you get, get some hot food into you, stay hydrated, and get some sleep. You'll need it.

"I'm changing the watch schedule so that Jessie, Rita and Will can stay below. It's just going to be us five deck apes up here for the duration. I'm going to call the five of us the deck crew, okay? So if you hear that the deck crew needs to do something—that means you. We'll do three-hour overlapping watches. You'll steer for an hour, be number-two for an hour, and then you'll be on standby for an hour. On standby you can be in the pilothouse or down in the galley, and you can strip off your foul-weather gear, but you have to be ready to come back up at a moment's notice to help deal with the next crisis.

"Here's the batting order for steering: Dan, Barry, Adam, Gino and Luke. There'll always be two in the cockpit and one on standby. Then, if you're lucky, you'll get a couple hours of sleep. The standby crewman wakes up the next helmsman, but he doesn't hit the rack until the new helmsman is in the cockpit and ready to take the wheel."

After last night, everybody understood the importance of waking up the next watch and doing a proper cockpit turnover.

"When Adam is steering, Barry is number-two and I'm on standby, see how it works? You steer an hour, you're number-two in the cockpit for an hour, and then you're on standby for an hour, and then you go to bed. When you're on standby is when you get something to eat. You won't have to make it—you'll just have to eat it. It's already being cooked right now.

"Now, as to foul-weather gear. Gino and I have our own. Adam, you have your green rain slicker, and it's good enough. Barry, Will's parka will fit you. I'll talk to him. He's not going to be on deck for this. Luke can use the yellow rain suit as long as it holds up. When we're finished here look after your gear and make sure it's ready. The rain gear won't really keep you dry, but it'll keep you from getting hypothermia. Don't wear cotton underneath, only wool or poly. If you don't have any, get some. Ask Sofia. We'll switch to the storm drill after my 1700 dog-watch with Will. Then at 1800 Barry will steer and I'll be his number-two.

"Then at 1900 Adam will steer, Barry will be number-two, and I'll still be on standby. At 2000 I'll wake up Gino, and then I'll hit the rack. See how it works? It's Dan, Barry, Adam, Gino and Luke. When you're on standby you can hang your foul-weather gear on the hooks inside the pilothouse, and get something warm to eat if you're hungry. It's going to get wet down below, but don't worry about that, it won't be the first time. We'll worry about getting dry when this is all over."

I gave the deck apes another looking over all around the cockpit. I didn't see fear or confusion on their faces, so I said, "Gentlemen, your sailing lessons are over. Now—it's war."

The waves were still marching in lines as we motor-sailed up and over them, with Gino at the wheel. We shared knowing nods, fist bumps, high fives and handshakes. We five, the deck apes, were going to take care of the others until it was over.

Then Adam said, "You know what? I sure wouldn't want to be out there in that little yellow raft right about now." Then he smiled briefly, revealing his crooked front tooth.

"Oh, he's fucked," replied Gino. We could all look at those steep waves and picture Mike in the toy dinghy. Up and over.

"Yeah," Barry added, "I wonder how that black umbrella is working out for him?" He mimed holding an umbrella sideways downwind, and then he high-fived Adam across the cockpit and we all laughed. Gallows humor was always a good sign that the troops were mentally ready.

Looking at my deck apes, I suddenly realized that I was no longer seeing young Adam Selfridge as any kind of a boy. Our assistant machine gunner still had smooth cheeks, but he was every bit of a man. They all were.

27

The first and last Barry-Adam watch on the regular schedule began at 1600, which was the first dog-watch. Among other things, this meant they would eat during the second dog-watch at 1700. Between the two of them Barry was the bigger, at maybe 150 pounds dripping wet. But just like when they were working together on the machine gun, I felt confident that the two lightweights would make up the difference with their team work. And they both had the energy of their youth.

Adam knew how to sail, but he didn't know about waves like these, so I gave them both some coaching while he was behind the wheel. Barry was on the high side of the cockpit just in front of the wheel, and he also had a hand on it.

"Always take the crests at an angle. You can't just steer a straight line across big waves, no way. You have to respect every one of them. You cross each wave at the best angle for the boat, and then you try to make up your overall course in between. You're steering one long S-turn after another. Now, it'll be different when the waves are bigger, and when they're behind us, but just remember this: you have to steer for every wave. Every single wave.

"You'll want to quarter them, because if we get caught broadside by a big enough breaking wave we can be knocked down or even rolled all the way over. And you don't want to take them straight on the nose or the stern either. If a wave is too big and steep and you're running straight down it, it can lift our stern and make our bow dig right into the water at the bottom of the trough. Yeah—instant submarine. That's called pitch-poling, and that's a real bad day. What I'm getting at is that you have to figure out every wave and try to quarter them. That's why you only steer for one hour on the storm drill: it's too tiring, and you need to be alert the whole time. Do you two think you've got it now? Is it safe for me to grab some chow?"

Adam said, “We’ve got it, Captain Kilmer. Motor-sailing is easy. Don’t worry—we’ll take care of your boat.”

“That’s right, captain,” Barry agreed. “We’re good to go. We’ve got it all under control up here.”

“I can see that you do, both of you. And you can call me skipper if you want. You’ve both earned it.” I put out my hand and they shook it, and then I turned and went inside and below before they could see my eyes. Captains can’t show their crew that kind of emotion. It gets in the way of hard decisions.

Before I sat down for supper, I inspected below decks from the bow to the stern. After Cape Hatteras my permanent crew was familiar with preparing Rebel Yell for heavy weather. Nothing looked like it would come loose, not even during a full mast-in-the-water knockdown. The cargo hold was always ready for a knockdown when we were at sea. The big timbers and their chains were taut on both sides of the passageway.

All the deck hatches except one were secured, with their inner handles turned and locked down. The one-foot-square deck hatch over the galley was cracked open for ventilation, a necessity for Tala and Sofia when they were working over the gimbaled propane stove in the galley alcove.

The scuttle hatch on the foredeck was also open in back to draw fresh air through the boat. We were still quartering into the waves, with only spray coming aboard, but as soon as we started taking solid green water over the foredeck it would be secured. And the pilothouse door was still latched open. That opening to the cockpit was always the last to be shut, because it was required for ingress and egress, and it was always close at hand to shut during an emergency. Like the foredeck scuttle hatch, the hinged pilothouse door was one of the ship-grade features on Rebel Yell, and a reason why I always thought her designer had a naval or a merchant marine background.

When I was ready to eat, a space was cleared and set for me at the dinette table as if by magic. My first mate had been training the new crew, and I could well imagine what he'd told them. The captain has to be firing on all cylinders and making good decisions at all times, so he has to be well fed and rested. Only after I sat did Gino sit across from me.

Hot chicken stew with lots of potatoes and carrots and cabbage was served to us in plastic dog bowls with non-skid bottoms. They weren't actually dog bowls, but that's what we sea-dogs called them. The vertical sides of the big bowls kept the food inside even when the boat was heeled far over. Our usual bowls and plates were for calmer weather.

I looked across the boat to the ladies in the galley nook. They would keep cooking for as long as they could, getting a day ahead preparing one-pot meals. Tala had already clipped the heavy lee-strap across the open end of the galley nook. Our angle of heel was not yet extreme, but when it was, the strap would keep them from being thrown down to starboard against the table. This was a good distance to fall, especially when the floors were wet. Since Tala and Sofia were strapped into the alcove, Jessie served us. Rita was watching the twins in the aft cabin. Will was in his hammock. All hands were accounted for. And Mike Ortega didn't count. Not anymore.

When I was finished eating I went back up to the cockpit to see how Barry and Adam were getting on. Barry was at the wheel. Adam was sitting in front of it on the high side with his legs braced across to the opposite cockpit bench, keeping his right hand on the wheel. He was teaching Barry how to carve long S-turns to take every wave without luffing the sails when turning into the wind, or risking a gybe going the other way.

The steady wind was over thirty and gusting much higher. The waves were becoming less orderly. The biggest ones were coming from the northeast, but the old ones were still coming from the east, causing them to rise, steepen and break where the trains collided. The wind shrieked and howled through the rigging, and hardware began to clatter and squeal.

"What's your best course now?" I asked them.

Barry said, "Southeast at about 130 degrees magnetic, but the compass is all over the place. I'd say we're averaging 130, but I'm steering up to 90 and down to 180."

"You gotta do what you gotta do. Take care of the boat, that's always number one. We have plenty of sea room. Get all the easting you can, but don't risk a knockdown." I looked all around the horizon and then at the speedo. "We're making six knots, so I'm killing the engine."

When the Cat was silenced I told them, "Now is when it gets *pure*. Just us, the boat, the wind and the waves. Barry, let me have the wheel for a minute, I want to get a feel for it." He slid to the side as I took over. We slowed to four knots under sail alone. My goal was to maintain control and steerage, not to make our maximum speed. We only had so much sea room before we'd run into the Bahamas.

I told them, "Don't get fixated on just one thing. Don't get tunnel vision. Keep your eyes moving. Fighter pilots call it 'the scan.' Look at the compass, the sails, and the next waves. Even the clouds might be trying to tell you something. Listen for anything that doesn't sound right. Most of the time before something breaks it gives you a warning. It's always different and there's always something to learn.

"Even if you're not on watch, anytime you're in the cockpit ask the helmsman if you can take the wheel for a while. He'll be glad to get the break, and you'll be better off when it's your next turn to take the helm. You always want to be ready for what's coming next; you never want to be taken by surprise. It looks like we'll be able to stay on port tack, but call me up on deck if we get a wind shift or any other changes."

After a few minutes of coaching them at sailing in waves, I let them take it again for the rest of their hour. I could tell by watching their eyes they were making an effort to shift their attention around, scanning all of their inputs. Adam was telling Barry what he was doing and why, explaining some of the esoteric principles of sailing, which he had obviously learned from his uncle, Captain Hilton Sapelo.

Will came up on his own at 1650, early for the turnover, wearing his big parka. I went over the new storm drill watch rotation with him. The last four-section two-hour watch was finished. Now it was going to be one-hour turns at the wheel by our five helmsmen, Dan, Barry, Adam, Gino and Luke.

Barry said, "D-bagel. Spell it out in your head and you won't forget it. D-B-A-G-L. Just use our initials, like they're written on the old watch schedule. D-bagel."

"That works for me," I agreed. "When I'm done at 1800 we're going into the storm drill, so Barry, you'll be right back up here after supper. Then Adam, and so on. D-B-A-G-L."

I steered the rest of the hour. Some of the crew came up to see the western sky turning silver and orange. Rebel Yell was riding over the waves beautifully, with no green water coming across past mid-deck.

Jessie came up with her mandolin in its case, and she sat in the front of the cockpit on the low side leaning back. When she was settled she brought out her instrument. I didn't bother to tell her that there was always a chance of catching a stray bucket of salt water at any time. She already knew the risk.

She said, "This is called the Wellerman song. It's about a whaling ship, and the Wellerman they're singing about was a resupply ship for the whalers. I forgot how much I liked it, and it just seemed like a perfect occasion." Then she began to sing and play her mandolin.

There once was a ship that put to sea,
The name of the ship was the Billy 'O Tea,
The winds blew up, her bow dipped down,
Oh blow, my bully boys blow
Soon may the Wellerman come,
To bring us sugar and tea and rum . . .

In mid-song a wave slapped the hull just right and sent spray across the cockpit. Jessie stayed dry because she'd been right behind the protection of the pilothouse, but the rest of us caught a respectable dose, including me full in the face with my hands on the wheel. Jessie cased her instrument and said, "Sorry, boys, this will have to wait for nicer weather—it's the only mandolin I've got." Her heart was certainly in the right place. Luke Hanahan had found a keeper. The last color was bleeding out of the western sky and the sunset party broke up.

Then it was just Will and me finishing the last hour of the two-man watch system. Scudding clouds from the northeast brought heavy rain, and the rain helped to lay down some of the breaking waves. I was in my foul-weather gear, including waterproof overall pants under my coat, so it was no problem for me, not with my hood up and the wind and rain coming more from behind. I was wearing my sodden boat shoes and not my rubber deck boots. Only Gino and I had real sea boots, so wearing them would have emphasized how poorly outfitted the rest of the crew were. It wasn't really so cold anyway. We were heading into the tropics, right?

Will huddled shivering in his big parka at the front of the cockpit against the pilothouse on the low side. Since the rain was increasingly being driven against the back of the pilothouse, I had Will close the door. The handle worked from inside or out, looking like an L from either side. The handle was pulled up to horizontal to clamp the door tight against its gasket. The band of rain passed and we opened the door again.

When 1800 came around, Barry came back up. It was his first go at taking the wheel for an hour during the storm but I was staying on as his number-two. He was wearing the old field jacket over his desert camo and the wool watch cap. It wasn't fully dark, but the entire sky was covered in overcast.

Without being specifically told, at least not by me, Will knew that he wasn't in the new rotation. He understood that he wasn't strong enough to steer in these waves. Before he went below he slid out of his parka and gave it to Barry, who put it on and zipped it up to his neck. Will showed him how to adjust the Velcro cuffs and some tricks with the hood string, and then he gave him a half-hug and went below. As a makeshift flotation device the parka had saved Will, so in our minds it had a lot of positive karmic energy.

The compass light was turned on, so all the nightlights on the same circuit down below were also on. I kept behind the wheel all through the 1800 turnover until it was just Barry and me in the cockpit. The military parka fit him well enough, and a lot better than it fit Will.

"Are you ready, Mr. Conway?"

"I'm ready, skipper. I've got the helm." I noticed that his hands were pale and chapped.

I slid around the pedestal and sat just in front of it on the high side with my feet on the opposite cockpit bench. My right hand could reach the wheel easily from there. This old sea-dog had learned this new teamwork trick by watching Barry and Adam on their first two-man watch.

Tala came up to see how I was doing. She sat beside me near the latched-open pilothouse door, ready to duck inside if spray came over. As long as the door was open, things were okay, things were under control. But bigger spray and some solid water was increasingly going across the deck.

When she moved to go back down below I asked her to see that the forward scuttle hatch was dogged down tight in the back. The horizontal slider on top could stay open for now, but somebody must always be alert to close it fast. The top of the scuttle hatch stood almost a yard above deck, and it could work something like a chimney or a snorkel, and so it could be closed later. Some rain might come down its open top, but not enough to matter. It was a constant tradeoff, the goal being to provide ventilation while keeping the serious water out.

If the two narrow vertical doors in the back of the scuttle were open, then solid green water from a wave breaking over the foredeck could send a hundred gallons down inside in a blink. The berths in the forward cabin would be drenched and almost unusable for days. On port tack, heeling to starboard, this meant Jessie and Luke's side was most at risk.

When Tala gave me a kiss and turned to go, I remembered Barry's hands, and I asked her to bring up our mesh bag full of sailing gloves. Rebel's wheel was covered in elk hide suede leather, and this gave the helmsman a better grip and just felt nicer on the hands than cold, hard, slippery stainless steel. But in these conditions gripping the elk hide was like squeezing a cold, wet sponge, and Barry had only been below for an hour before returning to duty.

Constantly wet hands would not only get prune-wrinkled, any slight scratch or abrasion would break the softened skin. Entire patches could slough off. What was a trivial cut on the land would not heal under the constant wet abuse, but would split, deepen and risk infection—without antibiotics.

When Tala returned with the bag of gloves I dug through them and selected a pair that I thought would work for Barry. Sailing gloves were heavy-duty leather but fingerless, so you could still tie knots, focus binoculars and do other fine work. Velcro straps across their backs cinched them in place, and joined each two in a pair when they were stored in the bag. Barry put them on while I steered from the side.

"Thanks, skipper," he said. "You know I'll never let you down, never. Not after what you've done for me." He took the wheel again, but now with his hands protected.

Adam came on at 1900, so Barry became the number-two and I was demoted to standby. I stayed in the cockpit anyway, to make sure they had it under control. Adam found a pair of sailing gloves for himself. His green hooded rain coat wasn't as big or rugged as Will's parka was on Barry, but as long as it held up it would protect roughly the same area. Staying dry was out of the question, but hypothermia had to be avoided.

“Adam,” I asked him, “did you check the barometer?”

“I did, captain. 983 millibars.”

I looked upwind at the waves to port and said, “We’re in for the shit now, boys, we’re in for the real shit. It’s blowing a hooligan and it’s hardly gotten started. I’d call it a steady thirty from the northeast gusting forty, and we’re only making south-southeast. But there’s good news with the bad. The wind seems to be backing to the north, so that means the storm is probably out to the east, and we’re on the weak side of it. If it was going under us, the wind would be clocking to the east.

“And the other good news is the moon. You can’t see it through the clouds, but we have a three-quarter-full moon out there tonight, and it won’t set until about an hour before dawn. This means it won’t get any darker than it is now, and we’ll be able to see the waves and steer for them almost like daytime. Let me tell you: on an overcast night with no moon, the waves sucker-punch you all night long.”

Barry and Adam had it under control, so I went inside the pilothouse on standby watch. I wasn’t quite ready to go down below, and I wanted to be close by in case I was needed. The pedestal chair was locked in position facing to port. It was always a pleasure to lean back in the padded pedestal seat in dry comfort while out of the wind and the watch the rain and spray lashing at the pilothouse windows.

I alternated scanning the windward horizon and looking back through the open pilothouse door to watch Adam at the wheel. Barry’s right hand was also on it most of the time. He wasn’t really steering, but then I’d hear Adam say “Hold!” and Barry would grip it tightly. Another band of rain came and the door was closed until it blew through and away.

At 1950 Gino came up to relieve Adam on the wheel. I knew that the boat was in safe hands with the first mate at the helm, so after peeling off my sodden foul weather coat in the pilothouse I finally allowed myself to go below. The galley was lit in red light to save the night vision of the watch crew.

I made my way around to the aft head and Tala helped me to disrobe and toweled me dry while I held onto the top of the raised bathtub. Then she helped me into a dry jersey and pants. I stumbled back to my bed, rolled against the lee cloth to starboard, and I was gone in a minute. The first mate was at the wheel with Barry and Adam backing him up. No worries. That was the beauty of the D-B-A-G-L watch rotation. Either Gino or I would be on watch in some capacity at all times.

I slept until Adam shook me awake by my foot while trying, unsuccessfully, not to awaken Tala. When he left she threw on a robe and accompanied me to the galley, pushed me into the dinette and put half a bowl of warm stew in front of me at the table. The food looked like blood under the red galley light as I spooned it up. The barometer pointed to 981 millibars.

I put my wet foulies back on in the pilothouse, then found my own pair of sailing gloves and stepped up and outside after thanking Adam for a job well done. Luke was at the wheel in his yellow rain suit. When I relieved him at the helm he would become my number-two and Gino would be on standby.

Luke greeted me with, "Hello, Captain Kilmer. It's 2200 hours by the wheel watch and I think that everything is more or less okay—but hey, the night is young. Wind is picking up a bit and coming from the north as near as we can tell. The waves are from all over the place, but mostly from our port quarter. Those are the big ones that I'm steering for, so we're just letting the smaller ones hit us on the side."

Gino said, "We closed the top of the scuttle. Every hatch on this boat is dogged tight except for the pilothouse door. We close it when rain comes through, then we open it again. So far we've had no boarding seas from behind."

"Roger that, Mr. Bracciano. Luke, I'm ready to take the helm, if you're ready to hand it over." The wheel and the compass were the center of our universe. The compass would appear to roll and twist inside its glowing glass bowl, but it was Rebel that was moving. It was the helmsman's task to steer an overall coherent course while carving one long S-turn after another to best suit the waves.

And so it went for the rest of the night. There would be an hour of intense concentration, of looking in every direction but mostly over your left shoulder for the next big one. The gray monster would loom up behind us, but at the last moment our stern would rise to meet it and let the wave sweep below our hull. The nameless Dutchman was who designed the schooner had made a real sea boat. Rebel Yell wasn't much for looks, to say the least, but she could take the waves.

Every five or ten minutes Rebel would find herself in an unlucky spot just when a big wave was breaking. Then we'd get hundreds of gallons of warm salt water dumped onto the aft decks and some of that rolled into the cockpit foot well, but it would quickly drain out. Nothing much of consequence made it into the pilothouse through the open door. They didn't need seawater down below, but they did need fresh air. This was one of the iron laws of ocean sailing tradeoffs.

One hour of steering was followed by one hour of calling the waves for Barry, and then another hour on standby while Adam steered with Barry as number-two, helping Adam with a third hand on the wheel. Then Gino is up and I can go below again, Tala finding me dry clothes and getting me into the rack a little after 0100. Then sleeping like a dead man until Adam shakes my foot again and he tells me it's getting on to 0300, and it's my turn to steer. Tala is not with me. I pull on the wet sweater that's hanging over the lee cloth and follow Adam up the passageway, our way lit by the tiny LED footlights.

The galley area is lit in red to save night vision. Tala is on her knees pushing old deck towels with both hands, drying the floors to make them less slippery for us. A parade of soaking-wet deck apes are leaving salt water and rain in their wake.

While the men fight their battle on deck, the women fight a different battle down below, but they fight it in an airless and windowless cavern that's pitching, rolling and lurching like a carnival ride. I'd take the deck anytime. Waves, spray and all.

I crouched and brushed her face with a kiss, then rose and grabbed the ladder again. I hear and feel the impact of a giant wave slamming against the port side of the hull and so I hang onto the ladder while Rebel is driven far over to starboard. The BOOM of the wave is followed by the waterfall sound of the wildly rushing sea, and then Rebel struggles back up.

Then I'm up the ladder and into the pilothouse and getting back into the sodden foul weather coat, not bothering with the farmer john overalls that are too hard to get my legs into on the slippery deck, an arm over the locked swivel chair so that I don't slip and fall on the wet floor while the boat is pitching and rolling like a mad, wild thing. I can't find my gloves, but it doesn't matter. It's 0300, so it's my turn to steer, and I'm almost late for my watch. Adam is with me, trying to help. He finds my gloves and he gives them to me by the light of the gooseneck lamp. Thank you, son, good job and good night.

Luke greets me behind the wheel, he's laughing, yellow hood back, his black hair and beard streaming rain and salt water. "I think I'm getting the hang of it, captain. I think I'm finally learning the rhythm. Catching the rhythm is always the key. You have to start turning *before* you really need to."

"Yeah, Luke, that's the trick all right. The rhythm. And I think it's time you started calling me skipper."

"I can do that, captain, I mean, *skipper*. I can do that. Hey, you look pretty tired, but I know I'm good for another hour."

"No, I'm good to go, I really am. I'm ready to steer. But if you spot the bad waves for me, that'll be a big help." Steering, you were mostly looking forward and at the lit compass, you couldn't help it. You needed an eye in the back of your head, so a number-two watching your six was a blessing. A number-two who could sing and tell jokes that made you laugh at the wind-driven salt spray in your face—that was even better.

28

The standby hour of my watch finished up in black darkness at 0500 after the moon had set. I was due back behind the wheel again at 0800. I woke up in broad daylight, so I had missed morning nautical twilight and any chance at a new celestial fix. The overcast would have prevented it anyway. The barometer was down to 979. I just wished it would stop dropping. The pilothouse door was shut but I could see Luke behind the wheel through its window.

After I got into the cockpit Gino shut the door behind me and dogged its handle over, sealing it tight. "We had to close it," he said, "We caught a good one a half hour ago. It fell on us like a mountain. That wave hit Luke so hard that I thought he was going to bend the wheel over and ruin it."

Luke said, "The first mate is exaggerating. It really wasn't that bad. Anyway, it caught me across the back with my hood up. But it got him right in the face—you should have seen it!"

Gino said, "I was sitting right here against the door, so it couldn't push me anywhere but back against it. Yeah, a lot of that one got inside, and after that one we closed it. When I go on standby I'll check the bilge. That was the only wave that swamped the cockpit, but it could happen anytime."

Luke said, "But on the other hand, there's some blue sky up there," and he pointed to the west. The hard wind made the sleeve of his cheap yellow rain suit chatter.

"The wind and the rain come in bands," said Gino. "It's not always steady up and down." This observation was meant for Luke. I knew it. In fact, I'd taught Gino. In his prior career he'd been a ship's engineer, not a bridge or deck officer.

I asked them both, "So right now, overall, do you think the wind going up, or coming down?"

"I'd say it's fairly steady," replied Luke, "and it's mostly out of the north. That's a good sign, right?"

"That's a very good sign. That means the system is tracking north and away from us. We're getting the weak-side bands. But the pressure is still dropping: it's down to 975."

Gino, transitioning to standby now that I was about to take the wheel, said, "While things are okay, I'd like to open the top of the scuttle and get some fresh air inside. It's stale up front and in the cargo hold."

"Okay, go ahead, but tell them they have to be ready to shut it fast." Gino went inside and I took the wheel from Luke. One big boarding wave in the cockpit in the last hour was not the worst thing. They needed fresh air down below. The top of the scuttle hatch was a yard above the foredeck. I'd risk a few gallons of rain or spray sneaking in with the new air.

The giant waves continued to rise behind us, the wind blowing the corners of their faces into streaming foam. They'd lift our stern and sweep below us, but they were increasingly being joined by a chaos of old and new wave trains colliding. Just because most of the twenty-something-footers were now coming from the north does not mean that the ten-and fifteen-footers from the northeast and the east have all disappeared.

Sailors called this the washing machine. When big waves from different directions meet at cross-angles, they can create super-node freaks that are way too steep and moving much too fast for them not to break and tumble. It was impressive to see instant waterfalls blasting out white avalanches of foam from a few hundred yards away. You just didn't want to be there.

Sometimes big waves caught Rebel broadside, heeling her past fifty degrees and briefly covering her decks with a foot of ocean and foam. You had to ignore the fifteen-footer taking aim at your beam to handle the bigger one sneaking up from behind. The steep fifteen-footers looked like walls of water as they rushed us from the side, but we always climbed up their faces and only took their breaking tops across our decks.

We spent three hours on and two hours off, but only one of the three hours was behind the wheel. My daylight rhythms kicked in and I felt reasonably rested. Hot coffee would have helped, or hot tea, but we had neither. This is how it had been in the Marines. You didn't whine, and you didn't moan. You just did your damn job no matter how little sleep you'd had. Lack of sleep was dismissed as a personal problem.

The day went on, three hours on, two hours off, but being on standby was practically as good as being off. At 1400 I was Barry's number-two, with Luke on standby in the pilothouse. Heavy rain and hard wind came in bands. They were mostly from the north but often veered to come from the northeast. Sometimes you could see streaks of blue sky and get a visual reference to the high-altitude bands that were fingers radiating far out from the distant storm's center. And rough weather was always more tolerable in the daytime, period.

On one occasion a ribbon of blue coincided with the angle of the sun, and for a few glorious minutes the wild ocean was lit like broken blue glass. Sunlight flashed through a hundred clear wave tops like blue-green prisms. Luke came back to the cockpit to share the experience. A platoon of porpoises chose that joyous time to join us. Squad after squad launched from the faces of the nearest waves in perfect alignment to obtain the best view of the strange sixty-foot interloper. Curious and unafraid, an interlude shared between seafaring mammals.

If they weren't showing off for the sheer fun of it, then the word fun has no meaning. The most amazing thing was to see porpoises kicking their flukes at full speed just inside the transparent faces of waves that were higher than Rebel's deck and only a dozen yards away. Wave tops so sharp and so clear that you could see the next wave through them. The Atlantic Seaquarium needed no human choreographer. That bottlenose tribe was taking advantage of the conditions to study us in detail. How long had they been shadowing us, waiting for the chance to say hello? Enjoying the rare sunlit sapphire storm waves just as much as us?

Then the clouds hid the sun again, the ocean returned to gun-metal gray, and our new friends were gone.

This was not the first time I'd shared magical moments with Atlantic and Pacific porpoises, and not to mention whales surfacing parallel to us, eyeballing us from twenty feet away. How long did they study the underside of the metal creature before surfacing to take a look at what was above the water?

Luke went below and then it was just me and Barry in the cockpit. He said, "I never imagined anything like that. Never. So, I guess we're over the worst of it, right?"

"I hope so."

"So, on a scale of one to ten for the worst storms you've ever been in, how would you rate this one?"

I had to think about this. "Storms at anchor, or storms at sea? Out on the ocean, I'd say about an eight. I might have said a nine last night. I think just wondering if it's a hurricane coming your way makes it worse. And if you're being driven onto a lee shore, then it's ten times worse—but we have some sea room, thank God."

"How long can it stay like this?"

"Now, if this was just a cold front, I'd say we've seen the worst of it, and it'll start getting better pretty soon. But if it's a tropical storm, well, then you never know what the limit is. They can even turn around and take another shot at you. But an actual hurricane out at sea? The eye passing right over you? Then you're probably going to die. At a certain point any boat can be overwhelmed. Big ships even, like the El Faro going from Jacksonville to San Juan. It's still November, and we're in the middle of hurricane alley. They've even had Christmas hurricanes. They're pretty rare, but they can happen. And who the hell knows what that Iceland volcano is doing?"

"Laki," said Barry. "I know it's dangerous, but I've got to tell you the truth: it's is pretty exciting too. The dolphins—that was just *crazy*. I never saw anything like that in my life, not even close. Anyway, it's better now than it was last night. I've never been surfing, but I'll bet it's something like this. When the big ones come from behind, they lift us up and give us a push. I've seen our speed over eleven knots, but we're making seven all the time with just those two little sails."

"When they push us like that, yeah, you could maybe call it surfing, but a heavy steel boat like Rebel Yell is never really going to surf. We have what's called a displacement hull, so we have a max hull speed. Racing sailboats and multihulls can take off and surf most of the time—planing like a motorboat—but I wouldn't want to be out here on one right now."

"Neither would I. Or a little yellow raft. So, I guess Mike has had it by now, wouldn't you say?" Barry wasn't smiling.

"Yeah, I'd say he's had it." I didn't need to explain why. When big waves broke they left an acre of churning sea foam in their wake. You might be able to hold your breath through a few of them, but those foamy acres would wear you down and you'd end up inhaling the frothy soup. Then lights out. And as far as the yellow plastic raft, well, that had probably flipped over and blown miles and miles away from Mike hours ago.

Around 1440, while Barry was steering, I was leaning forward against the back of the pilothouse. The door was latched open. My schooner was riding the waves well enough. We were still on port tack but not heeling over much because the wind was behind us and we only had a small amount of sail area up. If you averaged out all of the turning we were probably making south-southeast or about 150 or 160 degrees on the compass. Our speed went down to five and up to seven each time a big wave passed under us. Our depth sounder continued to read 500. The dead-reckoning plot from yesterday's noon sight was going to be an absolute joke.

Barry had also gotten a feel for the rhythm and he didn't need my extra hand on the wheel. The storm jib and reefed foresail sheeted in on the starboard side were holding up. Both appeared as stiff as metal against the wind pressure, and their sheet lines were like iron bars all the way back to the cockpit.

I was watching some frigate birds out plying their trade diving for fish among all the mayhem. Were our porpoises out there, sharing the feast? Then far to the east I noticed a section of the ocean that had gone completely white and was rushing toward us. I ducked and screamed into the pilothouse "Close the scuttle! Close the scuttle!" I slammed the pilothouse door shut and dogged its handle over to seal it. Then I yelled back, "Hard to port! Hard to port! Hang on, Barry!"

He could see it too. The white part of the ocean rushed at our port beam like a line of runaway snowplows blasting off the tops of the waves in front of them. Barry was cranking the wheel to the left but the wall of wind and water hit us before Rebel Yell was pointing her bow into it.

Solid ocean hit our hull side and flew across our decks as the wind blast heeled Rebel far over to starboard. Barry threw his right leg out against the back of the starboard side cockpit bench to brace himself while I wrapped my arms around the biggest winch on the port side cockpit combing. Rebel's two masts went over to ninety degrees and beyond while I was hanging down across the cockpit. The rushing foam, spray and blown-over wave tops continued for most of a minute and then my tired old schooner struggled to regain her footing. The lead in her keel was working to swing her back upright, her masts and sails streaming water. Green ocean poured off her decks as she struggled back up. She was going to make it!

I let go of the winch and grabbed for the wheel. Barry was there, his right leg braced out, his eyes wide, grinning at me. There were still two of us in the cockpit! Hallelujah!

Then I heard a bang, and I turned around and looked over the pilothouse just in time to see the foremast going over. It was following the wind and the waves down to starboard as Rebel

Yell rolled back up to port. I waited for the mainmast to follow its twin over. On its way down the foremast swung aft, and then forward, and I heard another bang, and the foremast fell into the ocean. The sea was much too wild to notice any additional splashing as it went in, but I heard a lot of creaking, scraping and grinding until it all came to rest. Our old rigging wire just couldn't take the punishment.

Rebel Yell's two mastheads were—had been—joined by a twenty-foot-long horizontal 'king-stay' wire meant to give them mutual support fore and aft. This benefit was balanced against the risk of losing both masts for a single wire failure on either. For that reason the king stay was only quarter-inch wire, like a fuse that was meant to break first. And my fingers-crossed who-really-knows theory had just been tested.

The mainmast still stood in front of the pilothouse, but the foremast, both sails and all the rigging wires and lines were in the water trailing over the starboard side. From knockdown to dismasting took less than a minute, but it's hard to keep track of time when everything goes into slow motion. Then Rebel Yell was back on her feet, but minus a mast, and with a junkyard dragging alongside.

Barry stammered, "Jee-sus Christ! Did I do that?"

"No, Mother Nature did it. Mother Nature and old rigging wire." Clear your head, Dan. First things first. "Barry, do you have control? Can you still turn the boat? Try for south and see what happens."

He spun the wheel to starboard. "She's coming over."

The pilothouse door was pushed open from inside and Luke was there, then Gino with Adam and Will behind him. I didn't have to explain what had just happened; they all could see it through the—thank God!—still intact pilothouse windows. Where there should have been two masts, now there was only one. And we had no sail up, in a storm. We weren't even running with bare poles; we only had a bare pole up, singular. And we couldn't start the engine because a vast tangle of trailing lines would immediately foul our propeller.

Gino said, "The top of the scuttle hatch was open and we took in a lot of water. A lot."

I replied, "Take Will and check the bilges. The pumps should be running but I can't hear them from up here. Have Will report back when you have a status report."

"Aye aye, skipper." Gino and Will disappeared below.

"Barry, you keep steering; you have the best feel for the conditions. Luke and Adam: come out and help. We need to assess the damage, but first we need to get forward support for the mainmast. The only thing holding it up is the wind from behind, but we can use the staysail halyard for a forestay."

This seldom-used spare mainmast halyard line raised the schooner staysail that we sometimes put up between the masts in light air. From time to time I also used the staysail halyard as a temporary forestay to support the mainmast from the front when the foremast was being lifted off the boat by a crane in a boatyard, so I knew exactly what we needed to do.

Adam and Luke followed me around the port side of the pilothouse to the still-standing mainmast. They had not taken the time to put on foul-weather gear. Adam was wearing a blue jersey, and Luke was in his red and black plaid shirt.

"Adam, I'm going to take the end of the staysail halyard forward. You'll have to ease it out carefully or the wind will grab it and it'll get wrapped in the rigging and we'll never get it out. If we mess this up there's no plan B. I'm going to clip it to the deck up on the bow. Once it's attached, I'll give you the signal and you winch it tight, okay? Luke, you come with me. Once we've got a temporary forestay on the mainmast we can take a look at what's left in the water."

Adam asked, "Are we going to cut the foremast loose?" He unclipped and handed me the halyard; it ended in a snap shackle. I wrapped the line around my hand.

"Cut it loose? Oh, I hope not. I hope we can salvage it."

"Salvage it?" Luke asked.

I said, "Where are we going to find a new foremast? We'll save it if we can, but first we need a new forestay or we'll lose the other mast too." All of this conversation took place on a rolling and pitching deck by the mainmast just in front of the pilothouse, with mad waves in every direction as far as you could see, with us grabbing onto any handholds we could find. Luke and Adam were soaked with spray in their first minute on deck. Luke was barefoot. Sand mixed into the final coat of white deck paint had optimistically qualified it as non-skid, but that had been years ago.

I looked aft over the pilothouse and yelled, "Barry, have you got it? We're going forward—do your best!"

He made an exaggerated nod and yelled back, "I will!" In those conditions he couldn't take a hand off the wheel. If we were caught broadside to one of the big ones, we'd be rolled again—and then we'd be done.

"Ready, Adam? Ready, Luke? Okay, let's go. Stay low."

I scurried forward. Whisper's canvas cover was gone. Our dinghy was heeled to starboard in her chocks but she was still there. The foremast's deck step was empty, obviously, and this was a disturbing thing to see, but I had to keep going. The further forward I could bring the staysail halyard for a wider angle the better it would support the mainmast. I went to the bow on all-fours and clipped the shackle to a stainless-steel ring welded to the deck behind the anchor windlass.

With the staysail halyard attached to the deck I raised and pumped my fist, and I felt the line going taut as Adam cranked it tight around its mainmast winch. It wasn't a stainless-steel wire, it was just old low-stretch rope, but it would have to do.

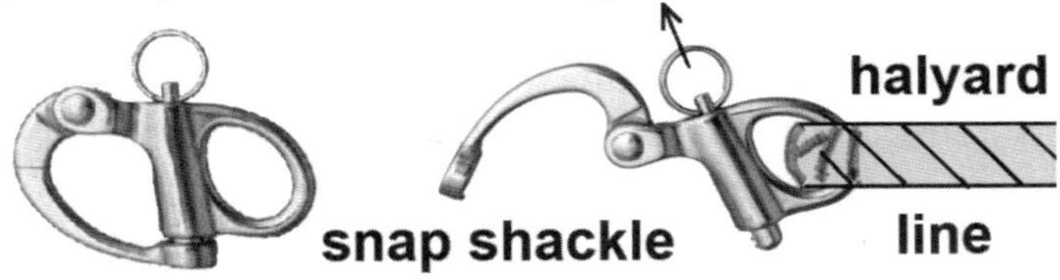

29

With that task accomplished, and the immediate risk of losing the mainmast behind us, Luke and I could study the wreckage of the foremast. It wasn't completely in the water. Its base was tangled in our starboard lifelines across the deck from the old mast step. The paint was scraped down to bare metal showing the path its foot had taken across the deck on its way down.

There had been four lower shroud wires attached to each of the masts. Now one mast stood, and one mast was down. The lower shrouds were meant to support the middles of the masts. They were attached to the masts halfway up, just below the spreaders, two on each side of both masts. These lower shroud wires descended to the port and starboard deck edges five feet ahead of and behind the masts, giving the middle of the masts side-to-side and fore-and-aft support. The lower shrouds supported the midsections of each mast so they could not bend or bow either front to back or side to side. The lower shrouds were especially important on Rebel Yell, because of her deck-stepped masts. Keel-stepped masts received added support where they passed through the deck.

To support the top half of both masts, cap-stay wires ran from the deck edge, then over the tips of the spreaders and all the way up to the mastheads. The foremast's port-side cap stay had failed while Rebel was recovering from the knockdown. The foremast was carrying the extra load of the two sails that had briefly been submerged in the waves. Twenty feet behind the foremast, the mainmast was bare of sails, so it swung back up to vertical without experiencing a rigging failure.

The port-side aft-lower shroud wire was stretched across the front lip of the cargo hatch, and then it turned and ran back to the foremast at the base of the broken spreaders. When the cap-stay wire failed, this lower shroud wire had prevented the entire foremast from being submerged in the ocean.

Rebel's lifeline stanchions were made of stout one-inch-diameter welded steel pipe. Between the stanchions a pair of quarter-inch stainless-steel lifeline wires ran horizontally at a yard and at eighteen inches above the deck-edge toe rails. The foremast's winches and halyard lines had become trapped and entangled between the stanchions and the horizontal lifeline wires as the aluminum spar had come down. Its boom and the triple-reefed foresail were trailing in the water to starboard. The storm jib was nowhere to be seen.

Even if I wanted to get rid of the downed foremast, boom, storm jib and reefed foresail, it would be quite a project. Just getting our bolt-cutters and clipping the lower port-side shroud would not be enough to set it all loose, because the foremast wreckage had snagged up between the lifeline stanchions on its way over, down and then back.

We worked our way along the horizontal spar, examining the destruction. The deck and toe rail were scraped through to bare steel in numerous places. Three of the lifeline stanchion posts were bent and twisted at crazy angles with the bottom of the mast wedged between them. And further back, what had been the top third of the mast was dragging the water.

Luke said, "It sure won't be easy to get it unstuck, not the way it's caught everywhere."

That was an understatement. Fixing this was going to be a major boatyard job, and there was no conceivable boatyard in our foreseeable future. And we still had a storm to deal with. At least Barry was keeping our stern to the big waves.

Adam said, "Can we lift it up? Not all of it, just the back of the mast. I mean the top of the mast, where it's in the water. With the mainsail furled down on the boom, the main halyard is available. I really think it could work."

It was so obvious, once he'd said it. Maybe the idea came to him first because lately he'd been our mast halyard guy.

"Good idea, let's try it." Luke followed me back to the cockpit while Adam stayed by the mainmast. The top third of the mast was trailing astern. The bent spreader bars were even with the pilothouse. Tangled knots and loops of halyards and sheets were everywhere. The masthead was in the water ten feet behind our transom and ten feet out to starboard.

I asked Barry, "How's she steering with all that drag?"

"I have to keep a half turn to port on the wheel, but I can hold a course. I can turn to starboard like a race car, but it's much slower turning to port. If we get another one of those white monsters, I won't be able to turn into it fast enough."

I said, "That's what they call a white squall. Most sailors never see one in their entire lives. That was my first."

Luke asked me, "What causes them?"

"I'm not sure. I think it's like a horizontal microburst. Some big stuff gets pushed together way out there and once in a while it shoots out a white squall. I think of it like squeezing out a watermelon seed between your thumb and finger. Maybe it's not scientific, but that's how I picture it. In 1986 a white squall knocked down the original Pride of Baltimore and she sank in about a minute because her hatches were open. And she was ninety feet long."

Luke asked, "How are we going to get a halyard onto it?"

"Grappling hook," I replied. "Sometimes there's nobody on a dock to catch your lines. We've saved boats from going aground with a grappling hook when they drug their anchors with nobody aboard. Every boat needs a grappling hook."

Will opened the pilothouse door from inside. "Mr. Bracciano says the pumps are working, most of the water is out and there should be no problem with starting the engine." Then he heaved some orange bile into the cockpit foot well.

"Anything else?"

"Rita and Sofia are real seasick. Much worse than me."

"Does Gino need you now? Would you rather come out here or stay down below?"

"Actually, I think my hammock would be the best."

"Okay, tell Gino I said you can hit the rack if he doesn't need you." Again I thought: give me the wind and the waves on deck. When it's bad outside, it can be *much* worse below.

I pointed to the grappling hook and its thirty feet of nylon line that were coiled and stowed on the port side of the stern pulpit. “Luke, that’s what you need. Catch the mast and we’ll tie its rope to the main halyard. Adam, you get the halyard.”

Luke tossed the hook underhand snagging the foremast’s remaining cap stay wire, and then he tied its line to the main-mast’s halyard shackle. Adam winched the mast up and out of the water until it was close enough for us to tie it to our toe rail cleats. This allowed us to get a short rope around the mast, and with a fresh purchase from the main halyard, we hauled the foremast up level with the deck and lashed it in place where it lay by the cockpit. The masthead of the fifty-five-foot aluminum tube was still about six feet out from our transom, and extended ten feet behind us. We left the halyard attached to the foremast to support its weight and hold it steady.

The bottom half of the foremast, now the front half with it lying horizontally,was enmeshed with the bent lifeline stanchions and needed no additional securing. With most of the excess water drag on the starboard side removed, Barry said that his steering ability was much improved.

It took another hour to mostly un-foul the downed mast’s boom and reefed mainsail. The best we could do with the submerged storm jib was to get it out of the water and lashed to the toe rail and lifelines. The outer jib’s roller-furling sail was still attached to the bowsprit so the outer forestay had failed at the top. The sail had been rolled up around the aluminum furling tube when it went over, and now the tube was bent in several places under the rolled-up Dacron. There was no way for us to remove the boom or the two sails without cutting the tangled knots of sheets, halyards and wires, and my goal was to salvage as much as possible.

Jobs that take a minute at anchor take ten when the boat is rolling and pitching in big waves, and this movement is even worse without the steadying effect of the sails. When I decided there was nothing more to do with the foremast and the rest of the mess we went back to the cockpit and collapsed.

Barry was still steering, and he had been since 1400. In a bit my first mate joined us, red-faced and pouring sweat as he came through the pilothouse door. His battles had been fought below. He announced, "The barometer is finally going up. It's showing 981. What about using the engine?"

"We can't take the chance until we sort out all the wires and lines in the water. Barry, how is she steering now?"

"It's hard with no sails up. I think the wind is going down, but the waves are still big. It's hard to steer but at least it's more balanced with the foremast out of the water."

"Okay. Luke and Adam, let's start up at the front again. We'll take a boat hook. If we can get every piece of line out the water and be sure about it, then we'll try the engine."

Adam asked me, "Can we put a jib on the new forestay?"

"No, it's only rope, and if anything happens to it we'll lose the mainmast for sure. But if we can get the boom off the foremast, that'll give us an eighteen-foot mast for a jury rig."

Gino said, "Maybe, boss, but what sail do we have that's going to fit on an eighteen-foot mast? So why don't we get all those ropes and wires cleaned up and use the engine?

I could not find any fault with his reasoning.

At 1600, just for the sake of the logbook, Gino pushed the start button on the engine panel and the old Cat diesel fired up like it was any other normal day. The deck crew was in the cockpit when I said, "Okay, Barry, idle speed, and then put her in gear." He had been standing behind the wheel through the knockdown and the dismasting, and I wanted him to see the job all the way through to getting Rebel Yell underway again.

He pulled the throttle back to slow the engine, pushed the shift lever forward and the transmission clunked into gear. The two handles were on each side of the pedestal under the compass. I put a hand on each lever from the front, ready to throw the engine back into neutral at the first sign of a line fouling the prop. After a minute I said, "Okay, let's see what she'll do at two grand," and I pulled the throttle ahead.

Will's speedometer had been reading between three and four knots on our single bare mast as the waves from behind alternately pushed us ahead and left us climbing their backs. At 2,000 RPM our speed rose to five knots, which I expected, but more importantly, no lines were sucked into the propeller.

"Barry," I said, "you've been at the wheel for two hours and you're due for a rest, but I want to stick with the storm watch rotation. Can you stay on as Adam's number-two?"

"No problem, skipper. I'll spot the waves for him."

Adam got behind the wheel as Barry slid around to sit on in front of the pedestal. There was no need for him to brace his legs across the cockpit because we were hardly heeling. The rolling, however, was another matter.

I stood behind the pilothouse and studied the horizon. There were widening streaks of blue behind us to the north. I spoke my thoughts aloud to them. "I think the wind is coming down. I think we're getting farther from the storm. It's going north and we're going south. If the wind is really dropping the conditions should get better. Will, Sofia and Rita are seasick, so we'll stick with the storm watch for tonight and see how it goes tomorrow. Now I need to check down below. Okay Gino, let's go. Show me what I need to see, starting in the back."

The sliding door to Rita's aft passageway cabin was half-way open. She was in her bunk lying on her back looking pale and miserable. There was a puke bucket by her head.

"How are you feeling?" I asked her.

"Terrible . . . terrible . . . When is this going to be over?"

"Tomorrow. One more night, but not as bad as last night."

Gino stayed with her while I continued to the aft cabin. Tala was sitting with the twins on their pallet between the desk and the bed. I knelt down and hugged them all together.

Chris said, "Daddy, you know we're not even a schooner anymore. If you only have one mast you're only a *sloop*."

"Don't worry; we'll be a schooner again. Now I have to go and look at the rest of the boat."

"Can we come with you?" asked Jonathan.

"No, not yet. I'm still working. You didn't get seasick?"

"We don't get seasick," he replied. "Not ever. We don't."

Chris said, "That's because we were born on a schooner."

Tala said, "No, you were born in a hospital. You had three days living in the world before you moved onto this boat."

I looked at them and said, "We'll be a schooner again, boys, I promise." Then I went up forward with Gino, passing through the galley toward the cargo hold. I was dreading the sight of it, imagining what had gone on in there while Rebel was knocked down past ninety degrees.

Gino said, "Some lids came off boxes of food. It's a mess but nothing too dangerous broke loose. And nobody got hurt."

I grabbed the timber planks in the back on both sides of the passageway and shook them hard. They were still locked in tight, held rigidly to the hull sides by their tensioned chains. Most importantly the four steel drums of gasoline and motor oil in the very back had not shifted. They did not only rely on the passageway timbers, but had their own individual chains securing them against the hull.

I moved up the passageway inspecting the cargo on both sides. There was some sloppy mush on the deck where some potatoes had gotten loose and been trodden underfoot. Mattresses, sheets and blankets from the forward cabin were spread on top of the cargo on both sides. The real cleanup would have to wait for calmer and drier conditions. Rebel was still rolling and pitching as each big swell overtook her, but now there was also the comforting thrum of the diesel driving her forward and giving the helmsman better steering control.

Will was in his hammock on the starboard side, his head to the front. He appeared to be asleep so we passed him quietly and entered the forward cabin. All the bedding was stripped off the top and bottom starboard berths, showing their white-painted wood construction. The teak ladder provided us secure handholds in the middle of the space. The scuttle hatch above us was wide open, both in back and on top, making a big skylight and ventilation shaft. This was fine as long as we didn't take another knockdown. Sofia was lying on the port-side lower berth, a plastic puke bucket tied to the side of the bunk near her head. Somebody was above her on the higher berth behind its canvas lee cloth, so that had to be Jessie.

Gino knelt and asked Sofia, "How are you doing, baby?"

She groaned and croaked out, "Ahh . . . ohh . . . I think I will live . . . maybe. But for how long must I suffer like this?"

"Dan says one more night, but not as bad." He kissed her pale cheek, then rose and turned to me and said, "It was a big waterfall up here when Rebel rolled on her side. The top of the scuttle was open and it was underwater long enough to let in a few thousand gallons. If she hadn't come back up fast like she did. . ." He gave me a look and mimed a diving submarine or a crashing airplane with his hand.

He continued. "Everything was underwater on the starboard side. The water was higher than the floorboards when she came up. Our crash pumps needed ten minutes to get the water under the floors. Everything is soaked. Even the guitars in their cases got wet. We're not going to really dry out until we can get to an anchorage and open everything up."

Jessie sat up on the top bunk and unclipped its lee cloth, letting it hang over. "Oh, Gino, I just hope they're not ruined. My mandolin stayed dry but both guitars were soaking wet. I didn't even know they were wet until I opened up their cases." She swung her legs over and slid down to join us. The uncased guitars were on the bunk to dry out. Jessie wiped her eyes with some bed sheets while her back was to us, then she turned to face us again and said, "Come on, you both must be starving." We followed her through the hold back to the galley.

I sat down at the table facing the barometer. It read 987. Gino sat across from me. I pointed to it and he said, "I know, I know, it's going back up—thank God."

"And thank God the crash pumps worked," I added.

"I'm not much of a ship's engineer if they don't."

Jessie brought us water bottles. I said, "Luke is with Barry and Adam. Can you bring him down here?"

She went up the ladder, and we both guzzled the South Carolina water. A combination of mental and physical fatigue was overtaking me. The difficulty of everyday normal activity was multiplied by the need to keep your balance on a platform that was pitching and rolling nonstop, moving from handhold to handhold with your body in constant tension. Just living was hard work. Even lying down in your bunk you had to use your torso muscles, especially when the boat was rolling from side to side downwind.

With each roll I could hear and feel the now-horizontal foremast sliding, scraping and banging against the starboard side of the hull just a few feet away on the other side of a quarter inch of steel. Every unseen dish and tool that had a few inches to slide from side to side in its bin or box or cabinet did so, and the combined clattering ruckus we heard on each deep roll added to our malaise.

Luke came down the ladder and I asked him to sit next to Gino. Jessie brought him water and I asked her to sit with us too. I was across from Gino, Luke and Jessie and I reached for their two outermost hands to make a circle and I put my head down to pretend to pray, but it was really to hide all the salty stuff leaking out of my face. I didn't have the words so Gino thanked the good lord for me. The storm wasn't over, but we were going to make it—as long as nothing else happened to us like the white squall monster that had knocked us down.

I collected myself, and when Gino finished I said Amen and we got back to business. The decisions would be made by Gino and me but I valued the judgment of Luke and Jessie. Everybody else was either busy or too seasick. Four heads are better than two. I wanted all the help I could get.

When we had joined our hands I noticed that Luke had a rag wrapped around his right fist. "What happened there?"

"I cut myself on a wire." He began to unwind the rag. The wad of cloth he'd been clenching was soaked with blood.

"Stop," I said. "Gino, get the first-aid kit."

He began to get up but Luke said, "It's fine, skipper; just please don't make a big deal out of it. It's only my strumming hand—it's my fret hand that matters." He pressed imaginary strings on the neck of a guitar with the fingers of his left hand. "I promise I'll take care of it right after this."

"Okay, right after this. Now we have some good news and some bad news. The good news first. We still have a mast, and the barometer is rising. The engine is running and nothing got in the propeller. The wind seems to be dropping so the waves should start dropping too. Okay? That's the good news."

Three sets of eyes burning into mine. It had been so much simpler when it had just been Victor, Hung and me. Bachelors with no dependents. Rootless oceanic nomads by choice. With a working autopilot that did most of the steering.

"Now, the bad news. We only have one mast and we can't use it for sailing, at least, not yet. Not with just a rope forestay holding it up. We only have enough diesel for maybe seven or eight hundred miles, so Argentina is not looking too good. We could motor back to South Carolina—but we're not."

They stared across the table, waiting for my next words.

"Our first priority is getting the foremast up on deck, not just hanging over the side, and getting a wire forestay up on the mainmast. Once we have a wire forestay we can put up the working jib, and then we'll be a big ugly sloop with its mast too far back, but at least we'll be a sailboat again. So we need to get to an anchorage where we can dry everything out and get some work done. And I have a few places in mind."

I turned and reached behind myself and grabbed a folded chart from the bottom shelf, then opened it on the table facing them. I used my finger as a pointer. "This is where we were at noon yesterday. I think we've run about a hundred and fifty miles south since then. Maybe south or southeast, it's all dead reckoning. We still have some sea room but it all depends on where we are right now, and we don't know. If our course was more southwest, then we'll be running into the Abacos, but if we've been going southeast, we'll have room to maneuver.

"We're going to stay on the storm watch routine while we have three of us down seasick. Everybody on deck has to keep their eyes and ears peeled for reefs up ahead. Breaking waves, white water, surf sounds, anything. And not just the on-duty watch—everybody on deck. We'll have an almost full moon tonight, and that's in our favor. That's a real blessing."

I spread my thumb and forefinger along the latitude ruler on the side of the chart to make a measurement of a hundred and fifty nautical miles, then I put my thumb on yesterday's noon position, and my finger to the south. "Here is my rough dead-reckoning guess, so we should still have sea room. We'll know for sure the next time I can get a celestial fix, but I think we'll be safe motoring southeast all night."

I penciled a circle around my fingertip. "Here" was about four hundred miles east of Orlando. Give or take fifty or more nautical miles in any direction. Plus or minus. We were almost off Chart 11009, Cape Hatteras to the Straits of Florida.

Then I said to Luke, "Let's take care of that cut. Cuts are no joke if they get infected." I didn't need to mention that we had no antibiotics on board. That was a given.

"I'll take care of the boy," said Jessie. "Trust me, I know all about patching this big sissy up, and it ain't the first time."

"I'm sure you can, but I need to see it. Let's unwrap it in the sink in case it's going to bleed again." I slid into the galley alcove with Luke and Jessie. When he unwound the rag and opened his hand it bled. He had a bad gash from the heel of his right palm and out across the base of his index finger.

This was a pretty typical wire rope "meat hook" wound. An almost invisible broken strand can stick out a quarter inch, and it will cut you like a razor as the wire rope slides through your grip. I'd been in too much of a rush to tackle the downed mast to remember our sailing gloves. Luke had had a hundred chances to get that cut while we secured the mast, but he'd hidden the injury. On the one hand this was commendable, he was a trooper and he'd play hurt, but it could also be foolish if it increased his risk of exposure to infection. This was a very bad way to die, and it had become common in the years since tetanus shots had become a thing of the past.

We had to clean the cut first, using soap and water and our "medicinal grade" high-proof South Carolina corn liquor. Eventually you run out of betadine, iodine, peroxide and even rubbing alcohol. The ninety-percent alcohol was in a black plastic bottle that had once contained peroxide. A bar of anti-bacterial Dial soap was reserved exclusively for medical use.

Keeping a supply of sterile bandages and wraps was the easy part. A more precious commodity was a diminishing but still-viable roll of stretchy surgical tape. I had some suture kits left from the Doctor Aleman era, but I decided to go with the surgical tape instead. I'd watched Victor deal with lacerations many times, on myself and on others. Accidents were a part of shipboard life, but hospital emergency rooms were not. I said a quick silent prayer for guidance, hoping I'd learned enough to do an adequate job for Luke.

The gash was three inches long, but under running water, soap and then alcohol it didn't look too deep. After drying his hand, and with Jessie keeping pressure on it with a bandage to stop the bleeding, I used scissors to cut tape butterflies. Jessie held the wound together while I stuck the butterflies onto his palm over the gash. Finally I taped a gauze dressing over the cut and wrapped his hand with his fingers curled over a rolled wad of cloth. This was to help the cut stay closed, but also to prevent Luke from using his injured hand, even by reflex, in any way that might open up the wound.

I looked at him and made this announcement in front of witnesses. “Luke, I’m putting you on light duty. No steering. No number-two on watch. Not even standby. You don’t touch a line or a winch handle until I say so. You have to keep that thing dry and we’ll look at it again tomorrow. I’m not kidding, dammit. You too, Jessie. We all know what can happen.”

A decade after the end of antibiotics we all knew why our ancestors had called infection *blood poisoning*. Gangrene, then a desperate attempt at amateur amputation, and then agonizing death could follow a simple everyday cut.

30

The conditions improved dramatically by Friday morning. The barometer was up to 992 and the wind was down in the teens. I was able to snag a pair of morning stars, Vega and Arcturus, and our celestial position put us far enough to the east that we didn't have to worry about the Abacos. In fact, we were fifty miles northeast of San Salvador Island, and off the chart that we'd been using since South Carolina. The new position was on Chart 27005, Key West to San Juan. It showed the Atlantic from Florida to Puerto Rico and down to Jamaica, including Haiti and the Dominican Republic, the Bahamas and most of Cuba. These were collectively known as The Greater Antilles.

It's difficult to explain the significance to an ocean sailor of switching to a new chart. For a week we'd been marking our positions on Chart #11009, Cape Hatteras to the Straits of Florida, which ended at the top of the Bahamas. When Chart 11009 was folded up and put away the Carolinas and Georgia were officially in our wake, in our past. Chart 27005 showed the entire northern tier of the Caribbean. A whole new world of sea and land was spread across the table before us.

With a new celestial fix we restarted our dead reckoning log, which had been overlooked during the storm. Will, Sofia and Rita were almost over their seasickness and could return to full duty. Based on the improving conditions, we returned to the old two-person watch system, with a helmsman and a number-two who were on for two hours and off for six. Jessie swore that she could steer under power as well as any man, and she'd keep Luke from using his bandaged hand, and keep it dry, so I let them stay together in the watch rotation.

A noon sight that put us level with San Salvador but forty miles to its east added to my confidence. My destination was under a hundred miles to the south-southeast, so we'd reach it the next day. There was no point in rushing, so we pulled the throttle back to make four knots, which still gave the helmsman easy control. Adam and Will put out their fishing hooks and lines. I didn't need to tell them that Will was up one fish to zero—they were bantering about it unprompted.

(Incidentally, it had been one week since Captain Hilton Sapelo had come aboard to adjust Rebel's compass, leading to his leaving young Adam Selfridge in our care. Just one week!)

The wind bands ran up and down between the teens and twenties, and while the swells had grown to more than thirty feet high measured by eye, they were just rollers with football fields between them. Yesterday's anarchy had conglomerated into smooth regularity. The big waves ate the small ones and became even bigger, but they were harmless and arriving in orderly rows. There wasn't even a whitecap, just some riffles. Our blood pressures went down as the barometer went up.

But we still had only one mast, a mast that we couldn't use, and not enough fuel to get us anywhere that would matter. First things first, though: we had to get to a safe anchorage to sort things out and become a sailboat again. I had a place in mind, and we had the fuel to get us there. I'd even been there before, on Rebel's first trip to the Caribbean after her rebirth.

We passed an uneventful night motoring south-southeast. Saturday morning was overcast again but it burned off enough to get a noon sight. Partly overcast is good enough for the sun, you only need to be able to make out its disc and drag it down to the horizon with your sextant's adjustable mirror.

Everyone on deck was under orders to keep their eyes peeled for the sight of terra firma or breaking waves ahead. Around 1300 Rita asked, "Is that land? Or just low clouds?"

I saw it too, but I was very happy to let her announce the discovery first. "That's got to be Mayaguana," I said. I had our Bahamas Out Islands chart in the cockpit, folded to the right section. I held it against the latched-open pilothouse door and used my finger as a pointer. “We’ve already gone too far for it to be Crooked Island or Acklins, and it’s way too big for it to be the Plana Cays, so it can only be Mayaguana.”

I had left Rebel Yell anchored on Acklins Island during our Castigo Cay operation a decade earlier. Victor and Hung took care of the boat while I’d gone to Florida. Now they were gone, and I was the only one left who remembered any part of that adventure. Just me and my friendly ghosts.

Unrelated to the land emerging ahead of us, behind us Will began to shout about some action on our trolling lines, and Adam yelled “Fish On!” Sailing gloves were lying around the cockpit drying out, and because it was the starboard-side line being stretched, Adam slipped on a pair and went to work. Something was slashing back and forth about a hundred yards behind us, but at least so far it couldn’t spit out the big hook, or cut the hundred-pound-test monofilament leader, or break the nylon cord tying him to Rebel Yell. This was meat fishing, and it had absolutely nothing to do with sport.

Adam stood on the aft deck and hauled in the line hand over hand, preserving his hard-won progress by dragging the cord through the one-way ratchet cleat on the stern rail. The entire crew was watching when he pulled the fish up near our stern. It was at least six feet long and shaped like a torpedo. Gino stood by the Dushka with our long-poled gaff.

Even before it was on our boarding platform I recognized it. “Barracuda—a big one. Cut it loose. It’s not worth losing a hand just to save a hook. I’m surprised he didn’t cut the leader with his teeth. I’m sorry, Adam, but that one’s not a keeper.”

Will said, “That thing is bigger than my wahoo. Just look at those teeth! I think he could eat a rabbit in one bite.”

Adam said, “Or take a rabbit-size chunk of meat out of you. Their teeth are razor-sharp and they interlock so they cut like scissors.” He pulled a folding knife from his pocket and the blade opened on the draw. He leaned over the rail, grabbed the monofilament leader and sliced it, letting the fish go. Then he turned to us and said, "Barracudas can kill you even when you're not in the water. They'll eat reef fish that eat poisonous coral. If you eat a big barracuda you can get something called ciguatera poisoning. There's no medicine for it, and there's no cure. It can take you a week to die, and you're in terrible pain the whole time."

"How do you know all that?" Rita asked him.

"My uncle told me. It's true. Just don't eat barracudas."

Then the other trolling line that was still out on the port side began to stretch, leading us to watch another fish trying to throw another hook a hundred yards behind us. This one made hopeless half leaps, wearing itself out running back and forth by the time Will pulled it up onto the platform. It was a bull mahi-mahi with the signature square forehead. Gino gaffed it and pulled it up and over the stern pulpit. I dispatched it with the fish billy while it was flashing iridescent green, purple and red, and finally in death it laid dull silver.

The big cutting board was brought out. I went straight to work with our fillet knife converting the mahi into meat. The crew kidded Adam about being skunked two-to-zero by Will but he took it pleasantly. No one mentioned who had filleted Will's wahoo in the same place just four days before. But how could any of us forget Mike Ortega?

The biggest fillets were the size of a man's arm. I sliced them into foot-long pieces so they would fit inside our pans. The meat went to the galley; the rest of the mahi went back into the ocean where it had been swimming a half hour before. The same ocean where Mike was in all likelihood fish food.

Mayaguana widened before us as more of it rose above the horizon. The island stretched 25 miles from east to west, but at no point was it more than 140 feet high, so sailors didn't get much warning before they were almost upon it. You can spot islands that are thousands of feet high many hours before you approach them, depending on the cloud cover. We had spotted Tenerife in the Canaries the evening before our arrival because it rose two miles above the Atlantic.

We upped our speed to six knots and adjusted our course to aim for the western tip of the island. I wanted to get around the end of Mayaguana so that we'd arrive before dark in order to have the sun behind us for entering the anchorage. When the sun is in front of you its reflection turns the ocean ahead into an opaque sheet of glare, but when the sun is behind you it pierces the water and shows the bottom in perfect clarity.

We rounded the western side of Mayaguana just a few miles off but with the depth sounder still indicating more than 500 feet below our keel. According to the chart the ocean in the middle of the Mayaguana Passage was over five thousand feet deep, with Acklins Island lying fifty miles to the west. If you drained the ocean, Mayaguana would be a steep mountain with a narrow 25-mile-long plateau on top.

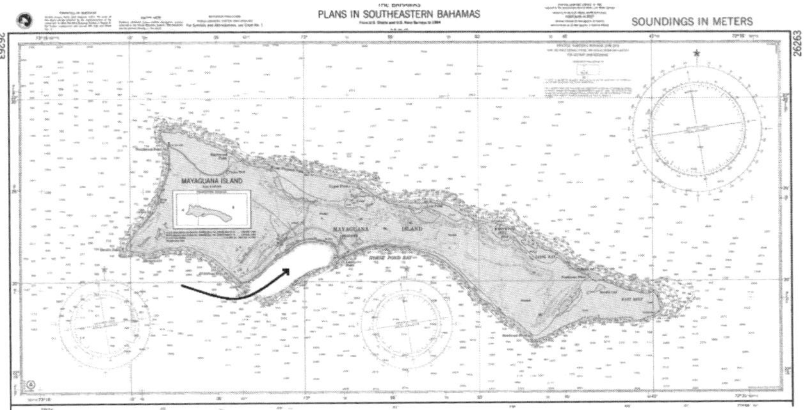

It was time to switch to an approach chart. I had a spiral-bound chart kit of the Bahamas dated from 1986 that I'd bought used in Miami when I was rebuilding Rebel Yell. This seventy-page collection of yard-wide chart reproductions was the state of the art for Bahamas navigation before the GPS era, and then again after GPS had disappeared. The charts included my own handwritten notes, plus my penciled arrows and anchor symbols showing where Rebel had spent a night on the hook.

Luke and Jessie were on watch but all hands were on deck, hungry to study the land we were motoring toward. The mahi could wait in the galley. Both pairs of binoculars were passed from hand to hand. We could make out trees on the shore but no people or vehicles. Devil's Point was unmistakable as we approached the sharply-turning southwest corner of the island. We could examine each palm tree, but our depth sounder was maxed at 500 feet and the chart said a thousand.

At my request Tala brought me my Polaroid sunglasses. They were saved for critical situations like these. Both of their hinges had broken years before, so I had glued their temple ear pieces in the open position. A string tied to their tips kept them attached to me even when they were not on my face. For safe-keeping they were kept in their own cigar box wrapped in a soft rag. Everybody knew I was serious when I put on my old Ray-Bans, with a long-billed ball cap to shade them.

We turned the corner around Devil's Point and continued motoring southeast toward the bottom of the island. Mayaguana was terra firm, but not by much. If it dropped 150 feet it would disappear. The crew was excited to see land of any sort, but I couldn't help but to compare this landfall to our far more dramatic approaches to Ireland and the Canaries. I didn't want to diminish the joy of my crew, so I kept my mouth shut.

When we were a half mile south of Low Point we were still off soundings, even as the western entrance to Abraham's Bay came into focus. Gino and I conferred on our tactics. I'd read the water from the bow and he'd steer and run the engine. The visual picture ahead of us matched the charts with my notes, arrows and anchors drawn on them. The short western leg of the bay's protective reef has a channel through it. As we approached the pass the two frothy areas of surf guarding the entrance became obvious, with the channel through the coral reef a smooth medium-blue. The chart said we'd have fifteen feet of water going into Abraham's Bay.

Once we broke 500 feet on our depth sounder the bottom came up rapidly, climbing from triple- to double-digit depths in only a few hundred yards. After a week off soundings it's shocking when the LCD numbers on the display drop from five hundred to ninety to nineteen feet in about a minute.

Gino steered and I went to the bow with the young crew to show them how to read tropical water. The sun was behind us making it a perfect teaching opportunity, so I just spoke my thoughts and observations aloud to them. Tropical water acts like a pale blue filter, and the deeper the water is, the darker the bottom appears. A foot of water over sand appears white, running through all the turquoise shades to indigo blue. Coral heads are generally brown, but they could appear black or mustard yellow depending on the type of coral and the depth of the water above them. A grassy bottom has its own unique color shifts. Passing clouds can trick you into seeing coral heads that aren't there. If a patch of coral seems to be moving, look up for a matching cloud casting a shadow.

Twelve feet—not fifteen—was the shallowest depth that Gino called out to us from the cockpit as we crossed through the opening. The ocean swell that had been wrapping around the island in the deep water disappeared. There was only a little wind chop, but not enough to push Rebel around.

Abraham's Bay continued in front of us to the northeast for five miles, with the shore of Mayaguana Island lying a half mile off our port side. The reef defining the bay lay a half mile to starboard and ran the entire five-mile length. The Bahamas Telephone Company BaTelCo radio tower was still standing just beyond the northeast end, marking the village named for the bay. I'd briefly visited years before, so I remembered that the village and the government offices were just a short walk beyond the end of the bay. The village at Abraham's Bay had practically been a ghost town, and the handful of garage-size government offices were rarely open. Even so, it was the biggest settlement on Mayaguana Island, and home to about half of the three hundred people living on it.

According to one of my old cruising guides, Mayaguana was 110 square miles in size. By comparison, New Providence was only 80 square miles, but it had a population of 300,000 people, as well as being the home of the national capital. More people lived around Nassau than in the rest of the Bahamas put together, and a dozen other islands were larger in area.

In decades past Mayaguana could have been a world-class scuba destination, but the wealth of beauty it had in abundance underwater was utterly lacking above. There were no dramatic bluffs, no hills from which to capture a dramatic view, it was, and is, just a flat, arid and wind-swept semi-wasteland. Live-aboard dive boats might have brought some tourism, but there were already many more accessible reefs in the region.

Mayaguana's only notable development had happened in the 1960s when NASA decided it would be an ideal location to build a missile tracking station. Long, flat and nearly uninhibited, with a giant bay to barge in heavy equipment, a 7,000-foot runway was laid down. This led to a brief boom with the population rising to a few thousand, followed by a decades-long bust when NASA and the U.S. Air Force pulled chocks and flew home for good after the Apollo program ended.

But the runway was still there, so a Bahamas Air flight came in twice a week, mostly so the handful of minor officials exiled to the remote "far-out island" could shuttle home. Without those two weekly flights, Mayaguana might have sunk into the ocean without the slightest notice from the outside world.

According to the rumors I'd heard when I'd visited, the little money that made its way into the local economy was the result of Mayaguana being a convenient drug transshipment point. There were miles of unnamed sandy beaches and a long runway that officially saw only two aircraft landings per week. The few constables assigned to keep the peace were notable for never being around when the drug loads came in across the beaches, or when an unannounced aircraft landed and took off again between midnight and dawn.

When I had visited Mayaguana I'd seen a few remarkably incongruent high-end 4-by-4s and big boat trailers customized with balloon tires for launching go-fast boats across a beach. It didn't take a NASA scientist to figure out what had been keeping Mayaguana's tiny population afloat. But that had been back when the American economy was flourishing, along with the American appetite for strong Jamaican ganja and the other narcotics flowing up from Central and South America.

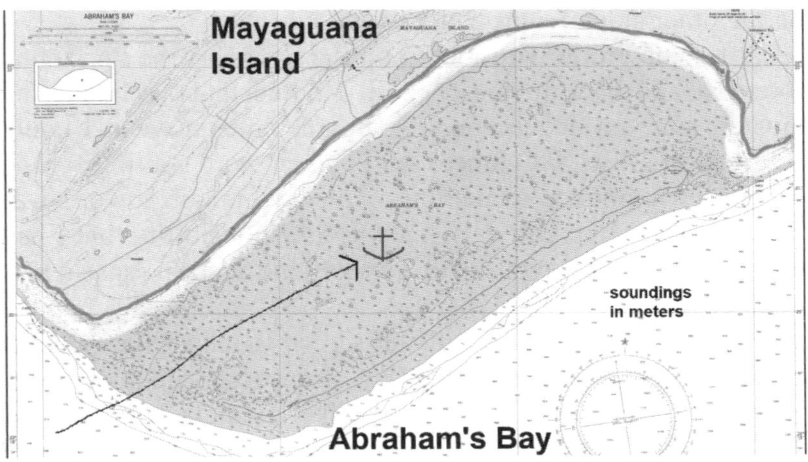

I stood at the bow and used arm signals to indicate the best path for Gino to steer while I continued with my water-reading class. There were no other boats at anchor; we had the entire five square miles all to ourselves. We motored halfway up the bay and dropped the hook in eleven feet of water, after making a wide circle to ensure that we had enough depth and no coral heads all the way around. I let Barry and Adam handle the anchor detail under my direction. Luke was on the bow too, but only to watch because he was on light duty. Will was there out of his own interest, and Rita was there because of Adam.

The hook was down by 1545. Following my hand signals Gino reversed hard a few times to make sure the anchor was well set, with our chain stretched out through the clear water. When I was satisfied I gave him the arm signal and he killed the engine. The Cat had been running non-stop for two days, and I mentally subtracted that much diesel fuel, running time and potential motoring distance from our reserves.

The silence and stillness were overwhelming. Rebel Yell was not moving through the ocean, there were no waves on the bay worthy of the name, and we were anchored next to an island that occupied half of our horizon. The open sea to our south was on the other side of a protective reef.

I led the group with me up on the bow past the horizontal foremast and back to the cockpit. I noted that we had a full muster, an even dozen souls on board. After a week I could count them all with a glance. All of them were waiting for the captain to announce something. And the captain's word was law: just ask Mike Ortega. This was a responsibility that I had to consciously endeavor not to abuse. In the deepest sense it was a sacred trust.

"Okay, gang, first of all, let's give thanks where thanks belongs for getting us through that storm to a safe anchorage. So thank you, lord, we know we didn't get here without your divine help." I heard a few amens, and the name of Jesus *not* being taken in vain. I was never a religious man, not in any formal sense, but I was a Christian, and if there was one thing life had taught me it's that we all need a good compass. Otherwise, you can steer off course and wind up on the rocks. And even much worse, you can take other people with you.

I made eye contact with all of them before speaking about our situation. "We have a lot to do, and we're going to get to it, but first I want everybody to take a deep breath and relax. We'll deal with the mast tomorrow. Today, I want everybody to just take it easy. And stay hydrated: we're in the real tropics now and it's summer all the time. You're going to see a lot of sun from now on, so wear hats and keep your skin covered. And if you don't like hats, I don't care. This isn't South Carolina. We're south of Havana, and the sun down here is no joke. Just the sun reflecting off the water is enough to burn you. I already see some red noses, so don't come crying to me later if you don't listen to me now."

I made eye contact with all of them again and continued. "Now, let's open every hatch on this boat and get some dry air down below. Get everything that's wet up on deck while we still have some sun left. Anything that might blow away once it's dry, weight it down or tie it to something or it'll be gone. And I want the big tarp set up over the cockpit. There's not much wind now because we're between systems, but most of the time here we can expect about twenty knots from the east. So let's get the big tarp up now before the trade wind comes back, okay? Gino will show you how we do it. From here on it won't be a matter of rain protection as much as sun protection, so stay in the shade as much as you can. Wear hats and keep your skin covered. If you don't listen to what I'm saying don't come crying to me about how bad it hurts or how your skin is all blistered. Take the sun seriously or you'll be damned sorry, and I'll be all out of sympathy."

I remembered Sergeant Major Tolbert giving us similar warnings about taking care of our feet back in Morocco.

"We're sticking to the two-man watch rotation, but now it's an anchor watch. I don't care who is on deck, but one of each pair has to be in the cockpit or the pilothouse at all times. We'll use the hand compass to take bearings on the shore, and I'll make a sketch map so we can tell if we're dragging. That's the number-one job of the anchor watch, letting us know if we're dragging anchor, especially at night. There's not much wind now, but it'll come, plenty of it, and there's no excuse for dragging anchor when we have an anchor watch, right? Now, let's open up all the hatches and bring the wet stuff up."

"All the hatches?" asked Adam. "Even the cargo hatch?"

"Yes, even the cargo hatch. *Especially* the cargo hatch."

"Then we'll have to move Whisper out of the way first."

"That's your job, dinghy master. You'll need a lot of help because we don't have the foremast boom to swing it out. You decide who you'll need and how you're going to do it. Splash the Whisper, open the cargo hatch and get everything wet up on deck. And now, if you will all excuse me, my next order of business is catching up on a little sleep. So if you can keep the noise down while you're putting up the tarp and launching the dinghy, I'd really appreciate it."

I went below to my cabin and kicked off my boat shoes, stripped out of my salt-damp clothes, put on a thin pair of dry shorts and crawled onto my bed. The lee cloth was still up but it didn't matter, because we were not heeling at anchor. Now it was just a privacy curtain between my double bed and the twins' pallet. Sunbeams drilled through the transom ports and made bright ovals on the back of the engine room and head. Tala must have opened the ports after we cut the motor. If they were open with the engine running, the aft cabin would fill with diesel smoke. Our exhaust would be sucked up our transom from its exit pipe under the swim platform and pulled in through the two ports. Engine on, ports closed.

Open transom ports, open deck hatches, and Rebel Yell is no longer battling killer waves and white squalls but riding gently at anchor in the afternoon sunshine with the engine off. This was a foretaste of heaven. Any problems we had were going to be solvable because Rebel was a strong steel boat and I was blessed with an amazing crew. We could fix anything and still go anywhere. Then I was out like a light and gone.

31

For a change I was not awakened by Adam grabbing my foot. The rudder was not groaning with effort as our stern rose to meet the next wave. Instead, almost beyond belief, I just woke up on my own. It was dark in the aft cabin and I had the entire place to myself. The aft-deck hatch above me was opened a foot to let in some breeze. The transom port was also open.

My wristwatch said it was nine-fifteen, or 2115 in voyage time. I turned on the lamp, and took my time getting up. Tala had laid a new outfit on the bed next me. Dry khakis, a dry t-shirt, and dry socks. Now if I could just get the body oils and sea salt off me . . . and especially out of my itchy scalp.

I went to the galley and nobody was there, but a plate was set for one. They'd let me sleep right through dinner. I pushed on the white galley light, no need to worry about preserving night vision at anchor. Two slabs of grilled mahi, home fried potatoes, cole slaw, a small bowl of dipping sauce, a fork, a cloth napkin and a glass of water. Somebody had made a place card out of a folded strip of white paper; it read *CAPTAIN* in a fantasy version of Germanic calligraphy. I recognized Rita's pencil art by its detailed edges and intricate shading.

The barometer was up to 997. My wristwatch was a few minutes ahead of the ship's clock. They'd both need to be set from the chronometer tomorrow, and the cockpit watch too. It took me only a few minutes to consume the food, most of this time spent staring at Rita's place holder card.

Then up through the cargo hold. Nobody there, but the big seven-by-seven foot hatch was wide open above me. The two hinged hatch leaves were standing upright on each side, held in place by skinny wooden poles forming an X at their front and rear. This arrangement kept the side decks clear and also prevented anyone from accidentally falling into the hold. When people become accustomed to freely roaming the decks, a massive new hole presents an unnecessary risk.

For a welcome change I could casually stand in the cargo hold passageway with my hands raised above deck level, and without bracing myself against the restraining timbers on the sides. This was my first look from the hold up at the sky with no foremast rocking gently against the stars. No foremast, no boom, no wire rigging, just the mainmast's staysail halyard clipped to the bow to hold it up. At least we still had a mast.

Then into the forward cabin, it was also empty. Then up the ladder to where Rebel's white decks were bathed in moonlight. Almost no clouds, just some high feathery cirrus. I studied the anchor windlass and chain where it led over the bow roller, and I looked down at the bottom. Below us Rebel Yell's moon shadow lay on the white sand, her bowsprit shadow a sharp finger pointing north. The chain was visible through the water and ahead of us to where it disappeared into the sand. My sixty-foot former schooner appeared to hover ten feet above the bottom. The chain could have been hanging through air.

Green phosphor trails zoomed and twisted all around us as predator sought prey. Fish that were leaping high to avoid being eaten left sparkling trails through the air and landed with a green flash. I knew that this was an experience land dwellers would never see or even imagine in their land-bound lives. But to be fair, landsmen also missed the prolonged terror of storms at sea. If we had stayed knocked down with our masts in the water for a full minute we'd have sunk, flooding through the open top of the scuttle hatch. That's how close we had come.

I grabbed the staysail halyard and followed it with my eye to the top of the mainmast. At least we still had one mast up. Luke and Jessie were sitting on deck in front of the open cargo hold and they rose when they saw me turning toward them. Jessie was wearing a light jersey, I knew by its logo that it was one of Sofia's, and it was pink in daylight. Luke was wearing a dress shirt that I had last seen on Victor. His black hair was tied back; Jessie's blonde hair was done in two braids.

Jessie said, "Honestly, captain, this is just about the most beautiful place I've ever seen. Here we are on Abraham's Bay, and I've never even heard of Mayaguana Island."

"This bay has a five-mile reef and a world-class dropoff wall on the other side, and nobody's ever heard of it. If it wasn't so remote, there'd be sportfishing boats and liveaboard dive boats anchored up and down the bay. Oh, and you don't have to call me captain, not unless you want to. Skipper is fine. So, how are your guitars doing?"

Luke said, "No water got inside them, but they were wet outside, especially where they were laying in the water inside their cases. We caught them before they started swelling. The varnish on my guitar looks milky on the bottom. We're drying them real slow because I don't want them to delaminate. We'll know in a few days."

Jessie added, "There's nothing wrong with my mandolin. Now that you're up and we don't need to tip-toe around, is it too late for a little music, captain? I've got that *urge* again."

"Too late for music? Not for me it isn't. What's the name of that song you were starting? The whaler man song?"

"The Wellerman song. Should I get my mandolin?"

"Yes, I'd like that." She dropped down through the scuttle hatch, and I advised Luke to never let go of that girl. Most of the crew were sitting or lying on deck while staring at the full moon and stars. Clothes and bedding were hanging from all of the lifelines and lay over the downed foremast. The tarp was over the mainmast boom and tied out to the lifeline stanchions making a tent over the cockpit.

I ran into Tala when I was coming around the back of the pilothouse, and after a quick kiss I asked her to please bring up a bottle of South Carolina moonshine. Not the medicinal-grade high-proof stuff that I'd poured on Luke's cut, but the sipping kind in the big square glass bottle. She gave me another kiss and went inside and below.

The compass light was glowing atop the steering pedestal, but the wheel was not moving, and in fact, it didn't even have a hand on it. I moved around the wheel and sat in the back of the cockpit on a cushion that was passed to me. Tala came up with the bottle and a stack of plastic tumblers and sat by me. The cups were green, but in moonlight they were gray.

In another era the bottle had contained 1.75 liters of Jack Daniels Tennessee bourbon whiskey. The bottle's black label was long gone back in Beaufort when I'd bought the new whiskey for silver coin. I looked around and I guessed that I was the only one who remembered Jack Daniels. Jack Who? Maybe Gino, but only maybe. Black Jack wasn't my favorite, it was not my taste, but it had been a famous brand that was internationally recognized by its square bottle and black label.

Now the clear bottle contained South Carolina moonshine from a Beaufort distiller of repute. So far, I hadn't gone blind, and it tasted all right. I'd only have dated myself if I asked my crew if they knew what had originally been in the bottle, so I didn't. "Hey—grandpa is telling a story about the olden days!"

I poured an inch into the top cup from the stack and I said, "The first glass is for my first mate and chief engineer—Mr. Gino Bracciano." I handed it to him; he toasted me, and drank it straight down. Next pour: "Luke Hanahan, this is strictly for medicinal purposes. It's only to keep your wound sterile from the inside out." He drank part of it, and set the rest down. Around the cockpit it went. Jessie took a cup with just an inch, sipped it and then put it down. Barry accepted an inch of the clear spirit, but he didn't move it toward his lips right away.

Once or twice a minute something big enough to make an audible splash slapped the water, reminding us that something even bigger had been chasing it down below. The moonlit bay was teeming with life. Adam Selfridge had surely earned a man's drink, but I remembered that Hilton Sapelo had said his mother was an alcoholic. He was sitting beside Rita on some drying piece of bedding, and they found another place to look while their captain was dispensing hard liquor. I knew Tala wouldn't take any, and Sofia shook her head no, so I poured a glass for myself and drank it down. Strong, yes, but not harsh.

A hint of peach, the Beaufort distiller's mark. Only their very best went into the old square Jack Daniels bottles.

If we'd had any beer or wine on board I'd have gone in that direction first, but we didn't, and so I couldn't. Our only choices were white lightning, or South Carolina river water aged in Rebel Yell's water tanks, and then run through Gino's homemade charcoal filter. I wondered if I'd committed a faux pas by bringing out the liquor, but I felt I'd earned a drink, and I wasn't going to sneak it, or have Tala see me drinking alone. Or the twins. No sir. Right out in the open, or not at all.

We'd all come through the storm together, so share and share alike, within reason. Call it decompression. Unwinding the built-up stress. And I also felt that teaching the young ones some of the seedier social graces had some merit, whether or not they partook. At least let them bear witness to responsible adults having a few drinks. I believed that throwing kids out into the cruel world without at least a passing familiarity with Demon Rum did them no benefit in the long run. This blind spot might leave them susceptible to falling all the way down through an unnoticed trap door to the bottom of the deepest pit of despair, far beyond any hope of recovery.

Well, anyway, that was how I rationalized it to myself. Will, Tala and Sofia all begged off the hard stuff, and Adam and Rita were too young. But if I'd had a bottle of chardonnay or merlot, I knew that Tala and Sofia would have enjoyed it with a connoisseur's appreciation. The drinkers finished their cups and passed them back for refills.

Jessie and Luke sat on cushions in the front of the cockpit against the open pilothouse door. Her blonde hair in braids; his black hair tied back. I had flashbacks of Victor because of his dress shirt. Everywhere that wasn't under the tarp was lit by stars, and the cockpit was lit by the compass. The wind had died, the bay was glassy, and the water was transparent with the full moon lighting the sand below and all around us. It was pure magic when Jessie began to play her mandolin and sing.

The Wellerman song was about the hardships endured by 19th-Century sailors who spent months at sea hunting whales and battling storms. Their only joy came from anticipating the arrival of a supply ship bringing them sugar, tea and rum. We had an approximation of rum, but no sugar. Or tea, or coffee, or other things that had not been available in South Carolina. When Jessie finished the song, I asked her if she remembered where she had been seven nights before.

"It's Saturday, right? Then we were playing in Beaufort in the pavilion. We had microphones, and amplifiers, and the whole place was wrapped around in electric lights. Oh, what a night! And that was the night we came aboard Rebel Yell."

Will said, "That was the night I came aboard, too."

"I was already aboard," said Adam. "By half a day."

Nobody mentioned someone else who had joined the crew on the night of the Beaufort Pavilion Electric Music Concert. I think we were all trying to forget Mike Ortega. I remembered Aikman and the machine gunner disappearing into the Beaufort River. Had their bodies been found? Probably, but what of it? We were long gone and never going back. Fujimo!

More songs by Jessie followed. Gino took over the square bottle and plastic tumbler duties. Adam brought out the PVS-14 to do some serious star and moon gazing with Rita and Will on the foredeck. At some point I realized that Luke had a guitar on his lap. He had an improvised guitar pick extending from inside his bandaged right mitt.

I remembered Jessie and Luke singing and playing songs from the past, but I didn't ask if anyone else remembered the tunes or the groups who had first recorded them. For the new generation they were fresh new songs. Luke was familiar with *Rebel Yell* as sung by Billy Idol, but not well enough to try to play it, not even with my vocal assistance and encouragement. Tala and Sofia may, or may not, have poured a little whiskey into their water as the night wore on, but I was unclear on this point. It was a magical, musical starry night, with my former schooner casting a single mast shadow on the moonlit sand.

32

When or how I got to my rack I don't recall, but when I woke up again daylight was filtering down inside the aft cabin. I had a headache and my mouth felt like it had been packed with dirt. I was in shorts and a t-shirt and I didn't remember getting into either. Tala was gone, and so were the twins. I headed forward to go to the cockpit to check out the scene, but Tala intercepted me in the galley, and she pushed me over into the dinette. She was wearing an old set of Victor's hospital scrubs so faded their pale green was almost white. According to the clock it was almost nine. I smelled bread baking in the oven.

"After you eat, Sofia is going to shave your beard down to skin. We can't stand looking on you. I would cut you but Sofia is better for shaving the beards, and you are the last. You look old and ugly with the gray beard, but maybe I will speak with you again when you have a clean face. And also—you stink." She planted a bowl of cereal mush and a glass of water in front of me, without making eye contact, and disappeared forward through the cargo hold.

Ho—ly—crap, I thought. I must have made an ass out of myself last night. Obviously there was no point in asking Tala what I'd done to piss her off. I'd get the real story from Gino. Not that it mattered. I was the captain, and Rebel Yell was my boat, and my boat was anchored out in the back of beyond. So where is she going to go? She'd get over it. She had no option.

But on the other hand, it would be totally wrong to take advantage of my advantage as the captain and boat owner. She was my wife, the woman I loved, and the mother of my sons. And I knew that she had a hundred ways to make my life a living hell if we ever turned against one another. Before I'd met Tala Abidar in Morocco these concepts had rarely entered my mind. That was back when only a very few girlfriends had lasted more than a couple months aboard Rebel Yell. Careful diplomacy was required to straddle the gap between tyrant and simp, while still retaining the favor of the beautiful French and Berber runaway with the burning amber eyes.

The chart kit was already on the table opened to the best Mayaguana chart, and I penciled a little anchor in the middle of the bay, with yesterday's date. I didn't need to break out the sextant, because I already knew exactly where we were. If I cared about our latitude and longitude, they were printed right along both edges of the chart. No wonder people on the land didn't care about transmitting a time signal on the radio anymore. They had maps, and they knew where they were.

When I finished the mush and I climbed up the ladder to go outside, Sofia was waiting to intercept me in the pilothouse. So that's why Tala had gone forward through the cargo hold: clearly the two were conspiring. Sofia pointed to the pedestal chair; it was facing to starboard to give her the most working room around it. I sat and she threw a musty deck towel around my shoulders. Everything else she needed was in reach behind me on the top of the chart cabinet where our single-sideband radio was also now residing. She was also wearing old scrubs.

She stood in front of me with her fists on her hips. "You know that Tala is very angry with you? You do know this?"

"What did I do? We were all having a great time. It was perfect—the moon, the stars everything. We were all singing, and I remember going swimming. So why is she angry?"

"Singing ? Going swimming? Just *swimming*? And is that what you remember?" Sofia whipped up some lather in a cup and applied it to one side of my week-old beard, and then she seized my chin and jaw and shoved my bristly face from side to side and up and down while making her appraisal. In her right hand, and in front of my face, she held up one of Victor's ancient German straight razors—opened full length.

"What's wrong with a midnight dip?" I asked her.

"What's wrong? Ha! Don't you move, not even one little inch, or you will have a cut like Luke—but you will have it on your face. Do you want another scar like the one you have? So don't move and be quiet. You made everybody so afraid, and this you don't even remember?" She stretched my left cheek and began to scrape away at my beard from the top down. This took a lot of scraping, because I had a week of new beard. She applied new lather, wiped the razor on my shoulder towel and began again, giving the same section from my ear to my chin another going-over.

"You dived over the side of the boat and you didn't come up—and this is what you call *a midnight dip*? Everybody was watching you diving from on top of this pilothouse in a big surprise, and then you didn't come up! Everybody is looking down in the ocean, and where is our captain? Where?"

Sofia wiped the razor against the towel and continued her attack with short hard scrapes while pulling my skin taut with her other hand. "We are looking down on the side where you dived into the ocean. One minute. Then two minutes. Maybe three minutes. We are all looking down on the side of the boat. Maybe four minutes. Rita is crying, and Tala is screaming, and nobody knows what we can do. And we are thinking maybe you are drowned because you are so drunk, or maybe a shark has taken you or maybe a barracuda, and then you are standing behind us, and you are *laughing* on us! All wet from the ocean and you are *laughing* on us!

"And you are doing all this for making a joke? *Hacer una broma*? So you swim under the boat, and then you wait on the other side, and maybe under the platform, while everybody is screaming and crying, and then you climbed up on the back. So okay, we learned about this later. The young boys think it's a funny trick after they see you again, but it's a very bad trick. *Un truco malo, un truco cruel. Insensible*. Especially it was so bad for Tala and Rita. You are gone down in the ocean more than three or four minutes! Gone down with all the sharks and barracudas in the world swimming in this bay! And this is why Tala is very angry on you now. This was a very bad joke, Dan, this midnight dip. A very bad joke. *Cruel*. Muy malo."

All the while Sofia was pushing and pulling my face, and slapping homemade shaving cream onto each new section in order to hack away at my beard millimeter by millimeter. But at least I understood why Tala was so angry at me. And there was no reason to say anything to Sofia. I had no case to make in my defense. Especially not with soap lather all over my lips.

She had to go over some parts of my face, chin and neck a few times. Even without the benefit of a mirror I knew that I had some shaving cuts. I'd felt the sharp stings, but I thought, if this gets me out of the dog house, it'll be worth it.

Finally, after wiping my face with the old deck towel, she announced she was done and told me to get out. *"¡Vete!"*

I didn't reply to Sofia. There was really no reply to make, so I just stepped up into the cockpit. What a difference between the boat out in the waves with sails up, and the boat at anchor with the tarp over the boom. Completely different worlds. Even the sunlight was different, filtered through the tan fabric.

Rebel was facing north, toward Mayaguana, and the wind was blowing at about fifteen, but the chop was negligible with only a half-mile of fetch from the land for waves to build up. Behind us the five-mile reef was visible but calm. I knew from my last visit that when the southeast trades built up big swells the entire length of the reef would be exploding in white fury, but even then Abraham's Bay would remain a safe anchorage.

Barry and Gino were both clean-shaven, but it looked like Gino was trying to grow a moustache. Luke's black beard was trimmed but still intact. Adam's cheeks had yet to feel a razor.

Barry's blonde hair was starting to fill in so he looked less like an escaped convict or boot-camp deserter. The salt air and salt water had healed his Beaufort face-plant scrapes. A paint-stained oxford dress shirt from the grab bag protected his arms from the sun and hid his burn scars from our eyes.

After a quick "good morning" in reply to their greetings I went to the stern-rail opening gate by the Dushka. Whisper was trailing astern by her bow line, but the shorter mast and red sail from Adam's pram were set instead of her usual rig.

I peeled off my shirt and dove into the water. We were anchored in only twelve feet so I grabbed handfuls of sand and scrubbed my hair and scalp and all of my body that I could reach. I made a few surface dives and repeated this until I felt like I'd been sandpapered. My body oils would be erased, and I wouldn't stink.

My facial cuts stung but the salt and minerals would stop the bleeding, and the sun would dry them out soon after that. Sharks and barracudas didn't worry me, not even at night, and certainly not in broad daylight. Outside of a few situations my policy was, *if you don't bother me, I won't bother you.* And if I can cut a brother a break, like with Adam's barracuda, I will. This was also my first chance to observe, from the water, the top of the downed foremast jutting out past the transom. Seen from any direction it's so out of place it's just crazy.

I rinsed the grit out of my hair while hanging back from the boarding ladder, which some thoughtful person had flipped down while I was underwater. It was somebody named Tala, because when I looked up she was waiting for me on the swim platform. She was wearing a form-fitting beige T-shirt dress that she saved for the tropics, and her hair was brushed out. Was I going to be scolded again? It sure didn't look like it.

But before I'd find out I had some business to attend to. "Get my mask and fins; I want to look at the bottom." These were kept ready in a cockpit locker and were passed to her. She dropped them down to me one at a time and I put them on while I was treading water. Putting a mask on my face and fins on my feet turned me from a clumsy ocean visitor into a functional marine mammal. Give me a sharp knife, and I could bite back.

The water was so gin clear I could have been surveying Rebel's hull high and dry in a boatyard. We sure weren't anchored on the Beaufort River with its one-foot visibility. The rudder and keel were covered with barnacle crust from our last careening and new barnacles were growing atop the old base. Between the keel and the rudder our big three-bladed bronze propeller looked okay. We would scrape the propeller before leaving the bay but the rest could wait. On the starboard side all of the ropes and lines from the dismasting had been pulled clear of the water and were secured to the downed mast.

Satisfied with my initial inspection I climbed the ladder up onto the platform across from Tala. I noticed a folded towel on the aft deck between the Dushka's legs. She examined my glistening body from my head to my heels. The aft deck and cockpit were strangely empty; the crew had all found someplace else to be. Neither of us moved closer.

She put her hands on her hips and tilted her face. Her eyes flashed amber in the sunlight, and her brown hair glinted with blonde streaks. "Sofia makes a good job of shaving. You have a good enough face when it's cut, but not when you look like the *vagabundo* with the gray beard. I am yet a young woman, and I will not be with an ugly old man."

She passed me the towel and said, "In ten minutes Adam and Rita are going sailing with the twins. Adam has already been sailing today."

"We don't have another dinghy to chase them if—"

"If nothing is going to happen. He knows how to stay up the wind from here. He is a very smart boy, and he has paddles and a little anchor. We lost his boat, and now he sails on ours. There is nobody on the island, not even one person do we see with the binoculars. Now you will come with me down below. I have some medicines and moisturizings for your face, and I have cologne perfume so you will not smell like a goat. After then I will decide if I still love you."

She went up the transom steps ahead of me in her tight dress. I gave her a good half minute before following her up. When I climbed up onto the aft deck and could see forward over the pilothouse, Gino was holding a meeting up on the foredeck. Except for him they were all sitting and facing forward. It was Sunday morning and the first mate was standing in the bow holding the Good Book. Calling meetings was one of his prerogatives, but we both knew who was really giving the orders, and it wasn't either one of us. I saw a flock of hats and covered arms, so they were taking sun precautions. Good.

Obviously an elaborate scheme had been plotted. The aft deck hatch was opened all the way back. Tala rose through it, standing on our bed in the twenty-inch-square opening, with her head, shoulders and waist appearing above deck level. She was not wearing her form-fitting beige t-shirt dress—or anything else. Then she disappeared back down inside.

I pulled the hatch closed behind me as I dropped inside, except for a few inches left open to let in some air. The tops of our hatches were dark Plexiglas, so they were opaque from above in the sunshine. We could see out but people on deck could not see down and in. This optical situation was reversed at night if a cabin light was on.

A few minutes later when we were entwined in the tub (and making an unauthorized use of a little fresh water via the handheld shower hose, shampooing our hair between kisses), we heard foot traffic and voices above us. Rita, Adam and the twins climbed down into the dinghy and cast off with the help of Gino and Sofia, who then went forward again.

I understood. All this effort wasn't just a bone thrown to an old sea dog, not even the captain. Oh, no, this was a plan to be repeated with the other *esposos*. Two other married couples were living up forward in a space the size of a twelve-foot box with irregular angles. On what were essentially bunk beds, two per side. With the forward ladder and scuttle hatch used by all the other crew planted right in the middle, and no private head with its own built-in tub. So please catch the message, skipper.

But had Gino or Luke hatched this plan? No. Clearly not in a million years. Not them, and not me. Then who? Who indeed.

While Rebel's ladies were more than happy to let the deck apes reef the sails during the storms, or butcher a bloody mess of fish, or scrape barnacles off the prop, or shovel thick river mud from the raised anchor . . . Tala, Sofia, and now Jessie, well, they unquestionably ruled Rebel Yell down below.

Not that I was complaining. Oh, no sir.

Their rule down below came with benefits.

We made love and we slept, and we made love and we slept, and I didn't know or care who was on watch or what time it was. The first mate and the crew could worry about all that. A raspy 12-volt oscillating fan spun a lazy breeze across our bodies. I woke up when I heard Whisper knocking against the boarding platform. I looked out through the transom porthole to see Barry, Adam and Will tying up the dinghy. They left the sail up but slackened, with the boat riding in our wind shadow.

My watch said it was almost three pm! My body was still catching up on lost sleep and recovering from the overload of stress. I left Tala sleeping and threw on a long-sleeved shirt and khakis so worn that even the paint stains were fading. The tropical sun will murder an untanned white man, especially if his ancestors hailed from the frozen northlands of Europe.

I filled my water bottle in the galley, grabbed my cap in the pilothouse and stepped into the cockpit to hear the news the dinghy sailors were clearly eager to share. We met under the shade of the tarp. After a week at sea and now at anchor they were able to tumble into comfortable positions around the wheel as easily as any landlubbers in their old suburban living rooms and man caves. Hats were tossed to the side and cockpit cushions were moved around to suit their preferences. They all had their water bottles. Life at anchor on Abraham's Bay was night-and-day different from the storm. It was *relaxed.* And it was Sunday, the day of rest.

Barry said, "We saw somebody on the shore. We sailed to within a few hundred yards of the beach."

This was not unexpected. About three hundred people had lived on Mayaguana during my last visit. Gino came back to join us in the shade. He had been working up forward on the downed mast, trying to untangle parts of the puzzle.

I said, "We'll get to the man you saw on the beach in a minute. So, Adam, how does our boat sail with your rig?"

"It sails good, I mean, it sails well. It's enough sail area for today, and I wouldn't want a bigger sail when it kicks up. That's why I used my rig instead of yours. Both of the masts are the same diameter at the foot so it went right in. It was no problem using my mast and sail with your boat's cleats and controls since they're both spritsails. Whisper has a nice tiller, and the centerboard works just like mine. I mean, like the one on my old boat. If it's my call, I'd keep my rig on it for now."

"It's your call, dinghy master. And it's really nice that we can see that red sail from way off."

"Yes sir, especially when there are white sails all over the place like back in Beaufort. You always know it's me."

I added, "And even here it stands out against the island. Okay, so Barry said you saw somebody. Tell me about it."

Adam nodded to Barry, who answered for the three. "We were tacking back and forth toward the land. Adam says that's the best way to practice sailing, and since the wind is coming from the land, that's the way we're going, you know, tacking back and forth. I was in the back steering with the tiller, Adam and Will did the sheet rope thing each time we tacked over. So we're about a couple hundred yards from land and I think Will saw him first. He looked like a black guy sitting on a log, or a boat that's turned over. He stood up and he waved his hat to us and we waved back. We didn't think it would be real smart to get any closer, in case he had a rifle and it was a trick. Like an ambush, I mean. And believe me—I've seen it happen."

Adam nodded and said, "We didn't think we should make the decision to make contact. We thought that was something you should decide on, not us. Then we sailed back downwind in one leg, and here we are, so he's probably still there."

"You did the right thing, guys, you did the right thing. Now that they know we're here, it'll be all over the island in an hour. If it's like it was back in Beaufort, or the way the Bahamas used to be, it'll be all over the VHF in no time."

Barry said, "We've been here since yesterday afternoon, so they probably know already. We're the only boat here."

"We should have been monitoring 16," I admitted. "It's been so long I didn't even think about the VHF radio."

Will said, "I'll turn it on." He rose to go inside.

"Put it on scan and turn up the volume," I told him. "If they're talking about us, we'll hear it."

"Should we bring any guns up, boss?" asked Gino.

"It can't hurt to be ready, and even just getting them out is good practice too. Let's bring up the elk gun, and one of the M-16s and a couple mags. Take these bilge rats with you and show them where everything is. If nothing else we can have a show-and-tell and get in some weapons familiarization. We'll start working on the mast tomorrow, early. It's Sunday, so we'll take it easy today."

Gino went inside followed by the other three, and they were back in five minutes with Barry and Adam each toting a long gun, and Will carrying the ammo boxes and mags.

"Anybody ever shot an AR before?" I asked them.

Barry answered, "I've handled them but I never shot one. I used a shotgun mostly, but I know how ARs work."

He passed it over to me and I held it horizontally in front, instructor-style. "This is an M-16A2. They were issued to the Army and the Marines in the 1990s. It works like a civilian AR-15, but it has a three-round-burst mechanism instead of just safe and fire on the selector. The peep sight is in the back of the carrying handle, see? We have two of them on board."

"If they're military, how did you get them?" Barry asked.

"It's complicated. The IRA smuggled them from Boston to Ireland back in the 1990s, and we wound up with two of them after Morocco." Every time I handled them I wondered if Pat Maguire and Sergeant Major Tolbert had ever made it out of Fort Zerhoun. Probably not, but there was a chance.

I handed the M-16 back to Barry and said, "Adam, you're holding a bolt-action Remington 700 in 7mm magnum, which also happens to be one of my favorite calibers. Go ahead and look through the scope. I was lucky to find this one for sale in Beaufort, and I was even luckier to get a hundred rounds of factory ammo with it. The scope is just a three-by-nine, but high magnification doesn't work on a boat anyway because you never have a steady rest. Your crosshair moves all over the place and you can't find what you're aiming at. On a boat, this is all the rifle you'll need for long-range work. Along with the Dushka and our new M-240 and a pair of M-16s and an AK-47—but this is the only one with a scope."

My next step was going to be to break down the M-16 to show the new guys how it worked on the inside, and let them each take a few shots out over the reef. Nobody was going to hear it from the beach a half mile in the other direction.

But then Will said, "Something is moving on the shore."

My binoculars were already in the cockpit just below the instrument panel. I stood up and leaned against the pilothouse with my elbows braced on its roof and gave the beach a careful scan. I was still in the shade of the tan tarp, which extended over the back of the pilothouse. The afternoon sun's angle put the sandy beach in a line of shadow so that it blended into the scrubby vegetation uphill, but there were a few places where white sand pushed up the slope through the brush. In a sandy opening I did indeed see some movement. Something big was being moved around by two men. They weren't turning over a boulder or a tree trunk but a boat, this became obvious when its hull came upright facing toward us.

Adam got the other binos from the pilothouse, stood next to me and said, “Now there’s two of them. They’re putting a boat on rollers. It has some kind of wheels in back.”

I could see them too. “The wheels are for pulling the boat across the sand. They’ll leave them on the beach. Looks like we’re going to have some company, gentlemen. It was good timing with the guns. We’ll keep them out of sight for now.”

“Should we load them up?” Barry asked me.

“Not yet. We’ll see how it goes. There’s twenty rounds in the mag for the M-16, and it’ll only take a second to load it.”

We kept on watching. The boat was rigged with a mast on the beach and then pushed out into the water. The two men got aboard and began paddling away from the shore, and then they raised a sail that appeared gray in that light. The wind was off the land, so they’d have an easy run down to us.

It took them five minutes to cross the half mile of water. The boat had a pointed bow, not a flat pram bow like Whisper. It had a triangular sail with a long boom, Bahamian-style.

Barry asked, “Shouldn’t we get the guns ready at least?”

I lowered my Steiners and said, “Approaching us in that little boat is like approaching a fortress. They have way more to fear from us than we have to fear from them, so I wouldn’t worry. These are real chilled-out folks who live out here. Most of them have never touched a gun in their lives, or even seen one. If they were going to get violent, knives and machetes are more their speed. This isn’t North Charleston.”

“I think the guy in front is white,” said Adam. “The other guy is black for sure, and he has a white beard, so he’s old.”

Will took the binoculars and said, “I think the man in front is half-white, maybe, but it’s hard to tell under that hat.”

“Salt and pepper team,” Barry observed. “I thought they were all black in these islands. I guess not.”

The wooden-hulled boat turned into the wind when it was fifty yards off. It was rigged as a catboat with the mast planted in the bow. The boat was fourteen or fifteen feet in length, a little shorter but beamier than Whisper.

33

The man in front held up a pair of string bags and yelled, "Ahoy there! We come bearing gifts! May we approach you in peace on this beautiful Sunday afternoon? Do you speak English?" He was wearing a wide-brimmed straw plantation hat, a white dress shirt and gray trousers.

I stepped across the aft deck and out from under the tarp, standing in the sun where they could see me easily—and see the Dushka behind me. "What's in the bags?" I asked him.

"I thought you'd never ask! Lemons and limes, and some oranges, and a few coconuts. And one very nice pineapple."

I could have sworn I smelled each one of their tart scents blowing down toward us. We had not tasted fresh citrus since the Atlantic crossing after leaving the Canaries. The twins had never seen an orange or a lemon in their short lives.

"You may approach our stern, sir, and come aboard. We will take your line." Then, quietly, I said, "Adam, go down and tie them off. Barry, cover the guns with those towels."

He gave me a questioning look but then he covered them. I knew that his South Carolina experiences had left him wary of traps and subterfuge. It could take a long time to readjust your mindset to expecting normal, decent human behavior and acting accordingly toward strangers. For a long time after that kind of trauma folks would always look for a hidden weapon, or for poison to be slipped into their drink, or a blade to their throat while sleeping. Thugees cozying up as fellow travelers.

But as the two neared us I could look down into their little vessel, and nothing warlike was visible. Just a pair of paddles, a rusty anchor with a jumble of line, and a bucket for bailing. An hour before, the boat had been upside-down on the beach. Both of them regarded our horizontal foremast with curiosity as they glided in toward our stern.

Adam climbed down onto the platform and took their line. A minute after getting permission to approach, their boat was tied to our starboard transom cleat. Adam moved Whisper to the port side so the two boats wouldn't bang into each other.

The man in front by the mast was indeed a Caucasian, but burnt dark by the sun. He swung the bags bulging with fruit over to Adam, who placed them up on the aft deck near my feet. The single pineapple was handed across by its top leaves. Then the man in front stood and stepped onto Rebel's teak boarding platform, waving off Adam's offered hand of help.

He was older than me, maybe in his fifties, and at least as tall, judging by where his shoulders rose above the level of the aft deck. He was a white man for certain by his facial features and the sound of his voice, but with cinnamon skin compared to his tillerman's near ebony. Our visitor's short beard was gray; the black man's was snow white. Both wore sunglasses.

The string bags of citrus lay on our aft deck like piles of emeralds and rubies. Our eyes and noses were pulled to them. Wahoo and mahi-mahi fillets were trash to be swept overboard by comparison. I know this was a manifestation of nutritional deprivation. We were stuffed full of fish protein, and we had plenty of potatoes and cabbages, but we were utterly lacking the magic fruit which had caused British sailors to be known as Limeys during the first age of sail. Avast, ye scurvy dogs.

The man looked up and studied the covered Dushka, and me. He was wearing a stylish pair of wraparound sunglasses beneath his plantation hat. He turned around and spoke to the older black man in the stern of the boat, and then he moved to cast off its bow line.

I asked the stranger, "Doesn't he want to come aboard?"

"What? Henry? No, no, it's really not his style. He says he gets seasick on big boats. Well, he doesn't actually *say* it; he can't really speak, you see. Not with words, anyway. But yes, he'll get seasick if he comes on your boat. In what part of his brain this syndrome arises, I have not been able to discern. He can articulate his thoughts to me only because we've spent so much time together. It's in his eyes, mostly. In his face and his hands, too. And posture, posture is also very important. He'll come back for me when I'm ready to depart this semi-dismasted vessel named Rebel Yell."

"How will he know when you're ready to leave?"

"Oh, he'll know. I might wave a flag, or you might flash your anchor light. Any number of means. Say, do you have an anchor light? I didn't notice one last night."

"Yes, we have an anchor light, because it's on the mast that's still standing—but I didn't see a reason to switch it on. We're the only boat on Abraham's Bay."

"So, you know where you are! Well, that's a good sign."

I thought this an odd comment. "What does that mean?"

"Mean? It means you're not shipwrecked. It means you're lucky you made it over the reef in one piece. And I'm thinking you came here by your own free choice and in full knowledge. I'm sorry for talking so much, but I've had nobody to talk with literally for years. I listen to the radio, but when I try to have a conversation they never seem to hear me. So please, forgive me if I run off at the mouth. I didn't used to, at least not as far as I can remember. But the way your crew is looking at those bags of fruit is exactly the same way that I want to talk to people. I'm starving for conversation, and I haven't seen three living white men in the same place in three years. Or three black men, for that matter. Conversationally speaking, I am holding back Niagara Falls. Forgive me if I tend to go on."

"I understand, don't worry about it. It's not a problem."

"Oh, by the way, my name is Perry Curtiss. Perry Curtiss with three R's and two S's."

"So welcome aboard, Perry Curtiss. Are you sure Henry doesn't want to come aboard?"

"Come aboard? No, no, that's not going to happen. And Henry's not really his name; it's just a name I gave him. We operate mostly on the non-verbal level. Sometimes I call him Henry, or Arthur, or Charlton, and I'm not quite sure why. . . but he doesn't mind any of them. But he won't step foot on your

Rebel Yell, he just won't, so don't think me uncaring for this." The tall stranger threw the line onto the boat and pushed its bow away with his foot. Out of our wind shadow, the old black man began to tack back toward shore.

I said, "Well, don't just stand there, Perry, climb on up. And welcome aboard my former and future schooner."

He was limber for his age and came up the transom steps like a teenager, grabbing the stern rails on each side of the opening by the Dushka to hoist himself the final way onto our aft deck. He removed his hat with his left hand, extended his right, and I shook it. Huge hands! It had been quite a long time since I'd had to look up at anybody aboard Rebel. Perry went six-four or five, and he had plenty of shoulder span on him from when he'd carried more meat on his bones.

While pumping my hand he said, "My name is spelled with three R's and two S's. Did I tell you that already? Well, now you'll never forget it. It's Curtiss with a hard C, and you can call me Curt. I never cottoned to Perry Ormond Curtiss." His gray hair was pulled back and tied in a ponytail.

I extricated my hand. "Are you by any chance related to Glenn Curtiss, spelled with two N's and two S's?"

"Do you mean the fastest man alive in 1907? The father of naval aviation? Yes, he was my great-grandfather. Say, do you have any tobacco on board? Spirits? Rum? Whiskey? By the pretty young faces lurking in your deck house I see that you have women aboard—and God bless you for that—but do you happen to also have the wine and song? I'm really after the trifecta. Please excuse my babbling but my mind is so full of ideas and I only have Arthur to share them with. You might say he is strong in the back but weak in the mind. But a very good man. Anyway, please do forgive me if I tend to dominate the conversation. It's the first one I've had in three years."

"Don't worry, Curt, I understand. My name is Dan Kilmer and my boat, as you have read, is named Rebel Yell. We'll get around to everybody else's names, but for now, Curt Curtiss, tell me, what the *hell* are you doing on Mayaguana?"

"*May*-aguana. Not *My*-aguana. I have it on good authority that the locals used to call their island *May*-aguana."

"So what do they call it now?"

"Call it now? They don't call it anything, Dan. They're all gone. Now it's just Henry and me. I mean Charlton. We're the last of the Mohicans. That is, the last of the Mayaguanans."

"Really? That's fascinating. So come on and get under the shade, Curt. Mind your head on the boom. Barry, let our guest sit there in the back. And everybody hiding in the pilothouse, you might as well come out too. And can somebody bring up a cutting board and a couple of kitchen knives?"

He had to duck under the tarp to join the party in its soft tan shade. I ushered our guest to the seat of honor at the back of the cockpit. He stepped down into the foot well, but before he sat he grabbed the leather-covered wheel with both hands and looked down into the compass, and then he stared over the pilothouse at his island, and back down at the compass again. He repeated this several times, sighed, and then dropped down to sit at the back of the cockpit, removed his sunglasses, and studied the details of the new world around him. Curt had a sharp nose and green eyes. He went silent, possibly overcome.

I sat on the port side near him, our bare feet close. My tan was just beginning, his was deep and permanent. We could look across the water at his island, or at each other, or shake hands or bump knees. I could tell that he was overwhelmed to be surrounded by so many people in such close quarters.

Gino sat across from me, the three oldest men on board forming a triad. The other deck apes moved to new positions around the cockpit and on the aft deck. Rita came out and sat on the aft deck by Adam. Curt looked at me, then at Gino and then at each of the crew around him. Without his sunglasses our guest had raccoon stripes around his sea-green eyes.

I thought his white button-down dress shirt and gray dress slacks were in good shape for a man who had been marooned for several years. His slacks were cut off short at mid-calf, and his wrists extended inches beyond the unbuttoned sleeves of his oxford shirt, meaning they weren't his clothes, or at least, not originally. If you get the waist and chest about right, the rest of the measurements don't matter, not when you're marooned on an island. And the mysteries were piling up.

"Say, Curt," I asked, trying to open him up again, "If you don't mind my asking, where did you find the cool shades?"

"These? Do you like them? Here, try them on."

"No, thanks," I replied. "I'm good. I already have a pair."

"We have more on the island, if anybody wants them."

"You have more? More sunglasses?"

"Sure. Nobody is left on the island but Arthur and me. We have our pick of what they left behind."

"When was this? What happened to them?"

"What happened to them? They all left, except for a few, but that was before I arrived. When I got here there were just a few remainers who wouldn't leave. They were too old to start somewhere else, so they were just going to trust in Jesus and take their chances. 'I was born here and I'm going to die here, and dying holds no fear for those who trust and believe.' They told me that from their own lips. That's what you call faith. I did what I could to help them, but they were very old to begin with. Very old. Eighties and nineties. They had refused to go.

"So, there were five people still on this side of the island when I arrived. Two couples and Arthur, I mean Henry. Did I say Arthur? I'm not sure why I do that. Sometimes I think I tried to create multiple personalities for him, so I could have more company after the others had passed. But his multiple personalities were all in my head, not his, and he never cared what I called him. I take turns, you see. Today he's Henry, so I speak to him differently than I speak to Charlton."

"So, Curt, why did they leave? What did the old couples tell you about that?" At that point I was thinking I have a kook on my hands, but a harmless one. Maybe it was a combination of too much sun and isolation from human contact.

"Well, Captain Dan, I'll just tell you what they told me. Mayaguana was always surviving right on the margin. Anybody born on the island with any brains got the hell off just as soon as they could. There was no economic activity, and the people on the island were just a welfare case for Nassau. They didn't say it in those words, but it's a reasonable inference. The only real money came from being a smuggling stopover, and Uncle Sam didn't approve of it and stamped it out. The government brought in enough fuel to run a generator so they had a little electricity, but it was all a subsidy. There was only one hotel on the island, up at Pirate Wells, and it almost never had a guest. It was just Nassau keeping the flag flying in the outermost of the Out Islands.

"Even the Haitians steered around Mayaguana. But what finally did them in was a long drought, just as simple as that. They caught rainwater for everything, and with no rain they were done for unless the government sent down a water barge, but they had to come and fetch it. There was no water system. Then there was a hurricane that took down their power lines, and the island's main generator failed and it had to be replaced again . . . and Nassau finally threw in the towel. The rest of the Bahamas already had enough problems and Mayaguana was one too many. It was written off. They told them that they'd be resettled someplace better, with health benefits and all that good stuff. They could leave on the mail boat or on the weekly airplane, free passage and no rush, but the electricity was off for good. Almost everybody took them up on the offer. I don't know what happened to them after they left.

"And do you know the craziest thing? It's been raining more than ever for the last two years. I guess it's that volcano up in Iceland they talk about on the radio. They used to need to water their fruit trees with what they caught off their roofs, but not anymore. So now when everything is growing like it's Florida or Hawaii, all the people are gone. Crazy, huh?"

Gino and I listened to Curt's story, but the others were more interested in making a happy mess behind us on the aft deck throwing a citrus party. Slices of lemons, limes, oranges and pineapple were tried with lip-smacking, moans of pleasure, and surprise that anything could taste so wonderful. The twins were ecstatic, with fruit juices running down their faces.

Sofia brought the three of us old men sitting in the back of the cockpit a sample platter of citrus and pineapple, along with chunks of white coconut meat. A husked coconut is only the size of a big peach, and a few of them had been packed in the string bags with the fruit. Curtis informed us that there was a nearly inexhaustible supply on the island, so eat all you want.

Because we were anchored on calm water the ladies had baked bread, and there was still some butter from the Beaufort market. The mahi leftovers went into cooking a big pot of fish chowder. This happened below decks while we men chatted about Nassau, volcanoes and other important world affairs.

Tala and Sofia informed us of the dinner arrangements and told us when to come below. The three married couples sat across the table from one another: Luke and Jessie in first, then Sofia and Gino in the middle seats, and finally me and Tala on the outside. Boy-girl-boy on my side, the opposite on the other. This was Tala's idea. Our tall guest sat on the stool at the head of the table. Gino took Jessie's and Tala's hands and the rest of us completed the circle. Curt took my hand and Tala's without hesitation, and his grip was strong.

Gino said the blessing, and after our amens I reflected that this was our Thanksgiving Supper on Abraham's Bay. When we were finished, we men were encouraged to depart for the deck so that the table could be cleared and made ready for the next sitting. Before we left I gave Tala a special request. After the previous night I wasn't sure if she'd go along with it.

We resumed our discussions in the cockpit, watching the western sky turn from orange to red to silver. The day rolled into night with the full moon rising at sunset. Finally most of the adults were present to hear Curt's story. The compass light was switched on. The compass was always our steady center.

Tala brought up a plastic pitcher and cups but she stayed inside the open pilothouse door, so I went to her. She said, so only I could hear, "This is what you asked for, and also it has some coconut milk." Her amber eyes narrowed to slits and she whispered, "But if you are again like as last night, I may kill you when you are sleeping."

I took the pitcher and cups and passed them to Gino, saying "Don't let me get like last night. Tomorrow's going to be a work day. Above all we have to get a wire forestay on the mainmast. We're going to turn-to at dawn. No, let's make it eight. Now pour me a drink—what are you waiting for?"

The pitcher held my suggested recipe of liquor, water and blended citrus juice, along with a little coconut milk. No ice, of course, but that had been the case for years. Jessie brought up her mandolin and sat beside Luke in their usual place at the front of the cockpit facing the rest of us. Without a word she began to play softly, just strumming chords at first.

I told Curt, "Wine, women and song—we have it all. We have everything except a vertical foremast."

Luke said, "Did you know that in the pirate days, cooks and musicians got a share of the loot even if they didn't fight? It's true. Good food and good music make life worth living."

"And worth fighting for," Barry added.

The moon was rising over the eastern end of the island. I could make out the unlit BaTelCo tower marking the deserted village of Abraham's Bay. "Curt, has the light been out on the tower since you got here?"

"Correct, it's been out. I never saw it, but they told me about it. It's how fisherman found their way home. There was a red light on top that flashed the Morse code for M, which is dash-dash. They said it could be seen from twenty miles out to sea. Every island big enough for a BTC tower had a letter. B was for Bimini, and so on. The locals said they knew it was all over for their island when BaTelCo shut down their operations. Then there were no more weekly airplanes, only charters, and the mail boat. The mail boat was what they called the supply ship. Near the end it only came once a month. It got harder and harder to live on Mayaguana until they all quit and left. All but the five remainers."

I said, "And you arrived after that."

"Yes. And not long after I got here the drought broke and it started raining practically every day. I think that sometimes Mother Nature has a wicked sense of humor. Or is it irony?"

"So what in the world brought you here?" I asked him.

"I was shipwrecked, but I can't start the story there or it won't make any sense. I was trying to get back to Florida from Antigua. It's quite a long story, are you sure you want to hear it? And young lady, you are magnificent on that instrument. Is that called a mandolin?"

"It is, Curt. And my name is Jessie, Jessie Hanahan, and the piratical-looking fellow next to me is my husband Luke."

Curt stood and reached over the compass to shake their hands. He had an impressive wing span.

Tala came out with a fresh pitcher and said, "Curt, you will sleep on our boat tonight. This is not a problem for us." She sat between me and the wheel, and Sofia sat by Gino.

She was right, of course. A half-mile open-water dinghy ride back to land in the darkness would be madness. Anything goes wrong with the rig, the sail or the tiller and you'd wind up on the five-mile reef and then out on the open Atlantic.

I said, "Curt, you were telling us how you got here."

"Yes, I was, but before I continue with that story I have a question for you. Captain Dan, did you build this steel boat?"

"I rebuilt her and I re-engined her and I renamed her, but she was built before I was born. In Holland, I think."

"That's what I should have done, gotten a boat, a sailboat. I often thought I should learn how to fly an airplane and how to sail, but I thought it would be simpler and easier to just hire a professional who was already an expert. That was a mistake, thinking I could always hire someone else to take care of my transportation requirements. But I had lots of money. Millions of dollars, in fact. So I thought that I could always hire someone else to get me from point A to point B. Big mistake."

He paused, and we all exchanged looks after hearing him mention his wealth. After a moment Gino asked him, "How did you come by millions of dollars, Curt?" Our guest looked like a weather-beaten and half-starved retired cowboy, not a trust fund beneficiary or a Wall Street hedge-fund brainiac.

"How? What? Oh, the money. I was an inventor. I worked the oil fields in my youth and my college years, and eventually all over the world. The mechanical stuff always fascinated me. I saved up to go to school and I got an engineering degree. I went back on the rigs but in management, and then I branched out into consulting and that paid for my post-graduate studies. I made my living where metallurgy and fluid dynamics meet. I shared the patent royalties until I figured out the business end. In my best years I made a fortune inventing little gadgets you could carry in your pocket, and big gadgets you'd need a crane to move. I just had a knack for it."

The image of the emaciated gray-bearded stranger sitting between us did not match the story, but his vocabulary and his diction raised the possibility that he was telling the truth.

Sofia asked him, "Are you married? Do have a family?" That night Sofia and Tala decided to sample the punch, and discovered that they enjoyed it. The clear corn whiskey was more to their taste when it was mixed with water and juice.

"I was married twice, but they didn't last. I have two families, maybe alive, probably not. Who knows? In Florida and Oklahoma, last I knew. I was trying to get back to Florida, but I'm getting ahead of my story. So, how did I wind up on Mayaguana? That's the question? Well, I was fifty years old and I decided to cash out. I had millions stashed in banks in three states and about a half million a year in royalties coming in. I bought a place in Oklahoma, a place in Montana, and a place in Florida. Spread the risk, right? They couldn't all turn out badly, could they? All three places were condos. Turn-key operations. You fly in, you have a place to stay and everything you need is already there. I didn't want to own a place I had to take care of from long distance. No lawns, no landscaping.

"But I'd also been bitten by the Caribbean bug when I was married to wife number two. We started taking cruises and it grew from there. We lived in South Florida, and Florida is cruise-ship-central. We cruised from Jamaica to Trinidad, but we bought a place in the Virgin Islands because they're American and that made it easier. We bought a condo on St. Croix, and I let her keep it when we got divorced.

"After we split up I wanted a little more elbow room in my primary location. Elbow room and privacy. Compensation, maybe, for being single again—and for good. Mid-life crisis? I don't know, maybe. But I wanted a real house, not just another condo, and I didn't want to be under American jurisdiction anymore, so the U.S. Virgins were out. I wanted a garden and fruit trees, and a swimming pool and a Caribbean Sea view. I looked at a dozen properties on a few different islands before I finally bought my place. Do you know where Antigua is?"

"Sure." I said. "In the middle of the Leeward Islands. It's a little country called Antigua and Barbuda. It was British, and if you pronounce it *An-tee-goo-ah* everybody knows you're a tourist. They pronounce it like you do: *AnTEEga*."

"Right. It was very strategic in the old square-rigger days because it has a few natural harbors. Not so much after that. I bought a hurricane-proof house that was also beautiful to look at. Stucco and tile work like you just wouldn't believe. Art and architecture, both. It was on a private road and each place had a name. My place was called Double Vision. My property was high up on a point with two different views of the Caribbean Sea, hence its name. Anytime I wanted to travel I could leave by water or by air; I'd just make a call or send a text. A fast boat, a slow boat, an airplane, a seaplane: whatever I needed.

And Antigua had an international airport with daily flights to North America and Europe. It was crawling with wealthy ex-pats. Mostly old British money; my spread was just middling."

"What about water?" I asked him. "Drinking water. The Leewards are pretty dry."

"I wasn't worried because I bought the slope uphill and I turned it into a rain catchment. The property above me was too steep to be buildable; so I bought it just for the water runoff. I designed it all and I drew the blueprints. I hired the contractors and I wrote the checks. I used local labor for the cement work, and I imported the pipes and filters and did that work myself. Double Vision already had a swimming pool, and that was my backup water cistern. The island's electric power was erratic so I brought in another backup generator and I put in a bigger fuel tank. I had enough money and you could still get things shipped in. The water catchment worked so well that during a good rain I could send the overflow to a few of my downhill neighbors, which they really appreciated.

"So there I am on Antigua, and I'm all set. Everything is in place, and I'm watching American cities burning down on my satellite television and on the internet. I was shifting my money around, putting more and more into cash and precious metals. That was my new preoccupation after I quit inventing better widgets. So no matter what happens, I'm all set, right? I have a ten-year supply of food and more water than I'll ever need. I'm a real genius, sitting there on the patio by the pool looking out over two views of the Caribbean. I'm a master of the universe, just waiting for America's final collapse. Then I'll fly home and buy everything I need. It's paradise, right? I mean, as long as you don't mind the lonely old bachelor part. With two ex-wives and grown kids you almost never see. But at least I could support them financially, and I did. Gladly."

Gino refilled his cup and then asked him, "So, Curt, what happened to paradise? It doesn't sound very happy."

34

“Paradise . . . well, it turns out Antigua had a few fatal flaws. I had enough water for all my needs on my two-acre habitat, but the rest of the island didn’t. Antigua is about a hundred times prettier than Mayaguana, but it’s only a third bigger and it had a hundred thousand people living on it. A hundred thousand people on land that couldn’t sustain ten percent of that number after you cut it off from the world. Just look at Mayaguana, and try to imagine sixty thousand people living on it! Without fresh water and electricity, Mayaguana couldn’t even support three hundred people.

“Ninety percent of Antigua’s food was imported. Eighty percent of the fresh water was made in a desalination plant by reverse osmosis, and that plant ran on oil. So after the tourism dollars dried up and the rich ex-pats started running away, it went to hell real fast. Antigua couldn’t pay for the oil to run the reverse osmosis plant, so there went the drinking water.”

From behind us Barry said, “It’s like pulling the plug on a tropical fish aquarium. I saw it happen in Charleston. To the whole city, I mean. To the people.”

“Indeed.” Curt continued. “Turns out the locals didn’t like the rich ex-pats as much as they pretended to when they were serving us in the bars and restaurants. And they knew about my private water catchment because local labor had built it. I tried to lay low, but everything was falling apart fast. Robberies, car-jackings, home invasions, all of that. Antigua is ninety-percent black with a long colonial history, including slave plantations, so it was finally payback time.

“Then I got word from my gardener that a new ‘people’s committee’ had decided that my water system was going to be ‘reallocated’ in order to the serve the common good. ‘All of Antigua’s water belongs to all of Antigua’s people’ was going to be the new policy and the law. I had no idea any of this was coming until my gardener told me. We were both living on the same island but in two different worlds, black and white."

"Even if the water was captured from rainfall?" I asked.

"Even if. When the rain hits the island, it becomes island water unless it sinks into the ground. They said, "How can you whites have swimming pools, when little babies are dying of thirst?" Hoarding island water was going to become a crime, and I was near the top of the target list. Being a rich white ex-pat went out of style fast. I couldn't go food shopping—it was too dangerous. And when you pay somebody else to shop for you, the word gets around fast. I could read the writing on the walls, I mean, literally on the walls around the island, and the writing said *kill whitey*. If I stayed, I'd be living under siege while I'm trying to hold off the natives until doomsday. One white millionaire splashing around in his swimming pool, against the rest of the island. Yeah, good luck with that.

"That's when I knew I had to get out. The problem was the international financial systems were all failing, and then you couldn't buy a plane ticket to save your life, or the flights were cancelled. I had two million dollars and euros in a pair of rolling suitcases, but what could I do with all that cash? Thank God I had my precious metals. And my satellite phone worked some of the time, and my sat text worked almost all the time, so I could still make some moves.

"A buddy of mine was a retired Brit, ex-military. Colonel Colin Fletcher. He was my private-road neighbor just downhill. I sent extra water his way, and he plugged me into the ex-pat network. He had a radio license and he played around on the short wave radio, so he could talk to people thousands of miles away. I thought this was just a hobby, an anachronism, but it proved to be quite useful. It was a mostly British scene on our end of Antigua, but it was falling apart fast—and not just on our island. He'd heard on a Caribbean radio net that there had been massacres of whites on Saint Thomas, Saint Croix and Saint Lucia, and that the massacres had come after food riots, and there were food riots starting on Antigua. We knew we had to get out or we'd be trapped and probably meet an ugly end. Colin was aiming for Jamaica, and I was heading to Florida.

"We decided to fly from Antigua to Providenciales in the Turks and Caicos, and then catch our next flights from there. He had to visit his safe deposit box. Provo is like the Cayman Islands; it's wall-to-wall banks. It was just five hundred miles so we chartered a light twin. I paid for it with two ounces of my gold. It took my gold and Colin's short wave radio to set up the flight. My gardener drove us to the airport in my Range Rover. We ducked down in the back and hid under a blanket. It wasn't safe for whites then. When he dropped us off I gave him my house keys and I wished him and his family luck."

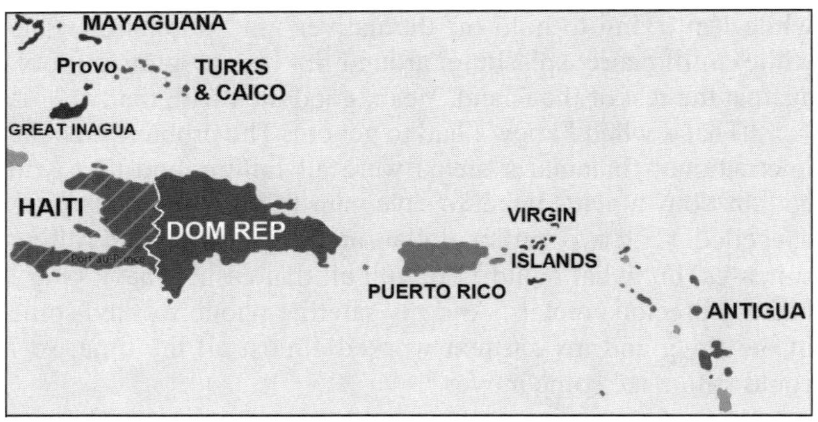

Gino asked him, "What did you do with all the cash?"

"I left it for my housekeeper and gardener, they were a married couple. The cash was too bulky and it was practically worthless by then. It was getting so that nobody on Antigua would take U.S. dollars. I hope they got to stay in my house. I hope they worked it all out with the people's committee. I like to think they're doing well, and their children too. Maybe the dollar bottomed out and the cash has some value, I just don't know, but I wish them well. Good people. Godly people. And I didn't leave all the cash; I brought about a hundred thousand because I just didn't know what to expect along the way. And some silver coins too—you don't want to flash Krugerrands.

"I was shitting bricks when that Beech Bonanza landed in Provo, but Colin had some old British spook connections there and we got out of the airport through a back gate. We never went through the terminal at all, but what we could see of it was pure mayhem, like the fall of Kabul. There was a British C-130 Hercules there, and some troops trying to keep order along with the local Turks police. The airport was still open but only for charter flights and only in the daytime. That morning two planes had collided right on the tarmac and everybody was flipping out because one of the planes burned with all the people in it. Scheduled airline service was finished and a lot of people were panicking, including me. Everybody was running around like maniacs waving wads of cash, but there weren't a lot of takers. The game had changed, and whites weren't at the top of the heap any more.

"But at least I had my hole card, my golden parachute. I'd been buying one-ounce gold coins for years and years. I kept them between clear sheets of plastic using a heat sealer. Six coins by six coins, with the plastic sheets melted between the rows going both ways. Eleven sheets makes 396 ounces with four left to make 400, plus some other loose ones. They were mostly Maple Leafs and Krugerrands. When I'd get another 36 I'd seal up another sheet. So I had 396 gold coins in a Pelican case, and I had that inside a backpack and I never let my hands off it for a single second. Twelve troy ounces make a pound, so each sheet of coins weighed three pounds. Thirty-three pounds in total. It all fit into a Pelican case this big."

He demonstrated the dimensions with his hands. The case he was describing was about as big as a shoebox, but square.

"Provo has an international airport, but everything was falling apart even with some British troops there. They came in the RAF Hercules that was parked off by itself with some soldiers standing guard around it."

I said, “The Turks and Caicos big shots must have had a lot of drag at Whitehall to get a C-130 sent over for them.”

“No doubt. Colin said they were sent there to pull out the British diplomats, and I suppose the British ex-pats with the best connections, but how many can fit on a Hercules with all the soldiers too? Not very many. So the rest of the rich ex-pat rats were trying to flee the sinking ship in time not to drown, but there were no more scheduled flights in or out.

“It was just wild at the banks in Provo. People were lined up on the sidewalks to get inside a few at a time. Hedge fund bosses, retired smugglers, swindlers, fugitives, British spooks, American spooks . . . it was an absolute clown show. Dodgy ex-pats from everywhere were trying to get into their deposit boxes. Arabs, Chinese, everybody. We got to Colin’s bank but it was closed. There were steel hurricane shutters rolled down over every window and door. People were trying to pull the shutters off the main door with a chain attached to a truck. We got away from there fast—it was just getting too crazy. It was pure mob hysteria. Colin never got to his safe deposit box.

“Colin had a ride to Montego Bay, but he said his plane was already over the head count and the weight limit, and no matter what they wouldn’t take me, and I didn’t want to go to Jamaica anyway. And I sure as hell wasn’t going to just jump onto some random stranger’s airplane to God-knows-where in all that madness and confusion. So what could I do?

“My sat text was working, so I could hire my own pilot to get me back to Florida with no questions asked. The internet was shot and the international phone service? Forget it. My sat phone was useless but the sat text worked most of the time. I’d hired so many pilots and chartered so many planes over the years I figured that I was a pro at it, and if it wasn’t going to be easy, at least it’d be possible. I tried some old numbers and I set up a ride with a pilot I’d flown with a few times. He was in Lake City, in North Florida. That place is all about general aviation—that means private planes and charter operations—and there were always hungry flyboys sitting around waiting to take your money—or your gold. You buy, they fly. Simple.

"He had his own Cessna 210. It's a single engine but it's long range. He has to carry enough gas to fly both ways, but that's no problem—the guy used to fly dope from Colombia. He was a real pro. I had no worries on his end. I basically had him on retainer; I'd already paid him plenty, and he knew I was good for my next ride. So he's confident, I'm confident, it's all set, two thumbs up. I'm as good as in Lake City, right? I'm doing all this on my sat text sitting at a table by the water drinking my last cold Heineken. But there's just one hitch—he won't fly into the Turks and Caicos. I mean, we're texting like mad. He's afraid he'll lose his plane if he lands in Provo, he's heard about the shit-show there, but he'll land on Mayaguana Island. The runway on Mayaguana is wide open, he knows the place. There's no tower, there's nobody's there at all. So I just need to get to Mayaguana, right?"

I leaned over and refilled Curt's punch. He drank half of it, closed his eyes and leaned back, and then he began again. He was on his third cup of white-lightning fruit punch.

"So we sat and put our heads together, and my British ex-pat neighbor and his British ex-pat spook friend recommended a little overnight sailboat trip. It's only fifty miles from Provo up to Mayaguana. Leave at night, arrive in the day, a piece of cake. It was all set. The cost of the ride to Mayaguana was two ounces of gold, the same as the airplane from Antigua. Colin knows I've got it, at least, he knows I've got some loose gold coins. He doesn't know exactly what I have in my pack, but I figure he can tell it's heavier than it looks like it should be.

"So the day after I leave Providenciales I'll be waiting on the tarmac on Mayaguana for my ride to Lake City. Maybe not on the first day, but for sure on the second or the third. That was the arrangement I made. Noon until two was my window. My plane will be there on one of those days, but only once. If I miss it, I miss it. My part of the deal was to be there waiting.

"Colin's friend recommended the boat and the crew. They had used them for extraterritorial work in the past. From Provo up to Mayaguana was a well-beaten path because it crossed an international boundary from the Turks and Caicos over to the Bahamas, but with no meaningful government presence there. It was the perfect place for moving people with no papers, or drugs, or guns, or the untaxed contents of safe deposit boxes. That's what they told me, and I believed them."

"Looking back, I was stupid. We were buying our drinks and dinners and taxi rides with hundred dollar bills and silver coins while fires were burning a mile away and you could hear gunshots. But I'm feeling fairly okay because all my gold is in a Pelican case. Thirty pounds isn't too bad, you can pretend that it's not very heavy when it's in a backpack. But even so, your hired captain and crew are going to wonder what's in the pack that the client never lets out of his reach for a second? What's in it that's so valuable that it will bring an airplane all the way out to Mayaguana to fetch him?

"But by then I was desperate. I suppose I was panicking. We'd gotten out of Antigua just ahead of the mob. Provo still had a veneer of civilization even if you could see the fires and smell the smoke. One more big adventure and tomorrow night I'm in Florida, and my gold will make everything okay again. And I've got more gold stashed in Florida and Oklahoma—I just have to get there! Just get there! And after Colin gave me a final hug, knowing that we'd never meet again, he's holding my hands and crying and begging me for two ounces of gold, or else they won't let him on the airplane to Montego Bay. We were way past any shame or embarrassment by then, so I gave him three of my last loose Krugerrands. Why not? After all, it was his radio that arranged our flight out of Antigua."

"What kind of a boat was it?" Gino asked him.

"The boat? It was a Jenneteau, or some French name like that. Under forty feet for sure. Much smaller than this one. We left after dark, around ten. Full moon like tonight. We slipped out of Sapodilla Bay with the tide and the wind behind us. There were just two of them, the captain and his brother. They were half white and half I don't know what, just typical island mutts. The captain was younger and smaller than his brother but evidently he was the smarter of the two.

"They didn't try to get all friendly with me, which I liked. They didn't offer to carry my pack, for example. I thought Colin's British ex-spook friend knew and trusted the crew and it would all go down like we planned. As soon as we were out in deep water they rolled out the sails and turned off the engine. Then they put the boat on the autopilot, and I heard them say it was about forty miles to Abraham's Bay, and they were steering 320 degrees on the compass, and it would be daylight when we got there.

"But I didn't trust anybody by then. I told them I was getting a little seasick and I wanted to go down below and sleep, and they were happy to hear this. No problem at all, boss. Make yourself comfortable. I went down and into the forward cabin because they couldn't see it from the cockpit. I unloaded my backpack up there on the bed. I couldn't turn on a light but enough moonlight came through the hatch to see. A full moon, just like tonight. In my backpack I had a rolled-up dry bag that I'd bought when I got the Pelican case. Like a rafting bag, it was gray vinyl rubber with a top that folds over and makes a seal. I put the Pelican case and a life vest I found in the cabin into the dry bag so I could be sure it wouldn't sink. So now I have two bags to haul around, but at least the gold won't sink.

"I also got out my pistol. Yes, I had a pistol. It was a little Ruger .380 smaller than Jessie's hand. I could have brought my Sig Sauer from Antigua, but I didn't know what to expect when we flew into Provo. But at least I had the .380."

Gino asked, "They let you have firearms on Antigua?"

"Of course not, but you can bring in anything if it's small enough, like the gold coins. When you're paying for the plane the rules are different. So I figured if they were going to make a play they'd do it sooner and not later. Why sail all the way to Mayaguana? Just dump the dead American overboard and take the loot back to Provo—and probably split it with the guy who set me up. So I was in that forward cabin on the V-berth, lying behind my backpack and my dry bag pretending to sleep, but I got into a place where I could see back into the main cabin. I couldn't see well, but well enough, and my hearing is sharp. And I pretended to snore.

"Sure enough, in no time here comes the captain's half-wit brother. I can hear floorboards creaking in the main cabin and then I see his shadow block the light from the cockpit so I know he's coming. I'm lying on my side behind my bag but I can just see around the end of it with my eyes slit open, and the pistol is in my right hand just behind the bag. The captain's brother has a flashlight in one hand and a big hammer in the other. I'm thinking, *well, it's your choice, pal.* You're not going to give me any warning, so turnabout is fair play. He had to get close to me because the bags didn't give him an easy angle to hit me with his hammer.

"Before he lifted that hammer all the way up I shot him in the middle of his chest from about a yard away. Shot him right through the slot between the backpack and the dry bag. Three or four shots—heart shots. He didn't get his hammer all the way up before he dropped like a load of manure. So now the captain is in the cockpit and he just heard the gunshots, right? I figured if they'd had a pistol the brother would have used it instead of a hammer, but who knows? So we have a standoff.

"I felt cornered, so I moved out into the main cabin and I crouched down behind a little table in the middle of the place. It was folded down; the top was folded down on each side. And then the captain was calling out for his brother, "Andre, what's up, mon? What up?" And then he gets real mad and he starts swearing at me to see if he'll get a reaction, but I stayed hidden.

And pretty soon he's coming through the hatch from the cockpit. That kind of hatch is a companionway, right?"

"Right, a companionway," I confirmed. "We have sort of a small ship's door, but I know what you mean."

"So there's the captain coming down the companionway. He's facing me, holding onto the ladder with one hand and he's got a machete in the other. It's not too smart of him after hearing gunshots, but I wasn't going to argue him out of it. So I aimed that little gun from behind the table and I emptied the magazine. He was further away than his brother, and the boat was rolling some and I hit him all over the place, and probably missed a few, but one got him in the neck. He was silhouetted against the moonlight in the companionway, and that's where he fell. So they were both dead."

Curt finished his spiked fruit punch and I refilled his cup.

"The boat was still on autopilot, the two sails were out on the left side, the port side. A nice breeze but the waves weren't too bad and I didn't get seasick at all. The dead captain and his dead brother had no more value to me. Keeping them was all downside. Who knows, some kind of coast guard might show up, or the U.S. Navy, or the Brits. Who knows? Unlikely, but it makes you think. So I dragged them out to the cockpit and I gave them the deep-blue goodbye. If you come at me at night with a hammer and a machete, what else should you expect?"

This was pretty much the way I felt about Captain Aikman and his machine gunner, but I let Curt tell his story.

"We're on autopilot, right? I found a Mayaguana chart on a little desk by the galley. The course line was marked to the western end of Abraham's Bay, and it showed the way in over the reef. There was a pencil line with arrows and the compass angles. And I'm sorry for monopolizing the entire night. I'm sure you have your own stories to tell, what with that broken mast strapped to the side, but please forgive me, I'm on a roll. Maybe it's the alcohol talking, or maybe it's having nobody with a three-digit IQ to talk to for so long. So, where was I?"

I said, "Sailing to Mayaguana, but minus your crew."

"Right. Mayaguana is twenty-five miles wide, so it's not like you can miss it from just forty miles away, even without GPS. I'd never steered a sailboat before, but I'd been on plenty, and of course I understood the principles. If the moron captain and his idiot brother can do it, it can't be that difficult, right?"

Curt laughed bitterly, drank some more punch, looked at each of us, and then continued.

"It was true, you can't miss Mayaguana. It was daylight when I came in sight of it. I started the motor; it wasn't hard to figure out. Key, start button, levers under the compass just like you have. The problem was that I had to navigate the boat into this bay, to get to the runway, to catch my plane to Lake City."

"I have a chart," I said. "We'll look at it tomorrow."

"Then you already know there's only one way into Abraham's Bay, through the reef from the west. Their chart was marked with the path; I just had to follow it. And that's where I came to grief. Came to grief on the reef."

"What time of day was it?" I asked him.

"Maybe nine in the morning? And my plane would land between noon and two. I still had time to make the pickup."

"So the sun was in the east, in front of you," I noted.

"At that time I didn't understand the significance of that fact. If I had, I would have motored around in circles until the afternoon before I tried to run into the bay. But I didn't even consider that because I was thinking about the airplane. I have to be there. So I thought I'd just motor right on in. I rolled up the sails so they wouldn't get in the way. You pull a rope and they roll up. So I just need to estimate where I am in relation to the path marked on the chart, and drive on into the bay. The line was drawn on the chart, and everything I can see around me and on the island looked exactly like it did on the chart.

"But the sailboat's keel hit the reef like it hit a concrete wall, and it all went downhill from there. So who's the idiot, huh? Who's the moron? Who's the fool? But at least I'm still on top of the water and I'm still breathing, unlike those two idiots I shot. So I pulled the gear shifter back into reverse, but it didn't do any good, it just hit the reef again. The boat kept banging its keel on the coral heads. They were all around. Full power in reverse, in forward, turn right, turn left—nothing.

"At some point the rudder must have broken on the coral, because the steering wheel didn't work at all. It went loose. So then what? I'm less than a hundred yards from the island. I'm looking around the boat for a raft, a dingy, a kayak, any damn thing that floats. There was a life raft in a yellow bag, the kind where you pull the rope and it inflates. But there was a picture of what it looked like when it was inflated on the case, and it was round, and I knew if I got in it I'd just blow away out to the west, out onto open water so that was no good. This also made me wonder how the crew expected me to get ashore on Mayaguana, and the answer was—they didn't.

"You could see the coral close to the top of the water in lots of places, so I figured I could walk across it to shore. The boat was moving back and forth in the waves and hitting the coral, it was leaning way over and grinding its hull. It'd lift up on a wave and then it'd come down and I'd hear the fiberglass cracking, so I knew I had to get off the boat and get on to land.

"At least I had good hiking shoes on. Ever since Antigua started going to hell I was getting ready for anything. I was in survivor mode. T-shirt, cargo shorts, boots. So I grabbed my backpack and the dry bag with the gold and I just slid into the water and stood up on the coral. The water was right up to the cockpit when the boat was on its side. Between waves the top of the coral was probably about two feet deep, and the waves weren't too big. It was walkable but the surge would push me over and I'd lose my footing and be floundering around until the water went back down. I was sure that I was going to have a heart attack dragging those two bags over the reef and trying to stay upright in the waves. My heart was going to explode.

"And then it got even worse. It turned out that reef wasn't anything even close to flat; it just looked that way from the boat. Halfway from the boat to the land there's a little canyon about eight feet wide and eight feet deep where the water goes through really fast. I fell right into it. So there I am, drowning, and I'm what, maybe a hundred feet from the beach?

"The dry bag with the pelican case had a life jacket in it so it was floating, and the pack with everything else in it was waterlogged and it weighed a ton. So, fast decision time. Keep the backpack *and* the gold, and drown right there in that coral canyon? Or let go of the backpack and try to swim with the gold? I chose the gold.

"I held onto that gray rubber bag for dear life and I tried to kick across the channel to where the reef was shallow again. I couldn't kick the water with hiking boots on, not while I'm hanging onto the dry bag, and now I'm being swept through the canyon back out to the west, out to the ocean, and then I'm a dead man for sure. *And*, I feel like I'm having a heart attack, *and* I'm drowning. *And* I'm going to miss my airplane ride—because I'm going to be dead."

Curt looked down, elbows on knees, and slowly shook his head before taking a deep breath, sitting up, and going on.

"So, I let go of the dry bag and I tried to swim across that little canyon to grab onto something before I'm swept out to sea. And I made it! I grabbed onto a coral head with my bare hands. It was like grabbing razor blades, or cactus, but I didn't care. After I got my breath I climbed up onto the reef to where I could finally stand up and look around. The dry bag is heading out to sea. The sailboat is leaning way over, it's trapped in the coral, and my backpack I can't see at all. Then in a minute or two I'm across the reef and I'm lying on a dry sandy beach staring up at the blue sky. My gold is heading toward Florida without me, but it'll probably wash up on some island in the Bahamas first. The sat phone and sat text are in the backpack.

I'm in shorts and a t-shirt, with boots on my feet and cuts and scrapes up and down my body but especially on my hands. My feet were protected or I probably wouldn't be here today. And that, my new friends, is how I came to arrive on Mayaguana Island. So now I must admit that you accomplished the feat much more skillfully, and far less painfully, than I did."

After a quiet period, Luke said, "You were scourged."

"Yes, black beard, I was scourged. I still have the scars."

"So what did you do then?" Jessie asked. She had stopped playing her mandolin a few minutes earlier to listen.

"I sat on a driftwood log staring at that sailboat lying on its side, and I gave my life a lot of thought. A lot. But I had a plane to catch. I knew from studying the chart on the boat that the runway ran parallel to Abraham's Bay, and it wasn't far off. I'd walk up the beach until I reached a short road that ran between the two. It was on the chart I'd seen on the boat. So I set off walking up the beach." He slumped forward again, his elbows on his knees, staring into his empty cup.

Jessie asked for all of us. "Well, Curt, and *then* what happened?"

He looked up and focused his gaze upon Jessie, and then Tala. "And then what happened? The rest of my sad tale of woe shall wait for another time. Tonight I had my very first taste of alcohol in several years, and I hardly know what I'm saying, but I fear that my tongue has been loosened beyond all reason. And despite your kind offer of hospitality, my dear captain's wife whose name escapes me. . ."

"Tala," she said, reminding him. "Tala Kilmer."

"Tala Kilmer, I'm afraid I'm not going to spend the night on your fine vessel, at least, not tonight. We'll have plenty of time for my story, and for yours, but not on this night."

Then he turned to me. "Captain Kilmer, a question: is the little boat with the red sail your sole means of transportation between the ship and the shore?"

"It is, Curt, but why do you ask? And you're staying right here tonight, it's been decided." I'd already asked him to call me Dan, but I would never insist on it. I was never offended by being called captain. It was also a pragmatic issue: every time I was called captain, it helped my crew to remember the chain of command—and their place in it. And sometimes that clear understanding was very important for all of us.

"A generous offer to stay the night was indeed made by your lovely wife, and thank you so much, but I never agreed. Henry will come for me when you flash your anchor light on and off. For him a full moon is as good as the high noon. But about your little boat with the red sail: do I understand that it has no engine? Or is there no more gasoline to be had?"

Gino said, "We had a little outboard until a week ago, but it was lost. It was a four-horsepower Honda."

Curt laughed. "All of four horsepower? Four horsepower? And is that the largest dingy you can carry on your ship?"

I replied, "We could fit an eighteen-footer between the masts—when we have two vertical masts—but there'd be no room to work around them. Sixteen feet is about the best for us. But it can't be too heavy. We lift them on and off with the foremast boom. That is, when we have a foremast."

"Less than eighteen feet, and not too heavy. And I'm also to assume that four horsepower is not your upper limit?"

"Our dinghy can take an eight or a nine-point-nine. I used to have a RIB with a seventy-horse Evinrude."

"I see. So, Captain Kilmer, do you have any gasoline on board? This is a moot point if there is no more gasoline. Gas that's fresh enough to run an engine, and not ruin it."

"Actually, Curt, we do have some fresh gasoline."

"In that case, Captain Kilmer, let me put a proposition to you: If you will give me five gallons of gasoline, I will return tomorrow with a better dinghy than the one you have, and an outboard motor that matches it. I will drive it here myself."

"For only five gallons of gasoline? That's a very generous offer. And what do you want in return?"

"What do you think I want in return? Isn't it obvious? I want you to end my exile here."

"But what about Henry?"

"Henry will never leave the island. He'll be content here as long as there is fruit on the trees and fish in the bay. If he's the last of the Mayaguanans, that's just how he'd want it."

"What kind of dinghy are you talking about, Curt?"

"You'll see it tomorrow . . . if you give me the gasoline."

We prepared the five gallons, pumping it from a drum in the hold into three jugs, and then we flashed the anchor light.

Our transom stern light was on when Henry steered his catboat toward our swim platform. Between the electric light and the moon reflecting off the sand below us, it could have been high noon for the tillerman. Curt stood and grabbed Rebel's wheel again, staring down at the lit compass and then at his island. He turned and stepped up onto the aft deck, crossed it in a few steps, and caught his neck on one of the tarp's paracord guy lines. He grabbed the line, ducked under it, found the opening through the stern pulpit, and climbed down the transom steps onto the swim platform. Once on it he turned to look up at us and proclaimed, "I shall return!" with both arms raised high.

I told Adam to go down and help him, and to make sure the gasoline jugs made it onto the boat safely. Henry bumped his boat's wooden bow against Rebel's boarding platform, under our transom light and next to the Whisper. Curt Curtiss saluted us again and turned around to board his water taxi. He put his foot across and then fell aboard, but he broke his fall with his hands. Adam was ready to leap to the rescue, but Curt rolled onto his back and waved off his offer of assistance.

A catboat's mast is practically right in its vertical bow, so Adam grabbed it with one hand while I passed down the jugs of gasoline and he swung them aboard. This was only possible because the bay was so calm, with just a light breeze from the northwest. A few days and nights before, we'd been dodging monster waves out in deep water. We had been knocked down by a white squall and we'd lost our foremast. The contrast was remarkable, or at least it was to me.

The catboat drifted back away from Rebel's cone of light. After some fumbling to haul in their boom and harden up their sail, all while drifting toward the five-mile reef, Henry steered them toward the radio tower miles up Abraham's Bay.

It was lit only by moonlight.

35

Gino had the working party dressed, fed and assembled on the foredeck at 0800. I stayed below while he got them sorted out. There's no reason to be the first mate if the captain is always hovering nearby to steal his wind. A mate needs opportunities to demonstrate his competence, and his authority, if he's going to make it stick when it counts during a crisis.

I spent the time at the galley table studying Chart 27005, "Key West to San Juan." Jamaica, Haiti, and the Dominican Republic were on the bottom of the four-foot-wide paper chart. I started measuring distances and writing notes because we had some important decisions to make. Members of the work detail made several trips down the forward ladder into the hold to extract the needed tools and supplies.

At 0830 I went up on deck to see how they were doing. The three cargo hold boys were there with Gino. They were all wearing sailing gloves, hats and long-sleeve shirts. There were boxes and tool carriers in front of the scuttle hatch that were full of pliers, screwdrivers, tape measures and wrenches. Gino had studied the mast tied along our starboard side and he knew what he needed. Our bolt cutters were next to a coil of spare rigging wire. The half-inch-diameter stainless-steel wire was so stiff that the coil was tied in a ring that was four feet across, but I knew it was no more than twenty feet in length.

Gino said, "Luke has the day off. His cut needs more time to heal. I have a plan for getting a forestay up to the mainmast. I drew it, if you want to look at it."

"If you drew it, I'm sure it's right. Just tell me the plan."

"I've got it right here." He pulled a paper out of his shirt pocket and handed it to me. I unfolded it while he spoke.

"I used your original rigging diagram to calculate the distance from the bow to the top of the mainmast, and it's 68 feet. Of course, nobody ever thought we'd lose the foremast and need a wire that long. We have to add more wire to one of the stay wires that went down and reuse it for the new forestay. We have some spare wire and we have a few end terminals, so we can add what we need to make the 68 feet. Our first job will be lifting the mast up a few feet and stripping it down. Then we'll see which old wire is the best to be part of the new forestay."

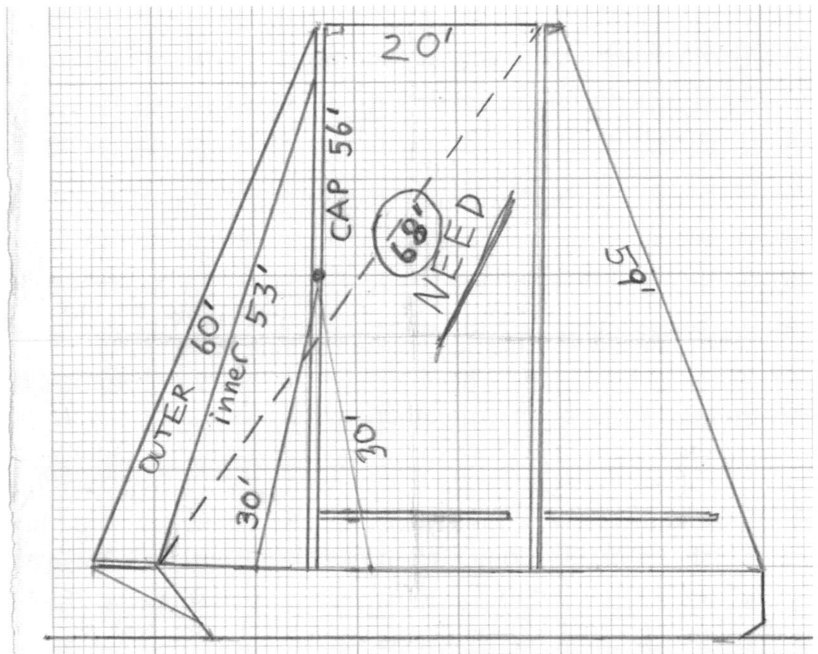

"Well, first mate, it sounds like you have a good plan. If you need me, if you have any questions, I'll be down below."

So I left them to do their work. It was torture to let them do this job without me. However, my personal discomfort was not as important as showing the new crew that Mr. Bracciano was a competent leader in his own right, and that even without the captain, they could plan and execute critical tasks.

Why? Because captains don't last forever.

All the deck hatches were open including the cargo hatch, so I could hear almost everything they were saying and doing, but I resisted the impulse to intervene. Forging a strong crew took precedence over demonstrating my mastery of rigging to them. If they were stumped by something, it wouldn't be hard to find me. Rebel Yell was only sixty feet long.

It took them a few hours of hammering, winching, pry-barring foot-stomping, metal-dragging, shouting and cursing to finish the job. Adam made several trips up the mast with our hundred-foot tape measure. We were all glad the mast steps were on the mainmast, which was still standing.

On his own he discovered Rebel's crow's-nest seat, where a radar unit had been located long ago. The stainless-steel tube that had protected the radar formed a circle above the seat to keep the lookout secured in place. The crow's nest perch was my own invention. The teak bench below the ring tilted twenty degrees either way and then locked into position, so that the lookout could sit level no matter how the boat was heeled.

On his final trip up the mast, Adam pulled the end of the new wire up with him and attached its eye terminal to the front of the masthead with a thumb-size stainless-steel clevis pin. Their cries of joy could have been heard across the reef. I left the pilothouse and pretended to be relaxing in the cockpit under the shade of the tarp when I heard Barry say, "I think it's finished. Should we get the captain?"

Gino answered, "Sure, go ahead and get him."

Barry and Adam came around the pilothouse, and Adam said, "It's all done, skipper, if you want to take a look."

"Sure, let's go see it." I didn't let on to them that I'd been following nearly every step of their work, looking up through deck hatches and out through the tinted pilothouse windows.

I followed them up to the foredeck.

Gino said, "It's all connected, but it's slack. I wanted you to check it first. We couldn't get the old wire out of the roller-furling tube. It's too damaged to do the job here. It's bent, and we can't get the sail off it or get the wire out of it. Fixing the roller-furler will be a boatyard job. We used the starboard cap-stay instead. It has a bend, but we don't have a better wire."

I examined the new forestay from the deck fitting welded on the bow up to the masthead. At the bottom, the adjustable turnbuckle was opened to its maximum length. The mainmast was still tensioned forward by the rope staysail halyard that ran parallel to the slack new wire. Close to the top, the two-part forestay was connected by mechanical end terminals. The wire had a dogleg halfway up where it had turned over the spreader bar in its last role. But we didn't have a better option.

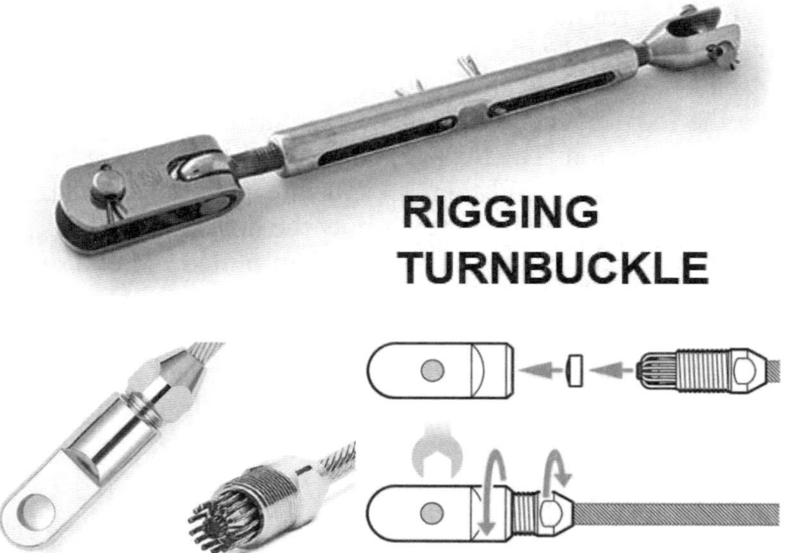

Sta-Lok mechanical end terminal for stay wires

So I said, "Well, at least it's wire. Crank it down, Barry."

He knelt at the bow and tightened the forestay by rotating the turnbuckle, turning it with a big wrench and drawing the two threaded bolts together. The kink straightened out as the forestay came under tension. I checked it by grabbing the wire at my shoulder height and shoving it from side to side. Nice and tight. The job was done. If not to my complete satisfaction, at least to my acceptance. The two-part forestay, made of salvaged wire and a remnant scrap, was the best we do under the circumstances. But it was wire, and it could carry a jib.

We shook hands all around, and I thanked each of them. Gino and I were of another generation, and we were the supervisors, so Barry, Adam and Will, the cargo hold boys, held their own celebration a little distance away from us. I don't know which of them said it first, but between all their high fives and fist bumps I heard them mention *the three amigos*.

There was still a lot of work for them to do in getting the bottom of the reefed foresail off its boom, and winding up all the wires that weren't being used, and coiling up the jib sheets and halyards and the many other lines and cords that had come down with the foremast. The foresail and the storm jib, both of them torn, were folded and sent below.

The outer jib was left wrapped around its roller-furling extrusion and laid along the starboard side deck. We all lifted the horizontal foremast and carried it forward so that it would not be jutting out past our transom. We lowered it to the deck inside all of the lifeline stanchions except the front two, where it protruded from the starboard bow like a second bowsprit next to the original, now bare and bereft of purpose. The bent stanchions were levered and pounded back into semi-vertical positions, and the wire lifelines were reinstalled. The hundred places where Rebel's paint had been scraped to bare metal would be red with rust in a week, but this couldn't be helped.

Gino said, "Okay, boys, let's put away the tools and bring up the working jib. We're lucky the storm jib was up when the mast went over. At least the working jib is still okay."

Adam said, "Now that the mast has a forestay, we can use the staysail halyard for other jobs. I know it's going to be for raising the jib, but when the jib is down we can use it for lifting the dingy up on deck. If we attach the foremast boom to the front of the mainmast, we can swing out the dinghy just like we did before. It's a little bent, but not enough to matter."

I asked him, "How will we attach it to the mainmast?"

"The same way it was attached to the foremast. There's a gooseneck that's attached with machine screws. If we take it off, we can screw it onto the front of the mainmast, and there's your new boom crane. Why not?"

A gooseneck is a universal joint where a horizontal boom is attached to a vertical mast. A gooseneck allows the boom to swing all the way out to each side and up and down in order to best trim its sail for the prevailing wind. I exchanged glances with Gino. I was thinking: *this kid will be ready to captain a boat before he's twenty.* If he can master celestial navigation, he'll have it all. If only Hilton Sapelo could see him now.

Will said, "I know where the electric drill is. If we have the right drill bits and taps to make threads it's an easy job."

I just said, "Then make it happen, gentlemen."

Luke came up through the scuttle hatch and joined us on deck, his right hand freshly bandaged. I checked my watch, it was after eleven. Luke was looking very relaxed, in a fresh t-shirt and clean cargo shorts. He was scrubbed and clean, his face glowing. His black hair was combed back and damp. I guessed where he'd spent the morning, and with whom. This was why Tala and Sofia had been hovering around the galley and guarding the passageway back to the aft cabin. And this is why Rita had been babysitting the twins up forward. Gino, Luke and I couldn't help exchange a few knowing glances, but we avoided making crass comments or throwing overt winks. And not because I'm a prude, mind you, but because it would have been unfair to our three young bachelors.

I told Will, "You know where the tap and die sets are."

Then Luke mentioned, "Oh, Gino—Sofia wants you."

After a few more furtive looks between the married men I said, "First mate, I don't think we're going to need you for this job, and I'm an expert at drilling and tapping. Go and see what Sofia wants. And crank up the generator for the drill."

"Sure, boss, I will." He answered casually, but he dropped down the scuttle hatch at roughly the speed of gravity.

In a minute I heard the generator come on. Will found the power cord and connected it, handing it up to Adam through the open cargo hatch. I showed Barry and Adam where I kept some of our other specialized tools and I left them to it.

My goal was to provide them nothing but advice, when asked, so that they could learn to do these jobs on their own. I could have done the job myself, blindfolded, but my greater objective was to build the crew and increase their confidence. Captains don't last forever. And neither do first mates.

At some point Rita appeared from around the pilothouse in a yellow sun dress, herding the twins up to the foredeck. It was hard to miss the flirtatious looks between Adam and Rita. The boys were bringing water bottles for us. They handed us the water and went straight to the new forestay wire and shook it like they'd seen me do so many times to check the tautness.

Chris muttered, "We're still just a sloop, not a schooner."

Jonathan replied, "But now at least we can put up a jib."

After they satisfied their curiosity, the three disappeared.

The gooseneck was being relocated onto the front of the mainmast and I was not touching a tool, and neither was Luke, who was with us now but was still officially on light duty. We stood back while the three amigos passed tools between them and shared ideas. I wondered if Luke's wound had gotten wet in the bathtub with Jessie. I glanced down at his new bandage.

He saw me look at it and popped me a quick wink.

Thanks for the private time with Jessie, skipper.

I just nodded back, while the three young bachelors were busy at their work on the front of the mainmast. So in one important area I was taking care of *los esposos*, the married couples, but what about the rest of the crew? It was Monday, and we'd all been confined to the same sixty feet since the Saturday before last. It wasn't just a matter of going stir crazy, but it was also a matter of health in many other ways.

There were miles of sandy beach on Abraham's Bay, and a runway that was just out of sight uphill and running parallel to it. I wanted to get them ashore for some exercise, to allow them to roam further than sixty feet, and give them time to be in their own groups. Or time to be a thousand yards away from anybody. This is why the navy called time off the ship *liberty*.

These were social issues I'd never confronted when it had just been Victor, Hung and me on Rebel Yell. Doctor Aleman would do anything he wanted anytime we were anchored near shore, with or without my unasked-for permission. Tran Hung rarely desired to hobble ashore, and then only to search for groceries and spices. I was thinking, when all the work is done and we're ready for sea again, I'll cut them loose for liberty.

When the gooseneck job was finished, and the boom was attached, now facing forward instead of aft, Adam clipped the staysail halyard to its end so we could see how it would work as a crane. Now we could pull Whisper up out of the water, or launch it, without manhandling and dropping it caveman-style.

Then it was time to put the working jib onto the new forestay. The wire was slanted further back at a lower angle, so we had to relocate the sheet turning blocks on the toe rails. This was so the sail would be pulled back and down at the optimal angle. This involved quite a lot of experimentation, frequently raising and lowering the working jib and making adjustments.

This was no problem with Rebel Yell facing into the wind at anchor, with the sail flowing harmlessly straight back. But it took considerable time to get just right, and this required a lot of discussion about all of the aerodynamic principles involved and how to maximize the lift and the drive from a jib with the wind on every different point of sail. All of these lessons took more than an hour . . . but only because I was stalling for time.

I abruptly dismissed the class when Gino reappeared back by the pilothouse. The jib was left on deck clipped to the new wire. Adam and Will disappeared down the scuttle, but Barry joined me and Luke for our short walk to the cockpit. Gino's hair was styled with some kind of fragrant oil, and he smelled better than any man ever should. He had also been closely shaved—after only one day—and his new mustache was gone.

Barry smiled at Gino but he poked Luke in the ribs and said, "Oh, you sly dogs. *Oh, you sly dogs*."

I pretended not to understand what he meant, but Luke winked at Barry and then at me, and I winked back at them.

To Gino I just said, "First mate, you look very nice. *Very clean*. And tell Sofia that I didn't like your moustache either."

Gino ignored my observation and said, "We're a sailboat again, boss. Wherever we need to go—we can sail there."

"*Almost* anywhere. The main and jib make only half our old sail area, but I've heard rumors the Caribbean is a windy place in the winter. It'll save us the trouble of reefing."

As I was ducking under the tarp into the shade Barry said, "A boat's coming, skipper. I'll get your binoculars."

He handed them to me without even taking his own look first. Rebel was facing east, riding on the anchor. I looked over the pilothouse: the land was to the left, the ocean reef was to the right, and the BaTelCo tower was straight up the bay. On the water beneath the tower a small boat was heading toward us.

Barry asked me, "Should I get a rifle, just in case?"

"No. That can only be Curt." I knew Barry was still wary of ambush and trickery. Part of me felt I should help walk him back toward feeling safe when confronting new situations. But what if he was right and I was wrong? The M-16 and the bolt-action had remained in the pilothouse since Sunday, the day before. Both rifles could be out and loaded in seconds.

By then Gino had the other binos. "It's Curt. He's alone."

The boat was approaching us bow-on, so it was hard to judge its speed, but it was moving fast. I could tell it was Curt driving by his gray hair, beard and wraparound sunglasses.

"Barry," I said, "go down and catch his line. You know what to do." Meaning, take care of the approaching boat. The captain has deemed it to be non-threatening, and you should too. This was also an exercise in trust building. Not everybody is trying to trick you or ambush you. You'll be okay. We'll all be okay. It's just a routine human encounter. Don't worry, be happy. Every new day is going to be better than yesterday.

Unless it isn't. It was often hard to know when to relax.

The boat didn't slow down as it approached our bow. It roared past us going at least thirty miles an hour, an incredible velocity in our world of single-digit boat speeds.

Curt was driving a silver V-hull with an outboard on its transom. He was in the back steering it with the engine's tiller. His hat was gone but his sunglasses were on, his long gray hair flying back. The aluminum boat had some cargo in its bottom. It left only a small wake in passing because it was so high up on plane there wasn't much boat touching the water.

He zoomed a few hundred yards out beyond our stern in a straight line and then began a wide turn at full speed, the boat leaning in. He made two circles around us and then began to slow down and turn in toward us, but he still approached our boarding platform at a fast clip. Barry squatted like a baseball catcher and caught his bow, stopped the boat and held it there until Curt twisted the throttle back to idle and killed the motor. Barry grabbed its bow line and secured it to a transom cleat.

The aluminum boat had a bench seat across the back, one across the middle, and another across the front a few feet from the bow. These bench seats were also made of aluminum, and were closed off by sheet aluminum on their fronts and backs. I understood why. Foam flotation was under the benches. Without the foam blocks, if it was swamped, the metal boat would sink like a stone. With the flotation you'd be able to bail it out.

Yeah, sure you could. Maybe in calm water. Good luck.

36

Curt stood and moved over his boat's cargo up to the bow, and then he stepped over onto the platform.

"Thanks for catching me," he said to Barry, who grabbed his arm. "It's the first time I've ever run it."

"No problem. It sure is fast." The aluminum V-hull was a little longer than Whisper, wider in the beam, and higher in its freeboard. The motor's gray engine cover said it was an Evinrude 40. My old Avon RIB had carried an Evinrude 70.

Curt looked up and said, "Captain Dan, I may be jumping the gun, but I think we should unload it. I'm not going back, so you're stuck with me. I said goodbye to Henry. He'll forget me by next week, or he'll think it was all a dream. I don't need to see that island again. And I don't know if you've had lunch, but I brought some things to eat."

"Then welcome aboard, Curt." And just like that we had a new member of the crew. And once again, we had a total head count of thirteen souls on board. Not Gino's even dozen.

Looking down I said, "Barry, let Whisper trail back, and then pull his boat sideways against the platform and tie it up at the bow and stern. It'll be easier to unload that way."

Curt had his sunglasses on but he was hatless. "So, what do you think of your new boat, Dan? Personally, I'd suggest not making sharp turns at high speed. There are lobster tails and grouper fillets in the white bucket."

"Lobster and grouper? You caught them since last night?"

"*Caught* them? No, captain, no, as a general rule we never catch them—they catch themselves. We trap them. They crawl in, or they swim in, and we just go out and bring them back. I tailed the lobsters and filleted the grouper before I came down the bay, but in the absence of any ice or refrigeration, I think the best place for them now is in your galley."

He passed the bucket to me. Adam and Will came up onto the aft deck and the boat was quickly unloaded. Soft luggage, tote boxes and more string bags of fruit were passed over the transom and set on the aft deck. The last item to be uncovered was a five-horsepower Mercury outboard. It was hard for me to contain my joy. Assuming it ran—and why wouldn't it?—we now had two dinghies with motors. This would open up many new logistical possibilities. When the metal boat was empty Barry let it trail astern parallel to Whisper.

Our guest and newest member of the crew was ushered again to the seat of honor at the back of the cockpit. He was given a glass of water, but now it was flavored with lemon. He pushed his sunglasses up onto his head and said, "I lost my hat coming here. And I think that boat will go just about as fast as you want it to go with only one person in it."

I asked him, "Whose boat is it?"

"Why, it's *your* boat, Captain Dan. It's your boat, and it's my passage fare. It's my paid ticket to wherever we're going."

"But whose boat was it *before* you brought it here?"

"Somebody who left Mayaguana Island years ago. But I can't see how that matters."

"It might matter to them."

"They're not coming back, Dan. They're never coming back. But it was me who made that Evinrude run again, and it was me who repaired and improved that boat in a dozen ways. It was me and Henry who dragged it to the water on a home-made wagon. It was me who kept the engines on a dozen cars and boats ready for their next drink of fresh gasoline. We kept up their houses, we tended to their fruit trees, and we planted more. We built new fish and lobster traps and a conch farm. The world's best protein swims into this bay, and it's here for the taking, but nobody ever came back. So now it's *my* turn to leave. The caretaker has retired. If we had a week, we could go and get a dozen boats and motors. We could tow them out in a line, but you said under eighteen feet and not too heavy."

“Curt,” I asked him, “How did you know the motor would run, if there was no fresh gas to test it?”

“I didn’t need to test it with gasoline to know it would run. It’s just physics, captain. Two plus two equals four. If it’s put together correctly, and it’s making a spark, it *has* to run. There was no fresh gasoline but there was plenty of motor oil, and oil doesn’t spoil. I took car and boat engines apart down to the smallest screws and springs, and I put them back together just to keep from going mad. I mean—to keep my mind busy. I had no doubt that Evinrude 40 would start. I polished all the moving parts, and I improved the carburetor over the factory specs. It fired on my second pull. It had to. It’s just physics.

“You said you wanted a light boat, so I knew you’d want a light motor for it, and that’s why I brought this one. It was buried in a shed, and I could tell by the dust on it that it hadn’t been touched in decades. The vertical rod that shifts gears from forward to reverse in the lower unit was broken. Not even the rod itself, just a rod coupling. That’s *nothing*. Somebody must have left it there and forgotten it.”

Luke said, “Maybe a son moved off the island, and he never came back. That happens a lot. The rest of the family starts piling other junk around it and they forget it. I’ve seen entire boats forgotten in garages. I’ve seen them piled up with junk until the family forgot there was a boat under it all.”

“Probably something like that,” Curt agreed. “Just don’t make any sharp turns at high speed. I think it’ll be safer with a few people in it to hold it down. But if you really need to go somewhere fast—you can. Just don’t make any sharp turns.”

I said, “Your great-grandfather would be proud of you.”

“Who? Oh, yes, I suppose so. Maybe he would be.”

In 1907 Glenn Curtiss built a V-8 engine, mounted it on a homemade motorcycle frame, and rode it at over 130 miles an hour on a Florida beach, making him the fastest man on earth. He accomplished this in his twenties, before he moved on to become a pioneer in aviation. It wasn’t hard to imagine where Curt Curtiss had gotten his knack for mechanical engineering.

Adam asked me, "Who's going to be in charge of it?"

"You're the dinghy master," I replied. "That's up to you."

He said, "I've driven *way* faster boats than that one back in Beaufort. How much gas is in the red tank?"

Curt said, "Over half, so almost three gallons. I ran it in a water barrel to make sure it would hold up at its full operating temperature. Especially the old rubber parts, like the hoses and belts and gaskets. I ran it for an hour. I trust it."

"Skipper," Adam said, "I'd like take it out with Barry and Will. We need to learn how to handle it, and I already know about not making sharp turns at high speed. So if you want to get Mr. Curtiss settled in, well, sir, I'd like to test it out."

I could see the wild eagerness in his young blue eyes, but he kept his lips pursed, hiding his joy and his crooked tooth.

"Stay away from the beach and the reef. There's at least a half hour of gas in that tank, and we'll bring up more, but for now don't wander too far away. Stay close enough to us to see people on Rebel Yell. Take lifejackets, but you don't have to wear them. Is there an anchor in that boat? There is? Good. If the engine dies, just anchor, and we'll come and get you."

"Yes sir, we will." In turn Adam said, "Will: can you go and collect three lifejackets? No, make it . . . five. Don't take them off Whisper because we'll want it to be ready too, so get them from down below. Barry: can you sort out that mess with the anchor? It needs to be ready if we need it. On a small boat your anchor is your last chance not to be swept out onto the open ocean if your motor craps out."

When these tasks were finished they went flying up the bay toward the radio tower, retracing Curt's path down to us. After a few minutes the boat made a wide turn and returned to our stern. Barry was on the engine and he put it into neutral far enough back from Rebel Yell that Adam was able to casually step onto the platform with the bow line.

He said, "Mr. Curtiss, we found your hat. It was floating because there's a piece of foam inside at the top. That's smart, making an unsinkable hat."

"Well, I could never stand a string under my chin and this one fits so well it rarely blows off. I would have gone back for it, but I was going so fast I was afraid of flipping the boat, and then the hat slipped my mind. So, how do you like it?"

"It was a blast," said Adam, stepping back onto the bow of the metal craft and pushing off. "We just came back to give you your hat. We still have some time, there's plenty of gas. We'll be back in a while. Will: it's your turn to drive."

After a brief consultation with Gino we announced our plans for getting everyone ashore for exercise and a mental health break. Curt didn't want to go, not even as a guide. Four years had been enough, thanks. He did look at our small chart of Mayaguana and advised us where to land the new dinghy to put people ashore. Groups of four were to stay in plain sight of Rebel Yell and return after an hour. Other than Curt and his companion Henry, we hadn't seen any sign of human activity on the beach, so I rated the danger as low.

Barry took Tala, the twins and me ashore on the first run. I brought a daypack with our water bottles as a way to carry my Glock while keeping it unseen. I wanted my family to be relaxed and not fearful, but I didn't want to be unarmed either.

The best feature of Abraham's Bay, whether seen from Rebel Yell or from the beach, was the radiant blue-green water itself. The sunlight reflecting off the sand and coral made the turquoise water shimmer and glow.

On the other hand, there was not much to recommend the beach or the island based on our short visit. The outer reef a mile across the bay took the energy out of the ocean swells, so there were no waves breaking on the miles of white sand. Upslope and inland the beach was bordered by dry scrub that was too high to see over and too tight to penetrate on foot.

There was not a sign of local human activity on the beach, but there were many signs of humanity on the sand and pushed up into the bush. Plastic bottles of every size and shape that had come from factories in vibrant colors lay fading above the high tide line and deep into the scrub brush where they had been pushed by storms. Trawler-size fishing nets were half buried in the sand and half rotting in the sun. Nets and ropes were tangled among timbers and parts of docks and piers that had been driven over the reef and up onto the land. There were wooden pallets, toilet seats and a thousand other discards of civilization. There were countless shoes, but never in pairs. We did scavenge a few pieces of useable lumber, and a refrigerator door for its hinges and hardware, but not much else.

One item was particularly ominous: a yellow-orange life raft, upside-down, deflated, and partly buried in the sand. It was at least a twenty-person raft by its estimated diameter. Who had launched it? Often life rafts are inflated during an emergency, but storm-force winds blow them away before the desperate sailors can board them. And if they are occupied, they can be capsized and rolled by storm waves.

Just to prepare this beach for new tourism would require a massive cleanup effort, and who would do it? And who would come as a tourist? That era was in the past. But at least there were no bright new detergent bottles recently dumped from a passing ship. I wondered about the half-life of civilization's detritus. Would it take a century for this beach to resemble the same strand a century earlier? Most of the rubbish was already deteriorating in the sun. The fishing nets and ropes crumbled into dust at the touch, but what would become of the plastic dust? Was it being taken up in the food chain? For how long, and with what consequences to new living organisms?

When we returned to Rebel Yell, Curt's appearance was transformed. He had noticed the trimmed haircuts and shaved faces of the adult men, and learned that Sofia was our barber. His face was pale where his gray beard had been, but he was all smiles about the result, happily stroking his bare chin. Nowhere was his gray hair longer than an inch, and it was tapered in the back and over his ears. Sofia was also pleased with her work.

After the last shore liberty party was recovered, I let the cargo-hold boys and Rita go out joyriding on the new dinghy. They had named the aluminum craft Metallica, and I saw no reason to overrule them. Barry and Adam seemed to have an affinity for driving the boat at high speed and they took turns steering, while Rita and Will were content to be passengers. The four made a fair test load for the boat. They'd roar close by Rebel Yell at full throttle, then carve a turn and cross their own wake to make the boat's hull slap across their own waves. I was happy to see them out enjoying themselves, their hoots and howls rising above the sound of the Evinrude 40.

Watching them, I thought Metallica would be a great boat for flat water, but I had serious concerns about taking it out in ocean waves. I could see it stuffing its sharp bow right into a steep wave face when running an inlet with the wind against the tide. This was a common enough situation, and often there is no plan B for getting to shore or returning to the mothership, so the tendency can be to push on into danger.

For handling real waves, my old Avon RIB with its fat inflatable tube construction was far superior, and safer—but on flat water I had to admit that the V-hulled Metallica was damn fast. The gasoline they'd burned was a small price to pay to add that capability to Rebel Yell. And since Barry and Adam loved to drive it, they'd master every aspect of handling it.

Dinner was served buffet-style as a mid-afternoon meal. There were not enough lobster tails for everyone, so Tala and Sofia made a lobster salad. The grouper was grilled with pineapple chunks and lemon and served with rice. There was still some bread from yesterday to spread with our last butter and jam.

The word for the day was relaxation. Our only mast had a wire forestay, and a jib clipped onto it and ready to raise. The horizontal foremast and the rolled-up outer jib were both secured on the starboard deck. The foremast boom had a new temporary location on the front of the mainmast, so we could crane our small boats aboard. We were ready to leave.

While Barry, Adam, Will and Rita were out on Metallica, I told Gino and Curt that we needed to have a look at the charts, because we needed to plan our next moves. We were using up our precious fresh water by the day. Nobody wanted to visit the beach again, so there was no reason to linger.

We cleared the dinette table and sat down. I faced the clock and barometer and Gino and Curt sat across from me. I pulled the folded chart off the shelf behind me and opened it up facing toward them. At four feet wide it covered most of the table.

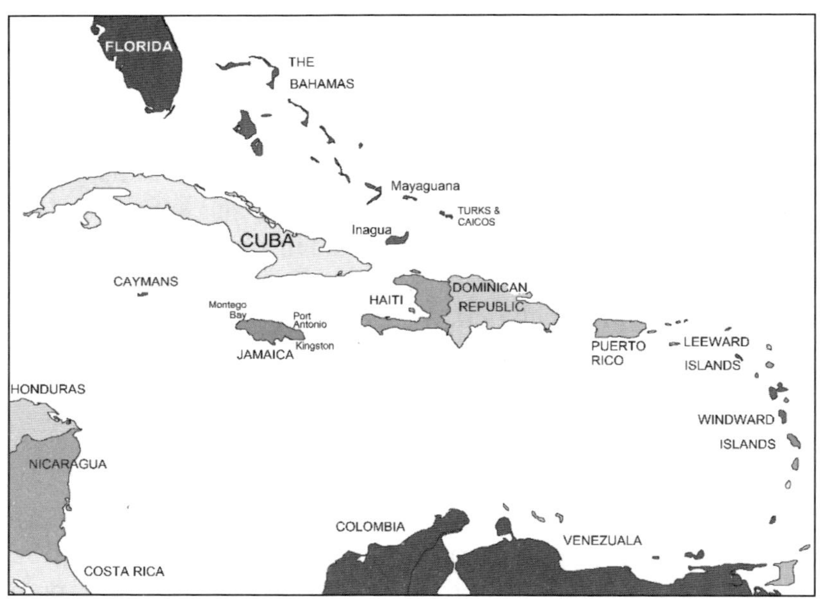

"Here's Florida, Cuba and Haiti, and here we are on Mayaguana." I moved my finger across the big map as I spoke.

Luke came down the ladder with an empty water bottle. "Well, well," he said to us. "The big chart is out for the gray hairs to study. So, where are we going, skipper?"

I replied, "Fill your bottle and have a seat, black beard."

When he did so, he sat next to Curt. Three to my one.

"Okay, here we are. Staying here and eating oranges and lobster and waiting for a miracle is not an option. Every day we're using up our fresh water. We have five or six hundred miles worth of diesel, and that becomes a factor depending on where we want to go. Our rigging wire is weak and not to be trusted, and we're only carrying half the sail area as before. With this setup we can't beat to windward. At the best we'll be able to reach or run downwind. There's no way we can sail east from here against the winter trades."

I had the full attention of the three men across the table.

"Our old plan was to get all of our easting from Beaufort up at thirty degrees north, and then turn south at sixty degrees east when we're past the Caribbean. Well, that's out, because we're already down here at twenty-two north, right in the trade wind belt. There's no way we can make it from here to South America on this jury rig. We're way too crippled for that.

"So, what are our realistic options? It's more than eight hundred miles back to South Carolina, and we could sail it, but we're not going to. If we sail northwest on the outside over the Bahamas we can aim for North Florida and try our luck there. That's six hundred miles, and it's all deep water. Now, if we go west from here and we follow the top of Cuba, it's five hundred miles to Miami—but it would be a bitch. Just look at the chart. We'd have to thread our way between Cuba and the Great Bahama Bank. Maybe we'd try it if we had GPS, but not with celestial, not when we're missing days between getting a fix. Only a fool would try to dead-reckon his way to Miami through the Old Bahama Channel." I slid my finger along the route. It was obviously out of the question.

Luke added, "I don't think we should go anywhere near South Florida, anyway. I talked to people who came up from there, and they said it was a zombie apocalypse from Miami to Tampa and Orlando. There were millions of people with no drinking water and no food. We can try North Florida, maybe, but I wouldn't go anywhere near South Florida. No way."

I compared what Luke was saying to Barry's story about the collapse of Charleston. At least the Charleston metro area was backed up by rural countryside and flowing rivers. South Florida's population existed on a strip of dry land between the ocean and the everglades. If you cut off their drinking water and food, then where would they go? Only north. There was a nuclear power plant south of Miami, but what had happened to it? Had it been shut down safely, or was it still operating? Or had it gone out of control, like Fukushima, or Chernobyl?

"I agree, Luke, South Florida is out. So are the Turks and Caicos—Curt told us what happened there. Going south from Mayaguana, Great Inagua is even worse than here because it doesn't have an all-around anchorage. That leaves Cuba and Haiti, and I'm ruling them out. I don't know what's going on in Cuba, and I'm not going to just pick a port on the chart and roll the dice. I'm ruling out Haiti, because it's always been a mess. They were already starving even before the collapse. So that leaves one other port we can sail to with our jury rig, and I've been there before. It's here, Port Antonio, in the northeast corner of Jamaica. It's only 350 miles from Mayaguana, and it'll be a broad reach or downwind all the way there. That's only three days of sailing." I traced the route with my finger.

Curt said, "Jamaica is where my buddy Colin was headed. He had friends there and he thought it was okay. I went there on a cruise with wife number two. Not to Port Antonio, but we stopped in Montego Bay and Ocho Rios on the north coast."

"I've never been to Jamaica," noted Gino, "but it doesn't have a good reputation. A lot of crime is what I heard."

"Port Antonio isn't like the rest of Jamaica," I replied. "It was always a stopover for boats going to the Panama Canal. It has a great natural harbor, but it's too small for cruise ships and freighters. Kingston and Montego Bay are big cities, but Port

Antonio is away from them in the northeast corner. It's only a little town compared to Kingston, but it's on the other side of the Blue Mountains. Port Antonio is nothing like most of Jamaica because of those mountains."

"That all sounds good," said Luke, "but even years ago I heard how dangerous Jamaica was, so I can only imagine how bad it is now, after the collapse. And we won't exactly be able to blend in—I think Jamaica is about ninety-percent black."

"Yes, it's black," I agreed, "but it's not like anywhere else I've ever been. It's hard to explain, but Jamaica is different. We can only guess what it's like now, but there are some great things about Jamaica that will never change. The mountains catch the clouds and it rains almost every day. It's nothing like the Bahamas: it's more like Hawaii, with rivers and waterfalls. Everything grows in Jamaica, so I don't think they would have starved. In Port Antonio we can fill our water tank, take baths, and wash our clothes. *Really* wash them. And Port Antonio has a boatyard with a crane that can lift our mast back up."

Gino said, "If they have the diesel fuel to run the crane."

"Well, if they don't, *we do*. And boatyards always have rigging wire. They order it by the five-hundred-foot spool. A boatyard like the one in Port Antonio is going to have what we need. Maybe even bottom paint, and we can get hauled out. I just feel good about the place. It might be like Beaufort. Port Antonio was always the best-kept secret in Jamaica."

I looked across at each of them. I was winning them over.

Gino asked, "So where would we go after Port Antonio?"

"If it's nice enough there, we might stay for a while. The hurricane season is over. Where we go after Jamaica depends on how much of our damage we can fix while we're there. If we can get the mast back up we'll have more options. Even at her best Rebel could never sail to windward against the winter trades. We could slant down to Cartagena and coast-hop eastward along the top of South America, but I have no idea about the situation down there. If our foremast is back up, we could slant northeast back through the Windward Passage and get all the easting we can out into the Atlantic. Then we'd turn south after we're past the Caribbean and try for Argentina again."

Luke asked, "But what if we can't fix the foremast? What if we leave Jamaica like we went in, with just one mast?"

"In that case we'll have to sail downwind. We won't have a choice. That could be anywhere from Honduras to Texas."

Curt said, "Do you know what else they have in Jamaica? Besides unlimited fresh water? Some of the best coffee in the world. Jamaica has the perfect climate and soil for coffee."

"If they have coffee," said Gino, "then I say let's go."

"And ganja," Curt added. "They grow a lot of marijuana. It's part of the Rastafarian thing. It's part of the Rasta religion. It's not exactly legal, but it's all over the place."

"Maybe it is," I said, "But we're not bringing any weed onto this boat. Especially not with kids on board. So, what do you guys think of our options? I think our only two realistic choices come down to North Florida, or Jamaica."

Luke said, "North Florida sounds too much like Georgia and South Carolina. It was okay in Beaufort, but the island wasn't typical. And North Florida got overrun by millions of refugees. I say we go to Jamaica and try to fix the mast there."

"I've never been to either place," said Gino, "but if they have a crane, and they have coffee, then I vote for Jamaica."

"That's two for Jamaica. What do you say, Curt?"

"Anywhere that's not here. It's your decision, captain."

"Then Jamaica it is. Let's bring in the new boat and have a crew meeting in the cockpit."

Gino stood beside me when I addressed the crew gathered in and around the cockpit. I'd brought up the chart.

I said, "As you may have figured out or heard by now, Mr. Curtiss is joining us as part of our crew. Curt, there's an empty hammock in the cargo hold, or you can make a sleeping pallet in there, it's up to you. In theory those hammocks can fit a man of your height, but you can check it for yourself." (I didn't mention how this hammock had come to be available.)

I held the folded chart against my chest. "We're here, and here's Jamaica, and that's where we're going. We'll have most of the full moon for the next couple of nights, and we're going to take advantage of it. Between here and Jamaica is the Windward Passage. The gap between Cuba and Haiti is forty miles across. From here to Jamaica it's 350 miles, so call it three days of sailing. Even with one mast. There's usually plenty of wind where we're going, and it's almost always from the east. It's called the Windward Passage because it was so hard for the old square-riggers to sail through it out to the Atlantic. But lucky for us, we're going through it the easy way, downwind.

"I've been to Port Antonio before, and they have a boatyard with a crane. If the crane works, and if we can find some more half-inch rigging wire, we can put the foremast up again after we do a little work on it. After that, we might be able to continue on to South America. It all depends on what kind of shape we're in after Jamaica."

Every face was looking at me, hanging on my every word.

"One great thing about Jamaica is they have more fresh water than they know what to do with. Jamaica is *nothing* like Mayaguana. *Nothing*. Jamaica is bigger than Puerto Rico—it's as big as the Big Island of Hawaii. A few million people live on it, or at least, they did, but they were mostly in a couple of big cities like Kingston. On this chart it might look close from Port Antonio down to Kingston, but right in between are the Blue Mountains, and they're over 7,000 feet high.

"So because they have so much water, and we'll be there in a few days, I've decided to relax the water restrictions for this afternoon. Adam, after this meeting we're going to bring the boats aboard, and then we're going to have a swim call and a freshwater rinse. You can soap up and shampoo your hair on the platform, and then jump into the bay to rinse it off, and when you're done swimming you can rinse off the salt water with fresh water. Tala will give you the soap that you need."

This announcement was met with smiles, high fives, fist bumps and other expressions of joy. We were all pretty much used to our collective stink, even down below in tight quarters, but you never get used to having itchy skin and a mangy scalp.

"After the swim call, and if Jessie and Luke feel like it, maybe we'll have a little music and watch the moon come up. But we're going to be up early in the morning, so this is going to be an early night. Tomorrow we're sailing to Jamaica, and if things go well, we'll be a schooner again."

I smiled and tried to project more confidence than I felt. We had another open-ocean passage in front of us, and crew morale was an essential element of success, hence the relaxed water restrictions. To the side I told Gino, "Tell Sofia that Rita can use the aft cabin tub. The swim platform is good enough for the boys and men. When Rita is done, I'll connect the hose extension and hang it out through the transom."

The boys brought Metallica around to the port side and tied it off. The same rope staysail halyard that had held up the mainmast now raised the boom for cargo handling. Gino and I showed them how to rig a block and tackle to the boom to pull the Evinrude up, swing it over the cargo hold and then lower it down inside. When that was done the two hinged leaves of the cargo hatch were folded inward and sealed tight for the ocean.

Next we lifted Metallica aboard and lowered her onto the port side of the deck. Then we all helped roll her over so she was bottom-up and pressed against the horizontal foremast. The mast lay on deck from the starboard side of the pilothouse to out past the bow where its base was lashed to the end of the bare bowsprit. So much paint damage had already been done to Rebel's deck during the dismasting that I didn't care about the new scrapes and gouges from man-handling the seventeen-foot metal boat, which weighed in the neighborhood of five hundred pounds. For a seventeen-footer she was a lightweight. Once we were a schooner again I'd whittle up a pair of custom chocks to fit the new boat, in order to stow it upright for easier launching. After our new metal boat was tied down, Whisper was hoisted aboard and stowed upright hard alongside.

After the dinghies were secured, I gave Barry and Adam masks, fins and scrapers, and I told them to clean the propeller down to the bronze, and to do what they could to de-barnacle the rudder. Christopher and Jonathan both declared to me that it was impossible to swim with lifejackets on, and life jackets were only for babies unless the boat was on fire or sinking and then everybody must wear them. I agreed with the twins over Tala's brief protestation. The other married couples showed no interest in the swim call after their recent tub baths. Curt also declined the offered plunge. He declared that the next time he swam in salt water it would not be in sight of Mayaguana.

By 1700, with the sun a hand-width above the horizon, everyone had gotten in all the swimming they desired, and had soaped-up and rinsed-off in fresh water. Jessie and Luke gave another concert in the cockpit, but because we were aiming for an early start, our South Carolina moonshine remained below. But even our tank water tasted better when we had lemon, lime and orange juice to add to our bottles. The ladies kept the rinds for water flavoring and for cooking, and there would be plenty more fresh fruit in Jamaica, only three days away.

Oh, happy day!

37

After first light I met with the four watch pairs in the cockpit. These were Luke and Jessie, Gino and Rita, Barry and Adam, and Will and me. The chart was on my lap facing toward them as they leaned in to hear my sailing orders.

"We have to make six knots all day. Whether we sail or we motor-sail, we have to make six knots, because we need to be in sight of Little Inagua before dark. We have to go east of the Inaguas, and the only way we'll be sure of where we are is if we see Little Inagua. Maybe we can push it a little because we have the NOD and there's a full moon, but to be safe, we need to see Little Inagua before sunset. And then we'll know where we are, and we can sail all night in deep water."

"Okay," said Gino, "So now it's time to get out of here—but first an Our Father." They say that there are no atheists in foxholes. Well, neither are they on a half-dismasted schooner at the start of an ocean voyage. After the prayer we fired up the Cat, and Barry and Adam raised the anchor up on the bow.

We made it out through the reef more easily than we'd come into Abraham's Bay. Gino steered while I read the water from the bow with my polarized Ray-Bans. In only a few minutes we were off soundings. I took the wheel, and we began our watch rotation. It wasn't 0800 yet, but Will and I were going to take it until ten, and then it would be Luke and Jessie.

The breeze was from the northeast at around fifteen. The depth sounder showed its maximum five hundred feet, but the chart said we were in seven thousand feet of water. I turned us into the wind and the deck apes raised our mainsail and jib. Sailboats don't get much simpler than sloops. Main and jib.

The seas weren't much, barely a whitecap, nothing bigger than six feet but averaging less. I steered 170 degrees, or just a hair east of south. We left the Cat in gear and made six knots with no strain on the engine, sails or rigging. Mayaguana was soon lost over the horizon behind us. I wasn't even going to try for a noon sight, because it wouldn't have been any more accurate than our D.R. position over that short of a distance.

With the wind from the northeast we were going to be on port tack all day, so I had them rig the small tarp to the boom and across the cockpit to the opposite-side lifelines. Shade is a necessity on a sun-blasted tropical day, and if a squall threatened it would only take a minute to pull it down. Despite my warnings, half the crew had sunburned shoulders and faces. This was par for the course south of the Tropic of Cancer.

With the watch set everyone was free to roam the deck, keep busy below, or get back in their rack or hammock. I still had my old Ray-Bans on from crossing the reef. While I was steering, I told Curt the story of our broken speedometer, and how Will had carved a duplicate of the white nylon impeller from a solid block of hard black Delrin plastic.

Curt was wearing his sunglasses, but he was hatless in the shade. He said, "It's hard to repair nylon plastic if it's cracked. Glue wouldn't have worked, and now all of the glue I've seen lately is no good. It's all gone hard or evaporated to crud. I'm impressed that Will was able to fabricate a new impeller."

"That's why I keep these sunglasses in their own box. If I break them again, we don't have any more glue. And we only have a little more surgical tape that's still sticky."

"Speaking of glasses," he said, "let me go get something."

Curt returned with a tote bin with a lid. It might have held two loaves of bread or anything else that didn't weigh much, judging by how easily he carried it.

He sat facing me with the bin on his lap and pulled off the lid, revealing the contents. "Here are all the glasses I found on the island. Sunglasses, reading glasses, and prescription eyeglasses. Believe me—I know how valuable glasses are. When I washed ashore I didn't have any readers. They were in my pack with my sat phone and my sat text. Captain Dan, I'm as blind as a bat for detail work, so reading glasses are incredibly important to me. I couldn't have begun to work on that Evinrude if I didn't have readers. I collected all the glasses I could find when we were out foraging for useful things like that outboard. There are fifty pairs of glasses in this box. Why don't I pull out the sunglasses for your crew to choose from?"

"Sure, Curt, good idea. Please do. And you said there are some reading glasses in there?"

He smiled at me. "Yes, there are. And why do you ask?"

"Well, lately I've noticed that the print in my navigational almanac tables seems to be getting rather small."

"It happens to all of us, Dan. Father Time marches on."

We motor-sailed to south-southeast all day. By 1600 we were scanning the forward horizon for the first hint of Little Inagua. We were using a magnetic compass on a steel boat, and even allowing for Hilton Sapelo's adjustment work, and factoring in magnetic variation and compass deviation, I only hoped that we would see land during daylight hours.

Barry was up in the crow's nest with the backup binoculars. He called down that he saw something off the starboard bow. "It's a sharp dot on the horizon, it's not just a gray smudge like Mayaguana. It's only a dot, but it's there."

In a few minutes I saw it too, with my Steiners. If I had to guess I'd have guessed it was a ship or a building, something tall with sharp edges. Condominium towers could also appear suddenly over the horizon, but they were usually in rows. A building was impossible on Little Inagua. For one thing, the island and its surrounding reefs had been a wildlife sanctuary, the biggest in the Bahamas. Ordinary people were not allowed to visit, only scientists, but who would want to study a treeless island with zero drinking water? The reefs would be another matter. With no fishing pressure they might be interesting.

So it had to be a ship. I shared the binos with Gino, Curt, and Adam. When Curt held the Steiners he said, "I can make out the top decks. It's at a forward angle to us, heading bow-on. I'd say it's a cruise ship, heading northwest."

Barry called down, "Oh, yeah, it's a cruise ship. It's not a container ship, and it's not a tanker. It's a cruise ship."

I took the Steiners again. I could see they were correct as more of it rose above the horizon. Every member of the crew down to the twins came on deck to observe the alien structure breaking the otherwise uninterrupted horizon. Then across the horizon behind the ship a gray line of land emerged. It had to be Little Inagua. Something unusual was happening around the ship that was blurring the sky near it. As we sailed closer this blur changed to the appearance of swarms of insects, and then at last into thousands of birds swooping and diving.

The chart showed a thousand feet of water almost up to Little Inagua, so we could motor-sail parallel to the stranded ship close enough for a good look. Finally we could all see it was a cruise ship with our bare eyes, but the binos continued to reveal more details. The ship's curved clipper bow and its giant satellite domes and its unique funnel topped by swept-back wings left zero doubt. It was slab-sided to squeeze into a Panama Canal lock, so it was about a thousand feet long. From its bow on up to the bridge the decks ascended in tiers like a wedding cake. Birds had taken up residence on every balcony, turning the cruise ship into a massive rookery.

I told Barry to come down. We could see the island and we knew where we were. With the crew all trying to get a turn on my binos there was no reason to keep the other pair up top.

Putting what I was seeing with my own eyes together with what I saw on the chart, it was clear that the ship had clipped the reef extending over a mile to the east of Little Inagua, and it had not moved an inch from that moment until our arrival.

Adam asked, "How could they not see an entire island? How could they run aground? How could they do that?"

"They grew up on GPS," Curt replied. "They never really learned any other way, or not enough to make a difference."

I said, "They just punched in waypoints and let the ship's navigational system take them there. They never learned old-school coastal nav. Currents and winds and tides didn't matter to them because the machines figured it out for them. Punch in where you want to go and you're all done. But when the GPS goes down and all you have is an autopilot, then you can really screw yourself. If you set an autopilot to steer due north, it'll steer due north till doomsday. Even if there's a strong current from the east, the autopilot will keep aiming north, but meanwhile the ship is crabbing to the northwest. If the navigators don't factor in the current and the wind, then it can happen."

This was a real-life navigation lesson for my young crew, so I continued. "They probably thought they'd clear the island by five or ten miles, but they got the current wrong. It's thirty miles of deep water over to West Caicos, so they wouldn't be worried. They'd probably made the run plenty of times before, but this time maybe it was at night, and in bad visibility, like hard rain. Hard rain can blind a ship's radar, especially with a low island like Little Inagua. There's not even a lighthouse on it. A ship like that has about a twenty-five-foot draft. If they plow into a reef at twenty knots, well, they're done.

"It even happened when they had GPS. A cruise ship ran aground in Italy in broad daylight, the Concordia-something. It had to be cut up in pieces and taken away on barges. There's no getting off when a ship drives onto a reef. It's over. Ships were the biggest moveable manmade structures ever built, and when a hundred thousand tons is going twenty knots, that's a lot of inertia. When they hit a reef, they became a part of it."

We passed close enough to study it with binoculars. The white hull was bleeding rust at its plate seams but we could read the name across the top of the flaring bow: Serenity of the Seas. A lifeboat near the stern hung vertically from one davit, evidence of a botched evacuation. The back of the ship was blackened by fire. There were a few lifeboats on the shore of Little Inagua, but no signs of recent human activity on the ship or over on the land. We were in its plain sight, but nobody was launching a flare, lighting a smoky fire or even waving a flag. Our VHF radio was turned on, but it remained silent.

We passed it starboard-to-starboard a half mile off. Our depth sounder was reading 500 and the chart indicated far more water below. Serenity had been heading northwest, and we were sailing southeast, but we were in deep water and she was a permanent reef fixture. As we passed her stern the extent of the fire damage became more evident. The steel was charred black and rusting to red-orange without its paint. Burnt ochre.

Will said, "I wonder if the fire happened when they hit the reef? Or maybe it was already on fire, and they steered for the reef so they wouldn't sink? It doesn't make any sense."

"The fire happened after they struck the reef," Curt said. "I went on cruises with wife number two. A ship like that could carry three thousand passengers and a thousand crew. That life boat by the stern was already hanging down when the fire broke out. Fires were always a big risk. Cruise ships ran entirely on electricity. Diesel generators made it, but they were all electric after that. Their electrical generating capabilities were impressive, like a small city packed into a metal box.

"Their engines weren't mechanically connected to their propellers. Instead, they had rotating azipods that could direct their thrust in any direction, so they didn't need tugboats going into harbors. Their propellers were powered by electric motors down in the azipods. As long as that ship had fuel they could keep moving and keep their systems running, but all their eggs were in the electric basket. But when the fuel ran out after they went aground, well, that's all she wrote. Lights out."

"What do you think caused the fire?" asked Will.

"Hmm . . . they probably had some safety issues that they ignored and they overrode. Once they were hard aground, they wouldn't have been able to shut down any of their systems for the routine required maintenance. I started out on offshore oil rigs, and I know all about complex systems. They need a lot of preventive maintenance. Something probably overheated and they kept it running, and there's your initiation point.

"Do you see the small portholes on the lowest level near the water? That's the crew quarters. The crew can move from there to the engineering spaces, but the passengers can't, not easily. The crew can lock and unlock anything. Turn the water on, or turn it off. The crew would have been able to keep the power on in one area and turn it off in another. They would have had to make a lot of difficult choices, like keeping all the freezers cold, or letting the food spoil. This would be balanced against trying to extend the operating time of the lights and the water, and who is in charge of deciding? Would they try to run everything as normal for one week until the fuel runs out, or try to stretch out the critical life-support systems?"

Our tall and now clean-shaved newcomer had a demeanor that commanded attention when he spoke on technical matters.

"And again, who decides? The sanitation systems would fail and there'd be no cabin toilets. Just imagine that one thing. And when the lights go out inside those ships you're in a black tomb. Their emergency lights run on batteries, but they'd only last about a day. The crew could have even become like prison guards, if you think of it that way. It would have been terrible after the water taps ran dry and the lights went out. Especially if the power and water distribution were being controlled by the crew, and the passengers knew it. They could have fought for control, but even if the passengers took over, that wouldn't bring the ship more fuel, and they wouldn't know how to run the systems. But maybe they were rescued. I sure hope so."

I said, "They were always impressive to watch at night. You'd see their loom before they even broke the horizon. Lit up like Christmas displays. Serenity is a big one, but not the biggest. She's about average. If you count the lower portholes, she has ten decks above the waterline, and she's a thousand feet long. That's as big as an aircraft carrier. Like you said, it's a floating city inside a metal box. Or it was."

Curt studied the chart. "Maybe they were sailing from Puerto Plata, here on the top of the Dominican Republic, and heading back to the USA. Or maybe from Puerto Rico, who knows? Any of the islands. I can't imagine many people were going on holiday cruises after GPS failed, but maybe the ship was just ferrying passengers, and not taking them on vacation. It would make sense if they were carrying people back to the states. After the tourism model ended they would have still been useful for moving people, a lot of people. Even refugees. I know how bad it was on the islands when the food imports stopped coming and they couldn't make fresh water. It takes fuel to run the de-sal plants, so no fuel means no fresh water—and people become desperate when there's no drinking water."

"Barry had it right," I said. "It's like pulling the plug on an aquarium. It had to be hell on that ship if nobody came to take them off. The stronger ones might have made it across the reef to Little Inagua, maybe in the lifeboats. But then what? There's no fresh water. There are a couple life boats on the island, but they might have just washed up there. And I saw a life raft up on Mayaguana that might have come from here. The ship had spots for a dozen covered life boats on each side, but that's not enough, and the one that's hanging down didn't even make it into the water. The life boats don't have much range; everything was based on waiting for rescue, but what if it doesn't come? The passengers could have gotten into the inflatable life rafts, but then what? What if nobody's coming? I think most of them would have stayed on the ship until the end. Fire and all."

Barry said, "How is that ship different from Charleston, or just about any city? Maybe the city people had a little more elbow room, but they still didn't have food or drinking water. And if nobody was coming to save them, well, then the people in the cities were doomed, just like the ones who were trapped there on doomsday reef. You fight over the last crumb of food, and then it gets even uglier. And I mean, a *lot* uglier."

Nobody said anything after that. I wondered if Barry had shared his story with anybody besides me and Will. His night watch testimony was etched in my memory, and I knew what he meant by "a lot uglier." He meant murder and cannibalism.

Then Gino said. "And now it's all just a bird farm. How did so many birds find it? There are five decks of balconies on each side and all the upper decks. That's one big bird farm."

It sure was. And the aft section of the ship had burned, so the rest had probably been filled with thick toxic smoke during the fire. Had the passengers and crew been rescued before the blaze? And if they had not been rescued, then what happened to them in that labyrinth of passageways, elevators and ladders when the lights went out? Before, during, or after the fire?

The sea birds in all their thousands were not saying.

Luke and Jessie took over the watch at 1600, and Luke took the wheel, but no matter who had the duty most of the crew remained on deck to observe the stranded leviathan while we motor-sailed past. Luke's hand was healing well and he could steer again. I laid the folded chart atop the pilothouse and held it down, getting oriented to the land I could see and trying to visualize the landmasses that lay ahead of us. Tomorrow we would enter the Windward Passage, but we would be sailing with the prevailing winds. Gino, Barry and Adam were also taking turns with the binos, so I used the opportunity to pass down the night orders. Luke was steering but he could see the folded chart as it was being passed around.

I said, "That ship is a sight we'll never forget, but at least we know exactly where we are. The east side of Great Inagua is all deep, so we're heading due south until midnight. That'll put us about here, and then we're going make our turn to the southwest for the Windward Passage. We've been running the engine so we'd be sure to see Little Inagua in the daytime, and we did. Now let's kill the motor, and let's see what we can do in this breeze with just two sails."

The Caterpillar went silent and our speed dropped to less than five knots. The stranded ship remained in sight through both dog-watches, until it was lost behind us in the dusk. We changed course at midnight when Luke and Jessie took over. The full moon overhead turned the moving ocean into molten silver. I explained to them why we were aiming for the center of the forty-mile gap between Cuba and Haiti. The currents through the passage usually—but not always—flow westward, moving in the same direction as the trade winds, but sometimes eddies and counter-currents can play devious tricks.

I said, "It's eighty miles from our current D.R. position, so we should be there tomorrow afternoon. If I get a morning star or a noon sight then we'll have a better understanding, but if we don't, our dead reckoning will have to be as close to perfect as possible. If we're lucky, we might sail on through and never see Cuba or Haiti. A lot of it will depend on getting a new celestial navigation fix. But once we're through the Windward Passage, it's an easy run to Jamaica. Just a few more days."

38

The sun did not shine Wednesday morning, one day south of Mayaguana. Instead, nimbostratus blew across the gray ocean from the northeast. There was some rain, but not much, and we were making an honest five knots under just our two sails. There was no need to rig the small tarp for shade. That was the good news. The bad news was not being able to get a dawn or a noon celestial fix. Nothing was guaranteed, not even a west-flowing ocean current. Cuba's Cabo Maisi is somewhere out there past our starboard bow—I think. In my mind's eye Haiti is closer, and its Cap du Mole is off to our left. I hope.

This is why Rebel's captain had set the course at exactly 225 degrees, more commonly known as southwest. This was to be manually steered using our magnetic compass, plus sixty feet of iron, minus Captain Sapelo's compass adjusting magic. So do you add the deviation and subtract the variation? Which is first? If you make a single mistake in any area you're ten or fifteen degrees wrong, and you risk becoming a permanent reef addition like Serenity of the Seas. With an extremely unhappy crew, and no serenity to be found. Doomed, in fact.

Beginning at noon Barry, Adam, Luke, Will and Rita took turns climbing up the mast steps to sit on the crow's nest seat. Adam suggested leaving the second pair of binoculars up there in a waterproof bag, instead of each lookout carrying them up and down hanging by the strap. Good idea.

The lookouts worked out their own watch system, with no input from the captain, and I was grateful not to have this on my plate. We only knew that The Windward Passage is Out There, and that Haiti and Cuba are the bookends, with forty miles of open sea in between. If we bowled a perfect strike on my guess-timated course and split the gap down the middle, the lookouts might never see land. *Bon chance.*

Keeping our little bubble of humanity afloat from day to day kept me busy in the best of times, whether we were back in Beaufort or sailing on the open ocean. Sailing through the Windward Passage promised to make that Wednesday a day to remember. And, God help them, the crew thinks I know what I'm doing. So please, God, help me. Just for their sakes.

From above Luke called out "I see land!" Luke and Jessie were on watch but she was more than happy to steer in these moderate conditions as long as another deck ape was around.

"Where?" I yelled back up to him, grabbing my Steiners.

"Port bow. There's a black line between the low clouds."

"I see it." I checked my watch, it was 1440. Land sighted. Remember it, log it. But just what land was it? Cuba or Haiti? I watched Jessie steering. She was looking up the mast at her husband more than down at the compass, and our wake was becoming serpentine, so I called up, "Come on down, Luke, somebody else can go up. You belong in the cockpit now."

Gino came out and stood next to me, also leaning against the back of the pilothouse. I gave him the Steiners while Luke clambered down the mast. Gino was looking ahead when Luke came around the pilothouse to the cockpit. He said to his wife, "I'll steer, Jess, you have a look." He took the wheel and she joined us, scanning ahead with the binos.

Will came out of the pilothouse and said, "I'll go up."

Our red-headed orphan was not much bigger than Rita, but he wasn't afraid to climb the mast, and he had sharp eyes with or without binoculars. He'd been keeping radio watch inside, sitting in the captain's chair with the headphones on. The single-sideband antenna between the mastheads had been lost when the foremast went down, and the reception on our non-transmitting SSB was reduced to a fraction, but he never quit scanning the airwaves for a station that was broadcasting.

The black line thickened and widened but it remained off our port bow. If it was Haiti, we could sail due west until we lost sight of it, and then turn to the southwest again. If it was

Cuba, it would grow like a continent in front of us. The lay of their coasts on the chart made me believe it was Haiti.

"Okay, Luke, steer west."

He turned to the new course, and I adjusted the sheets for the jib and main. The dark line on the horizon diminished, so we were sliding over the left shoulder of Haiti. According to Will's speedometer we were making five knots through the water, but what was the current doing to our speed over the ground, and in what direction? Just get away from Haiti, that's the main priority. It's forty miles across the passage to Cuba. Sail west for two or three hours and then turn for Jamaica. It's almost 1500 on my wristwatch, so we'll make the turn at dusk.

The line on the horizon disappeared but this might have been partly or entirely due to the thickening clouds. We sailed west for most of an hour. Haiti was gone. We had 360 degrees of ocean horizon, but it was not the sharp blue-on-blue line of a sunny day. Mid-level nimbostratus passed over us in lighter and darker sections, leaving some ambiguity.

Then Will called down from the crow's nest, "There's a sail off our starboard bow."

Oh, shit, I thought. "A sail? Can you tell its heading?"

"I don't know, captain. Maybe to the north?"

In a minute I could see it with my binoculars. It was a sloop with a small jib and a long boom. Local craft. Haitian.

Luke asked me, "What is it, skipper, a fishing boat?"

"Maybe—but maybe it's a spotter. A lookout. Everybody *please* stay out of sight. They could have binoculars too."

Our VHF squawked in the pilothouse. After Mayaguana it was left on to scan the marine channels.

"He's calling us in," I said. "That means he's a spotter."

Jessie brought out the cockpit speaker on its wire. A male voice was speaking rapid Creole, but none of us caught any of its meaning through the choppy static. We were sailing to the west, with the wind; the spotter was tacking to the northeast but making little progress. Holding his position. A charged 12-volt automobile battery could power a VHF radio for days.

We passed the open-deck wooden sloop about a mile off our starboard beam without changing our westward course. It was a thirty-footer, maybe less. With binoculars I could make out the shapes of people in it, and in turn they'd be seeing our pilothouse and deck boats, and of course our single mast and two sails. More chatter came from the speaker as the sailboat disappeared behind us. Would the encounter mean anything? We'd find out soon, or never find out at all.

Around 1630 Will called down, "Captain, there's a new boat behind us. It's not a sailboat this time."

I turned aft and saw it too, and it was coming fast. It was dead astern and bow-on to us. The spotter had earned his pay. When the boat was about three miles back a new voice from a more powerful transmitter came through the speaker. We were being hailed in Haitian Creole.

The last time I'd been in a comparable situation had been a few days before Morocco. Then, it had been a hundred-foot trawler converted to carry armed men instead of nets and fish. That encounter had ended in our favor, with the pirate ship on the bottom, and all of them dead. All of them except for Gino Bracciano, who had been captured by the sea-jihad pirates a few weeks earlier, and kept chained in their engine room.

I went back to the Dushka and unlaced the cords beneath it to remove its canvas cover. The first fifty rounds were in the breadbox-size metal can attached to its left side. 1979 was still legible among the faded Cyrillic letters. I hoped the 12.7mm ammo in it was not as old as the battered aluminum box, but it was the best we had, and I'd been lucky to find it in Beaufort.

After Morocco we'd been down to only a partial belt, less than fifty rounds. A few Dushkas had been brought home from Iraq or Afghanistan by the Marines for training purposes, and had soon been forgotten. Forgotten until somebody had seen a sales opportunity, and I had bought six boxes of their 12.7mm ammo in trade for drums of fuel back in Port Royal. One box had been expended to prove the stuff still worked.

I undid the rope that held its barrel in place for sailing and inspected the sleek steel antique. It was showing some surface rust here and there. Tran Hung had always kept the Dushka in immaculate condition. I was falling down on the job. I flipped the top of the ammo box open. A plastic bottle that had once contained Elmer's Glue was on top of the ammo belt, but now it contained motor oil.

The Dushka's swivel mount needed help in the lubrication department for it to swing freely. I squirted oil in a half dozen places inside the gun and its mount, and then I swung its barrel from side to side and in circles to loosen it up. What a journey the gun must have made since it had been manufactured back in the USSR! By what strange route did it come to be offered for sale at the marine flea market back in Beirut? The Russian Dushka with cooling fin rings around its barrel would *never* be mistaken for its American counterpart, the Browning M2 fifty-caliber—but both of them could launch finger-size fifty-gram projectiles at rifle velocities over great distances. Much further than I could see over its iron sights, that was for sure.

I grabbed the double grips and swung it to bear, taking a first look at our pursuer dancing on the tip of the front sight, the front sight that I had to move around by yanking the grips. The boat was pushing up a white bow wave and it was rapidly closing the distance between us. I flipped up the rear Vernier sight; it was set to a thousand meters on the sight ladder. The top of the front sight was a sharp inverted-V. The sights were capable of precision when fired from a steady rest on land, but none of that applied out on the ocean. On Rebel Yell, the sight was left dialed up to a thousand meters. For targets that were closer or further away I applied good old "Kentucky windage" (and elevation) and I watched my splashes to adjust my fire.

I told Gino, "Bring it all up, all of the twelve-point-seven. We've got five boxes of fifty, four not counting this one, and it won't do us any good down below. Bring up all the guns and ammo: the M-240, the M-16s, and the AK-47—but leave the pistols. Grab the deck apes—take whoever you need. I'll load the Dushka, but we gotta move fast."

Gino disappeared.

"Jessie, take the wheel—keep steering west. Luke, come here and watch what I'm doing. It's real easy to change these ammo boxes. These two slots match the ones on the gun when you lift it off. Once a new box is on, do what I do. First you lift the feed tray cover like this—it latches here—and then you open the top of the ammo box and flip the guide ramp against the gun. Drag out the belt, drop the first round here, and close the feed tray cover. Okay? You got it? Then you pull the charging handle all the way back to cock it. *All* the way back. It takes some muscle—this is a heavy machine gun. You do it."

I stepped away and Luke grabbed the handle from below the twin grips. "Like this?"

"Use both hands—it's got to go *all* the way back until it locks the bolt to the rear. That's it, good job—you just became my assistant machine gunner. The Dushka is ready to rock and roll. You aim off your splashes, just like on the M-240, so the spotter with binoculars is just as important as the gunner."

I wondered what kind of a gun was mounted on the bow of our tormenter. I supposed we'd find out when we took their incoming. The Moroccan pirates had a 20mm Oerlikon gun on their bow but it turned out to have no ammunition. In that case their bluff failed and our 12.7mm Dushka prevailed.

I went around Jessie at the wheel and fired up the Caterpillar. If it got to a shootout we'd want every means of prolusion to maximize our speed and our maneuverability. I pushed the throttle ahead until we were making eight knots, but I didn't want to risk the engine beyond that. They could outrun us and there was nothing we could do about that, not at the rate they were overtaking us. Another knot out of the Caterpillar would make no difference to the outcome of the chase, but it could prove fatal to us if we blew out the leaky main front seal.

The VHF squawked again, in English this time. "Sailing vessel, this is the Coast Guard of Haiti. You are intruding into the Zone of Exclusion of the Republic of Haiti. You must stop for the boarding and for the inspection. You must immediately stop for the boarding and for the inspection." After a pause the same message was repeated in French and Spanish. They were reading from a prepared script.

Jessie asked me, "Are you going to answer them?"

"No, no. It's almost always better to play dumb and bring them in close. Almost always."

This was not like the Spanish destroyer west of Gibraltar. In that situation we had folded our cards on demand and talked our way out of trouble. Not this time. The other ammo boxes for the Dushka were stacked in pairs in the back of the cockpit foot well behind Luke. I called for Will to come down, and to bring down the backup binoculars. There was no need for a lookout aloft—we could see the intruder from deck level.

Tala came through the pilothouse and said, "You made these for the ears and today you forget them." She handed me a plastic bag with the ear plugs I'd made from foam rubber. They might not have met the old OSHA or military standards but they were better than nothing. During the stress of a gunfight shooters will just blast away with no regard to their ears or to the ears of their buddies who are standing next to them. I took out two for myself and passed the bag to Luke.

I flashed back to a memory of Pat Maguire just before our battle with the Moroccan pirates, and his definition of a "grand battle." According to the old IRA man, this was when you had the chance to prepare your guns and put in your ear defenders prior to going loud. This was because you were the ambusher, and not the ambushed, "and 'tis better to give than to receive."

When all the weapons and ammunition had been brought up I told them, "Put in earplugs. If you don't, you'll wish you had. The Dushka is all ready, and there are fifty more rounds in each box. Luke knows how to reload it—he's my assistant machine gunner. Barry and Adam will cover us from the bow with the M-240. Load it up and put it on safe and be ready to fire to either side. Okay—go!" They disappeared forward with the gun and its ammo cans.

I looked at Luke. "You've shot ARs before, right?"

"Of course I have, skipper. I'm from South Carolina."

"Good. Jessie, you're going to steer. Luke, bring out both M-16s. The mags are in the canvas sack that's with them." They'd remained in the pilothouse since Mayaguana.

I scanned behind us again, my Steiners pressed to my eye sockets. The boat was growing bigger. Now there was a bridge deck visible, which I had expected, but there was something even worse in view. The vessel behind us was now flanked by a smaller boat on each side. *Oh, shit . . .*

"And then there were three." I handed the binos to Gino.

He looked and said, "They're on a line across. That's an attack formation."

"That's what it looks like to me, too. We'll know soon, because we're not stopping, no matter what they say or do."

"Do you think it's going to come down to gunfire?"

"Do you think that's the Haitian Coast Guard? Well, first mate, I don't give a shit if it is, or it isn't. Nobody's stopping us today, understand me? *Nobody* is stopping us today."

The voice from VHF speaker said, "Sailing vessel, this is the Coast Guard of Haiti: you must stop now for the boarding and the inspection or we will commence to the firing. You will not receive another warning." Again the message was repeated in French and Spanish. How many more lines were on their script? At what distance would they actually open fire on us?

Jessie was steering. Gino, Curt, Will, and Luke were in the cockpit. More details emerged through my binoculars, and I knew this worked both ways. I told them, "Okay, everybody, stay low and stay out of sight. We don't want them to see any activity. Let them think we're on autopilot and we don't have a radio, and nobody's noticed them yet. Let them get up close. As long as they're overtaking us and don't see any activity, I think they'll just keep on coming. They want us to surrender peacefully. They want to capture Rebel with no damage, but they're coming after us no matter what, whether it's the easy way, or the hard way. But we're not going to make it easy for them. No, not today. Oh, *hell* no. We're—Not—Stopping."

In a few minutes the smaller boats were close enough to see with our naked eyes. If the command vessel in the middle was a fifty-footer with a bridge deck, the two flankers were probably big outboard-powered boats. Considering that they were out on the ocean, they were probably in the class of the Beaufort Militia's 28-foot Mako with twin 200s, but it was hard to be sure when they were bow-on to us at that distance. The crew of that Mako could have chased Rebel Yell out onto the ocean, easily, if they'd wanted to. If they'd had the gasoline budget, and they had been ordered to stop us.

And now we had three supposed "Haitian Coast Guard" boats creeping up on us, and they were in an attack formation less than two miles behind. On paper, our 12.7mm Dushka had a two-kilometer effective range. That was firing at a stationary target from a stationary position—which we were not—and I was not going to waste our ammo on ineffective fire. I would not fire first unless they were within our effective range.

What clinched the matter was when the flankers began to separate from the main vessel and move out ahead of it, arcing wide apart while still keeping their distance from us. The two go-fasts were looping around to get out in front of us on both sides. Those boys meant business: I had to give them credit. They had a spotter on a sailboat. They had radio comms. They had a fuel budget. They had a tri-lingual radio script. And now they had their slow-moving prey in sight.

When the flankers moved out and around us, the die was cast. There was no bluff or ambiguity in their attack plan. No psyops. No head games. This was going to be straight-up gunfire, bloodshed and death until we surrendered or we sank, or until they gave up the hunt. All the women and children were already down below, except for Jessie behind the wheel.

I had Gino fetch Barry and Adam back to the cockpit to hear my battle plan while we still had a little time. All of the new guys were dressed in grab-bag hand-me-downs, mostly my old t-shirts and shorts that were not fit for wearing ashore, so I felt that connection. Jessie was wearing Tala's black leggings and a white blouse from Sofia. And I was leading them into a gun battle. My family, my crew, my friends. *My tribe. My people.*

"Look, gang, this is how it is. They know, and we know, that there's nobody who's going to pay a ransom to get us out of Haiti. Kidnapping for ransom is not even on the table for discussion. If they board us, that means we're captured, and captured means raped, tortured and murdered. I'm sorry to be so blunt, Jessie. Well, that's not going to happen. We're not stopping. We're not getting boarded. When any of those boats gets to within five hundred yards—and we're talking about a few minutes from now—we're going to open fire first. The speedboats can cross five hundred yards in nothing flat. Right now they're just loafing along, taking it easy, but don't let that fool you. When they come—they'll come fast. *Real* fast."

The crew took turns passing around both pairs of binos.

"The big boat is in charge, but the small boats have the boarding parties. We still don't know what any of them have for guns, not yet. Assume that they have AKs or M-16s at a minimum, and probably bigger guns than that. Now it looks to me like the speedboats have something in front of their center consoles that might be hillbilly armor. It's painted white but I think it's probably a piece of steel up against the front of the console. It can't be too thick, or it'd be too heavy. If it's steel armor the Dushka can probably penetrate it, but I don't know about the M-240. Probably not. My point is, don't waste your ammo on armor plate, if that's what it is."

I looked at Barry and he looked back at me and nodded.

"But to capture us the speedboats have to come right up to us, and then their boarding teams will either jump off their bows or they'll come alongside. Either way, they'll have to be exposed in the open right at the end. Shoot people, not armor plate. They'll probably both turn and make high-speed runs at the same time—that's what I'd do. Gino, I want you up on the bow with an M-16. Take the ammo bag and leave half of the magazines here for Luke. They'll use grappling hooks, so take the bolt cutters and plenty of knives. And if you see a guy with a grappling hook—shoot him first."

Our heavy-duty bolt cutters were kept in the pilothouse for cutting rigging wire or anything else in an emergency.

"If I'm hit, Luke takes over on the Dushka. Gino, Barry and Adam: stay up front. We always have to cover both sides from the bow. Jessie, you have to be ready to turn fast on my word, turn as fast as you can. And remember, pirates *always* fly a false flag to get in close, so don't feel bad if we open fire first. There's no Haitian Coast Guard, that's all just radio talk bullshit to let them get up close. They're just Haitian pirates, and we're not being boarded, and we're not being captured. So listen for my word of command, or for Gino's. Nobody fires before I do, but when I do fire, don't waste ammo just making noise. Only hits count—hits on people. Remember, the real weapons on the speedboats are the boarding parties, and it's going to get real close in a real big hurry. Barry and Adam: be ready to shift sides with your M-240, especially when we're turning fast. Gino will cover your six and support you with an M-16. Luke: haul in the main sheet like we're close-hauled; we can't have an unplanned gybe while we're running around on deck in a gunfight. Any questions?"

Luke asked me, "What about the pistols, the Glocks?"

"The ladies have the pistols down below. I'm not saying you're not a lady, Jessie, but nobody is going to be captured today. Nobody. *Nobody*. We're going to fight to the very end. No surrender, no defeat. Any other questions?"

Curt said, "Who gets the AK-47? Is that a spare cockpit gun? I've shot AKs before, and I understand how to use them. I don't want to be down below with the women and children."

"Alright, Curt, load the AK, chamber a round and put it on safe. It's only a semi-automatic. Push the safety bar down to fire. Don't shoot my boat and don't shoot my crew. Stay in the pilothouse unless they're in rock-throwing range, and then use your best judgment. We're not getting captured today."

When staring down a muzzle from a long way off, what you are looking at might not be readily apparent. I didn't bother with putting up camouflage. No deck towels over the barrel of the Dushka this time. Their closing rate was too fast for that. I had one knee on deck and both hands on the twin grips, my fingers over both triggers. I had the morbid thought that twin grips and triggers meant the machine gunner could keep firing even if one arm was shot off. Finish the belt. Oorah, Marine!

My main focus was on the boat astern as it grew from rice grain to pea size on top of my front sight. My target remained steady, but despite my best efforts the barrel did not, not on a boat pitching and rolling on the open ocean. And the gun was heavy and the mount stiff. Even on its tripod it took effort to control the beast, even after I'd oiled its friction points.

"Will," I said, "keep telling me what you see on all three boats; start with the big one in back. You're my eyes, son, tell me what you see. Does the big boat have a deck gun? Can you see people on it?" I knew he was behind me with the Steiners, leaning against something to hold himself steady.

"I can't see people on it, it's hard to tell, but I can see a narrower bridge house in the middle that looks higher than the main part, so I'd say it has two decks. I can't tell what's on the bow yet." After a pause he said, "The speedboat on our port side is passing our beam. Can you see it?"

Meaning could I see it with my bare eyes when I turned my head. My hands remained on the Dushka's twin grips. "I see it. It's about a kilometer out." I turned my gaze to starboard. "The other one is about the same. They're getting out in front but they're keeping their distance. They're bracketing us. Surrounding us. They're getting ready to attack. I can feel it."

Luke was sitting in the cockpit cradling an M-16, his wife steering. The scoped bolt-action rifle was on the cockpit seat in reach. I looked at it and he said it was loaded, chambered, on safe, and that a 7mm magnum should be able to take out an engine block if the opportunity presented itself. Then he asked me, "Skipper, can you hit them from this distance?"

"With the elk gun, or the machine gun?"

"The machine gun."

"I could, if I had all day and unlimited ammo. But they get a say too. Once the first rounds land in the water near them who knows what they'll do? They'll probably start dodging around, and then they'll be even harder to hit. When we open fire, I want it to count. If we're just making noise, we're just wasting ammo, and if we run out of ammo first, they win. We have to be smarter than them. Will, what do you see now?"

"The speedboats are out front and they're keeping about the same distance. I can see they have center consoles, I can see the drivers but there's something in front of the consoles, maybe it's an armor plate like you said. I can see some heads down low, so there are more people in the speedboats."

"That's their boarding teams," I said, stating the obvious.

"There's something above the sides of the two boats, I can't tell what it is, but there's something above the sides."

I could see with my bare eyes that the main boat behind us was slowly creeping up, closing the gap. The voice from the radio speaker repeated its warning to stop immediately.

"Will, go get Gino. I need to tell him something."

He was on the aft deck in seconds. "What is it, boss?"

"Take a look. We think there's armor plate in front of the consoles, and Will can see some heads above the gunnels."

Gino looked out to port through the Steiners. "I can see some heads. Hard to tell what's in front of the console? And there's something on the side. Something above the side."

I told him, "If there's armor plate in the middle, it's only meant to protect the boat driver from the front. The M-240 should be able to reach the men inside the hull. Fiberglass won't stop 7.62 NATO, but don't waste it either. The middle of the bow is super thick fiberglass so it might stop the 240 from the front. From the side fiberglass is like paper, so aim near the waterline to hit the men. If they're going to board us they'll use grappling hooks, so we have to be ready to cut their lines. The grappling hook lines could be rope or wire."

Gino said, "The bolt cutters and knives are ready."

We were both looking astern when a red meteor flare shot skyward from the original boat.

"This is it," I said. "They're coming. Go, Gino, go! Jessie: keep steering west but stay low and be ready to turn fast. Will: keep telling me what you see in the binos. Luke: you look all around in case we miss anything. Take the other binoculars."

Will said, "The boat behind us is making a bigger wave in front, like maybe it's going faster. And both of the speedboats are turning in toward us."

39

Splashes broke the water in a line down our port side but two hundred yards off, followed by distant muzzle reports at the same cadence. Their direction indicated the boat behind us had fired a burst on full auto, but the splashes did not erupt with the fury of a fifty caliber hitting the water. Then another row of splashes landed about the same distance to starboard but ahead of us. Maybe they were meant to be warning shots, or maybe they were intended to divert our attention from the approaching speedboats.

Or maybe they were going to lay the next one right down the middle—so I opened up. Waiting for them to get into our best effective range went out the window. They're shooting, so I'm shooting. The Dushka was so stiff it was like aiming a cannon. Sight picture, holdover, squeeze: B-B-BANG!

Damn, that was loud! "Will, can you see my splashes?"

The tracer compound in the ancient Russian ammo was dead. Splashes were all I had to go by.

"I didn't see the splashes, but the speedboats are coming fast! Shoot some more and I'll look for your splashes."

Luke yelled, "Your shots were off to the right and short."

B-B-B-BANG! I yelled, "Did you see them that time?"

Luke said, "A little higher and to the left—a little."

B-B-B-BANG! Another burst as I pulled the triggers.

"Right there is perfect!"

I tried to keep an image of that last holdover. I only fired when the rolling of the boat and the barrel were in alignment. B-B-B-BANG! Wait . . . wait . . . B-B-B-BANG! For an old sniper it was like trying to perform surgery with a hammer and an axe. Luke helped to keep my splashes around the target.

A new line of splashes appeared just to port, and I laid more bursts into our pursuer, taking as much care as I could with my aim. The Dushka's first belt ran out, its chain of black links on the deck. Luke removed the empty can and hoisted a new ammo box onto the slotted bracket. I loaded the second belt and then fired a long burst at the command boat.

Will yelled, "The speedboats are getting close, maybe five hundred yards!"

"Which one is closer?" I yelled back at him. Yelling was the only way to be heard at such decibels with ringing ears.

"Starboard side!"

"Jessie, hard to port!" I wanted to get the Dushka onto the closest boat. Our big gun had less than 180 degrees of traverse from side to side, so Rebel Yell had to be turned to bring it to bear. I kept firing at the boat behind, then I swung the barrel all the way over to starboard and saw the speedboat coming in fast. I went up on two feet and fired continuously, ignoring the sights and adjusting my aim by the splashes. At this range I didn't need the help of a spotter. The speedboat turned parallel to us and I laid a burst between its console and its outboard motor. The boat dropped off plane and stopped.

Luke yelled, "You nailed him! Oh, you nailed him good! Now, Jess, turn to starboard! Hard to starboard, Jess!"

Then Rebel was turning back the other way, and Luke was screaming into my face and pointing astern with his arm. "There, shoot right there! Shoot the big boat! The big boat!"

I'd lost focus on everything except what I could see down the barrel of my machine gun. The original command boat was in easy range, maybe seven hundred meters away, and I fired again. It was close enough for me to spot my own splashes and adjust my fire with each burst, sending more and more rounds into the vessel and fewer into the sea around it. The command boat turned sideways to us, offering me the perfect chance to rake it at the waterline, but the second box ran out of ammo. And now where was Luke? I threw off the empty metal bread box and turned around to grab the next ammo can by myself.

Rebel was still turning to starboard. The other speedboat was coming in fast on the port side from about eight o'clock, and I could hear our belt-fed M-240 just ripping away, and I could see its impacts shredding the boat's fiberglass hull as it swerved in toward us, thumping over the swells, spray flying. Shirtless black men were standing all along its starboard side leaning against something. The speedboat's bow slammed into Rebel's hull up forward and stopped, then fell back alongside us. They'd gotten their hooks into our lifelines.

I grabbed the next box of 12.7mm ammo from the back of the cockpit. Jessie was crouched behind the wheel. Luke was standing beside the pilothouse firing an M-16 down into the boat. He had extra mags in the back pockets of his cutoff jeans and he loaded a fresh one and kept firing. I put the third ammo box onto the Dushka and I reloaded it in record time. The command boat was turning away from us and I walked a long burst down its waterline and into its transom.

The M-240 went silent but somebody else on the bow was firing three-shot bursts from an M-16. I turned around toward the gunfight on our port side to see if I was needed there since the command boat was running away and the Dushka was not able to fire forward. The speedboat that was joined to us had a horizontal ladder attached to its starboard side to make it easy for the pirates to climb aboard. Their grappling hooks ensured that we'd be locked together until either one crew or the other prevailed. Luke was still firing his M-16. Curt was standing amidships firing the AK almost straight down into the pirates.

I finally heard Gino yelling "Stop firing, stop firing, they're all dead! Barry's been hit, we have to take care of Barry!"

"They're not all dead!" Luke yelled. He fired more shots into a pirate who was slumped over the wheel but still moving.

They were the last shots, and then it was over. Well, just look at them now, I thought. It was a black and bloody mess down inside their open boat. They should have stayed home.

I did a quick scan of the horizon all the way around. The big command boat's stern was to us, so it was either disabled or departing. The other speedboat was adrift hundreds of yards behind. Rebel had continued motoring west, even accounting for our turns to port and starboard and then dragging a thirty-foot pirate boat along for the ride.

I became aware that my ears were not working as usual. I could see people yelling but often I could not hear their words because high-pitched tones were blocking everything else out. Sometimes I could make out their words partly by lip reading.

Gino and Adam were up on the bow kneeling over Barry. I went forward to join them there, and in passing I told Luke to keep an eye out for anybody else in the pirate boat playing possum. I couldn't hear my own words, but I saw him put a new magazine into his rifle. We had a big speedboat attached to us but that was not my top priority, it would have to wait. Black bodies hung in our lifelines and on their ladder. That was not my concern either, because up on the foredeck, Adam and Gino were kneeling over one of my crew. My crew.

Gino looked up and said, "Barry's hit, boss. He's hit bad."

Some words I could hear, some I couldn't. I dug the plugs from my ears and that helped some. Barry was lying on his back in front of Metallica's upside-down bow.

"Will," I yelled, "get Tala and get the first aid kit—get the blowout kit! Get a tourniquet! Gino, where's the wound?"

"No, boss," he replied almost inaudibly, shaking his head. I sensed his meaning. He mouthed, "A tourniquet won't work. It went in under his collarbone and out his back." He widened both of his eyes to indicate the hopelessness of the situation. There was some blood on the front of Barry's t-shirt . . . but much more was spreading out on the deck beneath him.

I knelt by his shoulders, my knees in his blood. Blood ran thick across the deck. I had to see the exit wound for myself. I thought we should at least pack the wound on both sides and apply pressure. But when I rolled him a little to examine the exit wound, the mortal extent of the damage was evident.

Victor could not have saved him. Not even an old hospital trauma center would have been able to stop the bleeding. Will knelt down with us and helped to lift his head, and then he slid a folded cockpit cushion underneath. I took one of Barry's hands, Adam held the other, and Will stroked his forehead. He was deathly pale. This wasn't the first time I'd held the hand of a dying buddy during his final crossing over.

And it always sucked.

Barry opened his eyes. "Hey, skipper." He coughed out some blood. "Thanks for not putting me off the boat."

My hearing was coming back; the shrill whine was less exclusionary. "Why would I put my shipmate off the boat?"

"I'm not who you think I am. I'm a lot worse."

"Barry Conway, I think you're a good man. We all do."

He slowly shook his head at me. "No, captain, I'm not a good man. I'm not. I did much worse than I told you." He was aspirating blood in his effort to speak.

"It doesn't matter." His blue eyes were locked onto mine.

"Captain, can Jesus take me, the way I am? Can he? I'm much worse than you know. Much worse. Can he take me?"

"I *know* that he will. The only thing that matters to him is the man that you are right here and right now. A good man."

He smiled up at the faces looking down at him and said, "Thank you all. I loved . . . I . . . loved . . . every . . ."

In a minute his grip relaxed and his eyes went still. I felt for a pulse, found none, and closed his eyes. Adam and Will knelt over him, weeping and praying. They were the only two survivors of the original cargo hold gang, and the youngest.

I stood up, took a deep breath, and looked all around. The command boat was further behind us, showing us her transom, retreating. The other boat was dead in the water but I could see some movement on it. I went back to the cockpit and found my Steiners and gave it a look. Two men were crouching over the outboard motor. Its cover was off. If a Dushka round had gone through its block it was history. Good luck fixing that.

The disabled speedboat was going nowhere, and we were within the range of their rifles, but they weren't interested in taking pot-shots at us. They knew they were whipped and they didn't want any more of what we could dish out. They wanted us to keep on heading west and away from them.

West was where they were heading, too, on the winds and currents, but more slowly without an engine or sails. Maybe they'd brush close enough along the bottom coast of Cuba to be rescued, or maybe they were going all the way to Yucatan or Belize. The Caymans were out there too.

For a moment I considered letting Adam finish them off with the 240. Pirates attack civilians and they give no quarter, so they can expect no quarter in return. The rules for dealing with pirates are . . . no rules. No mercy. Adam could get a lot of satisfaction from machine-gunning them on behalf of Barry, but I pushed the idea from my mind. I didn't want to put more nightmares into Adam's head. He'd already seen enough.

And we didn't have any extra 7.62 ammunition to spare.

Considering our silent VHF speaker and the command boat's use of a red flare to initiate the attack, I figured that the crippled speedboat had no radio comms. Their bosses had fled the scene, abandoning them to their fates. I hoped that frigate birds would pick their bones clean on the long drift west to Central America. Or maybe some *Cubanos* would save them. Their fate was now in God's hands. I also hoped that I'd done a lot of damage to the command boat with the Dushka, and that I'd killed, crippled or maimed some of the Haitian pirate brass. Maybe even their pirate captain. Let it be a lesson.

I was standing on the port side of the pilothouse studying the speedboat that was still attached to our side. Many years ago it had been popped from a crude mold. Its fiberglass hull was patched and re-painted and showing the results of many old collisions and badly-executed modifications.

A white-painted steel rectangle was bolted to the front of the console. The armor plate would protect the boat driver from the front, but sooner or later pirates have to come alongside their prey and fight it out hand-to-hand the old-fashioned way. That is, if their prey decide to fight, instead of surrendering.

I noticed that things were happening around me without my direct input. Somebody put a bottle of water in my hand, and in Gino's too. Sofia and Rita pulled Will and Adam away from Barry, and led them down the forward hatch. Then Tala covered his body with a blanket, tucking it under him against the wind, and then she spread deck towels over his blood trail. The towels stuck to the deck. The things that you notice. . .

The speedboat's boarding ladder was about a dozen feet long from front to back and maybe four feet high. Its vertical and horizontal planks were nailed and screwed together from pallet wood, and it had longer legs at the front and back that were bolted to the boat's inner hull and gunnel.

The sailboat that we had seen had probably advised their bosses that they would need to bring their boarding ladders. A target vessel with less freeboard might not require extra help, or a small ship might require tall ladders with hooks at their tops. Different tools for different jobs, and the spotters would let their bosses know what to expect. They had a plan and they executed it, no doubt about that. They just didn't expect to take such effective return fire from their intended victim.

Gino said, "We lost one, but they lost at least eleven."

I snapped back to the present. "They're all dead?"

"All dead, unless one is hiding on the bottom. Their motor took a few hits, but we could lift the cover and have a look."

I asked him, "Did they turn it off, or did we shoot it?"

"I don't know, boss. The shifter is in neutral. A Yamaha 300 is worth a lot, but I'd guess it weighs at least 600 pounds."

"Yeah, that's a lot. I'd love to take it, but it's too heavy to salvage out here. We're rolling way too much, and their boat is beating the hell out of us. We could do it on flat water, but not out here. And we just killed a whole bunch of them, so I don't think we should hang around for too long. Maybe they threw everything they had at us, but maybe not. They might send out something bigger, or even an airplane."

Gino said, “Did you see their grappling hook? They didn’t use rope or wire, they used chain. That’s why we couldn’t cut them away. The bolt cutters could have cut it, but who’s going to stand there and use bolt cutters when bullets are flying?”

“They weren’t stupid,” I replied. “They had a good plan, but his time they were outgunned. Did we take any damage?”

“We have some holes in the hull. And, of course, Barry.”

“Poor Barry. Are any of the holes near the waterline?”

“No, they’re all higher up—at least as far as I can see.”

“Any damage inside?”

“I haven’t really checked. Nothing that’s obvious.”

“Put surgical tape over the holes to keep water out when we’re heeled to port. Tape will have to do for now.” The roll of tape we’d used on Luke’s hand was the last tape we had on board that would still stick to anything.

One of bodies of the pirates was tangled in our port side lifelines, a machete on deck beneath his bloody hand. Another was caught in their horizontal boarding ladder where his leg had slipped through when he’d been shot in the face and fallen backward. The rest of them lay dead inside the boat or against the ladder. Most of the pirates were shirtless in preparation for the final battle they must have expected on Rebel Yell’s deck. Most had been killed near where they lay, having never made it onto their boarding ladder. There were more machetes and a pair of AR-15 pattern carbines among their bodies.

Dead black bodies and gallons of blood and gore. Split-open skulls and faces are especially horrific. The opposite side of their hull caught a lot of it. Red on gray, dusted with fiber-glass particles glinting in the sun.

I worked backwards reconstructing what I had not seen while I was reloading the Dushka. The M-240 had raked and riddled the pirate’s hull before they slammed alongside and got their grappling hook into our lifelines. Their gunnels were a yard lower than ours, hence the improvised boarding ladder from the console forward. Barry had been hit right at the end when his machine gun had stopped, but Gino had kept firing his

M-16. There hadn't been time to get the M-240 back into action, because the action was over a few seconds later.

Luke, Gino and even old Curt had also laid into them as they turned in on their final run, but most of the killing work had been done by Barry on the belt-fed 7.62mm machine gun. At least a hundred black links and brass shells on the foredeck bore testimony to its heavy use. More must have gone into the water. At least a hundred 7.62mm slugs had gone through both sides of their boat and the now-dead pirates in between. The human destruction inside had mostly been Barry's doing.

The boat's fiberglass shell was barely concealment, not with many of their heads visible during their attack run, and it provided no cover at all. The only true cover was provided to the coxswain, where instead of a Plexiglas wind screen, there was a five- by five-foot square of half-inch-thick steel bolted to the front of the console. A crude viewing slit had been cut with a blow torch for the crouching boat driver to look through during his approach, but that steel plate could not protect the boarding party as the pirate boat came alongside. Bullets had rained almost straight down upon them when they swerved in and were fully exposed to our fire from above.

I told Gino, "Dump this guy into their boat. We'll take their guns and anything else we can use, but don't let anybody get their blood on them. Assume it's all infected ten different ways. Once we get the guns and those binoculars there on the console, cut it loose. Everything we take has to be disinfected. Clean their guns and check them. We'll motor-sail west until sunset, and then we'll cut the engine and turn to the southwest for Jamaica. You got all that, first mate?"

"I got it all, boss." Then he added, "You look tired."

"I didn't get much sleep last night. I'm going to make a quick inspection tour down below, but if I don't get horizontal I'm going to keel over. Take good care of Barry—we'll have his service tomorrow. Pull up the jib and let out the main. Put a lookout up the mast, and fetch me if there's a new contact."

40

Barry spent his last night above the world's waterline inside Whisper, where he had hidden during his first night on Rebel Yell. After dawn, Gino and I carried his wrapped body down onto the boarding platform. Wrapped in a blanket and then in folds of stiff sail cloth and laced up with cord, Barry's remains were easy to move. I remembered how Hung wrapped Victor, and I used that example as my model.

Luke and Jessie had the watch. Curt was awake and on deck and he helped where he could, mostly by keeping the rest of the crew away while we made the preparations on the back of Rebel Yell. Victor's remains had also briefly rested on the platform, before we carried him up the cliffs and interred him beneath a tower of stones atop Alegranza in the Canaries.

A week before Victor's death, Colonel Rainborow's ex-SAS medic had been given to the deep from the platform. For Barry's burial at sea service, I copied how Rainborow's British and Irish rescue team had said farewell to their comrade, who had also been felled by a pirate's bullet.

We tied four pieces of line around the outermost teak slat of the boarding platform. Their other ends were then passed up and over the stern rail. We placed Barry's remains above the ropes where they crossed the teak. I decided to cover him with our American flag, but it was only four feet long, the same as our blue Palmetto State flag. We had flown the blue flag in South Carolina waters, but this was mostly for local political expedience, and not out of any particular conviction.

On the other hand, the Stars and Stripes were a certified dead letter. The last time I had flown the U.S. flag from our stern had been on the way to Morocco, and only because a Spanish warship was breathing down our necks. Because our American flag was too short, I placed the South Carolina flag over him first, with Old Glory on top. This left blue on each end, with fifty stars to starboard toward the ocean. The inside corners of the two flags were tied to Rebel's transom.

Word was passed that the service for Barry would be held at nine. Curt, the new guy who scarcely knew him, steered the boat. This was an easy task with a following breeze in six foot swells. The crew gathered on the aft deck, and Luke and Jessie played their guitars. Jessie singing "Just a Closer Walk with Thee" was both heartbreaking and uplifting at the same time.

Adam and Will shared stories from the cargo hold, telling us all of Barry's kindness to them. Then I spoke of his journey from Charleston to Beaufort and to Rebel Yell, glossing over the worst details. Barry had endured an exceptionally hard life and had faced many difficult challenges, but he had overcome them all to become a fine man, a man who would lay down his life for his friends, and what greater love is there than that?

Gino told us all how Barry had fought up on Rebel Yell's foredeck. As the pirate boat had roared in, Barry continuously raised the stock of the M-240 machine gun, going up onto his knees and then his feet, exposing himself to the pirates' guns so that he could continue firing directly down at them. This was when he caught the bullet that ended his young life.

The way that we had rigged it, there were four cords leading from the aft rail down under the flags and under Barry. The flags were tied to Rebel Yell, but Barry was not. Gino and I took the outside cords, Will and Adam took the inner two by the still uncovered Dushka. They had both agreed to perform this duty at my suggestion.

When it was time I whispered, "All right, boys," and we pulled our cords and tipped Barry into the sea. I'd ensured that his remains were well weighted and his shroud ventilated, so he was instantly lost in our wake. According to the chart it was more than a thousand fathoms down to the sea bed, so nothing would ever disturb his sleep. Barry was buried over a thousand times six feet under, and that's well buried in anybody's book.

We all stared behind us, lost in our private thoughts. After a while I couldn't help but see Mike Ortega's yellow plastic raft disappearing in the distance. I wondered how many of us shared that week-old memory. I don't think I'd heard his name spoken aloud since we had expelled him from our community. It was a very different story with Barry. I can't remember when I had heard it first, but after his burial at sea, Barry the thief, Barry the runaway, Barry the stowaway, was always referred to as Machine Gun Barry. He had died so that we could live.

His death was not taken well or easily, and especially not by Rita and Adam. The twins took his departure rather calmly. The five-year-olds had not grown particularly close to him over the two weeks, and from their perspectives, grown-ups just showed up without explanation, and then they often left the same way. And the twins, who fought battles across the dinette table with Lego battleships, tanks and forts, knew that a real-life battle had taken place on the deck of their floating home, and that Machine Gun Barry had died defending Rebel Yell and its crew, including them. This meant that Barry was a hero—and heroes are the greatest men of all.

We had seen his earthly remains plunge down into the cold, dark sea, but I liked to think, I preferred to believe, that his eternal soul had already flown skyward on the afternoon before. I testified to this belief at his Christian burial service. His mortal body rested six thousand feet deep between Cuba, Haiti and Jamaica, but Barry Conway's everlasting soul rested in the arms of the Lord. That much I knew as a matter of faith.

Or as Will had put it to Barry and to me on a night watch earlier in the voyage, what are we without our Christian faith? Just animals that happen to walk up on their two hind legs? No. By the grace of God, we are so much more than that.

The clouds thinned at the right time and we were able to grab a noon sight. Adam and Will assisted, and for a quarter of an hour on both sides of twelve we passed the sextant, the new Japanese watch and the notepad worksheet between us, using the top of the pilothouse as our standing desk.

Our noon position that Thursday put us ninety nautical miles northeast of Port Antonio, plus or minus ten or fifteen miles in any direction. This was ocean navigation in the post-GPS era, and our position was that accurate only because we had been able to find a chronometer set to UTC on our last day in Beaufort. Without a trusted timepiece, we would have only known our latitude, but not our longitude. Sailing from South Carolina past the Bahamas to Mayaguana, and then between Haiti and Cuba, would have been like playing Russian roulette with an unknown number of bullets in the cylinder.

I wondered where Captain Stark's Battle Wagon IV was anchored or sailing that Thursday, the last day of November. I wondered how Harry Burton and his marine chandlery were doing back on Bay Street. A gold Krugerrand had brought us through the Windward Passage and into the Caribbean, even with missing entire days for clouds. No matter how skilled a celestial navigator might be, only God above can clear the sky.

Ninety miles to Port Antonio at noon on Thursday meant we'd see Jamaica on Friday. We were making six knots under sail in a fresh breeze from the east-northeast. Cumulous clouds marched across the sky toward the west like gigantic random cotton balls, each one casting a shadow on the sea below it. If we wanted a daylight arrival, we'd have to slow down.

We field-stripped, cleaned and checked out the carbines we'd salvaged from the pirate boat. They were both legitimate Colt military products with a full-auto capability, forerunners of the M-4s, but with carrying handles instead of rails for an optical sight. They'd been beat all to hell, and their bores were pitted, but they were serviceable. My guess was that they'd been transferred from the U.S. inventory to the Haitian police or military decades before they'd found their way into pirate hands. One of them had killed Barry, so while I recognized their potential utility, they carried a bad karma with them.

I came out into the cockpit after the one-hour mealtime dog-watches. The women were cleaning up in the galley after our suppers. They'd already seen hundreds of blazing red, orange and silver sunsets, and they didn't mind skipping a few. Will, as my number-two, was helping them with the dishes.

Adam was missing a watch partner, so I had Curt replace Barry. Curt had a half century and a head in height over Adam but neither cared. It was fascinating to hear an unschooled but well-tutored youth and a trained engineer discuss the aero-dynamic principles involved while trimming our two sails for the maximum speed. I wished that Adam's Uncle Hilton could have heard them. Gino and Luke were back in the cockpit too, so it was a good time to pass on the night orders.

"All right, boys—next stop, Port Antonio. We'll drop the main at midnight at the change of watch. That'll slow us down to under five knots. We don't want to get to Jamaica too early. And break out the NOD. Give the horizon a complete look all the way around with night vision at least every few minutes. Bring out the VHF speaker and leave it on scan. And get some rack time when you're not on watch—it's going to be a long night tonight, and a long day tomorrow."

Luke asked, "Should we put a lookout back up the mast?"

"No, I don't think so. Jamaica's not Mayaguana—it has big mountains we'll see from miles and miles out, and pirates aren't going to be looking for stray sheep at night. If there are any other boats out here, we'll see them with the NOD before they see us. But just in case, make sure all the mags are topped off and the guns are ready in the pilothouse. Leave the M-240 inside of Whisper. Wake me up if you spot a contact, or if we go back on soundings."

I was up and back in the cockpit around half past three. Adam was steering with Curt as number-two. A little after four the fathometer flashed numbers in the high 400s. According to the chart this meant we were about five miles off the coast, but even with a three-quarter moon above the overcast, and using the PVS-14, we couldn't see anything ahead but ocean. But because we were on soundings and getting close to Jamaica, I told Adam to change our course from southwest to south. We were making four knots under the working jib alone.

At around half past four Curt spotted land with the NOD. He was leaning against the back of the pilothouse for support. He'd extended the wire to the NOD's battery pack so that it could remain inside the pilothouse and away from salt spray or rain. I stood next to him and he handed me the monocular. It was unusual to have somebody significantly taller than me on Rebel Yell. The boom barely cleared the top of his head. The mainsail was down and furled and the boom was centerlined.

I couldn't see any lights on the shore, but this could have been due to the remoteness of the area, or because there was no electricity on the island. I asked Curt if he'd seen any lights yet and he said he hadn't, but we were still a few miles out.

"All right," I said, "we're close enough. It's time for the engine." I pushed the start button and the Cat fired right up.

We were studying the dark coastline as it grew ahead of us, taking turns with the NOD and the binos. The numbers on the depth sounder passed through the 300s and into the 200s. It wasn't anything like pitch black out, not with a three-quarter moon above the clouds, but the overcast was too low for us to see much past the shore.

Gino and Luke came up into the cockpit. They knew what it meant when the engine started. Land Ho . . . or trouble.

I passed my first mate the NOD. "There it is—Jamaica."

Luke went to the stern to take a leak and he said, "It's clearing behind us."

The clouds were racing overhead, but they were not as low or thick as before. There were some gaps where the moon turned the swells into rolling quicksilver.

I told Gino and Luke, "We just turned to south, and we're going to turn east when we reach the hundred foot curve. If the coast is running east to west, then we're near Port Antonio. If it's running to the southeast, then we've overshot it and we'll have to turn around. But either way . . . that's Jamaica."

Gino had the PVS-14 and was scanning ahead. He said, "Port Antonio has a lighthouse, right? Something is flashing ahead of us to the southeast."

"Flashing? Can you time it?" I asked him.

"It's blinking about every two seconds."

He handed me the NOD. It revealed more details on the shore, and a flashing light. I said, "According to the chart, if it's Port Antonio it's supposed to show one long white every ten seconds, but that's blinking like a strobe. And it should be visible from ten miles out."

Over the past day I had studied everything that was to be known about Port Antonio from every source I could find on board. I had gleaned minute details from several charts, pilot books, guide books, old logbooks, and even brochures I had filed away because they included a useful photograph or map. I included Adam and Will in this area study as part of their education as ocean navigators. This study also covered facts that I remembered about Port Antonio while we went through my old charts and files. For a navigator, there is no such thing as too much information. The detail that is missed or over-looked can land your ship on an unnamed doomsday reef.

Curt said, "A real lighthouse beam would require a lot of power. Maybe they changed it to a strobe to save electricity. A strobe light can run all night on a battery charged from a solar panel. A real lighthouse light would need full grid power, or a dedicated generator, and that would mean burning fuel."

“That’s true,” Gino agreed, “but we still don’t know if it’s Port Antonio. It could be anywhere on the north of Jamaica.”

From behind the wheel Adam said, “But it’s still a good sign that there’s a light, right? Even if it’s just a strobe light?”

“Oh, yeah,” I replied. “It’s a very good sign. It means that somebody is minding the store. Before GPS, lighthouses were considered critical infrastructure. They were how sailors found their way back to port at night, and how ships stayed clear of reefs and shoals, and steered around points and headlands.”

Will came out of the pilothouse into the cockpit, yawned, and stared behind us. Then he said, “Hey—look at the ocean.”

Sometimes clouds arrive in a line across the sky from horizon to horizon in a frontal passage, and sometimes they depart the same way, like a rug pulled across a floor. Behind us the Caribbean Sea was molten silver. The front edge raced across the water at the speed of the fleeing clouds. The line crossed us and we were bathed in light. The trailing edge of the clouds flew south across Jamaica, and then, visible to our night-adjusted eyes, the Blue Mountains appeared.

I thought: here was another experience land dwellers will never even imagine. I was elated to share that rare vision with my crew, and my spirit soared with their expressions of awe. We had a chart, and we knew the big island was there, but the moment was still breathtaking. What must it have been like for Columbus and his men to see Jamaica for the first time, a giant new Caribbean landmass; unknown, unnamed and untamed?

The depth sounder was showing numbers in the low 100s, so I told Adam to steer east, following the coast.

Assisted by the moonlight, the PVS-14 revealed all the details on the shore that we expected to see from studying the chart. We left the jib up as a steadying sail, and for the remainder of the night we tacked back and forth with at least a hundred feet of water below our keel, guiding off the blinking white strobe.

We dropped the jib at 0600 during the change of watch. I wanted to go in at first light. It was my turn to take the wheel, with Will as my number-two, but everyone was on deck to see Jamaica at sunrise. Port Antonio climbed the foothills. Homes and buildings lit by horizontal morning light were visible on the slopes. When the sun struck their windows at just the right angles they shone bright gold.

I said, "The big ones are the Blue Mountains, and they look just like the Blue Ridge Mountains in Virginia because they're both covered with trees. But Jamaica's mountains are higher, over seven thousand feet, and we're looking at them from sea level, and not from a few thousand feet up."

Curt explained, "The air acts like a blue filter. That's why the foothills are green, but the mountains appear to be blue."

Both pairs of binoculars were in heavy use. To our land-starved eyes Jamaica was a hundred times more alluring than Mayaguana, or even Beaufort. It was verdant green at the low elevations and covered with dark forests running up to the peaks of the mountains ten miles south of us. Mist and clouds hid parts of them. The morning sun made the folds and contours of the mountains appear in shadowed relief.

We had our yellow quarantine flag raised to the spreaders, and Old Glory on our stern. The mainsail was already stowed on the boom; the jib was down on deck. Our guns were ready, but they were concealed. The M-240 was in Whisper, hidden under Adam's red sail and sprit rig. The Dushka's barrel was swung to starboard above the stern rail and tied there, draped with towels. More deck towels were hung over the stern rails and aft lifelines as if to dry. This was all meant to appear as a normal sight on a sailboat coming in from the ocean. We were going into Port Antonio, but we were ready to turn around and run back out to sea at the first sign of ambush.

I stood behind the pilothouse with Gino and Luke, trading binoculars and observations. The lighthouse we'd seen in the pre-dawn hours was on the end of Folly Point to the east. As we approached Port Antonio we were close enough to see its three red and white horizontal stripes and make a positive ID of our location. Across the wide mouth of East Harbour lay the end of Navy Island, which protected West Harbour from the ocean waves. Just landward of Navy Island was the end of the Titchfield Peninsula, which led to the rest of Port Antonio.

Until we were close enough to make out the land features, Will had been steering south. He wasn't strong enough to steer under sail out in the waves, but he could steer under power in those conditions. Because of his short stature, in order to be able to see over the pilothouse he had to stand up high behind the wheel with one foot on each of the opposite bench seats.

I told him, "Just aim for the end of the point that's to starboard. That's the end of Navy Island."

We were transitioning from steering by the compass to using visual references on the land instead.

Curt asked, "Navy Island, like it's a navy base?"

Will replied, "It's called Navy Island because the British Navy had a base there back in the old square-rigger days. Now it's just palm trees, but it still protects Port Antonio." He knew this because I'd told him during our area study. We'd drawn a pencil sketch chart of the Port Antonio area, copying it from a four-inch map on a tourist brochure that I'd saved, and adding more details from my memory.

Luke had the backup binos and said, "There's somebody standing by the lighthouse. Maybe it's the lighthouse keeper. Maybe he's there to turn off the light."

He handed them to me so I could take a look. There was indeed somebody there facing us with his elbows jutting out. He was in the shade of the tower, with the rising sun behind it, so not easy to spot—and he was watching us with binoculars.

I said, "He has binos too. We've been spotted."

"Are we still going in?" asked Will.

I thought about it for a moment. "Yeah, we're still going in. Why not? Okay, Will, can you see the buildings on the end of the point between the lighthouse and Navy Island?"

"I see them. The buildings are the high school on the end of the peninsula. Before that it was a fort with cannons."

"That's right, Fort George. The channel runs between the point and Navy Island. Just steer right down the middle." As we motored in, the ocean swells diminished to nothing for the first time since we'd left Mayaguana Island.

Then a voice came from the VHF speaker. A female voice at that. "Vessel approaching Port Antonio, this is the Jamaica Coast Guard. Vessel approaching to Port Antonio, this is the Jamaica Coast Guard. If you hear this, please respond. Over."

In a way the call was comfortingly mundane and ordinary, but in another it was terrifying. Two days earlier, the Haitian pirates had called themselves the coast guard too.

Gino said, "Are we going to answer? I don't think we can ignore them. They know we're here, so if we're not going to answer them, we should turn around while we can."

I looked all the way around to see if a boat was moving to block us against the coast, but there was only empty horizon. If a trap lay further inside of West Harbour, why would pirates warn us that we'd been seen? And the green hills above Port Antonio looked so inviting. Here was a real town, a port that for centuries had been a crossroads of the Caribbean. The port had made its living by welcoming sailors flying every flag. In the modern era it had been too small for the cruise ships and too hilly for an airport, but it was the perfect size for yachts.

So I went into the pilothouse and picked up the VHF mic. "Coast Guard, this is the sailing vessel Rebel Yell, over."

"Sailing vessel, please switch to channel 14, over."

"Rebel Yell, switching to channel 14."

On the new channel I heard, "—your name, over."

"Coast Guard, this is the sailing vessel Rebel Yell, spelled Romeo, Echo, Bravo . . ." I recited the rest of the letters.

"Rebel Yell, what is your vessel's nationality, over?" Her English was clear, but her Jamaican accent was unmistakable.

"Coast Guard, we are an American-flagged vessel, over."

Our boat documents were nearly a decade old, but they were all we had, and so they were as valid as any other papers after the United States government had ceased issuing them.

"Sailing vessel, what was your last port of call, over?"

"Our last port was Charleston, in South Carolina, over." I'd expected this routine question. Odds were slim that they'd ever heard of Beaufort, and good luck with calling either city to check up on us. Our stop at Mayaguana wouldn't count as a port visit worth mentioning in anybody's book.

"Rebel Yell, what are your intentions here, over?"

"Coast Guard, we need to repair storm damage, over."

There was a long pause. "Yes, it appears that you have one mast standing, and one on the deck. Is that the damage?"

So they had eyes on us. A telescope on a tripod standing on terra firma would bring us into sharp focus. "Jamaica Coast Guard, yes, that is correct, that is the storm damage, over."

"Rebel Yell, have you been to Port Antonio before?"

"Affirmative, Coast Guard. Almost twenty years ago."

I heard a male voice in the background, and then, "Well, in that case, Rebel Yell, welcome back. Then you are familiar with the Errol Flynn marina? Over."

"Yes, I am familiar. We docked there before, over."

"Good. Now here's what you're going to do. Come in and tie along the outside of the marina's main pier. Someone will meet you there at nine o'clock. Nine o'clock. Do you copy?"

"I copy, Coast Guard. We'll tie up at the marina, over."

"Then that's it, Rebel Yell. Welcome back to Jamaica."

"Thank you, Coast Guard. This is Rebel Yell, switching back to channel 16 and standing by."

It might have been a trap, but it was still nice to hear a welcoming female voice on the radio, instead of threats from pirates. And there was just something about that accent that always raised my spirits. Through good times and bad, most of the Jamaicans I'd ever known were happy and positive people.

Gino asked, "Do you trust them? Once we go in, we're a fly in a bottle, and anybody can put in a cork. And then what?"

And then what, indeed? But sometimes you can't poll the gray hairs, or the deck apes, or your wife, or the whole crew. You have to go on your gut. I'd been to Port Antonio before, and they had not. So it was my call.

"I know all about putting corks in bottles, but we're still going in. Not everywhere is crazy like Haiti. Beaufort was all right, wasn't it? It wasn't perfect, but at least it was civilized."

Will was steering. "They treated me pretty good there."

"That's right," I agreed. "They treated us all pretty well."

Then Will added, "No, skipper, not all of us. I wouldn't say they treated Barry too good."

"No, I guess they didn't. Okay, son, start your turn and steer right down the middle."

Barry Conway still had the iron shackle of a V.I.W. on his leg when he'd snuck aboard Rebel Yell in Beaufort. No, they hadn't treated him too good.

"Gino," I said, "we're going to need fenders on the starboard side." He gave his instructions to the deck apes, and in a minute or two Adam and Luke shoved four of our biggest mismatched rubber fenders up through the forward hatch.

41

"I never saw a woman as beautiful as Port Antonio."
Errol Flynn

Red and green buoys marked the entrance to the Navy Island channel. We all watched the fathometer, but it showed nothing more shallow than forty feet, an astonishing natural depth for a channel into a small port. As we came around the end of the Titchfield Peninsula we could see across West Harbor to the town of Port Antonio rising from sea level up into the green foothills. The Errol Flynn Marina's dock jutted out from the land and turned south parallel to the shore, forming an upside-down L. It was drawn from memory on my sketch map.

My Steiners brought me in for a close, sharp look. There was a barred gate extending past both sides of the dock at its landward end. In the old times at similar marinas boat owners would have a number code to open it. The gate would only deter unauthorized visitors who wanted to walk onto the dock. At any marina a determined thief could paddle or swim his way in to rob a boat, but less easily in the daytime. Night or day, patrolling guards were the real security.

The side of the long main pier facing toward the harbor was empty except for a single gray boat moored at the north end, by the short leg of the L. The solitary boat was a military craft, about a forty-footer. JA COAST GUARD was painted in faded black across its hull. A pilothouse took up a third of its length. Antennas and a radar were mounted on a swept-back mast above the pilothouse. The boat was tied with its bow to the north, aiming out to sea, but the green scum and grass along its waterline said it hadn't gone anywhere recently.

On the landward side of the main dock there were a half dozen finger piers with a few boats tied to them, both power and sail. All of these pleasure craft were less than forty feet in length, and none of them appeared to be occupied.

"Okay, Will, let me have the helm. Gino, we're going in starboard-side-to, so we can run straight out. Only one dock line on the bow and one on the stern—but I don't want to be tied to their cleats. Just loop our lines around and bring them back aboard, so we can get out fast if we have to."

I made a few big circles while we were slowing down to docking speed. I was getting reacquainted with West Harbor while giving the crew their first look at Port Antonio. Now that we were so close, the Blue Mountains disappeared beyond the green foothills. None of the boats anchored in the harbor trailed a dinghy, indicating they were uninhabited. No hatches were open on them, indicating the same thing. On shore, no vehicle traffic could be seen moving on the roads visible along the shore or up into the hills. It was early Friday morning and there was almost no sign of activity at all. What did it mean?

Our last full circle brought us near a separate smaller dock further to the south of the marina. This dock was protected by a metal roof. It had not been there during my last visit. A boat was tied there, about a thirty-footer. Will had binoculars and he informed me that the boat had MARINE DIVISION on its side. It had a T-top, radar, antennas, and two big outboards.

I completed the turn and we coasted up to the empty side of the main pier. I stopped Rebel with a shot of reverse near its southern end. Adam and Luke jumped down onto the pier with our lines and passed them around dock cleats that were ahead and behind us. The top of the concrete pier was around four feet above the water, so they were able to climb back aboard with no difficulty. I killed the engine, and silence returned.

It was a little after seven by both my watch and the watch tied on the hub of the wheel. There was nobody visible on any of the boats in the marina, and no sign of the marina staff. There were a hundred yards of empty pier between us and the Jamaica Coast Guard forty-footer.

I called an all-hands meeting in the cockpit. Most of the crew was already there. “Let’s put the big tarp over the boom. It rains a lot here, and when it’s not raining the sun will bake you. Adam, when the officials show up at nine, I want you and Curt up by the dinghies. Just act like you’re getting ready to launch Whisper. If they’re going to storm the boat—which I don’t expect—you’ll cover us with the 240 while we haul ass. The Dushka is all set to go under the towels, and the rifles are in the pilothouse.”

Luke asked me, “Do you expect another gun battle? If it’s that dangerous, what are we doing here?

“No, I don’t expect that kind of trouble—but it’s better to be safe than sorry. I honestly don’t know what to expect. A lot has happened in twenty years.”

“Skipper,” he added, “they put people in jail here for *one bullet*. I don’t think they’re going to like our machine guns.”

“We have storm damage, and that gives us the right to come in and sort things out, even if we don’t clear customs. At least, that’s how it used to work under the old maritime law. But nobody is coming aboard to inspect Rebel Yell until we get a few things worked out first, and if they don’t agree to my terms, then we’re taking off. That’s why we looped our lines. They’re not going to force their way aboard. So if they come down the dock with a squad of police or soldiers, and they’re loaded for bear, then we’re leaving, and our guns will help them to decide to let us go—but nobody will fire before I give the order. Okay? Do you all understand what I’m saying? We’re playing it by ear. Hope for the best but prepare for the worst. Luke, you know how to shoot that Remington, right?”

“Oh, yes sir, I sure do. Ever since I was a boy.”

“I want it in the cockpit covered with towels. A hundred yards is basically point blank for that rifle, even offhand. Just keep it ready, with a round chambered and on safe. But if I tell you to shoot somebody, you’ll shoot them, right?”

“Damn right I will, skipper. Just tell me who and when.”

After our battle with the "Haitian coast guard," I had no doubt that he meant it. I'd seen him finish off the last pirate with an M-16. Luke was a Christian, a husband, a musician—and a killer. And there are times when you need killers.

"Good. Now, if they try to block us with police boats like the one under that covered dock, then we'll drive right over them, guns a-blazing. That's the worst-case scenario, but it's a possibility. But if they play nice, we will too. So get the guns ready, but keep them out of sight. You have to assume we're being watched every second. Every house up on those hills can have a telescope in a window. Okay? Good. Get on it."

I went below and cleaned up and shaved in preparation for an official visit at 0900. Being in the tropics, I figured this meant any time before noon. It felt strange to be inside the boat when it was perfectly still and tied to the land. For two weeks we had either been sailing on the ocean, or briefly at anchor. I put on khaki trousers, a short-sleeve button-down khaki shirt, and my last presentable boat shoes. My captain's uniform.

I gathered our boat documents, passports, driver licenses and other IDs in a zipper case. The boom tarp was up when I came topside again. We ate our usual breakfast of mush in the cockpit and we waited. Our cargo hatch was still down with the dinghies over it, but all the other hatches were open to let the trade wind breeze flow through the boat.

Both pairs of binoculars were passed from hand to hand. (The binos we'd taken from the pirate boat were trash, but I'd saved them to show the twins what was inside.) I knew from my last visit that the upscale marina occupied a few hundred yards of the best real estate along the West Harbor side of the exclusive Titchfield Peninsula. These acres were fenced off, and the marina had its own security force. Or at least they had.

On my prior visit, the two-story building across from the pier had contained the marina offices, some shops, a bar and a restaurant. In the old days the Errol Flynn Marina was where the local elite kept their sportfishing boats and other pleasure craft, and foreign vessels came in to clear through customs.

James Bond mega yachts had tied up on the same outside face of the pier where we occupied sixty feet in our forlorn glory.

Around half past seven a group of men and women walked north up the walkway along the harbor from the town heading toward the marina buildings. The path was inside the marina property, but it had been open to the public when I'd visited there before. The people seemed to be dressed for work. The long side of the pier ran parallel to the shore, and they stopped to stare at us across the hundred yards of water. A lady waved to us, and we all waved back. I took this as a very good sign.

Luke had the binos and said, "Well, at least the natives appear to be friendly. They look like restaurant staff, maybe?"

"Why are they staring at us?" asked Will.

I said, "Because we have the yellow quarantine flag up, and they know we just came into port. That probably doesn't happen every day." In past times gleaming super yachts worth millions of dollars, euros and pounds had been docked where we were tied that Friday. We were anything but gleaming with our old black hull faded and scraped, and our foremast down.

At quarter after eight there was activity at the end of the dock. Somebody opened the barred gate and two men walked through it. One was in a dark uniform, some kind of military utility fatigues. The other was wearing a white shirt and black trousers. We took turns with the binos until they made the turn onto the long leg of the pier and were coming directly toward us. So much for our 0900 or nine o'clock appointment.

"Okay," I said, "here they come. They're early, and that's unusual, but I still don't think we'll need guns. I'm going to meet them down on the dock. Everybody except for the deck apes needs to be in the pilothouse or down below."

I only wanted the shooters left topside.

"Gino: be ready to start the engine in one second or less."

He said, "You got it, boss. You know we'll be ready."

When the two were a hundred feet away, I hopped down onto the pier. I always preferred to do this. Otherwise, they might come aboard unasked, and once aboard there is no stopping them without getting physical. And in their country, not yours, getting physical will get you arrested. Or worse.

And meeting them on the dock is *far* better than meeting them underway out at sea, where they can slam their RIBs and other boats against your hull, while they scream orders at you over the VHF and with their loudspeakers, as they board you pointing pistols and carbines in your face. Far better.

Out on the ocean, at least in their eyes, any strange vessel is always a potential smuggler trying to violate their sovereign territory with criminal intent. A foreign boat could be bringing illegal narcotics, guns, explosives, or criminal aliens into their country, and they take a very dim view of this. If you resist their efforts to inspect your boat they can even shoot you, and if you survive, they will throw you into a filthy dungeon and lose the key, and you will never, ever see your boat again.

(If only America's former mis-leaders had protected her own borders with such an attitude of vigilant determination!)

When confronted at sea, you will almost always meet a testosterone-juiced junior officer or NCO with a raging desire to take a promotion-worthy scalp by busting a smuggler. And in a lot of the third world their hatred for white (and therefore presumably rich) American yachties is hard-wired from birth.

But when you greet the local officials down on the pier, or even better, in their shore-side offices, you are more likely to meet senior professionals with long years of experience. Men whose boat-boarding-at-sea days are long behind him.

The man in the white shirt was about my age, forties. The man in the fatigues was maybe a decade younger. There were three gold stripes on the older man's black shoulder boards, and he had a white and black combination cover on his head. It looked like an American naval officer's cover, but with a different gold insignia in front over the gold band.

The younger man was wearing camo utilities in a blue and gray digital pattern, and insignias that I didn't recognize at all. The cap on his head was in the same camo pattern. And he had a pistol in a covered holster on a web belt around his waist.

The officer had mocha-colored skin; the enlisted man was a little darker. Both were clean-shaved and had haircuts that would pass military standards. And they had the key to the marina's gate, or they knew its combination, so they were legitimate. But it was unusual to be met by the coast guard or the military—if that's who they were. Normally, the visitors would be from customs and immigration. And they were early.

I stepped toward them. "Good morning, gentlemen. It's great to be back in *Portie*." I used the home-town nickname for Port Antonio, with the accent subtly placed on the second syllable, Por-TEA, and both men smiled. I put out my right hand and shook the officer's first, with eye contact, and then the younger man's, but only briefly.

"My name is Dan Kilmer. I'm an American, and I'm the master and the owner of the schooner behind me. At least, it's a schooner when it has two masts up in the air. I have all the papers for the boat and for my crew." I raised the valise and then lowered it. The foremast, lying on deck and lashed to the end of the bare bowsprit, required no further explanation.

"Well, good morning, Captain Kilmer. I'm Commander Duncan of the Coast Guard of Jamaica. Welcome back to Port Antonio. You'll find it's not quite the same as before."

"Nowhere is quite the same as before, commander."

"No, no, I suppose not. Captain Kilmer, before we begin the process of clearing you in, I'd like to discuss a few matters with you on an informal basis. We have very strict quarantine laws in effect, and you may decide that they are too rigorous to justify your remaining here. Now I understand that your last port was Charleston, so if your crew would like to stretch their legs, they can walk on the pier if they stay near your boat."

"Thank you, commander, they'll appreciate that. And do these faucets on the power pedestals work? The last time I was here the water was the best I'd ever tasted this side of Ireland. We're running low, and I'd like to fill up our water tank."

"Of course. But let it run a while—the pipe under the pier hasn't been getting much use. After a few minutes it'll be safe to drink. God sends it down the mountains into our reservoirs, and then it's brought the rest of the way here by gravity."

I turned around and said, "Gino, did you hear all that?"

"Yes, sir, captain. We can fill our water tanks, and we can walk on the pier. We'll start on the water right away."

I turned back to the two Jamaicans. "That's my first mate, Gino Bracciano. We were in a storm and we lost our foremast, but we were able to save it. That's why we're here today."

The officer said, "Yes, I've seen a transcript of the radio call. Captain Kilmer, I'd like to speak to you privately, before we decide about your stay in *Portie*. I'm sure you understand."

This was an opening pitch that I was very familiar with.

"Oh, I do understand, commander. I most certainly do."

"Good. Then will you walk with me down to the end of the pier by our Coast Guard boat? There's a table there, and we can sit and relax while I look at your papers. I think that if we handle this informally at first, it may benefit both of us."

"And that would be my preference as well."

The enlisted man had a pistol, and I knew that once I was away from the boat they might drop the friendly pretense and try to arrest me. But sometimes you have to go on instinct, and my instinct was to trust them. And if not, Luke had binoculars and the scoped Remington, and I knew he was watching us.

We stopped by the gray forty-footer. It was tied where the L-shaped pier made its turn toward the land. It was dull gray aluminum, so it never needed paint. The Coast Guard boat was as close to the open ocean as it could be, combat-parked and ready to head out. Next to it on the pier was a wooden picnic table. None of the privately-owned boats on the finger piers on the other side of the main dock had a table.

"Here we are, captain. This is the flagship of Coast Guard Station Port Antonio. Chief, can you bring us some coffee?"

"Yes sir, commander." He walked away toward the gate and went through it. As quickly and as nonchalantly as he had answered his superior, I felt certain that this had been planned out between them in advance.

I sat down facing the land, and the commander sat across from me, removing his combination cover and placing it on the table. I unzipped the valise and removed our boat papers, passports, ID cards and other documents. The crew list was up to date and it included Mr. Curtiss, but he only had a hand-written affidavit as a form of identification.

The commander removed reading glasses from his shirt pocket and then spent some time flipping through the pages. My old U.S. Coast Guard documents went back twenty years. They told the history of the ownership of Rebel Yell since it had been relaunched. My passport had dozens of stamps in it, but none of them were more recent than six years earlier.

While he examined our papers I asked him, "Did anybody ever tell you that you look like Denzel Washington?"

He glanced up over his glasses. "Almost every day of my life. Denzel with green eyes. My wife said it's the only reason she married me." He said this in an American accent almost without any hint of Jamaican patois. He handed me back the stack of papers and said, in his Jamaican voice, "Thank you, Captain Kilmer. Taken all together it's quite a study, and the information is useful to me beyond the matter of granting you clearance or not. There's nothing newer than five years old, so it looks like we're not the only ones lost on a lonely planet."

He removed his readers and returned them to his pocket.

"Commander Duncan, I wish you would call me by my Christian name, Daniel, or Dan. I'm not one for formalities." I'd picked up on his comment about God bringing the water to the reservoirs, so as a believer, I reciprocated in kind.

He smiled, reached over the table, and we shook hands again. “Please, Dan, call me Harry. So, when you left Charleston, you were still a schooner. And when was that?”

“Two weeks ago.” I looked down the pier. Half the crew were off the boat. The twins were racing toward us, but they were chased down and turned back by Adam and Rita.

He noticed them too, and he smiled. “Your family?”

“Yes. My family and my crew. Twelve souls on board.”

“You’re a very fortunate man.”

“I’m more than fortunate. I’m blessed.”

We held more silent eye contact across the table.

“Dan, your vessel doesn’t look like a pleasure craft, and you don’t look like one of the idle rich that used to visit Portie. So, what did you do for a living in Charleston?”

“We carried small cargos around the Carolinas, and down to Georgia and Florida. The roads are still unsafe for travel.”

“I see. And then I take it that the laundry rack over your transom keeps you safe at sea? What is it, a fifty caliber?”

“Almost. It’s a Russian 12.7mm. How did you know?”

“We have a telescope in our office at the end of the point. One of my people studied that tripod, and how your laundry was blowing, but this was only a guess until you told me just now. But mounted on your stern, it’s clearly for defensive purposes.”

“Yes, clearly.” I held my tongue about its most recent use.

“And, so after leaving Charleston, what was your intended destination? Not here in Port Antonio, I’m fairly sure of that.”

“No. We were attempting to sail to South America.”

“South America? Why to South America? Are conditions so bad back up in South Carolina?”

“The conditions in some parts of coastal South Carolina weren’t too bad, but they were getting worse. I think this was because of the volcano up in Iceland. It was cold last summer, and it was raining almost all of the time this fall. The fields were flooded and a lot of the crops were ruined.”

He cocked his head and looked at me quizzically. “Dan, I think that volcano stopped erupting some months ago.”

"How do you know that?"

"We have an excellent radio section. Small but capable. And it helps having our antennas up on the mountain. Now the word is that the Iceland volcano has been quieting down."

"Our single-sideband blew a capacitor and it can't transmit. After that, I stopped listening very much. Its antenna was between our masts, and now that's gone too."

"And that broken mast is why you're here?"

"That's right, commander, that's why we're here. Portie has a boatyard with a crane . . . or at least it did. If we can find some half-inch rigging wire and we can use the crane, then we can put it back up. The mast will need a little welding, but then we can raise it back up and we'll be on our way again."

He shook his head no. "I'm sorry, Dan, but the boatyard is out of business, and their crane hasn't moved in years."

I'd anticipated hearing this. "Commander, Harry, I have two qualified mechanical engineers in my crew. If they can fix the crane, then everyone will benefit—even after we've gone."

He sighed. "I wish it were that simple. We have engineers in Portland Parish, that's not our problem. Our problem is we have no fuel. No gasoline, no diesel, almost no motor oil, and no hydraulic fluid. Qualified engineers, oh, those we have—but even they can't squeeze oil out of a stone. Not in Jamaica."

"Well, it wouldn't take much diesel to run the crane for an hour or two. We have enough fuel on board for that."

"But it's more complicated than just the fuel. I'm wearing my old uniform, but it's an unpaid position. Unpaid for seven years. But we still love our island. Oh, we love Jamaica! And we never quit. You can say we're holding the fort until things return to normal, but now there's not even a unified national government. We're almost on our own here in Portland Parish. We have water because God sends down the rain, and we have a little hydro power, just a little, and what people can get out of their solar panels. But now our biggest problem is we have no fuel. Even the boat behind you has no fuel. Not a single drop."

"It's diesel powered, right?"

"Yes, twin turbo diesels—but it's bone dry."

I knew where this was going. "How much can it hold?"

"More than a thousand liters, and this is why I wanted to speak with you off the record. A boat like yours, well, I don't know how much fuel you have on board, but I know that you motored into our harbor. Daniel, I don't know what happened back in Charleston, but it's been terrible here since the ships stopped coming. Today, a horse or a mule is worth more than a Ford or a Toyota. At least they can pull a wagon."

"Harry, I saw it in Ireland and Morocco too, horse-drawn wagons bringing the food. But it was *much* worse in America. There was mass starvation. Starvation and anarchy."

"We've had some very hard years here, and they're not over, but nobody starved in Portland Parish. By the grace of God we all pulled together, and nobody starved."

"And you kept the lighthouse on. We saw it last night."

"The lighthouse keeper telephoned us and reported you."

"Telephoned?"

"Hard-wired landlines use very little power. We maintain a lookout post and radio center in the Coast Guard office at the end of the peninsula. They spoke with you, and I heard their report. Dan, we haven't seen an American flag here in years. Years! You can't imagine what it means to see that flag again. I lived in the states. I went to the university in Jamaica, and I finished my degree in Virginia, and that scholarship led to my Coast Guard commission. I remember how it was in America, back in the good years. I have family up there, or at least I did, and we visited the states many, many times."

When he spoke of America, his accent diminished again.

"Harry, I remember the good years in America, too. But what you're telling me is that we can't fix our mast here?"

He shook his head slowly. "No, I'm afraid it's impossible. Here on the peninsula I have a bit of authority held over from the Coast Guard, but my authority doesn't even extend across the harbor to the boatyard. You see, our Coast Guard was—and is—part of the Jamaica Defense Force. The military. But the

Marine Division is part of the Constabulary Force, that's our civilian police. That's their boat at the dock under the roof, and the JCF police headquarters is a few blocks east of it."

He sighed again. "You see, the JCF was aligned with one party, and the JDF was aligned with the other. Even now, with no functioning national government, we're still divided into factions. It's our national curse. But all of our boats run on diesel, and all of their boats run on gasoline because they're powered by outboard motors. None of us have a drop of fuel for our boats, none of us. But even a few minutes of time away from the pier every day or two would make a big difference. When our boat moves again it'll be a signal to the people here. It'll be a visible, concrete step on the road back to normalcy."

The commander's motives sounded entirely altruistic, but I knew where this conversation was going. How much fuel do we have on board, and how can he get his hands on it.

"Oh, but Daniel, we're *so rich* in other ways. God must be laughing at us, but he also has his own mercies. We always had water, it comes from the rain and it runs by gravity, and we relearned how to grow everything we need to eat. No, it wasn't forgotten, the Maroons and the Rastafarians never forgot the old ways, never, but the old ways were overshadowed because there was more profit in importing food than growing it. But even after the last ship, nobody starved in Portie."

"Well, Harry, a lot of people starved in America. Millions starved when the trucks stopped bringing the food to the cities. The supermarkets were looted and everything went to hell. It was so bad there was cannibalism. Widespread cannibalism."

"Cannibalism? Oh, dear God. I read reports of it from our radio section, but you're the first person I've heard confirm it. There was cannibalism? Well, not here. Not here! No. As bad as it was, we pulled together, at least in Portland. There was a revival, a very strong religious revival, and we pulled together. The lack of food wasn't our worst problem—it was disease. We couldn't stop malaria and yellow fever. The mosquitoes are still our curse! Thousands died. Do you have screens?"

"For our hatches? Bug screens? Yes, we do."

"Use them, and tell your crew to stay inside at night. We lost half the parish, forty thousand lives. I lost my own dear wife and two of my children, but there was nothing we could do. Believe me, you don't want it. We're the survivors, and most of us will live with malaria for the rest of our days—but yellow fever is the worst. The absolute worst."

"Thanks for the warning. We'll be careful. So, this is the bottom line, there's no chance of our using a crane here?"

"No, not at the present time or the foreseeable future."

"Then what do suggest? Montego Bay? Kingston?"

"No, especially not Kingston! I'm not sure about Mo Bay, but Kingston is still very bad. That's why we maintain a watch on the ocean. We were repeatedly attacked from the sea until all their fuel ran out. You see, we still had food, and Kingston did not. We dynamited the road over the mountains, and we blew up the bridges, but we still have to guard against raids."

Then I noticed two men approaching the shore end of the dock. They opened the gate, came through and closed it again. One was the chief; the other man was pushing a cart similar to the one Will had back in Beaufort. The man pushing the cart was wearing a tan t-shirt and shorts. They stopped at our table.

"Thank you, Holden. Can you leave your wagon here for now? And chief, can you stay down by the gate?"

A lot of nonverbal communication was exchanged among them. Clearly this had all been planned since we'd been seen coming in. The two men left and walked back toward the land. The civilian who'd brought the wagon continued to the shore. The Chief closed the gate from our side, and while I watched, he wrapped a chain around the bars where it opened. He was standing guard and armed with a pistol. Whatever Commander Duncan had in mind, he didn't want us to be interrupted.

42

Harry took a deep breath, exhaled slowly, and said, "Dan, you must be wondering what's going on, why all the mystery. But you don't have to worry, not at all. I would never ask you for anything unless I could offer fair value in return. I'm doing what I believe I should do as the senior Coast Guard officer in Port Antonio. We don't have any fuel, and that's a real problem, but the Lord has blessed us in many other ways."

He stood and removed some of the contents of the wagon and placed them on the table, beginning with a stainless-steel thermos, and then a wooden box containing mugs and jars.

"First, before we talk business, let's have a coffee. Now, some people say that our Blue Mountain coffee is the best in the world, and from what I've heard, the only people who disagree are some Hawaiians who say that Kona coffee from the Big Island is just as good. Well, I've never been to Hawaii, so I can't say. But this sugar is local, and the cream is fresh."

Harry unscrewed the thermos and poured me a cup, steam coming off, and I tried it black. If I'd ever tasted better coffee, I couldn't remember when. Our last real coffee had been in the Canaries, and it had come from Africa. The chicory and mint tea substitutes back in Beaufort weren't worth mentioning.

Harry poured his own cup, added cream and sugar, and took a sip. The biggest jar remaining in the open box was full of ground coffee, and the smaller jars held other condiments. After drinking part of his cup he lifted a wicker basket from the wagon and set it on the table. It was full of something that was wrapped in cloth, and I guessed it was a few loaves of bread meant as a gift for our crew. Left in the bottom of the cart were two big sacks full of something that looked heavy.

"It's good coffee, isn't it?" he asked me.

"Yes, it's very nice." I finished my first cup and poured another, adding cream and sugar. We were in the bargaining phase, so I tried to downplay just how much I enjoyed it.

"I don't know what it's worth anywhere else, but it's very cheap here in Portie. The beans were always picked by hand, and that has never changed. Now we have lots of coffee but no export market, and that's what I want to discuss with you. These are twenty-kilo bags, and I can bring ten more today, or a hundred in a week. I don't know what it's worth in terms of diesel fuel, or how much fuel you have to spare, but I think we can work something out. But first, let's have a bite to eat."

He unfolded the cloth wrapping the contents of the basket and a truly scrumptious aroma escaped. Inside were stacks of what appeared to be pancakes, but almost an inch thick, light brown in color and about five inches across.

"These are *bullas*," he explained. "You can't get them any fresher unless you bake them yourself. These just came from the kitchen at the club. Some people like them with jam, but a lot of us think that avocado is the best."

I took another sip of coffee and tasted a warm bulla cake. Ginger, nutmeg and other spices overwhelmed my nostrils and my palate. I'm sure this was accentuated by the fact that we'd been eating the same drab breakfast fare since Beaufort.

I finished my second cup of coffee and then tried half of one smeared with fresh butter and the other half with red jelly, alternating bites. Harry told me the name of the local fruit the jelly came from, but I can't remember it. I only remember that it was absolutely delicious on a warm bulla cake.

I tried to lowball the effects of the coffee and the cakes to maintain my bargaining position, but it was no use. Palm trees waved along the marina pathway, and green foothills rose up to the Blue Mountains above Port Antonio. And every day, an inch of rain scraped by those mountains from the trade wind clouds fell to make everything grow like a Garden of Eden. And I'll have to admit that the coffee, after such a long abstinence, might also have affected my perceptions. I poured my next cup with a spoonful of brown sugar. I felt like a scoundrel for not sharing this bounty with Tala and the rest of Rebel's crew, but, always duty minded, I pressed on with the serious business at hand. After another long, appreciative sip of hot coffee.

"Harry, do you know that my boat once carried almost twenty thousand liters of diesel fuel? In ninety-six drums that were stacked two deep. Now, I think the last time I was here a pound of Blue Mountain coffee went for about twenty of the old American dollars. I'm just thinking out loud, but a gallon of diesel weighs about seven pounds, and when you add the weight of the steel drums, well, it all weighs a lot. I don't have anything like that amount of fuel on board, not even enough to fill the tank on your boat, but maybe a good part of it. So let's just say we're talking about these two burlap bags. You said they each hold twenty kilos of the good stuff?"

"They're jute, not burlap. Jute is stronger, and we grow it and make the bags here, but yes, they each hold twenty kilos of the top-grade beans. I had these two sacks brought from the club, the marina yacht club, so they're restaurant-size. But if you give me a week's notice we can fill your boat with fifty-kilo export bags—just as many as you can carry."

"You still have restaurants in Portie?"

"What? Sure we do. Don't look so surprised! We're rich in food, and we still have our wealthy families—but now the only money is silver and gold. So they enjoy a fine meal, and the people take their silver coins, and what's wrong with that? And it's not only the wealthy—it's all of us. Gold and silver, barter and trade—that's it. My Coast Guard position is valid, but it's unpaid. We're all businessmen now, and when you're ready, we can fill your boat with sacks of coffee beans."

"Okay, Harry, that's fine—but where can I sell that much coffee? You said we can't fix our mast here in Portie, so now I don't even know where we're heading next. So where do you suggest? Any ideas?" Apparently he knew more about the volcano than I did, so maybe he had other current information.

“Where? Well, Texas, that’s obvious. Texas or Louisiana. That’s where you’ll find fuel, and that’s where you’ll find a market for coffee. If you take even a partial load of coffee to Texas, you can bring back enough fuel to pay for a full load. And after your next trip to Texas with a full load the word will get around, and then we’ll have an export market again! And then we’ll have the fuel tankers coming. But Dan, we have so much more than coffee here—we just don’t have a market. We *have* to export to get things moving again.”

“We used to sail to Charleston to pick up drums of fuel. Louisiana was sending small tankers there, but it dried up.”

“Well, it didn’t dry up in Texas, not from the reports I’ve been getting. But who’s going to send a fuel tanker to Jamaica based on some rumors? They need samples to prime the pump, and when they try our Blue Mountain coffee, and they know it’s just waiting here, tons of it, then we’ll be able to kick-start our sea trade again. First here in Portie, then in Mo Bay, and then Kingston. And then Jamaica will be a country again!”

Harry’s belief in his own vision was infectious. The first boat always gets the best price, and Rebel Yell would be the first in Texas with coffee, and the first back in Port Antonio loaded with fuel. If we could only become a schooner again!

“That’s a great idea, and I think it can work, but I can’t give you more than five hundred liters. I can bring my boat up and tie outside of yours. We just have to decide how much a liter of diesel is worth in coffee beans. That’s it. Easy day.”

(I wasn’t ready to mention my last six gold Krugerrands. First I’d see how the coffee-for-fuel exchange went.)

He reached across the table, smiling, and we shook again.

I said, “I’m going to go tell them to move the boat. Do you mind if I take the ground coffee and the rest of the bullas? They’ve been eating mush for breakfast since South Carolina, and they haven’t tasted any real coffee in years. Some of my young crew have never tasted real coffee in their entire lives.”

“Oh, by all means, Dan. With my compliments.”

“And the cream and sugar and the rest of it?”

"Of course, Daniel! Of course!"

Walking down the dock, it struck me that the basket held more bullas than the two of us could possibly have eaten. I had always thought that I was a good short-fuse mission planner and horse trader, but I'd met my match in Harry Duncan. And he really did look like Denzel, but with hazel-green eyes and freckles. Especially when he was smiling, which was often.

The full force of the wind was blocked by the peninsula, and what breeze remained kept Rebel Yell off the dock, so we walked her up the pier by the fore and aft lines without using the engine. In minutes we were tied outboard of the Coast Guard boat, and fresh coffee was brewing down in our galley.

Normally we'd put the smaller boat outside the big one, but the sea breeze was holding us off and we weren't staying forever. One end of the hose went down into our tank and the other end went into his, with our 12-volt fuel transfer pump on our deck by the horizontal foremast. The pump had a meter to keep track of the liters. This wasn't the first time Rebel had played gas station, and both parties need to know the numbers. I told Harry that it wasn't a high-speed pump, and the job was going to take some time, but he didn't mind. Not while diesel fuel was running down into the Coast Guard boat's tank.

After some good-natured haggling we decided that a kilo of beans was worth a liter of fuel on that Friday in Portie. This was based upon nothing quantifiable, but we both liked round numbers. The value of a thing is the price it will bring, and we were each happy with our ends of the deal. When the fuel began to flow, the first two sacks of beans were carried across his boat and lifted up onto mine.

Five hundred liters would take a while to transfer, but this would also allow time for them to collect the rest of the coffee beans. Holden returned and then he went off with his wagon to gather more sacks, with the chief locking the gate behind him. We both understood that the day's rather puny deal was only intended to provide a salesman with product samples, in order to spur future transactions on a much larger scale.

The crew ate the rest of the bulla cakes, and when they were gone the twins were back on the dock running from end to end and exploring the finger piers on the landward side. The deck of the Coast Guard boat was midway between the level of the pier and Rebel Yell's deck so it was easy for Jon and Chris to escape again. Before that Friday, the last time they had been off the boat was on Mayaguana, and then only for an hour.

I asked Adam and Rita to follow them and keep them out of trouble, and to be ready to haul them back aboard when I whistled. Everybody wanted to stretch their legs, but we also needed to keep our guard up, so I had Luke and Will alternate turns on watch with binoculars, scanning all the way around.

The diesel had only been flowing for a few minutes when Luke reported that a group of men in dark blue uniforms were walking up the marina pathway from the south, the direction of town. He handed me the binos. There were five of them.

"Harry," I asked, "who are those guy? What's going on?" I stepped down onto his boat and handed him my Steiners.

He looked south along the shore. "Shit. They're from the JCF, the Marine Division. That's their boat under the roof."

"So, what do they want? What are they going to do?"

"I'm not sure. This marina is Coast Guard turf. Their dock is just south of the line. They must have heard about the coffee and figured out the rest. Excuse me for just a minute—I need to see my chief. I'll be right back."

Harry stepped across onto the pier and put his officer's cover back on. He called out to his subordinate and they met halfway between the gate and the Coast Guard boat. I whistled to get Adam's attention and waved them back. Everyone was on board before the police reached the gate. Harry returned but the chief stayed out in the middle of the short leg of the pier, about a hundred feet from the locked gate and an equal distance from the Coast Guard forty-footer.

"Gino," I said, "Everybody below except the deck apes. Stop the pump and pull out the hose—don't mind the mess—and start the engine. Luke, what do you see, are they armed?"

"They have pistols and belt gear. Cop stuff. Now they're trying to unlock the gate, but it looks like they didn't expect a new chain on it. It looks like they're pissed off. Angry."

One of the policemen left the group, jogging back down the walkway to the south. We could hear the police angrily yelling at the chief, but I couldn't make out any of the overlapping cacophony of their Jamaican patois.

I stood on the back deck of the Coast Guard boat next to Harry. The Caterpillar fired up behind us and I told him, "I'm sorry, but we can't stick around to see how this all plays out."

"You have to do what you have to do," he replied flatly.

I asked him, "Why don't they just climb around it?" The white bars extended about six feet out over the water on both sides of the gate. Even the twins could have gotten around it. There were no unsightly spikes or razor wire on the structure.

"They could do that, but then they'd look like criminals and they would lose face. If they come *through* the gate, then it'll appear as if they're on official business. Here's the bottom line: we are getting fuel, and they are not, so if they don't get any, then neither shall we. Pride and petty jealousy. Even now, it's always turf battles." Harry shook his head, disgusted.

I turned around. "Gino, how much fuel went over?"

"Almost twenty liters, boss."

Then Luke said, "One of them has his pistol out and he's waving it around. You say the word, and I can drop him."

We looked behind us. The Remington's long black barrel was sticking out between two of the cockpit winches. From up forward Adam said, "The machine gun is loaded and ready, skipper. Just say the word."

The Dushka couldn't be swung far enough around to cover the gate while we were tied parallel to the main pier.

Harry turned toward my crew, waving both of his hands, and said, “No, no, don’t shoot! Dan, tell them not to shoot!”

“You heard the man—no shooting. Not unless I say.”

Will, with binoculars, said, “The one who left is coming back and he’s running. He went to the police boat dock and it looks like he has some tools now. Bolt cutters, it looks like.”

I said, “Harry, if they come through that gate with their guns drawn, they’re not getting on this boat. There’s no way. We’ll stop them. Do you want your coffee back?”

“What? No, no, you keep it. We don’t need the coffee—we need guns! We only have one pistol against their five. We need guns, and then we can stand them off until you’re gone. I know you Americans: you *always* have extra guns on board!”

This was no exaggeration. He’d lived in the states, so he really did know us. “Gino, get the Haitian rifles, get them and then be ready to cast off.” I knew they were in the pilothouse.

Gino disappeared inside and returned with the two M-16 carbines, each loaded with an aluminum thirty-round mag. He looked at me, hard, and said, “Are you sure about this, boss?”

“I’m sure. Give them to me.” He handed them down by their barrels and I grabbed them by their carrying handles and spun around. “Harry, will these do the job?”

He reached for them, smiling. “Oh, they’ll do just fine.”

For long seconds we both had our hands on the rifles, and then I said, “I’m trusting you here, my new Jamaican friend.”

He replied, “And I’m trusting you too, my friend Daniel.”

Once he had the rifles he could aim them in any direction. Maybe he’d have a last-minute tactical change of heart, and decide to be on the side of the JCF marine police. He’d have to live with them long after we were gone. If we got away.

“We’ll cover your exit,” Harry said. He leaned the two carbines against the side of his boat’s pilothouse. Rebel’s side. I felt better with them out of his hands. Safer.

I asked him, “How are you going to explain all this?”

“Explain? My official report will state that I confiscated two illegal firearms from an American boat, but they escaped before the police could help us to stop them. Of course nobody will believe a word of it, but that's completely normal and expected here. The next time I see you, I hope you're bringing a lot of fuel—diesel *and* gasoline. So, good luck, Daniel."

"Good luck, Harry." We shook hands again.

Gino yelled down, "Get on, unless you plan to stay!"

Rebel Yell began to slide forward. I turned and climbed aboard. Gino was at the wheel, the channel out to the open sea lay ahead and to starboard. I went to the transom in case the Dushka might be needed, now that it could range across the entire marina and harbor behind us. Back on the pier the chief joined Harry on the Coast Guard boat and they picked up their Haitian pirate carbines and took cover behind its pilothouse. The gate swung open and the Marine Division police moved out toward the Coast Guard forty-footer. They were in a line across the wide pier with their pistols held out in front.

Then we were turning to starboard up the channel and I lost sight of the marina behind the palm trees and bougainvillea. I didn't hear any shooting, so I went to the cockpit. Adam, Will and Curt where there with Gino and Luke.

Luke asked me, "What was going on back there, skipper? I can't figure it out." He'd been watching the events through the bolt-action Remington's scope.

"Commander Duncan said it's a pissing contest between the police Marine Division and the Coast Guard. It's all about who's getting some fuel, and who's not. I think they'll scream at each other for a while and then they'll calm down. It'd be pretty stupid to get into a gun fight over a boat that's already gone, but hey, it's Jamaica, and it's a pretty crazy place. Who the hell knows what's going on back there?"

"Just another shitty day in paradise," Luke observed.

"Yeah, just another shitty day in paradise—and it's not even ten in the morning. So, did you like that Blue Mountain coffee? It's supposed to be just about the best of the best."

Gino replied, "I don't know where we're going, boss, but I'm going to be riding a caffeine buzz all the way there."

43

We raised the main and jib and motor-sailed to the northwest until the Blue Mountains dropped over the horizon astern, and then I called an all-hands meeting in the cockpit. After giving the crew a summary of what I thought had happened in Port Antonio, I announced that our new destination was Texas.

I recapped my dockside chat with Commander Duncan. He'd heard from his Coast Guard radio section that Texas was refining fuel again, and that a new economy might be starting up. This sounded plausible, because we'd traded for drums of Louisiana fuel back in Charleston. The small Gulf tankers and ocean barges had stopped sailing to South Carolina, but they had proven that some refineries were operating again. He'd also mentioned that the volcano in Iceland seemed to be quieting down, so maybe the worst of its weather effects were over.

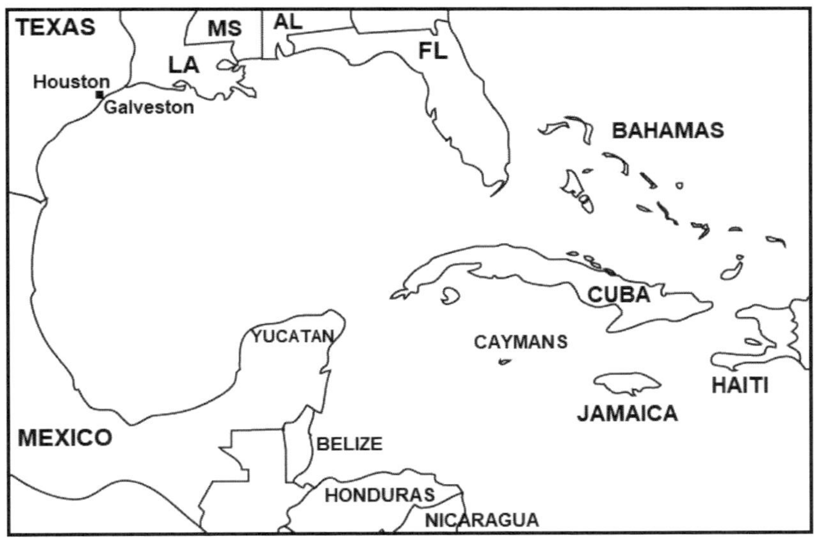

Galveston was the gateway to the Port of Houston, one of the biggest ports in America in the old days. I wasn't familiar with it, but I knew it was in the major leagues with Savannah and Charleston. This meant they'd have anything we'd need to fix the foremast and put it back up. After that, we'd play it by ear. I spoke with conviction and nobody questioned my choice destination. (I wasn't a hundred percent sold on Galveston, but captains must always strive to convey confidence, otherwise, who would follow them? And then what? Nothing good.)

After Jamaica, we sailed west for two days until we were past the Cayman Islands, and then we turned to the northwest toward the Yucatan Channel. It took us four days to cover the last five hundred miles to the end of the Caribbean Sea. It was downwind all the way, two days under the jib alone. Lack of a breeze was never a problem in the Caribbean in December.

Every night the moon was getting smaller and rising later, and we had clear horizons at each morning and evening twilight. Adam and Will learned how to shoot the stars, or at least the stars included in Kolbe's abridged long-term almanac.

The sun also cooperated and we obtained noon sights, so we were able to plot three positions a day. My student navigators and I worked out our own solutions independently, and they were getting closer together. Our accuracy was better than sufficient to avoid the Caymans and find the Yucatan Channel.

The gap between Mexico and Cuba was a hundred miles across, so over twice as wide as the Windward Passage. After working out our Tuesday noon sight I declared that we were through the Yucatan Channel. We were seventeen days out of Beaufort, and there was nothing between us and Galveston but seven hundred more miles of open water. We entered the Gulf of Mexico without seeing either country, but after our Haitian experience, where we had been discovered by a spotter boat lurking offshore, we were on high alert for a pirate attack. Our guns were all ready and we kept a lookout up the mast for two days and nights as we approached and went through.

The big excitement Tuesday afternoon was seeing a ship. We were sailing to the northwest, and the ship was heading the opposite way through the Yucatan Channel. Our closest point of approach (or CPA) was about four miles off our port beam. With binoculars we were close enough to identify the vessel as a small container ship with a red hull. The ship had its own cranes up on top, so it was built to serve smaller ports without their own cargo-handling facilities. It could have been heading to anywhere in the Caribbean or Central America.

Our VHF radio remained mute and I wasn't even tempted to break radio silence. In the old days, I'd hail a ship out on the open ocean to get a weather forecast, or even just to chat about our last ports and next destinations. Not this time. The chance of a third party hearing us was slight, but it could not be ruled out, and we might draw unwanted attention. Even so, seeing a ship was taken as a positive sign, and our binos got a workout during the half an hour that we were sharing the same horizon. The small ship was delivering fifty or sixty containers somewhere, so evidently a way had been found to conduct sea trade again. Nobody sends ships out on speculation. Deals are struck and contracts are inked before the crews are signed, the ships are fueled, and the first cargo container is loaded.

Also of significance was the fact that the ship was alone. It did not have armed escorts like the ones that accompanied the small tankers, ocean tugs and fuel barges up to Charleston before they had stopped coming the August before.

We skirted the Campeche Bank, which runs more than a hundred miles north of the Yucatan Peninsula, but the depth sounder never showed less than three hundred feet and then we were off soundings again. The Gulf of Mexico is no place for a sailboat to be during the hurricane season, but it's also dangerous during the winter when Northers can come blasting down from Canada once or twice a week. In the Gulf these Northers can create brutal square waves with vertical faces.

One thing that I had learned by hard experience was that Rebel Yell can't motor its way out of some sailing problems.

Our propeller's thrust pushes out from back under our stern, but square waves can strike our bow from the side. Our old diesel did not have anything like the raw power needed to turn into square waves slamming against her bow. Picture a ten- or fifteen-foot cement wall hitting your boat every five seconds. Sailors who have crossed the Gulf of Tehuantepec on the Pacific coast of Mexico, or faced the Papagayo winds off Costa Rica will be able to tell you all about square waves.

The widely-spaced thirty-foot swells after the big storm two weeks earlier were nothing compared to vertical walls of water smashing into you seconds apart. Their crests can come at you so rapidly that as soon as you make it over one you will plunge into the trough only to have your bow buried by the next, sending solid water all the way back to the pilothouse. They are not high enough to pitch-pole your boat end-over-end, but they are enough to stop your boat in its tracks like a right-cross to the jaw. And seconds later your boat is hit again. And again. Once you are beam-on to square waves, well, it's game over. In such a dire situation, our old diesel would be pathetically outmatched. And then our only option would be to turn and run away from them before being capsized.

I briefed Gino and the deck apes about the danger, trying not to unduly alarm them, but I'm sure that my fear showed through. I told them if we were hit by a Norther we'd have to run off to the south. We might lose days of progress toward Texas—but this was better than being rolled by an unrelenting train of square waves and sunk. And we might have to run off more than once, because Northers can come like clockwork.

There are two wind conditions out on the Gulf of Mexico: 1: not enough, and 2: enough to make square waves that can kill you. And the winter Northers will make you pine for the hurricanes that might miss a season and leave you wishing for more wind all summer and fall. Long story short: the Gulf is a psychotic bitch that will drive you mad from boredom—while waiting for the chance to murder you in your sleep.

To keep our speed up, and after consulting Gino, I decided to run the engine and motor-sail the rest of the way. The fewer days we spent crossing the Gulf, the less chance we'd have of encountering a Norther. We had enough fuel to run the entire distance, and we were going to a place where they made more. Under the main, the jib and the engine we were making almost seven knots of speed through the water most of the time. The Gulf Stream current flows north through the Yucatan Channel, so we were also picking up some of that.

The breeze held from the east and we made an estimated 170 miles between our noon sights on Tuesday and Wednesday, which was close to a 24-hour record for Rebel Yell, even motor-sailing. Given that our fixes in the post-GPS era were plus-or-minus fifteen or more miles, we might have covered more or less distance. But in any case, our navigation would be good enough to find Texas. Rhode Island, it is not.

And I knew that Adam and Will could each navigate by the sun and the stars. Our tightly grouped positions proved this to be true. I would have given them diplomas if I could have.

Wednesday was too overcast for evening stars. It doesn't get any blacker than a cloudy night with no moon and no stars. The chart said we had more than ten thousand feet of water under us in the deep middle of the gulf. This is where the Gulf Stream makes its giant meandering loop before heading back toward the Straits of Florida and the North Atlantic.

Will and I were scheduled to take the 2200 to midnight watch, and sometime before then I was taking a semi-nap in the aft cabin. I was in the same clothes I'd wear on watch, just drifting in and out of sleep, when somebody grabbed my ankle and shook it and I bolted upright. Adam was there, and I felt a surge of panic. The last time he'd been in the habit of shaking my foot had been during the storm that dismasted us. But the engine was running smoothly and we were still heeled gently to port, so what was the emergency? Had I overslept?

"What's the matter, son? Is there a contact? A ship?"

"No sir," he whispered. "Will found a Texas radio station. We didn't know if we should wake you up, but it's about time for you to come up anyway."

I looked at my dive watch: it was almost quarter before ten. "No problem. Just give me a minute." Adam departed.

I threw on an old flannel shirt. I knew it would be cool out in the breeze. We were already four hundred miles north of Jamaica, and in December this can mean a noticeable drop in temperatures. Continental weather instead of tropical.

Tala watched me get ready. "Should I come up too?"

"I'll let you know, honey. Probably not."

The twins were fast asleep in their nest.

In a minute I was climbing up into the pilothouse. There was only blackness through the windows. Enough light came off our lit-up single-sideband radio to see Will's face. He was sitting in the captain's chair with the headphones on. The only light out in the cockpit was the compass glow seen through the open pilothouse door. Tall Curt was behind the wheel, smiling at me and nodding. He had the duty with Adam.

Will noticed me come up. "We're getting a radio station from Houston, captain. It's coming in loud and clear."

"What frequency band?"

"It's on medium wave. Do you want to hear it?"

"Why don't we all hear it?" I pulled the jack for the remote speaker out of the VHF and plugged it into the SSB. A man's voice immediately spilled out. I said, "Let's take it outside."

Curt was steering, Adam was sitting with his back to the latched-open pilothouse door. I set the speaker down beside him and Will followed me out. We sat across from each other in front of the helm. With nothing to see past Rebel's decks, the compass was again the center of our universe. But now a male voice with a down-home Texas accent was joining our flight through the blackness of space.

"What part of Kansas are you talking at us from, Jim?"

"I'm from up near Wichita, but I'm not calling from there. I'm staying with kin in Norman. I'm on their HAM radio. You were asking about the road conditions, and I came down from Kansas two days ago. The I-35 was clear all the way down from Wichita. I hopped a ride with a state militia convoy."

"Folks, if you're just tuning in, we've got Jim in Norman, Oklahoma. He's patched in on the short wave so we can hear what he has to say. Jim, what did Oklahoma City look like?"

"We drove through at night. I didn't get a real good look, but it was dark. I mean, the city. There weren't a lot of lights on to see, but the highway was clear, clear all the way."

"So, Jim, what are your plans going forward? I'll bet it's getting mighty cold up there in Oklahoma about now."

"It sure is, Robbie. I'm coming down to Houston just like the last feller that called in. I'm not young enough to fight any more, or I'd head out to West Texas like him, but I'm a master electrician, and I know I can do some good down your way."

"Thank you, Jim, thank you. You hear that, folks? Do you hear that? They're coming from Kansas, they're coming from Missouri and they're coming from Tennessee! We even heard from Kirk and his brother and they're coming from Montana, and those boys rode most of the way on horseback! They're all coming to Texas because they want to be free, and if *you* want to live free, Texas is the only place to be! So stop *thinking* about it and get your rear in gear! You can't sit around *waiting* for good things to happen, you have to *make* them happen. We *make* things happen in Free Texas, and it all started right here in Houston, under General Jackson's leadership.

"Now, I see by the clock on the wall we're coming up on the top of the hour, and after the news that lovely lady you've all been waiting to hear will be behind the microphone, that's Kelly Fredericks of course, so you just sit tight and stay tuned. This is Robbie Del Rio saying sayonara, auf wiedersehen and adios amigos from the mighty Seven-Forty, blasting out fifty-thousand watts of radio power covering Texas and beyond! I'll be talking at you again in twenty-two hours—God willin' and the creek don't rise! Goodnight, Free Texas! Oh, yeah!"

Curt asked, "How far are we from Houston?"

I replied, "At noon we had about 550 miles to go."

"There was nothing all day," said Will. "I almost didn't turn it on, but when I did, the scan locked right onto that 740."

Curt said, "The ionosphere changes when the sun sets and you get the sky wave. At night a fifty-thousand-watt AM radio station can reach out five hundred miles easy."

"We can use it for a navigational beacon, too," I added. "We can use our radio direction finder. We can RDF it all the way up to Houston, and that's a beautiful—"

"Shhh!" said Adam. "Here's the news. Sorry, skipper."

"—Jackson held a third day of wide-ranging talks in Lake Charles with Louisiana President Phillip Beauregard. General Jackson stated that their talks have been productive, and that the details of the new Texas-Louisiana defense and free trade pact should be ironed out by the end of the week. The general also said that he is looking forward to making his first official visit to Baton Rouge in the coming weeks.

"A sticking point holding up the agreement had been the admittedly bitter fighting still taking place in El Paso County. However, with the Rio Grande Valley now pacified and under firm Texas Militia control from Brownsville to the Big Bend, President Beauregard stated that General Jackson was entitled to be recognized as the sole legitimate leader of all of Texas. Official recognition from Louisiana can only advance the talks that are already underway with the new leaders of Oklahoma and Arkansas as they also begin to rebuild."

The radio was never turned off after that first night. We could only receive it after sunset, but what we heard was enough to fuel discussions among the crew lasting the entire following day. Besides the news, AM 740 also broadcast nostalgic music and ten-minute prerecorded addresses from General Jackson. He had a resonant voice and a strong delivery. I heard a man in his middle years, but couldn't put a face on him.

Jackson's message was unambiguous. Free Texas would become an independent country when all 254 counties were under militia control, and there was only one left to bring back into the fold—El Paso County. The last drug cartel terrorists would be driven back across the Rio Grande before Christmas, and the new Republic of Texas would be declared before the New Year. Then a Texas constitution would be hammered out at a convention of counties, and Texas would never again be a vassal state subject to the irrational dictates of a distant and hostile godless empire. Texans would live free forever, or they would die fighting for their freedom. There was no other path forward, but the final victory was finally in sight.

Even if AM 740 was mostly propaganda, it was effective. The closer we got and the more we heard, the more convinced I became that Texas patriotism was real, and that it shouldn't be downplayed or dismissed. With this in mind, I asked Sofia and Rita to undertake a project that might prove helpful. We also ground enough coffee beans to fill a dozen plastic water bottles. (Thoroughly dried, of course.) These were meant to be handed out as gifts to smooth our entry. Our old coffee grinder had been quiet for years but now it was back in heavy action.

While the Gulf of Mexico is very deep in the middle, it has a continental shelf that extends far offshore from Florida around to Mexico. Our Friday noon position put us 280 miles southeast of Galveston. We were still off soundings, but Curt warned us that the gas and oil platforms had been planted out at least that far, and there were hundreds of them, both large and small, and the small low ones were the most dangerous because they were harder to see. We spotted two of the big platforms just before twilight a few miles off from our course, and they were more than enough to convince us to slow down. Scanning ahead with the PVS-14 NOD was incorporated into our nighttime watch-standing routine.

Saturday morning we were steering northwest, riding the AM 740 radio beam toward Houston. It was too hazy to get a morning sight, but our dead reckoning put us about 150 miles from Galveston. The haze did not prevent us from getting a noon sun sight, and this position put us about 110 miles out.

The wind clocked to the south and nearly quit. The diesel was doing all the work and so we dropped the sails. When the speed from the motor outruns the available wind, the sails just flap and the boom swings and the sheets go slack and then the sails will slap out and snap. This is called slatting, and it's not only annoying, it's also very hard on old sails and rigging, so I elected to go with the motor alone until the end of the voyage.

Our handheld RDF was left in the cockpit. This mid-20th Century analogue relic had always been powered by a 12-volt cigarette-lighter plug and never a battery, and it still worked perfectly after a decade in its box. The radio direction finder looked like a toy ray gun with a disc on top, and you literally turned it slowly from side to side until your target radio station was at max volume. My young crew marveled at its simple but effective technology.

Saturday night and on into Sunday morning we slowed to four knots to reduce our chance of running into a gas or oil rig. We were on soundings, with the depths in the mid-200s. Curt warned us that the number of abandoned rigs and platforms were only going to increase. I couldn't sleep so I stayed in the cockpit. At least it was dry, and the temperature wasn't bad.

In spite of searching ahead with the PVS-14, we passed a platform just a hundred yards to port. Black is black, and light amplification fails when there is zero light for the NOD to amplify. There wasn't even time for us to turn. Luke put our spotlight on it as we went past. A basketball-court-size deck loomed a hundred feet above the water, all supported by steel columns. We had missed it only by luck.

Curt said, "The fishermen loved them: they'd catch *huge* red snappers. The companies were glad not to pay to remove them. They'd take off all the equipment they could use somewhere else, and just leave the rest of it. It was a win-win."

"Yeah," I replied. "It's all a win-win until you hit one."

44

Sunday morning's dawn was too overcast to find a star and pull it down to the horizon, but we were riding the radio beam and the depths were only in the seventies, so even without an approach chart we knew we were close. We passed abandoned gas and oil rigs, but at least we could see them, so I kicked the speed back up to six knots.

The watch schedule was essentially forgotten. There were more of the crew in the cockpit and on deck than were needed because everyone was eager to see Texas. We could smell the nearness of land. The water color was changing, and the seabirds included common gulls. I remembered our courtesy flag and Rita brought it up. It had been easy for her to hand-stitch a three-foot-wide Lone Star flag, simplicity always being one of its virtues. Adam ran it up to the starboard spreaders under the yellow quarantine flag. We flew the blue South Carolina flag from our transom.

Luke and Adam were both leaning against the pilothouse with binos to their eyes. Nobody was up in the crow's nest. It wasn't necessary. Pirates were not our concern. The Dushka, the M-240 and most of the rifles were stowed in the hold. Two rifles were inside the pilothouse just as insurance.

At 0725 Adam said, "A boat is coming."

Luke said, "I see it. Bow-on. Right on the nose."

For the purpose of the log, the Hanahans were on watch. Jessie was steering, her long blonde hair tied in her customary wind-proof braids, even when there was no wind. She wore a pair of Curt's gifted sunglasses under a pink ball cap.

She asked me, "Now what, skipper?"

"Just hold your course. Everybody please stay loose."

Adam handed me my Steiners as I stepped up next to him. A boat with an odd pilothouse that looked like a mushroom at that distance was racing toward us and throwing out spray.

I said, “Here’s the welcome wagon.”

A voice came out from the cockpit speaker. “Northbound vessel approaching Galveston, this is the Texas Coast Guard. Maintain your course and speed, and prepare to be boarded. Everybody needs to get on the bow except the captain. Everybody else get up on the bow. You copy that? Over.”

In a second I was inside the pilothouse and on the mic. “Texas Coast Guard, this is Rebel Yell. We will maintain our course and speed and comply with all instructions, over.”

Gino went in with me and I told him, “Get everybody up on the bow, except Tala. I have a different plan for her. Jessie can keep steering, and I’ll meet them.”

They swerved away from us and circled back to parallel our track while dropping off plane. It was another aluminum forty-something-footer, but very different from the Jamaican model. It had low freeboard, a square pilothouse that was even uglier than ours, and a fat orange fender rail wrapped around its hull. TEXAS COAST GUARD was painted on its side.

A man on the bow was standing behind a pintle-mounted machine gun. A black patch covered an eye. He kept its barrel aimed toward us, but high. It was an M-240 like ours. There was another machine gun on the stern, also with a man behind it, and there were three other men on the aft deck, two with carbines slung over their backs. They were all wearing the old Army ACU uniforms, that grayish digital pattern. It matched their gray aluminum boat. They wore gray inflatable life vests over them. No body armor, no combat vests. All of them wore ACU boonie hats, but cowboy style with their sides turned up. And all of them appeared to be Caucasians.

The boat narrowed the distance between us. A voice from a loudspeaker said, “Rebel Yell, prepare to be boarded. Stand aside, and keep your hands out where we can see them.”

I stood behind the pilothouse and waved to the men on the boat, trying to appear friendly. Jessie was steering, everybody else except for Tala was mustered on the bow. The ocean was calm enough that this was not a problem for our crew or theirs. They drove parallel to us ten feet off while studying the rather large crew on our bow. I could see their men outside on deck, but not who was inside steering and talking on the loud hailer.

They had heard our name on the radio, and seen it painted on our transom when they circled behind us. We had a South Carolina flag on our stern, and the yellow quarantine flag over the Lone Star flag of Texas raised to the mast spreader. They eased over until their hull was pressed against ours, matching speeds. Both M-240s were directed toward us, but with their barrels aimed high above us at the sky.

I’d been approached by coast guard, customs and military vessels dozens of times, but seeing TEXAS COAST GUARD painted on their hull was a new twist. The Beaufort Militia had never claimed to control all of South Carolina’s smaller coast.

To equal our slow speed their engines were almost at an idle, so it was quiet enough to allow conversation between us. I went to our side and said, “Mind your step—this busted mast should be up in the air, but now it’s in everybody’s way.”

Our deck was a good yard above theirs, but the lifeline gate was open, and one at a time they grabbed the stanchions and pulled themselves aboard. The first man had a black chevron insignia sewn to the front of his hat. Three points up and two rockers made him a sergeant first class. He had a pistol on a belt, but the two men behind him carried M-4 carbines, slung barrel down on their backs. They were corporals according to their two chevrons. The youngest was clean shaven, one had a short beard, and the sergeant had a brushy mustache and was overdue for a shave. None of the three had gotten a haircut in at least a few weeks.

When they were all aboard I said, “Good morning, gentlemen. My name is Dan Kilmer, and I’m the captain and the owner of this boat that should be a schooner.” I put my hand out to the sergeant and he shook it over the downed foremast, flanked by his subordinates. Their M-4s remained slung over their backs. The machine guns on their boat ensured our good behavior.

“Captain Kilmer, I’m Sergeant First Class James Boylan, and I’m in charge of that boat. Nice to meet you, captain. I assume that you’re aiming for Galveston Bay?”

“Yes sir, that’s where we’re aiming for. Galveston.”

“Okay, then, I want you to follow my boat.” He waved to them, and pointed his arm forward. The boat crept ahead of us and when it was in front it slowed so that we could keep pace.

“You’re coming from South Carolina?” he asked me.

“Yes, sir, we heard the call to arms from General Jackson. Sergeant, have you had any coffee this morning? How would you and your men like a hot cup of Joe while we get down to business? Tala, can you bring out some coffee?”

She was waiting for her cue in the pilothouse. They could not see her through the tinted windows, not with the morning sun on the Plexiglas. I was ignoring one or two of their orders, and taking a calculated risk. There was a tray of ceramic mugs and a bowl of sugar at the front of the cockpit by the latched-open door. (We had no cream or milk.)

After my recent Jamaican experience with Commander Harry Duncan, I knew what a cup of fresh coffee would mean to men who might not have tasted any in months or even years. And I knew that seeing a couple of pretty faces instead of the usual crusty old salts would also positively affect their dispositions. And this is why I'd kept Jessie behind the wheel instead of Luke: she looked much better in braids wearing a denim skirt and a pink blouse. Jessie understood the game.

Tala leaned out of the pilothouse with our biggest thermos and said, "Please sit down, boys, we have some hours of time before we see the land. Please, sit, it's only coffee, I promise." She was wearing a snug sapphire-blue sweater, her hair pulled back in a ponytail. She began to fill the cups on the tray.

Their eyes flickered between Tala, Jessie and the mugs of coffee. Their nostrils flared and their lips twitched. Finally the sergeant said, "Well . . . I can't see any harm in having a cup."

Judging by their Pavlovian response they had not smelled or tasted genuine coffee in a long time. I had probably looked the same way to Harry in Port Antonio. I sat down at the front of the cockpit across from their senior man and I showed him the documents I'd shown Harry across the table in Jamaica. The other coast guardsmen sat behind Jessie. The younger of them had a clipboard and a pen, and he recorded our names and other information after the sergeant examined each page and passed them back to him. As they finished their coffees, Tala refilled their cups. She had a very nice figure and I didn't resent their glances at her—not when it was a planned psyop.

"Sergeant," I asked him, "Can the rest of my crew move off the bow? None of them are criminals or fugitives, not in the least. They're all good people, or I wouldn't be bringing them to Texas."

"What? Oh, sure. No problem. Go ahead. Cut 'em loose."

I stood and waved to Gino. After a few years we didn't need words to communicate at that short distance. In seconds the twins had galloped back to the cockpit.

Jonathan asked me, "Daddy, are they Army soldiers?"

"These are your sons?" the sergeant asked me in turn, and I nodded yes to him.

He said, "No, boys, we're militiamen, not soldiers. Texas doesn't have an army. Texas has a citizens' militia."

Christopher went around behind them and pointed to one of their M-4s. "We have guns like yours, but ours are bigger."

"Especially our Dushka," added Jonathan. "Way bigger."

Oh, great, I thought. Thanks, boys. Thanks a whole lot.

The sergeant laughed it off. "Kids—what can you do?"

I asked him, "Is it a problem, our having guns on board?"

"Are guns a problem in Texas? You're Americans, right? From South Carolina? No, guns are not a problem in Texas."

The bearded corporal asked me, "What goes on that tripod back there? I don't think it's rigged up for deep-sea fishing."

"No, it's not," I replied. "It's for a Russian machine gun, about like a fifty caliber. That's the Dushka. It's down below."

"Did you ever have to fire it in anger?" he asked.

"A few times. We were attacked by Haitian pirates almost two weeks ago. And like my son just said, we have some more guns, too. I have a list of them all, if you want to see it."

The sergeant waved this offer away. "No, I don't need to see a list. Everybody here has guns. It's what people do with their guns that matters. Texas wouldn't be free without guns."

"Sergeant, I'm wondering why the Texas Coast Guard is using Army ranks? I thought that the Coast Guard used Navy ranks? And Tala, can you take the twins below, and bring up some more coffee?" She left with them.

He replied, "It's because the Coast Guard is a branch of the Texas Militia now. The old Coast Guard base is on the end of Galveston Island. I guess it didn't make any sense to repaint everything on the base and on the cutters and on the boats, so they just painted Texas anywhere that it said U.S. Like on my boat." He laughed again. "I was a chief petty officer in the Navy, and now I'm a sergeant first class in the Texas Coast Guard. Same pay grade, but not the same pay. Crazy, huh? So, y'all came from South Carolina to join our little fracas?"

"That's what we did, sergeant. We heard the call."

"That's good, the more the merrier. We get a couple boats a week coming in, but mostly they're from Florida. A lot more people walk in and ride in. They say about a thousand a week. So, did you make any stops after South Carolina?"

"We anchored at an island in the Bahamas after we were dismasted. And after that we couldn't sail to windward, so we headed to Jamaica to see if we could fix our mast there, but we couldn't. That was in Port Antonio, in the northeast corner."

"Jamaica? Now, we don't have a problem with guns, but drugs are a whole different matter. If you stopped in Jamaica, I have to ask you this: do you have any narcotics on board?"

"Just the coffee we're drinking. We were only in Jamaica for two hours, and we never made it past the dock."

"Only two hours? What happened?"

"We got into the middle of a feud between the police and the coast guard. We were transferring diesel fuel into a coast guard boat in trade for coffee, and the police showed up. Port Antonio has no fuel at all. None. The police and the Coasties were pulling guns on each other and we took off. But we did manage to come away with a couple sacks of beans. It's Blue Mountain coffee, and they say it's world class."

The clean-shaved corporal was furiously writing notes.

The sergeant asked, "Skipper, do you know how long it's been since any of us have had any real coffee? Years. So, is it your intention to become Texas residents?"

"Yes, sir, it is. That's why we came. We all think General Jackson is a hero. We're ready to fight for Free Texas."

(We had listened to enough Texas radio to know what to say. By then most of the crew were sitting around the cockpit to study our guests, who had relaxed and unslung their rifles.)

Rita said, "I made the flag up there. I sewed it myself, all by hand. I had to make the red stripe out of three pieces that didn't really match, and that's why it looks a little funny."

Sergeant Boylan said, "Well, darlin', it looks just fine to me. We're coming up on the sea buoy, and that's the start of the Houston ship channel, so we're twelve miles out. At this speed, it'll be at least two hours before you get to Galveston. Okay, captain, let's take a look around your boat, and then I can check 'perform vessel inspection' off my list."

The boarding party gave Rebel a less-than-cursory look during their walk-through down below. Then the sergeant waved for his boat to come alongside, and called for the machine gunners to come aboard so that they could take the tour and get some coffee. Their machine guns were left unmanned after that. The bearded member of the original boarding party left to relieve the coxswain at the wheel in their pilothouse, so that he could come over and have a cup or three of hot Jamaican coffee.

The sergeant said, "So, Captain Kilmer, I guess your first order of business is going to be getting that busted mast fixed and standing back up in the air?"

"That's right, if it's fixable. Please, call me Dan. I was an enlisted Marine, so hearing captain before my name always sounded pretentious." (I often took this approach with NCOs like Sergeant Boylan. It helped us to relate on an equal basis.)

"Okay, fine by me. Now, Dan, if you don't have a yard in mind, for a boat this size I'd recommend the Sea-Lake marina and boatyard up in Seabrook. Do you know where that is?"

"I've never been to Galveston in my life. I don't have a chart or even a road map. I have nothing at all for Texas."

"Well, I know they have a big Travel-Lift there. You can get hauled out, fix your mast—anything you need."

I asked him, "Do you know if they have paint, especially anti-fouling bottom paint?" There was no hiding the faded, scraped, and, in some places, rusted condition of Rebel Yell.

The sergeant asked one of his men, "Do they, Parker?"

He was the bow machine gunner with the eye patch, but now he was sitting at the back of the cockpit sipping his coffee while admiring Jessie's blond braids and slim curves. He was about the same age as the sergeant, both in their thirties, but he only had a single chevron on his hat. Private Parker.

"Bottom paint? Oh, I'm sure they do, Sarge. I don't know how good it is, but I see boats get hauled out there, and when they go back in the water they got red paint on their bottoms, so I'm sure they got all kind of paint. Hey, you know, Sarge, I could pilot them up to Seabrook, and then I could hop a ride back on the base shuttle. It runs every two hours on Sunday."

"Hmmm . . . that's a good idea, Parker, since they haven't got a chart and they don't know the water. You can pilot them up there, but then you can take the rest of the day off. It's 35 miles from here to Seabrook, and that'll take most of the day. I'll count it as official duty. Just try to make it to the muster in the morning—so try to stay out of those Kemah dive bars."

"I will, Sarge. I'll spend the night on a buddy's houseboat on Clear Lake, and I'll catch the first base shuttle at 0600."

The sergeant laughed. "Yeah, Parker, I'm sure you will."

"I'll make it to muster, Sarge, I will this time. You'll see."

Sergeant Boylan turned back to me. "Dan, you don't need to follow our boat, and we sure don't want to spend the next two hours out here going six knots, so we'll be saying adios. Private Parker knows the way. And so if you're all done with South Carolina, and since you're applying for residency, why don't you haul down that yellow quarantine flag, and put that homemade Lone Star on your stern? I'd kind of like to see it there before we take off. We might be jumping the gun, but I won't mind if you don't. Nobody will question it. Nobody."

This was a pleasant surprise. "Well, thank you, Sergeant Boylan. Adam, go ahead and bring them down."

He went to the flag halyard on the starboard side of our mast and pulled the two flags down while Luke removed the staff from its stern-rail mount and untied the blue Palmetto flag. Adam tied Rita's Lone Star flag to the wooden pole and re-mounted it onto the rail. The Texans all stood at attention while this was being done, and so we did too. It was a rare moment, and it gave me chills. It had been many years since I'd stood at attention facing the Stars and Stripes, and we'd only flown the Palmetto flag in South Carolina waters as a matter of political expediency. After this brief informal ceremony was over, the sergeant and I sat down again in the cockpit.

I asked him, "Does this mean we're officially cleared in?"

"You will be just as soon as we both sign the papers and I stamp them. Two copies for you and two copies for me. Now it's Sunday, and there's only a small watch section on duty at the base, but after I turn in my report, I'm thinking some folks from the intel shop might want to talk to you. Just leave your radio on for a few days, but if you don't hear from us, assume everything's cool. Somebody might come out to see you, but only to pick your brain about South Carolina and Jamaica and that Haitian pirate situation. You can find out at the boatyard what you need to do to apply for residency. And that's it, Dan. Welcome to Free Texas." We shook hands again.

The clean-shaved corporal handed him the clipboard and a rubber stamp, and we made our signatures and it was done.

Tala said, "Sergeant, we have too much coffee, so if you want, you can take some for your men and for your wife and your friends." She handed him a bag containing plastic bottles filled with ground coffee. In an hour Jamaican Blue Mountain coffee would be brewing all over their base. Then the Texas Coasties would love us, and the word would spread around Galveston, possibly leading to profitable business ventures.

The sergeant was the last to depart. He shook my hand again and hopped down onto his deck. He disappeared inside the pilothouse and his boat roared away, its turbines whistling in a cloud of diesel smoke. There was no fuel shortage here.

45

Private Parker moved to the front of the cockpit to sit across from me, taking his sergeant's place. He'd been their machine gunner, and he didn't bring a buddy or even a sidearm for the run up Galveston Bay. The Lone Star flag was flying from our stern. They had welcomed us to Texas, and they trusted us. It would take me a while to understand it all. More than anything else, I wished Machine Gun Barry was with us to meet Private Parker. They could compare notes on the M-240.

Parker said, "That fella with the black beard said that you were in the Marines. When was that?"

"What? Oh, that was in the early 2000s. I was in Iraq."

"Iraq? What did you do there? What was your M.O.S.?"

I never brought up this part of my past unless I was asked. "Well, private, as a matter of fact, I was a scout-sniper."

"No shit! Hell, I was too! Well, I'll be goddamned. Don't let the patch fool you, I'm still a dead shot. But I'm right-eyed, at least I was, and now I can't do rifle scopes. Now machine guns, I'm still as good as ever, and that's why I'm in the coast guard now. They could have shit-canned me after San Antonio, but they moved me to the coast guard instead. And it wasn't just for the eye. No, I got in some other trouble too. Drinkin' too much, fightin' too much, and shootin' the wrong people sometimes—or so they say. But a damn fine colonel transferred me down here where I can't do too much harm—at least according to some—and I can still count all my time toward my bonus."

"What bonus, Private Parker? I'm not following you."

"It's just Parker—skip the Private. Say, Cap'n—that scar under your eye: did you get it the same way I got my patch?"

"Yeah, and I'd have a patch too if I hadn't been wearing eye-pro when that big fucker exploded." He stared at me with his blue left eye. There but by the grace of God—and eye pro.

"Well, we didn't have any eye protection where I was at. I'm not bitchin'—you win some, you lose some. Just look at me now, just kickin' back out here on the Gulf! Easy days in the sunshine, rackin' up good weeks for my bonus. And now I'm drinkin' my first honest-to-God coffee in years—so I say God bless Rebel Yell, and God bless Texas and General Jackson!"

Will was sitting on top of the pilothouse scanning ahead with binoculars and he called out the landfall just before 0900. "There it is, everybody—Texas!"

It had been nine days since Jamaica had dropped behind us over the world. We passed the binos between us all and studied the shore. Some high-rise buildings broke the low coast. A thin trace of orange smoke smeared the horizon.

I said, "You know, Parker, we have our papers now, and the Lone Star flag is flying back there, so I'm thinking that maybe this calls for a little celebration. You're the only Texan on board, so you're our guest of honor. How'd you like to have an Irish coffee with me? I just hate to drink alone. We still have a little South Carolina moonshine left, and I'd like to make a toast to celebrate our safe arrival in Free Texas. I know you're on duty, sort of, but what do you think?"

He slapped his knees and grinned. "Irish coffee, with real coffee and South Carolina 'shine? What do I *think*? I think it's five o'clock somewhere—so I say bring it on! Oh, *hell* yeah!"

"Sofia, can you—" She was passing by the pilothouse.

"Oh, I know *exactly* what you want, *captain*."

She would never call me captain unless it was to impress an outsider. Gino's wife was a team player, and she knew we had hours of motoring ahead of us. In a minute she was back with the square bottle that was a third filled with clear liquid. She gave me her warning glare while handing it to me, slowly.

The purpose of all of this was, of course, to further loosen Private Parker's tongue. His presence among us was a golden opportunity for intel gathering, and *in vino veritas*. (At least this was how I rationalized breaking out the bottle well before the sun was over the yardarm.) This was rare aboard Rebel, but it's a rare day when you declare allegiance to a new flag. Signed and stamped in front of witnesses. A rare day indeed.

"Adam," I asked, "can you steer for a while? And Jessie, if we're going to celebrate arriving in Texas, do you think that you and Luke could maybe get some music going on?"

She removed her sunglasses and said, "Music? I believe we can arrange that." She winked at us, and they went below.

I poured a few ounces of liquor into Parker's half-filled mug, but I put only a splash or two into mine. As the captain I was always on duty when Rebel was underway. A dollop went into Gino's cup when Sofia wasn't looking. We clinked mugs and I said, "To Texas: may the Lone Star Flag fly forever."

More toasts followed. Luke and Jessie brought out their instruments and sat with their backs against the latched-open pilothouse door. She had her mandolin and he had his guitar. At my suggestion, after Jamaica, they'd worked out the lyrics and practiced a few new songs. They started with The Yellow Rose of Texas, and then they played and sang Dixie.

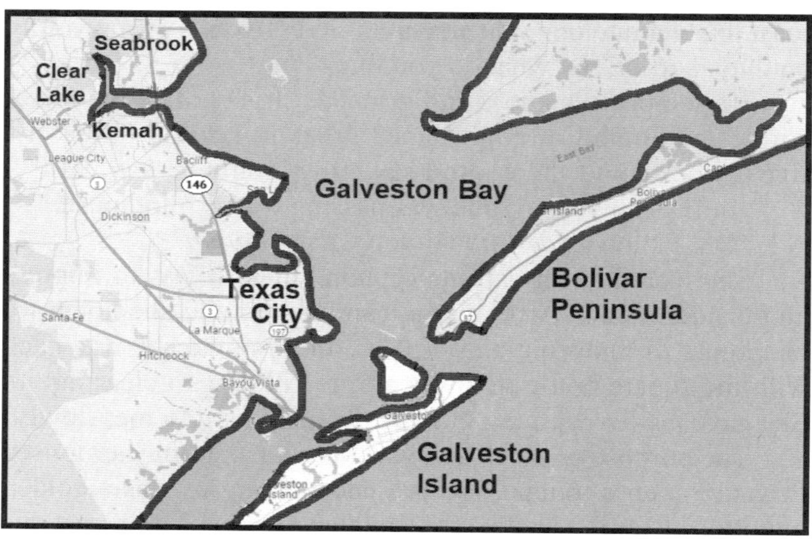

Soon we were coming through the pass, land spreading out to each side. Parker said it was two miles from Galveston Island over to the Bolivar Peninsula to the north. It was low country like Georgia and the Carolinas, but spread out much further. More high rises broke the land horizon to the south. The last ocean swell flattened out as we entered the inland waters. The blue sky was garnished with herringbone cirrus.

Parker said that most of the old channel buoys were still in place, and he was glad he had not been assigned to the buoy tender. On his 45-foot Medium Response Boat he could stand behind a machine gun like a real Texas militiaman. Mexicans cruised up to poach Texas fish from around the oil rigs, or to remove parts for metal scrap. It was an easy mission, and it got him out on the water with his face in the wind and the sun.

As we entered the miles-wide pass Parker said, "The coast guard base is over there on the north end of Galveston Island. We were on standby duty when we got the call."

"Who called you?" I asked him. "Who spotted us?"

"We have observation posts out on the oil rigs. They have radar and night vision. Two days on, and four days off. It's easy duty, and you catch fish like you can't even believe. Did you ever hook and cook a twenty-pound snapper in the same hour? After San Antonio, duty in Galveston is like heaven."

Will said, "There's a ship, or something, up ahead."

I rose to look. A long, low motor vessel was crossing a few miles ahead of us. I asked our guest, "What's that?"

He stood up to look over the pilothouse. "That's the ferry. It runs across from the Bolivar Peninsula to Galveston day and night—and it's free. It's a hundred and fifty miles around by road without the ferry, and it didn't start running again until last September. Now we have three refineries in operation and things are improving by the day. Do you see the smoke over Texas City? We *love* that smoke. We just *love* it."

Our course up the Houston shipping channel took us to the northwest, but after we were through the wide entrance and past the Bolivar Peninsula to the north, no other land was visible to the east, only another salty horizon. Galveston Bay was an inland sea compared to Charleston Harbor, and South Carolina's biggest seaport was a mere puddle in comparison.

"So, Parker, what's this bonus you're talking about?"

"What? The bonus? Well, you see, when General Jackson kicked off the reconquest of Texas, there was no money left around. I mean, seriously, there was *no money*. Old American paper dollars? Well, maybe you could wipe your ass with 'em, or light a fire. There was *no money*. No banks, no economy, no nothing. Just barter and trade, that's it. That is, if you were one of the lucky ones who was still alive. Now just imagine you're General Jackson. How are you going to motivate folks to fight for an idea like Free Texas, when there's no money? No—money! Well, you gotta promise people *something* right? That's where the idea of re-homesteading came from. That's the bonus. And God bless General Jackson for thinking of it!"

Gino asked him, "What's re-homesteading?"

"Re-homesteading means we'll get a house and property, free and clear, if we fight for Texas for five years. Fight in the Texas Militia, or serve in the Texas Engineering Corps—but that takes longer to earn the bonus. That's the main bonus, re-homesteading. After you get your house, if you live in it for twenty years, it's all yours, free and clear, forever. No bank note, no mortgage, no nothing. Oh, you have to understand, there's a metric shit-ton of empty houses now. There used to be seven million people living in the Houston metro area, and now it's under a million. It's the same in Dallas and Austin, it's the same everywhere, and that's a lot of empty houses—but most of them need a lot of work.

"So what they do is, they take a subdivision and they pick the best houses, the ones that don't need too much rehab. Then they bust down the other ones for parts, like the lumber and hardware and wires and pipe, and they fix up the best one. Oh, it's only after they got water and electric power going in there.

"But if you take a house for your bonus you can't sell it and you can't rent it out for twenty years. You can only do an even trade to move somewhere else. But if you don't want a house you can take your bonus in silver, but most people think a house is the best deal, especially if they're married.

"Oh, and you have to plant food on it, but they'll give you the seeds and teach you how, or they'll bring you fruit trees, whatever works best there. And the weather in Texas has been great for the last few years. Plenty of rain, and not too hot in the summer, and no hurricanes at all. But you can only get the bonus if you're a citizen of Texas. A house, or the silver."

Gino asked him, "But what about that volcano in Iceland? I thought the volcano messed up the weather?"

He shrugged. "Not in Texas. The weather's been great."

I asked him, "What if somebody still lives in a house?"

"Well, sure, if people still live in it, and they can prove they owned it, then they can keep it, I mean, of course."

Curt asked him, "What if they still owe money on it?

Parker laughed. "Owe money to who? The banks were all wiped out. Don't even talk about banks in Texas—it's a good way to start a fight. There's no banks, at least not for now, not during General Jackson's war economy. That's what they call it, the war economy. Maybe next year. They're talking about a new constitution after we get all the counties back."

Then Luke asked him, "What if people were just renting, but they couldn't pay the rent? What happens if the landlords come back and want to evict their tenants?"

"That's a good question—it happens—but if somebody's been keeping a place up and living in it, well, that counts too. Places that were abandoned went downhill real fast. There are some complicated cases, but now we have property courts."

I asked him, "How can they have property courts, if you don't have a government?"

"The same way we have a war economy, I suppose. Every county has a commission put in by the militia. The judges are appointed by the commission. They're all local to the county, and mostly they're old preachers. But I'd say in general that a person who's lived in a place and kept it up has a claim on it too. What I mean is that the old landlord can't just kick you out if they finally show up again. Most of them are dead. Most of *everybody* is dead, I mean. And the landlords were usually paying on a bank note too, right? Well, all of that bank paper went up in smoke when all the banks failed. If you can prove that you've been living in a place since before the collapse, and if you can show some old utility bills and property taxes, I think it'll hold up. After we get a new constitution like they're talking about, who knows what's going to happen? But I trust General Jackson. He won't screw us over. I know it's a leap of faith, but we're all leaping together. So get used to hearing this a lot: *God bless Texas*."

Parker raised a toast and emptied his mug. Tala refilled it.

Gino asked him, "So, what do people use for money? I mean, day-to-day money to pay their bills, and to buy their food?"

"The money around here is silver. One ounce of silver is the most common money. Everybody takes any kind of silver coins. Or gold, if they have it. Fifteen ounces of silver counts the same as one ounce of gold. The old American silver quarters weren't pure silver so it takes five of them to make an ounce. Don't worry; you'll get the hang of it real quick.

"I earn sixty ounces of silver a month as a private, but it's mostly in escrow until I get my five years in. If I don't take a house, my bonus will be double what they kept for me. I get two ounces a week in hard cash money, but I eat for free and I live in the barracks. I ride the bus free too, if I'm in uniform. You get paid more if you're married and you have kids and you live off-base. But hey, it's what we call the war economy, and believe-you-me, we ain't in it for money."

He reached into a pants pocket and pulled out a plum-size leather bag, and dumped its contents into his hand. All of the crew who were gathered around leaned in to see. There were mostly pre-1964 American silver quarters and dimes and some nickels, but they were dominated by one large coin.

He said, "This one is one ounce of silver. You can read it, see? It says 'One Troy Ounce, .999 Fine Silver."

He handed the big coin to me. I still had some that were similar; they were called silver rounds. They weren't any government's official currency. They were privately minted, and they were just exactly what they said they were: one ounce of silver, a bullion coin. Being made of a lighter metal, they were a little bigger than gold coins. One side showed a flag with a lone star, a cannon, and the words "COME AND TAKE IT." The other side showed the state of Texas, and the years 1836-1986. Except now Texas wasn't a state, so I had to adjust my thinking. Now it was Free Texas, and soon it was going to be an independent and sovereign nation. Or maybe it already was.

Will asked him, "But what if it's fake? What if it's just a silver coating on the outside and something else inside?"

"Well, son," Parker said, "That would be a real good way to get yourself an appointment with the hangman. But it'd be pretty hard to fake one. You can tell that it was made in a real mint, and there are people who keep track of all the real ones."

Will wasn't done. "What if you didn't know it was fake?"

"Oh, they'd figure out where it came from originally, and then the counterfeiters would get hung. That's the same reason we don't have a lot of robberies, or, excuse me ladies—rapes. We don't tolerate that shit in Free Texas. We hang criminals, and they know it. We're a very well-armed and polite society. That's called 'Heinlein's Law.' You ever hear of it?"

I said, "I heard of it. It's a quote from Robert Heinlein."

"He's the guy who wrote Starship Troopers," Luke noted.

Adam asked him, "How old do you have to be to join the Texas Militia?" He was sitting by Rita on the downed mast.

Private Parker asked Adam, "How old are you, son?"

"I'm fifteen—but I'm big for my age."

"That's too young for the militia, but you can apprentice in the Texas Engineering Corps. I believe that apprentice deal is two years, and then you'd be old enough to join the militia. Or you could stay in the T.E.C. as an engineer. I think by then we'll need more engineers than militiamen! You're all going to be Texas residents, right?"

Everybody nodded or said yes. Including me.

Parker continued. "And that's all fine, residency is a good first step, but the bonus is only for Texas citizens, and that's only if you got five good years in the militia, or a few more in the T.E.C. The bonus is only for citizens, and for voting when we have elections. General Jackson's real clear on that point: only Texas citizens will get a say in how Texas is going to be run. Now, in the coast guard I'm still in the militia—and they could have shit-canned me—so I know I got a good deal. Two more years and I'll qualify for the bonus, but I'll probably take the silver instead of the house. I sure ain't got no wife or kids. Just look at me, ladies—do I look like husband material?" He threw his head back and laughed, and then he drained his cup.

"The bonuses are paid out in the order we signed up, and I got a low number because I signed up early. But I don't want a house to take care of, so I think I'll buy a fishing boat with my bonus, and I'll live on it. But that ain't hardly the reason why I'm in the militia. No sir, that ain't hardly why we do it."

I asked him, "But what if General Jackson can't deliver on his promise? What if they don't have enough silver, or if a new Texas congress passes a law and they won't pay it off? What if there's no bonus waiting for you at the end of the rainbow?"

His one blue eye opened wide at me. "What did you say? You shut your mouth! He wouldn't do that—he's a great man, he's a great Texan! I'd give my life for General Jackson and Texas! You think we're just fightin' for a house, or for silver? Man, you don't know *shit*! Goddammit, we're fightin' for *Texas*!"

Whew! “I’m sorry, Parker, I guess I just don’t understand everything yet. We came from South Carolina, and we haven’t even stepped foot on Texas. I guess I have a lot to learn.”

“You're damn right you do, and you'd better start now!”

To cut the tension, Luke and Jessie began to play a song they had practiced after hearing it a few times on AM 740. They had barely heard of Glen Campbell, but they’d had a few days to work out the lyrics and the chords crossing the Gulf.

Galveston, oh Galveston
I still hear your sea waves crashing
While I watch the cannons flashing
I clean my gun, and dream of Galveston

Parker closed his eye and leaned forward, sighing deeply. I could see that he had something to get off his chest, and who better to tell than strangers? Newcomers from South Carolina?

But he started his story with the oil refineries. According to Private Parker, almost everything boiled down to fuel. Once General Jackson had enough fuel, and the militia had airplanes that could fly again, they put spotters up in the sky. And that’s why General Jackson and his original volunteers had started in Texas City by taking over the old oil refineries, fuel farms and chemical plants. Jackson’s corps of engineers, mostly former oil industry workers, protected by unpaid militia volunteers, had gotten the flat-lined heart of Texas pumping once again by turning raw petroleum into new fuel.

Armories on the old military bases had been liberated, so mortars, machine guns and ammo were available to the Texas Militia. Once enough fuel was available, military trucks and light armored vehicles were put into service, and they became a powerful force multiplier against the disorganized bands of outlaws who were occupying Texas farms, towns and cities.

The militia had cleared Austin block by block, and then moved on to San Antonio. Most of both cities’ inhabitants were already dead from starvation, disease, and the rampant Mad

Max criminality. Most of the survivors in San Antonio and the surrounding counties weren't even Americans. Instead, they were foreign invaders from third-world nations who were more used to the so-called new normal conditions, subsisting on ditch water, stolen crops, poached livestock, and human flesh.

But that all changed when General Jackson stood up the militia and Texas was producing fuel again. The militia's rules of engagement were: 1. We win, you lose and 2. We live, you die. Parker's fellow militiamen had zero tolerance for the alien invaders who had occupied the homes and farms of the Texans who had not survived the years of collapse. In many cases, the foreign squatters had murdered the owners to take possession.

It was even worse in the cities. After a few years without potable water, without electricity, and without any food being brought in, the cities were practically depopulated. Only the toughest foreign invaders had survived the medieval conditions, but only until the even tougher Texas Militia had arrived on the scene, with small planes giving them eyes up in the sky, and trucks and buses carrying troops where they were needed.

At long range, past four or five hundred yards, anybody with face tattoos was shot on sight, along with anybody near them. They were assumed to be drug cartel soldiers, and they were killed on the spot. At close range, war dogs were used to flush out the hidden holdouts. You just can't hide from a trained dog, Parker explained. You just can't. The militia planes high overhead kept track of the runners, and directed the vehicle-borne militiamen to the most effective ambush locations.

There were so many Chinese communist spies and agents who had been let in under the traitorous Biden regime that at times, and in some places, it was hard for Asians to be taken alive—and no doubt mistakes were made—but this was war! Among the militiamen there was seething anger against the Chinese infiltrators, after their coordinated sabotage attacks had done so much damage at the beginning of the collapse. Invaders from the Middle East were treated the same way.

It helped that the Chinese agents and the jihadists almost always clustered in sizeable groups on the stolen farms and in the buildings they had captured and occupied. Twenty or thirty armed foreign fighters had been enough to dominate the local terrain during and after the collapse they had helped to cause, but they were no match for platoons of furiously angry Texas militiamen. You can't argue with 81mm mortar shells dropped down the tube almost four miles away. You just can't.

At surrender distance, anyone who couldn't speak English did not get the chance to seek an interpreter. General Jackson had declared English to be the official language of Texas, and that was the end of that. Anybody who could not explain—in English—where he had been born, and just how he had come to be occupying the place where he was then living, and then to prove his ownership, well, he was not asked a second time.

According to Parker this was called "Rule Five-Five-Six," or, on the radio, "carrying out deportation orders." The "dearly deported" illegal foreign invaders were referred to as Foxtrot Tango Foxtrot, or FTF, which stood for Free Texas Fertilizer. I understood that Rule 556 referred to 5.56mm ammunition, the most common caliber used in their rifles and carbines.

Flame throwers and Molotov grenade launchers—a Texas invention—destroyed the hideouts of dead-enders. "When in doubt, burn 'em out" was the militia's standard operating procedure. Children and the elderly were few and far between in the areas occupied by foreign invaders. Most of the American children and old folks had already starved, died from all the diseases, or had been killed outright, sometimes for food.

High rises and apartment buildings had long since become death traps, and General Jackson was against them on general principal. He believed that free Texans were meant to live on their own land, and not in beehives like insects. It was hard to argue this point. Everybody knew what had happened to the inhabitants of the hives when the power, water, and food had stopped flowing in. In any case, there were more than enough vacant single-family homes. I was reminded again of Barry's aquarium analogy, and the burnt cruise ship that was stranded forever on Doomsday Reef.

As the reconquest of Texas had rolled on, the militiamen developed calluses over the calluses on their hearts. They were seizing the red-hot iron of destiny with their hands in order to pass something of lasting worth to the next generation. They were retaking Texas for the Texans, and nobody promised that it would be pretty. It was viciously cruel, and there were many terrible excesses, but in the end, only Texans with Texas roots were still alive in Austin and in San Antonio. Those two cities and the land between them were the extent of Parker's war.

Then he lost his right eye to an explosion.

Private Parker had been a sergeant before being busted down to private when some of the stories from San Antonio caught up with him in the field hospital. But at least he hadn't been court-martialed or shit-canned. He had been transferred to the Texas Coast Guard, and he had kept his bonus years.

"God Bless Texas, and God Bless General Jackson!"

More hours passed as the day wore on and the Cat continued to purr. We put the tarp over the boom to make an island of shade. Parker told us we'd make our turn to the west when we reached Green 61, the Houston channel buoy that marked the exit to our destination. After we turned, the bottom came up from the thirties to around ten feet. Private Parker steered us past a half-sunk tugboat, a stranded barge, a sunken sailboat's mast and then finally a pole with number 2 on a red square. This marked the channel to the Kemah Cut into Clear Lake.

Our binoculars were again in constant demand as the land features defined themselves. There was a big highway bridge ahead of us. Parker said it was the Bayport Boulevard Bridge, Highway 146, and it ran from Houston through Seabrook and Texas City and then down to Galveston over another bridge. As we approached the cut it seemed like we were driving right into the dry land, but the water continued to part in front of us until we had land both to port and starboard. This was the cut.

Parker said, “On the south is the town of Kemah. It has a marina but it’s mostly bars and restaurants. You see that Ferris Wheel? There used to be a big amusement park there, but now it’s mostly bars. That’s where Sergeant Boylan thinks I’ll wind up tonight, but I won’t.” He laughed. “Well, maybe I won’t.”

“How high is that bridge?” I asked him. Not possessing a chart or even local knowledge, we were at Parker’s mercy.

“Over seventy feet—how tall is your mast?”

“Not that tall,” I replied. “Seventy feet is enough.”

Parker spoke to Adam, who was still behind the wheel. “As soon as we’re under the bridge, slow down. The boatyard will be the first place on your right.”

There were actually two parallel road bridges, both with tall concrete pillars on each side of the boat channel. The last bridge that we had motored beneath had been in Beaufort, three weeks earlier. It felt like three lifetimes. Actually, it had been: Mike, Barry and Curt. Minus two and plus one. And then we were through. On the west side of the two bridges we motored under power lines, high ones sagging between giant towers.

Parker said, “So now it’s all Clear Lake for miles ahead. Slow down some more, son, your marina is the first opening on the right. My buddy’s houseboat is about a mile west.”

“Once we get tied up,” I told him, “we’ll launch our boat and take you there. Good job, Parker. Thank you very much.”

I meant to ask Tala to get some bottles of ground coffee for him, but things were happening too fast. It was always my instinct to take the wheel when we were docking Rebel Yell. But how would Adam ever get the experience that he needed if I took the wheel right then? When it really counted?

Parker stood up and leaned over him and said, “That’s it, son, now, see the blue shed with the gray roof? That’s on the far side of the cut into the boatyard. Good, that’s it, slow down now, real slow, one knot is plenty. Good. Now make a sharp turn to starboard after those first boats on the right, then hard left. Good—good—perfect! That's the haulout pier with the Travel-Lift. And we're in luck—there's only one boat on it. Go neutral now, that's good, now give it some reverse. . ."

I bit my tongue and I let Adam handle Rebel's wheel, the throttle and the gear shifter until we were stopped against the dock. I couldn't have done it any better myself, and what if he *had* crashed the dock? Rebel Yell was a half-century-old steel scow of a former schooner. Who would notice more scrapes?

Gino and Luke jumped over with our lines and tied us up. We'd forgotten to put out our fenders, but it didn't matter. For the first time since we'd left Port Antonio, we were absolutely motionless. A Travel-Lift that could pull us out of the water was just two-hundred feet up the dock. Gino killed the engine.

I told him, "Fine job, Adam. A damn fine job. Your uncle would be proud. And here's your next job: launch Metallica, put its motor on, and take Private Parker wherever he wants to go. And thank you, Parker, and not only for piloting us here, but for getting us up to speed on Texas. Oh, Tala, can you get some coffee for him to take with him? Okay? Good. Gino—let's walk up to the office and see what we can find out about this place."

This was where having the Lone Star flag hanging off our stern, instead of the blue South Carolina flag, made a huge difference. Our yellow quarantine flag was already down and put away. We didn't have to call anybody on our VHF radio, or go around searching for a customs or immigration official. Why? We had already been cleared in by the Texas Coast Guard. In an important way, we were already Texans. *God Bless Texas!*

46

The heart of a boatyard, the essential element of its existence, is the haulout slip and the giant four-wheeled Travel-Lift that pulls a boat out of the water on a pair of giant nylon straps, and then carries the boat, at a walking speed, to the spot in the boatyard where the work will be done up on the dry ground.

Gino and I hopped down onto the pier and walked up the dock. The other boat was closer to the land. The yard's Travel-Lift was poised over the haulout slip, its straps hanging slack. It was a mild December Sunday afternoon, but we didn't hear any power tools. Weekends were usually busy at boatyards.

We neared the forty-foot cruising trawler, its bow to land. Doubtless waiting to be hauled out next. The name on the back said *My Time*. A man was sitting on a chair reading a book. A white toy poodle ran in circles yapping, and the man looked up.

I said, "Well, hello, good morning, nice pooch. Looks like a great boat dog. Hey, are they open? The office, I mean."

"Oh, I seen ya come in. No, the office is *not* open today. There's no haul outs on Sunday, or I'd be getting hauled out. If you can believe it, they don't work on Sundays here." He was paunchy and balding, and he had a thick New England accent. A Yankee—but not from Captain Peter Stark's tribe.

"So, nobody is in the office?" I asked him.

"Isn't that what I just said? Go see for yourself. The office is up there on the right side of the main building."

I noticed a yellow power cable running from his cockpit to a dockside pedestal. "Do they have shore power working here?" I felt stupid as soon as the words left my mouth.

He replied, "Do ya think I'd be plugged in if they didn't?"

"No, I guess not." The last time Rebel had been plugged into shore power had been in the Canaries, five years before.

We walked past the Travel-Lift that was waiting over the haulout slip. It was a big one, at least a hundred-ton job, big enough to lift boats considerably bigger than Rebel Yell, and it appeared to be in good working order. The building was faded blue, two stories high, with big hangar doors that were closed. Boats were blocked up on both sides of the building, pleasure and commercial craft from thirty to a hundred feet in length.

A yellow mobile hydraulic crane was parked by the water over to our right. Its boom was down and telescoped inward, but if it was extended and raised, it was obvious that it could lift our foremast with plenty of feet to spare. We walked up to the building and found the office door. As expected, it was locked. No cars parked in front, no signs of activity nearby.

The hours were posted on the door: Monday to Saturday, 8 to 5, closed Sunday. Below this was a note: *Please no power tools on Sunday*. Above the door was a four-foot-wide hand-painted sign. Somebody with calligraphy talent had drawn it.

SEA-LAKE MARINA AND BOAT YARD
HAUL, BLOCK & LAUNCH........................25C PER FOOT
PRESSURE WASH & SCRAPE.....................10C PER FOOT
LAY-DAYS IN YARD....................................6C/FOOT/DAY
TRANSIENT DOCKAGE................................4C/FOOT/DAY
ELECTRIC POWER (30 AMP).......................1 OZ PER DAY
YARD LABOR RATE..................................1 OZ PER HOUR
SKILLED LABOR RATE.............................3 OZ PER HOUR
BOATYARD CRANE..................................3 OZ PER HOUR
BOTTOM PAINT....................................3 OZ PER GALLON
No DIY bottom work. Bottom paint MUST be bought here. Outside labor MUST be approved and MUST check in at the office each day. All payments due MUST be received before scheduling launch. In God We Trust. All others pay cash.
—NO CASH—NO SPLASH—NO EXCEPTIONS—

Gino and I studied the sign. He'd brought a pencil and paper to take down information. Every boatyard from Quebec to Cape Town had a similar sign stating their rates in the local currency, and laying down their house rules. This place looked tidy and organized. There were no long-term "bum boats" that I could detect. This boatyard appeared to be all business. Haul out—do your work—pay in cash—launch.

I told Gino, "Just getting hauled will cost fifteen ounces of silver. Cleaning the bottom, that's another six ounces. We'll need at least ten gallons of bottom paint, and with their paint and their crew doing the work, a bottom job is going to cost at least fifty ounces. I figure we'll need at least two weeks on the hard to fix the mast and paint the hull sides and the deck, and I'm always off by at least a half, so call it a month of lay-days. Six cents a foot times sixty feet is almost four ounces of silver a day just to stay in the yard. What are we up to so far?"

"Over a hundred and fifty ounces. And divided by fifteen, that's over ten ounces of gold. Boss—we just don't have it. Not unless you have an emergency fund I don't know about."

We were both silent for a minute or two, studying their rates, trying to figure out a way for us to proceed. Finally I said, "You know that we don't. And it always costs more than we estimate. And we haven't even counted deck and hull paint. 'No cash, no splash' means they'll own Rebel Yell if we can't pay the yard bill. Shit! Okay. If we stay in the water, and we skip the haulout and just use their crane, maybe we can fix the mast ourselves on the boat. If it needs any welding that's three ounces an hour for labor, and that's assuming we can fix the mast at all. This place sure ain't cheap. First Mate, I wish we were still back in the Canaries. We should've never left."

"We were heroes there, because of saving the Irish girls. They don't know us here. Here, we're nobodies. Nobodies."

"So we can forget about getting hauled out. We just don't have the money. But if we can just get the mast back up, we can anchor out somewhere and scrape our own bottom in the water. Then we could sail to Port Antonio and buy some coffee."

"Buy some coffee with what?" he asked. "And we'll need to pay for new rigging wire, assuming we can fix the mast at all. We'll need to take fuel to Jamaica to pay for a load of coffee, and we'll be lucky if we can repair the mast and put it back up. And don't forget, we'll still need money to buy food."

I said, "We still have most of the forty kilos of beans. If we're clever how we spread them around, maybe we can find an investor to front us the fuel for a trip back to Port Antonio."

"Who'd give us a load of fuel and then just let us sail off? We'd need to leave some collateral for an investor to front that much fuel. But we don't have any collateral, not unless we left somebody here. Left them here like a hostage."

"Who?" I asked. "Not our families. So, then who? Adam? Luke and Jessie? Should we ask them if they'd be willing to be signed over as human collateral until we return? Do they do that here, like in Beaufort? 'Voluntary indentured servitude?' What if we don't come back? What if something happened to Rebel Yell during the voyage? They'd be left in bondage like Barry.

No way. No way. Gino, you cut the shackle off him. And I cut the chain off of your foot."

"Barry's shackle and my chain. I remember *everything*."

"I wouldn't ask them to do it. I couldn't. There's no way." Barry's shackle rivet was in the cigar box with the key from Fort Zerhoun's dungeon, Victor's snub-nose S&W revolver, the old speedo impeller, and some other small items.

"Then what, boss? We're cutting it close to the bone."

"How much silver can we get for the coffee we have? If we just pay for the crane and do the mast, we can buy as much fuel as we can with whatever gold and silver we have left. Or maybe we can find some investors who won't demand collateral if we offer them most of the profit. They might even pay for the boatyard work, but we'd have to sign a contract with them."

Gino said, "Then they'd put their own men on the boat to make sure we come back, and then who's the boss? Who's the real captain? No, I don't like the contract idea."

"I don't either. But the first step has to be getting the mast back up. We'll know more tomorrow when the office is open."

I heard Curt from behind us. "Hey, Captain Dan—change of plans." I turned around. He was with Parker. Tall Curt was carrying a hand bag he'd brought aboard in Mayaguana. He was wearing a pair of my old blue jeans and a frayed and stained sweatshirt from the grab bag. The bottom hems did not reach his sandals, and the sleeves of the sweater did not reach to his wrists—and these rags were his Sunday best. Curt Curtiss was a tall scarecrow with a white plantation hat and cool sunglasses.

"I'm heading to Oklahoma to see if I can find my family, and try to find some other things I left up there too. Mr. Parker used your VHF radio and he arranged a seat for me on a Texas Militia convoy heading north. That's all set for tomorrow, but now I'm going with him to get some warmer clothes at the Salvation Army. Yeah, they're open on Sunday. I'm going to stay with Parker tonight, and I'll be heading north in the morning. I already said goodbye to Tala and Sofia and the rest of your crew. Now we're going to walk to a place by the highway where people share rides . . . so I guess we'll be on our way."

"Curt," I said, "I just didn't expect this. It's so sudden. You know that you're welcome to stay on the boat for as—"

"And I appreciate that, Dan, I do, I really do. It was a hell of a ride from Mayaguana, wasn't it? But I have to know what happened to my family in Oklahoma. If I come back, I'll look you up. I think you have a lot of work to do, and you'll be busy for a while. So this is adios, Captain Dan . . . Gino."

I shook hands with him, and then with Parker, and so did Gino. They turned and walked off around the building toward the boatyard's front gate and they were soon out of sight. The highway he'd spoken of was not far off, the twin bridges we'd motored under loomed above the boatyard just to the east.

Gino said, "Well, I sure didn't see that coming. Damn."

"Neither did I. Curt's a strange one. A good man, but an odd duck. Let's go back to the boat, have another coffee, and discuss our options with the rest of the crew. We'll have until the office opens tomorrow to decide what we're going to do. At the most, they'll charge us for a night at their dock. Maybe there's a cheaper boatyard somewhere. I know it'll work out."

Even with Gino I had to fake a brave smile. It would not have helped our cause if my first mate knew just how hopeless I felt then. We walked back out the dock and climbed aboard. Adam, Will and Luke were standing by the mainmast.

Adam said, "We put Whisper in the water to make room to launch Metallica, but then Curt said he was leaving the boat with Parker to get a ride somewhere, to Oklahoma I think, and then we got sidetracked with all the goodbyes and whatnot. So if you two don't mind, give us a hand. We were about to roll her over, but it'll be easier with all five of us."

"Aye-aye, dinghy master." We took our places with them.

They had pushed the upside-down aluminum boat away from the horizontal foremast and over the closed cargo hatch to give them room to stand along it. We all grabbed its gunnel near the deck, and then on Adam's 1-2-3 count we heaved it up and over with clatters and bangs. Metallica's hull came to rest tilted to port. More scrapes inflicted on Rebel Yell's once-white deck would not make any appreciable difference.

"Did you know that Curt was leaving?" I asked them.

Luke said, "Not until he just told us. He said he's going to try to get up to Oklahoma because he had family there. Parker was going to swing him a ride north with the Texas Militia."

"Before he left," said Will, "Mr. Curtiss told us he wished that he had sons like us, and he shook our hands and wished us all good fortune. I just didn't expect him to leave so soon." Our ginger-haired starveling got misty-eyed and looked away.

Adam said, "Oh, and just before he took off, he told us to look under the seat. But what seat was he talking about?"

Metallica had aluminum bench seats near the bow, in the middle, and near the transom. Thin sheet metal went from the hull's bottom up to the sturdier aluminum benches. Below the seats and hidden by the sheet metal were flotation blocks. The blocks of foam had qualified the boat as unsinkable according to the U.S. Coast Guard requirements of many decades before.

"Now, that's pretty weird," Adam said. "The front seat and the middle seat are riveted to the hull, but the one in the back is attached with machine screws."

"They look like 10-24s," Will noted. "Philips heads on the outside, and little hex nuts on the inside. I'll get the tools." He dropped down the forward scuttle hatch and quickly returned.

Instead of factory-installed rivets, there were aspirin-pill-size machine screws on each side of the bench attaching it to the hull. On the insides, the threaded ends of the screws were flush with the tiny hex nuts, so their difference from the rivets attaching the other seats had not been noticed. Will removed the machine screws and we all pried up the bench. The foam block left below it was dry, brown and crumbling with age.

On top of the block of hard foam were four clear vinyl sheets, each with six rows of six gold coins, with the plastic heat-sealed both ways between them. This concealment work had obviously not been done aboard Rebel Yell on the upside-down metal skiff, but two weeks earlier on Mayaguana Island.

Oh, Curt Curtiss. *Thank you. Thank you. Thank you.*

AFTER THOUGHT BY HENRY ARTHUR CHARLTON

While filleting a grouper on a table in the shade of the tin-roof tiki-hut near the old boat landing

At last they are all gone, and I can wander my island in peace, instead of always having to stop to help everyone else. But I know that God wanted me to help them all, and so I did, and happily! And isn't it funny that the last one to leave was a white man, who was also the last to arrive? Oh, how God plays His jokes! If only I was younger, and if there was a young woman for me, we could begin again now that the rains have returned. Alas, I am the end of my people, and when I lay down for my final rest Mayaguana will be a home only for our spirits, and I will join the elders in the eternal world. But until that day, just *look* at how Abraham's Bay shines like a jewel in the sunlight! And, God willing, there will be others who will come after me to see it, to live here, and to harvest God's magnificent bounty.

Texas historical note: 19th-Century Texas Rangers were paid approximately sixty dollars per month, in silver, depending on their position. For that princely salary, Rangers were expected to supply their own horse, saddle, and firearms. Ammunition and food were provided when available. Rangers routinely went unpaid. They were not in the fight for the money, but for Texas.

Matthew Bracken was born in Baltimore, Maryland, in 1957, and graduated from the University of Virginia and UDT/SEAL training in 1979. He is still happily married and lives in Florida.

For signed copies of Matt's novels, send $24 per book to:

STEELCUTTER PUBLISHING, INC
PO Box 65673
Orange Park, FL 32065

For PayPal orders: **paypal.me/steelcutter48**

All seven titles, signed and inscribed: **$140**

Cases of 16 unsigned novels, any titles: **$180**
Cases of 16 flat-signed novels: **$200**

(Shipping & handling included on all orders)

Preview the first 100 pages of each novel at:
www.EnemiesForeignAndDomestic.com

Also available on Amazon Kindle and Audible